French Tales of
Mad Scientists
(Vol. 2)

FROM THE SAME PUBLISHER

French Tales of
Mad Scientists
(Vol. 2)

by
**Michel Corday, André Couvreur,
Jules Janin, Maurice Renard,
Edward Rod** and **Jacques Spitz**

Translated by
Brian Stableford

A Black Coat Press Book

English adaptations:
Jules Janin: *The Magnetized Corpse* (1845)
Edward Rod: *Dr Z***'s autopsy* (1884)
Michel Corday: *The Mysterious Dajan-Phinn* (1908)
Maurice Renard: *Doctor Lerne, Subgod* (1908)
André Couvreur: *An Invasion of Macrobes* (1909)
Jacques Spitz: *Dr. Mops' Experiment* (1939)
Copyright © 2024 by Brian Stableford.
Introductions Copyright © 2024 by Brian Stableford & Jean-Marc Lofficier.
Cover illustration Copyright © 2024 by Stephan Martiniere.

TABLE OF CONTENTS

Introduction

Here are more French science fiction stories featuring the character of the mad scientist in all of its wicked, dangerous aspects.

We outlined an history of this most fruitful theme that runs through French science fiction like a live wire in our first volume; and therefore, refer our readers to it.

Here, we shall mention some of the most common features of the character:

Usually bearing the title of doctor or professor, the mad scientist is competent in many sciences and techniques at the same time; he is both an Albert Einstein with revolutionary ideas, and a handy Gyro Gearloose, capable of putting his crazy theories into practice.

The mad scientist usually displays obsessive behavior and use dangerous or at least unconventional methods to achieve his goals without the least regard for destructive or ethical consequences. He may be motivated by revenge, trying to punish a real or imagined slight, often related to his work. This narcissism and excessive pride generate a megalomania which leads him to want to overcome the laws of Nature, to despise human beings, to "play at being God" and to ne unable to maintain normal human relationships, which can lead him to live as a hermit.

Visually, his laboratory is generally cluttered with Tesla coils, Van der Graaf electrostatic machines, Jacob's ladders, perpetual motion machines and other spectacular scientific instruments, not forgetting test tubes and distillation equipment where brightly colored liquids bubble, from which disturbing vapors emanate.

I'll conclude with a real-life anecdote. Already in the 18th century, when alchemists and sorcerers were not yet forgotten, Professor Guillaume-François Rouelle, a French chemist and apothecary, demonstrator at the *Jardin du roi* (current National Museum of Natural History) warned his students:

"Do you see this cauldron on this brazier, gentlemen? Well, if I stopped stirring the mixture it contains for a single moment, an explosion would ensue that would make us all jump into the air!"

A moment of distraction, and his prediction came true: a terrible explosion was heard, all the windows in the laboratory were shattered, the chimney collapsed, and the incorrigible professor's wig was removed to the ceiling!

Jean-Marc & Randy Lofficier

Jules Janin: *The Magnetized Corpse*

Jules Janin (1804-1874) came to Paris to prepare for a career in law, but gave scant attention to his studies. Having twice been a schoolfellow of Edgar Quinet, his law studies briefly overlapped with those of Honoré de Balzac, and like them, he became avidly involved in the capital's literary life.

Janin wrote articles and stories for several periodicals during the 1820s, including Le Figaro *and the two key periodicals of the burgeoning Romantic Movement, the* Revue des Deux Mondes *and the* Revue de Paris; *he was an unusually prolific writer. His first shot at fame was when he published* L'Âne mort et la femme guillotinée *(tr. as* The Dead Donkey and the Guillotined Woman) *in 1829, causing something of a sensation. The work was subsequently hailed by critics as the culminating specimen of* roman frénétique *[frenzied fiction], that being one of the labels invented in parallel with the English notion of "Gothic novels" for application to French products associated with the fad. The story tracks the career of an unfortunate young woman spoiled and corrupted by the struggle for existence in French society, who follows an inexorable path of misfortune and moral degradation all the way to the guillotine.*

Janin entitled his first collection of short stories, published in 1832, Contes fantastiques et contes littéraires. *Within the French Romantic Movement that gathered momentum in the 1820s and enjoyed its first heyday, E.T.A. Hoffmann was then a very popular and influential writer and Janin was by no means the only French writer to take considerable inspiration from him. No one else, however, took the same strange kind of inspiration that he did. Janin wanted more than anything else not to do things the way that other people did them. He wanted to be different, perhaps in the unique sense of the word, to be* fantastique.

"Le Mort magnétisé" (initially published in 1845 in the Revue Pittoresque; *here translated as "The Magnetized Corpse") had been dismissively reviewed in the* Journal du Magnétisme, *which dutifully reported that the experiment described had been tried, and had not produced the indicated result. Yet the story is of some historical significance, because it was published several months before Edgar Allan Poe's "The Facts in the Case of M. Valdemar," which has an identical theme, appeared in the December 1845 issue of the* American Review.

The possibility of any direct influence of Janin's story on Poe's seems remote, and the idea is one that might have occurred to anyone at the time, but the coincidence is all the more striking because Poe, assisted by Charles Baudelaire's translations, was the writer who supplemented and displaced Hoffmann in the affections of the French Romantics and their Decadent and Symbolist successors.

B.S.

With regard to good stories, here is one that was told to me by a trustworthy man, who claimed to be the friend of a friend of an eye-witness who played a significant role in the drama that I am about to relate to you briefly, not without making the ardent wish that the story in question might be honored before long by an adaptation for the theater—which is, as everyone knows, the greatest honor that can be desired nowadays.

Not six weeks ago, a young Englishman named Belfort was dying, quite simply from a bad chest and a few crazy years recklessly spent. The young man, although he was nearing the end, did not regret losing his life too much, for he had had his fair share of amours, duels, bad debts, picnics, and even fine sermons—in short, his fair share of all the Parisian joys.

One of his friends, a man of science but a good enough fellow regardless, seeing that Charles Belfort would soon render his last breath, came to say to him, in his softest voice: "If it wouldn't displease you too much, my dear invalid, I'll use my abilities to magnetize you, and I'll choose the moment when you render up your soul; it seems to me that it will be a fine experiment, and that there's nothing about it likely to displease you. What do you say?"

"Not only doesn't your experiment displease me," the other replied, "but it seems to me to be very amusing and interesting, and I thank you for having thought of me for the proof, which will be decisive. Count on me, my dear doctor; you'll be content with my patience, I hope, and I'll be sure to let you know when the moment comes."

With those words, the two friends shook hands and separated, saying that they would see one another again soon. They were both full of hope, and it would have been difficult to decide which of the two was the more content, the moribund or the magnetizer.

Two days went by—two centuries—while the magnetizer waited impatiently for the final agony, which did not seem to want to arrive for good and all. The dying man, for his part, lost patience, and he said to his friend: "Damn it, my dear chap, it's not my fault if death is treating me with such ill-will, but what consoles me is that you won't lose anything by waiting, and I'll be a magnificent subject."

On the night following this conversation, the sick man had a final crisis and fell into a comatose ecstasy; he started sketching fantastic spider-webs with his finger, and yet, in the midst of the most abominable grimaces, he still had the presence of mind to say to his comrade: "You have to lift my head, to hide the light that is hurting my eyes."

The other obeyed. He propped his moribund up in a sitting position, took away every importunate light and set about the operation; which is to say that never, absolutely never, had such beautiful passes and counter-passes—the whole customary apparatus, in short—been performed. The magnetizer was in the swim; but in the end, when he had enveloped the moribund—who lent himself to it with exemplary willingness—with his all-powerful fluid, and saw that his subject had arrived at magnetic perfection, the magnetizer started to interrogate him.

"How are you doing, Belfort? Where are you?"

"My dear friend," the other said, "I'm just dying; you've caught me just at the moment when the breath was leaving my body, and now it depends entirely on you to let me finish the job or to keep me here, suspended between being and non-being, which doesn't seem to me to be a disagreeable state, so far."

"Let's wait," said the magnetizer. "There's no hurry, Belfort, my friend." And with that, the magnetizer went to dinner, without taking the trouble to demagnetize his friend.

The next day the maker of magnetism reappeared in the mortuary chamber; everything was in its place, including the cadaver.

"Belfort," said the scientist, after a few preliminary passes, "what have you been doing since you died?"

"In truth, my dear chap," the dead man replied, "I've been obliged to follow you everywhere you went."

And with that, the dead man told the living one everything that the latter had done the day before: he had dined in a cheap eatery, and from there he had gone to stand on the steps of the Café de Paris; he had been given a ticket to the Vaudeville and he had seen some young women who were pretty enough, but some of whom sang out of tune; finally he had gone back home, and read a little of a novel that he had picked up on the way.

"And if you'll permit me to make an observation," the dead man said, "so long as I'm attached to you by a thread that only you can break, eat better, I beg you, remembering that I'm sharing the experience. You know that I like music, so don't expose me to hearing quavering voices that would spoil the most beautiful faces. All alone here, I'm getting bored, and I wouldn't be sorry if you were to read a good novel from time to time, but at least, for pity's sake, read it all the way through. Finally, if you please, don't go to bed so late; I become irritated not sleeping, because for twenty-four hours, I ought to have been sleeping eternally."

With these words, the man slumped back, and the magnetizer left the room, slightly discomfited by the strange spy that was dogging his heels.

The next day, the living man came back, and found his dead man a trifle numb. He warmed him up with a further dose of magnetic fluid, rendering him, if not life, at least a little color and the ability to speak.

"Ah!" said the dead man, raising himself up. "You're not showing me any charity. What! You go to see such hideous sick people, and I have to hear them coughing, spitting, howling, moaning and all the rest! In the street you follow a horrible woman reeking of musk, a woman in old shoes and a dirty skirt, and I have to keep you company counting the holes and the stains of the filthy creature! Then you go to meet up with some young people, and you tell them about your good luck! You make the streetwalker into a duchess, and a cotton apron into a silk skirt! When you're dead, you know, lying makes you feel ill. And what makes you feel even worse, when you're dead, is stupidity—some quip that would have made me laugh when I was of this world appears to me to be utter nonsense now that I can hear your mind with the ears of my own. So try to talk better my dear chap, and, if it's all the same to you, I'd be obliged if you didn't get drunk on adulterated wine; my throat's been torn apart by the alcohol you've swallowed."

Who do you think pulled a face? It was the living man, who was beginning to think that his dead man was damnable hard to please—because, after all, the previous evening's indulgence hadn't been deserving of such scorn. As for the lady with the worn-out shoes, the living man hadn't noticed the shoe, but only the foot and a little bit of the leg. However, he was fond to his dead man, and he resolved to keep a better eye on himself, in order not to give poor Belfort further reason for discontentment.

When he came back two days later, he found the deceased in a state of incredible excitement. The dead man was sweating copiously, with indignation legible on his distressed face.

First of all, the magnetizer set about trying to calm that anger; he blew his most soothing breath upon those irritated nerves, and appeased that motionless and frozen heart as best he could, which beat in memory.

"What is it, Master Belfort? Who's upset you? And for God's sake, what's the matter with you?"

"What's the matter with me?" replied the cadaver, after a long pause. "What's the matter with me, imbecile that you are? A curse upon the brazen threads that attack me to a fool like you! What's the matter with me! But my dear chap, for two days you've been going from one stupidity to another. The day before yesterday, it's true, you were well-groomed and well-dressed, but you'd fastened your belt too tight and I nearly choked. Your boots—or, rather, our boots—were well-polished, but they were too small, and if I could still walk, I'm sure that I'd be limping with my right foot.

"I've nothing to say about the lovely salon to which you took me; it was pleasant and it was calm; the clothes weren't at all garish; the mature ladies kept to their place, leaving the foreground to the young women; no one played the slightest sonata or read the slightest sonnet; people only spoke in even voices, neither too loud not too quiet, and said the nicest things—trivial but light, benevolent and sonorous. In brief, had it not been for your belt and our footwear, I would have blessed you for having taken me to such a beautiful place. But good heavens! Could you have been any more gauche, maladroit and absurd?

"In a corner of the little room to the left, a more beautiful woman than I ever saw with my mortal eyes was sitting; by dint of attention and will-power, via your terrestrial intermediation. I had attracted the benevolent interest of that amiable lady; already she was looking at me with a certain tenderness, and she was about to smile at me; our two souls were no longer any but one, and we were about to fall in love, when you turned your head like an idiot to greet I don't know what starchy spirit. Then the image of my beautiful lady fled, and if you live for a hundred years you won't find either another face as beautiful or another heart as noble.

"Idiot that you are, having done that, what do you do next? You know that I've left some glaring debts, and that I don't even have a tomb. You haven't a sou yourself; you live from hand to mouth; your rent hasn't been paid and never will be; in brief, you're as poor as a poet and an actor rolled into one—which is to say, abominably poor! Well, you sit down at a card-table, tremulously risk a wretched pistole, and, having won the hand, you pocket the money and run away like a thief!

"Now, do you know what you did there, Monsieur Idiot? You renounced getting your hands on a round sum of four lovely thousand louis d'or, for you'd have won the next thirteen hands, my son! With your four thousand louis you'd have had a carriage and I'd have had a first-class funeral. You'd have had a new suit and I'd have had an embroidered shroud. You'd have gone to seek your supper in the chorus of the Opéra, and I'd have gone to look for Monsieur Gannal.[1]

"Damn your feeble intelligence—you can't make use of what little sense you have, but you amuse yourself dragging another man's intelligence around with you. Go away—you make me sick, wretched living individual that you are!"

When our magnetizer finally understood that whatever he did would surely attract criticism or sarcasm, he fell silent. Now that he felt that he was being followed and observed at close range by some invisible entity that he had retained on the boundary between the two worlds, the scientist dare not take a step in the street; he scarcely dared answer yes or no to the simplest questions that were addressed to him; if was as if he were deaf and dumb. At times he wondered whether he might be the magnetized man and the magnetizer that great motionless—but not speechless—cadaver, the mere sight of which had ended up making him shiver.

An idea, a thought, is such a powerful thing, even independent of life! An idea pursues you, obsesses you, more tenacious than a shadow, as eloquent as remorse or hope, full of starts, excitations and perils!

---

[1] Jean-Nicolas Gannal (1791-1852) was the pharmacist and inventor who founded and developed the modern techniques of embalming in the early 1830s, winning the Prix Montyon three times by virtue of the benefits thus provided to human society. In 1837 he obtained a patent for his embalming fluid and set up a commercial laboratory in the Rue Saint-Hippolyte.

However, our man went back to his friend Belfort three days later. This time, once again, a great change was evident in his inanimate face; pure and simple scorn had replaced indignation and anger. The half-closed eyes seemed to be saying: "Away with you!" The tight lips were expressing an indescribable disdain. Every muscle, taut from top to bottom, held a contempt suspended from every thread connecting it to the soul.

"What's the matter now, my friend?" cried the living man, "You seem dazed. You can't say this time that I've done or said anything stupid, because I've stayed at home, alone, entirely given over to my thoughts."

"Oh, my dear fellow," the dead man said, "it's the contemplation of your thoughts that's giving me nausea. Motionless as you were, I was forced to look into the depths of that chaos you call your soul. But what kind of animal are you to occupy yourself with so many ignoble, frivolous and shameful things? When I was alive and I called you my friend, everyone said that you were a gallant fellow; you had a reputation for keen, even eloquent wit; you were credited with philosophy, probity and tact.

"For three days, unable to help it, I've been watching you very attentively—but my dear fellow, you're a complete mess! What you know, you know poorly; what you don't know, you replace with words as empty as your head. Your generosity is a certain organic weakness that ends up making your eyes red, and that's all. Your intelligence is represented by a few mechanical cog-wheels that rotate of their own accord like the wheel of a water-mill incessantly repeating the same tick-tock. Your courage—I've seen all the way its depths, your courage!—is a cardboard mask that frightens children. Your probity—let's talk about your probity!—is written in the margins of the commercial Code and the penal Code.

"Shame upon your vices, those of a badly brought-up child! I wouldn't give four sous for your vices; they make me sick, your wicked shameful vices: they're like a kind of boasting! As for your virtues, they're so worthless I wouldn't even give them to my lackeys; there's something limp and vain about your virtue, which bears some resemblance to a badly-cooked broth. Oh, I advise you not to lay bare the inside of your brain and your heart—it's not a pretty sight, although, on the other hand, it's very sad.

"And what ideas you have about other men! What thwarted ambitions! And I don't envy your work at all, my poor sir! What! You aren't ashamed, even of your castles in Spain, when you amuse yourself rambling on for entire hours in petty daydreams?

"Anyway, Monsieur, let's leave it at that—but I'm damnably sorry that I ever called you my friend!"

It would not have taken much on this occasion for the magnetizer to destroy his work and liberate himself from the unwelcome thought that was obsessing him. He left the mortuary chamber in a very bad mood, and on the way home he said to himself that it was, after all, quite an accomplishment to have stopped Belfort's discontented soul half-way.

Then again, the living man said to himself, sadly, *what good has it done me to have retained that dead man in the edge of his grave? To have myself told such rude home-truths, to hear the story of my everyday life told in such a cruel and grotesque fashion, no longer to be alone with my conscience, my thoughts, my ambitions, my self? If the clairvoyant that sees everything were, at least, to indicate some unknown science to me—a remedy for the gout or some hidden treasure easy to extract—I'd be rewarded for my troubles, but no! For having carried out the most difficult task, the most excellent miracle that magnetism has ever accomplished, here I am dragging behind me a bilious inquisitor who isn't content with anything, and who'll end up making me disgusted with myself.*

Thus the clever man reasoned; he was very annoyed, and firmly resolved to put an end to his dealings with such a miscreant, no matter what it cost.

As he was unable to sleep, the magnetizer went back to Belfort's house that same evening, at midnight.

Belfort watched him come in, and without waiting to be interrogated—for the magnetic fluid becomes, it seems, a habit, and replaces life as a well-lit candle replaces with winter sun—the dead man cried: "I'll tell you what you've just done, amiable doctor! You've quite simply decided to murder me! Yes, you're jealous of this artificial life, you're furious at my revelations, and you've decided to extract me abruptly from magnetic sleep in order to return me to dust and silence!

"That's handsome of you, Monsieur, it's glorious, what you're doing, coming to murder...a dead man! Coming to trouble a cadaver in his coffin! Attacking the thought of a man because the man, having become, thanks to you, a part of eternal life, is no longer able and no longer wants to flatter you!

"Well, get on with it, then, and turn me to dust—but that dust, when you've cast it to the wind, will summon to its aid another, bolder thought, to follow in your tracks, another gaze, even more clairvoyant, to read the depths of your soul, another avenger, even more implacable: remorse!"

At these threats the magnetizer fled, but, in his distress, he left the door ajar.

The neighbors of both sexes, who had initially kept their distance, took the chance, one after another, and finally all together, of coming to greet and interrogate the dead man, and picked up, here and there, some of those fine verities—I mean a few of those eternal, ever-living truths—that only the dead know how to voice appropriately. Husbands, wives, children, tenants, owners, masters and servants, the rich and the poor, all the way to the porter, each obtained a parcel of justice addressed to them.

The dead man spoke true words and expressed true notions, and what he said was, admittedly, cruel. If you asked him where fortune lay, he would point out a wart on the end of your nose; if you mentioned ambition to him, he would

15

talk to you about modesty, economy and bonhomie. The female neighbors found him so ungallant that they slammed the door violently.

That was all that the late Monsieur Belfort wanted.

A week went by without the magnetized and the magnetizer seeing one another again; they were sulking, but it was obviously not up to the dead man to make the first move. The scientist finally understood that, and came back to his subject's bedside.

"I've thought about everything that has happened," Belfort said to him, "and I'd be glad if you were to carry through the plan you made the other day. You're right: wake me up, so that I can finish dying quietly. It had made such a good beginning, when you came along to disrupt it, that I'd already be devoured by worms and returned via the thousand pores of universal decomposition into the ocean of life and light. Wake me up, then, and I'll die entirely—and joyfully, for, this time, I'll amuse myself by gazing, not at your soul, which isn't beautiful, but at your body, which is very ugly.

"Only the other day—I caught you in that agreeable occupation—you were telling yourself how fortunate you were before, but please, where are these women who can look lovingly at an ape like you? You're badly-formed; you always have one shoulder higher than the other, this one over that one or that one over this one. Your hair started falling out a long time ago, and what's left is hanging on to rotten roots, like last year's thatch after the winter. Your eyes can still see, but I can see some sort of pellicle extending over your line of sight that doesn't augur anything good.

"Oh, if you could see those layers of yellow chalk encrusted in the joints of your fingers, which are corrupting your bones and are going to break them bit by bit, like the boot of torture, but more slowly, more insidiously and with a more obstinate verve!

"Your heart is swollen, my dear chap, and the point is being torn by some viscera or other that is wounded in its turn. Your left lung isn't much better than my right lung. Gradually infiltrating between your skin and your softened tendons I can see layers of thick fat which makes you resemble some sort of sea-cow. Your teeth are already turning yellow; they're loose in their bloody cavities. In your brain I can see veins swollen with apoplectic blood, ready to burst. You're doomed, you see, and—give me your hand—you're dead!"

On hearing those lugubrious words, the magnetizer begs the magnetized for mercy, pity and forgiveness. And, in order to free himself from the vision that is obsessing him, to expel from his mind that voice, which is pursuing him with such bruising stubbornness, in order not to remain exposed to that mockery and those prophecies of misfortune, the magnetizer sets about countermanding the magnetic fluid and destroying that artificial life.

The dead man resists, but in vain; it is necessary that a corpse, which is dead, should yield to a man who is still alive.

Gradually, the voice fades away. It utters one last gasp, and then Belfort, so eloquent a little while before, is no longer more than I don't know what, that which I don't know how to name in any language...

It was, in fact, for three weeks already that death had had possession of the cadaver, and now the magnetic breath had ceased, corruption and the worm took hold of their prey again and did not let go.

One shivers at the mere idea that the magnetizer might have died before having demagnetized his friend Belfort. How long eternity would have seemed to the latter then—unless his thought, obedient all the way to the abyss, or to Heaven, had followed the soul of magnetizer.

That would be another trial to attempt!

Edouard Rod: *Dr. Z***'s Autopsy*

"L'Autopsie du docteur Z***," *translated as "Doctor Z***'s Autopsy,"
by Édouard Rod (1857-1910), is a* conte philosophique. *As in the classic Vol-
tairean tales in that vein, it employs a fantastic literary device as a narrative
lever to bring a philosophical question into clearer focus; albeit, in this instance, somewhat perfunctory (the experience related, ostensibly as a result of
the "autopsy" in question, is conspicuous in its failure to mention any such autopsy being carried out).*

*There is a sense in which "L'Autopsie du docteur Z***" belongs to a se-
ries of French stories raising the issue of whether consciousness might persist
for a while after death, most of which feature scientists conducting experiments
on freshly-guillotined heads—one of the most famous, Villiers de Isle Adam's
"Le Secret de l'échafaud"[2], had been published in* Le Figaro, *to which Rod was
also a contributor, in 1883, and might well have inspired Rod's flight of fancy.
Rod's story is remarkable, however, in assuming that the residue of consciousness might last for days or weeks rather than mere seconds, and is not at all
concerned with the mere question of whether or not the hypothesis might be
true. Instead, it is intensely interested in the existential thought-experiment of
how the consciousness of being dead and the experience of slow post-mortem
extinction might affect one's attitude to the life one has lived. As such, it is highly unusual and quite fascinating in its suppositions.*

It is worth noting that Rod's story qualifies as roman scientifique *in both
senses of the term, and can be regarded as a contribution to the school of "neo-
Naturalism" that followed from Zola's Naturalism, and were differentiated by
its substitution of more up-to-date psychological theories of biological heredity
and their analyses of human behavior and consciousness.*

B.S.

*For myself, knowing nothing and holding dreams in doubt,
I believe that after death, when union is achieved,
The soul then recovers clarity of sight,
And that, judging its work with serenity,
Understanding without obstacles and explaining without difficulty,
Like its sisters in heaven it is powerful and regal,
Measures its true weight, knowing manifestly*

---

[2] tr. as "The Secret of the Scaffold" in *The Scaffold*, Black Coat Press, ISBN
978-1-932983-01-2.

> *That the breath, falsified by the false instrument,*
> *Was neither glorious nor vile, not being free,*
> *That the body alone prevented equilibrium;*
> *And calmly, it resumes, in ideal bliss,*
> *The holy equality of the Lord's spirits.*
> Alfred de Vigny, "The Flute."[3]

Perhaps you will still remember the noise made in the scientific world some thirty years ago by the discoveries of Doctor Z***, which suffered the fate of many discoveries and was universally denied. When he finally decided to publish the results of his patient research, Dr. Z*** was living in Bordeaux, where he enjoyed the renown of a good practitioner. The pamphlet for which he bore the expense, *Observations on Some Phenomena of Cerebral Existence*, provoked a general outcry, and he gradually lost his clientele.

It should also be said that the pamphlet in question—an octavo of about a hundred and twenty pages—overturned all received notions, simultaneously threatening by its indirect consequences science, morality and religion.

In effect, the physiologist claimed that the life of the brain is not extinguished at the same time as that of the body; that, on the contrary, it continues for a period that varies between seven and ten days after the last sigh—except, of course, in cases when the brain itself has been directly attacked by a disease, as in meningitis, encephalitis, general paralysis, softening, ataxia, etc.

He went further than that; he affirmed that, while during life the cerebral cells consumed by thought are incessantly reformed, they are irrevocably destroyed after death, with the result that the brain, still intact and fully active when the heart ceases to beat, although already detached from sensation by the wastage or weakness of the interior nervous centers, gradually declines in that final labor.

A good technologist as well as an excellent chemist, Dr. Z*** constructed an apparatus himself—which, so far as I can remember, bore some resemblance to the instrument invented more recently named the photophone[4]—with which he was able, for four or five days after death, to track the activity of brains in the process of decomposition.

He destroyed that instrument, as he burned his records, when he saw that no one believed him, and that the most indulgent were treating him as a madman

---

[3] "La Flûte" was first published in 1843.

[4] The photophone, involving the transmission of speech by means of a beam of light, was invented by Alexander Graham Bell and Charles Sumner Tainter in 1880; Bell thought it by far his most important invention, but its range was far surpassed by Guglielmo Marconi's wireless transmission system, and it was superseded, although it was the ancestor of modern transmissions via fiber-optic cable.

and the rest as a charlatan. Nothing, therefore, remains of his great work, and when science has finally deciphered the enigma of death, no one will be able to tell whether the obscure practitioner from Bordeaux was a pioneer or a trickster.

For myself, who knew him, who saw him at work, who listened on many an occasion, in his laboratory, to his conversations full of luminous perceptions, his reasoning was irreproachable, departing from the most scrupulous observations to rise to the heights where thought can finally detach itself from the tyranny of facts, and were his deductions, all the links of which were connected by the most rigorous logic. I have always regarded him as one of the beacons that ignorance and human stupidity too frequently take it upon themselves to extinguish, for fear of seeing the darkness of their routines illuminated.

I do not intend to explain Doctor Z***'s theories at length here, nor to recount his personal history. That might be instructive, but it is, I think, appropriate to leave it in the obscurity to which fate has relegated it, and to which he resigned himself without difficulty. But it was given to him once, to read with absolute clarity, an instance of that last period of life, which he alone has known, and I want to recall the circumstances of that strange case.

A ship-owner of Bordeaux, Dutch by origin, Monsieur van Gelt, committed suicide in 1854. His family took a great many precautions to hide that catastrophic event, of which malevolent rumor did not take long to circulate in society, where Monsieur van Gelt had been highly esteemed. The secrets of his private life, which had transpired long before, gave that gossip a certain consistency.

The family requested an autopsy, and Dr. Z***, then still looked on favorably, was given the responsibility. He communicated his surgical observations to the law, but he kept to himself the psychology of the dead man, which he had read as if in a book in the scarcely-drowsy brain.

The ship-owner, van Gelt, was evidently a man of high intelligence and great heart, so his posthumous ideas presented a character of superiority that Dr. Z*** had never encountered before. He collated his notes lovingly, conserving their personal form. On the day when he communicated them to me, reading his manuscript as an author might read a chapter of his novel, I was amazed: the dead man lived—so to speak—his strange cadaveric existence before me.

I begged my friend to let me have a copy of his notes, and he agreed, on the express condition that I did not publish them before he had published the great work to which his observations were only the preface. I have described the fate of his writings. He is dead now, and I can therefore regard myself as released from my promise and free to deliver this curious document to the public. If I am not mistaken, it will one day cast new light on the presently unfathomed mysteries of eternity. The only element that I shall permit myself to introduce into it, which appears to me to be necessary to the understanding of the script, concerns the ordering of the facts; I have brought together in the early pages details relating to the circumstances of the suicide, which are dispersed in the notes as if at the hazard of memory.

...I have exhausted what it is appropriate to call the calyx of suffering; for some time, catastrophes and misfortunes, superposed upon me like heavy stones on a man being walled up alive, have been pursuing me with a tenacity almost incredible in the force of its ferocity.

First of all, it was my only son, twenty-six years old, who fled with some creature after having robbed me in the manner of a treacherous accountant. Then my daughter died of typhoid fever at the moment when I was about to marry her to a young man she loved.

Soon afterwards, I discovered that my second wife—whom I had married without a dowry, for love, foolish old man that I was!—was deceiving me with one of my nephews, to whom I had given a position in my business, and whom I regarded, alas, as a second son. Rendered cowardly by that love, almost senile and almost ridiculous, whose roots stifled my courage, I accepted with interior tortures my role as a deceived husband, begging the wretch for the refuse of her tenderness, striving to conceal a wound that was getting larger every day.

Worn out by so much emotion, I became ill. I consulted a physician; he recognized that my morbid state was caused by the first symptoms of a cancerous infection of the stomach. Finally, after a disaster that coincided fatally with a financial crisis in Lyon, I saw the moment arriving when I would no longer be able to meet my obligations. At sixty-two years of age, at the end of an honorable career, having worked hard and done good, I thus found myself surrounded by dishonest affections, cuckolded, ill and poor.

Among the few idea that could still germinate within my brain, raked as if by the claws of birds of prey, a comparison was insinuated between my fate and that of Job. And I found myself even more unhappy than the patriarch: he had God, while I, throughout my overworked existence, had paid no heed to supernatural matters, which inspired an insurmountable mistrust in me, and even a little of the disgust that men of action have for the reveries of the contemplative.

At that moment, removed from all activity, forced into bitter contemplation of myself, meditative for perhaps the first time in my life, I began to desire faith, which the unfortunate regard as the supreme panacea. To acquire it, however, would have required time; and even then, would I ever succeed in vanquishing my deep-rooted skepticism? Would not my innate need for truth always triumph over the suggestions of my sentimentality? Certainly, in spite of my efforts, doubts would subsist in me, poisoning the consolations of the priest.

That refuge was thus refused to me. There remained one other, more reliable: death. I accepted it.

The fear of bankruptcy vanquished my last hesitations. At another time, I would have tightened my muscles, stiffened my will and struggled until the final defeat, but I felt paralyzed by a definitive lassitude, like a shipwreck victim whose limbs have become heavy, who loses consciousness and abandons himself. I did not even wait for the certainty of my disaster to be absolute; the probability was sufficient for me, and I bought an American revolver.

...I went home; I locked myself in my study and there, while parading my eyes over the files filled with papers in which my entire activity was stagnating, over the curiously-wrought old furniture with which I liked to surround myself, and the few valuable paintings hanging on the walls, I slipped into a long reverie. My life passed before me in images whose colors sang with strange symphonies; I started going back over the course of time, stopping at unforgettable dates.

I arrived at the distant years of youth when I had battled furiously to live, my heart swollen with immeasurable ambitions, tormented by insatiable appetites; and I lingered there with delight while certain charming details gradually emerged from the monotonous tint of the past, like holes of light in a fog.

One memory, above all, pursued me for some time and made me smile. It was in the month of May; I had left the obscure mansard in the Rue de Jeûners to which I went home after my long days of work; I went for a walk in the woods of Meudon with my first mistress, a blonde milliner, slim and cheerful, who loved me as I loved her, without any hidden agenda, without any thought for the morrow, just for the pleasure that we gave one another. We had a little money and we drank warm milk at a farm. Suddenly, she started, the milk spilled over her beautiful Sunday dress. She was distressed. We were hidden by a bushy arbor; I kissed her for a long time, and she forgot her chagrin. Her name was Marguerite. There were flowers everywhere....

...The clock, chiming midnight, extracted me from my reverie. The intervals between each of the strokes seemed long to me; the chime, metallic and sonorous, was lugubrious. I understood that the hour in question really does have something solemn about it; on hearing it fall into the heavy silence of my last night, I understood why it is designated for crime. And I told myself that it was necessary to finish it. In any case, I had nothing more to do: no testament, since my succession would probably be swallowed up by a deficit; no letters, since those I loved did not love me and would learn of my death with dry eyes.

I only wrote, on a piece of paper that I left in a prominent place: *Today, 26 June 1854, I have killed myself.* I signed it. As midnight had just sounded, I had hesitated slightly before writing the date.

[That piece of paper, which had initially gone astray, was found by the judiciary investigation *several days after Dr. Z*** had communicated his notes to me*, and removed all doubts concerning Monsieur van Gelt's demise.]

My decision was firmly made. I retained all my calmness, but it seemed to me that I was acting in a dream, that nothing that was happening was definitive, that I might suddenly wake up with new horizons before me, as in a splendid dawn—and without having to do anything for that.

Then I sank back in my armchair, my eyes glued to the weapon, the barrel of which was gleaming in the lamplight, hypnotizing me. A great torpor invaded me. Increasingly vague visions floated before me, occasionally making me smile. I would have liked to stay like that eternally, letting time go by without losing consciousness of its duration and yet without feeling any more, without thinking any more....

Then, suddenly, the memory of the resolution I had to carry out returned to me; reality reasserted itself. I shook myself, like a man about to go to sleep who suddenly remembers something he has forgotten to do and makes an effort to chase sleep away.

It was almost mechanically that I opened my jacket, my waistcoat and my shirt. I sought the location of the heart, which started beating violently under my hand, as if to affirm by its precipitate beats the strength of its life. At the same time I felt a glacial chill running through my veins; I believe that my teeth were chattering, although my brow was inundated with sweat. I made gestures of anguish; I was suffering like a patient on whom some painful operation is about to be carried out, who is afraid but desires to proceed even so, and who is pushing away the surgeon while crying to him: "Do it, then!"

Will-power triumphed, however, over the last revolts of instinct in a supreme contest, so rapid and passionate that it seemed to me to be a spasm; I was able to take the revolver, the ivory butt of which was burning my hand. I placed the muzzle slightly above the place where my heart was pounding, taking care to leave a little space between my flesh and the barrel of the weapon, which was trembling so much that I was obliged to steady it with my left hand. Finally, in a shudder of my entire being, dominated by a frightful terror of the unknown that loomed up before me, suddenly gripped by a desire to live as poignant as remorse and by regrets sharper than any pain, I pressed the trigger.

Truly, I believe that my will-power, at that precise moment, was annihilated, consumed as it had been by its final effort: the abandoned nerves simply carried out the action of their own accord, and movement commenced.

I felt an atrocious pain, but did not lose consciousness; undoubtedly, I had only broken a rib; I had to start again. But I was seized by a kind of delirium: mechanically, I pressed the trigger twice more without hearing the sound of the detonations. The last shot struck home, for I felt my heart stop beating, my blood pause in my veins, and a great rigidity stretch my limbs, like the hand of an invisible giant....

...I'm dead, there's no doubt about it. By what miracle, then, are Thought and Sensation obstinate in persisting within me? My eyes can no longer see, but I have a marvelously precise vision of what surrounds me; my ears can no longer hear, but the slightest sounds—the fluttering of a moth trapped in the room, the distant murmurs from outside, the sputtering of the lamp on the brink of going out—seem to me to be reverberating within me by virtue of a crystal clear echo; my limbs are already stiff, but I feel, scarcely muffled by a thick carpet,

23

the hardness of the parquet onto which I've slid; I can even perceive the odor of powder that fills the room.

I analyze my situation with a lucidity superior to any I've ever deployed before. "Undoubtedly," I say to myself, "this state won't last long; my thoughts will gradually stop, as my limbs are becoming cold and stiff"—that double sensation of cold and stiffness is excessively painful to me—"and my entire being will fall asleep in a benevolent final repose."

The memory even returns to me—for my faculties continue to operate as they did a little while before, perhaps better—of having heard in a lecture an account of the effects of curare poisoning, and I think that a phenomenon of the same kind is taking place in me, that I'm not dying in an instant, that it's necessary to be patient....

...But no! No appreciable diminution in my physical suffering, not the slightest disturbance in my reasoning; and that cold, the terrible cold that chills me to the marrow without my being able to shiver as I once could, when I was young and went to bed in a room without a fire!

And now those sensations are becoming more precise, as a poignant anxiety is added to them: what if this is the immortality of the soul that people talk about? What if it's necessary to remain like this throughout the cycle of the eternal ages, simultaneously dead and alive, Thought persisting in a stiff, cold body that is decaying? Who can tell? Perhaps God exists; perhaps this is the last torture that He inflicts on us; perhaps He punishes in this fashion those who have been unable to glimpse His infinity or who have transgressed His mysterious laws? Are there prayers that might touch Him...?

...The minutes and the hours elapse with an indescribable slowness. I start thinking about cataleptics who are buried alive, who wake up in the grave with howls stifled by the earth, gnawing their firsts, and convulsed by the pangs of asphyxia. What if, by virtue of some strange lesion that has never been produced before, of which surgery has no suspicions, I'm only in a state of catalepsy? What if I wake up in three or four days, or a week, convulsively, with an immutable weight on my chest...?

But no, it's impossible. I'm dead; I'm really dead. The human body is submissive to precise laws; it has been dismantled piece by piece, like a machine whose smallest mechanism is familiar. I felt the bullet pass through my heart; hence, I have nothing more to fear; my ideas will gradually calm down, silence will fall within me. My present state is logical; doubtless all the dead experience it, all of them have experienced that same anguish—and all of them have calmed down, as I shall calm down....

...Meanwhile, daybreak is beginning, in wan gleams that are trailing over me. There are noises outside in the street, reaching me as if through a thick wall. A few more minutes and my manservant, accustomed to waking me up early, will knock on the door, and, on receiving no reply, will come in. He's a worthy man, who has served me for ten years. I've been good to him in several circumstances; perhaps he'll miss me....

Then my wife will enter in her turn, and my nephew....

And I feel a frisson pass through me at the idea that I'll soon be able to measure their affection irrevocably....

Someone knocks on the door; for ten years, the same raps have been struck every morning, and it was my voice that replied. As no response is forthcoming, the knocking is repeated, more loudly.

The door opens.

Jean goes as pale as I must be, stifles a cry, makes a movement to go out, hesitates on the threshold, comes in and closes the door *carefully*....

He comes over to me, puts his hand over my heart, listens....

He carries me to my bed. Why is he looking at me with such a fearful expression? Why is he turning me to face the wall? I can see regardless, since my faculties are in some way disengaged from my senses, since I'm living a superior and independent life, since my vision is vaster in spite of the fixity of my eyes....

What is he going to do?

He goes to my writing-desk, to which I've given him a key. He opens it. He rummages in the drawers, striving to release a secret compartment whose mechanism he doesn't know, where the money is kept. I hear the dry click of gold coins in his hand....

And, the theft accomplished, although his legs are unsteady, although his teeth are still chattering with fear, utterly distressed, he runs out of the room shouting for help. People will say: "The domestic was very fond of his master, very faithful; one doesn't find his kind any more today...."

After all, he's a poor man. He would never have had the courage to steal from me while I was alive, and perhaps never had any such idea—and yet, the sight of my cadaver frightened him more than the law, to which he gave no thought. He must, therefore, be driven by a very powerful motive; undoubtedly he has immediately deduced the causes of my suicide, he has been struck by the sudden and clear awareness of his situation; he's no longer young, he was counting on remaining in my service for as long as I could provide him with a small income, or, if I died before him, that he'd be provided for in my testament. Instead of that, the hazard of seeking employment is emerging; all of the placid arrangement of his life has been disturbed....

Then again, who knows what school he has passed through previously; who knows what circumstances have rendered him sinful or defiant? Perhaps days devoid of bread have developed appetites in him stronger than his conscience, which would have bent him sooner or later to their irresistible domination. He has lived with me for ten years without my ever asking him about his life; perhaps he was abandoned as a child, or his father beat him without a reason, or his mother didn't love him....

And then, after all, I have no further need of the money that he's taken. It requires an effort of memory for me to recall that I've worked all my life to earn it, that I've killed myself because I was about to lack it, that others kill themselves for the same reason and live as I am living.

Two days ago, if I'd found the slightest irregularity in Jean's conduct, I'd have fired him without hesitation; for the slightest misdemeanor, I'd have dragged him pitilessly before the courts, because I was rigid, one of those who regarded it as a duty for honest men to pursue the guilty. Now, I'd like to be able to get up in order to tell the man, whose conscience is doubtless in torment, that I forgive him.

It's likely the beginning of detachment, or perhaps things are appearing to me in a different light?

My wife comes into the room, and says: "Leave me alone."

Now we're face to face, the torturer and her victim, and death has inverted the roles: she's the one who's suffering now. I can see the traces of her emotions and here remorse passing over her face; it's me who is placid and tranquil now.

She approaches me slowly, as if fascinated; she closes my eyes, whose fixity doubtless makes her feel uncomfortable; then she steps back....

I'll never know what she's thinking.

Perhaps I, who wanted her to be happy, made her unhappy. I remember how sad she was before the marriage, and that it didn't worry me; I said to myself: "It's the unknown of her new life that's troubling her...." Her parents forced her into it, I'm sure. Perhaps she was in love with someone else, with the omnipotent chastity of first love, and I doubtless wounded her virginal delicacies as I overturned her young woman's dreams. She must have cursed me....

She draws closer to me, very pale. She touches my hand. She recoils again with a movement of dread, as if that icy hand had burned her....

I don't reproach her at all, though, because I acted like other men: egotism blinded me; I thought I'd make her happy by taking her; it's a common illusion. She suffered because of me; what does it matter? Nothing remains of her tears any more than anything will remain of her regrets. I, too, have wept for her; already I can scarcely remember...and who knows...?

The door opens again; it's my nephew.

He stops a few paces away from her; then he comes closer. They're both grave. I've never calculated their struggles, never thought that their sin has doubtless cost them dear; that they loved one another, and took account of what they called their infamy, but that love conquers all, in accordance with the law of nature; that the things that the living find monstrous would appear quite natural to them if the passions of the moment didn't blind them....

Meanwhile, she rests her head on his shoulder with the gracious movement of a woman soliciting protection; and, her throat full of sobs, she says "He was very good, though!"

Was I good? I don't believe so. I only applied, no more and no less, whatever the circumstances, the rule that measured my actions against the common standard. I gave to beggars and I let the poor starve; according to the caprice of circumstances, I felt my heart ready to melt with pity, or as hard as stone; I respected the law, but I also made use of it for the defense of my interests; between two courses of action, I always chose the one to which I was more forcefully driven by the motives tyrannizing my will.

In sum, now that I can judge my life in its entirety, I don't regret any of what I've done and wouldn't want to have done anything differently—and yet, my activity seems to me to have been limited, futile and fatal.

After a silence, my nephew replies: "He was a true father to me."

I was mistaken on his account, therefore. I thought him ungrateful; he was unhappy.

She continues: "My God, how guilty we are!"

And they stand before me, ashamed.

Then she throws herself into his arms, weeping....

Oh, I wish I could get up and say to them: "Love one another! Love one another! Certainly not for the enjoyment of love, which isn't worth the pain, but because it isn't worth the pain, either, of struggling against one's desires!" They're young, they're handsome, the blood is seething in their veins; what right do I, an old man who has already had my share of joys, have to want to separate them...?

...The hours go by. It seems to me that a modification has taken place in my condition; I no longer feel any physical discomfort; the sensation of cold has disappeared; I even think that I'm enjoying lying down, as if after heavy fatigue, and the ideas that continue to pass through me no longer trouble me.

People come: old friends who mourn me. One of them, my oldest friend, stayed by my bedside for a long time without saying anything, shaking his head from time to time, doubtless thinking that it would soon be his turn, and dreading it. The indifferent have composed themselves at the door as they rang the bell, putting on distressed expressions as they took off their hats. The employees of the company have filed past one by one, buttoned up in worn frock coats and poorly gloved. They've been told that it was an apoplectic fit; they seemed anxious.

Candles are burning; a nun mumbles prayers by my bedside, which she interrupts with a sulky expression every time someone arrives....

I remember that once, when I was out walking, I sometimes saw a swarm of gnats swirling, flying in all directions like specks of dust, and didn't know whether they were following a common goal or whether chance alone determined the sum of their movements. Truly, it's the same for so many comings and goings, for those contradictory anxieties that I read on all the faces, for the warmth of the hands that touch mine fearfully and leave me with a vague impression of fever.

The human face no longer strikes me as anything but a distant memory; the people who pass around me seem like shadows moving in a mist. When I compare their agitation to my immobility, the sound of their footfalls, which they stifle as if they were afraid of waking me up, and the murmur their voices, with my silence, and the animation of their eyes with the fixity of mine beneath my permanently lowered lids, I wonder where the reality of existence is. Between their condition and mine, between being and non-being, is there really such an imperceptible nuance?

I contemplate life as a traveler who has just passed over a mountain and casts a glance behind him; he has been walking for a long time, his feet have been bruised by sharp stones, he has hesitated before many obstacles; but now, the torrents that barred his path are only thin white lines beneath his feet, the rocks that loomed up before him are black dots, he can no longer see the chasms into which he nearly fell, and the distance traveled seems to him to be such a little matter that he thinks he could touch the nearby peak with his finger.

Then, the shadows of evening rise up, everything is drowned and disappears into a uniform shade; space no longer exists.

Night falls. My wife has decided to keep vigil with the nun. They've both fallen asleep. In the efforts of their respiration, I hear painful thoughts, poorly allayed, or heavy dreams pursuing them. The idea of their actions, which they're judging sinful in their imperfect consciences, is still troubling them, and also concern for things that they believe to be important.

In my slumber, which is better than theirs and devoid of nightmares, nothing similar is happening. Of forgotten cares nothing remains in me but indifference, and I understand irresponsibility....

...At times, my brain stops: I'm no longer thinking....

...The second day begins. My vision of the things surrounding me is not as clear; the golden dots of the candle flames are fading. Noises are muffled; and the sensation of blindness and deafness that is invading me, instead of being painful, is full of charm.

My son has arrived. He has fallen into a chair at the foot of my bed, without speaking. I don't know where he has come from, or how the news of my death reached him; perhaps he learned about it from a newspaper in some café. Anyway, I have no curiosity in his regard, although I judge him differently as well. Instead of letting his youth develop, I compress it, wanting him to work as I had worked, without taking account of the difference in our situations, "on principle," as I put it. I opposed him in his inclinations, to the extent of preventing him from pursuing the career of his preference. From childhood, I measured out his pleasures sparingly, under the pretext of showing him the miserliness of life's joys. Was it astonishingly that his youth burst forth?

He had, all things considered, no reason to love me, but he's mourning me; his conduct was the fatal result of circumstances for which he is not culpable, but he's deploring it; it's the illogicality of every thought that life crushes. While vain remorse torments him, I understand him and I absolve him—to tell the truth, without afflicting myself with his condition, without sympathizing with his undeserved anguish, without my stillness being in any way troubled by his grief, for afflictions are frozen along with the blood.

With the supreme intelligence of things that I feel within me, I also feel the supreme indifference. In the same way that I have escaped all the laws of human morality, and now finally understand relativity, I have fled the tyranny of the heart. I have no more hatred for those who made me suffer than gratitude for those who have loved me. The good and bad hours that I owe to the commerce of human beings are now too distant for me to be able to make any distinction between them.

Every day, in life, does one not experience agreeable or painful sensations of which one does not retain any memory? No one, for example, thinks for days on end about the pleasure he had experienced in a scented bath, or a good meal, or entering into a warm room after having suffered from cold, any more than the pain caused by a pinprick or bumping into a door. Well, my great joys and my great pains, those that caused me to wander the streets with my chest on the point of explosion, those which made me, an adult, weep as a child weeps, all of that is as distant, as faded, as depleted as the thousand fugitive impressions that every day bears away and replaces. How, then, can the slightest rancor against those who have afflicted me subsist in me, since the pain has gone? And how can the slightest affection, since the memory of individuals no longer awakens anything within me...?

...My son and my wife have always detested one another. This morning, a few hours before the burial, they seemed to be reconciled by their common mourning and remorse; they wept together. But the crisis of despair passed; they started talking about ordinary things, about me, and suddenly, in response to something my wife said, an argument burst forth. They blamed one another reciprocally for my death.

"You're the one that killed him!"

And I learned, thus, new details regarding both of them. While I was alive, by virtue of a kind of tacit complicity, they closed their eyes to their respective faults, helping one another if necessary, in spite of the fact that their intimacy was less powerful than their self-interest. Now the common enemy is no longer there; they can tear one another apart at their ease. They display before me their improper actions: how the adulterous affairs began; by what methods of dissimulation they kept them hidden for a long time.

"Your chambermaid knew everything; at what price did you buy her silence?"

I learn that my son's theft was not the only one he committed in my employ; that when he started on that path, he was driven by a long series of dishonorable faults.

29

"Wasn't it me who paid for your first mistake? You didn't ask me then where I got the money?"

I also learn about my own defects: I was too demanding for everyday life; I complained needlessly about unimportant things; I had ridiculous manias, the manias of an old man of which my wife made fun; I frightened everyone around me with my severity...what do I know now?

Perhaps all that was true—but what does it matter?

The quarrel continues, although the time is approaching when they will come to fetch my body. I know them better now than I ever did, better than I knew myself. I see that, even just now, I was entertaining illusions on their account; their tears deceived me; perhaps they were false; perhaps they were putting on an act and juggling their sentiments in order to fool themselves.

And yet, I persist in my judgment: they're neither better nor worse than anyone else; human beings are malleable dough, which things fashion and soil at their whim; they're passive mirrors in which images leave their reflection, sometimes pleasant to behold and sometimes repulsive; the bed of an eternal stream over which filth and flowers flow. It's life that forms them; life alone is guilty and dirty.

Questions of money come up incessantly in their dispute. Suddenly, my wife goes pale, struck by a sudden idea: she has been wrong to irritate my son.

"My God!" she cries. "What will become of me if he hasn't made a will?"

My son replies: "What good is a will? He's ruined." And he adds: "It's your expenses—you, who came into the house like a beggar...."

She interrupts him, standing up in front of him: "Didn't you leave it like a thief?"

They're white with anger, both trembling; their sadness and their remorse have disappeared.

He moves toward her, his arm raised. She doesn't recoil.

"Oh, hit me! Hit me! You're cowardly enough for that. But be careful! I'll defend myself!"

She picks up a knife that happened to be close at hand. Are they going to fight, here and now, without waiting for me to be taken away?

My son retreats slowly. He stops on the threshold and says: "Hurry up and marry one of your lovers, so that we can be rid of you!"

He says that very loudly; if any servants were passing in the corridor, they would have been able to hear it. My wife has drawn closer to me, as if to ask for protection....

...It seems to me that I can hear, very distantly, a storm. The same rumbling that might perhaps make passengers on a ship howl in terror, lulls me like a gentle murmur. The wind, which is tearing sails and breaking masts out there, is a fresh breeze brushing my face like a beloved breath. Because of the distance, the sea seems to me to be scarcely rippled, and I take the vessels, tossed and twisted, overturned, for motionless dots. The anguish of the unfortunates struggling desperately finds no echo in me, so replete am I in the sentiment of my security....

...I am no longer paying any heed to the miserable quarrels in which I once took part, and it will not be long before I'm separated forever from human beings by the earth heaped on top of me....

...That desired moment is approaching; the supreme ceremony is beginning.

I can hear the sound of sobbing; anger has given way once again to tears, more appropriately. There are whispers. People are there.

The lid of my coffin is lowered. I can no longer see anything. I can scarcely perceive the noises in the room. The nailing begins; at the first blow of the hammer all the voices have fallen silent, as if frightened by that harsh sound, which is imprisoning me in the supreme solitude. Then, that task finished, footsteps resume, a dull agitation. How many times I have waited, in bereaved houses, for the signal to follow the coffin, in the crowd of relatives and guests; and almost always, thoughts of matters other than death followed me....

...I am hoisted onto the hearse, slightly astonished not to feel any shock; it appears that I am separated from material sensation, without having lost all consciousness of what is happening around me. The procession sets off; the noise of horses' hooves, wheels and footfalls is only a muted buzz for me. It requires a mental effort for me to imagine myself being transported from one place to another; the notion of movement no longer exists. All of space seems to me to be constituted by this tiny corner that I occupy, in which everything is without any movement. If I did not have memories and experiences, I could easily believe that the world is rotating, and that while it rotates, specific objects remain eternally in place....

...Prayers for the dead are chanted, which the organ accompanies with its purring. From time to time, the halberd of a Swiss Guard sounds a dry click on the paving stones, or the hand bell instructs the assembly to kneel down....

When I was alive, I had fits of atheism in which I wanted to overthrow the Church. I detested its religious ceremonies, which I found puerile to the point of derision. Well, I judge them differently now; I don't feel any need for God, of course; I have no more idea than before whether He exists or not, in Heaven or elsewhere. It seems to me, however, that those monotonous chants might soothe and appease the dolor of the living, that they might engender vague hopes—deceptive but consoling—in hearts still full of doubt. As for the dead, that last echo of human voices that reach them, those genuflections that they represent in memory, the movements of the costumed priests...all of that summarizes admirably the nullity of their lives, and all life; if any regret for the things left behind still subsists, it will fade away completely into that supreme solemnity.

I am carried away, and we walk for a long time. My thoughts still wander over religious questions. I can't make up my mind whether God is a useful or a harmful invention; undoubtedly, He doesn't matter, like everything else that humans have found.

I am lowered into the ground; the spadefuls of earth that are thrown down rattle on my coffin. This is the moment when all the affection that there is in living human hearts for the dead feels stirred to the depths by the dry thud that a slightly larger pebble sometimes renders sonorous. Among the murmur of those desolations, the priest resumes his prayers...I know that, although I cannot hear them; I can no longer hear anything. The separation from the living is accomplished; I can no longer even perceive the noise that the people I loved are making as they leave; I have no knowledge of the final tears that are being shed for me....

...Time has moved on, but nothing can any longer allow me to distinguish the minutes or the hours, the seasons or the years. I shall not know when the flowers bloom whose roots will soon plunge into my being. I shall not feel the warmth of the summer sun; I shall not be cold when the snow extends over the dead grass like another shroud; in spring, I shall not hear the chirping of the birds in my cypress, in which the sap is rising. And I experience a kind of voluptuousness in thinking about the confusion of everything into which I am disappearing. There was a time when, although I remained motionless and awake, the minutes seemed long to me; now, the minutes melt into one another to form eternity, as drops of water do to make a river, and they draw me gently into their flow....

...Gradually, my memories dissolve. I can scarcely recall my life. It seems to me that I can see a long way, and very high. I am no longer merely the traveler whom the mirages of arrival deceive as to the distance covered; I am the aeronaut suspended in space, at heights that humans have never reached. He no longer sees the cities, the mountains seem to him to be imperceptible pimples, the seas puddles, and of all the noise that creatures make, no murmur reaches him; above the drifting and disintegrating clouds illuminated by strange light, he floats as if in a new element.

The events of which my life was formed are gradually erased: my poor childhood, my youth full of struggles, my years of prosperity, the sadness of my latter days, all draw away and melt into a uniform hue. I forget the differences between pleasure and pain. I no longer know that I once loved; no memory of any kind whatsoever can trouble my thoughts, which continue to flow nevertheless, but slowly and with an exceeding limpidity, like a body to which nothing can form an obstacle.

One last concern remains in me—or rather, one problem whose solution still interests me: I seek to know by what series of successive impulsions my will had determined my suicide, which required so much effort.

I rediscover the motives, by an effort of memory, but I no longer understand how the dread of ruination, regret for a dead woman, fear of malady, the dolor of being deceived—all those abstractions—were able to change into a brutal fact, to provoke a positive resolution and a real suffering.

Certainly, I don't regret having killed myself; in the space where I am, there is no room for regret; but I can't explain to myself how the motives for my action were able to emerge from the indifferent monotony of things and act upon me to the point of making me exchange one condition for another. The acuity of the sorrow, the force of affections, the tenacity of anguish—those are the notions that escape me. The veil that, at a time that I can no longer measure, already enveloped and hid my memories of time past, and has thickened. Everything that once happened to me appears as material objects appear, in an increasingly profound darkness. Vague forms move heavily in my thoughts; I imagine that during the long nights of the Arctic regions, the blocks of ice move in the same way....

...At times, I amuse myself with efforts to recover the details of my life or the faces of those I loved, and the very futility of those evocations satisfies me. When I was alive, it sufficed for me to close my eyes immediately to see faces that had long disappeared, and so clearly that I could have believed myself to be beside them. At present, in this obscurity in which my eyes are always closed, I seek in vain; the images are no longer designed; and it's without the slightest regret that I observe the flight of those shades, however dear.

Thus, everything fades away, as if Time, which marches on without my hearing it, were destroying gently, one by one, the impressions engraved within me....

Indeed, I remember that a few hours ago—or a few minutes, or a few days; I no longer know—certain events of my past became exact to me again, preoccupying me. At present, I can no longer locate them; I am, therefore, escaping myself; the sentiment of my own personality is fleeing me, like the memories, like all fatiguing impressions. I no longer know exactly what my *self* is; I seems to me that I'm melting into millions of beings, that I'm disappearing into things, that I'm no longer anything but one with a formidable unity....

If humans succeed in imagining that which cannot be seen, cannot be heard and cannot be felt; if, above all, they have a presentiment that one only arrives by a slow gradation at the conditions of which I'm on the brink, disaccustoming the self to past habits...they would no longer fear Death. That king of terrors, as their sages call it, would bring them an unalterable peace, the delights of a slumber whose duration is unmarked, on a bed so soft that it cannot be felt. In the great silence and the great obscurity of the tomb, nothing exists but soothing sensuality, which becomes ever more gentle, like fading gleams, like dwindling harmonies....

I sense that my brain is still alive—but my thoughts are deliciously asleep....

33

Michel Corday: *The Mysterious Dajan-Phinn*

"Le Mystérieux Dajan-Phinn,"—*translated as* "The Mysterious Dajan-Phinn"—*first appeared in two parts in the April 14 and May 15, 1908 issues of* Je Sais Tout, *one of a new generation of French "middlebrow" magazines, which was specifically modeled on the English periodical* The Strand. *Like it,* Je Sais Tout *gladly played host to several flourishing genres of popular fiction, giving pride of place to detective fiction, including stories featuring Maurice Leblanc's famous gentleman-burglar Arsène Lupin, but by no means scorning scientific romance—although, as with* The Strand, *its editors soon decided that scientific romance was insufficiently popular and gradually de-emphasized it.*

The author of the present story, Michel Corday (1870-1937), was a prolific contributor to periodicals of that sort, but he soon learned that it was more profitable to concentrate on more popular genres, although he retained an interest in the genre in spite of the difficulty in marketing it, producing an offbeat thriller in collaboration with André Couvreur, Le Lynx *(1911; tr. as* The Lynx*)[5] and two quasi-Utopian futuristic fantasies.*

There is a sense in which "Le Mystérieux Dajan-Phinn" *harks back to the 1860s boom in the popularization of science, in that it refers to one of the great controversies of that decade, brought to a head by a presentation made to the Académie des Sciences in 1864 by Louis Pasteur, who claimed to have demolished Frédéric Pouchet's alleged experimental demonstration of the spontaneous generation of life by a process of "fermentation." Although it was a spectacular coup in terms of public relations, and is still held up today as a triumphant victory securing the "germ theory" against its inept competitor, the extent of the consequences of Pasteur's demonstration remained questionable, and modern commentators tend to forget that his primary motivation was his hatred of Darwinism, which he supposed to be dependent on spontaneous generation and which, therefore, he thought he had demolished along with the latter.*

Corday's story is interested in the way in which "orthodox science" rejected the theory of spontaneous generation so conclusively that it began to dismiss any argument in favor of it a priori, regardless of any experimental support that such arguments might claim. In developing this theme, however, it is very noticeable that Corday is still working with the same assumptions that underlie others' stories, regarding the psychology of scientists and the incompatibility of scientific obsession with the joys of domestic life, and using those assumptions to generate the narrative tension of his melodrama.

B.S.

---

[5] Tr. as *The Lynx*, Black Coat Press, ISBN 978-1-61227-273-3.

It is 9 a.m. on a cool April morning, on the platform at the Gare de Lyon; scattered groups are awaiting the arrival of the express from Marseilles. All faces are turned toward the luminous access-route, amid a view encumbered by signals and motionless trains, watching for the first glimpse of the engine. If all the foreheads are orientated by the same gesture, however, how diverse are the thoughts that they conceal! What varied motives these seemingly-identical impatiences have!

Examine the little group of two ladies and three gentlemen who have advanced to the very edge of the platform. These five people have come to meet Doctor Bro, returned from Borneo after an absence of seven years. How disparate their sentiments are, though! To grasp them, it will be necessary to know the man who inspires them.

It would, it's true, require a fine mind to define Dr. Bro exactly. When he left for the Orient, at 45 years of age, his contemporaries had the most contradictory opinions of him: an unsound mind; a universal intelligence; an innocent; a charlatan; a semi-lunatic; a superman. His life had been hectic. As a naval physician, he had once traveled the world with an avid curiosity and a relentless ardor. He wanted to try everything, to know everything, to exercise himself in all the directions of human activity. Then, at about 30, during an extended stopover in Malaya, he had become enamored of a young orphan in the Dutch colony and had married her. Renouncing his naval career, he seemed to want to settle in Borneo, to devote himself to personal endeavors within the tranquility of the family. After two years, however, his wife had died giving birth to a little girl.

Bro threw himself violently into pure science. Having returned to France, he confided his little Suzanne to the care of a nurse, then to the protection of a boarding-school, and plunged himself entirely into his work. For more than two years he divided his time between his laboratories and research stations of marine physiology where attempts were being made to wrench the secret of organic origins from the oceans.

Finally, he published the results of his research on the living cell. Picking up the theory of spontaneous generation after Traube, Leduc and Raphael Dubois,[6] he claimed, with evidential support, to be able to create life. He displayed

---

[6] Moritz Traube (1826-1894), Stéphane Leduc (1853-1939) & Raphael Dubois (1849-1929). If anyone doubts the force and scope of the scientific "orthodoxy" that set out to crush and annihilate the theory of spontaneous generation, they only have to consult the on-line biographies of these scientists and observe how their championship of the notion has either been expunged from the record of their careers or radically downplayed. We now know for sure, of course, that the theory is false, but in their day, the evidence was still weak enough to permit controversy, and there was no shame in their espousal. Modern readers of this

artificial vegetation made with his own hands. The manufacture and the experiments, the news of which expanded beyond the scientific world to reach the crowd, were passionately contested.

By a singular hazard, his most redoubtable adversary was his best friend. This Bro, in whom brutal grief and the empery of science seemed to have dried up the wellsprings of affection, had remained faithful, throughout his turbulent life, to one adolescent friendship—but Ruchard, whom he had known during his student years, had followed a straight line. Now a famous professor, he defended orthodox theories with authority, from the height of State-approved chairs. Exasperated by the sight of his old companion compromising himself with pursuits that he deemed chimerical, he castigated him in private and pursued him in public. The contest was too unequal; Bro was vanquished. His doctrines were reduced to the rank of alchemical dreams and his experiments to the dimensions of puerile games.

Perhaps the defeat was all the more painful because it was inflicted by a friend. Nevertheless, he let nothing of that sort of that show. He did not fall out with the triumphant Ruchard. Shortly afterwards, however, he went into exile. His brother, the landscape-painter César Bro, had just got married. He entrusted Suzanne to the young household. As for himself, he applied for and obtained a post in the zoological gardens of Borneo.

It was thought, by those around him, that he was going to try to forget his disappointments in the country where he had got married, and where he had spent a few happy and peaceful years. For seven years, his letters—rare and brief—remained mute regarding his work, his leisure and his inner life. Detached from his relatives, indifferent to the questions that had impassioned him, in retreat from the world, he seemed to have accomplished a sort of moral suicide.

An event came into prospect, however, from which he could not disinterest himself: his daughter's marriage. If it had been a matter of some random fiancé, no doubt he would have left the matter to the clairvoyance of those he had placed in charge of Suzanne and given his consent, nothing more. But could he accept for a son-in-law, without protest, the son of Dr. Ruchard? Such was the man, in fact, to whom it would be necessary for him to give his daughter, according to the two young people in question—for they were in love with one another. Each appeared to the other as the living promise of honor.

Let no one see in this choice one of those fatal hazards which, in novels and plays, throw heroes destined to avoid one another together. There was nothing simpler and more logical than the circumstances of which the affinity was born. Professor Ruchard, although he had acted in the contest according to his scientific beliefs and in the interests of his friend, had experienced remorse over

---

story may find it advantageous to reassume an open mind temporarily, in spite of the certainty of hindsight.

his excessively complete victory. He deemed himself partly responsible for the exile in which his old companion had buried himself alive. He had tried to repair the damage to the extent that was possible, and he had taken an interest and developed an attachment to the young girl who, without him, might perhaps have retained a father.

A widower himself, Ruchard found favor in the family in which the girl lived. That intimacy became greater still when Henri Ruchard, the professor's son, who was gifted with a considerable talent as a painter, took César Bro as a tutor. Thus the two young people were able, for years, to enjoy the benefits of one of those frank and healthy friendships in which temperaments and characters are revealed and tested, which ought to be the veritable school of marriage.

Warned by a letter from his brother—a small masterpiece of prudent diplomacy and emotional eloquence—Dr. Bro said that he might give his reply in two months' time. By the hundred-and-twentieth day, they were watching out for it with every mailboat from the Far East. Finally, a telegram came from Borneo: *Am returning.* Nothing else. And by means of a telegram dated the previous evening, from Marseilles, Bro had announced his return for that very morning.

One can now imagine the mental dispositions of the two young people and their family standing on the platform of the railway station.

The most excited, by far, is Suzanne Bro. She is going to see her father again. Oh, certainly, a father with whom she had hardly ever lived, whom she recalls in her schoolgirl memories, always feverish, quivering with the tension of thought, always about to leave. She does not hold that semi-abandonment against him. He must have suffered so much...having been left alone after two years of marriage, and then experienced so much unjust disappointment. Yes, unjust. Her knowledge of the great quarrel in which her father and Professor Ruchard were involved is somewhat confused, but she feels, and is sure, that her father was right. She has faith in him. And it is precisely because he was right that he was able to forgive his fortunate rival.

As for thinking that her father, in consequence of those old differences, might oppose his daughter's marriage, she refuses to believe it. Besides, will she not be able to vanquish him, to seduce him, if he makes any sign of resistance? One knows one's power. One is 20 years old. One is not too repulsive. And is there not a joy that must override and efface everything, for a father who has left an indecisive little girl to recover a fully-grown young woman, neat and blonde in the typical Dutch manner, with eyes of a blue so limpid that they seem to instill a desire to bow down before them?

One person who is not bringing so much forbearance or confidence to the station platform is young Henri Ruchard. He cares very little about the living cell, its opponents and defenders. It is sufficient to observe his energetic and harsh features, his face contracted with jealous passion, to divine that he would gladly have left in Malaya the restless fanatic on whom his happiness depends.

Professor Ruchard, by contrast, is standing tall, with his broad shoulders and his flourishing rosette, his handsome head serene and magnanimous. He is glad to have come to wait for his old friend to jump down from the train, effacing by that amicable step any possible rancor.

César Bro, slender and placid in appearance, is thinking sadly about the older brother from whom the vicissitudes of life have so often separated him and whose daughter has become almost as dear to him as his own children. The common memories of their childhood have, however, woven bonds between them that the imminent return causes to vibrate. And, with the instincts of a painter and the weakness of a man, he is apprehensive of the signs of age with which the last seven years have inflicted on both of them and which they will discover in one another's faces at the first glance...

His wife, a cheerful and tender individual, a little bit romantic, in the full glory of 30 years of age, is awaiting the traveler she hardly knows with the avid curiosity of an audience-member anticipating the denouement of a play. Not that she has the slightest doubt about the outcome of the adventure. She would like to see someone get in the way of the marriage of the two young people, whose idyll she has nurtured with so much benevolence! But who knows whether some unforeseen plot-twist might not emerge?

The train! Here comes the train!

Indeed, tall and dark, coiffed with a plume of white smoke, the engine surges forth amid the motionless trains that cramp the horizon. The black caterpillar of carriages undulates, seems to hesitate, even to draw away, but finally plunges into the station, drawing slowly level with the platform, and its doors open.

Gazes meet and search for one another. Hands wave. Muffled exclamations are heard, like moans of happiness. Already the most agile have leapt down to the ground. Some slip into the crowd, as if in a hurry to disappear and plunge into the city. Others are immediately seized, imprisoned by effusions.

Suzanne has discovered her father, leaning out of a window. "There he is!"

Everyone follows her.

Dr. Bro brandishes his traveling cap. An unforgettable vision! Beneath the overhanging brows, pitted by wrinkles and swollen with projections, in the hollow of blue-tinted and profound ridges, his mobile eyes have a phosphorescent yellow gleam. The abrupt nose displays the black holes of the nostrils. Sparse, indecisive hair, red, blond and white at the same time, frames the rictus of his mouth, curling over the jutting chin, climbing the thin cheeks, quivering alongside the faun's ears, and evaporating down on its shapeless and tumultuous skull. And that chaotic, almost simian face, soiled with dust and carbon-grease, is resplendent with intelligence.

With a bound, elbowing people out of the way and bumping into suitcases, indifferent to collisions, Dr. Bro surges toward his relatives. A white scarf is around his neck. A discolored waterproof overcoat envelops his short figure. In the confusion and emption of the first contact he lavishes awkward kisses and nervous handshakes, stammering neutral words from tremulous lips.

Suddenly, he takes off, plunges into the crowd, and then reappears, holding the arm of a tall and handsome young man with an exceedingly pale complexion and an exceedingly brown beard. In a familiar manner, amicably clapping the unknown on the shoulder, he introduces him, in a voice clear, musical and a trifle vulgar, whose charm is surprising: "My laboratory assistant Dajan-Phinn, a very distinguished fellow, a native of Borneo, who wanted to come with me and continue to render me his assistance."

The stranger slowly takes off his hat. Heads and upper bodies incline. But this unexpected presence alarms and embarrasses the intimate little group, and that malaise increases in the family omnibus that carries everyone to César Bro's house, where a lunch is to celebrate the return of the absentee. The painter has been obliged to invite Dajan-Phinn, for the doctor has clearly expressed the intention of not being separated from his pupil.

In the racket of the rattling windows, everyone falls silent. No allusion to the past, or the imminent future. No effusiveness, no surges of affection. Nothing is exchanged but glances. Bro contents himself with scrutinizing faces.

The presence of the unknown is not sufficient on its own to explain the general mutism, but his appearance is fascinating. The gaze is fatally attracted by that extraordinary beauty, that nacreous complexion set within that coal-black beard, that face in which one searches in vain for an imperfection, in which nature has not committed any sin of color or design, in which every feature, taken in isolation, compels admiration and gives an impression of the ideal realized. In him, all is harmony, from his slender but solid build and his delicate joints to his careful and discreet bearing.

And yet the mind does not experience a complete satisfaction. What secretly irritates it is being unable to penetrate the mind that lives behind that admirable mask.

Does he feel lost, out of his element, transported to the other side of the world, among people he does not know, the swarming of the city? But on that face of triumphant beauty, which one would like to see animated by a flame as beautiful as itself, there is nothing to be seen but a slight astonishment, like the amazement of being alive...

César Bro lives in a villa near the Boulevard Pereire, a discrete house nestling in the depths of a garden. It is on the threshold of that pleasant swelling that the little company disembarks, still numbed by the long journey through the city.

After a rapid and summary refreshment, Dr. Bro launched forth on an exploration of the house, with which he was unfamiliar. Accompanied by the silent Dajan-Phinn and his brother, he bounded upstairs to the studio, which occupied the entire second floor. Running around, pausing and rummaging, he offered an appreciation of every canvas in precise terms, whose justice the painter was obliged to admit. Then he plunged down to the ground floor and sprawled on a sofa, head back, arms on the cushions and legs crossed, praised the painter for having combined the drawing-room and dining-room, took an interest in the Louis XV furniture, judged it authentic while pointing out a restored side-table, savored the old rose and pale blue wallpaper, gallantly declared that its flowery tints suited blondes and that his sister-in-law and daughter resembled, among these delicately-woven fabrics, golden bees at the heart of a corolla.

At that point, the painter's two children returned from their morning stroll; Bro took possession of them, set them on his knees, promised Chinese dolls to the three-year-old Lise and a Malay kris to the seven-year-old Claude, inspected their teeth, ears, palates, the inner surfaces of their eyelids and enumerated, very exactly, a few weaknesses of their complexion, prescribed a regime, assured himself of their knowledge and, as they were learning English with their governess, began to sing a minstrel refrain to them in a hearty voice.

Half an hour after his arrival, he knew the house, objects and people alike, as if he had always lived there.

At table, he was liveliness personified. Occupied in talking, he ate and drank whimsically. Sometimes, he forgot a dish on his plate, and then dispatched it in two or three mouthfuls in order to make up for lost time. Sometimes, he returned to a dish, not out of greed, but out of distraction, not realizing that he had already served himself once. He left all his glasses full, then emptied them one after the other, mixing the vintages and the colors. And above that incoherence and massacre his gestures fulgurated and his flavorsome speech sang.

Between the hors d'oeuvres and dessert, Bro re-lived his seven years in the Far East. He sculpted anecdotes, launched witticisms, mimed scenes, sketched locations. He was malicious, subtle, ingenious and profound. In accordance with an evident premeditation, however, he abstained from any allusion to his own work, to any scientific development, either by virtue of the skill of a conversationalist who fears boring his audience, or because he was firmly resolved to avoid any controversy with Ruchard, by awakening old questions that had been laid to rest.

He only interrupted himself to take Dajan-Phinn for his witness. The young stranger expressed himself in a very pure French. Doubtless unfamiliar with our language, however, he hesitated momentarily, with his mouth partly open, before speaking. Then, once released, his sentence would flow like a spring. Bro never took his eyes off him, encouraging him vocally and by gesture.

"Dajan-Phinn is a modest fellow," he declared. "He speaks six languages admirably: French, Dutch, German, English, Spanish and the Malay idiom most commonly used on his island. It's the embarrassment of choice that paralyzes him. Come on, don't be afraid. You're among friends."

At first, the young man abbreviated his replies, restricting them to the strictly necessary. Gradually, however, he gained in confidence, and when the meal was over, Dajan-Phinn had almost raised himself to the cordial tone that

Bro's verve and good humor had given to the reunion. The doctor's gaiety seemed, in fact, to bode well. How could a man so full of zest be contemplating opposition to the wishes of his entire family?

Henri Ruchard, however, did not share this happy mental disposition. As everyone rose from the table to take coffee he isolated Suzanne Bro in a corner of the room. Her face radiant, she was already getting ready to rejoice with him with regard to the favorable omens, but he shook his head.

"I understand your confidence, but I don't share it. Now that our fate is about to be decided, I'm afraid; I'm not reassured..."

"Why?" she interjected, swiftly.

"Because your father manifests no bitterness, does it follow that he doesn't experience any? Do we know what he's thinking, de down?"

"But..."

"The proof that he's capable of hiding his true thoughts is that he has let none of them show for seven years. Certainly, the blow was hard: ten years of work, a whole assembly of doctrines; a whole set of experiments that would have revolutionized the world, all reduced to nothing, to less than nothing, by a few weeks of controversy. What a disappointment, what a blow! And yet, your father has never shown mine his resentment. By his exile, he seemed to abandon the contest—but has he renounced all hope of revenge?"

Many times already, before Dr. Bro's return, the two young people had broached this redoubtable question—but it seemed to be resolved by the very attitude of the traveler. That was what the young woman could not help opposing to her companion.

"Oh, come on! Does he present the appearance of someone who's been nursing a resentment, or who's considering causing us any difficulty? Look at him."

He obeyed. At the far end of the room, beside the fireplace, Dr. Bro, with his hand set familiarly on Dajan-Phinn's shoulder, was standing in front of Ruchard, who was sitting beside the lady of the house—and the animated cheerfulness of his old companion lit up the haughty and tranquil face of the professor with a smile.

The young man remained anxious, however. With his head bowed, he resumed: "Yes, perhaps you're right—but it doesn't matter. Why that long silence, then this abrupt return? There's something abnormal and mysterious about all this..." Then, suddenly revealing his true dread, he went on: "And look—this Dajan-Phinn. Do you find his presence natural? What is this tenebrous beauty, black and white like a domino, as multilingual as a hotel porter? We don't know where he comes from, or what he's come to do here. Have you noticed your father's insistence on praising him highly, on showing him off? Are you sure that he doesn't have plans for that dear pupil, that he isn't the fiancé he has in mind for you?"

This time, Suzanne burst out laughing. "What an idea! And what under-handed thoughts you're crediting to my poor Papa!"

Henri loosed a gesture of annoyance with himself. "Yes, I was wrong to tell you all that. But you mustn't hold it against me. If I'm anxious, it's out of dread. I'm so afraid of seeing some obstacle rise up between us, at the very moment when our fate seems settled. There are moments, you see, when I'm almost tempted to go find my father, and ask him not to talk to yours today, if he has any intention of doing so, so fearful am I of knowing, so preferable does doubt sometimes seem to certainty..."

Moved by this anguish and wanting to hide her own anxiety, she said, jok-ingly: "But I forbid you to do that. I feel so sure of the result." Then, suddenly becoming serious, she added: "Besides, it's too late. Look."

He turned round. Ruchard had risen to his feet and was leaning toward Dr. Bro's ear. The latter, acquiescing with a nod of the head, confided Dajan-Phinn to his sister-in-law. Laughing graciously, she invited him to sit next to her. The two men left the room.

They went up to the studio. Behind the imposing mass of the professor, who made the narrow oak-wood staircase creak, Bro climbed with an uneven and hurried gait—and he contrast between the two individuals was further in-creased in the bright crisp daylight that descended from the skylights. His solid clean-shaven face fully lit, his handsome plump white hands on the arms of his armchair, Ruchard seemed to be posing for his portrait. Incapable of keeping still, astride a chair one moment, throwing himself on a divan whose springs re-turned him to his feet the next, Bro tried hard to relight a stout cigar, which, moistened and reduced to pulp, fell apart.

In a voice habituated to the professorial chair, but humanized by benevo-lence, Richard opened fire.

"My dear friend, I'll get straight to the point. You know why I've brought you here. Our children are in love. I only have my son. You only have your daughter. We both want them to be happy. Let's marry them. Your brother has written as much to you, and I hope that I don't have to see in your delay in re-plying as an indication of opposition, and especially not the residue of old quar-rels that once..."

Bro, who had stopped moving momentarily, bounded toward his friend and waved a peremptory hand in front of the professor's august lips.

"Shh! Shh! Let's not talk about that, let's say nothing about it. It's neces-sary not to confuse the issues. The happiness of our children has nothing to do with our laboratory disputes. I lost the game. I even think that I've been a rather good sport. But, after all, you beat me. That's understood. And it's not the mo-ment to reopen the debate..."

"In that case...?" Ruchard began.

Bro was following his own train of thought, though. "Now, if I haven't re-plied to César's letter, it's because, as soon as I received it, I decided to return to

France—but I'd undertaken a project that I absolutely had to finish before my departure. I was overwhelmed by work. In brief, I kept putting off from one day to the next the joy of bringing my reply myself..."

"So it's favorable?" the professor interjected.

Bro gripped his hands. "Can you doubt it, my dear friend? Such a project honors me and fulfils my desires..."

Ruchard got to his feet and breathed out expansively. "Mine too, believe me! And the proof is that your silence made me dread some snag. Without reproach, since you were decided, you might have spared the loving couple a two-month delay..."

A shadow of embarrassment passed over Dr. Bro's noble features. In an uncertain voice he said: "I couldn't...I didn't want to...in sum, I wanted to bring my reply in person."

"Let's not leave them in suspense any longer, then," said Ruchard, heading for the door. "As for the practical arrangements, in which we can't be uninvolved, I've discussed them with your brother. I know that he touched upon them in his letter. I hope that we're entirely in agreement in that respect too..."

"Perfectly, perfectly!" declared Bro, precipitating himself downstairs.

Professor Ruchard follow him ponderously. Had he exaggerated his anxieties during the months of waiting and incomprehensible silence? Had his son's impassioned disquiet gradually infected him? But his prompt and facile victory disconcerted him. It was the unease of deliverance, anguish in triumph, the state of mind of an assailant who believes a redoubt to be strongly guarded and finds it empty.

Henri Ruchard went swiftly through the garden in front of César Bro's house. It was May. New leaves were bursting forth on all sides: that Paris verdure which hastens to blossom as if it knew that it would die young in the July heat. But Suzanne Bro's fiancé seemed indifferent to the external world. Familiar with the house, he went straight up to the studio.

The pensive painter, one eye half-closed by the smoke of his cigarette, was sketching beside a box of charcoal. His wife was writing at a little table. They were alone.

While he shook hands with them, in a warm but slightly abrupt fashion, she said to him: "Have you seen Suzanne?"

Distractedly, he replied: "No, but I'm not displeased to find you alone first."

He seemed so worried that she became grave. "No trouble, I hope?"

"No trouble, strictly speaking, but the sort of dull irritation that you can prevent from bursting out, and can even dissipate." He let himself fall into a chair and twisted his hat in his hands. He attempted a meager smile, which contracted his energetic face, and went on: "You'll think me very demanding to complain since, in spite of our apprehensions, Monsieur Bro has granted me his daughter's hand without any difficulty and we're to be married in a month's time, but, sincerely, don't you think all the same that there's something abnormal about my situation? Why, we've been engaged for three weeks, and living under the same roof as my future wife is a young man endowed with all the qualities, handsome enough to turn heads in the street—in a word, perfect from every point of view! Me, I only come here as a visitor. He lives in complete intimacy with Mademoiselle Suzanne. Don't you find it natural that I take umbrage and want to see it ended?"

César Bro interrupted him in his tranquil voice, without ceasing his sketching. "I beg your pardon, my dear friend, but remember first of all how these things came about, and agree that they could hardly be arranged otherwise. It was natural on my part to offer hospitality to my brother for a sojourn that, he has told me, will not be prolonged beyond your marriage. Now, he has expressed to me his formal desire not to be separated from that young man. You know how forcefully and vehemently he has explained his reasons. The boy has never been to France; he is literally lost among us. My brother, who has brought him, has assumed responsibility for him, and does not want to abandon him. I could do no less than offer to accommodate both of them, since I have enough room. And take note that if my brother had refused, you would have lost out, for he would have taken his daughter away without letting go of his ward. All three of them would have been living together, instead of being disseminated among us."

As the young man, far from being convinced, became even sulkier, Madame Bro ventured in her turn: "Besides, aren't they living alongside one another in the most complete indifference? Monsieur Dajan-Phinn manifests an insensibility, a coldness, for everything touching matters of sentiment. Nothing seems to move him—the grace of a young woman no more than the extended arms of a little child. Have you ever caught a word or a gesture on his part to which you could take offense...?"

"That's all that's lacking" exclaimed the fiancé.

"As for Suzanne," she continued, "don't you know that for a woman in love, there is but one man in the world—the one she loves? The others don't exist. She doesn't notice them; she doesn't see them. It's the very sign of affection. Have you seen her pay the slightest attention to Monsieur Dajan-Phinn?"

"No, no," said Henri, swiftly. "And that's why I didn't want to complain in front of her. There would have been something indelicate about explaining my annoyance to her—but that doesn't prevent it from being well-founded. This cohabitation irritates me, wounds me. And whatever you say, there's a means of putting an end to it. Since this Dajan-Phinn is so intelligent, he'll assimilate our customs rapidly. There's no need for him to remain on the leash any longer, like an exotic animal that can't be set free. Let him live near his master, but not in the same house. And I beg you to say a few words to Monsieur Bro, since he thinks himself so far above these wretched details...if, however, it's out of disregard for consequences that he's inflicting this unpleasant ordeal on me..."

"What do you mean?" Madame Bro interjected, sharply.

Evidently embarrassed by the presence of the painter, Henri continued: "Nothing. I don't want to say anything about which I'm not certain. I might be wrong. Anyway, will you accept the commission?"

"I promise," she said.

He got up, relieved.

She escorted him as far as the door and there, lifting up the curtain while he set off down the stairs, she said: "How anxious you are, and what chimeras you conjure up. Can't you enjoy your engagement in peace?"

"It's exactly because I want it to be unshadowed, protected from any incident and any complication, that that I beg you to send away the overly handsome souvenir of Dr. Bro's voyage."

"The poor boy," she said. "He's no trouble though."

He raised his head and wagged his finger at her while going down the stairs. "Oh, I suspect you of having a little weakness for him."

Leaning toward him and laughing, she admitted: "That's true."

In her generosity, she felt drawn toward him by maternal instinct. He seemed to her as isolated as a lost child. Dr. Bro remained mute as to his protégé's origins, but she knew that he had no family and no ties. His admirable features retained the astonished mildness of early infancy, but they were gradually becoming charged with melancholy. On seeing him, one thought of a beautiful lily bowing on its stem—and the hesitation that marked the beginning of his speeches, which left his mouth partly open and his eyelids hesitant for a moment, added a further measure to his touching timidity.

Not that he was embarrassed in his movements, or ignorant of our customs. On the contrary, he possessed every finesse. In addition, he occasionally revealed a surprising erudition.

"So you know everything, Monsieur Dajan-Phinn!" Madame Bro sometimes exclaimed.

In fact, his culture was very extensive. No human knowledge seemed entirely strange to him. He was certainly a worthy pupil of Dr. Bro. Far from deriving vanity from his knowledge, he seemed confused by it. In order for him to give proof of it, one was obliged to press him and interrogate him, as one turns the pages of a dictionary to extract its science. In the same way, being clever with his hands, capable of putting on paper a sketch, or even a water-color, of playing a piano pleasantly, he disdained his gifts. In brief, he had no passion for anything. He lacked the internal fire of enthusiasm.

Madame Bro attributed that lack of ardor and indolence to homesickness. She had tried to distract the young foreigner, but her attempts had scarcely been encouraging. In vain, she had put into his hands novels of which she was very fond. In vain, she had taken him to the theater. Books and plays nourished by love did not move him, did not draw him out of his melancholy. She was, in consequence, apprehensive about abandoning him to himself, as Henri Richard wished. Nevertheless, faithful to her promise, she explained the umbrageous fiancé's request to her brother-in-law that same evening.

At the first words, Dr. Bro manifested a wild gaiety. His eyes shining, he jeered; "Oh! The young man is jealous of Dajan-Phinn! Look at that! But it's perfect, perfect..."

"What?" queried Madame Bro, somewhat nonplussed.

He went on: "But that proves, quite simply, that he loves my daughter. Besides, it's of no importance whatsoever. An amorous fantasy. Don't insist, my dear friend, don't insist. I intend to keep Dajan-Phinn with me, you know, and nothing will separate me from him."

She dared not press the point. Her very duty as a hostess obliged her to be discreet. As her husband had remarked, the whole set-up would only last until the departure of the doctor and his protégé. Momentarily, she thought of having a word with Dajan-Phinn himself, but in case of success she would have arrived at an identical result: if the pupil left, the master would follow. She therefore renounced that vain and delicate step.

She was not very proud, therefore, when Henri Ruchard asked for news of her embassy two days later. Everything was conspiring to exasperate the suspicious young man. The professor and his son, who were bringing the engagement ring, had arrived a few minutes in advance of the agreed time. Suzanne had not come back. And—an aggravating circumstance—she had gone out in company with her father and the inseparable Dajan-Phinn.

Madame Bro received the two men in the Louis XV drawing-room. Sincerely affected, as a woman who, in her generosity, only wanted to see smiling faces around her, she allowed the admission of her failure and Suzanne's absence to be extracted from her by degrees.

Henri controlled himself, but his features contracted with anger. Through clenched teeth, he said: "That's all right. I'll have a word with Monsieur Bro myself."

Madame Bro made one last conciliatory effort. "Don't you fear poisoning everything? Remember that in a month, you'll be married, and you'll laugh at these petty nothings."

She turned to the professor in quest of his agreement, but he maintained a severe expression and sketched an evasive gesture. He certainly did not approve of his friend's behavior.

At that moment, Dr. Bro's loud voice became audible in the vestibule. He came in alone, extending his hands.

"Ah! Here's Henri, seething with impatience. His fiancée is behind me. She's..."

Henri cut in: "Pardon me—a word before she comes in. Madame Bro tells me that you've refused my request. Agree that it appears more legitimate than ever, on the day when you have gone out with your daughter and Dajan-Phinn...in such a way that someone in the street might be deceived and mistake that handsome young man for Mademoiselle Suzanne's fiancé!"

Dr. Bro, perched on his short legs with his hands in his pockets, swayed back and forth between his heels and his toes, jovially, and retorted: "What difference can that make to you, since she isn't deceived about it?"

Henri started. "I can see nothing in your inappropriate joke than your desire to push me aside, but I won't allow myself to be deflected from my goal. Monsieur Bro, you know that I'm anxious and jealous, rightly or wrongly—and yet you have no hesitation, by actions like today's excursion, in provoking me further. Such conduct certainly has its reasons. I beg you to tell me what they are."

"And what if I don't want to?" Dr. Bro said, mockingly.

"Then I'll tell you what they are myself and you'll be forced to recognize that I've seen through them."

"I'm curious to hear them."

"You'll be satisfied," he young man declared, dryly. "From the first day, your attitude has seemed strange to us. I say *us* because my father shares my anxieties and suspicions. Your very consent, following your long silence, appeared to him too facile not to have any hidden motive. You forgot your former grievances against him too easily. As for me, the presence of this so-called laboratory assistant has always seemed shady. How can you explain it, if not by your desire to make your daughter love him? He's the fiancé of your choice! Thanks to his prodigious beauty, and his merits, of which you boast incessantly, and the continued intimacy that you maintain between him and Mademoiselle Suzanne, do you not count on him supplanting me? You would already have succeeded had she been less constant. And you would have succeeded, had I not seen through your ruse. Oh, it was a good plan. This way you would have evicted me while avoiding the annoyance of a direct refusal—and your vengeance would have been even more complete and more refined. You would precipitate me from a higher position, since, after having given me your daughter, you would have had her stolen away by a rival."

Dr. Bro's attitude was incomprehensible. He laughed, rubbed his hands, and seemed overwhelmed by jubilation.

"Ha ha! You've worked all that out by yourself! Or rather, you've done it together. My compliments. Well, my lad, you're on completely the wrong track..."

Disconcerted, Henri stammered: "But...if I'm mistaken...which I hope with all my heart...at least justify your conduct..."

Very gravely, the professor lent his support. "Yes, Bro, explain yourself. Explain to us why you have bought back that individual, why you keep him under your roof, and why you persist even when you know that your daughter's fiancé is suffering..."

Bro was no longer laughing. He walked toward to two men. His phosphorescent eyes were gleaming in the hollows of their blue-tinted orbits. His obstinate head swelled up. His entire face was grimacing with malice and intense satisfaction.

"Oh, you both want an explanation! Well, so be it—you shall have one. It wouldn't have been long delayed anyway. Since you offer me the opportunity, I'll take it. On one sole point you've seen clearly. Yes, it's true, I haven't forgotten the past. The defeat that you inflicted on me, Ruchard, is as sensible to me as on the first day. I lost my case thanks to your speech, but not without appeal. Except, as I told you, the happiness of our children has nothing to do with our quarrels. No, my lad, I haven't plotted to evict you. Beaten on the scientific battleground, it's on the scientific battleground that I wanted my revenge. But it had to be absolutely crushing. My adversaries had to be annihilated forever. Well, I have it, I have the means..."

He was excited. Uplifted, magnified by triumph, he was fearful to behold.

"Ha ha! You're jealous of Dajan-Phinn, angry Henri. And you share his dread, grave Richard! You see in my pupil a rival worthy of you, umbrageous fiancé. You do him the honor of hating him. You're afraid of him. Well, you've both fallen into the trap I set for you, which I've been preparing for you for seven years...and you've fallen into it even more deeply than I dared to hope. Oh, one can't make life! Oh, it's impossible for a man to create an organism! Oh, my plants were just puerile games! Well, know then that the odious Dajann-Phinn emerged from my hands, that the detested rival is artificial, and that, to sum it all up in one word, Henri is jealous of an automaton!"

Dr. Bro wanted to annihilate his adversaries; he had succeeded. The painter's wife and the two Ruchards stood there, overwhelmed by amazement. The professor was tragic; one might have thought him a felled oak. He was, however, the first to speak, saying: "What? You claim that this Dajan-Phinn..."

But Suzanne came in then, animated by happiness. Suddenly confused by those petrified faces, she murmured: "What's the matter?"

The doctor, radiant, stroked her cheek and said: "Your fiancé will tell you that." Then, taking the arm of his friend Ruchard, he drew him toward the garden. On the threshold, he turned round and said, authoritatively: "Not a word to Dajan-Phinn, all right?"

Scarcely had he closed the door to the garden when Madame César Bro went upstairs to tell her husband the sensational news. The two young people remained alone.

"What's happening?" Suzanne said. "Tell me quickly."

Glossing rapidly over his own suspicions, Henri repeated the astonishing revelation. It was the young woman's turn to stand there astounded. Her fiancé had to repeat the doctor's last words to her. In her, however, admiration was soon mingled with surprise.

"I was sure that he would end up triumphant, that he'd never ceased being right. What a reply, and what a revenge!"

"You're certain, then, that this Dajan-Phinn emerged from his hands...?"

She cut him off, with a reproach in her limpid eyes: "Since he says so..."

"Oh, for my part," he protested, "I'm not in any doubt..."

Indeed, everything encouraged him, everything drove him to consider Dr. Bro's unexpected assertion as true. It reduced to nothing his jealous anxieties. It explained everything. The web of intrigue that he had thought woven against him, the rival by whom he believed himself threatened—all that disappeared.

But what about his father? Would the professor accept the miracle as easily? A champion of scientific orthodoxy, victor in the first round, utterly convinced of the justice and the grandeur of his cause, would he given in without a fight this time? If, on the contrary, he resisted, the contest between the two men would be resumed, more bitterly and violently than ever.

And as the young woman, slightly intoxicated with filial pride, tried to imagine the resonance of such a discovery, he gazed distractedly through the window, following the two scientists as they strolled around the garden.

Dressed casually in a yellow suit, coiffed with a shapeless straw hat baked by the sun, Bro was hanging on to his companion's ample frock-coat. From an inside pocket he had taken a thick portfolio, and he was parading an entire series of pieces of paper before his friend's eyes. From time to time, they paused. Bro's gestures became more pressing. The professor slowly passed his hand over his forehead, like a man seeing to dissipate the smoke of his dreams.

Dusk crept up on them in the garden. Henri was burning with the desire to know the result of that long conversation. So, as soon as he found himself alone again with his father in the street, he interrogated him with a word in which all his haste was concentrated:

"Well?"

"That man makes one dizzy," murmured the professor. "One loses one's footing. One is submerged beneath the flood of his words. Seven years, according to him, he's been keeping his secret! For more than a month he's been resisting the temptation to deliver it to us. Then he overflows, explodes."

"Finally, do you believe in this discovery?"

The professor, ordinarily sober in his gestures, waved his arms desperately. "I don't know any more...I don't know. It's necessary to believe everything, or believe nothing."

"What did he tell you?"

"He told me that he's been preparing his great work for seven years. He intended, in the case of success, to bring his Dajan-Phinn to France, to make him live among us, and, when we had taken well and truly taken the bait and believed in the reality of the individual, to reveal his nature to us. He had almost reached his goal, it appears, when our petition for marriage reached him. It was a trump card in his game. The period of engagement would bring us closely together, and put us in continual contact with his Dajan-Phinn. But he still wanted to be perfectly sure of his success, to be absolutely ready—hence his delay in replying to us, still according to him. Finally, he made the decision to take the boat. And once in France, the anxiety and irritation that the unknown inspired— and which Bro claims to have anticipated—would complete his ambition. Your jealousy was a homage to the perfection of his work..."

By the tone in which his father reported his friend's words, the young man sensed that her was hesitant, undecided. He persisted: "But after all, has he explained his method, furnished with technical details?"

Again, the tearful professor raised his hands toward the heavens. "Technical details! But to follow that man, it's necessary to forget everything one knows, to rid oneself of all one's convictions. One flounders in the unknown, the fantastic. Yes, he's explained his method to me. Yes, he's shown me photographs of his experiment at different stages. The only witnesses, moreover, for Bro claims to have acted alone, with no other auxiliary than a Hindu, a sort of semi-artist, semi-sorcerer, who only aided him from the plastic viewpoint. Oh, he has an answer for everything, naturally—but on what can one found a serious controversy when one advances on inconsistent ground, in an atmosphere as dark, beyond the solid ground and clear sight of science."

"So?"

"So, either we're confronted by the boldest trickery, and Bro is nothing but a poor madman unhinged by his past disappointments, or...he's telling the truth."

He pronounced the final words in a slightly ashamed voice, as if he blushed—he, the orthodox scientist, the famous professor—to admit the possibility of such a prodigy even momentarily.

"In the end, how can we know?" Henri queried.

"By studying Dajan-Phinn at close range now that we're aware of Bro's stupefying affirmation. By subjecting him to a rigorous close investigation that will end up revealing the truth to us."

Then, life in César Bro's house took a singular turn. With a common accord, the initiates had decided to keep the secret. Professor Ruchard had been particularly insistent that no news of the events should be spread outside. He dreaded, in the case that the investigation should turn out to his friend's disadvantage, the mockery of his colleagues. What! The grave Ruchard had been able to consent to examine such ridiculousness—and, in consequence, to take it seriously for a moment. What outbursts of laughter! And if, on the contrary, the implausible was true, would it not be better for the professor to be the first to announce his conversion, with considerable ceremony, before his colleagues could take possession of the question and constrain him to admit that he had been defeated.?

As for Dr. Bro, sure of his conclusive victory, indulgent to the last resistance of his old companion, he accepted with a good grace the examination demanded by Ruchard. He declared that, having waited for seven years, he could easily be patient for a few more days. Relatives and friends, touched by his faith, would become ardent disciples during this interval—and the news would break all the more violently upon the world for having been longer contained.

Even Dajan-Phinn—Dajan-Phinn especially—ought to remain in ignorance, for he knew nothing about his mysterious origin. Dr. Bro explained that very clearly. Before Dajan-Phinn became the object of discreet investigations, he had emphasized this point heavily.

"I've always hidden his origin and we all have an interest in maintaining the same discretion, To reveal his true nature to him would be to falsify his attitude, take away his ease and, if I dare use the expression, his naturalness. He would become my accomplice, he would hide his secret from you. While he believes himself to be similar to the common run of men, he acts as they do effortlessly, and does not suffer from being a prodigious exception. Oh, Dajan-Phinn, interrogated by you, will not fail to tell you that he lived until adolescence with two old people who brought him up on the outskirts of the city, near the gate, until the day when I took him to live in the zoological garden. He will describe to you very succinctly the surroundings of his childhood monotony: the hut, the nearby forest, the school to which he went every day. Why? Because, to give him the illusion of a normal life, I was obliged to create memories for him, as one furnishes a modern château with ancient objects to give it the appearance of age...."

And as those most inclined to believe the doctor could not repress signs of astonishment, he added: "What is there in that to surprise you? Have you not witnessed and admitted more extraordinary phenomena? Have you not seen, during a séance of hypnotism and suggestion, the operator leave stronger imprints in the consciousness of subjects, persuading them that a potato is a delicious fruit, that all the vowels are missing from a newspaper they're reading, or even constraining them to commit a theft or some other crime in the waking state? And he is acting on a fully-formed organism—a task more difficult than making an impression on an entirely new substance."

Fixing a few images in a brain was, was nothing for Dr. Bro. The most outstanding aspect of his work, in that order of ideas, was to have created in Dajan-Phinn a heredity of sorts, to have slipped instincts and knowledge into his skull as one injects sera under the skin. It was necessary to see Dr. Bro striving to make that comprehensible. As his listeners, with the exception of Ruchard, had been unable to follow him with regard to technical developments, he deployed an untiring patience in initiating them—adapting science for the usage of ordinary people, as he put it. He explained the cerebral localizations, pointed out the seat of each function in his head, struck himself on the cranium—everything but open it up to display the white substance and the grey matter—and, like a genial cook revealing a recipe, enumerated and measured out the notions and sentiments with which he had endowed Dajan-Phinn.

To model a character as one models a statue! To carry out an instruction, an education as one packs a trunk! To choose oneself the moral and physical qualities that ought to compose the idea being! So many exciting problems...but there was no time to linger over them. Dr. Bro carried everything away in the torrent of his loquacity.

Professor Ruchard was right: the man made one dizzy. On listening to him, one no longer knew whether one was living in a hallucination or reality. And he was always ready with a riposte, as Ruchard had also observed.

If one timidly expressed astonishment that a task s prodigiously complex had not required more time, he folded his arms beneath his chin and cried: "What! What! You admit without discussion, on the basis of a traveler's tale, that a fakir can make a seed grow, within half an hour, into a plant covered with flowers, but you won't admit that seven years have been enough for me to complete my work?"

Or, striking minds by means of analogy, he cried: "Living beings! But your industry has almost created them, and by the thousand. Do you think than an automobile is so very different from an animal? Add to it an organ of vision like a photographic apparatus, and an organ of audition like the telephone, which would alert it to dangers on the road, and react against them, and you would have an embryonic being capable of guiding itself and steering itself unaided."

Every time he launched into these fantastic comparisons, Professor Ruchard protested, shaking his head gravely.

"Yes, yes, I know," Bro anticipated. "The very principle of life is lacking, the energy inclusive in the seed, in the cell. The fact of having isolated and reconstituted that energy evidently constitutes the heart of my discovery.

Letting himself off the bridle briefly, he launched into vast considerations, affirmed that mineral, vegetable and animal matter each had a unique essence, represented as a condensation of forces, grabbed some random object, depicted it as an agglomeration of tiny worlds incessantly in vibration....

Then, having perceived a few signs of lassitude in his audience, he sketched some witty observations about Dajan-Phinn—a name that he had made up on a whim, for any trace of which one could search the world's records in vain. He imagined the automaton, alerted to his true origin, disconcerting an employee of the civil service with the unexpectedness of his replies, asserting that he had neither father nor mother and concluding with the prodigious affirmation that: "I was born at the age of 20."

Naturally, the young foreigner was never present during these conversations. As soon as he appeared, the subject was changed. Everyone did his best to dissimulate that abrupt leap and to adopt a cheerful tone—efforts more praiseworthy than successful. For, since Dr. Bro's revelation, the mere presence of

Dajan-Phinn provoked an anxiety among all the participants that they could not suppress.

It must be agreed that their situation was quite unique. To live in the company of an individual whose origin is unknown, and unknowable! About whom one demands, on talking to him, listening to him and looking at him: "Is he a man or an automaton?" Certainly, he is human in appearance—but a scientist, a genius or a madman, has sprung forth and proclaimed; "He's an artificial being, emerged from my hand!" And from then on the mind doubts, alternately rebelling and submitting, and losing balance in those overly abrupt oscillations.

In the little group that was upset and impassioned by the enigma set before them, however, Dr. Bro immediately found two convinced partisans: his daughter, blindly rallied by filial faith; and his sister-in-law, seduced by the attraction of the marvelous. Nothing could any longer tear Madame Bro away from the conviction that she was playing hostess to an automaton. Into the ardent discussions that where whispered in corners in Dajan-Phinn's absence, she had even thrown a weighty argument, calculated to have an impact on the mind.

"Come on!" she said. "Is his absolute insensibility that a of human being? Have you ever seen him take any interest in the slightest adventure, imaginary or real, of which love might be the motive? Has he ever sat Lise or Claude on his knee? Have the funny little things they say, their mannerisms and caresses, which delight us and bring tears to our eyes, ever had a softening effect on him? The joy of Suzanne and Henri on seeing one another surprises him. Their impatience to be married is incomprehensible to him. Does he not lack what the doctor calls, in his scientific language, the affective faculties? And is not that imperfection in his work also the mark of its authenticity?"

Bro took on a contrite air. He confessed that, indeed, that was the weak point of his creation. He had, however, paid particular attention to those affective instincts so necessary to a human being, which are the sweetness of life. What cause had vitiated his cultures, caused the development of those faculties to be abortive? He did not know. Along with Dajan-Phinn's speech defect—the difficulty of release that delayed the beginning of each sentence on his lips—they were the two flaws in his work...

But such arguments were not sufficient to compel all conviction. Among the experts poring over Dajan-Phinn, two remained undecided: César Bro and Henri Ruchard.

Since his brother's shattering revelation, the painter had not ceased examining the young foreigner from the corner of his eye. And he found—but might it not be the effect of a kind of suggestion?—something artificial in the nacreous translucency of his complexion and the mineral gleam of his beard and hair, and an extra-natural perfection in the beauty of his lines and contours. At the same time though, as soon as he was inclined to believe, an instinct of prudence and pride rebelled within him and cried out to him to deny the miracle of science.

To that ancient horror of reason for everything unknown, Henri Ruchard was equally submissive, and it counterbalanced in him the impulse that, from the very first moment, had thrown him on to Dr. Bro's side, inclining him to the solution most favorable to his cause, the only one capable of putting a conclusive end to those wearying quarrels. In fact, if the artificial origin of Dajan-Phinn were to be proven and recognized, all controversy ceased. If, on the contrary, that origin were contested, the discussion remained open indefinitely.

Alas, Professor Ruchard did not appear to be close to giving in. In the little group, he represented the opposition, but a defiant, hostile opposition. In his dread of being duped and set up for mockery, he redoubled his gravity—and he set about studying Dajan-Phinn with concentrated but discreet attention: the attention reserved for a selected invalid to whom one does not wish to reveal his illness.

What about Dajan-Phinn? If he was insensitive, Dajan-Phinn was, at least, very intelligent, and it could not take him long to perceive that he had become the center of attention of the little society in which he lived. Once put on his guard, none of the signs of that metamorphosis could any longer escape him: neither the silence, nor the awkward transitions that marked his entrance; nor the hesitant hands and fugitive fingers that were extended toward him at moments of greeting; nor the gazes that lingered on his face: the ponderous gaze of Professor Ruchard; the sly and pensive gaze of César Bro; the limpid and marveling gaze of Suzanne Bro. He could not be unaware of the instinctive gesture with which Madame Bro sometimes drew her children away from him, as if she were pulling them out of the way of a moving machine. He could not fail to perceive the change of attitude on the part of Henri Ruchard, once somber and sulky, seemingly inclined to avoid him and even treat him with hostility, but who now interrogated him cordially about his childhood and youth. It was impossible not to notice the sudden solicitude of Professor Ruchard, who, indifferent at first, now sounded his chest and examined him minutely at the slightest sign of indisposition...

Evidently, Dajan-Phinn had to take note of all these symptoms and seek and explanation for them. For, if they did not cause him any emotion—given that nothing seemed to cause him any emotion—the mystery that he sensed around him had to appear to him as a problem of sorts, which his lucid mind would strive to solve.

Now, the solution offered itself. This period of intense but discreet inquisition had been going on for about a fortnight. The banns of the imminent marriage had been posted.

One afternoon, Dajan-Phinn went into the dining-room at an indolent pace in order to fetch a book that Madame Bro had forgotten. In the painter's house, the room in question was only separated from the drawing-room by a light curtain that was drawn during the day. Dajan-Phinn heard his name pronounced on the other side of that veil. He recognized Henri Ruchard's voice. He stood still and listened.

"...I told you that he would be our evil genius. You see, Suzanne, that my presentiments did not deceive me. Without him, this accursed quarrel would be dead. On the contrary, it's nourished by him—and now it's poisoned, in a state of acute crisis. What good does it do to hide it? My father's conclusions are injurious to yours. It's the most wounding denial, the most insulting suspicion. Oh, Suzanne, my dear Suzanne, will it be necessary for us to separate, so near to our union, to being together? And all for this adventure in dementia..."

"Please calm down," pronounced Suzanne's voice. "Don't demoralize me in my turn. We need all our composure. So, your father has made his decision, in a firm manner. There's no means of making him relent in his determination?"

"I've tried everything, but in vain. Nothing will deter him any longer from talking to your father imminently. His verdict is without appeal. Disconcerted momentarily by the prodigious assertion, he had gradually pulled himself together. Oh, I'm certain that he's undertaken the most scrupulous examination, with absolute probity. Be sure that if he had conserved the slightest doubt, he'd have admitted it frankly...but he no longer has any. For him, Dajan-Phinn is a mere mortal..."

"Then your father won't hesitate to accuse his old friend of lying?"

"I believe that objection has held him in check longer than the apparent proofs provided by your father—but he explains and excuses the trickery. For him, Dr. Bro's mind has been stricken, even disturbed, by the premature death of his wife, by excessive labor, and above all by his very defeat. And in consequence of that final shock, the idea developed within him of obtaining revenge at any cost, by means of this implausible but troubling fable.

"My father," Suzanne interjected, sharply, "will not admit the excuse of madness. He would consider that one more insult. But, all in all, is Monsieur Ruchard not struck by the singular signs that make Dajan-Phinn an exceptional being, beyond humanity?"

"You can be sure that I've struggled, that I've used every weapon at our disposal—I, who ask nothing more than to be convinced, who have so much interest in the miracle being real. That hesitation he displays at the beginning of every statement? It appears that it's quite common."

"The photographs that your father has seen?"

"He's sure, in the final analysis, that they're fake. One can express anything one wishes by means of photography—and Dr. Bro had as many models as he might desire among the anatomical specimens in the zoological gardens of Borneo."

"That excessively perfect beauty?"

"Why should it be the work of a man rather than that of nature?"

"That almost absolute insensibility?"

"Does one need to be an automaton to be heartless? How many human beings are ignorant of tenderness? No, for my father, Dajan-Phinn is a poor foundling, exceptionally endowed, like those little Alpine shepherds who are prodigious calculators, whom Dr. Bro must have discovered, cultivated and even subjected to suggestion. Come on—all these proofs are fragile, and break against reason. We can't avoid an explosion. Oh, one sometimes has to ask oneself whether people who attach themselves to nothing and are indifferent to everything might be better off. They don't have our anxieties…"

"Would you change places with them?" she asked, softly.

Stricken, he replied: "No, no. You're right—but I'm like one of those bad-tempered horses enraged by any hobble, you see. I blasphemed. Certainly, it would be insane to despair, since we love one another, since I have you close to me, sure and faithful, and since I only breathe for you. To love, to be loved…oh, that really is the secret of all effort, all energy, the motto of happiness, and the flower and perfume of life. Yes, we'll fight. Nothing will ever separate us."

"Have we not," she went on, "undergone many other ordeals already: the waiting, the uncertainty…the worst of evils, it's said, because it contains all of them."

"Dear Suzanne, I admire your smiling valor. Yes, for us the past answers for the future. There are already so many shared memories…that's a chain which nothing can break. You remember, last year, when we still didn't dare to admit anything to one another…taking little Lise for our confidant, who couldn't understand, and, leaning over that two-year-old child in her crib by turns, we told her…everything that we would have wished to say to one another…"

"Yes, that was the time when my uncle César, from whom you were taking lessons and who made you work on a portrait from a living model, exclaimed: 'That's odd—all your women resemble my niece Suzanne!'"

Thus they poured out the cordial of memories for one another in advance of the impending battle. They lowered their voices. Sometimes, even the slight murmur paused, and from the silence, the noise of a kiss emerged, as soft and gentle as that of a drop of water falling into a bowl. Then the tender litany rose up again, replete with murmured oaths, praises, reminiscences and plans, acts of grace and acts of retreat, words to lull, or to cajole, puerile words, words as old as humankind, but which always seem new to those who pronounce them and those who hear them, words akin to kisses which, like them, take on a new savor in passing over the lips…

Dajan-Phinn had heard everything: that he was or was not an automaton. No more shattering revelation had ever struck an understanding. To know that his origin was being discussed! To sense that he was on the frontiers of humanity! And, to the disarray into which such a dispute must have thrown his mind, was doubtless added the sadness of surprising that loving duo, of glimpsing the promised land in which he would never set foot.

That day, he was more silent than usual. The next day, he was hardly to be seen. He shut himself up in his room. During dinner, at which the Ruchards were guests, he remained concentrated within himself. A sort of anguish weighed over the table in any case. The professor maintained a grave and ominous expression. The two fiancés were apprehensive about their fate. Only Dr. Bro was dazzling. One might have thought that he had scented the coming conflict and was becoming intoxicated in advance in an atmosphere with a whiff of gunpowder.

After the meal, the guests spread out in the drawing-room, the door of which was open to the garden. The rain-soaked foliage was exhaling its green moist scent into the belated dusk of June. Dajan-Phinn wandered along the pathways. In common with the flowers that retained a certain phosphorescent gleam in the twilight, like a memory of day, his beauty was radiant and luminous. He stopped in front of Dr. Bro, who was camped on the steps of the perron, lighting his cigar.

The young man opened his mouth slightly, and his eyelids fluttered. Then he began, softly: "Doctor, why have you always hidden from me what you have said about me to those surrounding us? Tell me the truth. Am I truly a sort of machine forged by your hands, designed to astonish the world, to proclaim your merit?"

Bro threw away his match violently. "Everyone here will be my witness that I kept silent as much in your interest than in mine. And I would like to know who has permitted..."

Dajan-Phinn raised his arm to interrupt the doctor. After a brief hesitation, he said: "I alone committed an indiscretion. No one said anything to me. I overheard...oh, my master! However it was done, I am what you have made of me. I owe you everything. But you have always been good to me. Don't leave me in ignorance..."

"It's precisely out of goodness that I left you there," Bro replied, rudely. "I wanted you to avoid the embarrassment, the shame, of feeling that you were on the margins of society, an exceptional being..."

Ruchard, who had been sitting in the drawing-room, had risen to his feet. The carpet muffled his footsteps. Bro did not hear them. The professor placed a hand on his shoulder.

"You don't have the right to torture a poor human creature to this extent, for the sole satisfaction of your insane pride!"

Beneath the sudden weight and the rude interjection, Bro started and turned round. He directed the disquieting fire of his yellow pupils at the professor. At the same time, his features expressed absolute amazement. Had he, until the very last moment, nurtured the certainty of bringing his adversary round?

Ruchard continued: "Bro, in the name of our old friendship, in the name of all that is sacred to you, in the name of our children, I beg you to admit the truth."

Bro straightened, rising up, so to speak, against his old companion. "What are you saying?"

Everyone—the two fiancés, César Bro and his wife—surrounded the two men. Dajan-Phinn had remained at the bottom of the steps, his face bright against the dark background of the garden.

"I'm saying," Ruchard went on, forcefully, "and I'm affirming, that Dajan-Phinn is a human being like all of us here: that your entire story is nothing but an elaborate hoax."

Bro folded his arms. The corners of his mouth were quivering. "Nothing can convince you, then—not the documents I have shown you, nor the proofs that I have put within your reach, nor the oath that I am ready to renew?"

Ruchard made a chopping gesture with his extended hand. "Nothing. And if you're acting in good faith, it's because you're the dupe of your own imagination."

"Not one word more!" howled Dr. Bro.

He was so terribly excited that Henri Ruchard drew nearer to his father. "Don't insist, I beg you."

"Come on, then!" Ruchard shouted. "It's necessary to be done with this once and for all, to nip this legendary impiety in the bud, to annihilate this execrable lie."

"Don't challenge me, Ruchard—don't push me too far!" Bro brandished his fist. He seemed to be suffering a paroxysm of exasperation. Saliva was running from his lips. His inflamed eyes were bulging from their orbits. Vainly, his daughter exhorted him to be calm, her gestures imploring.

The professor shrugged his shoulders. "Play-acting," he murmured.

Bro took a step back. He gathered himself together. He put his hands in the pocket of his capacious jacket. "That's it," he hissed. "You won't believe me?"

"No."

In a firmer voice, all the more frightening in consequence, Bro went on: "You believe me capable of a deception?"

"Yes."

"But you don't believe me capable of a crime?"

Ruchard did not hesitate. "No."

"But you admit," Bro continued, "that a sculptor has the right to smash his statue, that an inventor has the right to break up his machine?"

Ruchard made no reply, fearful of comprehension. There was, for all those watching, an interminable moment of absolute anguish.

Then, speaking and acting at the same time, Bro said: "Well, the proof that Dajan-Phinn is my work is that I am destroying him!"

Three gunshots punctuated this sentence. With a revolver withdrawn from his pocket, he had fired at Dajan-Phinn, standing at the bottom of the steps.

Amid the cries of horror and panic, Ruchard hurled himself upon his puny adversary, seized his wrist and disarmed him. Bro shouted full in his face:

58

"Well, that's what you wanted! That's where it has led me, orthodox science! To destroy my masterpiece! Ha ha! Orthodox science!"

Dajan-Phinn suddenly collapsed, turning as he did so to fall face down. Aided by the servants brought running by the noise, Henri Ruchard and César Bro carried him to a settee in the drawing-room. Lamps were brought.

While the two women went up to calm the children woken up by the detonations, who were uttering screams of fright, the professor examined the wounded man. He shook his head. Dajan-Phinn had received two bullets full in the chest. His condition seemed hopeless.

Indifferent to his victim, Dr. Bro strode back and forth in the drawing-room, filling it with his gestures and vocal outbursts. He declared that he was going to surrender to the law, that the instruction of his trial and the sensation at the assizes would compel the entire world to recognize the truth of his affirmations, the excellence of his doctrines and finally render him justice.

The professor, who was listening, left Dajan-Phinn momentarily. He drew his son and the painter into a corner of the room. It was, on the contrary, necessary to avoid the scandal of such a trial. Bro had evidently acted in a fit of madness. He, Ruchard, would do his utmost to prove it—and he would use his influence to cut short any pursuit. He begged the two men to aid him in this plan. They would pretend to accede to the murderer's desire, but instead of accompanying him to the commissariat, they would take him to a nearby lunatic asylum kept by one of their mutual friends, where he would receive all the necessary case, and where the court would be able, the following day, to proceed with the customary inquiries.

A quarter of an hour later, Dr. Bro left the house with his two bodyguards, convinced that he would be turned over to the law and launching one final sarcasm and one final challenge at his adversary...

The hours went by, slowly, at Dajan-Phinn's bedside, in the drawing-room from which they had not dared to remove him. Madame Bro kept watch, while Professor Ruchard took a little rest in a neighboring room. The celebrated physician still offered no hope. The unfortunate victim would doubtless soon take the secret of his origin away with him forever.

Meanwhile, he had recovered consciousness—and as the good Madame Bro, wiped a tear from the corner of her eye with a fingertip, Dajan-Phinn murmured: "Don't cry. I don't regret disappearing. Yesterday, in this room, I heard your fiancés. I became conscious of my real misfortune, my true destiny. Whether or not I was born like other men, I would always have lacked the only faculty that makes life worth living, that reveals its charm and attraction..."

"And that is?"

"Love."

Maurice Renard: *Doctor Lerne, Subgod*

Le Docteur Lerne, sous-dieu, *here translated as* Doctor Lerne, Subgod, *was initially published by Mercure de France in 1908. Although clearly influenced by Wells's* The Island of Doctor Moreau *(1896), it is a strikingly original work, which succeeds in its earnest desire to be shocking in more ways than one. It was not the first story to assume that recent advancements in the technologies of "grafting" might soon realize the age-old fantasies expressed in such mythical figures as the chimera and the Minotaur, but it was the first to grasp that nettle firmly.*

Sadly, the book does not seem to have sold very well, but it did receive significant critical praise from several fellow writers, and undoubtedly contributed to the success of the literary salon that Renard began to host not long afterwards. Guillaume Apollinaire was happy to echo its subtitle in classifying it as a pioneering specimen of the roman sub-divin *[subdivine novel]. Georges de la Fourchardière, then at the beginning of a long and august career, wrote that its publication represented* "un événement scientifique et littéraire d'un ordre prodigieux" *[a scientific and literary event of a prodigious magnitude]. Such omens anticipated the fact that the novel would eventually be hailed as one of the landmark works of French speculative fiction.*

Maurice Renard (1875-1939)'s first collection of stories, Fantômes et fantoches *[Phantoms and Marionettes], was published in 1905 under the nom de plume of "Vincent Saint-Vincent;"* Le Docteur Lerne *was his second book and his first novel. His next "scientific marvel novel," as he called it,* Un Homme chez les microbes *[A Man Among the Microbes], followed almost immediately afterwards, but Renard could not find a publisher for it for a long time. Then another collection of stories appeared,* Le Voyage immobile *[The Motionless Journey] (1909), published by the Mercure de France.*

His next book was the novel Le Péril bleu *(1911; tr. as* The Blue Peril*), which caused something of a stir, and was eventually to be established as Renard's second landmark contribution to the history of French speculative fiction, a masterpiece even more considerable than* Le Docteur Lerne. *His publisher, Louis Michaud, also released Renard's third collection of short stories,* Monsieur d'Outremort *(1913).*

In August 1914, Renard was mobilized as a cavalry officer, and did not return to civilian life until January 1919; he was fortunate to survive the numerous battles in which he was involved, but four years of warfare took a heavy toll not only on him but his marriage (he finally divorced in 1930). To complete the personal damage inflicted by the war, the invading Germans had destroyed his

Château Saint-Rémy residence and devastated the estate attached to it, dealing a dire blow to his financial security.

Renard's first new novel after the war was the offbeat thriller Les Mains d'Orlac *(tr. as* The Hands of Orlac*), (1920) which became a commercial and critical success. That too has a scientific marvel component, in that it deals with the grafting of a new pair of hands onto the wrists of an injured concert pianist, but the device is used simply as a premise to set up a highly ingenious and magnificently paranoid thriller. The novel was translated into English and filmed twice, the first time in Germany in 1925—a movie that became one of the key works of German expressionist cinema—and the second time in the USA, as* Mad Love, *in 1935.*

Although the version of Un Homme chez les microbes *that was eventually published in 1928 incorporates some material that reflects the legacy of the war, that material could not be credited, by any stretch of the imagination, with the slightest morale-building potential. Indeed, Renard's subsequent reflections on the war, as expressed in his fiction, strongly suggest that, in spite of his dyed-in-the-wool patriotism, he was too embittered and disillusioned ever to have been interested in writing facile propaganda.*

One significant factor in the death of Renard's ambition to popularize scientific marvel fiction was that the brief fashionability of Wellsian scientific romance had waned, publishers realizing that many French readers found it too alien for easy reading. The experience of war further concentrated minds forcefully on the vicissitudes of the immediate and the material, at the expense of the imaginative and the hypothetical. Although British scientific romance made a slow recovery, enjoying a new flicker of energetic endeavor and modest commercial success after 1930, its French equivalent remained longer in the doldrums.

Ironically, as Renard observed, it was in Germany, the nation worst affected by the war, that utter despair with present circumstances boosted exaggerated hope for future possibilities based on new technologies, and the fortunes of propagandistic fiction associated with those hopes. In America, the seeds of a revolution had already been sown in 1928, and the term "science fiction" was invented a year later (replacing the earlier "scientifiction"), eventually to take root so firmly that, when France was flooded with American cultural products after World War II, it was the borrowed American label that was eventually to catch on, where all of Renard's suggestions had conspicuously failed. [7]

B.S.

---

[7] Black Coat Press has published five collections of Maurice Renard's genre work: *The Blue Peril* (ISBN 978-1-935558-17-0), *Doctor Lerne* (ISBN 978-1-935558-15-6), *The Doctored Man* (ISBN 978-1-935558-18-7), *A Man Among the Microbes* (ISBN 978-1-935558-16-3), and *The Master of Light* (ISBN 978-1-935558-19-4).

To Monsieur H.-G. Wells

I ask you, Monsieur, to accept the dedication this book.

Of all the pleasures that its invention has given me, that if dedicating it to you is certainly not the least.

I have conceived it within a category of ideas that is dear to you. I would have liked it to be more closely akin to yours, if not in literary value—which I could not claim without seeming ridiculous—then at least in that reader-friendliness that all your works possess, which permits intelligences of the most virginal sort as well as less accommodating minds to acquaint themselves with your genius, without which the best minds of our epoch would find its charm attenuated.

When fortune, good or ill, caused me to happen upon the subject of this novel, in the form of an allegory, I did not think I ought to set it aside on account of a few temerities that its faithful expression would involve, and which an abridged development—a misdemeanor of literary conscience, so to speak—could only sketch out.

You know by now—you will doubtless have guessed—what I would like people to think about my work, if by chance anyone renders it the unexpected homage of thinking about it. Far from wanting to provoke in the reader's instinctive self a delight in shocking imagery, it is addressed to the philosophical lover of Truth, in the guise of marvelous fiction, and retains an orderly method within the artificial riot of its narrative twists.

That, Monsieur, is why I ask you to accept it.

M.R.

Preface

This happened on a certain winter's evening, more than a year ago. It was after the last dinner party I gave for my friends, in the Avenue Victor Hugo, in a little house that I had rented fully furnished. Nothing apart from my restlessness having motivated the change of residence, they celebrated my farewell as joyfully as they had my house-warming party at the same address. When the time for liqueurs arrived, along with that of whimsical sallies, each of us attempted to show off our brilliance—especially, naturally enough, Gilbert Marlotte, a clubman devoted to dirty jokes, paradoxes and playing the fool, and Cardaillac, our official practical joker.

I don't remember exactly how it came about that, after an hour of smoking, someone switched off the electric light and gathered us around a small table in the darkness, insisting on the urgency of doing a little table-turning,. It should be noted that the person in question was not Cardaillac—but Cardaillac might have recruited him as an accomplice, if Cardaillac had a hand in it at all.

There were exactly eight of us: eight unbelievers sitting at a tiny table whose single pillar split into a tripod and whose round top was burdened by our sixteen hands, joined according to the rituals of occultism. It was Marlotte who informed us as to these rituals. He had once been curious about spirit manifestations and was familiar with gyratory tables, but only as a layman. As he was our usual buffoon, when we saw him take over the organization of the session, everyone lent himself to it with good grace, in expectation of some good fun. Cardaillac was sitting on my right. I heard him strangle a laugh in his throat and cough.

The table turned, though.

Then Gilbert asked it questions, and—to Marlotte's manifest amazement—it replied by means of dry clicks, analogous to those of warping wood, corresponding to the esoteric alphabet.

Marlotte translated, in a shaky voice.

Then everyone wanted to question the table, which demonstrated considerable sagacity in its replies. The audience became serious; no one knew what to think any longer. The questions hastened to our lips and the replies to the foot of the table—somewhat in my direction, it seemed, and to my right.

"Who will be living in this house a year from now?" the person who had proposed the séance asked, in his turn.

"Oh, if you ask it about the future," cried Marlotte, "you'll get nothing but lies, or it'll shut up completely."

"Let it be!" Cardaillac put in.

Someone repeated: "Who will be living in this house a year from now?"

The table clicked.

"No one," said the interpreter.

"What about two years?"

"Nicolas Vermont."

Everyone was hearing that name for the first time.

"What will he be doing at this time, two years from now?"

"He's beginning...to write on me...his adventures."

"Can you read what he's writing?"

"Yes, and also what he will write afterwards."

"Tell us...the beginning, just the beginning..."

"Tired. Alphabet...too long. Provide typewriter, will inspire typist."

A murmur went around in the darkness. I got up and went to fetch my typewriter, which was placed on the table.

"It's a Watson," said the table. "Don't like it. Am French, want French machine. Want a Durand."

"A Durand?" said my left-hand neighbor, in a skeptical tone. "Does that brand exist? I've never heard of it."

"Me neither."

"Nor me."

"Nor me."

We were in distress by virtue of this disappointment when Cardaillac's voice said, slowly: "I never use anything but a Durand machine. Would you like me to fetch it?"

"Can you type without looking at it?"

"I'll be back in a quarter of an hour," the other said—and he went out, without answering.

"If Cardaillac's mixed up in this," said one of the guests, "it's going to be amusing."

Meanwhile, the re-illuminated chandelier showed faces sterner than was reasonable. Even Marlotte was pale.

Cardaillac came back after a very brief lapse of time—astonishingly short, one might say. He sat down at the table in front of his Durand machine. Darkness was restored, and the table unexpectedly declared: "No more need for others. Place your feet on mine. Write."

The tapping of fingertips on the keys was heard.

"That's extraordinary!" exclaimed the typist-medium. "Extraordinary! My hands are acting of their own accord..."

"Pfft!" whispered Marlotte. "What a fake!"

"I swear to you...I swear..." Cardaillac repeated.

We stayed there for a long time, listening to the noise of the typewriter, punctuated from moment to moment by the bell marking the end of a line and the scrape of the carriage-return. Every five minutes or so, another sheet was delivered to us. We made the decision to retire to the drawing-room and read them aloud as Gilbert, having received them from Cardaillac, handed them to me.

Page 79 was deciphered in the light of morning. The machine had just stopped. But what it had printed seemed sufficiently captivating to us for to beg Cardaillac to be kind enough to do it again the following evening.

He did so. And when he had passed many nights sitting at the table at his graphic harpsichord, we possessed the complete adventures of the aforementioned Vermont. The reader will make their acquaintance shortly.

They are bizarre and scabrous. Their future writer will feel obliged not to commit them to print. *He will burn them* as soon as they are finished—with the result that, were it not for the obliging table, no one would ever have read them. That is why, convinced of their authenticity, I deem it urgent to publish them in anticipation. For I take them to be veridical, even though they have a far-fetched and caricaturish quality and are somewhat reminiscent of a medical student's whimsy, penned in the manner of a comment on the margins of an engraving of a personification of Science.

Are they apocryphal? Fables have the reputation of being more seductive than truth, and Cardaillac's will not seem inferior to many others. I would nevertheless prefer *Doctor Lerne* to be a faithful revelation of actual vicissitudes, because, in that case, since the table has played a prophetic role, the hero's tribulations have not yet begun, and they will doubtless be unfolding at the same time as the book will divulge them—a strangely intriguing circumstance.

I shall, of course, know in two years' time whether Nicolas Vermont is resident in the little house in the Avenue Victor Hugo. Something tells me that he will; how can one believe that a serious and intelligent fellow like Cardaillac would have wasted so much time making up such a crazy story? That is my principal argument in favor of its sincerity. At any rate, if any punctilious reader wishes to enlighten himself, let him go to Grey-l'Abbaye. There, he will be informed as to the existence of Doctor Lerne and his habits. Personally, I don't have the leisure myself, but I beg that eventual seeker to let me know the truth, being strongly desirous myself of bringing the matter into the light and knowing whether the following story really is one of Cardaillac's tricks or whether it really was typed by a turning table.[8]

I. Nocturne

The first Sunday in June was drawing to a close. The automobile's shadow extended in front of me, getting longer with every passing minute.

Since the morning, people with anxious faces had been watching me go by as if they were watching a scene in a melodrama. With the leather helmet that made my head seem bald, my round-lensed goggles, like the orbits of a skull, and my leather-clad body, I must have looked to them like some infernal and macabre seal, or one of St. Anthony's demons, fleeing the sun and hastening to meet the night in order to enter the darkness sooner. And, all things considered, I nearly did have the soul of a reprobate, for such is the condition of a solitary voyager who has spent seven consecutive hours in a racing car. His mind takes on a nightmarish character; obsession preys upon him in the guise of thought. Mine was a short imperative sentence: *Come alone and give advance notice—*

---

[8] Renard inserts a footnote here: "We have not modified so much as a syllable of the original text of *Doctor Lerne*, as dictated (?) by the table to Cardaillac. There are liberties that may not be taken with respect to an unknown author, when one is already publishing without authorization. The reader will therefore be kind enough not to attribute Monsieur Vermont's often-prudhommesque style or his sometimes-Biblical audacity to us. At any rate, he will generously forgive them, in view of the terrible trials to which the young man's common sense must have been subjected during the confession of this memoir." The adjective *prudhommesque* refers to the protagonist of Henri Monnier's *Mémoires de Joseph Prudhomme* (1857), an archetype of unwonted self-satisfaction and unconscious banality.

which harassed my solitude, wearied by trepidation and speed, like some tenacious hobgoblin.

The bizarre injunction to *Come alone and give advance notice*—which my uncle Lerne had underlined twice in his letter—had not struck me as excessively odd at first. Now that I was acting in conformity with it, though, rolling toward the Château de Fonval, alone and without having told anyone, the inexplicable instruction was, so to speak, insistent in displaying its strangeness. My eyes saw its ominous terms everywhere, and my ears sounded them within every noise, in spite of my efforts to chase the obsession away. Would I like to know the name of a village? The indicative plaque announced to me: *Come alone. Give advance notice*, traced the flight of birds. And the car's engine, indefatigable and exasperating, repeated thousands of times over: *Come alone, come alone, come alone, give advance notice, give advance notice, give advance notice…*

I asked myself why my uncle wanted that, and, being unable to think of any reason, became all the most enthusiastic to arrive, in order to solve the mystery—not so much because I was curious, to tell the truth, about a reply that would doubtless be banal, as because I was annoyed by the excessively despotic question. Fortunately, I was getting close, and the increasingly familiar countryside reminded me so strongly of times past that the haunting began to relax. The populous and busy town of Nanthel slowed me down, but on emerging from its suburbs I finally perceived, as a vague and distant mass, the heights of the Ardennes.

Dusk is falling. Wanting to reach my destination before dark, I step on the gas. The automobile roars, and the road is swallowed up beneath it vertiginously; it seems to be entering into the car to roll up inside it, as meters of flexible ribbon roll up on a reel. Its speed makes the wind of its progress whistle in my ears; a swarm of mosquitoes pepper my face like particles of lead, and all kinds of tiny creatures splash on my goggles. I have the Sun to my right now. It is on the horizon; the road takes me down, then bears me up again very rapidly, obliging it to set several times in succession and then rise again for me. Eventually, it disappears. I race through the twilight as fast as my brave machine can carry me—and I don't believe that a 234-XY has ever been overtaken. At that speed, the Ardennes are less than half an hour away. Their mass is already taking on a green tint, the color of forests, and my heart leaps. Fifteen years! It's 15 years since I last saw them, those dear large woods! My old vacation friends!

For it is there, in their shadow, that the château hides, at the bottom of its enormous basin. I remember it very clearly, that basin, and can already distinguish the location, marked out by a dark patch. In truth, it's the most extraordinary ravine! My late aunt Lidivine Lerne, who was besotted with legends, claimed that Satan, furious at some setback, had hollowed it out with a single sweep of his gigantic claw, but that origin is dubious. In any case, the image paints a rather vivid picture of the place: an amphitheater with steep walls, with no other exit than a large defile opening on to the fields. To put it another way, the plain penetrates into the mountain like a terrestrial gulf; it hollows out a cul-de-sac there, whose sheer walls rise up more steely the further it extends, and whose far end is broadly rounded—to such an extent that one arrives at Fonval on the level, without climbing the slightest slope, in spite of its location in the heart of the mountain. Its grounds are the floor of the amphitheater and the cliff serves them as a wall, except on the side of the gorge. The latter is separated from the estate by a wall in which a gate is set. A long avenue extends therefrom, very straight and bordered by linden-trees. In a few minutes I shall be going along it...and shortly afterwards, I shall find out why no one must follow me to Fonval. "Come alone and give advance notice!" Why those instructions?

Patience. The mass of the Ardennes divides into individual blocks. At the speed I'm traveling, they all seem to be moving. The outcrops slide past one another rapidly, approaching and drawing away, descending only to rise again with wave-like majesty, and the spectacle varies continuously, like that of a titanic sea.

A bend in the road unmasks a village. I know it well. Once upon a time, in the month of August every year, it was at the village railway station that uncle's carriage, harnessed to his horse Biribi, waited for my mother and me. We used to go back there in order to return. Hello, hello, Grey-l'Abbaye! Fonval is no more than three kilometers away. I could find it with my eyes shut! And here's the direct road, which will soon plunge into the woods and acquire the title of avenue.

It's nearly dark. A peasant calls out to me—probably insults. I'm used to it. My horn replies to his mournful and menacing complaint.

The forest! Ah, it's powerful aroma! The perfume of holidays of yesteryear! Could their memory bring back any other scent than that of the forest? It's exquisite. I'd love to prolong my nostrils' feast...

Decelerating, the automobile moves forward slowly. Its roar becomes a murmur. To the right and left, the walls of the long corridor begin to get higher. If the light was better I'd already be able to see Fonval at the end of the straight avenue. Hang on! What's the matter?

I've almost crashed; contrary to my expectation, there was a bend in the road.

I slow down further.

A little further on, another bend, and then another...

I stopped.

The stars were coming out one by one, like luminous dewdrops. The spring night permitted me to see the jutting crests above me, and the direction of their slopes astonished me. I started to back up, and discovered a fork in the road that I had not noticed as I passed it. Having taken the right-hand road, it presented me with a new fork after a few bends, as if it were setting me a riddle. There, I headed in the direction of Fonval, after taking my bearings from the cliffs whose height increased nearer to the château—but a further crossroads nonplussed me. What had happened to the straight avenue? I was utterly confused.

I switched on the headlights. By their light, I wandered through a tangle of lanes for some time without being able to figure out where I was, because there were so many intersections and blind alleys. It seemed to me that I had already passed a certain birch-tree. The walls, moreover, still had the same height. I was, therefore, moving through a veritable labyrinth, without getting any further forward. Had the peasant from Grey been trying to warn me? Probably.

Nevertheless, I pursued my exploration, counting on luck and annoyed by the circumstance. Three times the same junction presented itself within the radiant field of my headlights, and three times I exited from it by different routes, facing the same birch-tree.

I tried to summon help. Unfortunately, the horn malfunctioned and I had no means of sounding an alarm; as for my voice, the distance that separated me from Grey in one direction and Fonval in the other prevented it from being heard.

Anxiety took hold of me then. What if I ran out of gas? I drew to a halt at a crossroads and checked the level. My tank was almost empty. What was the point of draining it by going in hopeless circles? After all, it seemed easy enough to reach the château on foot, through the woods. I tried it—but a wire fence hidden in the bushes prevented me from passing through...

The labyrinth was obviously not a playful enterprise mounted at the entrance to a garden but a defensive contrivance deliberately complicating the approach to a retreat.

Considerably put out, I set about examining the question.

I don't understand you at all, Uncle Lerne, I thought. *You received notice of my arrival this morning, but here I am, trapped in the slyest of all adventures in landscape gardening. What eccentric whim caused you to have it done? Have you changed even more than I supposed? You would never have contemplated such fortifications 15 years ago.*

Fifteen years ago, the nights doubtless resembled this one. The sky sparkled in the same way, and the toads were already punctuating the silence with their strident, abrupt and soft croaking. A nightingale was trilling, like that one. That old evening was delightful too, Uncle. My aunt and my mother had both just died, though, within a week of one another, and with the two sisters gone, you and I were left with one another, one of us a widower and the other an orphan...

And the man of that era appeared in my memory as the town of Nanthel then knew him: a surgeon, already famous at 35 for the dexterity of his hands and the good fortune of his audacity, but who remained faithful to his native town in spite of his renown; Doctor Frédéric Lerne, clinical lecturer at the Ecole de Médecine, associate member of numerous scientific societies, recipient of many awards and—to leave nothing out—tutor to his nephew Nicolas Vermont.

In fact, I had not spent much time with the new father imposed on me by law, for he never took vacations and only spent his Sundays at Fonval in the summer. Even those he spent working ceaselessly, in isolation. Indeed, on those Sundays, his passion for horticulture, suppressed all week, kept him shut up in his little hothouse with his tulips and his orchids. In spite of the rarity of our meetings, though, I knew him well and loved him dearly. He was a strong, calm and sober fellow, perhaps a trifle cold, but very kind. Irreverently, I referred to his clean-shaven face as an old woman's face, but my joke rang false, for he would sometimes adopt an antique expression, haughty and grave, and sometimes one of subtle mockery in the Regency style. My uncle was one of the few modern beardless men whose head legitimated that affectation, by means of a nobility suggestive of ancestors clad in togas and grandparents clad in satin, which permitted their scion to wear the costumes of his ancestors without insult.

At present, Lerne appeared to me clad in a rather ill-fitting black frock-coat, in which I had seen him for the last time before leaving for Spain. Being rich, and wanting me to be rich too, my uncle had sent me to be a cork-trader, in the employ of the Gomez Company in Badajoz. My exile had lasted 15 years, during which the professor's situation had surely improved, to judge by the sensational operations he had undertaken, rumor of which had reached me even in the depths of the Estremadura.

As for me, my affairs had not prospered. After 15 years, despairing of ever having my own business selling lifebelts and corks, I had just returned to France to seek another profession when fate procured me independent means. I was the million-franc jackpot winner on the lottery who wished to remain anonymous. In Paris, I obtained comfortable but not luxurious accommodation. My apartment was simple and convenient. I had what I needed, plus an automobile, but minus a family.

Before founding a new family, it seemed to me to be appropriate to renew contact with the old one—which is to say, with Lerne. So I wrote to him—not that we had not stayed in touch more-or-less continually since our separation. At first, he had given me wise advice and shown himself politely paternal. His first letter even told me about a will in my favor, hidden in the secret drawer of a desk at Fonval. After the formal completion of his duties as a tutor, our relationship remained the same. Then, abruptly, his letters had changed, their tone becoming fractious, then cantankerous. Their banal subject-matter had become vulgar and his phraseology coarse; even the handwriting seemed to change. These features became more accentuated with each passing missive, until I had to limit myself to sending him my good wishes once a year, at Christmas. My uncle replied with a few scribbled words. Wounded in my only affection, I was desolate.

What had happened? A year before this sudden change—five years before my return to Fonval and getting lost in the labyrinth—I had read in *Epoca*:

Our Paris correspondent has informed us that Professor Lerne is bidding farewell to his patients in order to devote himself to the scientific research he has already begun at Nanthel hospital. With that end in mind, the excellent practitioner is retiring to his Château de Fonval in the vicinity of the Ardennes town, fitted out for that purpose. He has been joined by a few enlightened collaborators, including Dr. Klotz of Mannheim and three laboratory assistants from the Anatomical Institute founded by the latter at 22 Friedrichstrasse, which is now closed. When shall we see the results?

Lerne had confirmed this news in an enthusiastic note, which did not add anything to the bare facts of the article. I repeat that it was a year later that his sudden change of character had taken place. Had 12 months of work ended in frustration? Had a bitter disappointment affected the professor seriously enough to make him treat me like a stranger, almost an annoyance?

In spite of his hostility, it was with the greatest possible affection and respect that I had written the letter from Paris in which I told him of my good fortune and asked for permission to visit him. Never was there an invitation less warm than his. He asked me to notify him of my arrival, in order that he could send a carriage to meet me at the station. You will presumably not stay long, he added, for Fonval is not a pleasant place to stay. We work hard here. *Come alone and give advance notice!*

But I had given advance notice, damn it, and I was alone! I, who had considered my visit as a duty! Well, yes, it was simply stupid! I stared at the meeting-place of the pathways, which the exhausted headlights was no longer brightening much more than a night-light, in a bad temper. I was surely going to spend the night in that sylvan jail; there was no way of getting out of it before dawn. The toads in the pool near Fonval could call all they liked, and the church bell in Grey vainly chime the hours to signal an alternative refuge—for bell-towers are sonic lighthouses—but I was a prisoner.

Prisoner. That made me smile. How frightened I would have been, once. Prisoner of the Ardennes! At the mercy of the cavernous shadow of the monstrous forest of Broceliande, darkening a world between its two edges, one beyond Blois and the other in Constantinople![9] Broceliande! Theater of epic tales

---

[9] The actual Broceliande was a forest that once covered much of Brittany; its modern remnant, Paimpart Forest, is near Rennes. This location ensured that its mythical equivalent became the setting for much early French chivalric romance, including many Arthurian romances. The wry reference to its extent reaching almost to Constantinople is ultimately derived from the romance of Huon of Bordeaux, whose encounter with Oberon—a god of the underworld subsequently reconfigured, in consequence of this fateful meeting, as the king of fairyland—obviously takes place in the generic forest but is alleged in the text to occur in Syria. When Oberon was re-employed by Shakespeare in *A Midsummer Night's Dream* the setting was allegedly "a wood near Athens," but a subsequent

and puerile legends, fatherland of the four sons of Aymon and Petit Poucet, the forest of druids and goblins, the wood in which Sleeping Beauty slept while Charlemagne kept watch! What slightly fantastic story did not have its thickets for a setting, and were its trees not characters themselves?

Oh, Aunt Lidivine, I murmured, *how you were able to animate all that nonsense every evening after dinner. A fine woman! Did she ever suspect how much influence those tales had? Did you know, Aunt, that all your wonderful puppets invaded my life as they passed through my dreams? Do you know that a magical fanfare still sounds in my ears, sometimes—you who made the nights I spend at Fonval echo with the sounds of Roland's Oliphant and Oberon's horn.*

At that moment, I could not help feeling a surge of annoyance; the headlights had just gone out after one last dying flicker. For a few seconds, the darkness was absolute, and, at the same time, there was such a profound silence that I could have believed I had suddenly gone blind and deaf.

Then my eyes adapted gradually, and a crescent Moon soon appeared, snowy in the cold night. The forest lit up with a frosty whiteness. I shivered. While my aunt was alive, it would have been in terror; in the mists creeping through the darkness I would have seen dragons slithering and serpents crawling. An owl took flight. I would have made it into the winged helmet of an enchanted paladin. The straight-boled birch tree gleamed like a lance. An oak— perhaps a descendant of the magic tree that espoused Princess Laelina — quivered. It was enormous and druidic; a ball of mistletoe hung from its main branch, and the moon cut through it like a shiny sacred sickle.

The landscape was certainly hallucinatory. For want of anything better to do I studied it. I did not understand any better today than I had then why I had felt all its power of suggestion, and had only gone outside reluctantly after nightfall. In spite of its countless flowers and its beautiful winding pathways, Fonval itself was, I think, a most forbidding place. An ancient abbey transformed into a château, its arched windows, its surrounding precipice and its Hellish entrance all rendered it strange, even in daylight, and it was hardly surprising that everyone tried to understand it by means of fables. That must have been its true language. At least, that was how I spoke and—even more so—how I acted during my vacations.

For me, those vacations were one long fairy tale, which I acted out with imaginary or artificial bit-part players, more often than not living on the water, in the trees or underground. If I raced bare-legged over the lawn, it was obvious, by my attitude that squadrons of knights were charging behind me, in illusion. And the old rowing-boat! Masted for the occasion with three broomsticks, from which colored flags fluttered, it served me as a sailing-ship, and the pond be-

---

reference makes it clear that Renard considers the generic "Shakespearean forest"—including the moving wood in *Macbeth*—to be a version of the mythical Broceliande.

came the Mediterranean bearing a crusader fleet! Pensively staring at water-lily-islands and grassy peninsulas, I proclaimed: "There's Corsica and Sardinia! Italy's in sight! We're doubling Malta!" A minute later: "Land Ho!" We landed in Palestine. "Montjoie et Saint Denis!" I suffered both land- and sea-sickness in that boat; Holy War intoxicated me; I learned enthusiasm and geography therein...

More often than not, though, the other actors were simulated. That was more real. The memory came back to me then—for every child has a Don Quixote within him—of the giant Briareus, who was the summer-house, and, especially, a barrel that became Andromeda's dragon. Oh, that barrel! I had made a head for it with the aid of a squint-eyed pumpkin, and vampiric wings with two umbrellas. With the apparatus lying in ambush round the bed of a pathway, supported by a terracotta nymph, I went in search of it, more tremulous than the actual Perseus, armed with a beanpole and prancing on an invisible hippogriff—but when I discovered it, the pumpkin looked at me so strangely that Perseus almost took flight, and it was due to that excitement that the umbrellas were smashed into pieces in the yellow blood of the facetious vegetable.

My mannequins, in fact, made a deep impression on me by virtue of the roles I gave them to play. As I always kept that of protagonist, hero and conqueror for myself, I easily overcame that dread by day, but by night, although the gallant knight became that little scamp Nicolas Vermont again, the barrel remained a monster. Cowering under my bedclothes, my mind tormented by whatever story my aunt had just finished, I *knew* that the garden was populated by my fearful fantasies, that Briareus was still standing guard there, and that the terrifying barrel, restored to life, clenching the claws on its wings, was watching my window from afar.

At that age, I despaired of ever being like everyone else and being able to confront the darkness; and yet my fear had vanished—leaving me impressionable, to be sure, but not a coward—and it really was me who now found himself unafraid while lost in a deserted forest that was, alas, devoid of fairies and enchanters.

I had reached this point in my reverie when vague noises became audible in the direction of Fonval: an ox bellowing; something akin to the long mournful howling of a dog. That was all; calm was restored. A few minutes went by, and I heard a barn-owl hooting between myself and the château. Another, less distant, took flight; then others followed suit, at increasingly close range. One might have thought that the passage of some creature was frightening them. Indeed, the faint sound of footfalls—the repetitive trot of a quadruped—became audible and drew nearer, striking the hard ground of the pathway. I listened to the animal for some minutes as it went back and forth in the maze, perhaps also going astray there—and then it suddenly surged forth before my eyes.

By virtue of its widespread antlers, the proudness of its neck and the delicacy of its ears, it was unmistakable; it was a ten-point red deer stag. Scarcely had I thought that, however, when it caught sight of me and ran away, making an abrupt about-turn. Then—had it braced itself for a leap?—its body seemed curiously small and slim. It also seemed to me—was it a trick of the light?—that it was white. The animal disappeared in the blink of an eye, and its constricted gallop drew away rapidly.

Had I mistaken a goat for a deer, at first glance? Or had I subsequently mistaken a deer for a goat? It must be admitted that I was powerfully intrigued, to the extent that I wondered whether I might be about to rediscover the childish state of mind that I had left behind at Fonval. A little reflection, however, persuaded me that hunger, fatigue and drowsiness, aided by the moonlight, can easily deceive one's sight, and that a single ray of moonlight striking at an awkward angle was not a phenomenon.

I regretted it, however. Although my fear of the marvelous was in the past, I had conserved my love of it. It still held me captive. As a child, I had seen it everywhere; as a young man, I was content to suppose it in the inexplicable, gladly presuming the bizarre effect of any unknown cause as supernatural. To borrow the philosopher's phrase, "When water curves a staff" it is unacceptable to me that "my reason straightens it"[10] and I would have preferred not to know that the archer Phoebus would have been unable to draw his mighty and charming rainbow without the decomposition of solar light.

And yet, amid everything that tends to dispel the illusion of the marvelous, is it not necessary to take note of its innate attractiveness? One says to oneself; "Perhaps it's there, but that's only a conjecture; I'd prefer, in order to enjoy it more, to see it more clearly, with certainty…" As one approaches, the truth becomes clearer and the prodigy is eclipsed. Thus, like all men of my stripe, when confronted by a mystery made all the more seductive by virtue of being veiled, even at the risk of worse deception, I try to unveil it…

At the end of the day, though, that animal was truly extraordinary…

Wandering through the incomprehensible labyrinth, it seemed to me to be an enigma wrapped up in a puzzle, and my curiosity was piqued by it. Weighed down by weariness as I was, though, I soon fell asleep, thinking about the trickery of detective stories and the subtle methods of logical investigation.

I woke up at daybreak. Immediately, I glimpsed a means of escape from my imprisonment. Not far away, in fact, men were chatting as they walked, hidden by the undergrowth. They moved back and forth, like the stag—if it had been a stag—doubtless following the twisting pathways. Once, still hidden, they passed within a few meters of the car, but I could not understand their speech. It seemed to me that they were chatting in German.

---

[10] The quotation is an epigram formulated by the fabulist Jean de La Fontaine (1621-1695).

Finally, they came in sight, at the same place as the animal. There were three of them, bending down over the ground as if following a trail. At the spot where the beast had turned round, one of them uttered an exclamation and showed the others that it had turned back. They had seen me, though, and I advanced toward them.

"Gentlemen," I said, doing my best to smile, "would you have the kindness to show me the way to Fonval? I'm lost…"

The three men studied me without replying, slyly inquisitive. They were an unusual trio. The first had a rounded and unfortunately flat face atop a massive but squat body; his thin and pointed nose was mounted on that disk like the gnomon of a sundial. The second had a military bearing, and was twisting his Imperial Germanic moustache; his chin stuck out, more like a ship's figurehead than the toe of a shoe. The third was a tall old man with gold-rimmed spectacles, curly grey hair and an unkempt beard. He was eating cherries noisily, the way a county bumpkin eats tripe.

They were definitely Germans, doubtless the three laboratory assistants from the Anatomical Institute.

The old one spat out a salvo of cherry-stones in my direction and one of those Teutonic phrases in which a machine-gun rattle of words is mingled with countless other sounds toward his comrades. They exchanged a few remarks in this fashion, like so many broadsides, without paying any heed to me; then, having conferred among themselves—their mouths having skillfully imitated the noise of a battle fought beside a cataract—they turned on their heels, leaving me stunned by their rudeness.

It was, however, necessary to get out of there! This expedition was becoming more ridiculous by the minute. What did it all mean? What kind of comedy was this? In sum, I was being played for a fool! I was furious. The presumed secrets that I thought I had detected now seemed to be mere childishness, products of tiredness and darkness. I had to get away! I had to get away immediately!

Angrily, and without thinking, I pressed the ignition-switch that started the car, and its eighty-horsepower engine came to life under the hood, buzzing like bees within a hive. I seized the gear-stick, but as I did so, an outburst of laughter made me turn round.

With his cap tilted over his ear and his bag of letters slung over his shoulder, a blue-shirted postman was looking at me, triumphant in his hilarity. "Ha ha!" he drawled. "I told you last night that you were on the wrong road!"

I recognized the villager from Grey-l'Abbaye, but my ill humor prevented me from answering him.

"Are you really going to Fonval?" he went on.

I fulminated against Fonval in rather impolite terms, which consigned it, along with all its inhabitants, to Hell.

"Because," the postman continued, "if you're going there. I'll take you myself. I have to go there to take the post. Hurry, though. There's twice as much today; it's Monday and I don't come here on Sundays."

So saying, he had taken some letters from his sack and was sorting through them.

"Show me that!" I cried excitedly. "Yes, that yellow envelope..."

He looked me up and down suspiciously and showed it to me from a distance. It was my letter—the announcement of my arrival, which had followed it by one night rather than anticipating it by one day!

That misfortune excused my uncle and dispelled my rancor.

"Get in!" I said. "You can show me the way...and we'll have a chat."

The car moved off into the new day.

The mist was fading away, as if the sun, having bleached the darkness, had still to dissolve it, and as if that condensation, now almost gone, were its lingering foggy shadow: a vaporous residue of night in day, the fading specter of a vanished phantom.

II. Among Sphinxes

The automobile slowly wound its way through the labyrinth. Sometimes, confronted by a crossroads, the postman hesitated momentarily.

"How long is it since these zigzags replaced the straight road?" I asked.

"Four years, Monsieur—about a year after Monsieur Lerne took up permanent residence at the château."

"Do you know their purpose? You can tell me—I'm the professor's nephew."

"Bah! He's...well, he's an eccentric."

"What does he do that's so extraordinary?"

"Oh, my God, nothing...we hardly ever see him. That's what's so strange. Before he took it into his head to build this maze, we often ran into him—he took walks in the countryside—but since then...all he does is go to catch the train in Grey once a month."

In sum, all my uncle's eccentricities had started at the same time: the maze and the different style of his letters dated from the same era. Something had profoundly affected his mind at that time.

"What about his companions, the Germans?" I went on.

"Oh, them! Invisible men, Monsieur. What's more, although I go to Fonval six times a week, I can't recall when I last cast a glance over the grounds. Monsieur Lerne comes to the gate in person to pick up the mail. Oh, what changes there've been! Did you know old Jean? Well, he's gone, and his wife too. It's just as I tell you, Monsieur: no more coachman, no more housekeeper...no more horse!"

"Four years ago, wasn't it?"

75

"Yes, Monsieur."

"Tel me, postman, there's a lot of game hereabouts, isn't there?"

"My word, no. A few rabbits, two or three hares...but there are too many foxes."

"What, no roe deer or red deer?"

"Never."

A strange joy made me quiver.

"We're here, Monsieur."

Indeed, after one hast hairpin bend, the road opened out on to the former avenue, of which Lerne had kept the stump. Two rows of linden trees marked out its borders and at the very end of their line, Fonval's gate seemed to be coming toward us. In front of it, a semicircular esplanade broadened out the avenue, and behind it, the blue roof of the château stood out against the green of the trees, while the trees stood out themselves against the dark flank of the gulf.

In the middle of a wall connected to the cliffs, still coiffed by its tiled roof, the gateway had aged; the stone of its frame was eroded and the worm-eaten wood of its panels was crumbling to dust in places—but the bell had not changed. It rang from the depths of my childhood, so cheerful, so clear, and so distant that I could have wept on hearing it.

We waited for a few moments. Eventually, clogs clattered.

"Is that you, Guilloteaux?" said a voice with an accent from beyond the Rhine.

"Yes, Monsieur Lerne."

Monsieur Lerne? I looked at my guide, my eyes wide. What? It was my uncle who was speaking in that fashion?

"You're early," said the voice.

Iron bolts were withdrawn, then a hand was extended through a narrow gap.

"Give..."

"There you are, Monsieur Lerne...but there's someone with me," insinuated the postman, suddenly timid.

"Who is it?" exclaimed the other—and he appeared in the crack left by the partly-opened door.

It really was my uncle Lerne—but life had affected him strangely, afflicting him with premature old age and turning him into a wild and unkempt individual whose overly long grey hair made his collar greasy. He stared at me as if I were an enemy, his eyebrows furrowed above his hostile eyes. "What do you want?" he demanded, rudely. He pronounced his *w*s as if they were *v*s.

I hesitated momentarily. That Siouxesque mask, hairless and cruel, no longer bore any similarity to the face of an old woman; as I looked at it, I experienced the contradictory sensation of recognizing it even though it was not recognizable.

"But it's me, Uncle," I finally stammered. "I've come to see you…with your permission. I wrote to you—except that my letter…there it is…we've arrived together. Excuse my stupidity…"

"Ah! Well…you should have told me. It's me that asks forgiveness of you, my dear nephew." The change was sudden. Lerne blushed in confusion, becoming eager, almost servile. This embarrassment, unnecessary so far as I was concerned, surprised me. "Ha ha!" he added. "You've come in a mechanical carriage. Hmmm…there's enough room to get it in, isn't there?"

He opened both panels of the gate. "Here, one often has to be one's own servant," he said, while the ancient hinges creaked—and my uncle laughed dully. I would have wagered, given his perplexed expression, that he had no desire to do so, and that his thoughts were far from frivolity.

The postman had gone on his way.

"Is that still the coach-house?" I said, pointing at a brick shed to the right.

"Yes, yes…I didn't recognize you because of your moustache. Hmm…yes…your moustache. You didn't have one before…ha ha? How old are you now?"

"31, uncle."

At the sight of the coach-house, my heart slipped a beat. The carriage was moldering, half-buried under bundles of firewood, and the stable next door, which was full of bric-à-brac, was covered in cobwebs, old and new.

"31 already!" Lerne went on, without conviction, his mind obviously distracted.

"Address me as *tu*, as you used to, uncle."

"Eh? That's right, my dear…er…Nicolas, isn't it?"

I was very embarrassed, but he seemed no more at ease than I was. My presence was clearly unwelcome. It's always intriguing for an intruder to discover why he's intruding; I grabbed my suitcase. Lerne noticed the gesture and seemed to come to a sudden decision.

"Leave that!" he instructed, rather imperiously. "Leave it, Nicolas! I'll have your luggage sent up shortly. Before then, we must have a chat. Let's go for a walk." He took me by the arm and drew me toward the grounds. He was still reflective, however.

We went toward the château. Nearly all of the shutters were closed. In many places the roof was depressed, sometimes even cracked, and the leprous walls, whose plaster was coming away in large flakes, were displaying their masonry in places. Potted shrubs still framed the edifice, but there was no doubt that the vervains, pomegranates, orange-trees and laurels had not been taken indoors for several winters. Rotting where they stood in their broken tubs, they were all dead. The sandy drive, once kept carefully raked, might have been taken for a coarse meadow, so extensively had the grass invaded it, mingled with stinging-nettles and hemlock. It might have been the Sleeping Beauty's manor-house, when the prince arrived.

Lerne held my arm as we walked. He said nothing more. We went around the sad dwelling, and the grounds appeared before my eyes: a mess. No more flower-beds or broad and winding sandy paths. Except for the lawn in front of the château—which had metamorphosed into a pasture, enclosed by steel wire, and given as grazing to a few cattle—the vale had resumed its wild state. The pathways were still marked out by shallow depressions, but young saplings were growing amid the grass. The garden was now no more than a large wood strewn with clearings and criss-crossed by verdant footpaths. The Ardennes were re-claiming their stolen domain.

Carefully, Lerne stuffed a large pipe with a feverish finger and lit it. We went into the wood, along one of the cave-like lanes.

As we went past, I looked at the statues with disillusioned eyes. A former proprietor of Fonval had erected them in profusion. These magnificent bit-part players in my dramas were, in fact, poor modern castings, commercially copied from Rome or Greece by some magnate of the Second Empire. The concrete tunics swelled out like crinolines, the cloaks hung down like shawls, and the divinities of the woods—Echo, Syrinx, Arethusa—wore hair-nets in the Benoiton style. Today, these tawdry simulacra of exquisite fantasies, forest-dwellers' fancies transmuted into dryads, were more timely in their mantles of virginal vines and clematis, although certain heroes were no more than men of ivy, whose mossy expressions were imagining Diana.

After walking for some time, my uncle made me sit down on a stone bench covered with a layer of lichen, in the shade of a flowering hazel-tree. There was a little cracking sound within its crown, immediately above our heads. Lerne started convulsively, and raised his head. It was merely a squirrel, which was watching us from a high branch. My uncle glared at it ferociously, as if he were taking aim at it; then he started laughing, in a reassured fashion. "Ha ha ha! It's only a little...thing," he said, unable to find the right word.

In truth, I thought, *how odd one can become as one ages. Environment, I know, explains a great deal of evolution; one acquires the appearance, and even the accent, of one's intimates. The company Lerne keeps is sufficient to explain why my uncle is badly-dressed, expresses himself awkwardly, talks with a German accent and smokes that huge pipe...but he's stopped liking flowers, no longer looks after his estate and seems, at present, to be astonishingly nervous and preoccupied. If we add in last night's incidents, all that seems less natural.*

Meanwhile, the professor was staring at me in a disconcerting manner, studying me as if he were weighing me up, never having seen me before. I was confused. A lively debate was going on within him, reflected in his face in alternatives of various resolutions. Our eyes met continually, finally meeting steadfastly, and my uncle, unable to keep silent any longer, appeared to make up his mind for a second time.

"You know, Nicolas," he said, patting me on the thigh, "I'm ruined!"

I understood what he was trying to do, and rebelled.

"Be frank, uncle—you want me to go away!"

"Me? What an idea..."

"Definitely. I'm sure of it. Your invitation was rather discouraging, and your welcome is hardly hospitable—but you have a very short memory, uncle, if you think me greedy enough only to have come here as your heir. I can see that you're no longer the same man—your letters had alerted me to that, anyway—but it surpasses all understanding that you've invented this gross subterfuge designed to chase me away. For myself, I haven't changed in 15 years! I've never ceased to respect you wholeheartedly, and I deserve better that those icy epistles and—Great God!—this insult!"

"Now, now...take it easy..." said Lerne, profoundly irritated.

"In any case," I continued, "do you want me to go? Say so straightforwardly, and I'll say goodbye. You're no longer my uncle!"

"Never pronounce such a blasphemy, Nicolas!" He said that in such a fearful voice that I attempted intimidation.

"And I shall denounce you, uncle—you and your acolytes and your mysteries!"

"You're mad! Mad! You'd better shut up! What an imagination!" Lerne burst out laughing—but his eyes frightened me, and for some unknown reason I regretted what I'd said. "Come on, Nicolas," he went on. "Don't get carried away. You're a good lad. You'll always find in me your old uncle, who loves you. Listen—no, it isn't true, I'm not ruined, and my heir will certainly receive something...if he does as I wish. Honestly, though, it seems to me that it would be better if you didn't stay here. There's nothing here to interest a man of your age, Nicolas; personally, I'm busy all day long..."

The professor was able to talk now. Hypocrisy was evident in every sentence; he was no longer anything but a Tartuffe unworthy of consideration, fair game for deception. I had no intention of leaving until my curiosity was completely satisfied, so I interrupted him. "There you go again," I said, "still playing the inheritance card in order to make me leave Fonval. You obviously don't trust me..."

He denied it with a gesture. "No, uncle," I continued, "permit me to remain in order that we can get to know one another again. We both have need of one another."

Lerne frowned, then joked: "Do you persist in disowning me?"

"No," I said, in a bantering tone, "but if you don't let me stay here, you'll hurt my feelings, and I won't know what to think..."

"Stop!" said my uncle, forcefully. "There's nothing of which to be suspicious—far from it!"

"Of course. Nevertheless you have secrets, and that's your right. If I mention them to you, it's because I need to assure you, firmly, that I shall respect them."

79

"There's only one!" said my uncle emphatically, becoming animated. "Just one secret—and its purpose is noble and salutary! One alone, you understand! That of our work: beneficent, and glorious too, and worth a lot of money! But it's still necessary to keep it quiet. Secrets? The whole world knows we're here, that we're working! The newspapers have said so; there's no secret in that!"

"Calm down uncle, and tell me the rules I must follow in your house. I'm at your disposal."

Lerne resumed his internal debate. "Well," he said, when he raised his head again, "that's agreed. An uncle such as I have always been to you could not possibly send you away. That would be giving a lie to my entire past. Stay then, but on the following conditions: we're conducting research here that has almost reached its conclusion; when our discovery is an accomplished fact, the public will learn of it at a stroke; until then, I don't wish to inform it about certain trials whose revelation might alert rivals capable of anticipating us; I don't doubt your discretion, but I would prefer, nevertheless, not to put it to the test, and I beg you, in your own interest, not to try to discover anything, rather than be forced to conceal it.

"I said *in your own interest*. That's not only because it's easier not to pry than to keep silent, but also for other reasons, which are these: our business is fundamentally commercial; a businessman with our experience could be useful to me; we shall be rich, nephew—millionaires—but it's necessary to leave me in peace to forge the instrument of your fortune; you must show yourself henceforth to be the tactful man, respectful of my orders, that I need as an associate.

"Besides, I'm not alone in this enterprise. You might be made to repent your actions, if they transgress the rules that I lay down...repent cruelly, more cruelly than you can imagine...so practice indifference, my dear nephew. See nothing, hear nothing, understand nothing, in order to achieve wealth, and to stay...alive...

"Oh, indifference is not such an easy virtue, at least at Fonval...there are now things outside, since last night...things that should not be there and are only there by virtue of carelessness..."

As he pronounced these final words, an unexpected anger took hold of Lerne. He waved his fists in the air and muttered: "Wilhelm! Imbecilic ass!"

I was now sure that the secrets were important, and would be very surprising once they were winkled out. As for the doctor's promises and threats, I didn't believe them, and his speech hadn't aroused either covetousness or fear, by which two means my uncle would have liked to guarantee my obedience.

"Is that all you ask of me?" I enquired, coldly.

"No. But this prohibition is of another sort. Shortly, Nicolas, at the château, I shall introduce you to someone. It's someone to whom I'm giving shelter...a young woman..."

I started in surprise, and Lerne divined my inference. "Oh!" he cried. "She's like a daughter, nothing more. In spite of everything, her friendship is precious to me, and it would hurt me to see it diminished by a sentiment that I can no longer inspire." He added, very quickly, with a certain shame: "In brief, Nicolas, I demand that you swear an oath not to pay court to my ward."

Distressed by such debased thinking and even more by such a lack of delicacy, I nevertheless thought that there is no jealousy without love, any more than smoke without fire.

"What do you take me for, uncle? The fact that I'm your guest is sufficient…"

"That's good. I know my physiology, and how to make use of it. Can I count on you? Do you swear it? Good." With a thin smile, he added: "As for her, I have no worries for the time being. She has recently seen how I treat suitors…I advise you not to try it."

Having risen to his feet, with his hands in his pockets and his pipe between his teeth, Lerne looked me up and down, mockingly and provocatively. This physiologist inspired me with an indomitable aversion.

We continued our tour of the grounds.

"By the way," said the professor, "do you speak German?"

"No, uncle—only French and Spanish."

"Nor English, either? That's a bit thin for a future merchant prince. You have not been very well-educated."

Tell that to the marines, uncle! I thought. *I've begun to keep these eyes, which you ordered me to close, wide open—and I can see your satisfied expression belies your criticism.*

Going along the cliffs, we arrived at the far side of the grounds, facing the château, which seemed from there to be extending its two wings toward us, outdoing the undergrowth with its dilapidation—and it was at that exact moment that my attention was attracted by an unusual bird: a pigeon, which was spiraling rapidly through the air, flying ever more rapidly as its circles tightened.

"Look at those roses on the ground, on that long briar stem," said my uncle. "Pretty, and interesting. Free of cultivations, they've run wild."

"What a strange pigeon!" I remarked.

"Look at those flowers," Lerne insisted.

"One might think it had a lead pellet in its head. That sometimes happens during a shoot. It will climb up and up, and die at the greatest possible height."

"If you don't watch your feet, you'll trip up among the thorns and break your neck, my friend!" This useful warning was muttered in an entirely uncalled-for tone of menace.

Up above. The bird reached the center of its spiral, and began not to climb, but to descend, fluttering madly, and whirling around. It struck a rock not far away and fell, inert, into a thicket.

Why had the professor suddenly become anxious? What motive was causing him to accelerate his pace? That was what I was asking myself, when the large pipe dropped out of his mouth. Leaping forward to pick it up, I could not retain an exclamation of amazement; it had been cut clean through by an angry clench of the teeth, which ended in a German word, doubtless an oath.

As we went back toward the château, we saw a corpulent woman running toward us, overflowing her blue apron. The gymnastic pace was visibly exceptional and contrary to her inclination, for it shook her dangerously, and while trotting she supported herself by means of her arms and hands, as if she were hugging some precious, awkward and enormous burden. On seeing us she stopped dead—which seemed impossible—then appeared to want to go back. She continued on her way, however, very sheepishly, with an expression on her kindly face like that of a schoolgirl caught misbehaving. She was anticipating her fate.

"What are you doing here, Barbe!" said Lerne, angrily. "You've forgotten that I forbade you to go beyond the pasture. I'll end up sending you away, Barbe—after punishing you, of course!"

The fat woman was very frightened. She forced a simper, pursed her lips as if she were about to give birth, and made her excuses. She had seen the pigeon fall from her kitchen and thought she might add it to the menu. "We always eat the same dishes," she said, and added, stupidly: "Anyway, I didn't think you were in the garden, I thought you were in the lab..."

A brutal slap in the face interrupted the last syllable, which I inferred to be the first of *labyrinth*.

"Oh, uncle!" I cried, indignantly.

"You can hold your tongue or hop it! It's quite simple, eh?"

The terrified Barbe was no longer weeping. Her repressed sobs made her hiccup. She was very pale, and the print of Lerne's bony hand on her cheek was still red.

"Go and get Monsieur's bags from the coach-house and take it up to the Lion Room."

That was a room on the first floor of the west wing. "Won't you let me have my old room, uncle?" I asked.

"Which one?"

"Which one? But you know very well...the one on the ground floor, the Yellow Room, in the east wing."

"No," he said, sharply. "I'm using that one. Go on, Barbe!"

The cook moved off ahead of us as quickly as she could, gathering up her forefront in both arms, while her backside, confided to versatile destiny, wobbled freely.

To the right, the pond was stagnating. The reflection of our taciturn passage moved along it like a lethargic dream. I was prey to a gradually increasing amazement. Even so, I contrived not to seem overly surprised at the sight of a new and spacious grey stone building backing on to the cliff. It comprised two residential blocks separated by a courtyard. A high wall, pierced by a carriage gate—presently closed—hid the courtyard from view, but the clucking of poultry escaped therefrom, and a dog that had scented us started yapping.

Boldly, I sent out a probe. "Will you take me to visit your farm?"

Lerne shrugged his shoulders. "Perhaps," he said. Then, turning toward the house, he called: "Wilhelm! Wilhelm!"

The German with the face like a sundial opened a small window and the professor spoke rudely to him in his native tongue, so violently that the poor fellow trembled from head to toe.

Well, I said to myself, *it's evidently thanks to his inadvertence that there were things abroad last night that should not have been.*

When that job was done, we went alongside the pasture. It contained a black bull and four variously-colored cows. The herd escorted us, for no particular reason. My terrible relative became jocular. "Nicolas, may I introduce Jupiter. This is the white Europa, Io the russet, Athor the blonde and Pasiphae, comfortably clad in a milk-white dress stained with ink—or of charcoal stained with chalk, if you prefer, my friend."

This memorial to libertine mythology made me smile. In truth, I would have latched on to any pretext to cheer myself up a little; I had a physical need to do so. I was also feeling so hungry that assuaging my appetite would soon become the only matter of interest. The château became uniquely attractive—it was where I would get something to eat!

That attraction almost prevented me from examining the château's neighbor, the greenhouse. That would have been a pity. The old flower-house had been augmented by two new compartments whose bulbous forms flanked the original rotunda. Beneath its caparison of lowered blinds, the construction appeared to me to be "state of the art". It was like a cross between an exhibition hall and a bell-jar, and was possessed, if I dare say it, of a certain highly-unexpected grandiosity.

A greenhouse of that sort in this jungle! I would have been less astonished to find a love-potion in the depths of a monastery!

In my aunt's day, regrettably long past, the Lion Room had been a guest-room. It had—and still has—three windows with bays as deep as alcoves. One overlooks the greenhouse and has a balcony. A second opens on to the garden; I could see the pasture from it, and, more distantly, the pond—and between the two, the summer-house that had been Briareus. The third casement faced the east wing; from there, I could see the window of my old room—which was closed—and the entire façade of the château, sideways on, blocking the view to the left.

In that room I might as well have been in a hotel. Nothing there had any memories attached to it. Jouy wallpaper, marbled with damp and hanging loose in one corner, covered the walls with a host of red lions, each stopping a cannonball with its paw. The curtains on the bed and the windows deformed the same images within their pleats. Two engravings hung on the wall: *The Education of Achilles* and *The Ravishment of Deïanera*, in which damp had stained the faces of the four subjects red and dappled the hindquarters of the centaurs Chiron and Nessus.[11] There was also a rather fine Norman clock, like a coffin stood on end, both an emblem and a measure of time. It was all commonplace and out of date.

I washed my face in cold water and gladly put on clean underwear. Without knocking, Barbe brought me a bowl of rustic soup. She made no response to my condolences regarding her swollen cheek, and slipped away awkwardly, like some enormous sylph.

There was no one in the drawing-room, unless shades count. Little black velvet armchair with two yellow tassels, shapeless crouching puffiness, so aptly called a toad, could I remember you as you were without evoking the storytelling shade of my aunt upon your batrachian form? And my mother's chair—more austere, about which I cannot joke—will she not always be leaning on your back in my memory, for as long as you're an armchair, if ever you really were one?

Not a single detail had changed. From the ineffable white wall-paper, on which garlands of flowers trussed up in wreaths hung down, to the lambrequins of sulfur-yellow damask draping their fringed basques in a row, the work of a former owner—a contemporary of crinolines—had proved admirably resistant. Exaggerated padding still puffed up the sofas and settees, and nothing had succeeded in deflating the swollen chairs or the emphysemic poufs.

All along the wood-paneling, my dear family smiled at me: my ancestors from pastels; my grandparents from miniatures; my father as a schoolboy from a daguerreotype. On the mantelpiece, appropriately decked out with frayed bouffant frames, a few photographs were propped up in front of the mirror. One group, in a large format, solicited my attention. I picked it up in order to examine it more easily. It depicted my uncle surrounded by five gentlemen, next to a huge St. Bernard dog. The picture had been taken at Fonval; the wall of the château formed a background, which included a laurier-rose in a tub. It was an amateur print, unsigned. There, Lerne was radiant with generosity, strength and intelligence, similar in all respects to the scientist I had expected to find. Of the five gentlemen, three were known to me: the Germans; I had never seen the other two.

At that point, the door opened, so suddenly that I did not have time to put the group back in its place. Lerne ushered in a young woman.

---

[11] Renard evidently expects his readers to know that the two images form a morally contrasted pair, Achilles' tutor Chiron being the epitome of a virtuous centaur, while Nessus, Deïanera's attempted rapist and the eventual murderer of Hercules by means of the poisoned shirt he subsequently gave her, is an archetype of malevolence.

"My nephew, Nicolas Vermont, Mademoiselle Emma Bourdichet."

Mademoiselle Emma, according to all appearances, had just endured one of those sharp reprimands that Lerne distributed so prodigally. Her fearful expression testified to it. She did not even have the courage to make the conventional grimace customary in circumstances of forced amiability, awkwardly sketching a nod of the head.

As for me, having bowed, I dared not raise my eyes, for fear that my uncle might read my soul therein.

My soul? If one means by that, as one usually does, the assembly of faculties from which it results that man is the only animal slightly superior to others, it might be better, I think, not to involve my soul in this affair. Oh, I'm not unaware of the fact that, although all love—even the purest—originates in the bestial rut of the sexes, esteem and amity are often added into it to ennoble the unions of human beings. Alas, my passion for Emma still remained in its primordial state.

If Fragonard were to set out to commemorate our first encounter and wished, in the manner of the eighteenth century, to paint the love that presided over it, I would advise him to symbolize it as a little Eros with a goat's feet and legs, a faun-like Cupid, devoid of wings and a smile; his arrows would be made of wood, set in a quiver of bark, and bloody; he might, without impropriety, be named Pan. He is the universal love, the unintentionally fecund pleasure, the insidious instigating vice of childbirth and paternity, the sensual master of life, who preoccupies himself with equal solicitude with pigsties and eyries, burrows and middle-class beds...and who impelled us toward one another—Mademoiselle Bourdichet and me—like crazed rabbits.

Are there degrees in femininity? If there are, I have never seen a more womanly woman than Emma. I shall not describe her, having seen her more as a state of being than an object. Beautiful? Undoubtedly. Desirable? Most certainly. I remember her hair, though—it was the color of fire; dark red, perhaps dyed—and the image of her body has just reappeared to my moribund desire. Having blossomed with rare perfection and reached its culmination, it had those seductive contours for which wise nature, careful of selection, has put a taste in masculine brains, to the detriment of flat-chested women. Emma's clothing did not flatten those curves at all, and, animated by a meritorious scruple, left transparent what certain clothes would have covered up, just as sculptors and painters lay them bare and show them off in spite of couturiers.

Now, the charm of this adorable creature had just reached the height of its perfection. My pulse beat strongly in my skull and an enraged jealousy suddenly took hold of me. In truth, I would willingly have renounced that young woman, provided that no one else would ever touch her. Already displeasing, Lerne now became odious to me. I was now determined to stay, at any cost.

Meanwhile, we did not know what to say. Disturbed by the suddenness of the incident, and wanting to hide my confusion, I stammered in desperation: "I was just looking at this photograph, uncle..."

"Ah, yes! My assistants—Wilhelm, Karl and Johann—and me. And here's MacBell, my pupil![12] It's a good resemblance, wouldn't you say, Emma?" He stuck the print under his ward's nose, pointing out a short and slender young man, clean-shaven in the American style, with a distinguished bearing, who was leaning on the St. Bernard. "A handsome and witty fellow, eh?" said the professor, teasingly. "The cream of Scotland!"

Emma, still fearful, did not flinch. She merely articulated, with difficulty: "His Nelly was very amusing, with her circus-dog tricks."

"And MacBell?" sneered my uncle. "Was he amusing too?"

I saw Emma's chin quiver, a symptom of imminent tears. "Poor MacBell," she murmured.

"Yes," Lerne said to me, in response to my puzzled expression. "Donovan MacBell had to give up his position in the wake of some unfortunate incidents. May Fate spare you such unpleasantness, Nicolas!"

"And the other man?" I asked, in order to change the subject. "The gentleman with the moustache and dark sideburns—who's he?"

"He's gone too."

"Doctor Klotz," said Emma, who had drawn nearer and collected herself. "Otto Klotz. Oh! There's..."

Lerne silenced her with a terrible stare. I don't know what punishment it promised, but the young woman suffered a spasm that rendered her rigid.

At this point, Barbe introduced her opulent form sideways, and muttered that dinner was served. She had only set three places in the dining-room. The Germans, I imagined, must live in the grey building.

The meal was a morose affair. Mademoiselle Bourdichet did not venture another word, nor did she eat anything, but I could not work out the reason for it, terror equalizing all creatures with the same appearance.

In any case, I was overcome by drowsiness. As soon as we had finished dessert, I sought permission to go to bed, asking that I be allowed to sleep until the following morning.

In my room, I began to get undressed without delay. Quite frankly, the journey, the previous night and that morning had worn me out. All those puzzles irritated me still, first because they were enigmatic, and then because they pre-

---

[12] The Macaulay translation changes MacBell's name to Macbeth, perhaps in tacit recognition of a veiled reference to that play in the narrator's subsequent dream. Although I have not followed suit in that instance, I have followed the earlier translator's example in altering the spelling of the character's Christian name to "Donovan" rather than retaining Renard's highly unlikely "Doniphan."

sented themselves so confusedly. It was as if I were within a cloud in which uncertain sphinxes were turning their vague faces toward me.

My braces were just about to come off...but they did not.

In the garden, Lerne was heading for the grey buildings, accompanied by his three assistants.

They're doubtless going to work in there, I told myself. *No one's watching me; they haven't had time to take many precautions; my uncle thinks I'm going to sleep. Now's the time to act, Nicolas, or never! Where should I start? With Emma? Or the secret? Hmm...the girl was utterly petrified today...and as for the secret....*

Having put my jacket back on, I went from window to window, mechanically.

Then, between the wrought-iron bars of the balcony, the greenhouse exposed its mysterious extensions. It was closed, forbidden, attractive....

I went out stealthily.

III. The Greenhouse

Once outside, and exposed, it seemed to me that everything was spying on me, and I threw myself precipitately into a little wood next to the greenhouse. Then, fighting my way through a tangle of brambles and creepers, I headed for my objective.

It was very warm. I went forward with great difficulty, with a thousand precautions, in order to avoid revelatory scrapings and stumbles. Finally, the central dome of the greenhouse and one of its lateral bulges loomed up in front of me. It presented itself side-on. Discretion demanded that I make some initial observations without emerging from the wood.

What struck my immediately was its tidy appearance, its state of perfect maintenance; there was not a single displaced flagstone in the surrounding pavement, not a single broken brick in the foundation. The carefully-fitted blinds had all their slats, and in the narrow gaps between them, the windows glistened in the sunlight.

I listened. No sound reached me from the château or the grey buildings. In the greenhouse, there was silence. Nothing could be heard but the immense chatter of a hot afternoon. I plucked up my courage. Having approached furtively, I lifted up one of the wooden blinds and tried to look through the window-panes—but I couldn't see anything; they had been coated on the inner surface with a whitish substance. It was becoming increasingly probable that Lerne had diverted the greenhouse from its original purpose and was now using it for a very different cultivation than that of flowers. The idea of vats of microbes, simmering beneath the warm lights, seemed quite plausible to me.

I went around the greenhouse. Everywhere, the same coating—of varying thickness, it seemed—intercepted my sight. The partly-open ventilation panels were high up, out of reach. The wings had no door; one could only get into them from the central part, at the back. As I continued going round, scrutinizing the brickwork and glass that was no less opaque, I soon found myself on the château side, facing my balcony.

That location, being too exposed, was perilous. Being war-weary, I thought it best to go back to my room, abandoning the ostensible exhibition-hall of bacilli without visiting its façade. I limited my investigation, therefore, to a dejected glance, which unexpectedly informed me that the mystery was open to me. The door had only been pushed to, but the fully-extended bolt testified that some stupid person had imagined that he had locked it. Oh Wilhelm, you priceless scatterbrain!

As soon as I went in, my bacteriological hypothesis was obliterated. A gust of floral scents greeted me—a warm and humid gust, with a hint of nicotine.

I stopped on the threshold, wonderstruck. No greenhouse—not even a royal one—had ever given me the impression of unbridled luxury that I felt immediately. In that rotunda, surrounded by all those sumptuous plants, the first sensation was that of being dazzled. The entire gamut of greens was played as a chromatic scale on keys of foliage, amid the multicolored tints of flowers and fruits, and those splendors were magnificently stages on the steps ascending toward the cupola.

My eyes nevertheless became accustomed to it, and my admiration gradually faded. Certainly, in order for the winter garden to have made such an immediate impact, it had to be composed of plants that were quite remarkable in themselves, for, in reality, no harmonic artistry had been put into their arrangement. They were grouped according to their classification, not under the dictation of a spirit of elegance, like some Eldorado confided to the care of a policeman. Their groups were brutally separated from one another, into so many categories; the pots were lined up in military ranks, each one bearing a label that was more suggestive of botany than gardening, exhibiting less art than science. That circumstance provided food for thought. After all, could I admit for a single instant that Lerne was still a gardener for his own pleasure?

In pursuit of information, I paraded my hypnotized gaze over all the marvels, incapable in my ignorance of putting a name to any of them. I tried, nevertheless, mechanically—and then that luxury, which a collective examination had shown me in the capacity of rarity, perhaps exoticism, began to appear as it really was....

Incredulous, and gripped by a feverish curiosity, I inspected a cactus. In spite of my lack of knowledge, I could not be mistaken about it, but its red flower confused me. I examined it minutely, but my perplexity only increased. There was no possible doubt: that fanatical flower with the insolent gaze, that firework that shot up green to burst into fiery stars, was the flower of a geranium!

I went on to the next plant: three bamboo stems rising from the soil, whose colonnettes, in the guise of capitals, were coiffed with dahlias!

Almost fearful, breathing distorted perfumes in short inhalations, I interrogated my surroundings and their miraculous incoherence was suddenly obvious. The reigns of spring, summer and autumn were combined there, and Lerne had doubtless eliminated winter, which snuffs out flowers like candle-flames. All sorts of flowers were there, alongside all sorts of fruits, but not one had sprouted on its native plant or tree.

Clusters of cornflowers garnished a stalk abdicated by hollyhocks, which now brandished a blue thyrsus. The bristling branches of an araucaria now bore the indigo petals of gentians. And along a trellis, among nasturtium leaves and on the network of its serpentine stem, camellias became the siblings of varicolored tulips.

Opposite the entrance door, a clump of bushes rose up against the glass wall. The tallest of the shrubs attracted my attention. A few pears were hanging from it, although it was an orange tree. Behind it, two vine-stocks worthy of Canaan garlanded a trellis, their giant grapes as disparate as the stems; one bore yellow fruit, the other purple, but every product of one of them was a Mirabelle plum, and of the other a damson.

Then, on the branches of a minuscule oak on which several rebel acorns were obstinately forming, walnuts and cherries were visibly keeping company. One of them was an abortion; neither nut nor cherry, it formed a grey tumor streaked with pink, monstrous and repugnant.

Instead of resinous cones, a fir-tree was studded with chestnuts like radiant stars, and flaunted a strange contrast as well: oranges, the suns of Oriental orchards; and medlars, like the posthumous fruit of tress that have died of cold.

Not far away more fully-fledged miracles crowded together. Flora was jostling Pomona there, as the worthy Demoustier might have put it.[13] The majority of the constituent plants were unknown to me, and I only remember the most common, whose names are familiar to everyone. I can still see an astonishing willow, a bearer of hortensias and peonies, peaches and strawberries—but the prettiest of all these hybrids was surely the rose-bush with asters for flowers and little red apples for fruit. One bush in the middle of the rotunda mingled the disparate foliage of holly, lindens and poplars; pushing them aside, I was able to verify that all three emanated from a single stem.

It was the triumph of grafting, a science in which Lerne had made prodigious strides in the last 15 years—so much progress that the spectacle of his results had something disquieting about it; when he improves on life, man produces monsters. I felt a kind of malaise.

By what right does one disturb Creation? I wondered. *Is it permissible to turn the age-old order upside-down to this extent? Can one play this sacrile-*

---

[13] Charles-Albert Demoustier (1760-1891) was the author of *Lettres à Emilie sur la mythologie* [Letters to Emily on the subject of Mythology], which mingled verse and prose but always retained a pretentiously colorful style of expression.

gious game without committing treason against Nature? If these doctored sub-
jects were even in good taste! Deprived of genuine novelty, though, they're noth-
ing more than bizarre alliances: varieties of vegetable chimeras, floral fauns,
half one thing and half another. On my honor, whether this work is graceful or
not, it's impious—and that's all!

Whatever he had wrought, though, the professor must have toiled long and hard to bring this work to completion. The collection proved that, and there was other evidence of the scientist's labor; on a table, I perceived a number of vials, sharp grafting-knives and gardening-tools, which glittered like surgical instruments. Their discovery sent me back to the flowers, and on closer inspection I understood all the indignities to which they had been subjected. They were plastered with various sorts of gum, wrapped around by ligatures that were almost bandages and streaked with notches that were almost wounds, from which dubious fluids leaked. There was a gash in the bark of the pear-bearing orange tree. It looked like a gently weeping eye.

I was becoming irritated. Would one ever have thought it? I was assailed by a ridiculous anguish as I gazed at the surgically-modified oak...because the cherries put me in mind of drops of blood.

Plop! Plop! Two of them, having ripened, fell at my feet like the first drops of a rainstorm.

Already, I was no longer possessed of the calm necessary to consult the labels. They only informed me of a few dates, and that Lerne had covered them with indecipherable Franco-German terms, further obscured by erasures.

With my ears pricked and my forehead in my hands, I needed a moment's rest before recovering my composure, and I opened the door to the right wing.

A little aisle extended in front of me. Its glass ceiling filtered the daylight, attenuating it into a blue-tinted twilight, which was singularly cool. My footsteps resounded on the tiled floor.

There were three aquaria gleaming within the room: three tanks of crystal glass so clear that water seemed to be holding together of its own accord in three geometric blocks.

The two aquaria to either side contained marine plants. They did not appear to be much different from one another. The rotunda had, however informed me as to the methodical way in which Lerne classified everything, and I could not believe that he had separated two absolutely identical tanks. I therefore looked attentively at the algae.

Their fronds combined to form the same submarine landscape on either side. To the right and the left, arborescences of every color encrusted the rocks with their rigid and bifurcated stalks. The sandy bottom was strewn with stars reminiscent of edelweiss, and sheaves of chalky rods sprouted here and there, at the end of each of which sprouted a sort of fleshy chrysanthemum, yellow or violet. I can't describe the host of other corollas; they often resembled unctuous calices of wax or gelatin; the majority offered indefinable hues and imprecise contours; sometimes they were mere edgeless nuances in the midst of the water. Bubbles emerged by the thousand from an internal tap, and their tumultuous pearls raced madly along the dendrites before rising up to burst at the surface. On seeing them, one might have thought that it was necessary to sprinkle that aquatic garden with air.

Having summoned up my schoolboy memories, they informed me that the two floral displays, dissimilar only in detail, were composed exclusively of polyps: equivocal creatures such as corals and sponges, which naturalists consider intermediate between vegetables and animals. Their ambiguity never fails to excite interest. I tapped the left-hand tank.

Immediately, something unexpected appeared, swimming by contraction, like an opaline Venetian goblet that remained malleable. A second, purple in color, crossed its path. They were two jellyfish. The tap of my finger had, however, provoked other movements. Like yellow and mauve pompoms, the sea-anemones withdrew into heir calcareous tubes, then re-emerged to blossom rhythmically. The arms of the starfish and spines of the sea-urchins undulated lazily, grey, crimson or saffron yellow in color. As if stirred by an eddy, the entire aquarium came to life.

I rapped on the glass of the right-hand tank. Nothing moved.

That was conclusive. The division of polyps into to receptacles permitted me to obtain a better grasp of the link they constituted—which, uniting the animal and the vegetable, makes humans relatives of blades of grass. At this junction between two organized kingdoms, the active creatures on the left formed the base of their own scale, and the inanimate ones on the right the summit of theirs. The former were beginning to turn into animals, while the latter were settling for being plants. Thus, the gulf that seems to separate these two antitheses of the world is reduced in structural terms to slight, almost invisible divergences—distinctions less striking than those between the wolf and the fox, which are doubles and almost brothers.

Now, that infinitesimal distinction of organization, which science regards nevertheless as insurmountable because it separates inertia from spontaneous movement, *Lerne had bridged!* In the tank at the back, *the two sets of species were grafted on to one another.* I observed there some sort of gelatinous leaflet of the impassive sort, grafted on to a mobile stalk, which was now also able to move. *The grafts adopted the estate of the plant that supported them*; penetrated by a vivifying sap, indifference became animate, while activity was paralyzed by the force of a rigidifying sap.

I would gladly have made a careful inspection of the various applications of this principle, but a jellyfish, this time linked to some sort of seaweed, was struggling madly within that mossy net, and I turned away, prey to disgust. This final stage of grafting, in spite of the difficulties, completed the profanation in my estimation, and my eyes searched the blue twilight for less disturbing visions.

The professor's apparatus was ready for his use. A dresser accommodated an entire pharmacy. Four tables with unsilvered glass tops alternated with the aquaria, carrying an arsenal of knives and torturers' pincers...

No! Lerne had no right! It was as infamous as murder! More, even. The odious operations he performed on virginal Nature combined the horror of murder with the ignominy of rape!

As I abandoned myself to that righteous indignation, I heard a noise. Someone was knocking. Ah! That will be the hellish torment of my ears: to hear, beyond the grave, that tiny little tapping! In a flash, I felt every nerve in my body. Someone was knocking! With one bound, I was in the rotunda—and my face must have been a terrible sight, for the fear of an adversary drove me, instinctively, to make it frightful.

There was no one on the threshold, and no one in the grounds.

I went back in. The noise started again. It was coming from the wing I had not yet explored. Losing my head, I ran toward it, heedless of my temerity, at the risk of finding myself face to face with peril.

I was so overexcited that I bumped my head on the door as I jerked it open. Enervation and extreme fatigue had reduced me to that weakness—and I still wonder today whether they might have hallucinated me slightly, and caused things to seem even more bizarre than they actually were.

An intense light flooded the third hall and permitted me to reassure myself without delay. On a workbench there was a cage, set upside down, which was jumping about, thanks to a rat imprisoned within it. When the rat jumped, the cage jumped—whence came the noise. On seeing me, the rodent became quiet. I did not attach any importance to that interlude.

This place, less tidy than the preceding ones, looked like an ill-kept greenhouse. Bloody towels thrown on the floor, however, and scalpels lying randomly amid unemptied test-tubes, testified to recent work that might excuse the confusion.

I started my investigation. The first two witnesses to appear did not tell me much. They were two modest plants in ceramic pots. Their Latin names have vanished from my memory—which I regret, for they would give my narrative more authority as well as more resonance—but who, on hearing their common names, could not conjure up a picture of a spray of plantain and a tuft of hare's-ear?[14]

The former, it's true, is an exceptionally long and supple species. As for the second, there's nothing odd about it; following the example of its name-

---

[14] The French name for hare's-ear, *oreille-du-lapin* [rabbit's-ear], is more apt in context, given the subsequent reference to a rabbit, but the plant known in English as rabbit-ear, *Linaria vulgaris*—also known as toadflax—is clearly not the one to which Renard is referring; the Latin name that the narrator cannot remember is *Bupleurum rotundifolium*.

sake—a very successful counterfeit from which it takes its apt name—it conscientiously produces imitations of a dozen large auricular lobes. On two of these silvery hairy leaves and one of the plantain stems, at the base, a bandage displayed its bracelet of white cloth, seemingly stained brown by tar.

I sighed in relief. *Very good!* I said to myself. *Lerne has inoculated them. This is only a repetition of what I've already glimpsed, or perhaps even a preliminary experiment—simple, timid and awkward, if I'm not mistaken—a step on the way to the eventual phenomena of the rotunda, which prepares for them as they prepare for the atrocities of the aquarium. To follow Lerne's progress, I should have started here, continued through the central Eden, and concluded with the polyps. Thank you, God! I've seen the worst...*

My train of thought was running on in this fashion when the plantain stem twisted like a worm. At the same time, an iridescent grey mass made a jerky movement that betrayed its presence behind the workbench. There, in the middle of a pool of blood, lay a rabbit with silvery fur. It had just died, *and nothing was left of its ears but two bloody holes.*

A presentiment of the reality of the situation covered me with sweat. It was then that I touched the furry plant. Having palpated the two treated leaves, so similar to ears, I felt that they were *warm and tremulous.*

My recoil hurled me against the workbench. My hand, clenched in revulsion, was shaking with the memory of the contact, as if it had touched some hideous spider; it collided frantically with the rat's cage, which fell over. At once, the rat leapt up inside its cage, writhing, biting and struggling furiously, like a creature possessed. And my bulging eyes went incessantly from the plantain to the animal and back again, from the stem that was still quivering *like a slender black snake* to the rat that *no longer had a tail*. Its wound had healed, but, following its somersault, the poor beast was dragging a sort of slack belt after it—a vestige of another experiment—which was attached to its side by a green shoot that had been inserted there.

That shoot, moreover, appeared to me to be etiolated.

Lerne was, therefore, going further up the scale of living beings! Now, he was grafting parts of superior animals and plants of various sorts on to one another! Infamous, but increased in magnitude, my uncle inspired in me the disgust and admiration due to a criminal god. His work was, however, less estimable than repulsive, and I had to pull myself together violently in order to continue my exploration.

It was worth the trouble, even if it was only an exploration of hallucinations. What remained for me to discover surpassed the nightmares of a madman: frightful, to be sure, but also comic, by virtue of a certain aspect of sinister burlesque.

Among the patients, which one displayed that horror most starkly: the guinea-pig, the frog or the shrubs?

All things considered, perhaps the guinea-pig was not so very remarkable. Might its pelt not have been green and grassy by virtue of the reflection of all those plants? That's possible. But what about the frog? The shrubs? What could one think of them? The frog the color of grass, its four paws buried in humus, planted in the middle of a pot like a plant with four roots, its eyelids closed, its attitude insensible and bleak? The dates that had not moved at first, and which no wind stirred—of that I'm certain—and yet, when they did move, moved in every direction? Their palmate leaves swayed very gently...it seemed that I could even hear them, but I wouldn't swear to it. Yes, the trees swayed, and came closer together with every oscillation, and suddenly gripped one another with all their green-fingered hands, and embraced convulsively, in anger or affection, either to do battle or to make love—how do I know? It's the same gesture, always brutal.

Beside the frog was a white porcelain dish filled with a colorless liquid in which a Pravaz syringe was submerged. A similar dish containing a similar syringe was set next to the shrubs, but there the liquid was red and was coagulating. I deduced that they were sap and blood. The dates having let go of one another, my trembling hand advanced toward them, and I counted the beats, as rhythmic as a pulse, that were perceptible beneath the bark...

Since then, I have told myself that one can feel one's own pulse when taking someone else's, and that fever was doubtless making my fingers vibrate with its measured flux—but at the time, how could I doubt my senses? Besides, the continuation of the story does not tend to incriminate my lucidity at that moment; instead, it testifies in its favor. I don't know whether the intensity of memory, in a case of possible hallucination, is an argument for or against that morbid state; at any rate, I recall the image of those monstrosities, emerging from the disarray of bandages and bottles amid the scattered gleaming scalpels, very clearly indeed.

Was there anything else to see? I checked the corners. No, nothing more. I had followed me uncle's work step by step and—as chance would have it—in the same order as its stages and its progress, rationally speaking.

I returned to the château without hindrance, and then to my room. There, the artificial vigor that had sustained me died away. While I undressed I tried, unsuccessfully, to recapitulate my campaign. It was already taking on the semblance of a bad dream, and I no longer believed in it. Could the vegetable kingdom be fused with the animal kingdom? How absurd! Even if plant-polyps are nearly animal-polyps, what do an insect and a leaf for example, have in common?

Then I felt a sharp pain in the thumb of my right hand; a little white dot, ringed in pink, was protruding there. While I had been going through the wood, something had stung me—but I was unable to decide whether it was the vengeance of a nettle or an ant. That sting having recalled my sense of possibilities, I had no further pretext for not accepting those accomplished by my uncle, and I continued my reflections along the following lines:

To sum up, Lerne has attempted to amalgamate vegetables and animals and to contrive an exchange of their vitality. His methods, judiciously progressive, have succeeded. But are they ends or means? What does he want to get out of it? I can't see that his experiments are susceptible to any immediate practical application, uses that a speculator could exploit; therefore, they aren't ends. It seems to me, moreover, that their succession is directed toward some further improvement, which I can imagine vaguely without being able to distinguish it clearly. My aching head seems to be stuffed with cotton wool. Let's see...perhaps the professor is also carrying forward other research projects converging on the same goal as these, knowledge of which would clarify the ultimate object. Come on, come on! A little logic! On the one hand—Lord, I'm tired!—on the one hand, I've seen vegetables grafted on to one another; on the other hand, my uncle has begun to mix plants and animals...oh, I give up!

My overtaxed brain refused to reason any further. I glimpsed, confusedly, the fact that in the matter of grafting, an entire branch of study had been neglected, or, at least, that the greenhouse was not its location—but my eyelids were heavy. The more I attempted to induce or deduce, the more confused I became. Last night's apparition, the grey buildings and Emma loomed up, aggravating my bewilderment with anxiety, curiosity and desire.

In brief, never had a feather pillow been the haunt of such gibberish.

It was a riddle.

Yes, certainly: a riddle!

Although the sphinxes still surrounded me, however, I could now distinguish them more clearly through the smoke—and as one of them had the lovely face and breasts of a young woman, I feel asleep with a smile on my face in spite of everything.

IV. Hot and Cold

Sleep nourishes. My slumber lasted until the following morning. I had never slept so badly, though. The trepidations of the automobile journey had haunted my hips, and I felt the repercussions of revenant jolts and the twists of spectral bends for a long time. Then I was visited by dreams in which a prodigious world came to life: Broceliande, the Shakespearean forest, was on the march; amid the host of its branches, mostly walking arm-in-arm in pairs, a birch tree that had the appearance of a lance made a speech to me in German— which I could scarcely hear, because many of the flowers were singing, many of the plants were yapping insistently, and, from time to time, the tall trees howled.

On awakening, I remembered this wild hunt with phonographic exactitude, to the point of being alarmed, and scolded myself for not having made a more thorough examination of the greenhouse; a calmer and less hasty study of its

95

contents would doubtless have been more edifying. I passed a severe judgment on my haste and irritation of the day before. But why not try to make up for it? Perhaps it wasn't too late.

With my hands behind my back, a cigarette between my lips and seemingly going in no particular direction—as an idle stroller, in sum—I wandered past the greenhouse. It was locked. I had, therefore, spoiled the only opportunity to instruct myself in that regard—yes, I sensed it, the only one. Fool! Fool!

In order not to arouse suspicion, I went through the prohibited region without even pausing, and the pathway now took me toward the grey buildings. A new path beaten through the grass that covered the old one testified to frequent usage.

After a few strides, I saw my uncle appear in front of me; he had undoubtedly been on the lookout for my emergence. He was very cheerful. When he smiled, his dull face bore more resemblance to his youthful face of long ago. That affable expression restored my serenity; my escapade had passed unnoticed.

"Well, nephew?" he said, almost amicably. You agree with me, I'll wager. The place isn't recreational. You'll soon have had your fill of your nostalgic strolls through the depths of this old dump!"

"Oh, uncle, I've always loved Fonval, not for its scenery but as an old friend—an ancestor, if you like. It's family. I've often played on its laws and among its branches, you know; it's a grandfather that has dandled me on its knees, rather like—if you'll forgive the cajolery—rather like you, uncle…"

"Yes, yes," murmured Lerne, evasively. "All the same, you'll soon have had enough of it."

"You're mistaken. Fonval's grounds, you see, are my Earthly Paradise."

"You said it! It's certainly that," he confirmed, laughing. "The forbidden tree grows within its bounds. At any moment, you might run into the Tree of Life and the Tree of Science, which you mustn't touch…it's dangerous. If I were you, I'd go out from time to time in your mechanical carriage. Oh, if only Adam had owned a mechanical carriage!"

"But there's the labyrinth, uncle."

"I'll go with you, then, and guide you!" the professor cried, merrily. "Besides, I'm curious to see one of these…er…machines in action…."

"It's called an automobile, uncle."

"Yes: one of these automobiles." His Teutonic accent gave the word, already somewhat lacking in velocity, the amplitude, gravity and immobility of a cathedral.

We were walking side by side toward the coach-house. My uncle, mustering his courage in the face of ill fortune, had obviously reconciled himself to my intrusion. Nevertheless, his persistent good humor only served to irritate me. My planned indiscretions seemed less legitimate. Perhaps I might even have abandoned them there and then, if desire for Emma had not encouraged my hostility to her despotic jailer. Then again, was he sincere? Was it not merely to incite me to keep my sworn oath that he said to me, as we arrived at the improvised garage: "Nicolas, I've given it a lot of thought, and I really do think that you might be very useful to us in future. I'd like to get to know you better. Since you'll be staying here for a few days, we'll talk a good deal. I don't do much work in the mornings, so we'll spend them going abroad, whether on foot or in your carriage, and chatting. But you haven't forgotten your promises?"

I nodded my head. *After all*, I thought, *he really does seem to want to publish the unknown solution he's pursuing, some day. Why should it not equitable, even if the endeavors needed to attain it are not? It's doubtless those alone that he intends to keep hidden until they bear fruit; he reckons that the brilliance of the latter will justify the barbarity of the former, and grant him absolution for them. As long as the end does not betray the means, and that those means can remain unknown forever. On the other hand, Lerne really might be afraid of competition. Why not?*

I ruminated thus while emptying a can of gasoline that I had been lucky enough to find in the trunk into the tank of my lovely car.

Lerne got in beside me. He pointed me in the direction of a straight road that ran alongside one of the encircling cliffs—an ingeniously-concealed short cut. I was astonished, at first, that my uncle should have shown me this recourse, but, all things considered, was he not showing me the way that I might leave? And wasn't that, deep down, what he desired with all his heart?

Dear uncle! He must have led a very reclusive or very absorbed existence, for he retained a touching ignorance on the subject of automobiles, of the sort that scientists often have for subjects outside their specialties. My physiologist was not strong in practical mechanics. He had only a nodding acquaintance with the principles of the automobile's docile, flexible, silent and speedy locomotion, which filled him with enthusiasm.

"Can we stop here, please?" he said, when we reached the edge of the forest. "Explain the machine to me—it's marvelous. This is where I usually terminate my excursions. I'm an old eccentric! You can go on alone afterwards, if you wish."

I began my demonstration, and perceived then that the slightly-damaged horn could be repaired in a trice. Two screws and a piece of wire restored its deafening force. On hearing it, Lerne's face lit up with ingenuous delight. I went on with my lecture, and as I talked my uncle listened with increasing attention.

In truth, the subject was well worthy of interest. During the last three years, although motor cars have scarcely changed in respect of their elementary structure and principal components, their adaptation has progressed in compensation, and their constituent materials have been employed more judiciously. Thus, no wood had been used in the construction of my car, whose racing-seats had been reduced to a minimum. My eighty-horsepower engine was a luxurious and precise little factory, entirely made of cast iron, steel, copper, nickel and aluminum.

The great invention of the era had been applied to it—I mean that it did not rest on four pneumatic tires but on admirably elastic spring-mounted wheels. Today, that seems perfectly ordinary; a year ago, my steel rims still provoked a great deal of surprise.[15] But the most remarkable thing about the 234-XY, in my considered opinion, was the improvement that the engineers had obtained so gradually that one hardly perceived it on a day-to-day basis: automation.

The first "horseless carriages" had been cluttered with levers, pedals, knobs and steering-wheels necessary to control it, and taps and grease-guns indispensable to the functioning of the engine. Each generation of automobiles had, however, dispensed with more of them. One by one, almost all these manual controls requiring incessant and multiple human intervention had disappeared. In our day, its component parts having become automatic, the mechanism is self-regulating. A driver is no more than a pilot; once in action, his mount maintains its own progress; once awakened, it only goes to sleep again on command.

In brief, as Lerne remarked to me, the modern automobile enjoys all the properties that a spinal cord might confer upon it: it has instincts and reflexes. Spontaneous movements are produced there, alongside the voluntary movements provoked by the intelligence of the driver—the latter becoming, so to speak, the vehicle's brain. It is from that intelligence that the orders for willful actions depart, to be transmitted by metallic nerves to muscles of steel.

"Besides," my uncle added, "there's a striking resemblance between this carriage and the body of a vertebrate."

At this point, Lerne was getting back to his own subject. I lent an attentive ear. "We already have the nervous and muscular systems," he continued, "represented by the control rods, the transmission and the working parts. But what is the chassis, Nicolas, if not the skeleton, to which the bolts attach them like tendons? Gasoline blood, the vital element, circulates in copper arteries! The carburetor breathes; it's a lung. Instead of combining air with blood, it mixes it with gasoline vapor, that's all! The hood is the thorax within which life beats rhythmically. Synovial fluid plays the same role in our joints as oil in these. Shielded by the resistant skin of the bodywork, here are the tanks, stomachs that grow hungry and are replenished. Here are the eyes, phosphorescent like those of cats, but thus far deprived of sight: the headlights. The horn is a voice. Here is the exhaust-pipe, whose comparison would seem offensive to you, Nicolas. All in all, your vehicle lacks nothing but a brain—for which yours sometimes stands in—

---

[15] The notion that pneumatic tires might have given way to wheels of solid steel by 1910—two years after the novel's publication—inevitably produces even more surprise 100 years later, when the pneumatic tire is still secure in its empire of the road. Renard's anticipation of the progressive automation of the automobile, and the elimination of wood from its make-up, is, however, far more accurate.

in order to become a huge beast, albeit one that is deaf, blind, insensible and sterile, deprived of the senses of taste and smell."

"A full set of infirmities!" I remarked, bursting into laughter.

"Hmm!" Lerne retorted. "In other respects the automobile is better equipped than we are. Consider this water, which cools it: what a remedy against fever! And how long an engine might last, if used in moderation! For it is infinitely reparable...it can always be cured. Haven't you just restored its power of speech? You could replace its eyes just as easily..."

The professor was getting carried away. "It's a powerful and redoubtable body!" he cried, "but a body that allows itself to be put on, a suit of armor whose wearer finds himself amplified beyond all expectation, multiplying his power and speed! Why, inside this you're neither more nor less than one of Wells's Martians in its three-legged cylinder! You're no more than the brain of an artificial and vertiginous monster!"

"All machines are like that, uncle."

"No, not as completely. Except for its form—which has no similarity to any animal, of course—the automobile is the most adequate automaton we have ever contrived. It is more aptly made in our image than the best clockwork man-ikins made by Maelzel or Vaucanson, the most human of androids—for, beneath their anthropomorphic envelopes, the latter conceal a turnspit organism, which can't compare with the anatomy of a snail, while this..." He stepped back, en-veloping my motor car with a tender gaze. "A superb creature!" he exclaimed. "How great is man!"

Yes, I said to myself, *there's far more beauty in the act of creation than in your sinister assemblages of ancient flesh and immemorial wood! But it's good of you to acknowledge it!*

Although it was getting late, I went on to Grey-l'Abbaye to fill up with gas—and, in spite of the fact that he was a creature of habit, Lerne, infatuated with the automobile, went beyond the traditional limit of his walks and insisted on accompanying me.

Then we took the road to Fonval again.

My uncle, prey to neophyte ardor, leaned over the hood in order to take the machine's pulse, then dissected one of the grease-nipples. In the meantime, he questioned me, and I had to inform him of the smallest details regarding the car, which he assimilated with incredible accuracy.

"I say, Nicolas, sound the horn, would you? Now slow down... stop... set off again... quicker... enough! Brake... reverse now... halt! That's colossal!"

He was laughing. His darkened face underwent a sort of beautification. On seeing us, anyone might have supposed that we were the best of friends. Perhaps we were, in fact, for the moment—and I glimpsed the possibility that Lerne might one day take me into his confidence, thanks to my two-seater.

He conserved that gaiety all the way back to the château. The recovered proximity of the mysterious workshops did not alter it at all; it only disappeared in the dining-room. There, Lerne suddenly darkened again. Emma had just come in—and the husband of my Aunt Lidivine seemed to vanish with my uncle's smile, leaving behind a peevish old scientist between his two guests. I understood then how little his future discoveries mattered to him by comparison with that woman, and that he only wanted to acquire wealth and glory in order to keep a better hold on that charming girl.

He certainly lusted after her, as I lusted after her too: in the manner of a hunger, a corruption, a burning desire of the epidermis, a thirst of the skin. He was greedier; I had more appetite—that was the difference between us.

Come on, let's be frank. Elvire, Beatrice, ideal lovers,[16] you are only coveted pastures to begin with. Before you are given rhythm in verse, you are desired in a non-literary way, like—why search for hypocritical metaphors?—like a plate of lentils, or a cup of fresh water. But harmonious phrases were found for you, because you were able to become venerated lovers, and from then one you were cherished with that perfected tenderness that is our involuntary masterpiece, our slow and exquisite retouching of Creation. Certainly, as Lerne put it, man is great! His love is a delightfully gilded lily: the most beautiful graft in our gardens; an essentially artificial work of art, with a cleverly sweetened aroma.

Alas, it wasn't that aroma that Lerne and I were breathing, but the curt, simple and primitive corolla in which the perpetuation of the species is allegorized, and whose anticipated fruit is its sole *raison d'être*. Its imperious odor intoxicated us: a poisonous perfume, weighted with luxury and jealousy; the scent of Nature's tenebrous designs, in which it not so much the love of a woman that pulses as a hatred for all other men.

Barbe came and went like a jack-in-a-box, serving the meal. We ate silently. I avoided the pleasant spectacle of Emma, convinced that my gaze, if it lighted upon her, would carry an implication of kisses, about which my uncle would not be mistaken.

Now entirely at ease, she feigned indifference. With her chin in her hands and her elbow on the table, her bare arms emerging from short sleeves, she looked out of the window at the meadow, whose occupants were lowing.

I would have liked, at least, to look at the same thing as my beloved. That distant and sentimental communion would, it seemed to me, have appeased my base ambition for more intimate encounters. Unfortunately, the meadow was invisible from where I was sitting, and my eyes wandered idly, always perceiving, in spite of themselves, the whiteness of bare arms and the uplifts of a bosom that was palpitating faster than might have been expected.

---

[16] Elvire and Beatrice were the young girls appointed—unwittingly—as sources of extravagant inspiration by the poets Alphonse de Lamartine (1790-1869) and Dante Alighieri (1265-1321); Renard is presumably correct to argue that their selection as muses was a matter of the pretentious sublimation of sexual desires, but it was still conventional at this time to idealize the feelings in question.

Faster than might have been expected.

As I interpreted that agitation in my favor, Lerne, hostile and taciturn, called an end to the session. As I went past the young woman, brushing her, I felt that she was entirely vibrant; her nostrils were quivering—and a great delight transported me. Could I doubt that I had moved her?

We were going past the window when Lerne tapped my shoulder and whispered to me, in the quavering tone in which, I imagine, satyrs laugh: "Ach! There's Jupiter up to his old tricks!" And he pointed at the bull, standing lecherously amid his harem, in the meadow.

By the time we were in the drawing-room, my uncle had already recovered his surly manner. He told Emma to go up to her room, and, having given me a few books, he advised me in a categorical tone to go and read in the shade of the forest.

I could not do otherwise than obey. *Bah!* I said to myself. *For exhorting me to submission, he's to be pitied more than anything...*

What took place that night significantly chilled that pity. The incident troubled me all the more because, far from seeming to contribute to the clarification of the mystery, it seemed inherently incomprehensible.

This is what happened.

I had fallen asleep peacefully, my mind occupied with Emma and the delightful hopes associated with her. Instead of taking me into some indecent and entertaining phantasmagoria, however, sleep brought back the previous night's absurdities: roaring and baying plants. The intensity of the dream increased incessantly. It became so sharp, the noises so real, that I woke up abruptly.

Sweat inundated my body and my hot sheets. The last vibrations of the echo of a recent cry were fading away on my eardrums. It was not the first time...no...I had heard that cry before, from the labyrinth, in the distance, in the direction of Fonval...hmm...

I raised myself on my hands. A ray of moonlight lit the room. There was nothing to be heard except the rhythmic march of Time within the clock, the oscillation of his scythe. My head fell back on the pillow.

Suddenly, though, with a sudden twitch of my entire body, I buried myself under the bedclothes, with my hands over my ears. The sinister howling was coming from the darkness of the grounds, but it was extraordinary and supernatural. It really was the stuff of nightmares, and the dream was intruding upon reality. I thought of the huge plane-tree growing next to the château...

With a superhuman effort, I got out of bed. It was then that the yapping started...a stifled sort of yapping; very stifled...

Well, what of it? All that could have come from the mouth of a dog, damn it!

From the window overlooking the garden, there was nothing to be seen...nothing but the plane-tree and the other torpid trees, in the moonlight...

The howling began again, however, over to the left—and from the other window, I saw something that seemed to me, momentarily, to explain everything. One thing that was certain was that it was reality that had nourished my dream in an auditory sense, actual sounds having suggested the vision of imaginary screamers in my sleep.

There was a huge but emaciated dog out there, with its back to me. It had placed its forepaws on the closed shutters of my old room and was uttering long wails at intervals, with all its might. The other barking sounds—the stifled ones—were replying to it from inside the house. Was the latter really barking, though? What if my hearing, now suspect, were still deceiving me? One might have thought that it was, in fact, the voice of a man imitating a dog. The harder I listened, the more convincing that conclusion became. Yes, certainly, it was impossible to mistake it—how had I been able to hesitate? It leapt to the ears: some joker, installed in my room, was amusing himself by tormenting the poor dog. Furthermore, he had succeeded; the animal was giving signs of increasing exasperation. It modulated its clamor terribly, giving it a more extraordinary intonation every time, as if in desperation.

In the end, it scratched the shutters furiously, and bit them. I could hear the wood cracking between its jaws.

Suddenly, the beast froze, its hackles raised. A storm of abuse abruptly broke out inside the apartment. I recognized my uncle's voice, without being able to grasp the meaning of the reprimand.

The admonished joker immediately fell silent. But the dog, unaccountably, whose frenzy ought to have diminished, was now beside itself. Its back bristled like a wild boar's. Growling, it began to run along the wall of the château, toward the middle door. Just as it got there, Lerne opened the door.

Fortunately for me, I had taken the precaution of not drawing back my curtains. His first glance was at my window.

In a low voice, with suppressed anger, the professor scolded the dog. He did not move forward, though, and I realized that he was afraid. The other drew nearer, still growling, its eyes glinting within its vast head.

Lerne spoke louder: "To your kennel, vile beast!" A few foreign words followed; then he went on in French as the animal kept coming: "Go away! Do you want me to beat you? Do you?"

My uncle seemed to be going crazy. The moonlight exaggerated his pallor.

He'll be torn apart, I thought. *He doesn't even have a riding-crop.*

"Back, Nelly! Back!"

Nelly? This was expelled student's bitch, then—the Scotsman's Saint-Bernard.

Indeed, the foreign words that poured forth then informed me, to my utter astonishment, that my uncle also spoke English. His guttural invective resonated in the nocturnal silence.

The dog gathered herself, about to pounce—whereupon Lerne, at the end of his tether, threatened her with a revolver, while using the other hand to indicate the direction in which she was to go. While out shooting, I had had the opportunity to see a dog put to flight by a rifle, the murderous power of which it knew. Facing a pistol, the thing seemed to me less banal. Had Nelly experienced the effect of that weapon before? It was plausible, but I thought it more likely that she had a better understanding of English—MacBell's language—than my uncle's revolver. She was gentled as if by the voice of Orpheus, crouched down, and took the path toward the grey buildings, as indicated by Lerne, with her tail between her legs. He ran after the dog, and the darkness swallowed them both.

From the depths of my clock, the imperishable Reaper mowed down a few more minutes. In the distance, doors slammed. Then Lerne came back. There was nothing more.

There were, therefore, two unsuspected individuals at Fonval: Nelly, doubtless abandoned by her master in the course of his precipitate flight, whose lamentable appearance scarcely suggested that she was happy there, and the practical joker. For the latter, logically, could not be either of the two women or any of the three Germans; the nature of the buffoonery betrayed the age of its author: only a child cold amuse himself at the expense of a dog. But no one, so far as I knew, was lodged in that wing...

Ah! Lerne had told me that he was using my room. Who, then, was living in it?

I would find out.

If the hidden presence of Nelly in the grey buildings invested that already-intriguing location with new interest, the closed apartments of the château were becoming a supplementary target. My objectives were finally becoming clearer!

As the prospect of the mystery-hunt excited me, a presentiment warned me that I would be wise to follow it to the death, and break Lerne's first commandment before violating the second. "Let's get to the bottom of things first," said the voice of reason. "They're complicated. Afterwards, we can make provision for the bagatelle in peace."

If only I had heeded my own advice! But the voice of reason speaks softly, and who, I ask you, can hear it, when passion starts bawling?

V. The Madman

A week later, I was lying in ambush behind the door of my old room—the Yellow Room—with my eye to the keyhole. I had been there already, two days before, but had not had time to observe...

Oh, it wasn't easy, at least in appearance! Fonval's left wing had never been so jealously guarded since the days when the monks were cloistered there.

How had I got into it? In the simplest possible manner. The Yellow Room is connected to the central vestibule—through which anyone could pass freely—

by a sequence of three rooms; the vestibule connects to the large drawing-room, which connects to the billiard-room, which itself opens into a boudoir, which has the Yellow Room as the next room on the right, going in the direction of the grounds. Now, two days before, taking advantage of a moment of independence, I had tried keys that I had stolen from various other doors in the lock of the drawing-room, one by one. I was not confident, but the tongue of the lock suddenly yielded. I opened it and perceived the entire sequence of rooms, unimpeded, in the half-light of closed shutters.

As I went from one threshold to the next, I recognized the particular odor of each room, all a little mustier than of old—odors that the past would exhale if one could travel into it. There was dust everywhere. On tiptoe, I followed a trail that many boots had left behind in their dry mud. A mouse ran across the drawing-room carpet. On the billiard table, the black, red and white spheres described an isosceles triangle; mentally, I calculated the shot, the impulse required and the angle of the second ball. And the boudoir surrounded me; the hands of its stopped clock indicated noon, or midnight. I felt marvelously receptive.

Scarcely had I had time to see the closed door of the Yellow Room, though, when a noise made me return precipitately to the vestibule....

It was no joking matter! Lerne was working in the grey buildings, but he knew that I was in the château, and on such occasions, he had a habit of returning frequently without warning, to keep watch on me. A postponement of the enterprise seemed prudent.

An hour of liberty was indispensable. I formulated a plan. The next day, I took the automobile to Grey-l'Abbaye and bought various items of clothing, which I hid beneath a bush in the forest, not far from the grounds. The day after that, at lunch, I told Emma and Lerne: "I'm going to Grey this afternoon. I hope to find certain items there of which I'm in considerable need. If I can't, I'll go on as far as Nanthel. Is there anything you'd like me to do?"

Fortunately, there wasn't; otherwise it would all have come unstuck.

By that means, a fifteen-minute run would permit me to recover my purchases from the bush, as if I had gone to the village for them. The duration of the journey from Fonval to Grey and back could be reckoned at an hour and a quarter, with time added on to visit the grocer and the haberdasher's, so I had an hour at my disposal—Q.E.D.

I went out, left my car in a thicket not far from the bush where the things were hidden, then climbed over the wall into the garden; the ivy on one side and a trellis on the other simplified the task. Creeping along the wall of the château, I reached the vestibule.

So here I am in the drawing-room, with the door carefully closed behind me. In case I have to cut and run, though, I thought it prudent not to lock it. The keyhole is broad. With respect to what I can see through it, it forms a frame in the shape of a loophole, through which a keen draught is blowing. And what can I see?

The room is dark. Cutting laterally through the shutters, a slanting sunbeam seems to be propping up the window with its dazzling spray, in which particles of dust float like orbiting planets. On the carpet, the shutter's laths are designed in shadow. In the gloom: a hovel, a bohemian's lair; a few cloths scattered here and there. On the floor, a plate with leftovers, and next to it, something filthy. One might think it a hermit's den. The bed....Ah! What's that moving?

There he is: the prisoner!

A man. He's lying on his belly amid a mess of pillows, a bolster and a quilt, his head resting on his folded arms. He's wearing nothing but a nightshirt and trousers. His beard, several weeks long, and his rather short hair are pale blond, almost white.

I've seen that face before...

No. Since I heard that cry the other night I've been a little crazy. I've never seen that swollen bearded face, that stout body. I've never met this plump young man...never. His eyes seem quite benevolent, though, stupid but benevolent...hmm! Especially that indifferent face He must be a lazy fellow!

The prisoner is taking a nap—rather uncomfortably. Flies are annoying him. He swats them away with a sudden clumsy hand-gesture. His indolent eyes follow their flight, between two intervals of drowsiness. Sometimes, in a sudden fit of anger, smacking his lips with a sudden thrust of the head, he tries to snap up the annoying insects as they pass by.

A madman!

There's a madman in my uncle's house! Who is he?

My eyelid touches the keyhole. My eye is cold. The other, brought to bear in its turn, is slightly myopic. My vision is unclear. The peep-hole is too narrow! Damn it! I've bumped into the door, noisily!

The madman has leapt to his feet. How small he is! He's coming toward me...what if he tries to open the door? Good, he's thrown himself down next to the door, sniffing, growling...poor fellow! It's a painful sight...

He hasn't divined anything. Crouching in the sunbeams now, striped by the shadow of the shutters, he's more open to inspection.

His hands and face are speckled with little red marks, like old grazes. One would think that he's been in a fight. More seriously, there's a long purple streak beneath his hairline, extending from one temple to the other and around the back of the head. It bears a singular resemblance to a scar. This man has been martyrized! I don't know what treatment Lerne has subjected him to, or what vengeance he's exacting upon him... Oh, the torturer!

An association of ideas is instantly formed: I compare my uncle's Indian profile, Emma's unusual hair, that of the madman—so blond—and the green pelt of the rat. Can Lerne be seeking a means of grafting hairy scalps on to bald heads? Might that be his enterprise?

I immediately realize how stupid my hypothesis is. There's certainly nothing to corroborate it. Then again—and this is the decisive argument—this madman hasn't been scalped; were that the case, the scar would describe a complete circle. Why shouldn't he have gone mad in the aftermath of an accident, a perfectly simple backward fall?

Mad—but not raging. Inoffensive. He has a decidedly pleasant expression. His eyes, in fact, sometimes light up with a sort of intelligence. He must know something. I'm sure that if I question him softly, he'll reply. Should I take the chance?

The door is only secured by a bolt on my side. I draw it back with my thumb, carefully. But I'm not yet inside the Yellow Room when the recluse hurtles forward, head down, goes through my legs, knocks me over, gets up and runs away, making the canine yelps that caused me to mistake him for a practical joker the other night...

His agility surprises me. How was he able to make a fool of me like that? What an idea, to go between my legs! In spite of the brevity of the adventure, I stood up as quickly as I fell down, dazed and confused. That lunatic released by an idiot, whom he'll ruin! Toasted, Nicolas! Toasted! There's not a shadow of doubt about it! Wouldn't it be better to make oneself scarce rather than run after the fugitive? What good will that do now? Yes, but what about Emma? And the secret? Good God! Let's try to capture him, damn it!"

And here I am, hot on the unknown man's heels.

Just as long as he doesn't go near the grey buildings! Fortunately, he's gone in the opposite direction. It doesn't matter! Someone might see us at any moment. My deserter is drawing away in leaps and bounds, quite merrily. He plunges into the wood. God be praised! The animal's no longer crying—that's something! Is someone there? No—it's a statue. I must catch up as quickly as possible. If he takes an unfortunate turn, we'll be seen, and I'll be done for...

How joyful he seems, the cur! Damn! If he continues along his path, we'll make a tour of the grounds and the pursuit will pass in front of the grey buildings, under Lerne's windows! Bless the trees that are still hiding us! Quickly! And what about the drawing-room door, which I've left open? Quickly, quickly! The man doesn't know he's being chased; he isn't looking behind him. His feet, hurting by virtue of being bare, are slowing him down. I'm gaining on him...

He stops, sniffs the air, sets off again. But I'm much closer. He jumps into the undergrowth on the left, toward the cliff...me too. I'm ten meters behind him. He charges through the brambles, heedless of the thorns. I follow in his wake. The lashes of the stems are flagellating him; the thorns are hurting him; he cries out in pain as they dig into him. Why not push them aside, then? He could easily avoid their talons...

The cliff isn't far away. We're heading straight for it. Word of honor, my prey seems to know exactly where he wants to go...I can see his back...but not always...I have to track him by means of the crackling of branches...

Finally, his narrow head stands out against the rocky wall, unmoving.

Silently, I glide forward... Another second and I'll throw myself upon him...

But his unexpected action stops me on the edge of the clearing that encircles him, bordered on one side by the cliff.

He's on his knees, scraping the soil furiously. The work is tormenting his fingernails, to the point at which he whines, as he did a little while ago among the sharp points of the hawthorns and mulberries. Earth flies up behind him, as far as me; his clenched hands work obstinately, with rapid and regular thrusts. He digs while moaning in pain, then, from time to time, plunges his nose into the hole as deeply as he can, snuffling and jerking his head back and forth, and then resumes the absurd task. The scar is clearly visible, like a livid crown. Hey! I don't care about his nonsensical behavior—it's the propitious moment to jump on him and carry him off!

I emerge from the thicket stealthily. Hold on! Someone's been digging here already: a heap of overturned earth testifies to that; the blond man is only taking up some old abandoned task. Bah!

My heels flex; I get ready to pounce.

The man releases a groan of pleasure then—but what's that I see in the depths of the cavity? An old shoe, that he's just laid bare! Oh, wretched humanity!

Ha! I've jumped, I have him, the rascal! Good Lord! He's turned round, pushing me away, but I'm not letting go! Bizarre...how awkward he is with his hands! Aargh! So you bite, cretin!

I wrap my arms around him, bone-crushingly. He's never done any wrestling, that's evident. I haven't got the upper hand yet, though...

What have I done? A false step—it's the hole...I'm treading on the old boot. Horror! There's something inside it! Something holding it to the ground! I draw breath. Nothing fits a shoe better than a foot...

I have to finish it, once and for all. The minutes are priceless...

My adversary and I are face to face, with our arms wrapped round one another, pressed against the rock, panting, equally strong...I've got an idea!

I open my eyes terribly wide, as if it were a matter of intimidating a child or subduing an animal; I adopt the domineering expression of a master. And the other loosens his grip, subjugated and repentant. Look how he's licking my hands as a sign of obedience!

"Let's go—come along!"

I drag him away. The shoe—an elastic-sided slip-on—stands up, its toe in the air. It doesn't have the lamentable appearance of dead shoes abandoned on the highway, but it's even more repulsive. Whatever is fixing it in the soil is partly disengaged. All that's visible is the end of something knitted. A sock? The madman also turns to look at it.

"At the double, my friend!"

My companion remains docile, thanks to my magical stare, and we run off at top speed.

Oh Lord! What's been happening at the château during this escapade?

Nothing at all.

As we went into the vestibule, however, I heard Emma and Barbe in conversation on the floor above. They were beginning to come down the staircase when the famous drawing-room door closed behind us, putting an end to my anxieties—only to give rise to new ones.

Once the unknown man was back in his room, how was I to get out again without being seen by either of the women?

Having returned furtively to the drawing-room, I put my ear to the door and listened, in order to make out which way the two worrisome individuals were heading. Suddenly, though, I retreated to the middle of the room in alarm, searching for a hiding-place, a screen, making the gestures of a drowning man, my throat swollen with suppressed cries....

A key had been inserted into the lock.

Was it mine? My key, left behind in the door and filched during my absence? No, that one was still there, making a bulge in my waistcoat pocket. I'd put it there as I came back in.

What, then?

The verdigris-stained handle turned slowly. Someone was about to come in. Who? One of the Germans? Lerne?

Emma.

Emma, who could only see an empty room. Perhaps one of the large damask curtains moved, as if trembling. She did not see it.

Barbe was standing behind her. The young woman said to her, in a soft voice: "Stay there and watch the garden. Do as you did the other day—that was good. As soon as the old man comes out of the laboratory, warn me by coughing."

"It's not him I'm worried about," Barbe replied, visibly frightened. "He's quite confident now, I tell you. We won't see him again before dusk. As for Nicolas, that's something else. He might turn up, you know."

So the grey buildings were called *the laboratory*! That was the word that had caused the professor to gag the servant with a slap in the face. My knowledge was increasing...

"There's no danger, I tell you," Emma continued, in an exasperated tone. "Come on! Is this the first time?"

"Nicolas wasn't here then..."

"Come on—do as you're told!"

Reluctantly, Barbe went to stand guard.

Emma stood still for a few seconds, listening. Beautiful! Oh, as beautiful as the vampiric demon of luxury! And yet, she was only a silhouette in the luminous rectangle of the door, a motionless shadow...but as subtle as if she were moving, for Emma in repose always seemed to have paused in mid-dance, and even to be continuing the dance by means of some unknown black magic, so harmonious was the sight of her: the harmony of bayaderes who can mime nothing but love, unable to swing their hips, undulate, quiver or lean over, nor shake their tresses, nor sketch the slightest gesture, without one imagining them in sensuous ecstasy...

Life was seething within my body. An exaltation overwhelmed me, an omnipotent age-old passion. Emma! Her, in the madman's room! All that paradise for that brute! The slut! I could have killed her!

Are you thinking that I didn't know anything? That I was making gratuitous suppositions? You're not familiar, then, with the impulsive gait and the crafty and avid attitude of those women who are coming to a man on the sly? Look: she had started walking again. Well? Was it necessary to look at her twice to guess what she was about to do? Everything about her was crying it out. Everything confessed that hope and that pathological need, which is already a pleasure. But I don't want to describe that demonically-possessed body, nor translate its indecent language. Don't expect me to fill out the shameful portrait of a lustful woman. For, sordid though it is to write, that is what she was. There are moments of perception so sharp that, under the influence of a vision or a domineering flavor, a man becomes a monster and is no longer anything else but a huge eye, or a mouth, and nothing more. Just as a man who hears an extraordinary piece of music can only see with his hearing, listening with his eyes, his nose and his entire being, so that enamored woman was no longer, in her entirety, anything but the radiation of sex, a minor function aggrandized and personified: Aphrodite herself.

And that drove me mad.

The pretty girl, hastening toward the ignoble scene, brushed my curtain with a swish of her skirt.

I barred her way.

She emitted a loud gasp of fear. I thought she was about to faint. Barbe's eyes widened, and she fled in panic. Then, stupidly, I revealed the reason for what I had done. "Why are you going that way, to the madman's room?" My voice, blank and artificial, was rough and halting. "Tell me! Why? Good God, tell me!"

I had flung myself upon her and I twisted her wrists. She moaned softly; her entire adorable body shuddered, as if a ripple had passed through it. I squeezed the soft, firm flesh of her arms as if to strangle two doves, and looked down into her agonized eyes. "Why? Tell me! Why?"

Did I have to be so candid? Addressed in that tone, she straightened up, looked me up and down, and challenged me.

"So what?" she said. "You know full well that Monsieur MacBell was my lover! Lerne as good as told you that in my presence, on the day of your arrival..."

"MacBell? That's who the madman is?"

Emma made no reply, but her astonished expression informed me that I had made another mistake in disclosing my ignorance.

"Do I no longer have the right to love him?" she went on. "Do you, perchance, think you can forbid it?"

I pulled at her arms as if they were bell-cords. "Do you still love him?"

"More than ever, do you hear?"

"But he's a brute beast!"

"There are madmen who think they're gods; he, from time to time, imagines that he's a dog; perhaps his lunacy in the less serious. And then, after all..."

She smiled mysteriously. One might have sworn that she wanted to push me to the limit. That smile and her words had imposed a cruel vision on me. "Oh! Slut!"

I gripped the girl round the neck to strangle her, spitting insults in her face. She must have thought that she was a dead woman—and yet, though suffocated, she continued to smile...

It was me that it was mocking, that mouth which another man used at his whim! All my rage was concentrated upon it. Ha! I'd provide it with a fine accompaniment, her smile! It would be redder and moister, yes! My jaws had an urge to bite. I was worse than a madman! I understood every kind of madness, at that moment. I hurled myself upon those mocking lips—which would soon be bloody and torn, would they not? Ah! There! There! Our teeth clashed, and there was a kiss—similar, undoubtedly, to humankind's first, long ago, in some cave or rude and primitive lakeside hut; less a caress than a blow, but a kiss all the same...

Then a voluptuous penetration unclenched my teeth, and the sequel to that savage kiss was so refined that it revealed in Emma not merely a considerable natural disposition to games of debauchery, but also a consummate experience.

This confusion of our selves suggested another, and appealed for it. That day, however, we were only to experience the most vulgar of preludes. I mean the distant carillon which, in a double descent, makes the springs of old sofas ring—to chime, I suppose, the shepherd's hour.[17]

Barbe, simultaneously untimely and opportune, came running. She coughed as if her guts were splitting. "Monsieur is coming!"

Emma freed herself from my embrace. Lerne's empery dominated her again. "Get away!" she said. "Hurry up! If he knew...you'd be done for...and

---

[17] The expression "*l'heure du berger*" [the shepherd's hour] is used to signify a propitious moment for lovers; it is nowadays best-known as the title of a poem by Verlaine, which was set to music and became a popular song.

110

me too, probably, this time! Oh, get out! Run, my little darling. Lerne's capable of anything!" And I sensed that she was telling the truth, for her dear hands had grown cold, and were shivering in mine, and beneath my softly amorous lips, her mouth was babbling in terror.

Still moved by an imbecilic joy that multiplied my strength and agility ten-fold, I scaled the trellis nimbly and leapt down on the other side of the wall.

I found my vehicle in its garage of verdure. My parcels were piled into it in a rush. I was blissfully happy. Emma would be mine! And what a mistress! A woman who had not recoiled from the duty of bringing a friend who had become repulsive the consolation of her visits, the treat of her agitated charms! But it was me that she wanted now, I was sure of it. Love MacBell? Get away! She had lied to rouse my passion. She merely pitied him…

With respect to that, though, how had madness taken hold of the Scots-man? And why was Lerne hiding him? My uncle had affirmed that he had left. Why was he keeping his Saint Bernard bitch locked up? Poor Nelly! I under-stood her dolor, at the window, and her rancor against the professor: a drama had unfolded before her, involving Emma, Lerne and MacBell, doubtless in the wake of their being caught in the act. What drama? I would soon know; one has no secrets from one's lover, and I would become Emma's. Come on! Everything was falling into place marvelously!

My joy generally manifests itself in the form of song. It was, if I'm not mistaken, a seguidilla that I hummed as I went along—whose gangling melody I interrupted abruptly, because the macabre memory of the old shoe had surged forth into my reverie, like the Red Death in mid-ball.

Instantaneously, my mood darkened. The sun set in the depths of my thoughts; everything became black, suspect, menacing. An excessive reversal showed me the most sinister suppositions as certainties, and—even the image of the ardent Emma having been unable to resist that funereal light—I fell prey to fear of the unknown as I reached that château-madhouse and that garden-tomb, where the ghoul of vice was waiting for me between a madman and a cadaver.

VI. Nelly, the Saint Bernard Bitch

A few days went by without anything happening that was capable of satis-fying my lust or my curiosity. Lerne—was he suspicious?—contrived things so that my time was fully employed.

In the mornings, he asked me to accompany him, one day on foot, another in the automobile. He spent these excursions treating some scientific matter or other, and in questioning me as if he really wanted to assess my aptitudes. In the automobile, we made long journeys. On foot, my uncle made a habit of taking the straight road leading toward Grey; he stopped continually in order to hold forth more easily, and never went further than the edge of the woods. Often, in mid-dissertation or at the very outset of a walk or a car-journey, Lerne decided to return unexpectedly, mistrustful of the individuals left behind at Fonval.

He also organized the use of my afternoons. Sometimes, sent to fetch something from the town or the village, or forced to go out alone to undertake some designated excursion, I had to fill the gas-tank or put on my boots without delay. Lerne watched me leave, and in the evening, posted on the doorstep, he demanded an account of my day. According to the circumstances, I had to render an account of a message or describe a location. Now, it's true that my uncle was unfamiliar with the majority of the locations to be described, but I couldn't tell which ones; in those circumstances, any resort to bluff would have been perilous. So I conscientiously beat the forest and the countryside from dawn to dusk.

I would much rather, however, have got closer to Emma's room! By counting the number of shuttered and unshuttered windows, I had calculated its location within the topography of the château, which I knew in detail. The entire left wing remained constantly closed. As for the right wing, quotidian life utilized its ground floor. Of the six upper rooms, only three remained open: mine, in the forward part, and, at the other end, Aunt Lidivine's room, opening on to the central corridor and connecting with Lerne's. Emma, therefore, could only have succeeded my aunt in her own bed or be sharing my uncle's. The latter hypothesis set me beside myself, and I was impatient, in order to test it, that I might be left alone to check it out in a few strides: one push of a door, and I would know what I was dealing with.

But the professor was on the lookout.

Under the thumb of his pitiless tyranny, I only saw Mademoiselle Bourdichet at meals. We both affected a detached attitude. I had audacity enough to look at her, but I dared not speak to her. She persisted in the most absolute mutism, to such an extent, that for want of her conversation, I was forced to estimate her condition by her manner.

I admit that, gross as the human means of alimentation by means of dead animals and withered plants might be, there are two kinds of female eaters. She willingly picked up a chicken-bone or a cutlet in her fingers, and every time she put it down, it seemed to me that I heard her say "my little darling" in her proletarian accent. But I ask you, how close is civility to libertinage, and what has the table in common with the bed-alcove?

Between Emma and myself, Lerne fidgeted. He reduced pieces of bread to crumbs and tapped his fork. Muffled fits of wrath brought his fists down on the tablecloth, or made the glass and china rattle.

One day, by mistake, my foot made contact with his. The doctor suspected that innocent foot of stupidity, credited it with telegraphic intentions, and, mistakenly convinced that he had detected some pedestrian madrigal via the toe, immediately decided that Mademoiselle Bourdichet was unwell, and would take her meals in her room in future.

Immediately, two passions took possession of my thoughts, in the form of a double need to engender pain or pleasure in someone else: hatred of Lerne, and love of Emma. And I resolved to do my utmost to satisfy both of them.

On that same day, my uncle told me point-blank that he wanted to take me to Nanthel on the following day, where he had business to attend to. I glimpsed an opportunity to escape his surveillance. That following day, a Sunday, Grey was holding its annual festival. I thought I might take advantage of it.

"With pleasure, uncle," I replied. We'll leave early, in case of a possible breakdown."

"I'd prefer to take the car to Grey, and get the train to Nanthel there…that will be the safest way to make the journey…"

That suited me admirably.

"As you wish, uncle."

"The train leaves Grey at 8 a.m. We'll come back on the 5:15 p.m.; there isn't an earlier one."

As we arrived in the village we heard a muted sound of voices intermittently punctuated by the lowing of cattle. A horse whinnied, and sheep were bleating nearby. I had some difficulty clearing a path across Grey-l'Abbaye's main square, which was transformed into a fairground, already thronged by a placid and slow-moving crowd.

Cattle for sale were penned in the gaps between the shooting-galleries and other paltry stalls; coarse hands were testing the weight of their udders, parting the jaws in which their age could be read during a yawn, and sliding hands along their muscles to judge their vigor. In full view of everyone, a young girl was quite unselfconsciously verifying the sex of a rabbit held in her lap. Horse-dealers were bragging. Between two rows of meek peasants, grooms were trotting massive Percherons and heavy work-horses. A fusillade of stock-whips sounded on the horses' rumps. The first drunkard of the day tripped up while calling me "citizen."

We went on. In the semi-silence of the market, the inn was already resounding, but no brawling had broken out as yet. The church-bells were ringing a prelude to the mass and a small white wooden kiosk in the center of the square, decorated with foliage, promised that the municipal band would soon add its simplistic racket to the hubbub of the festival.

We stopped in front of the station. That was the moment at which I intended to make my move.

"Need I escort you during all your peregrinations in Nanthel, Uncle?"

"Certainly not. Why?"

"In that case, Uncle, having an aversion to cafes, taverns and public houses, I beg you to leave me here, where I can wait for you just as well as in a brasserie in Nanthel."

"But you're under no obligation to…"

"To begin with, Grey's festival is seductive. I'd like to observe a gathering of this sort for a while longer; the customs of a people are vividly revealed there, and I feel the spirit of an ethnologist within me today..."

"You're joking—or it's a silly whim."

"Secondly, Uncle, to whom can I entrust my motor car? The innkeeper? The alcoholic landlord of some dive full of drunken boors? You don't think I'm going to leave a 25,000-franc car exposed to the clowning of a whole village on the spree for nine hours, do you? No—I'd like to keep watch on the automobile myself!"

My uncle was not convinced of my sincerity. He wanted to thwart any stratagem that I might have concocted in order to get back to Fonval, either by automobile or on a borrowed bicycle, with the intention of returning to Grey by 5:14 p.m. And that was exactly what I had planned to do. The accursed scientist nearly ruined everything.

"You're right," he said, coldly. He got down and, amid the flood of passers-by in their Sunday best, lifted the hood and inspected the engine carefully. I felt ill at ease.

My uncle took out his knife, dismantled the carburetor, and stuck some of its parts into his pocket. In the meantime, he said to me: "That's your vehicle immobilized. As you might make yourself scarce by another means, though, I'll give you something to do. On my return, you'll show me the complete carburetor, refitted with parts you've manufactured. The blacksmith hasn't closed his forge; he'll lend you an anvil and a vice—but he's a poor fool, unable to assist you. That will keep you amused until 5:14 p.m..."

Seeing that I made no objection, he went on in a self-conscious tone: "Forgive me, Nicolas, and be assured that all this has no purpose other than to guarantee your future and safeguard the secret of our work. Goodbye."

The train bore him away.

I had let him go without any sign of disapproval, and without feeling any. Being not much of a mechanic, detesting grease and bruises on my hands, and constrained by my uncle's demand to deprive myself of a chauffeur, I had brought numerous spare parts in the trunk, including an entire carburetor ready to be fitted. Ignorance had served me better than the skill of a professional would have done. I set to work without delay, anxious about the inhabitants of Fonval, left to their own devices.

A short time afterwards, having parked the motor car in a copse, I climbed over the wall into the grounds. I would have gone straight up to Emma's room if a lugubrious barking had not resounded from the direction of the grey buildings.

The laboratory...Nelly...

The singular circumstance of a dog being kept in a laboratory made me hesitate between the tug of the mystery and the attraction of Emma. This time, the instinct of self-preservation awakened by the unknown, and the danger that one always associates with it, was bound to hold sway. I headed for the grey buildings. In any case, the Germans would certainly be there; their presence would prevent me from staying long. It was, therefore, a mere matter of stealing a few minutes from the commerce of gallantry; reason only triumphs feebly.

As I went past the Yellow Room I listened at the shutters, in order to assure myself that MacBell was alone. He was—which swelled my heart with an immense and vile satisfaction.

A few silver-white clouds were floating in a raw sky. The wind was blowing from Grey-l'Abbaye through the gorge, carrying the monotonous sound of the bells to my ears. They were endlessly repeating the same three notes, thus executing the carillon from *L'Arlésienne*.[18] I felt cheerful, and whistled the profane orchestral melody to that holy accompaniment—a combination inherently reminiscent of a modern statue on a Gothic plinth. Lerne's absence was a definite relief to my perpetual constraint; I was able to indulge in idle whims and my mind surrendered itself to the most unreflective digressions...

Facing the laboratory, on the other side of the path, there was a wood. I sneaked into it, having made my battle-plan. In the middle of the wood there was an old friend of mine: a fir-tree whose radiating branches formed a spiral stairway. It overlooked the buildings; there could be no better-situated or more easily-accessible observatory. I had once played there, pretending to be a sailor among the yardarms.

The tree offered me a perch, a trifle short but still bushy. On the higher branches, a memory awaited me, made of ropes and rotten planks: the cow's-nest! Who would have thought that I, who had once pretended to discover continents and archipelagoes—so many plausible fantasies—from that vantage would one day be on the lookout there for sights as fabulously real?

My gaze plunged downwards.

As I've said, the laboratory consisted of a courtyard between two blocks. The one on the left was pierced y large bay windows on its ground floor and its single upper story. It appeared to me to be merely a superimposition of two vast rooms. I could only see the upper one, furnished with complicated apparatus: an apothecary's cupboard, marble tables charged with flasks, bottles and retorts, open boxes full of shiny instruments, and two indescribable items, of glass and nickel-plated metal, whose appearance recalled nothing analogous, except perhaps—vaguely—the pedestal-mounted spheres on which waiters in taverns hang their napkins.

The other block, too far away for me to be able to see into it, seemed from the outside to be an ordinary dwelling, evidently that of the three assistants—but

---

[18] *L'Arlésienne* originated as a play by Alphonse Daudet, premièred in 1872, for which Georges Bizet wrote the incidental music. The music eventually become far more famous than the play; it was reorganized into a four-movement suite, the fourth part of which is "Carillon," featuring the chime to which Nicolas is referring.

what I had taken for a farmyard on the day of my arrival captured all of my attention.

A wretched farmyard! Its walls were equipped with cages of various sizes piled one atop another up to a man's height. In these cages, each surmounted by a label, rabbits, guinea-pigs, rats, cats and other animals that I could not identify because they were too far away, moving plaintively back and forth or lying down half-hidden beneath the straw. One such layer of straw was agitated, but I could not see the cause—a nest of mice, I presumed.

The last enclosure on the right served as a henhouse. Contrary to custom, the poultry were locked up there. The whole scene was mute and melancholy. Four hens and a cockerel of a common sort were, however, more lively and alert, cackling as they strutted around the concrete floor, pecking at it obstinately, trying to discover grain or worms there, but in vain.

In the middle of the yard, a grating inscribed a large square. In front of their lined-up kennels, philosophers both cynic and peripatetic, resigned dogs paced back and forth: frightful traveling salesmen's poodles, poachers' mongrels, concierges' watch-dogs and pimps' lap-dogs, degenerate mutts and bastard lurchers; in brief, an entire pack of curs, good for nothing but fidelity. They were roaming around, thus completing the courtyard's resemblance to the playground of a veterinary hospital.

It was at this point that things took on a more sinister appearance. Of all these beasts, I fact, very few seemed to be healthy. The majority sported bandages, whether on their backs, around their necks, on the napes of their necks, or—most frequently—on their heads. There were hardly any to be seen through the wire-netting of their cells that did not have pieces of white linen rolled into bonnets, cowls or turbans. And the procession of miserable dogs, comically coiffed in linen like tuaregs or abbesses, with labels dangling from their necks, formed a masquerade of the most funereal kind. It seemed that nearly all of them were lame; one of them fell on its muzzle at every step; another was limping; a third was shaking with a senile palsy. One stumbling mastiff, whining without any perceptible reason, suddenly unleashed a long howl, of the sort that people call deathly.

Nelly was not there.

I noticed a silent aviary in a shadowed corner, devoid of fluttering. As far as I could make out, the birds belonged to the most commonplace families; sparrows were swarming there. Even so, the majority belonged to a white-headed variety that my knowledge of ornithology did not permit me to recognize at such an altitude.

An odor of phenol rose up to meet me.

Ah! Lovely farmyards fragranced by dungheaps, the cooing of pigeons on the tops of mossy tiled roofs, cock-a-doodle-dos, the yapping of a dog tugging at its chain, squadrons of geese charging back and forth without rhyme or reason with their wings outspread...I thought of you as I confronted that infirmary. A miserable farmyard indeed, with its discipline and its invalids, labeled like the plants in the greenhouse!

Suddenly, there was a stir. The dogs went back into their kennels and the poultry sought refuge beneath a stone rough. Nothing moved any longer; the aviary and the cages seemed to contain stuffed animals.

Karl, the German with the Kaiseresque moustache, had emerged from the building on the left. He opened one of the cages, reached out for the bundle of fur huddled within it, grabbed it and drew out a monkey. The animal—a chimpanzee—struggled. The assistant dragged it away and disappeared with it the way he had come.

A mastiff uttered a long howl.

There was a commotion in the room with the apparatus then, and I saw that the three laboratory assistants were just coming into it. One stretched out the monkey, which was now bound, on a narrow table, and tied it down firmly. Wilhelm thrust something under its nose. Karl pricked the chimpanzee's side with a morphine syringe. Then the tall old man, Johann, approached. He adjusted his gold-rimmed spectacles with a hand that was holding a scalpel and bent over the patient. I cannot explain the rapidity of the operation, but in no time at all, the chimpanzee's face was no more than a shapeless red mass.

I turned away, seized by a nauseating malaise: the vertigo of blood.

What I had behind me, then, was a vivisection laboratory: one of those terrifying institutions in which philanthropy tortures brave and healthy animals in the hope of curing a few more sick people. Science there assumes a highly contestable right, which, in confrontation with the drama of bloodshed, seems impossible to sustain—for, if the executioner of a guinea-pig is assured of always torturing innocence, and often blissful happiness, the savior of a man, ten times out of twelve, can only delay the death of a guttersnipe or a wretch. In addition, to devote one's existence to vivisection is almost equivalent to supporting oneself by eating living creatures. One can claim otherwise when one is chatting by the fireside, but not from a critical position like mine, in the very presence of the horrible thing and in the midst of tenebrous perils—which might, perhaps, involve it.

I could not redirect my rebellious eyes toward that thing, in spite of all that it might possibly have told me. My gaze *would not* quit the trunk of the fir-tree, nor the red insect with a shield-like carapace dotted with black that blazoned its bark, providing it with a small and incorrect coat-of-arms with fifteen sable points strewn on a crimson field.

Finally, I turned back—too late. The sunlight struck the windows, and their gleam obstructed my vision.

In the courtyard, however, the dogs had left their kennels, and Donovan MacBell's bitch, Nelly, was now walking among them. She was coughing. Her threadbare fur was no longer reminiscent of the beautiful fleece of a Saint Bernard. The superb hound was no more than a large carcass, whose thinness contrasted with the relative plumpness of her companions. Nelly too bore a bandage on the nape of her neck. What scheme had Lerne been able to hatch to make her suffer since the night of their altercation? What diabolical invention had he tested on her?

The bitch seemed to be reflecting, so distressed was her appearance. She kept herself apart from the other dogs. When a certain rather fragrant bulldog accosted her, with lewd eyes and a tail declaring his intent, the bitch leapt up, accompanying the gesture with a gaze of such ferocity and a hoarse cry so terrible that the other retreated to the back of his kennel, while the pack raised their carnivalesque heads in alarm.

The bashful Nelly continued on her way.

What was I still doing there? In spite of my haste to cut that reconnaissance short and hurry on to other pastimes, something held me back...something inexplicable in the behavior of the bitch, which I could not quite make out.

At that moment, a quickstep played by the Grey-l'Abbaye band reached Fonval on the wings of the wind. My fingers spontaneously tapped out the beat on the branches of my observation-post, and I perceived that Nelly had accelerated her progress. She was moving in step, following the rhythm of the tune.

I remembered that Emma had made allusion to dog-tricks with reference to the bitch. Was this a circus routine that MacBell had taught his Saint Bernard? It did not seem to me that such a "turn" was performable in the absence of a trainer, or that an auditory sensation could provoke in an animal those mechanical movements that have always been our prerogative, resulting from habits more complex than those of instinct.

The music faded away as the wind eased. The bitch sat down, looked up— and saw me. Damn! She was about to bark, to raise the alarm!

Not at all. She looked at me with neither fear nor anger, with an expression that I shall remember forever. Then, shaking her huge shaggy head, she began to moan softly, very softly, her paw moving in a gesturing manner. Then she resumed her walk, still murmuring and darting furtive glances, as if she had wanted to make herself understood without attracting the attention of the Germans. Obviously, this is a mere manner of description, but all the same, one might have imagined that the bitch wanted to talk, so varied were the inflections of her modulated plaint. She was almost emitting the rudiments of a long guttural sentence, uniform and confused, in which the syllables "aicboul, aicboul" recurred incessantly. The whole thing sounded like an extended gargle...rather like badly-pronounced English words.

The entrance on stage of the three laboratory assistants interrupted the phenomenon. They went across the courtyard, and all the dogs, with Nelly in the lead, headed for shelter. As he passed the fence of the kennels, Wilhelm threw over a piece of skinned but hairy meat, to which the monkey's body was attached. It fell heavily; it was dead. The Germans went into the block on the right, whose chimney immediately started smoking.

Then, one by one, the dogs came to sniff the chimpanzee. The bulldog was the first to bite into it, and the whole pack immediately joined in, snarling threateningly and voraciously. The cripples' muzzles grew red, and their spiteful fangs tore that pitiful caricature of a child's corpse to pieces. Only Nelly, her paws crossed in the doorway of her kennel, disdained the feast, gazing at me with lovely profound eyes. I realized that I had discovered the reason for her thinness.

A window opened above all that, through which I perceived a dining-table fully set for three. The assistants sat down to a meal facing my wood; it was high time for me to leave.

Then, I made an unpardonable blunder. I should have set forth to investigate the old shoe—that's elementary. It seemed to me, falsely, that I had made supreme concessions to prudence, and that an elastic-sided shoe had every right to be considered nothing more than an elastic-sided shoe and not as a buried man, or even a buried leg. To a warm heart, at the end of the day, a beautiful girl certainly holds sway over all the footwear in the world—so, fortified by these reasons, with which I duped myself, it was toward the château that I went.

My Aunt Lidivine's room was now a store-room. One might have taken it for a courtesan's dressing-room. Several wicker-work mannequins, clad in extremely elegant costumes, formed a gathering of armless and decapitated coquettes. The mantelpiece and side-tables were a milliner's display-cases, in which feathers and ribbons concoct those minuscule or vast assemblies that only turn into pretty hats once they are on someone's head. A battalion of dress-shoes embellished shoe-trees, and a thousand feminine baubles were heaped up everywhere, in the midst of a delicate and depraved scent—which was Emma's.

My poor dear aunt, I would have preferred that your bedroom was further profaned, and that it was Mademoiselle Bourdichet's own bedroom, rather than hearing laughter from the next one—your husband's—for that left me with no illusions.

When I appeared, Emma and Barbe were stupefied. The young woman understood immediately, and burst out laughing. She was having lunch in bed. With a flick of the wrist, she twisted the flame of her hair into the coiffure of a bacchante. In that movement, I saw the shadow of her entire arm through her sleeve, and her chemise fell open. She made no attempt to close it again.

A table loaded with plates and carafes had been pushed up against the bed. Barbe, who was serving her mistress, was cutting marmoreal slices from a ham. My first thought was that Barbe and the table were going to be a considerable hindrance.

I gazed at the white throat—modeled it seemed, by a double caress—where a hint of pink was beginning to show next to the lace.

"What about Lerne?" Emma said.

I reassured her. He would not come back before 5 p.m.; I guaranteed it.

She made that slight cluck that is the sob of joy, and Barbe, who was obviously very devoted, cheered up with such jubilation that her entire body partook of it, each of her bosoms heaving with laughter on its own account in the general hilarity.

It was 12:30 p.m. We had four hours at our disposal. I suggested that time was short...but Emma said: "Would you like to have lunch with me, you rascal?"

I had nothing better to do for the moment, because of Barbe and the table, so I sat down facing the young lady. "As you wish—but quickly, then!" I said, in a prayerful tone.

She took a drink. Her vague murmur of acquiescence was stifled by the glass into a comic groan and her eyes peeped slyly over the crystal rim. She served me with her pale hands, the nails of which were painted.

My wit and appetite were both lacking. Nothing could emerge from my mouth any more than penetrate it. Eros was strangling me.

Emma! We measured one another with our eyes. In hers there were a great many promises and not a little irony. She was eating asparagus, making a noise like gluttonous kisses. Sometimes, when she leaned toward me, her chemise opened further, and the vision was then so prodigiously stimulating that it invaded my entire being through my pupils and gave my hands a sensation of softness...

"Emma..."

But she had already straightened up, almost nude, laughing at her own beauty as if at some great stroke of luck—and never, surely, had the infallible art of instinct made the most of such perfect plenitude and exact freshness with so much genius.

I was definitely not hungry, and nothing passed my lips; I settled for contemplating Emma without further persistence. She was in no hurry, teasing me—deliberately, I assume—in order to excite my desire to frenzy.

She ate her light meal in an Epicurean spirit. I had not yet seen her at ease. The act she put on in the perfumed warmth of the bedroom was, in my opinion, singularly accomplished, and the trailer gave birth to an irresistible desire for the full performance. I diverted myself by supposing the invisible from the visible, according to the secret relationship that charms that are made public are said to bear to those that are held in reserve. Emma's nose was a highly expressive little individual, and her narrow mouth had red fleshy lips whose very silence—a silence of tremors, smiles and moues—was lively speech...

She stretched herself. The batiste molded her contours, judiciously slender or appropriately curvaceous, and two points—one of which escaped as if it were a ruby star suddenly lighting up in a dazzling sky, astonished to find itself there.

My involuntary start shook the table. A strawberry rolled into the milk-bowl.

"Take all this and go away, Barbe!" said Emma.

When the servant had gone she curled up under the bedclothes as if sensitive to the cold. She wore the expression of someone who has just heard good news.

And for the moment that followed, a priapic god would have given his eternal life...

Afterwards, Emma remained inert for longer than normal. Her stiff body was embellished by a disquieting pallor, and I could not unclench her mouth in order to make her drink a little water.

I was about to call for help when a brief convulsion shook her. She released a sigh, both soft and hoarse, opened her eyes and sighed again, but with more coaxing grace. Her mind seemed still to be far away; she was looking at me from afar, from lost Cytherean shores from which she was returning slowly.

Suddenly bashful, I rearranged the bedclothes over her perfect nakedness—more naked and more perfect than any other—because, fateful and fastidious echoes of the tresses that determine, in collaboration with them, an inevitable diamond shape, the three previously-glimpsed reflections, previously seen as somber gleams, were no longer inflamed.

Emma twisted a wisp of hair overhanging her forehead into a curl. She became animated again...she wanted to talk. The statue of ice and fire was about to come back to life and conclude the adorable act, the act of acts, with an adorable word...

And she said: "Just as long as the old man don't find out—that's all we have to do, ain't it, darling?"

VII. Thus Spake Mademoiselle Bourdichet

That sentence was a great disappointment to me.

A few minutes earlier, I wouldn't even have noticed it. On the one hand, its author had committed many other vulgarities, and on the other, I knew that the dread she manifested that my uncle might discover our transgression was ill-founded—but the time of satiation is that of virtue and good manners, remorse and anxiety.

However, according to the custom of such encounters, we each contemplated one another's respective physiognomies. They were in conformity with the rules in force for many millennia, hers imprinted with a rather irrational gratitude, mine denoting the most ridiculous pride.

The mutism of my slang-babbling Cypris[19] was a stroke of luck. I wished it might be prolonged. Fortunately, as the habit often adapts itself to the monk, the

---

[19] Cypris, whose literal reference is to the island of Cyprus, was sometimes used in literary diction to refer to Aphrodite, just as "a voyage to Cytherea"—the "amorous isle" to which passing reference has already been made and will be made again—was routinely used as a euphemism for sexual intercourse.

foundation can correct the form, and she moderated her language somewhat in order to express the grave matters that had now begun to torment me. She continued her train of thought.

"My darling," she said, "now that we've got there, there's no use trying not to do it again—but I beg you, no recklessness; we need to be completely safe! Lerne, you see...Lerne! You've no suspicion of the dangers that threaten us...that threaten *you*, you most of all."

I understood that she was recalling tragic scenes to mind.

"What dangers?"

"That's the worst of it—I don't know. I don't understand anything of what's happening around me—nothing at all...except that Donovan MacBell has become a madman because I loved him...and I love you too!"

"Come on, Emma, calm down! We're allies now; between the two of us, we'll discover the truth! When did you arrive at Fonval? And what has happened since then?"

She told me about the ups and downs of her life then. I shall reproduce them as best I can, for the sake of clarity, but in reality the story was scattered through a dialogue in which my questions guided the story-teller, who was ever-ready to digress and loquacious in matters of unnecessary detail. The conversation was, moreover, pleasantly augmented by intervals that interrupted it delightfully—like a drama interwoven with songs—and that is the main reason why I shall refrain from transcribing it in full, to spare my sensibility the remembrance of transports that were never completed. One cannot conserve a very coherent manner with an intemperate mistress when she is exceedingly beautiful, clad only in bedclothes, especially if she loses track of what she is saying every time she gets up to her old tricks.

Sometimes, too, a creak or some other noise would interrupt our talk or our frolicking in mid-sentence or mid-kiss. Emma would stiffen then, fearful of Lerne, and I could not help shivering at the sight of her terror, for it only required an ear at the door or an eye at the keyhole for the somber anecdote to have been re-enacted with respect to me.

One way or another, I learned the details of Emma's origin and early life. They are irrelevant to this story, and can be summed up as a tale of "how a foundling became a whore." During this confession, Emma gave evidence of a sincerity that one might have charged with cynicism in anyone less candid.

She continued, with the same frankness: "I met Lerne five years ago—I was 15—in the hospital at Nanthel. I had entered his employ. As a nurse? No. I'd got into a fight with a comrade, Léonie, over Alcide, my man...well, what of it? I'm not ashamed of it. He's superb. He's a colossus, my darling—he could juggle with you. My belt was too narrow to make a bracelet for him. Anyway, I'd got a stab-wound...well deserved, I assure you. Just look!"

She threw off the bedclothes and showed me a livid triangular scar in her armpit, the handiwork of the execrable Léonie. "Yes, go on, you can kiss it," she went on. "I nearly died of it. Your uncle looked after me and saved me, it must be said. At that time your uncle was a nice chap, not stuck-up. He often talked to me. I found that flattering, myself. He preached me sermons as fine as those in church, on my life—it was wicked, I ought to change, and all that stuff—and all without seeming disgusted with me, so seriously that I began to be thoroughly disgusted with myself, and not to want to go back to being a whore, or to Alcide...being ill, you know, calms your blood....

"Then Lerne says to me one day: 'You're cured. You can go wherever you want. But it's not enough to make good resolutions; you have to keep them. Would you like to come to my house, as a laundry-maid, and earn a living far away from your old companions? All perfectly honorable, you know!'

"Well, that startled me. I said to myself: *All this talk is just to jolly me along. Once I'm in your home...goodbye platonic relationship! To hear you before, I'd never have thought it—but there are no more saints; no one offers to keep a woman for love of the art...*

"All the same, Lerne's kindness, his status, his renown, and a certain indefinable style magnified my gratitude, making it into a sort of affection, you see? And I accepted his proposition willingly, along with the consequences I expected. Well, not at all! There was still one saint: him. He didn't touch me for an entire year.

"I'd gone with him in secret. The idea that Alcide might find me again kept me awake at night. 'Don't be afraid,' said Lerne, 'I'm no longer a surgeon at the hospital; I'm going to do research work; we'll go live in the country, and no one will come looking for you there.' Indeed, he brought me here right away. Oh, you should have seen the château and the grounds! Gardeners, domestics, carriages, a horse...nothing was lacking here. I was happy.

"When we arrived, workmen were finishing off the extensions to the greenhouse and the laboratory. Lerne supervised the work. He was constantly joking and repeating: 'The work will go well in there! The work will go well!' in the same way that schoolboys shout 'Hurray for the holidays!'

"The laboratory was furnished. Lots of boxes went in, and one morning, when it was all finished, Lerne left for Grey in the open carriage. The avenue was straight then. I saw your uncle come back with the five travelers and the dog that he'd gone to fetch from the station: Donovan MacBell, Johann, Wilhelm, Karl, Otto Klotz—you remember him, the big dark man in the photograph—and Nelly. The Scotsman had met up with the Germans in Nanthel. I'm sure he hadn't met them before.

"The assistants were lodging in the laboratory, and MacBell was given a bedroom in the château, as was Dr. Klotz. That one frightened me from the start. I couldn't help asking Lerne where he'd found that jailbird. My question amused him greatly. 'Don't worry,' he answered. 'You see Monsieur Alcide's henchmen everywhere! Professor Klotz comes from Germany. He's very knowledgeable and very honorable. He's not a subordinate but a collaborator, whose main task is to supervise the work of his three compatriots...' "

"I beg your pardon, Emma," I said, interrupting her, "but did my uncle speak German and English at that time?"

"Very little, it seemed to me. He practiced every day, without any great result. It was only after a year, all of a sudden, that he succeeded in speaking it fluently. Anyway, the assistants already knew a few words of French, and Klotz more, as well as a little English. As for MacBell, though, he only understood his own language. Lerne told me that he'd only let him come to Fonval on the insistence of his father, who wanted the young student to work under his supervision for a while."

"Where did you sleep, Emma?"

"Next door to the laundry." With a smile, she added: "Oh, a long way away from MacBell and Klotz!"

"What attitude did all these men have to one another?"

"They seemed to be good friends. Were they sincere? I don't know anything about it, and it's not impossible that the four Germans were jealous of MacBell from the start. I noticed a few dirty looks. At any rate, Donovan wouldn't have had to tolerate their close company, since he didn't work in the laboratory with them but in the château and the greenhouse. Besides, at first his studies consisted of picking up French from books. We ran into one another frequently because I was always coming and going about the house. He was always polite and respectful—in sign-language, of course—and I was obliged to be pleasant...

"Those little flirtations were, I'm sure, the cause of a muted antipathy between him and Klotz. I soon noticed it. Although they hid their animosity successfully, Nelly, incapable of disguising hers, never lost an opportunity to growl at the German—and that wasn't the only sign I could see that a storm was brewing. But your uncle didn't see anything, and I didn't dare disturb his happiness with woeful prophecies. I didn't dare...and on the other hand, there was nothing in that rivalry to displease me. In spite of all my promises to Lerne to live virtuously, the jealous desire of the two adversaries ended up exciting me. I didn't know how it was going to work out, when our circumstances changed abruptly. We'd been here at year, so it was four years ago..."

"Ah!" I cried.

"What's up?"

"Nothing, nothing! Go on!"

"Well, four years ago, Donovan MacBell left for Scotland, in order to spend a few weeks' leave with his parents. On the day after his departure, in the morning, Lerne left. 'I'm going to Nanthel with Klotz,' he told me. 'We'll be there all day.'

"That evening, Klotz came back alone. I asked him about Lerne. The professor, it appeared, had received important news requiring a trip aboard, and would be gone for about three weeks. 'Where is he?' I asked. Klotz hesitated, and finally replied: 'He's in Germany. We'll be alone here all that time, Emma...'

"He put his arm round my waist and looked me in the eyes...

"I couldn't understand why Lerne, careful of my promised virtue, could have left me, without warning, at the mercy of a foreigner. 'Do you like me?' Klotz asked, pressing me against him without more ado. As I've already told you, Nicolas, he was big and strong. I felt his muscles and abandoned myself to him without wanting to. 'Well, Emma,' he said, 'let's love one another today, for you'll never see me again!'

"I'm not a coward. Between you and me, I've been caressed by hands that had just committed murder, and I've even been subjected to possessions that were akin to murders. My first lovers made love as if they were stabbing you to death...they weighed down heavily and hammered hard; you're a victim to them, you don't know whether you're experiencing more fear than pleasure. It's not unpleasant—but that's nothing. That night with Klotz was awful. It left me with an impression of rape. I'll always remember the terror and the fatigue.

"I woke up late the next morning. He was no longer beside me, and I never saw him again. Three weeks went by. Your uncle didn't write and his absence was prolonged. He came back without warning. I didn't even see him come in. He told me that he had gone to the laboratory as soon as he returned, I saw him when he came out, at about midday. His pallor worried me. A great sadness seemed to be weighing him down. He walked slowly, as if behind a hearse. What had he learned? What had he done? What cataclysm had overwhelmed him?

"I questioned him gently. His awkward speech retained the accent of the country he had just left. 'Emma,' he said, 'you like me, I think?'

" 'You know that very well, my dear benefactor; I'm devoted to you body and soul.'

" 'I'm only interested in the body. Do you think you're capable of liking me...of loving me?' He sniggered. 'Oh, I'm no longer a young man, but after all...'

"What answer should I have given? I didn't know. Lerne frowned. 'That's all right!' he snapped. 'From tonight on, my bedroom will be yours.'

"I admit, Nicolas, that it seemed more natural that way. But I had no inkling of the suspicious and wrathful Frédéric Lerne that was about to be revealed. He took hold of both my hands; his eyes were amazing. 'Now,' he cried, 'there's no more laughing, no fooling around, eh? You're mine, *exclusively*. I'm very well aware of what's been happening here, and that those dandies have been sniffing around you. I've got rid of Klotz. As for Donovan MacBell, beware! If he carries on, his account will be settled! Take care!'

"Then Lerne, having sacked the domestics, engaged poor Barbe as his only servant, and built the labyrinth.

"On the appointed day, MacBell, bewildered at finding the forest turned inside out, came back to the château in his turn, followed by his dog. Lerne accosted him while he was still holding his suitcases, and finished up dumbfounding him by admonishing him, with so many gestures and an expression so malevolent, that Nelly started to growl, with her hackles raised and showing her fangs.

"What was bound to happen, happened. In consideration of the age and quality of our host, MacBell and I should probably have respected his roof, as they say, but it was no more than a matter of deceiving an angry and tyrannical greybeard—which we did.

"Meanwhile, the professor became more despotic and more irritable every day. He lived in a state of indescribable overexcitement, not going out, working without rest, a genius perhaps, but a sick man for certain. The proof? He was losing his memory. He was subject to fits of total forgetfulness and often questioned me about his own past, only having precise memories in matters of science.

"No more laughing! That was true. And no more happiness with him! On an assumption, Lerne would scold me; on a suspicion, he would beat me. I'm not averse to insults or blows, I admit, but only when the former make me weep and the latter draw blood, when the insulting mouth is that of someone I love and the fist that strikes is solid, able to carry it through to the end. I told the feeble old wreck that I'd had enough of loneliness and poverty. 'I want to leave,' I declared. Oh, my darling, if you could have seen him! He fell at my knees and hugged them.

" 'What! What! Stay, Emma, I implore you. Wait! Wait two more years! Afterwards, we'll leave together, and you'll live like a queen. I'll be rich, extremely rich. Be patient! I know perfectly well that you weren't made to live like this indefinitely, as if in a convent. Believe me, I'm on the way to making an incalculable fortune. Two years of petty bourgeois existence, for the life of an empress!'

"Dazzled by the prospect, I didn't leave Fonval. But the years went by, the term elapsed, and of luxury there was none. Even so, I waited, having confidence in Lerne's own confidence, and in his genius. 'Don't be discouraged,' he told me, 'we're getting close. Everything will happen as I have prophesied; you'll have billions...' And to brighten up my idleness, he had dresses, hats and all sorts of trinkets sent from Paris every season. 'Get used to wearing them, learn your part, and rehearse the future...'

"I lived like that for three years, between Lerne and MacBell, treated roughly and insulted by the former, then adored like a Madonna and heaped with useless finery, and taken on the sly by the other, here and there, as the hazard of circumstances permitted, on a sofa or a carpet.

"At that time, Lerne went off on a long journey—two months, during which your uncle sent MacBell back to his family, on the pretext of a vacation.

They came back on the same day. I think the professor and he had met up at Dieppe. Lerne was depressed and incensed. 'You'll have to wait a little longer, Emma,' he said.

" 'What's the matter? Isn't it going well?'

" 'The general opinion is that my inventions aren't sufficiently perfected—but there's nothing to fear! I'll get there!'

"He resumed his researches in the laboratory…"

Once again, I broke into Emma's narrative. "I beg your pardon," I said. "Did MacBell also work in the laboratory at that time?"

"Never. Lerne gave him projects to do in the greenhouse, where he imprisoned him, my friend! Poor Donovan! He would have done better to stay away. It was because of me that he came back from Scotland. He gave me to understand that, in his gibberish. 'For you! For you!' He didn't know how to say much more. For me! Great gods, what did he become, for me, a few weeks later!

"Listen—this is where the madness come in.

"It's winter, and it's snowing. After lunch, Lerne takes a nap in an armchair in the little drawing-room next to the dining-room; at least, he pretends to go to sleep. Donovan winks at me. Pretending to go for a walk in the falling snow, on a whim, he goes out through the vestibule. He's heard whistling a tune outside. He draws away. As for me, I go back to the dining-room, as if to help the maid clear the table. Donovan rejoins me there by the door opposite the little drawing-room, which remains open to permit us to listen for Lerne's movements. He takes me in his arms; I embrace him. A silent kiss.

"Suddenly, Donovan goes green. I follow the direction of his gaze. The door of the little drawing-room is fitted with a glass plate—what they call a finger-plate, you know—and in the depths of that dark mirror, *I see Lerne's eyes spying on us!*

"Here he is, upon us! My knees bend, MacBell is very short. Lerne has knocked him down. They fight. Blood runs. Your uncle stops at nothing—feet, fingernails, teeth. I cry out, snatch at his clothes. Suddenly, he gets up again. MacBell is unconscious. Then Lerne bursts into wild laughter, lifts Donovan on to his shoulder, and carries him off toward the laboratory. I'm still screaming, but then I have the idea of calling: 'Nelly! Nelly!' The dog comes running. I point at the pair of them, and she runs after them just as Lerne disappears behind the trees with his burden. She disappears too. I listen. She barks—but suddenly, all I can hear is the whisper of the snow.

"Lerne had played me for a fool. It required all the credibility of his word, and all my assurance in a sumptuous future, to prevent me from running away that day. Besides which, having seen me being unfaithful, didn't he love me all the more ardently?

"Days passed…I scarcely dared hope that MacBell had suffered the same fate as Klotz and been sent away. Neither he nor the dog reappeared. Finally, the professor asked me to have the Yellow Room made up for the Scotsman. 'Is he still alive, then?' I said, without thinking.

" 'Half alive,' Lerne replied. 'He's mad. A sad epilogue to your sin, Emma! First, he thought he was the Eternal Father, then the Tower of London; now he thinks he's a dog. Tomorrow, he'll doubtless suffer from some other delusion.'

" 'What have you done to him?' I stammered.

" 'My child!' cried the professor, 'No one's done anything to him! Remember that, and bite your tongue if you're ever tempted to talk drivel. When I carried MacBell away after our scuffle in the dining-room, it was in order to care for him—you could easily see that he had been taken ill. As he fell, he seriously injured his head. That caused a lesion, and that led to madness. That's all, understand?'

"I didn't say anything else, convinced that if your uncle hadn't killed Donovan, fear of his family and judicial consequences were the only reason.

"They brought him back to the château that same evening, his head swathed in bandages. He didn't recognize me. I still loved him, and I visited him in his hiding-place. He healed rapidly, but internment has made him fat. The MacBell of the photograph and the MacBell of the Yellow Room are quite dissimilar, to the extent that you didn't recognize him there, Nicolas...' "

"Emma," I murmured, "how were you able to caress that madman?"

"Love has no need of intelligence; on the contrary, I read in a novel that Messalina, who was a very passionate queen, disdained the service of poets.[20] MacBell..."

"Ah! Shut up!"

"Stupid!" she said, "Since you're my little man, and you alone."

Indeed, I thought. Aloud, I said: "Tell me, though—do you know anything about Klotz? What fate did my uncle have in store for him? You mentioned being sent away, a little while ago."

"I've always been certain that he was sent away. His attitude when he returned from Germany with Lerne convinced me of it."

"Has he a family?"

"I believe he's a orphan and a bachelor."

"How long did MacBell remain in the laboratory?"

"About three weeks...or a month."

"Was his hair as blond before this setback?" I asked, in pursuit of my old hobby-horse.

"Of course—what a strange thing to ask!"

"And Nelly—what did they do to her?"

---

[20] The reference is probably to Alfred Jarry's *Messaline* (1901), a calculatedly-scandalous *avant-garde* text published in the same year as the same author's similarly-eroticized scientific romance *Le surmâle* [The Supermale].

"The day after the brawl, I heard her uttering heart-rending howls, presumably because she'd been separated from her master. According to your uncle, when I asked him about it, she was with other dogs in kennels. 'The right place,' Lerne added. She hasn't come out, until the other evening. Perhaps you heard her? Poor Nelly! How quickly she found MacBell! She often howls at night. Her life isn't a happy one."

"Finally," I said, "what can we conclude? What's at the bottom of all this? Where's the truth of it? Do you believe that the madness resulted from the fall?"

"How do I know? It's possible—but I suspect that the laboratory contains hideous things, the sight of which would be sufficient to drive you mad. Donovan had never gone into it. He must have witnessed some abomination..."

I remembered the chimpanzee and the violent impression that its death had made on me. Emma might have been right. The monkey's fate lent support to her hypothesis. Instead of searching for the key to that particular mystery, though, was it not necessary to go back four years, to the critical phase when so many problems had originated? Was it not necessary to scrutinize the mysterious era in which so many doors had been closed, in order to find the key that would open them all?

A little foot emerged from the coverlet, white and pink on the yellow silk, like an absurd jewel in its casket. "Good God, Mademoiselle! Do you really walk on that little soft thing, with its toenails painted and polished like Japanese coral? That living and sensitive jewel that a moustache puts to flight? What magnificent imprudence!"

The foot retired into its large parcel. Nimble and dainty as it was, though, and so tender, it reminded me by contrast of another: the one in the clearing, the macabre shoe-tree whose shoe, I was now convinced, was on the foot of a carcass. All of a sudden, it seemed to me that I was alone in a darkness full of ambushes.

"Emma! What if we were to leave?"

She shook her Maenad's tresses, and declined. "Donovan suggested that to me. No. Lerne has promised me opulence. In addition to that, on the day of your arrival, he swore that he would kill me in the event of deceit or escape. I've known for a long time that he's capable of carrying out the first threat, and I feel sure now that he'd carry out the second..."

"That's true—when he introduced us to one another, Emma, you had death in your eyes!"

"Now," she continued, "we can conceal our love, but not our flight. No, no—let's stay here and keep our eyes open. Let's be prudent, but let's also make the most of the time."

And as time was getting on, we made the most of it.

The clock was chiming 4:30 p.m. when I left my insatiable mistress to take the road back to Grey-l'Abbaye. Emma was in no condition to bid my goodbye;

sighing and stretching like a she-cat, she was nonchalantly dreaming of the amorous isle.

VIII. Temerity

I went back along the road to Grey at top speed. The festival was in full swing there and the crowd, in a festive mood, abused me with insults and quips. The clock on the platform showed 5 p.m. I took advantage of the respite to do a little scene-setting, in order that my uncle might fall more readily into the pitfall that he had laid for his own feet by demanding the repair of a mechanism of which I possessed an entire specimen. With a mechanic's blue overall on my back, and my hands and face dirtied, having taken the tools out of the trunk and strewn them around, I put a dent in the new carburetor with a few gentle hammer-blows and smeared it with grease. A few strokes of a file, drawn randomly across it, completed the task of giving it the rough-hewn appearance of a newly-forged item.

The train stopped.

When Lerne touched me on the shoulder, I was exerting myself with feigned efforts to tighten a screw that was already perfectly secure.

"Nicolas!"

I turned a coal-heaver's face to my uncle, as peevish as I could make it. "I've just finished," I muttered. "That was a nasty trick you pulled there! Making people work for no reason!"

"Is it back in order?"

"Yes; I've just tried it. You can see that the engine' hot..."

"Do you want to fit the parts I took away back into the carburetor?"

"Keep them as a memento of your nice day, uncle. Let's get in. I've been here long enough, myself.

Frédéric Lerne was uneasy. "No hard feelings, eh, Nicolas?"

"No hard feelings, uncle."

"I have my reasons, you know. Later..."

"Don't worry. If you knew me, you'd be less suspicious...but your conduct today is in accord with our agreement. I don't have any cause for complaint."

He made an evasive gesture. "You're not angry, that's the main thing. In sum, you understand how things are."

Lerne was evidently worried that he had annoyed me and that, if I resolved to leave in the wake of such vexation, I might divulge the existence of important secrets at Fonval, even without being able to tell anyone their exact nature.

All things considered, the presence in his home of a stranger at liberty was a matter of constant alarm to my uncle. It seemed to me that in his place, obliged to receive a third party because he was related to me, I would certainly have preferred to make him my accomplice as soon as possible, to ensure his discretion.

After all, I said to myself, *why would my uncle not have thought of that? Before the uncertain, and perhaps illusory, date when Lerne will have to initiate me, there will be a long period of torment for him in which he will have to exercise his double role of analyst and policeman. What if I anticipate his plan? He will doubtless hasten joyfully to an instruction as sacred as a confession, which would unite the master and the disciple in the same conspiracy.*

I can't see why my anticipations would be unwelcome, for, in the two possible circumstances—whether Lerne's promise to initiate me into his enterprise was or was not given in good faith—the situation has only two possible outcomes: my departure, which might even now have revelatory consequences, or my connivance. Now, Emma and the mystery retain me at the château, so I won't leave. There remains, therefore, the simulated comedy, which would have the further advantage of enabling me to solve the puzzle. Who else but Lerne will expose it to me, since Emma knows nothing and, if I were to search for it on my own, every problem solved would bring another into view? Wise diplomacy would certainly convince my uncle to make an imminent revelation. That's all he needs to do—but how can I induce him to do it?

It's important to suggest to him that his secrets won't frighten me, even if they're criminal. Thus, it would be wise to represent myself as a resolute man, who is not scandalized by contact with crimes, and who would refrain from denouncing them because he would commit them himself if need be. That's it—perfect. But how do I pick a crime that Lerne would be capable of perpetrating, which I might declare to be natural, and which I might commit if the opportunity arose? Of course! Make use of his own misdeeds, Nicolas! Admit to him that you know about one of his most reprehensible actions, and that you approve, not merely of that action but also of all others of the same sort, in which you're ready to aid him! Then, in the face of such a declaration, he'll loosen up, and you'll find out everything, ready to make good use of the confidence later, as your own interests dictate! Meanwhile, be cunning; let's not speak to my uncle unless he's in a good mood, and if the old shoe doesn't tell us anything.

I reasoned thus as I was driving Lerne to Fonval. The satiation of my desire impoverished my thinking; I thought my mind was calm and clear, but I was very tired. It was obvious; under the powerful influence of the surroundings, Lerne's unproven crimes preoccupied me more than anything else, and I imagined them to be detestable and countless. I forgot that his surreptitiously-plotted work, shielded from duplication, might really have an industrial aim. Impatient as I was to satisfy my curiosity, and relaxed by the satiation of my lust, that strategy seemed to me to be cleverly conceived. I had no sense of the enormity of the fictitious confession that I would have to make before obtaining anything in exchange.

More reflection would have indicated the danger I was running, but adverse fortune dictated that my uncle, satisfied by my replies and content that I "understood how things were" affected an entirely unexpected joviality. No opportunity more appropriate to my plan was ever likely to present itself...

Stupidly, I seized it.

As usual, enthused by the motor car, my uncle had me execute various maneuvers as I went through the labyrinth, and it was while describing these curves that I had been deliberating.

"Colossal, Nicolas!" he said. "I repeat, this automobile is prodigious! A beast—a veritable organic creature...perhaps the least imperfect! Who knows the heights to which progress might take it? A spark of life therein, a little more spontaneity, a scrap of brain...and you'd have the finest creature on Earth! Yes, finer than us, in a sense—for, remember what I told you: it's perfectible and immortal, virtues of which human physical being is pitifully deprived.

"Everybody renews itself almost entirely, Nicolas. Your hair, for example"—why the Devil was he always talking about hair?—"isn't the same as the hair you had last year, but it grows back older, thinner and less dark. The automobile, on the other hand, changes its parts *at will*, and is rejuvenated every time, with an entirely new heart, fresh bones, designed with greater ingenuity or resistance than the original organs. In 1000 years, therefore, a Jeannot[21] vehicle—an automobile, never having stopped improving—will be just as young as it is today, if it is regenerated on a regular basis, piece by piece.

"And don't say: 'It won't be the same, since all its parts will have been replaced.' If you raise that objection, Nicolas, what must you think of a human being who, in that race to death that we call life, is subject to transformations just as radical, but in a decadent fashion? You would therefore have to conclude, strangely: 'The old person who dies is no longer the one who was born. The one who has just been born, and cannot last forever, will not die—or, at least, will not die all at once, but progressively, scattered by the four winds of Heaven as organic dust, over a long period during which another will slowly form in the same location, which is that of the body. This other person, whose birth is imperceptible, develops in every one of us without our being aware of it, as the earlier one subsides. The new person supplants the old day by day, modified incessantly at the behest of the dying and recreated cells of which it is the sum — and is the one who will be seen to die.'

"Such would be your conclusion, which anyone would judge accurate; and the latter would add: 'It's true that the mind seems to persist, immutable in the midst of all these evolutions; nevertheless, that isn't proven; for if the traits of the infant generally linger in those of the old person, the mind is sometimes al-

---

[21] Jeannot, the French equivalent of the English "Johnny," has a wide potential range of reference, but a French reader would immediately think of the one in Voltaire's moral fable "Jeannot et Colin," whose circumstances enjoy a remarkable and rapid improvement, whereupon he forgets his former friends—until he suffers a rude reversal of fortune.

tered to the point that we can no longer recognize it as our own. Then again, can the elements of the brain not renew themselves, molecule by molecule, without thought being interrupted, in the same way that one may change the elements of an electric pile without the generation of electricity being interrupted?'

"At the end of the day, though, what does the question of personality *in extremis* matter to the human being?[22] And what use would it be to imperishable automobiles—in which humans direct, like a demiurge, the development of the individual and the evolution of the species—to retain a tedious identity through the phases of their reformation? That's arrant nonsense! Would they be any more admirable for it, these colossi of iron that are almost alive already?

"I tell you, Nicolas, that if, by some miracle, the automobile were to become independent, man might as well pack his bags. His era would be approaching its end. After him, the automobile would be the monarch of the world, as the mammoth reigned before him."

"Yes," I said, distractedly, absorbed by my own speculations, "but that sovereign would still depend on a human constructor."

"A fine argument! Are we the slaves of the animals and the plants that sustain our construction with their flesh and their tissue?" My uncle was so pleased with his paradoxes that he shouted them out, wriggling in his seat and waving his arms in the air frantically, as if he were grabbing handfuls of ideas therefrom. "In truth, nephew, what a splendid decision you made in bringing this motor car! It has cheered me up no end! You must teach me how to drive this animal. I'll be the mahout of the mammoth to come, eh? Ha ha ha!"

When this outburst of hilarity occurred I had just finished my own reasoning, and it was the laughter that decided my immediate—and imprudent—attack.

---

[22] Renard inserts a footnote here, attributed to "the transcriber:" "Monsieur Vermont is reporting Dr. Lerne's words with more grandiloquence than fidelity. The latter, so meticulous in the explanation of his slightest divagations, must certainly have perceived and mentioned the importance that attaches, in the matter of responsibility, to the verification of so insane a theory. One can hear him asking himself: 'Are adults bound to make amends for the sins of their youth? Have they the right to refuse, on the grounds that it was someone else who committed them?' To put it another way: Could the king of France legitimately dismiss the creditors of the Duc d'Orléans? Are old grudges valid? Should gratitude wear away over time? Etc. Monsieur Vermont tells us that he was distracted. We can see that easily enough—for he is too inexperienced in the art of writing for us to suspect him of having cut this paragraph deliberately, in order to lighten a chapter that is already too anarchic, in which he has simply reproduced the authentic confusion of life instead of distributing things in that good order whose artifice is the writer's glory." Sternly disregarding the sarcasm of the final sentiment, the translator of the Macaulay version not only cut the footnote but the entire paragraph to which it is attached.

"How amusing you are, uncle! I'm delighted by your cheerfulness—I recognize you again. Why aren't you like this all the time, instead of mistrusting me—the person who, on the contrary, merits your full confidence?"

"But you know full well," said Lerne, "that I've committed myself to telling you when the time is right."

"Why not right away, uncle?" And I recklessly launched into my blunder. "Come on! We're cut from the same cloth, you and I. You don't know me at all. Nothing astonishes me. I know more about it than you think. Well, uncle, know this: I share your opinions; I admire your actions!"

Slightly surprised, Lerne began to laugh. "And what is it that you know?"

"I know that one can't rely on the present law to take care of one's own affairs. Has someone wronged you? It's safer to get rid of him oneself, and imprisonment, in such a case, is legitimate even though it remains illegal. One fortuitous incident has convinced me of this. In brief, uncle, if I were named Frédéric Lerne, Monsieur MacBell would not have got off so easily. You don't know me, I tell you."

"Well," he said, "that's news!" The professor's tone, however, made me conscious of my gaffe. He defended himself in a manner that I thought hypocritical. "What an imagination! Are you really the rogue you claim to be? So much the worse, then. As for me, nephew, that's not my way. MacBell is mad, but that's nothing to do with me! It's regrettable that you've discovered him—it's a sad spectacle. The poor man! Me, imprison him? What nonsense, Nicolas! What will you say next? It's just as well, however, that you mentioned it to me; it has opened my eyes. Appearances are, indeed, against me. I was waiting for an improvement in the invalid's state of mind before informing his relatives, in order that they might be less affected by a less obvious illness...but no! To hesitate further would be too dangerous; my own safety requires it. At the risk of causing them more grief, I must inform them! I'll write to them this evening to tell them that they must come to fetch him. Poor Donovan! His departure, I hope, will dispel your shameful presumptions. They sadden me greatly, Nicolas..."

I experienced a considerable confusion. Was I mistaken? Had Emma lied? Or did Lerne want to allay my suspicions? In either event, I had made a bad error; whether he was an honest man or a scoundrel, Lerne would hold me accountable for having accused him, falsely or otherwise. It was a defeat, and the only reward I had was a new doubt, with respect to Emma.

"In any case, uncle, I swear to you that chance alone led me to discover MacBell..."

"If *chance* leads you to discover other reasons to slander me," Lerne replied, harshly, "don't neglect to inform me; I'll clear myself without delay. Nevertheless, the strict observance of your promises would prevent you from assisting any *chance* that would enable you to discover madmen...or madwomen."

We had arrived at Fonval. "Nicolas," said Lerne, in a softer tone, "I feel a great affection for you. I wish you well—so obey me, my boy!"

134

He wants to soft-soap me, I thought. *He's wooing me. Beware!*

"Obey me," he continued, in a honeyed tone, "and help me out in the meantime, by your patience. Intelligent as you are, you must understand that nuance! The day isn't far off, if I'm not mistaken, when I'll be able to tell you everything. You'll see the great thing of which I've dreamed, nephew, a part of which I'm saving for you...

"In the meantime, since you know about the MacBell business—here, this is testimony to the faith for which I ask—come with me to visit him. We'll decide whether he's sufficiently well to cope with the journey and the crossing."

After a brief hesitation, I followed him to the Yellow Room.

At the sight of him, the madman arched his back and retreated into a corner, growling all the while, his pose fearful and his eyes resentful.

Lerne pushed me in front of him. I was afraid he was going to imprison me.

"Take his hands. Bring him into the middle of the room."

Donovan allowed himself to be drawn. The doctor examined him thoroughly, but I noticed that the scar attracted his most careful attention. In my opinion, the rest of the inspection was merely a pretence intended to deflect my suspicions.

That wound! An incised diadem, half-hidden by the long hair; a wound extending around the head—what fall on what kind of floor could possibly have produced it?

"Excellent health," my uncle pronounced. "You see, Nicolas, he was violent at first and scratched himself grievously...hmm...all over. In a fortnight, he won't look so bad. He can be taken away." The consultation was concluded. "Your feeling is that I should get rid of him as soon as possible, Nicolas?" he continued. "Give me your opinion—I value it highly."

I congratulated him on his resolution, although so much kindness made me wary.

Lerne sighed. "You're right. The world is so wicked! I'll write straight away. Would you like to take my letter to the Post Office in Grey? It will be ready in ten minutes."

My nerves relaxed. I had wondered, as I came back into the château, whether I would ever leave it again, and the demon of evil dreams sometimes gives me the madman's room as a prison to this day. The ogre was definitely putting on a show of being paternal and benign. With my liberty at his disposal, being able to incarcerate me, he was sending me for a cross-country run, which I might decide to end by fleeing. Was it worth taking advantage of an opportunity so gladly conceded? Not being so stupid, I would not make use of it.

While Lerne wrote his letter to the MacBells I went for a stroll in the grounds—and I witnessed an incident there that was most strange, at least in the impression it made on me.

Dame Fortune, as you will have observed, was playing with me unrelentingly, jerking me back and forth like a marionette between tranquility and turbulence. This time, in order to upset me, she made use of the slightest pretext. Had my mind been calm, I would not have attributed a mysterious character to what might have been no more than a freak of nature, but the marvelous was in the air; I scented it everywhere, and one of Lerne's observations was still ringing in my ears. *Since the night of my arrival, there had been certain things outside that should not have been there.*

Furthermore, what I saw in the grounds that day—which, I insist, would not have amazed everyone as they did me—seemed to me to be a lacuna in my documentation of the Lerne question, the cycle of his studies having, so to speak, been closed in that respect. It was quite indistinct. Thanks to its uncertain evidence, I even caught a glimpse of a solution to the whole set of problems—an abominable solution!—but my tumultuous and extravagant ideas were not sufficiently precise for self-expression. For the duration of a second, however, they acquired an unimaginable violence, and if I shrugged my shoulders after the short scene that gave birth to them, it must be admitted that it had scared me half to death. I shall describe it.

Having planned to employ my ten minutes in an investigation of the old shoe, I went along a path where the evening dew was already visible in the tall grass. The twilight was already beginning to darken in the wood. The chirping of the sparrows was becoming sparser. I think it was half past six. The bull bellowed. As I passed the pasture I only counted four animals—Pasiphae was no longer parading the demi-mourning of her variegated coat—but that was of no interest.

I was walking deliberately when a riot of hissing, mingled with little cries—a cluster of sharp squeals, if I might put it thus—brought me to a halt.

The grass was undulating.

I drew nearer without making a noise, craning my neck.

There was a duel in progress: one of the countless combats which make every pathway a sink of iniquity; a criminal battle in which one of the adversaries is condemned to perish in order that the other might be fed—the duel of a little bird and a snake.

The snake was a rather imposing viper, whose triangular skull bore a large black mark of the same shape. The bird...imagine a blackcap, with the rather significant difference that its head, unnaturally, was white: a variety, doubtless artificially bred, which I could describe less awkwardly if I were better versed in natural history.

The two champions were facing one another, one of them advancing toward the other. Imagine my surprise, though: it was the blackcap that was causing the snake to retreat. It was advancing jerkily, in abrupt and periodic little leaps, without fluttering its wings, with a hypnotic appearance; its staring eyes had the magnetizing gleam that shines in the eyes of a hunting dog. The viper was recoiling from it awkwardly, fascinated by the implacable gaze, while fear drew choked hissing sounds from it.

Damn! I said to myself. *Has the world turned upside-down, or is my mind topsy-turvy?"*

Then I made the mistake, in order to witness the outcome, of getting too close—which modified it. The blackcap noticed me and took flight; as its enemy slid into the grass, the wake of its escape ran through it in zigzags.

The ridiculous and excessive anguish that had gripped me was already dissipating. I scolded myself roundly. *I'm seeing things...it's a matter of maternal affection, that's all. The heroic little animal is defending its nest and its eggs. The fortitude of mothers is incalculable...that's it, damn it! That's it! What else could it be? No, I'm being silly. What else could it be?*

"Halloooo!" My uncle was hailing me. I retraced my steps—but the incident bothered me. In spite of my attempt to convince myself that it was perfectly ordinary, I didn't mention it to Lerne.

The professor had an engaging manner, though: the cheerful appearance of a man who has just made a big decision and found himself quite pleased about it. He was standing at the château's main door, his missive in his hand, contemplating the boot-scraper with interest.

My presence having failed to interrupt his ecstasy, I thought it only polite to study the boot-scraper as well. It was a sharp blade sealed in the wall, which dynasties of shoes had hollowed out, curving it like a billhook, almost a sickle, by the force of their scraping. I presumed that the meditative Lerne was gazing at the blade without seeing it. Indeed, he seemed to wake up abruptly. "Well, Nicolas, here's the letter. Forgive me for putting you to the trouble."

"Oh, I'm used to it, uncle. Automobilists are messengers, whether they like it or not. Gladly assuming that they're ready to drive for no reason at all, many a lady asks them, many a time, to drive for a purpose...and to carry quantities of extremely urgent and very heavy parcels. It's a tax levied on our sport...."

"Come on—you're a good lad. Go—dusk is falling."

I took the letter: the heart-rending letter that would make MacBell's madness known in Scotland; the benevolent letter that would separate Emma from her degraded lover.

Sir George MacBell
12 Trafalgar Street
Glasgow
Scotland

The handwriting of the address gave me pause for thought. Only a few vestiges of the former cursive rendered it recognizable and still revealed Lerne's pen. The majority of the characters, the emphases, the punctuation and the general appearance denoted a "graphic intelligence" diametrically opposed to that of old. Graphology is never wrong; its conclusions are infallible. The author of that script had changed out of all recognition.

Now, in his youth, my uncle had exhibited all the virtues. What vices, therefore, were presently absent in him? And how he must hate me, having once loved me so much!

IX. The Ambush

MacBell's father came to fetch him without delay, accompanied by his other son.

Since Lerne had written to him, nothing new had occurred at Fonval. The mystery dragged on, and dispositions against my person had been multiplied. Emma no longer came downstairs; I heard her, from the small drawing-room, devoting herself to her futile pastimes in the room with the mannequins, repeatedly clicking her heels on the ceiling.

My nights were sleepless. The idea of Lerne and Emma together, one a sadist and the other compliant, tormented my insomnia. Jealousy tends to enrich the imagination; it made me see scenes of unbearable ingenuity. I certainly promised myself to act them out for my own pleasure as soon as I was able to do so, but I was haunted by the obsessive vision of Lerne as the master of my mistress, savoring the bloodshed of his tortures and sating his desires with sophistications that redoubled their succulence.

Once, I tried to go out for a walk in the cool night air, as far as the edge of the wild part of the grounds, and thus to tire myself out like a hard-worked animal—but the doors on the ground floor were locked. Lerne was keeping me confined!

The imprudence that I had committed in revealing my discovery of Mac-Bell to him had, however, had no other apparent consequence than a recrudescence of his amity. During our walks, which became more frequent, he seemed increasingly pleased with my society, endeavoring to ameliorate the rigor of my closely-observed life and retain me at Fonval, whether in genuine preparation for an association or to avoid the risks of an escape.

His precautions annoyed me. This was a period when, without it seeming that I was being closely watched, I was watched more closely than before. My days were filled against my will. Impatience was gnawing at me. While sounding the depths of my love and those of the mystery—both of which were prohibited—I hardly noticed that if, in practice, love called to me in the form of an inaccessible pretty woman, the mystery that attracted me just as imperiously was represented primarily by a no-less-approachable old shoe—grotesque alternatives!

That elasticated garbage served as a basis for all the hypotheses I constructed by night, in the hope of calming jealousy with curiosity. It constituted, in fact, the sole clearly-determined goal at which my indiscretion might be aimed. I had taken note that the tool-shed was in the vicinity of the clearing; that was convenient for unearthing the boot...and the remains, if necessary. Under the yoke of his affection, however, Lerne kept me away from it mercilessly, along with the greenhouse, the laboratory, Emma and everything else.

I yearned with all my heart, therefore, for some event, some new fact that, by disturbing our *modus vivendi*, would permit me to evade the vigilance of my guardians: a trip to Nanthel on Lerne's part, or an accident, if necessary, no matter what, of which I might take advantage.

That windfall was the arrival of the MacBells, father and son.

My uncle, forewarned by telegram, told me about it with an explosion of delight. Why was he so pleased? Seriously, had I cast light on the danger of keeping the invalid Donovan without his family's knowledge? I found it damnably difficult to believe that—but then again, Lerne's laughter, though sincere, seemed to have something nasty about it, and might well originate from some evil plan.

At any rate, I followed the professor's example in cheering up, and without any imposture, for I had good reason to do so.

They arrived one morning in a brake hired in Grey and driven by Karl. They resembled one another closely, and they both resembled the Donovan of the photograph. They were stiff, pale and impassive.

Lerne, perfectly at ease, introduced me. They shook my hand coldly, keeping their gloves on. One might have thought that they had put gloves on their feelings. Introduced into the small drawing-room, they sat down without a word. The three assistants were there. Lerne made a long speech in English, abundantly illustrated with demonstrative gestures, and singularly emotional. At one point, he imitated the backward fall of a person who has slipped. Thanking the two men by the arm thereafter, he led them to the château's central door facing the grounds. We followed him. There, he showed them the billhook-shaped boot-scraper and repeated his mime. Undoubtedly, he was explaining that Donovan had injured himself by falling backwards, and that his head had struck the curved blade.

That was, of course, a novelty!

We went back to the drawing-room. My uncle completed his speech, wiping his eyes, and the three Germans attempted to sniffle, to indicate a valiantly-repressed need to weep. The MacBells did not bat an eyelash. They gave no hint of grief or impatience.

Finally, Johann and Wilhelm, having absented themselves on an order from Lerne, brought Donovan. He was clean-shaven, with his hair pomaded and parted to one side, looking like a fashionable young aristocrat, even though his worn traveling costume was coming apart at the buttons and his overly narrow collar was reddening his plump good-natured face. His greasy hair almost hid the scar.

At the sight of his father and brother, the madman's eyes became radiant with intelligent happiness, and his smile lit up his previously-apathetic features with affectionate kindness. I thought he had recovered his reason…but he knelt down at his relatives' feet and began licking their hands and barking inarticulately. His brother could not get anything out of him but that. His father was similarly frustrated. After that, the MacBells got ready to take their leave of Lerne.

My uncle spoke to them. I understood that they were declining an invitation to stay, at least for lunch. The other did not insist at all, and everyone went out.

Wilhelm put Donovan's suitcase on to the seat of the carriage.

"Nicolas," Lerne said to me, "I'll go with these gentlemen to the station. You stay here with Johann and Wilhelm. Karl and I will come back on foot." He added in a cheerful tone: "I entrust the house to you!" And he gave me a brisk handshake.

Was my uncle making fun of me? A fine sovereignty, under the authority of two watchers!

They got into the brake, Karl and the trunk in front, Lerne and the lunatic facing the lucid MacBells in rear.

The gate was already open when Donovan suddenly stood up, with a terrified expression, as if he could hear Death sharpening his scythe; a long howl, recognizable to us, went up from the laboratory. The madman pointed in that direction and replied to Nelly with a prolonged bestial screech, the horror of which made us grow pale. We waited for it to end, as if for deliverance.

Lerne, his eyes forceful and his speech gruff, snapped: "Vorwärts! Karl! Vorwärts!" And he shoved his pupil down on the seat, unceremoniously.

The carriage moved off. The madman, moving closer to his brother, looked at him in a distraught fashion, seemingly in the grip of an incomprehensible misery.

The frightful unknown gripped me again. It was all around, getting closer and closer; this time, I had felt it touch me.

In the distance, the howling redoubled. Then, in the moving brake, MacBell senior exclaimed: "Hey! What about Nelly! Where's Nelly?"

"Alas," my uncle replied, "Nelly's dead."

"Poor Nelly!" said MacBell senior.

Duffer as I was, I knew enough English to translate this elementary textbook dialogue. Lerne's lie made me indignant—how dare he claim that Nelly was dead, that that voice was not hers? What a mockery! Oh, why did I not shout to those phlegmatic individuals: "Halt! You're being swindled! There's something terrible about this!"

Yes, but what? I didn't know. The MacBell's would have taken me for another lunatic…

Meanwhile, the hired nag was trotting toward the gate, where Barbe was standing, ready to close it again. Donovan had sat down again. Facing him, the MacBells retained their measured dignity, but as the carriage turned into the gateway I saw the paternal back bend suddenly, shivering more than was warranted by the jolting of the cobblestones...

The ancient and creaky halves of the gate came together.

I'm sure that the brother would not have been much longer in breaking into sobs.

Johann and Wilhelm went away.

Were they relieving me of their company? I trailed them alongside the pasture, as far as the laboratory. Nelly persisted in her lamentation; they probably wanted to force her to shut up. Indeed, she fell silent as soon as the assistants went into the courtyard. In spite of my fears, instead of coming back to the château to shut me in, the odd couple, having lit cigars, shamelessly made preparations for an apparent siesta. Through an open window of their lodgings, I saw them in their shirtsleeves, smoking like chimneys in their swaying rocking-chairs.

When I was sure of their intention—without wondering whether they were acting in defiance of Lerne's instructions or with his permission, and a thousand leagues from thinking that in displaying themselves at the window they might be carrying out his orders to the letter—I went to the tool-shed.

Soon, I was digging up the soil around the old shoe—or, as I was now able to say, around *the foot.*

Toes upwards, it extended from the bottom of a crater in which the marks of Donovan's nails were still visible among other, more ancient signs of scraping. Except that the latter, made by powerful clawed feet, testified that the first digger had been a dog of large stature—presumably Nelly, at the time when she had wandered the grounds in total liberty.

A leg was attached to the foot, superficially covered in earth. I clung to the possibility that it might be anatomical debris, but without conviction.

A hairy torso followed the leg. An entire cadaver, scantily clad, in a very poor state. It had been buried slantwise; the head, lower than the feet, was still embedded. It was with a quivering spade that I uncovered the chin, the near-blue side-whiskers, then a thick moustache, and finally the face...

I now knew the fate of all the individuals grouped in the photograph. Otto Klotz lay before me, half-exhumed, with the top of his head in the soil. I identified him without hesitation; there was no need to disinter him completely. On the contrary, it would be better to fill in the hole, in order to leave no evidence of the escapade.

Suddenly, though, I took up the pick-axe again, frantically, and resumed hollowing out the ground beside the dead man. A rounded bone emerged therefrom, like a venomous mushroom, its apophysis blanched and already spongy. Oh! Were there...other graves here?

I dug...and I dug...I was feverish. White spots fluttered before my eyes and, a Pentecost to my maddened retina, it seemed to me that it was snowing tongues of fire...

I dug...and I dug...and I discovered an entire cemetery blossoming in the soil—an animal cemetery, thank God! Some were skeletons, others still had their fur or feathers, shriveled or purulent: guinea-pigs, dogs, goats, sometimes whole, sometimes reduced to mere fragments, the rest of which had fed the dog-pack; a horse's leg—my dear Biribi, it was hers!—and, beneath a freshly shifted layer of earth, butcher's offal packed up in a varicolored skin: Pasiphae's hide.

A fetid stench filled my throat. Exhausted, I leaned on my filthy pick in the middle of the charnel-house.

The sweat streaming down my forehead pricked my eyes. I was panting hard.

At that moment, my gaze chanced to fall on the skull of a cat. I picked it up immediately. It was a veritable pipe-bowl—which is to say that there was a large circular hole where the top had been taken off. I picked up another—a rabbit's, if I remember rightly—and found the same singularity. Four, six, fifteen others: all the skulls displayed their gaping holes, with some diversity in their position. Here and there, osseous lids strewed the clearing with their large or small, deep or flat bowls. One would have thought that all these creatures had been killed in the same way, in a precise hecatomb, a reasoned sacrifice....

And suddenly, an idea struck me: an atrocious idea!

I knelt down by the dead man, and I finished clearing the mud from his head. Nothing abnormal in front: close-cropped hair; but behind, enveloping the occiput from one temple to the other—like MacBell's scar—a horrid incision exposed the split skull...

Lerne had killed Klotz! He had murdered him, because of Emma, in the same fashion that he destroyed the lives of birds and beasts, when he had exhausted their strength to endure his experiments! It was a surgical crime. I reckoned that the mystery was pierced from top to bottom.

In my judgment, I thought, *MacBell's madness originates from the fact that Lerne did not complete his work, and from the fact that the poor fellow, at the sight of the frightful death awaiting him, lost his mind. But why did my uncle not complete his work? Doubtless, in the course of the funereal labor—which he had started thoughtlessly, guided by his blind fury and lust-clouded mind—he suddenly saw more clearly, and became fearful of the reprisals of MacBell's family. According to Emma, Klotz was an orphan and a bachelor—so here he is! And it's the same fate that waits me—and perhaps awaits her, if he catches us together! Oh, we must flee, no matter what the cost, she and I! Flee, that's the only reasonable thing to do! Right now, circumstances are in our favor. Will the opportunity ever arise again? We have to leave and go through the forest to the station, in order to avoid Lerne and Karl as they come back along the direct road. But what about the labyrinth? Would it be preferable to use the automo-*

bile and run them over? I don't know...we'll see...shall I arrive in time? Quickly, for God's sake, quickly!

I ran, losing my breath, racing against rapid, nimble, invisible Death. I ran, falling down twice and getting up twice, gasping with the terror of being overtaken....

The château! No Lerne yet—his felt hat wasn't hanging on its usual peg in the vestibule. I'd won the first leg. The second consisted of our escaping before his return...

Having climbed the staircase, crossed the landing and bounded through the dressing-room, I irrupted into Emma's bedroom.

"Let's go!" I stammered. "Come, my love! Come on! I'll explain. There's been murder at Fonval. What's the matter? What?"

She remained rooted to the spot in the face of my agitation, quite rigid.

"How pale you are! You're frightening me..."

Then, and only then, I perceived that terror possessed her, and that her poor corpse-like face was signaling to me with terrified eyes and a bloodless mouth to be silent, betraying the imminence of great peril close at hand...too close for her to be able to warn me with her voice or a gesture without the enemy on watch exacting vengeance upon her.

Nothing happened, though. With a glance I scanned the placid room. Everything there seemed mysterious to me; the very air was a hostile fluid, an unbreathable sea in which I was shipwrecked. The thought of what might be happening behind me terrified me.

I expected some legendary apparition—and the sight of Lerne sauntering out of a cupboard was more terrible than the appearance of Mephistopheles in a lightning-flash. "You've kept us waiting, Nicolas," he said.

I was dumbfounded. Emma collapsed, foaming at the mouth and writhing, knocking over items of furniture as her fit continued.

"*Jetzt!*"[23] cried the professor.

There was a noise of rustling fabric in the next room. I heard mannequins falling over. Wilhelm and Johann threw themselves upon me.

Tied up. Captured. Doomed. And the fear of torture rendered me cowardly.

"Uncle," I begged, "kill me straight away! I implore you. No torments! A revolver-bullet, say, or poison! Anything you want, my dear uncle, but no torments!"

Lerne sniggered, and slapped Emma's cheeks with a wet napkin.

I felt myself going mad. Who could tell whether MacBell's sanity had given way in a similar situation? MacBell...Klotz...the animals...hallucination caused me to experience a cutting pain, which sliced my skull from one temple to the other...

---

[23] "Now!"

143

The assistants took me downstairs, Johann taking my head and Wilhelm my feet. *Perhaps they're merely going to put me away in a locked room. A nephew, damn it, can't have his throat slit like a chicken...*

They took the path leading to the laboratory.

In a faint, my entire life flashed before me in the space of a heartbeat, one day at a time.

The professor rejoined us. We went past the Germans' block and along the courtyard wall. Lerne opened a cart-door on the ground floor of the left-hand block and I was deposited underneath the operating theater, in a sort of laundry-room, as bare as a tomb and covered from top to bottom in white tiles. A curtain of thick canvas, suspended on rings from a rod, divided it into two sections of similar dimension. The atmosphere was pharmaceutical. It was well-lit.

A little camp-bed had been set up against the wall, which Lerne pointed out to me saying: "Your bed has been made for a long time, Nicolas..."

Then my uncle gave instructions in German. The two assistants untied me and undressed me. Resistance was futile.

A few minutes later, I was lying down comfortably, with sheets up to my chin and the edges tucked in. Johann was watching me, alone, sitting with his legs apart on a stool, the only ornament in the place, the austerity of which I examined.

The curtain, drawn to one side, disclosed another door with two battens, opening into the courtyard. Facing me, through the bay window, I could see the branches of my friend the bay-tree.

My depression increased. I had a bad taste in my mouth, as if it could already sense its own impending decomposition. Oh, to think of the disgusting chemistry that would probably soon be a prelude to that!

Johann was toying with a revolver, aiming it at me periodically, delighted with the excellent joke. I turned to the wall, which enabled me to discover an inscription engraved in coarse letters in the varnish of the tiles with the aid—at least, I thought so—of a stone mounted in a ring.

GOODBYE FOREVER, DEAR FATHER. DONOVAN

I understood the meaning of the English words. Poor fellow! He too had been laid on this bed...and Klotz as well...and what proof was there that my uncle had only murdered those two before me? But I cared little about that...very little....

Dusk fell.

There were hurried comings and goings above us. The darkness caused them to slow down and cease. Then Karl, having come back from Grey-l'Abbaye, relieved Johann at his post.

Almost immediately, Lerne had me plunged into a bath and forced me to drink a bitter beverage. I recognized magnesium sulfate. There was no more doubt; they were going to butcher me. These were the preliminaries of an operation; no one is unaware of that any longer, in this century of appendicitis. It would take place the following morning. What would they try out on my body before finishing it off?

Alone with Karl.

I was hungry. The murmur of the wretched farmyard, not far away, was audible: a susurrus of shifted straw, fearful clucking, hushed barking. The cattle were lowing.

Darkness.

Lerne came in. I was extremely agitated. He took my pulse. "Are you sleepy?" he asked me.

"Brute!" I replied.

"Good. I'll give you a sedative."

He offered it to me. I drank it. It reeked of chloral.

Alone with Karl again.

The croaking of toads. The twinkling of stars. Moonrise. The elevation of its ruddy disk. Mystical assumption of the heavenly body, from star to star... All the beauty of the night.... A forgotten prayer, a small child's orison, rose from my distress toward Paradise, the myth of yesterday, the present's certainty. How could I have doubted its existence?

And the Moon wandered through the firmament like a halo in search of a head.

It was a long while since my eyelids had not closed on tears...

I became drowsy, prey to delirium. A buzzing sound took on the proportions of a din. Almost imperceptible sounds sometimes seem to be the thunder of very distant cataclysms. Straw was being scattered. That farmyard was deafening! The bull was bellowing. I even had the illusion that it was bellowing more and more loudly. Was it brought in every evening, along with the cows, to some byre in that strange farm? Bah! Good God, what a racket!

It was while my mind was wandering in that fashion under the influence of the narcotic, irremissibly condemned to death or doomed to madness, that I drifted off into a crushing artificial sleep that lasted until morning.

Someone touched my shoulder.

Lerne, clad in a white smock, was standing next to the bed.

The sensation of having my throat cut was instantaneously reborn, clear and complete.

"What time is it? Am I about to die? Or is your work done?"

"Patience, nephew! It hasn't even started."

"What are you going to do to me? Are you going to inject me with the plague? Tuberculosis? Cholera? Tell me, uncle. No? What, then?"

"Come on," he said, "no childishness!"

Having stepped aside, he revealed an operating table, which, perched on narrow trestles fashioned like a lattice, looked like an inquisitorial rack. Sets of instruments and bottles glistened in the light of the rising sun. A cloudy bundle of absorbent cotton-wool was set on a side-table. Two nickel-plated spheres, on the tips of their supports, swelled out like the helmets of diving-suits; a sprit-lamp was burning beneath one of them.

My stupor prevented me from fainting.

To one side, someone was busy behind the curtain, which was now extended and quivering. A penetrating odor of ether came from it. Secrets! Secrets until the very end!

"What's behind that?" I exclaimed.

Karl and Wilhelm came through between the curtain and the wall, leaving the space thus isolated in the other half of the room empty. They too had put on white smocks. They were only assistants, then...

But Lerne had taken hold of something, and I felt the cold touch of steel on the back of my neck. I uttered a scream.

"Imbecile!" said my uncle. "It's just hair-clippers."

He cut my hair, then shaved off the remaining fuzz. At every stroke of the razor I thought I felt the edge cutting into my flesh.

Afterwards, my skull was soaped gain, then rinsed, and the professor covered my bald head with cabalistic lines, drawn in soft pencil with the aid of dividers.

"Take off your shirt," he told me. "Be careful—don't smudge my reference-marks."

They helped me up on to the table. I was attached to it securely, with my arms beneath the tabletop.

Where was Johann, then?

Without any warning, Karl put a sort of muzzle on me. A flow of ether penetrated my lungs. *Why not chloroform?* I thought.

"Breathe deeply and regularly," Lerne recommended. "It's for your own good. Breathe in!"

I obeyed.

A pointed syringe in my uncle's fingers...aieee! He had pricked me with it, in the neck. I bit down; my tongue and lips were leaden. "Wait! I'm not asleep yet! What's that...virus? Syphilis?"

"Merely morphine," said the professor.

The anesthesia was taking effect.

Another prick, very sharp, in the shoulder.

"I'm not asleep! Wait, for God's sake! I'm not asleep!"

"That's what I wanted to know," muttered my executioner.

For some moments, a consolation had been ameliorating my torture. Didn't the cranial preparations demonstrate that they were about to kill me without further delay? MacBell had survived the trepanning, though...

I withdrew into myself. Silvery bells were merrily tinkling a celestial chorus, which I have never been able to recall, although it seemed to me to be unforgettable.

Another prick on the shoulder, hardly perceptible. I wanted to repeat that I wasn't asleep, but the effort was in vain; my words resonated dully, submerged in the utmost depths of an invasive sea. They were already dead; I alone could still distinguish them.

The rings clicked along the curtain-road.

And without any pain, on the threshold of the artificial nirvana, this is what I seemed to intuit:

Lerne makes a long incision from the right temple to the left, via the occiput—an incomplete scalping—and he pulls down the excised flap over my face in one piece, the skin of my forehead making a hinge. From in front, my head must be seen as the bloody mess that I remarked on the chimpanzee...

"Help! I'm not asleep!"

But the silver bells prevent me from hearing my appeals. Firstly, they're too far under the sea, and secondly, the bells are ringing with full force now, like church bells pealing mightily. And it's me who is sinking, in my turn, into the ocean of ether...

Am I or am I not? I am...I'm a dead man conscious of being dead.... More than that...

Oblivion.

X. The Circean Operation

I opened my eyes again upon hermetic darkness, in which a silence of odors also reigned over a desert of sound. I wanted to repeat: "Don't start! I'm still awake!"—but no speech resonated. The delirium of the previous night was extended; it seemed to me that the bellowing had drawn even closer, to the point of being audible within me. Impotent to master the riot of my senses, I kept quiet.

And then the certainty grew that the mysterious operation was complete.

Little by little, the darkness dissipated. The ataraxia came to an end. As my blindness was cured, ever-more-numerous odors and sounds emerged like a joyous host. Bliss! Oh, to remain, to remain thus...!

But that death-agony in reverse proceeded regardless, and life took hold of me again.

Objects, though now distinct, nevertheless remained shapeless, two-dimensional, and bizarrely colored. My vision took in a wide space, a vaster field than before. I recalled the influence of certain anesthetics on the dilatation of the pupil, a phenomenon that was doubtless responsible for these visual perturbations.

I observed, however, without overmuch difficulty that I had been lifted off the table and laid on the ground on the other side of the room, and in spite of my eyes, which were functioning in the manner of distorting lenses, I succeeded in surveying the situation.

The curtain was no longer extended. Lerne had his assistants, grouped around the operating table, were devoting themselves to some task that their juxtaposed bodies hid from me—probably cleaning the instruments. The grounds were visible through the wide-open door. Scarcely 20 meters away, there was a corner of the pasture, where the cows were gazing at us, ruminating and lowing.

Except that I could have imagined that I had been transported into the most revolutionary painting of the Impressionist school. The blue of the sky, without losing its lucid profundity, had been transformed into a beautiful orange tint; instead of being green, the pasture and the trees seemed to me to be red; the buttercups in the meadow strewed the vermilion grass with violets. Everything had changed color, save for things that were black or white. The four men's black trousers remained obstinately as before; it was the same with their smocks—but those smocks were soiled with stains...green ones! There were pools, similarly green, gleaming on the floor—but what could that liquid be, if not blood? And why should it be surprising that it appeared to me to be green, since verdure gave me a sensation of red? That liquid exhaled a violent aroma, which would have made me run far away if I had been capable of movement—and yet its scent was not the one that I was accustomed to attribute to blood...I had *never* breathed it in before...any more than any of the other perfumes...any more than my ears remembered having welcomed sonorities such as those....

And the phantasmagoria persisted, the aberration of my senses not dissipating at all with the etheric vapors!

I tried to fight the numbness. Impossible.

I had been laid out on a litter of straw...obviously straw....but *mauve* straw.

The operators had their backs to me, except for Johann. From time to time, Lerne threw cotton wool soaked in green blood into a basin.

Johann was the first to notice that I was awake, and he told the professor. There was a movement of general curiosity in my direction then, which, by breaking up the group, permitted me to see a naked man tied to the table, his hands beneath the tabletop, lying motionless, white, waxen and cadaverous, a black moustache further exaggerating his pallor, with his head enveloped by a bandage spotted with...well, with green smears. His breast was rising and falling rhythmically; he was breathing air by the lungful, his nostrils twitching at each inhalation.

I took some time to accept that THE MAN WAS ME.

When I was certain that no mirror was sending back my own image—easily checked—it crossed my mind that Lerne had duplicated my being, and that there were now two of me...

Or was it not more probable that I was dreaming?

No, certainly not. Up to this point, however, the adventure had not surpassed the bizarre; I was neither dead nor mad—and that realization cheered me up no end. Protest if you will against the certainty I had that I was in full possession of my sanity—the future was to confirm that rash judgment.

The patient on the operating table shook his head. Wilhelm untied him and I watched my other self wake up. Having opened blind eyes, he nodded his head idiotically, stroked the edges of the table, and sat up. He seemed extremely awkward. I could not believe that my simulacrum could manifest such animal stupidity.

The invalid was laid down on the camp-bed. He allowed himself to be stroked. Soon, though, painful surges of nausea caused him to retch, proving the complete absence of any connection between the two of us, since I was not suffering any discomfort, except mentally, due to the effect of a perfectly natural compassion toward a gentleman so very like myself.

Wait, though! Like me? Was that merely a replica of my body? Or my actual body? Bah! Absurd! I could smell, see, hear—quite badly, admittedly, but nevertheless sufficiently to be convinced that I possessed a nose, eyes and ears. I strained, and cords cut into my limbs; I had flesh, therefore, slack and numb, but flesh...my body was here, not there!

The professor announced that he was going to untie me.

The network of hemp loosened. Impatience spurred me. I was standing up in a trice, and a complex impression spread terror through my entire being, upsetting it. God, how heavy and short I was! I tried to look down at myself; there was nothing beneath my head. And as I leaned further forward, with great difficulty, I saw, instead of my feet, two cloven hooves terminating black knobbed legs covered in dense hair.

A scream swelled my throat...but it was the bellowing of the previous night that burst out of my mouth, making the building shake and echoing repeatedly from unscalable walls of rock.

"Shut up, Jupiter!" said Lerne. "You're annoying poor Nicolas, who needs rest!" And he pointed to my body, sitting up in the bed in alarm.

I was, therefore, the black bull! Lerne, the detestable magician, had changed me into a beast!

He was greatly amused. The three servile scoundrels were holding their sides, guffawing, and my bovine eyes learned how to weep.

"Well, yes," said the enchanter, as if replying to the debacle of my thoughts, "you're Jupiter. But you have the right to ask more. Here are your identity papers. You were born in Spain, in a celebrated ganaderia, the progeny of famous parents, of which the male posterity died gloriously, with a sword in his withers, on the sand of the arena. I rescued you from the toreadors' banderillas.[24] As your pedigree suited my purposes, I paid dearly for you, and the cows. You cost me 2000 pesetas, not including the cost of transportation. It's been five

---

[24] A ganaderia is a Spanish ranch specializing in the breeding of bulls for bullfighting; a banderilla is a barbed dart employed in the sport.

years and two months since you were born; you might live as much again, but not more...if we let you die of old age. In sum, I acquired you in order to perform a few experiments on your organism. We've only just started."

My witty relative was seized by a fit of wild laughter. When he had exhausted his excessive good humor, he went on: "Hey, Nicolas—it's good, eh? Not too bad, I'm sure. Your curiosity, son of Eve, your infernal curiosity must be sustaining you, and I'll wager you're less annoyed than intrigued, eh? Come on, I can be magnanimous, and since you're now discreet, my dear pupil, hearken to the enlightenment for which you're so avid. Didn't I tell you that the time was approaching when you'd know everything? Nicolas, you shall know everything. Anyway, I wouldn't like to be mistaken for a demon, a thaumaturge or a sorcerer—I'm neither Belphegor, nor Moses, nor Merlin, but simple Lerne. My power doesn't come from outside; it's mine, and I'm proud of it. It's my science. The most one could say by way of correction is that it's humankind's science, which I've continued in my lifetime and of which I'm the most advanced pioneer, the principal possessor—but let's not quibble. Are the bandages blocking your ears? Can you hear me?"

I nodded my head.

"Good. Listen, then, and don't roll your eyes; everything will be explained—we're not in a novel, damn it!"

The assistants were polishing and rearranging the instruments. My sleeping body was snoring. Having drawn up a stool beside me, Lerne at down, at my level, and made the following speech:

"First, my dear nephew, I was wrong to call you Jupiter just now. Strictly speaking, I haven't transformed you into a bull, and you're still Nicolas Vermont—for a name describes, first and foremost, a personality, which is the soul rather than the body. As, on the one hand, you've retained your soul and, on the other, the seat of the soul is the brain, it's easy to deduce, in the presence of these surgical instruments, that I've simply exchanged Jupiter's brain with yours and that his now inhabits your human rag.

"That is, you might tell me, Nicolas, a rather dubious joke. You haven't yet divined either the grandiose objective of my work or the sequence of ideas that led up to it. From that sequence, however, this little comic renewal of Ovid is derived. It may be, though, that that means nothing to you, for I've only devoted myself to it occasionally. If you wish, we'll call it a theatrical skit. No, my goal doesn't manifest itself to me in this form—comical and malicious, you'll agree, but puerile and devoid of social or industrial consequences of an exploitable nature.

"My goal is that of the *transposition of human personalities*, which I have attempted to obtain, in the first place, by the exchange of brains.

"You're familiar with my inveterate passion for flowers. I've always cultivated them obsessively. My early life was absorbed by the exercise of my profession, interrupted on Sundays by that recreation: a single day of gardening.

Now, my hobby had an influence on my profession, grafting on surgery. At the hospital, I began to devote myself increasingly to animal grafting. I specialized in it, and became passionate about it, reproducing the enthusiasm of the greenhouse in the clinic. Even at the outset, I had dimly anticipated a point of contact between animal and vegetable grafts—a hyphen that my logical endeavor soon clarified...we'll come back to that.

"When I became infatuated with animal grafting, that branch of surgery was languishing. We might say that it had remained stationary since the ancient Hindus, the first known grafters. Perhaps you've forgotten its fundamental principles though? It doesn't matter. Learn them again. It's based, Nicolas, on this fact: that every animal tissue enjoys an individual vitality, and that the body of a living animal merely provides the appropriate environment for the life of these tissues—an environment from which they may be removed, surviving thereafter for a variable length of time.

"You're not unaware of the fact that nails and hair continue growing after death. That's because they're still alive. A man dead for fifty-four hours, who has left no descendants, still fulfils the principal condition for remedying that omission. Unfortunately, other essential faculties are lacking...but I'll continue the series of examples.

"In certain conditions of humidity, oxygenation and warmth, a rat's tail has been kept alive for seven days, an amputated finger for four hours. After these lapses of time, they die, but during those seven days and four hours, if skillfully reconnected, they would be able to continue living.

"That's the procedure employed by the Hindus, who thus reintegrated noses cut off by way of punishment, or, if the appendages had been burned, replaced them with noses made from the skin and flesh of buttocks—previously extracted, my dear Nicolas, from the victim's own backside.

"The operation thus effected belongs to the first category of animal grafting, which consists of transplanting a section of an individual to another part of his body. The second consists of uniting two animals by means of two wounds, which weld themselves together. One can then slice from one the part of its body adjacent to the weld, which will continue living on the other thereafter. The third consists of transplanting a part of one animal into another, without an attachment, in such a way that it preserves its own life therein. That's the most elegant of the three; that's the one I found seductive.

"The last-named operation was reputed to be risky for many reasons, of which the principal one is that a graft becomes less likely to take the further removed the two subjects are in the scale of relationship. Grafts prosper marvelously on the same animal less well between father to son, and increasingly less well from brother to brother, cousin to cousin, stranger to stranger, German to Spaniard, Negro to white man, man to woman and infant to old person.

"When I entered the arena, the exchanges in question invariably failed between different species and, for even stronger reasons, between orders and classes. A few experiments, however, were exceptions on which I based my own, wishing to accomplish the most difficult task in order to succeed better in the least, to intergraft a fish and a bird before concentrating solely on humankind.

"I mentioned a few experiments. Weismann[25] had removed a canary-feather from his arm, which he had transplanted a month earlier, and which left a small bloody wound. Boronio[26] had grafted the wing of a canary and the tail of a rat on to a cockerel's crest. That wasn't much, but Nature itself encouraged me. Birds interbreed shamelessly, and produce numerous hybrids, which gave me evidence of the possible fusion of species. Then again, if one gets further away from humans, vegetables have a considerable plasticity. Such, reduced to its simplest expression, is a summary of the situation that I found and on which I counted.

"I came here to work more easily, and almost immediately carried out some fine operations. They became famous, none especially. You'll certainly remember it. Lipton, the tinned goods king, the American billionaire, had only one ear, and wanted a pair. Some poor devil sold him one of his for 5000 dollars. I performed the little ceremony. The ear only died when Lipton did, two years later, of indigestion.

"It was then, while the world was applauding my triumph—just at the moment when the unexpected arrival of love incited me to make money so that Emma could live in luxury—that I had my great idea, the fruit of the following reasoning. If that billionaire, discontented with his physique, was prepared to pay 5000 dollars for the satisfaction of a slight embellishment, what would he not have given to change it completely *and acquire for himself—for his brain—a new body?* An abode full of grace, vigor and youth, instead of a sickly and repulsive old cast-off? On the other hand, how many paupers of my acquaintance would surrender their splendid anatomy in exchange for a few years of the good life!

"And let us note, Nicolas, that the purchase of a juvenile body would not only furnish the pleasures of flexibility, warmth and endurance, but also the enormous advantage that the transferred organ would be regenerated and rejuvenated in a young environment! Oh, I'm not the first to have thought of it, and Paul Bert[27] had already admitted the possibility of grafting an organ on to several bodies consecutively, as each of them grew old—with the result that, by virtue of a series of rejuvenations, he anticipated that one might cause a single

---

[25] The German biologist August Weismann (1834-1914), nowadays better known for his contributions to evolutionary theory.

[26] The Italian biologist Giuseppe Boronio (1759-1811) was the first person to perform a successful skin graft (in a sheep) in 1803 but he revealed the limitations of xenotransplantation in his more adventurous experiments.

[27] Paul Bert (1833-1886) was physiologist whose fame turned to notoriety when he became a radical statesman.

stomach or a single brain to live indefinitely inside a series of successive bodies. That was to declare that *a personality might live indefinitely* by means of a series of avatars, a voyage through different carcasses, discarded as appropriate.

"The discovery to be made surpassed my initial hopes. I was not only in pursuit of the choice of a pleasing appearance; I was after *the secret of immortality*. The encephalum being the residence of the *ego*—for you're aware that the spinal fluid in merely a transmission mechanism and a center of reflexes—it was no longer a question of anything but the ability to graft.

"To be sure, there's a considerable difference between an ear and a brain—but they're only separated by matters of degree: firstly, that between cartilaginous substance and nervous tissue, and secondly that between an accessory article and the principal organ. Logic supported my assurance, and the logic in question was founded on famous antecedents, officially verified.

"In addition to their grafts of mucous membranes, skin, spurs and so on, Philippeaux and Vulpian replaced the nervous tissue in an optic nerve in 1861. In 1880, Gluck replaced a few centimeters of the sciatic nerve of a chicken with those of a rabbit. In 1890, Thompson removed a few cubic centimeters of brain tissue from various dogs and cats, and introduced into the cavities thus created similar quantities of cerebral substances, collected from dogs, cats *and other species*. Thus we pass from cartilage to nerve-tissue and from the ear to fragments of brain. Let us now occupy ourselves with difficulties of the second order.

"Gardeners can easily graft entire organisms. In addition to fingers, tails and paws, Philippeaux and Mantegazza have grafted more important organs: spleens, stomachs, tongues. They made a hen into a cock, on a whim. They even tried to graft a pancreas and a thyroid. In New York in 1905, Carrel and Guthrie proposed that it would be possible to substitute the veins and arteries of animals for those of humans. We have now bridged the difference between the accessory and the principal. Finally, Mantegazza claimed to have grafted the spinal cords and brains of frogs. These observations provided abundant proof that my projects might be realized. Therefore, I would realize them.[28]

---

[28] The names cited in the previous two paragraphs are all taken from published research papers. The more celebrated names include those of the neurologists Alfred Vulpian (1826-1887) and Paolo Mantegazza (1831-1910)—the latter was also a pioneer of Italian scientific romance—both of whom published papers in collaboration with J. M. Philippeaux. Two other minor figures cited signed their work T. Gluck and W. G. Thompson. The most interesting reference is the one to Alexis Carrel (1873-1944) and Charles Claude Guthrie (1880-1963), who were at the beginning of their respective careers; the work cited won Carrel a Nobel prize in 1912, which many observers thought should have been shared with Guthrie, but the notoriety of Guthrie's attempts to transplant heads probably cost him the nomination. Carrel went on to do classic experiments in tissue

"I started work.

"One obstacle stopped me: the employment of a pedicle being impracticable, it transpired that either the body or the brain, or both, once separated, died before being placed in contact with their new companions. Here again, though, the facts emboldened me.

"As regards the body, an animal can live perfectly well with a single cerebral lobe. You've seen a pigeon deprived of three-quarters of its brain flying in circles. A decapitated duck often flies away, for as much as a hundred meters from the chopping-block where its severed head remains. A grasshopper has survived without a head for a fortnight. A fortnight! That's a verified experiment. As regards the organ, there are the depositions already cited. That led me to think that the brain and the body, suitably treated, would each be able to live independently for the few minutes of separation necessary to the operation.

"Be that as it may, the slowness of the trepanning led me, in the first instance, to exchange heads rather than brains, knowing, thanks to Brown-Séquard,[29] that the head of a dog injected with oxygenated blood had survived severance for a quarter of an hour.

"Various heteroclitic creatures date from that period—a donkey with a horse's head, a goat with a deer's head—which I would have like to conserve, because the animals making them up are rather distant from one another, while belonging to the same families: a distance that I was never able to increase by that procedure. Alas, on the night of your arrival, Wilhelm left the gates open, and those monsters, worthy of Doctor Moreau, took the opportunity to escape, along with many other specimens under observation. You can boast of having arrived in Fonval like a spaniel in a game of croquet...

"I'll go on, but to avoid overtaxing the attention of a convalescent, I'll skip over such details as the abandonment of that first method, the discovery of the Lerne ultra-rapid circular trepanning saw, that of the brain-preserving globes or artificial meninges, that of the nerve-connecting ointment, the recognized utility of the injection of morphine prescribed by Broca[30] for constricting the blood-vessels and minimizing blood loss, the accepted use of ether as an anesthetic, the manipulation of encephala for the purpose of fitting them exactly to skulls, etc...

"Thanks to all that, I transposed the personalities of a—oh, I can never remember the name of it—a...squirrel and a wood-pigeon, then those of a warbler and a viper, and then those of a carp and a blackbird—warm blood and hot blood; that was perfect. In comparison with these prodigies, my goal of human substitution became child's play.

---

culture, which inspired such skeptical scientific romances as Julian Huxley's "The Tissue-Culture King" (1926).

[29] The physiologist Charles-Edouard Brown-Séquard (1817-1894).

[30] The neuroanatomist Paul Broca (1824-1880).

"At that point, Karl and Wilhelm offered themselves for the crucial experiment. It was epic. Otto Klotz had... hmm... left me. MacBell wasn't trustworthy. I operated alone, with the help of Johann and automatic machinery.

"Success.

"Oh, those brave men! Who would imagine that their entire bodies had been amputated? And yet each of them, to this day, inhabits his friend's carnal housing. Look!"

He summoned his assistants and, lifting up their hair, brought the purple scars to light. The two German were smiling, and I couldn't help admiring them.

Lerne went on. "My fortune was made, therefore, and I had ensured, at a stroke, my glory and Emma's happiness and love—which is my most inestimable possession, Nicolas!

"Once the discovery was certain, however, it was necessary to apply it. To tell the truth, one point of obscurity troubled me. I mean the influence of the mental on the physical, and vice versa. After a few months, my patients were modified. If I had endowed a body with a mentality finer than the original, the latter spoiled the former, and I've seen, among others, pigs with the brains of dogs become sickly and thin, dying very rapidly. On the other hand, intellects coarser than their predecessors allow themselves to be dominated by the corporeal, and the composite animal then becomes more bestial and fatter. It's an invariable rule. Sometimes, too, the imperative flesh refashions the mind according to its brutal material instincts—one of my wolves, my dear chap, instilled cruelty in the brain of a sheep! But was that inconvenience not bound, in my future clients—humans—to be reduced to slight differences of health or character? It was derisory, and did not interrupt me at all.

"Not wanting to leave MacBell with Emma, I sent him to Scotland, and I set out for America, the land of audacities, billons and the grafted ear—which appeared to me to be the best soil to cultivate. That was two years ago.

"The day after my disembarkation, I had 35 scoundrels at my disposal, resolved to divest themselves of an impeccable constitution to the benefit of 35 generous billionaires I had yet to introduce myself, indoctrinate and convince.

"Check!

"I began with the ugliest and those closest to death. Some treated me as a madman and threw me out. Others were annoyed and, while looking me up and down with a majestic and suspicious eye, thrusting out their weak and wheezy chests, or raising themselves up on their rickety legs, expressed astonishment that anyone could think them ugly. The moribund were certain that they would be cured, more certain than they were that they might die under the anesthetic. There were some who took fright, saying that it was tempting God. They recoiled from me as from the Devil, and a few wanted to have me sprinkled with holy water. I raised the objection that a man is modified more completely in the course of his life than he would change beneath my scalpel, and that religious tolerance has come a long way since 1670, when that Russian whose skull had been patched with canine bone was excommunicated[31] ...but it made no difference.

"Many of them also recited: 'A bird in the hand is worth two in the bush.'

"Would you believe it? I was almost saved by women! Whole crowds of them wanted to become men. Unfortunately, my blackguards, save for a couple of the most intrepid, categorically refused to adopt the female sex.

"Despairing of my cause, I offered them the alluring perspective of indefinite life, renewing its vigor at each new incarnation. 'Life,' septuagenarians replied, 'is already too long as God has set its limits. We no longer have any desire but to die.'

" 'But I'll restore all your desires at the same time as youth!' I said. 'Many thanks,' they replied, 'but the fate of desires is to be unsatisfied.' I often heard adults reply: 'The charm of acquired experience is worth preserving from any lessening, and its diminution should not be risked by naïve impetuosity and the temerity of adolescent blood.'

"There were, nevertheless, a few would-be emulators of Faust ready to sign a pact of youth—but all those wary nabobs raised the same objection: the danger of the operation, the unreasonableness of risking life in the covetousness of life. You see, Nicolas, only young people on the point of death and conscious of their condition would unhesitatingly submit to the operation.

"Having understood the necessity of overcoming the perceived danger, I was ready to undertake further studies—oh, greatly disillusioned, knowing thereafter how few clients I would have in the event of a second discovery, but also knowing that there would be enough of them to establish my fortune and my happiness—but they were postponed indefinitely.

"I returned to Fonval, bitter and taciturn, with rage in my heart. Emma and Donovan could only encounter the most implacable of judges. I caught them; I took my revenge. You've guessed, haven't you? Yesterday, the two MacBells took away Nelly's brain, and Donovan's soul resides in the Saint Bernard. The same punishment awaited the two of you for the same sin. Solomon could not have passed a better sentence, nor could Circe have executed it any more adeptly.

"Well, nephew, I have been working hard and—in spite of your intrusion and the surveillance that I was forced to exercise over your actions—in a few days' time, probably, I shall inaugurate the transfer of personalities *without surgical intervention.*

---

[31] Although this anecdote is reproduced incessantly, with slight variations, in modern books and articles dealing with xenotransplantation, it is clearly apocryphal. The incident is alleged to have been reported by the Dutch surgeon Job van Meekeren (1611-1666); some sources give the date as 1668 rather than 1670, but van Meekeren was already dead by then.

"I was intelligent enough, you see, not to abandon vegetable grafting. I have taken all its developments much further, and that education, combined with my zoological experiments, constitutes an almost universal study of grafting. It's the combination of that science with others that has revealed the probable solution to me. There can never be enough generalization, Nicolas! Besotted with specialization, parceling knowledge up into ever-more-minuscule subdivisions, we have a mania for analysis and we live with our eyes riveted to the microscope. In half of our investigations we should employ another method, revealing wholes: an instrument of optical synthesis, a synoptic telescope—or, if you prefer, a megaloscope.

"I anticipate colossal discoveries...

"And to think that without Emma, disdainful of finance, I would never have aimed so high! Love has fostered ambition, which fosters glory! By the way, you nearly put on the features of Professor Frédéric Lerne. Yes! She adores you with such a fine ardor, my lad, that I thought of dressing up in your appearance, in order to be loved in your stead! That would have been the best revenge, and was very tempting—but I still have need of my contemptible antiquity for some time yet. We'll see about discarding that decrepitude later. Your captivating exterior will still be at my disposal, won't it?"

At these sarcastic words, I wept more copiously. My uncle affected commiseration, and continued.

"Oh, I'm abusing your valor, my dear invalid. Get some rest. The satisfaction of your curiosity will, I hope, allow you a reparative slumber. Oh, I forgot! Don't be alarmed about perceiving the external world otherwise than before. Among other novelties, things must seem as flat as a photograph. That's because you can only look at the majority of objects with one eye at a time. Thus, one might say, playing with the terminology, that many animals are no more than doubly one-eyed; their sight is not stereoscopic. Other eyes, other visions; new eardrums, new sounds—and so on. It's trivial. Among humans, every individual has his own way of perceiving things. Habit informs us, for example, that we should call a certain color 'red', so we do—but some who call it red receive an impression of green—that's quite common-and others an impression of yellow-green[32] or dark blue...

"Well, goodnight!"

No, my curiosity wasn't satisfied at all—but I took account of that without being able to determine the points that my uncle had not elucidated, for an exaggerated unhappiness was overwhelming me with sadness. It was as if the Circe-

---

[32] The term Lerne employs here is *merdoie*, whose literal meaning is "goose-shit," but as that English equivalent is not used to describe a particular color it would strike a slightly discordant note, so I have employed a more literal description.

an operation had left me impregnated with ether, the vapors of which were disturbing both my human understanding and my taurean heart.

XI. In the Pasture

During the week of my convalescence in the laboratory, bandaged, sedated and treated with various drugs, I was subject to the alternation of great sorrows: fits of despair followed by periods of exhaustion.

After each interval of somnolence, I thought that I had dreamed the misadventure, Now, it's important to note that the sensations of my awakenings confirmed me in this immediately-falsified error. It is, in fact, well known that amputees suffer a great deal of pain, and attribute that pain to the peripheral extremities of the severed nerves—that is to say, to the limb that is no longer there, and which they imagine they still have. The arm or leg that has been removed still hurts. If you consider that my entire body had been amputated, you will understand that I experienced pain in all its parts—my distant hands, my human feet—and that the pain in question seemed to me to be evidence of the continued possession of that of which I had been deprived.

This phenomenon was gradually ameliorated, and disappeared. My misery did not decrease as quickly. Those who have amused their fellows with tales of similar farces—Homer, Ovid, Apuleius, Perrault—did not know what tragedies their fictions would become once realized. What a drama Lucian's *Ass* is, deep down![33] What a martyrdom that week of starvation and forced inaction was for me! Dead to humankind, I awaited without courage the tortures of vivisection or the old age that would put an end to everything within five years.

In spite of my misery, I healed. Having established that, Lerne had me placed in the pasture.

Europa, Athor and Io gamboled around me. Ashamed as I am of it, honesty compels me to say that I found an unexpected gracefulness in them. They surrounded me amiably and, no matter what my soul did to repress it, a sovereign instinct—doubtless a property of my accursed spinal cord—infatuated me. But the heifers made off, probably astonished not to receive a response in some occult language, or frightened by some presentiment.

Long days would not have sufficed for me to domesticate them, long days and all the guile that humans employ in that regard. A good kicking, in the end, subjugated them to my sovereignty. The incident would provide rich fodder for a philosopher, and I would definitely surrender myself to the joys of a digression

---

[33] *The Ass*, a prose romance attributed (perhaps unreliably) to the Greek satirist Lucian, whose protagonist is transformed into the eponymous animal by a witch, provided the model that the Roman satirist Apuleius expanded considerably into the much better known prose romance *The Golden Ass*.

if such awkward morsels did not break up the flow of a story with superb but inapt obstacles.

At the time, in spite of the welcome the three horned ladies gave me, and only desirous of their commerce with valetudinarian ardor and stumbling technique, I set about grazing the meadow-grass peacefully.

Then began a period of great interest: that of my observations of my new condition. It was so absorbing that I succeeded in considering the body of the bull as place that I was passing through in the course of a voyage: a station of exile, certainly, but an unexplored station full of surprises, from which hazard might perhaps extract me—for it is sufficient that a place be not unpleasant for one to envisage the risk of being expelled therefrom.

For as long as that accommodation of my human mind within the body of the beast lasted, I was really quite happy. It was, in effect, as if an entirely new world had just been revealed to me, along with a taste for the herbs that I grazed. Just as my eyes, ears and muzzle sent my brain unexpected visions, auditory sensations and olfactory indications, the exotic papillae of my tongue furnished me with wholly original gustatory sensations. The herbs released countless savors of which our human palates have no suspicion. Gourmet cuisine cannot offer as many pleasures in a dozen courses as a bull obtains from a square foot of meadow. I could not help comparing the taste of my forage with that of my former aliments. There is more difference between Lucerne and clover than between a fried sole and a haunch of venison with *chasseur* sauce. All kinds of spices season plants for a herbivore's mouth: buttercups are a trifle bland, and thistles a little too peppery, but nothing equals the multiple scents of hay...

Pastures are continuously-served feasts, to which perpetual hunger commits their gourmet guests.

The water in the trough changed its taste according to the time and the weather, sometimes being acidic and sometimes salty or sweet, light in the morning and syrupy in the evening. I can't describe the delights of drinking it, and I suspect that the late Olympians, in a vindictive and ironic will, while leaving men nothing but laughter, left other animals the rare privilege of tasting ambrosia in lawn-grass and drinking nectar from every spring.

I was initiated into the delights of rumination, and I understood the seriously epicurean concentration that oxen affect during the activity of their four stomachs, while an entire pastoral symphony fills their nostrils with rural scents.

By virtue of experimenting with my senses and testing my faculties I obtained strange impressions. The happiest memory that I retain is that of my muzzle, center of tactile sensation, subtle and infallible touchstone of good and unhealthy grain, advertiser of enemy presences, pilot and counselor: a sort of authoritarian and dogmatic consciousness, an oracle concise in approval and denial, never in default, always obeyed. It is a mystery why the god Jupiter, having adopted the form of a bull for the benefit of Princess Europa, was not more charmed by his muzzle than the rest of that rather disgusting rape...

I was, at any rate, wise to make these observations without delay, for my deteriorating health robbed me of the calm of mind necessary to their clarity as well as the desire to continue them. I suffered the ravages of headaches, colds, toothaches...the whole series of indispositions typical of citizens of the 20th century. I grew thinner. I harbored dark thoughts. It was caused, firstly, by the predominance of the soul over the body that my uncle had mentioned, and secondly, by two incidents that occurred and which immediately aggravated my illness.

After a period of absence—occasioned, I presumed, by an illness consequent to her great terror—Emma reappeared. Without emotion, I saw her at the windows of her apartment, then those of the ground floor, and then outside. She went out on the arm of the maid and walked around the grounds, avoiding the laboratory in which Lerne and his assistants were working tirelessly. I had expected her features to be less drawn, and her eyelids less red.

She walked slowly, her complexion pale and her gaze fixed, displaying a hint of moonlight to the sun, and eyes that open in the dark. A pathetic widow, she showed off her rebellious love in mourning, and the fervor of her regret, in a rather noble fashion. So she loved me still and, not seeing me anymore, supposed my fate to be that which she attributed to Klotz—not that of MacBell, which she had, in any case, misunderstood. In her mind, I could only be dead or a fugitive. The truth was beyond her understanding!

More piously with every passing day, I followed her progress for as long as I could. Separated from her by a thread of barbed wire, I attempted mimes and speeches—but Emma was afraid of the bull, of its pirouettes and its bellowing. She understood none of it, any more than I had understood Donovan's canine machinations. Sometimes, when the intention of an overly human gesture made my quadruped mass totter, the young woman was amused by it...and I found myself staggering in order to see her smile.

Thus, little by little, love reasserted its rights as a tormentor. It could not return without the escort of jealousy—and it was that jealousy, in the second place, that accelerated my decline. It was accompanied by an extraordinary sensation...

Situated between the pasture and the pond was a hexagonal building: the summer-house; the ex-giant Briareus. In order to annoy me, Lerne lodged my former body there. I saw his assistants bring in some basic furniture, and then the creature...and from that day on he was always there, his face stuck to one of the windows, looking at my stupidly.

His hair was growing again, his beard growing longer. Having become dim-witted and chubby, his flesh was bursting out of his clothes. His eyes—those almond eyes of which I had been so proud—were rounded out in a bovine fashion. The man with the bull's brain assumed the expression I had remarked in Donovan, but even more bestial and less god-natured. My poor body had retained the habit of certain familiar gestures: an incorrigible tic made him shrug his shoulders from time to time, with the result that the miserable creature seemed to be mocking me through the windows of the summer-house. Often, he cried out in the twilight; my beautiful baritone voice broke out into long discordant clamors, the howls of a gorilla. Then, in the laboratory, MacBell howled with the throat of a sick dog, and an irresistible need to lament in unison made the Fonval basin resound with the echoes of a monstrous trio.

Emma eventually noticed that the summer-house was inhabited. That day, she and Barbe were going alongside the pasture. As usual, I had accompanied them as far as a certain arbor through which the path led, and waited for them at the opening of the tunnel, where turtle-doves were cooing.

They came out, only to come to an abrupt halt.

Emma was transfigured. She had taken on an animated expression that I recognized: nostrils flared, half-closed eyelids fluttering, and bosom heaving. She squeezed Barbe's arm. "Nicolas!" she murmured. "Nicolas!"

"What do you mean?" said the servant.

"There! There! Can't you see?"

And while the stifled laughter of the turtle-doves emerged from the foliage, Emma pointed out the creature behind the window of the summer-house to Barbe.

Having made sure that they could not be seen from the laboratory, Emma made a few signs, and blew a few kisses. The creature had excellent reasons for not understanding them. He opened his round eyes wide let his lip droop, and made the external appearance that I missed so much into a perfect type-specimen of cretinism.

"Mad!" said Emma. "Him too! Lerne has made him mad, like MacBell!"

Then the kind-hearted girl sobbed with all her heart, and I felt anger rising within me.

"Above all," the servant told her, "don't take it into your head to go near that summer-house—it's visible from every direction."

The other shook her lovely tresses, dried her tears, and settled down on her belly in the grass, in the stance of a sphinx, with her head in her hands and her rump thrust upwards. Lovingly, she contemplated that young male body, from which her own had drawn so much pleasure. The brute seemed much more interested in that pose than her previous one.

Such a scene exceeded the bounds of the grotesque and the horrible. That woman, infatuated with my form, in which I was no longer contained! That woman, whom I adored, lusting after a beast! How could I accept that with a tranquil mind? And I knew, from the history of MacBell, that Emma's passions would not recoil from madness, and that my former body, being more athletic, would therefore please her even more!

My wrath burst forth. It was the first time that I yielded to the domination of my violent flesh. Mad with rage, panting, snorting and foaming at the mouth,

161

I ran through the meadow in every direction, ripping up the soil with my hooves and my horns, possessed by a murderous fury...

From that moment on, hatred poisoned my dreams: a ferocious hatred against that supernatural brute, that stupid Minotaur who made Broceliande into a parody of Crete with his forest labyrinth! I cursed that body which had been stolen from me; I was jealous of it, and often, when Jupiter-Me and Me-Jupiter looked at one another, both prey to nostalgia for our cast-off clothing, the fury possessed me again. I charged back and forth, bellowing as if in a corrida, tail upright, nostrils fuming, head down, ready to commit murder and as desirous of doing so as for sex in springtime. The cows protected themselves as best they could; all the creatures in the grounds dreaded the raging bull. One day, Lerne, who happened to be passing that way, fled as fast as his legs could carry him.

Life weighed heavily. I had exhausted all the pleasures of observation, and my new dwelling no longer caused me anything but distress and repugnance. I continued getting thinner. The forage lost its aroma, the spring became insipid and the company of the heifers became odious. On the other hand, old desires imposed themselves upon me in the guise of morbid whims: the desire to eat meat and...to smoke! Priceless isn't it? But other considerations were no laughing matter. The dread of the laboratory made me tremble every time an assistant approached the pasture, and the fear of being tied up during the night prevented me from sleeping.

That wasn't all. I nursed the conviction that I would go mad in my ruminant's skull. The fits of uncontrollable wrath would be the cause of it. They were becoming more frequent—and Emma's conduct was not helping to make them any less frequent.

In fact, the pretty walker prowled assiduously in the vicinity of the summer-house, and desire drew her toward the Minotaur. In truth, he had the appearance of a complete humanity at such moments, so similar to brutes does lust render us! Emma gazed complacently at that cruel face, none of whose features moved, in which the eyes glittered above inflamed cheeks: that abject expression which I had already observed in true men in the course of some debauchery, which would have sent an equivocal frisson through the wisest of virgins...

Can it be that such an avaricious and murderous expression is the face of Eros? And is it surprising that so many women in love shut their eyes beneath the kisses of that deity?

Emma, therefore, gazed complacently at that vile physiognomy, and did not see Lerne watching her, laughing up his sleeve at her misapprehension.

Laughing—but philosophically, and in order not to cry. My uncle was visibly suffering. He seemed to have understood that Emma would never love him, and the professor was not taking his disappointment well. He was growing old, killing himself with work. Machines had been installed on the terrace of the laboratory and the roof of the château, whose deployment interested me greatly. They were surmounted by characteristic antennae and, as bells were continually

162

ringing in the two dwellings, it was my opinion that they had been transformed into wireless telegraph and telephone stations.

One morning. Lerne sent a little boat out on the pond—a toy torpedo-boat. He controlled it from the bank with the aid of an apparatus that was also equipped with antennae: telemechanical apparatus. That was conclusive: the professor was studying communication at a distance with no solid intermediary. The new method for transposing personalities? Very probably.

I lost interest in it. A fortunate outcome of my tribulations now seemed an impossible miracle; I would therefore know nothing of that future discovery, nor of any other secrets blackening the past of my uncle and his assistants. It was by means of the meditation of these latter mysteries that I countered the anxious insomnia of my nights and the idleness of my days, but I found nothing. Perhaps, though, my mind was growing dull, for, among the daily occurrences that I have just narrated, there were some that it was unable to retain, to which certain of Lerne's confidences lent a cardinal importance, and the reasoned examination of which would have given me cause for hope of deliverance.

So, in mid-September, that deliverance was accomplished without my having anticipated it, in the following circumstances.

For some time, the platonic acquaintance of the Minotaur and Emma had being growing firmer. They were savoring an increasing intoxication in contemplating one another from afar. The monster, having become accustomed to my body, gesticulated. His pantomime was lascivious and simian. As for Emma, unable to refuse these apelike gallantries, she had adopted the tactic of remaining hidden in the small arbor. There, invisible to everyone except for that horrid booby who parodied my role in deplorable buffoonery, she was able in total liberty to lock gazes with him, send him kisses from the rosy tips of her white fingers, as from a dainty imaginary catapult, and swear her passion by means of mummery and grimaces, as ballerinas do. At any rate, I can't believe that she sketched any other declarations or other promises than those...and yet, they were sufficient to unleash the beast's rut.

Yes, that vile occasion arrived.

One afternoon, while I was attempting to catch sight of my beloved through the bushes where she was leading on the false Nicolas, a racket of breaking and falling glass suddenly broke out. The Minotaur, his patience exhausted, had jumped through the window of the summer-house. Without the slightest care for my unfortunate physique, he ran forward, bruised, lacerated and covered in blood, howling in pain in a terrifying manner.

It seemed to me that Emma uttered an exclamation and tried to escape—but the creature had already plunged into the little wood.

Then behind me, I heard the sound of someone running. In response to the noise of breaking glass, Lerne and his assistants had emerged from the laboratory; they had seen the escape and were racing toward the fateful arbor.

Unfortunately, the assistants were fearful of coming too close to me, and the detour they were making to avoid me, outside the pasture, was delaying them. Lerne, intrepidly, had taken a short cut, climbing over the wire fence, and was heading straight across the enclosure, his frock-coat ripped by the artificial thorns.

Alas, he was old and slow...they would all get there too late. Atrocious! Atrocious!

No! It must not be! I launched myself at the frail barrier and crashed into it, breaking it in spite of the little spikes that lacerated my skin. With a single bound, I smashed through the wall of foliage....

The scene that confronted me was worthy of admiration.

The sunlight coming through the vaults of leaves striped the undergrowth with light. I saw Emma stretched out on the edge of the slightly sunken path, pale and huddled, with her jeweled undergarments alluringly displaced. She was moaning voluptuously, and her hoarse, feline plaint was too familiar for me to hesitate for an instant as to its nature. Standing in front of her, more bewildered than ever, the ignoble creature was not hiding the ridicule of his assuaged and now-inoffensive virility.

I did not have the time for a longer look. All the stars of midnight blazed between him and me. In a rush of blood, I was drunk. Unmanageable wrath hurled me through that dazzling curtain, horns poised. I struck something that fell; I trampled it with my four hooves and, turning back upon my victim, I stamped, and stamped, and stamped....

Suddenly, my uncle's breathless voice screeched: "Hey! You're committing suicide, my friend!"

My dementia evaporated. The stars went out. Everything reappeared.

The beautiful girl, emerged from her luxurious coma, was sitting on the ground, blinking her eyes uncomprehendingly. The assistants were watching me warily, each one behind a bush—and Lerne, leaning over my inert and injured former body, was lifting up his head, bloodied by a large wound.

And it was me—me!—who had committed the indescribable stupidity of damaging myself!

Having felt all the parts of the wounded man's body, the professor formulated his diagnosis: "One arm dislocated; three ribs broken; fractures of the left clavicle and tibia; they're not mortal—but the horn-thrust to the head is more serious. Hmmm! The brain has been reduced to pulp. It's ruined. Nothing will save it. In half an hour, *finita la commedia!*"

I had to lean against a tree in order not to collapse. So my body, my ultimate fatherland, was going to die! It was over. Banished forever from my annihilated dwelling, I had eliminated the first condition of my deliverance. It was over. Even Lerne had admitted that he could do nothing. Half an hour! The brain reduced to pulp! But...but...that brain...

He could...

On the contrary, he could do everything necessary. I drew nearer to him. It was my last throw of the dice.

My uncle, who had turned to the young woman, said to her sadly: "You must love him very much, to love him still in such a degenerate state! My poor Emma! I must be extremely unlovable, for you to prefer such a wreck to me!"

Emma was weeping into her hands

"She must love him," Lerne repeated, looking at the sinner, the dying man and me in turn. "She must love him!"

For a few moments, I surrendered myself to uncouth entrechats and attempts at vocalization, intended to express my thoughts. My uncle was wrapped up in his own. Without quite realizing that his clouded brow must be harboring some stormy conflict of interests and passions, dominated by the imminence of a catastrophe that he might be able to prevent, I redoubled my objurgations.

"Yes, Nicolas, I understand what you want," my uncle said. "You'd gladly donate your brain to its original envelope, which might save it, since you have put Jupiter's beyond use…well, so be it!"

"Save him! Save him!" implored the adulterous mistress, who had only grasped that one word. "Save him! I swear to you, Frédéric, I swear to you that I'll never see him again!"

"Enough!" said Lerne. "On the contrary, you'll have to love him with all your heart. I don't want to cause you any more grief. What good is it to struggle against one's destiny?"

He called the assistants and issued curt orders to them. Karl and Wilhelm took possession of the Minotaur, who was gasping. Johann had already left the clearing at a run.

"*Schnell! Schnell!*" said the professor, and added: "Quickly, Nicolas—follow us!"

I obeyed, torn between the joyful prospect of recovering my body and the dread that it might die before the operation.

It was a complete success.

Nevertheless, deprived of precautions preliminary to the anesthesia, which urgency did not permit us to be given, I experienced and instructive but painful ether-dream.

I dreamed that Lerne, by way of jest, instead of restoring my own figure, had given me Emma's. What a purgatory that ravishing form was! I missed that of the bull. My soul found itself assailed therein by nervous demands and impetuous instincts, which mastered it. A natural desire, more powerful than the will, dictated my actions, and I felt that the resistance of my masculine spirit was reduced to a minimum. To be sure, I was dealing with an exceptional temperament in which lust was a chronic malady, but, all the same, considering the ordinary conduct of men and the power of Venus over so many women, how many of you, my brothers, were to you change sex while retaining your brains, would make honest girls rather than loose women?

It might be, though, that ether is a poor professor of gynecology, and that my dream had abused me—for it was nothing but a vain nightmare. It probably lasted for a quarter of a second, the time to experience a single tooth of a biting saw, or the trenchant blade of an ill-sharpened scalpel.

Twilight fills the laundry with a vermilion half-light. On lowering my eyes, I perceive the tips of my moustache.

It is the resurrection of Nicolas Vermont.

And it is also the end of Jupiter. The black mass in which I have sojourned is being cut up at the back of the room. In the courtyard, the squabbling dogs are already fighting over the first morsels that Johann is throwing to them.

My broken leg is hurting, and the clavicle too. I've returned to a painful armor.

Lerne is watching over me. He's delighted. At least, he should be. Isn't he at peace with his conscience? Hasn't he atoned for his sins against me? How could I feel resentful toward him? It even seems to me that I owe him some gratitude...

It's very true that nothing simulates a good deed like the voluntary reparation of a misdeed.

XII. Lerne Changes Tack

I had sworn, while I was in the bull's hide, that if my original form were ever returned to me, I would flee immediately, with or without Emma. Autumn was coming to an end, though, and I had not left Fonval.

That was because my treatment there was the inverse of what it had been before.

First of all, I could use my time as I wished. The first usage I made of that liberty was to go to the charnel-house in the clearing and to erase every trace of my visit. Some favorable deity had dictated that no one had gone there during my bucolic phase in the meadow, so that none of the assistants had noticed the violation of the grave. Either they had changed their cemetery, or my uncle was no longer vivisecting any but tiny creatures of which the dog-pack left nothing, or the experiments *in anima vili*[34] had been completely abandoned.

I observed, that day, a detail that took a great weight from my heart. I had feared that the soul of the unfortunate Klotz might have been transferred to some carefully-isolated animal, but his remains—although magnificently evocative of a Baudelairean poem—refuted that hypothesis. The dead man's brain, beneath his wound, was engraved with numerous and deep circumvolutions, still visible.

---

[34] "On living animals."

Their number and depth testified to their humanity, proof of a pure and simple murder—thank God!

Thus, I enjoyed considerable independence.

Besides, an affectionate and repentant Lerne had been manifest at my beside during my convalescent. Oh, not the Lerne of yesteryear, my aunt Lidivine's cheerful companion—but, all the same, no longer the sullen and bloodthirsty host who had welcomed me as if he wished that I would go away. When he saw that I was back on my feet, he summoned Emma, and told her in my presence that I had been cured of a temporary imbecility, and that she was to adore me.

"As for me," he continued, "I renounce an exercise that was no longer appropriate to my age. Emma, you shall now have your own room, next to mine; the one in which you keep your finery. I only ask that you do not leave me. Sudden loneliness would augment the distress that you can easily imagine and that both of you will pardon. It will pass; work will get the better of it. Don't be afraid, my girl, the greater part of the profits of my invention will be yours. Nothing has changed in that regard—and Nicolas will be no less provided for in the deed of partnership and my will for having been in your bed. Love one another in peace!"

Having spoken thus, the professor took himself off to his electrical machines.

Nothing astonished Emma. Confident and naïve, she had accepted my uncle's tirade by clapping her hands. Personally, knowing what an actor he was, I might have been able to tell myself that he was feigning generosity in order to keep me in his house, whether because he was afraid of what I might reveal or because he was hatching some new plan—but the two Circean operations had disturbed my memory and my intelligence somewhat. *Why*, I said to myself, *should I suspect a man who has, of his own free will, rescued me from the darkest situation imaginable? He's following the right truck now! All is for the best!*

A new life therefore began, pleasant and immoral: a life of love and liberty on the one hand, and of work and apparent abnegation on the other. We were all discreet, in our own fashion, Emma and I in our effusions, my uncle in his regrets.

Judging by the professor's laborious and familial behavior, who could have believed in his victims? In the trap that he had set for me? In the murder of Klotz? And in Nelly-MacBell, who never ceased howling at the clouds or the stars that frightful torment that I had endured myself? For she was still there. That puzzled me—the fact that Lerne was perpetuating the punishment of a sin whose gravity must seem to him to be considerable attenuated, now that Emma no longer held sway over his heart. I resolved to confess my surprise to my uncle.

"You've put your finger on my greatest concern, Nicolas," he replied. "To re-establish the order of things in that situation, it's absolutely necessary that

MacBell's body should return here...but what stratagem would make his father decide to send him back? Try to think of one. Help me. I promise to act without delay as soon as we've found one."

This reply dissolved my last doubts. I didn't ask myself why Lerne had undergone such a complete metamorphosis from one day to the next. In my opinion, the professor had finally mended his ways, and, though lacking other virtues—which would doubtless reappear one by one—his old rectitude seemed to me to have been reborn, the equal of that science which he had never abandoned, and as evident.

And Lerne's science was almost unlimited. I was increasingly convinced of it as the days went by. We had resumed our walks, and he took advantage of them to entertain me learnedly about everything we encountered. A leaf gave rise to the entirety of botany; entomology developed with regard to a woodlouse; a raindrop unleashed for my delight a deluge of chemistry; and by the time we had reached the edge of the forest, I had heard an entire professorial college from Lerne's lips.

But it was just there, on the border of the woods and the fields, that he really came into his own. Once the last tree was past, he stopped. Inexorably, hoisted himself up on to a boundary-marker, and held forth regarding the universe, in confrontation with the earth and the heavens. He described things so ingeniously that, to listen to him, you thought that Nature was explaining herself, opening herself up from the depths of the earth to the end of space. His words were as capable of hollowing out hills in order to lay bare the geological strata as of bringing the invisible planets closer, in order to discuss them more easily. They were able to analyze the vapor of clouds and to reveal the origin of a wind, to evoke prehistoric landscapes and just as easily prophesy the future of the region, for centuries to come. He scanned the immense panorama with his eyes and his mind, from the nearby hut to the horizons that distance painted blue. Everything was defined by a word, clarified by a commentary, and as he made great sweeping gestures to designate, by turns, some river or bell-tower, the span of his arm seemed to prolong itself along the line of sight and describe the countryside with the luminous and salutary gesture of a lighthouse.

The return to Fonval was usually accomplished less scientifically. My uncle continued speculations in private which, I suppose, he esteemed too abstruse for my intelligence, and he hummed his favorite tune as he went along, which he had probably picked up from his assistants: "Rum ti tum, ti tum..."

Then, as soon as we were back, he hastened to the laboratory or the greenhouse.

We alternated these walks with automobile trips. Then, my uncle bestrode another hobby-horse. He assigned my vehicle its place in the classification of animals, exposed the beasts of today, those of yesterday and those of tomorrow, in the midst of which, no doubt, the automobile would take its place—and the prophecy concluded with an affectionate hymn of praise to my eighty-horsepower machine.

He wanted to learn how to drive the machine. It was an easy task. In three lessons, I made him a past master. He always drove me thereafter, and I made no complaint, because my eyes tired very quickly with sustained attention since the double section and the two consequential sutures of the optical nerve. My left ear had not yet recovered the desirable sensitivity, but I dared not confess that to Lerne, for fear of adding a further remorse to the number that he appeared to have already.

It was after one of these sporting excursions that while cleaning my car—I had to do it myself—I happened to find a little notebook between the back and the cushion of Lerne's seat, which had slipped out of his pocket. I stuck it in mine, with the intention of giving it back to him—but curiosity moved me when I reached my room without having been able to see the professor again, and I examined the find.

It was a diary crammed with notes and hasty diagrams sketched in pencil. It appeared to be the day-by-day record of some research project: a laboratory journal. The figures held no significance for my eyes. The text consisted mostly of German words, with some French ones, one or other language being chosen at the hazard of inspiration. The whole told me nothing. However, under the previous day's date, a piece of writing less chaotic than the others was displayed, which I thought I recognized as a summary of the preceding pages.

The meanings of some French words, and the sense they acquired when put together awoke in me, at a stroke, the incurable detective and a newborn linguist. These substantives, linked to one another by Teutonic words, were: *transmission, thought, electricity, brains,* and *piles.*

By means of a dictionary lifted from my uncle's room, I deciphered the quasi-cryptogram, in which, luckily, the same expressions recurred frequently. A translation follows; I reproduce it for what it may be worth, unskilled as I am in such tasks, and impelled to haste as I was by the necessity of returning the notebook as soon as possible.

CONCLUSIONS AS OF THE 30TH

Goal pursued: the exchange of personalities without the exchange of brains.

Basis of research: old experiments have proved that everybody possesses a soul. For the soul and life are inseparable, and all organisms, between their birth and their death, enjoy a more-or-less developed soul, according to whether they are themselves more-or-less organized. Thus, between humans and mosses, passing through polyps, every living being has its own soul. Do plants not sleep, breathe, digest? Why should they not think?

This demonstrates that there is a soul even where there is no brain. Thus, the soul and the brain are independent of one another. In consequence, souls must be capable of being exchanged without the transposition of brains.

EXPERIMENTS IN TRANSMISSION

Thought is the electricity of which our brains are the piles, or the accumulators—I don't know that yet, but what is certain is that the transmission of the mental fluid works in a fashion analogous to that of the electric fluid.

The experiment of the 4th proves that thought can be transmitted through conductors, that of the 10th that it is transmitted without conductors on etheric waves.

The experiments that have followed indicate the defect that I describe here.

A soul that is projected into an organism unknown to the latter compresses, so to speak, the soul that is already there without being able to expel it, and the projected soul—soul removed from its body—remains inexplicably connected to its own organism by some sort of *mental pedicle*, which nothing, thus far, has been able to sever.

If the two beings are consenting, the reciprocal transmission fails for the same reason. The major part of each soul installs itself securely in the organism of its partner, but the troublesome mental pedicle prevents each of them from completely quitting the body from which it is attempting to detach itself.

The simpler the destination organism is, relative to the projecting organism, the easier it is for the latter to enter into the receptacle, whose previous contents are so slight, and the pedicle connecting it to the projecting body is, so to speak, *thinner*—but it still exists.

On the 20th, I introduced myself mentally into Johann's body. On the 22nd I incarnated myself within a cat, on the 24th, an ash-tree. Access became easier each time, the invasion increasingly complete, but the pedicle remains.

I thought that an experiment on a cadaver might succeed, because no inconvenient fluid would already be present in the recipient to be filled. I had not considered the fact that death is incompatible with the soul, the inseparable companion of life itself. The result was unsatisfactory, and the sensation abominable.

Theoretically, what is required for the pedicle to be destroyed? A destination organism that has no soul at all—in order that one can lodge one's own soul there entire—but which is not dead; in other words, *an organized body that has never been alive*. That's impossible.

Thus, in practical terms, our efforts must be devoted to the destruction of the pedicle by means of some indirect expedient that I have yet to perceive...

Not that the experiments of this period haven't yielded interesting results, since we've made the following observations.

Firstly, the human brain discharges itself almost entirely into that of a plant.

Secondly, between humans, *with mutual consent*, an almost complete transfer of personalities is effected, apart from the matter of the pedicle, which makes the souls siblings of a sort: mental Siamese twins...

Thirdly, between humans, *without mutual consent*, the subsidence of the destination soul under the pressure of the other produces, in spite of the imperfection of the procedure, a partial and temporary avatar of the projecting individual—a very interesting avatar, for it already satisfies some of the criteria of desirability that need to be fully satisfied if I'm to attain the envisaged goal.

It seems inaccessible.

This, therefore, was the aim of the universal studies that my uncle had extolled so extravagantly!

The theory was disconcerting. I should have been dumbfounded. There was a curious tendency to spiritualism therein, anomalous in a materialist like Lerne, and the new doctrine was presented in such a phantasmagoric light that it would have made many a learned eye widen behind its spectacle lens, erudite pince-nez or peremptory monocle. As for me, I did not discover all the subjects for admiration therein immediately, being still slightly unwell at the time. Nor did I realize that I had translated a Franco-German *mene mene tekel upharsin* relevant to myself.[35] My attention was concentrated on two facts: that *the organized being that had never been alive* did not exist and that, on the other hand, the professor doubted that he would be able to destroy the pedicle. Thus, he had failed. Given his former prowess, I expected all kinds of miracles on his part; one thing alone could astonish me: his impotence.

I went in search of my uncle in order to return his notebook. I ran into Barbe, her bosom bulging over her belly, who told me that he had gone for a walk in the grounds. I did not find him there, but I saw Karl and Wilhelm on the edge of the pool, gazing at something in the water. I had conceived an aversion for the two rascals because of their interchanged brains; their presence usually caused me to draw away, but on that day, I was curious to see what they were looking at from the water's edge.

The thing that they were looking at leapt out of the water, with a splash of diamond droplets; it was a carp. It shook its fins as it leapt up, beating the air as if they were wings. One might have thought that it was trying to fly away....

The unfortunate creature! It really was trying to do that! I had before me the fish that Lerne had endowed with the soul of a blackbird. The captive bird,

---

[35] The quoted prophetic words, which appeared during Belshazzar's feast in *Daniel* 5:25, gave the phrase "the writing on the wall" its conventional metaphorical meaning.

prey within its scaly flesh to the aspirations of its original species, and weary of its blue diet, was launching itself toward the impossible heavens.

Finally, in consequence of a more desperate leap, the animal fell on the bank, its gills panting. Then Wilhelm seized it, and the assistants drew away with their catch. They were abusing it and amusing themselves with it like grown-up guttersnipes, whistling a parodic version of the blackbird's song. Then, in the guise of laughter, a loud whinny emerged from their throats, and, without being aware of it, they rendered a imitation of a horse's call much better than that of the winged flute.

I stayed there, thoughtfully contemplating the pond: that liquid cage in which the enchanted monster had suffered haunting dreams of flight and nostalgia for the nest. The fluid sheet, momentarily disturbed by its bounding fury, would only have resumed its dull flatness when the creature was dead. Its martyrdom would end in the frying-pan. How would that of the other victims end? The animals that had escaped...and MacBell? Oh, MacBell! How might he be saved?

The final ripple extended its circle on the calm, torpid water, and the abysm of the firmament was hollowed out in its reconstituted mirror. The evening star was shining in its utmost depths, millions of leagues away...but it was sufficient to make the effort to imagine, on the contrary, that it was floating on the surface. And the variously-shaped foliage of the water-lilies—circles, semi-circles and crescents—seemed to be reflections of the moon in its successive phases, which had remained there, trapped in the sleep-frozen water.

MacBell! I thought, again. *What can be done for MacBell?*

At that moment the bell at the distant front gate rang. Someone calling at this hour! A visitor? No one ever came...

I went back to the château at a run, asking myself for the first time what would become of Nicolas Vermont if agents of the law mounted a raid on Fonval.

Hidden behind the corner of the château, I peeped out. Lerne was standing in the doorway, reading a telegram he had just received. I came out of hiding.

"Look, uncle," I said, "here's a notebook that belongs to you, I think. You left it in the automobile."

The rustle of petticoats caused me to turn my head. Emma was coming toward us, utterly radiant in the light of the setting sun, from which her hair seemed to draw a new provision of red gleams every evening. She came with a tune on her lips, like a rose between her teeth, and her lithe step was almost a dance. The sound of the bell had intrigued her too. She asked about the telegram.

The professor made no reply.

"Oh, what's the matter?" she said. "My God, what is it now?"

"Is it really so serious, uncle?" I asked in my turn.

"No," Lerne replied. "Donovan's dead, that's all."

"Poor chap!" said Emma. Then, after a pause, she added: "But isn't it better to be dead than mad? It might be for the best, after all. Come on, Nicolas, don't make faces like that...come here!"

She took my hand and drew me toward the château. Lerne went off in another direction.

I was devastated. "Let go of me! Let go of me!" I cried, all of a sudden. "It's too horrible! Donovan! The poor wretch! You don't understand, you can't understand...just leave me alone!"

A frightful dread had overtaken me. Having got free of Emma, I ran after my uncle and caught him up at the entrance to the laboratory. He was talking to Johann and showing him the telegram. The German disappeared into the house just as I accosted the professor.

"Uncle, you haven't told him anything, have you? Anything at all—to Johann?"

"Yes. Why?"

"Oh! But he'll repeat it to the others. He'll tell them that MacBell is dead...and Nelly will know, uncle! That's certain! They'll tell her. Oh, you have to understand me: Donovan's soul will learn that it no longer has a human body! It mustn't! It mustn't!"

With irritating calmness, my uncle said: "There's no danger, Nicolas. I guarantee that."

"No danger? Is that what you think? These men are scoundrels; they'll spill the beans, I tell you. Let me avert...the risk...time's passing...let me in, I beg you! Please! Let me in...just for a moment...I beg you. Damn it, I'm coming in!"

I took advantage of lessons learned from the bull; I charged, head down. Butted in the stomach, my uncle fell flat in the grass, and I opened the door, which stood ajar, with a blow of my fist. The worthy Johann, who was on watch behind it, collapsed with a bloody nose. Then I went into the courtyard, firmly decided to take the bitch away, whatever the cost, and never to be separated from her again.

The pack piled into the kennels. I saw Nelly immediately. She had been given a separate kennel. Her huge, emaciated, hairless, pitiful body was lying alongside the fence.

"Donovan!" I called.

She did not move. The dogs; eyes gleamed in the depths of their dark hovels. A few growled.

"Donovan! Nelly!"

Nothing.

I had an intuition of the truth. Here, too, the grim reaper had plied his scythe.

Yes. Nelly was cold and stiff. A chain, twisted around her neck, seemed to have strangled her. I was about to make sure of it when Lerne and Johann appeared on the threshold of the courtyard.

"Brigands!" I cried. "You've killed her!"

"No—on my honor, I swear it!" my uncle declared. "She was found this morning, exactly as you see her."

"Do you think, then, that she did it deliberately? That she has killed herself? Oh, what a horrible end!"

"Perhaps," said Lerne. "There's another possibility, though, that's more likely. In my opinion, it was a final convulsion that twisted the chain. The body was very ill. Hydrophobia became manifest several days ago. I'm not hiding anything from you, Nicolas; I'm not exonerating myself in any way—you can see that."

"Oh," I murmured, fearfully. "Rabies!"

Calmly, Lerne continued: "There might also be another cause of death that we don't know. The bitch was found at 8 a.m., still warm. Death must have taken place about an hour earlier..." The professor consulted the telegram, and added: "And MacBell died at 7 a.m., at exactly the same instant."[36]

"Of what?" I said, in a choked voice. "Of what did he die?"

"Of rabies, likewise."

XIII. Experiments? Hallucinations?

Emma, Lerne and I were in the small drawing-room after lunch when the professor had a dizzy spell.

It wasn't the first time; I'd already noticed similar disturbances in my uncle's health—but this one was clearly characterized. I was able to observe all its details, and the bizarre symptoms accompanying it. That's the main reason why I mention it.

A witness who was not forewarned would have attributed these accidents to intellectual stress. In truth, my uncle had been overworking. The laboratory, the greenhouse and the château, were no longer sufficient for him; he had annexed the grounds too. Now, all Fonval was bristling with complicated poles, abnormal masts and unusual semaphore-towers. When some trees hindered his experiments, a crew of woodcutters was commandeered in order to fell them. The joy of seeing freedom of circulation restored to the property consoled me in respect of this sacrilegious act.

---

[36] Lerne is presumably correcting for the one-hour time difference between France and Scotland; MacBell must, of course, have died at 6 a.m. GMT to coincide with Nelly's death at seven, in terms of the European time-zones standardized in the late 19th century.

The professor was seen moving feverishly back and forth through the basin, now an immense workshop, from one building to another, from one machine to another, doggedly determined to destroy the fatal pedicle. Sometimes, however, he weakened, under the influence of one of these exceedingly peculiar fits of dizziness to which he was subject.

The attacks always occurred while he was thinking deeply, his eyes fixed on some object, while his brain was fully active. He would then become paler and paler...until the color gradually came back into his cheeks of its own accord. These crises left him devoid of energy and strength. They robbed him of his sturdy confidence, and I heard him complaining after one of them, murmuring in a discouraged tone: "I'll never get there—never, never, never!" I had often been on the point of speaking to him about it; that day I made up my mind to do so.

We were drinking coffee. Lerne was sitting in an armchair by the window, with his cup in his hand. We were chatting, in an increasingly desultory fashion. For want of any worthy subject, the conversation languished; little by little, it died away, like a fire going out for lack of fuel.

The clock chimed, and we saw the woodcutters going past on their way to work, their axes on their shoulders. I imagined the as ragged but stern lictors, on their way to arrange the execution of the trees.[37] Which of my old comrades would perish today? That beech? That chestnut? I could see them from the window, laden with all the blond shades of autumn, from the deepest copper to the palest gold, each one displaying its patches of brown or russet among the variegation of all those yellows. The fir-trees were getting blacker. Leaves were falling of their own accord, for there was no wind.

The leafless summit of a colossal poplar loomed above the crowns like a cathedral spire. I had always known it thus—monumental—and its contemplating stirred up my childhood memories. A panicked flock of small birds suddenly burst forth from it. Two crows flew away, croaking. A squirrel leapt from branch to branch, taking refuge in a neighboring walnut tree. Some stinking beast, climbing up the tree, had doubtless frightened them. I could not make it out; besides, a clump of bushes concealed the lower part of the poplar from me. I was painfully surprised, though, to see it shudder from top to bottom and shake once or twice, slowly swaying its branches. One might have thought that a wind had risen, blowing for it alone.

I thought about the woodcutters, without forming a very clear impression of the role they might be playing in the drama. *Has my uncle*, I wondered, *ordered them to execute the poplar—that venerable patriarch, the king of Fonval? That would be too much!* And it was then, wanting to ask Lerne about it, that I perceived that he had fainted.

----

[37] The lictors of ancient Rome were assistants to the magistrates, who served as their bodyguards and agents ensuring that their sentences were carried out.

Immobility, pallor, fixity of gaze—I verified the distinctive signs of his illness, and succeeded in determining that he was staring with somnambulistic persistence. Now, what he was staring at was the poplar, that *animated* tree, whose present appearance was so frighteningly reminiscent of the amorous or battling date-trees in the greenhouse. I remembered the notebook. Might there not be some significant connection between the *absence* of the man and the *life* of the tree?

Suddenly, the sound of an axe on a trunk rang out dully. The poplar shuddered, twisted...and my uncle started. He dropped his cup, which broke on the floor-tiles, and while his cheeks regained their color, he quickly reached down to his ankles, as if the axe had struck the man and the tree with the same stroke.

Lerne gradually recovered, however. I pretended that I hadn't seen anything, except for his fainting, and I told him that I he should take better care of himself, or these repeated fits would end up laying him low. I asked him if he knew what caused them. My uncle nodded his head. Emma was fussing his armchair.

"I know," he said, eventually. "Palpitations... syncopes... cardiac problems... I'm treating them."

That was untrue. The professor was not treating them. He was racing through life in pursuit of his chimera, with no more heed for his skin than for an old work-jacket that was to be thrown away as soon as the task at hand was finished.

"You ought to go outside," Emma advised him. "Fresh air would do you good."

He went out. We saw him heading for the poplar, smoking his pipe. The blows of the axe were falling faster. The tree tilted, and fell...its collapse sounded like an earthquake. The branches whipped my uncle, who had not stepped aside.

Now, deprived of its natural bell-tower, Fonval sank even lower into the bottom of the valley, and I sought to repair the void left in the devastated sky by the tree, already forgotten, and its height, already legendary.

Lerne came back in. He had no suspicion that he had committed an imprudence. His recklessness sent a shiver down my spine when I thought that he might be undertaking experiments of the most hazardous sort—to wit, the transfusions of the soul he had mentioned in the notebook...

Was it one of those attempts that I had just witnessed? I thought about it with a measure of apprehension, with the bizarre sensation I had experienced so frequently at Fonval, like that engendered by groping one's way through unfamiliar surroundings in the dark. Was there more than mere coincidence between Lerne's fainting fit and the tree's agitation, or did some mysterious link unite them as the axe fell? The arrival of the woodcutters at the foot of the poplar would certainly have been sufficient to put the birds to flight. As for the tremor, why should the tree-feller not have produced it by climbing the far side of the trunk in order to fix the traditional rope to it?

Once again, the crossroads of possibility offered me different answers, like so many alternative paths. But my intelligence lacked perspicacity: the deleterious effect of the Circean operations persisted, and the regimen of intensive love-making demanded by my mistress and fostered by my uncle was no tonic.

Lust being my drug of choice, I could no more deprive myself of Emma than an opium-smoker of his pipe or a morphine addict of her syringe—I beg the latter delightful creature to forgive me the impoliteness of such a comparison, in view of its accuracy. I had even become bold enough to join the inspirer of my ecstasy in her bedroom on a frequent basis. Lerne had caught us there one evening, and had taken the opportunity the following day to restate the terms of our contract: "She has free license to love you, on condition that she does not leave me; otherwise you'll get nothing from me." Having said that, he said the equivalent to Emma, for he knew it to be an irresistible argument so far as she was concerned.

It was a matter of astonishment—which plunged me into a gulf of perplexity—that I had accepted that shameful arrangement so easily…but a woman surpasses the most adept enchanter: a wink, a roll of the hips, and there we are, transformed in our most intimate personality more radically than any magic wand or skillful scalpel could contrive. What was Lerne by comparison with Emma?

Emma! I had had her every night, in spite of the scientist's proximity. He would be breathing there, on the other side of the partition wall; he could hear us in his imagination, see us through the keyhole…God forgive me! I found an excitement in that, a wicked spice for our orgiastic scenes—and yet, what feasts they already were, every night more sumptuous than the one before!

Emma, an ingenuous woman and an ingenious lover, was able to contrive an infinite variety in the antique nuptial ritual, whose foundation is immutable, by means of new rites that parodied them until their outcome. She always did honor to her desire differently, not by means of those classical arrangements that are numbered, catalogued and fastidiously calculated, but by grace of an indescribable, unexpected and charming originality. She multiplied herself in love, and was, without being aware of it, knowledgeable by instinct, making herself a tyrannical mistress and a docile victim by turns. Her body, it's true, her insidious and versatile body, was admirably prepared for the caprices of these diverse physiognomies, for if it became, in action and by natural gesture, that of a frantic courtesan, some sudden willful modest grace, or its immobility, would render my lover into a simulacrum of a young girl already perfect in her form. Oh, the body of a crazed virgin, with a strange pre-pubescent nudity!

I have gone on long enough, it seems to me, about our amusements to establish the value I placed on them, and to demonstrate that, if I were obliged to interrupt them, the motive for doing so would have to be irresistible.

That motive I discovered in the following humiliation, which I would doubtless have attributed to my nervous condition had it not been for my acquaintance with the notebook. I would then have dismissed it as "a pathological consequence of the operations" and Lerne would have made a fool of me until the end. Fortunately, I divined his stratagem at the first assault.

One evening, as I was going through the rooms on the ground floor, as usual, on my way from my own bedroom to Emma's, I heard a chair being dragged across the floor in the room above the dining-room—my uncle's. At that late hour, he was accustomed to rest, but that tiny detail left me quite indifferent. Without muffling the sound of my footsteps, I continued an expedition that was authorized, not clandestine.

Emma had just finished curling her hair for the night. Amid the coquettish aromas of the bedroom, the odor of the scorched paper with which the heat of the tongs is measured was floating, a symbolic mingling of the Devil's scent with the perfume of scantily-clad pretty girls.

To the side, all noise had ceased. As an extra precaution, I drew the small interior bolt that locked Lerne's door, so that we need have no fear of an unexpected entrance on my uncle's part—not dangerous, of course, but untimely. There was no light showing through the keyhole. I had never taken so many precautions.

All a-tremble, her nightdress silky and her flesh even silkier, Emma drew me toward the bed.

Two bright lamps were burning on the mantelpiece, for the delight that we were about to enjoy is a fine spectacle, not to be scorned, and it is appropriate to thank Nature, which dictates that each of our senses has a part to play in her wild games, and that, on this occasion alone, their number is six.

Emma gradually activated them all. My joys lit up with hers, and stoked up their increasing flame. With her, the divine comedy became a complete plot. Nothing was lacking therein—prologue, dramatic twists, *coups de théâtre*, dénouement—just as in the most excellent plays, in which the events that one desires to happen always do, but in an unexpected fashion.

To begin with, Emma liked to allow herself to be caressed...

Then, judging that the introduction had lasted long enough, she adopted the position of a heroine, and wanted, on that particular evening as on so many others, to go for a fantastic nuptial ride, at the gallop.

But then, as she raced toward the abysm of satisfactions like an expert Valkyrie, something surprising and terrible occurred. Instead of climbing the voluptuous slope towards the implored paroxysm, it seemed to me, on the contrary, that I was descending it, passing from one pleasure to a lesser one, sliding by degrees towards indifference. I was still conducting myself valiantly, an increasing ardor animating the fury of my body, but the harder it played the game, the less contentment my mind experienced...

This poor result distressed me. And that distress, too, diminished...

I tried to stop my diabolically-possessed physique. Pffft! Hopeless! My will diminished to the point of being powerless, I sensed my faculties being continuously reduced, closing down and my soul, having become Lilliputian, was as impotent to govern my muscles as to receive the sensation of their maneuvers. I could scarcely take account of my body's actions, and register that it was giving evidence of an entirely exceptional zest, for which Emma was visibly grateful.

In the hope of cutting the phenomenon short, I concentrated the force of my authority. It was in vain. One might have thought that another soul had invaded the seat of my own, directing my conduct in its stead and savoring the reward of the resultant delights via my nerves. That personality had driven my own ego back into a corner of my brain. An intruder was cheating me with my mistress, who was deceived herself, by means of a detestable trick!

These microscopic reflections agitated my dwarf soul. It became so meager at the instant of the couple's apotheosis that I was afraid I might feel it vanish.

Then it expanded, grew, blossomed, and progressively reoccupied its domain. My ideas resumed their former proportions. I was able to feel the great joyful fatigue that is Eros' rear-guard, and a cramp in my right calf. A pressure on my shoulder became gradually heavier: Emma's head was supported there, and her inevitable swoon was pressing down on my bosom the double pain of her extended throat.

I completed my self-repossession. It took a long time. My eyes had not yet blinked; they were fixed on a particular point, and I realized that, throughout those extravagant minutes, they had never ceased staring at Lerne's keyhole. Even now, they could not detach themselves from it.

They were suddenly able to do it. I detached myself from my lover's grip and, unexpectedly...a chair creaked in the next room, behind my uncle's door—the sound of someone getting up from a sitting position and moving away on tiptoe....

The keyhole had the appearance of a tiny dark window, opening in to the very heart of the mystery...

Emma sighed. "You've never reached such heights, Nicolas, except for once...shall we go again? Say the word..."

I fled, without making any reply.

I could see clearly now. Had the professor not as good as told me: *I'm thinking of assuming your appearance, in order to be loved in your stead*? His eagerness to save my stricken body, the methodology explained in the notebook, and the incident of the poplar all came together in my mind to form a belief. The apparent fainting fits took on the aspect of experiments, in which Lerne, by means of a sort of hypnotism, was injecting his soul into various other beings. With his eye at the keyhole, he had transfused his ego into my brain, using the power that his incomplete discovery gave him to effect the substitution of the most implausible personalities! It might be argued that that very quality of implausibility should have made me hesitate as to the accuracy of my reasoning, but at Fonval, incoherence was the rule, an explanation having a proportionately greater chance of being correct the closer it approached the absurd!

Oh, that eye of Lerne's at the keyhole! It was pursuing me, as all-powerful as the eye of Jehovah that struck Cain down from the height of its triangular peephole!

Although I can joke about it now, I had perceived the new danger, and my only thought was how to avoid it. After a rather long deliberation, I reached the only reasonable decision, which I should have taken long before: to leave. To leave with Emma, of course, for now, nothing in the world would have persuade me to leave her to my uncle, who could assume a man's lust for a woman along with his anatomy.

But Emma was not one of those women who can be abducted against their will. Would she consent to abandon Lerne and the promised wealth just like that? Certainly not. The poor girl could not see the disagreeably-modernized fairy tale unfolding around her; her mind was fully-occupied by future splendors; she was foolish and avaricious. In order to convince her to go with me, it would be necessary to assure her that she wouldn't lose a centime...and Lerne alone could make a valid declaration to that effect.

It was, therefore, the professor's consent that had to be obtained!

There could be no question of a consent obtained by force, of course—but intimidation might do the job admirably. If I could make skillful use of the murders of MacBell and Klotz, my fearful uncle might talk to Emma in accordance with my wishes, and I would be able to take my lover away...at the expense of depriving Monsieur Nicolas Vermont of an inheritance that as doubtless considerably eroded, and Mademoiselle Bourdichet of riches that were probably chimerical in any case.

The details of my plan were soon complete.

XIV. Death and the Mask

But the plan was never put into action.

That was not because I hesitated to put it into action. I was still determined to do it, and if any doubt arose with regard to the peril to be run, it was only after my projects were no longer practicable. While they seemed so, on the other hand, I waited impatiently for an opportunity to accomplish them, and will even admit that my haste to activate them was motivated by an ever-increasing fear...

Danger presented itself to my hallucinated eyes on all sides, all the more perfidious and mysterious because there was often nothing to fear. Emma spent her nights in my room. The keyholes, the cracks in the doors, and every other issue by which the redoubtable voyeur might infiltrate his line of sight, were blocked. In spite of the security of the location, Emma complained about my coldness; I dared not allow myself to be distracted. On the one occasion I tried, her strange terminal swoon was provoked more rapidly than usual; I suspect today that that was caused by the preliminary abstinence, but at the time, that precipitate *absence* made me suspect a new misfortune; might it not be Emma that the foreign soul had just possessed momentarily? And the horror of having sated old Lerne's sadism under the auspices of my companion robbed me conclusively of her accolade.

I no longer took the risk of looking my uncle in the face. Vanquished by fear, I lowered my eyes and avoided those of others—even those of portraits, whose gaze follows us everywhere. The slightest thing made me jump. I was fearful of any creature with a white head, of any plant swayed by a breath of wind, of any voice lent by a bird to a tree...

You will understand that it was high time to leave, and that I wanted to do so with all my heart—but I had resolved to choose a moment when Lerne might listen to my proposition with an accommodating ear, in order only to use threats as a last resort. And that moment was slow in coming. The discovery did not want to hatch out; continued failure preyed upon the professor's mind. His fits—or, rather, his experiments—hastened his deterioration considerably...and his temper reflected it.

Only our excursions retained the prerogative of reviving him; he still sang "Rum ti tum" as we walked and stopped every ten meters to pronounce some scientific verity—but the automobile enchanted the enchanter more than anything else.

So, in spite of the poor result obtained in the same conditions several months before, I had to take the decision to talk to him during an outing in the eighty horse-power machine.

And I would have done so, had it not been for the accident.

I happened in the woods at Lourq, three kilometers from Grey, as we were returning to Fonval from an automobile trip to Vouziers. We were going up a shallow slope at high speed. My uncle was driving. I was mentally rehearsing the speech I was going to make, repeating the long-prepared sentences for the hundredth time, and apprehension was drying up my tongue. Since our departure, I had been continually putting off the moment when I would have to speak to my tyrant in the firm tone that would intimidate him. Before every village, every turning, I told myself: *That's where you must speak*; but we had passed through all the villages and rounded all the beds without my pronouncing a syllable. Scarcely ten minutes remained to me. Come on! I would open fire at the top of the hill. No more delay!

My first sentence was ready at the entrance to my memory, awaiting expression, when the car made a sharp swerve to the right, then swerved again to the left, skidding sideways. We were going to turn over!

I grabbed the steering-wheel, braked as hard as I could with the footbrake and the handbrake...

Gradually, the automobile's lurching leased, and it slowed down, stopping just short of the crest of the rise.

Then I looked at Lerne.

He was leaning out of his bucket-seat, his head swaying and his eyes haggard behind his goggles; one of his arms was hanging down. A dizzy spell! We'd had a narrow escape! In that case, though, these fainting fits must be genuine syncopes. What had I been thinking, with my stupid ideas?

He was not recovering, however. Having taken off his safety-helmet, I saw that his clean-shaven face was as pale as candle-wax. His hands, once his gloves were off, had the same waxen tint. Knowing nothing about medicine, I slapped them vigorously, as people do to actresses in the theater suffering from the vapors. The sound of applause broke out in the quiet countryside. Sonorous and funereal, it welcomed the exit of the great ham.

Frédéric Lerne had, in fact, ceased living. I deduced that from the chill in his fingers and the lividity of his cheeks, his soulless eyes and his stopped heart. The cardiac disease in which I had refused to believe had killed him, according to the custom of such maladies, without warning.

Stupefaction, and the nervous reaction to the crash that I had just avoided, nailed me to the spot. So, within a second, nothing remained of Lerne but vermin fare and a name to be forgotten—nothing! In spite of my hatred for the noxious man and my relief in the knowledge that he was harmless, the swiftness of his death, spiriting away that monstrous intelligence like a conjuring trick, was inevitably frightening.

Like a puppet deprived of the hand that gives it life, a marionette prostrate on the edge of the stage, Lerne was limp, his arm hanging slackly down toward the ground, and death added further whiteness to his funereal clown's face. As the liberated genius drew further away into the unknown, however, my uncle's corpse seemed to me to become more beautiful. The soul is so lauded by comparison with the flesh that it is astonishing to see the latter adorned at the latter's expense. I followed the progress of the phenomenon in Lerne's features. The great mystery illuminated his forehead with a divine serenity, as if life had been a cloud whose complete passing unmasked some unknown sun—and the face took on the sheen of white marble; the mannequin became a statue.

A tear blurred my vision. I took off my helmet. If my uncle had perished fifteen years before, in the fullness of his happiness and his wisdom, the Lerne of yesteryear could not have been more handsome...

But I could not extend that intimate reverie indefinitely, on a busy road, with a cadaver. I therefore took hold of him, reluctantly, and seated him on the left. The straps from the luggage-rack attached him firmly to the bodywork. Once his gloves were back on and is face was hidden beneath his readjusted headgear, his goggles and his scarf, he seemed to be asleep. We departed, side by side.

No one in Grey noticed my neighbor's stiffness, and I was able to take him back quietly to Fonval, full of admiration for the dead scientist and pity for the amorous old man who had suffered so much. I forgot the offences in confrontation with the offender's death. He no longer inspired anything in me but an immense respect and—need it be said?—an insurmountable repugnance, which made me draw away from him as far as possible within my seat.

Since our encounter in the middle of the labyrinth on the morning of my arrival, I had not spoken a word to the Germans. I went to look for them in the laboratory, having left the automobile and its sepulchral chauffeur in front of the main door, in the charge of the housekeeper.

The assistants understood immediately from my gesticulations that something extraordinary had occurred, and followed me. They had the worried expressions of guilty men who foresee disaster I the slightest event. When they were certain of the misfortune that had struck them, the three accomplices did not hide their disappointment or their anxiety. They held a vociferous conference. Johann exerted his authority; the other two became obsequious. I awaited their pleasure.

Finally, they helped me to carry the professor up to his room and lay him down on his bed. Emma saw us, screamed and fled; the Germans left with no further ado. Barbe and I remained alone with my uncle. The fat housekeeper shed a few tears—in honor I suppose, of death envisaged as an entity, rather than to satisfy her master's guardian spirits. She considered him from the heights of her corpulence. Lerne had changed; his nose was pinched and his fingernails were blue.

"We have to lay out the body," I said, suddenly.

"Let me do that," Barbe replied. "It's not a pleasant task, but I know how to do it."

I turned my back on the mortuary dressing. Barbe had the knowledge of old peasant women, who are all part-time midwives and undertakers. She soon announced: "It's done, and done properly. Nothing's lacking, apart from holy water and the decorations I don't have..."

Lerne was so white on his entirely white bed that they seemed to me to blend together and take on the appearance of an alabaster sarcophagus with its commemorative effigy, hewn from the same block of marble. My uncle, with his hair carefully combed, wore a dress shirt with a white cravat. His hands, so very pale, were joined, with a rosary passed through his fingers. A crucifix formed a shiny breastplate. His feet and knees stuck out of the sheets, like very distant pointed snowy peaks. On the nightstand, behind the bowl devoid of holy water, in which a superfluous sprinkler lay in vain, like a dry twig, two candles were burning. Barbe had made the item of furniture into a kind of altar—and I reproached her sharply for that inconsequence. She retorted that it was customary—and with that, closed the shutters. Shadows were hollowed out on the dead man's face, anticipating the future and creating a premature marbling effect.

"Open the window very wide!" I said. "Let the daylight in, the birdsong and the scent of the garden."

The servant obeyed me, even though it was "contrary to custom", and then, when she had received my instructions for the obligatory formalities, she left, as I asked her to.

A powerful aroma of dead leaves was coming from the grounds. That odor is infinitely sad; one breathes it as if one were listening to a funereal hymn. Crows were flying past, croaking as they do in edifices, and their passage imitated an enormous and prodigious flight from a basilica. The approach of dusk was darkening the daylight.

I inspected the room, in order to look at something other than the bed. Above the writing-desk there was a pastel drawing of my Aunt Lidivine, smiling. It is a mistake to make portraits smile; they are doomed to so many heart-rending sights—so the colored Lividine, having smiled while seeing her spouse fornicate with a whore, was smiling still in confrontation with his deplorable remains. The picture was 20 years old, but the powder of pastels, which resembles the dust of the ages, gave it an appearance more ancient still. Every day, moreover, darkened it further and seemed to age it more. It therefore removed my aunt and my youth into an even more distant past. I didn't like it. I tried to interest myself in other objects: in the falling dusk, the first bats, the baubles in the room, the candles that—regrettably—lit it feebly, the dancing gleams....

A wind that was rising was able to hold my attention momentarily; it sent an invisible torrent roaring through the foliage; to hear it in the hearth, moaning as it clove the darkness, one might have thought that one was hearing the passage of time. With one more forceful gust, it extinguished a candle; the other flickered. I slammed the window shut; staying there without light was not an attractive prospect.

Suddenly, I became sincere, and no longer sought to dupe myself; I needed to look at the dead man, to survey his impotence. I lit the lamp then, and placed Lerne in a flood of light.

He really was handsome. Very handsome. Nothing was left of the sullen physiognomy that I had found after fifteen years of absence—nothing...save perhaps an errant irony about the mouth, the shadow of a sardonic smile. Did my late uncle still have some afterthought? Dead, the man who had retouched the Great Work still seemed to be defying Nature...

And his work appeared to my mind, with all its sublime audacity and criminal boldness, which were as worthy of the pillory as a pedestal, the birch-rod and the palm at the same time. Once, I had known him worth of the latter and would have sworn that he would never deserve the latter! But what mortal adventure had made him become, for nearly five years, a châtelain who murdered his guests?

I asked myself that. Meanwhile, the phantoms of Klotz and MacBell seemed to be screaming under their torture from the depths of the windswept hearth. The squall, having turned into a tempest, was whistling through the cracks in the doors; the candle-flames were restless; a curtain swelled out and fell back again with a discouraged gesture. Lerne's white wispy hair flew about, parted by the storm-wind, which drew it back for a long time, brushing it in every direction...

And as the imponderable hand of the squall played among the tresses, I stood leaning over the bed, frozen in astonishment on seeing the continual appearance, beneath the silvery wisps, of *the violet scar that circled Lerne's head from one temple to the other!*

A frightful demi-crown, the indication of the Circean operation! It had been carried out on my uncle. By whom?

Otto Klotz, of course!

The mystery was clarified. Its final veil, a shroud, had been snatched away. Everything was explained! Everything: the professor's abrupt metamorphosis, coinciding with the disappearance of his principal assistant, with MacBell's journey, and the effective eclipse of Lerne! Everything: the hostile letters, the altered handwriting, the failure to recognize me, the German accent, the losses of memory and, in addition, Klotz's reckless character, his temerity, his passion for Emma, his reprehensible endeavors, the crimes perpetrated upon MacBell and myself. Everything! Everything! Everything!

Recalling my beloved's story to mind, I was able to reconstitute the history of an unimaginable crime.

Four years before my return to Fonval, Lerne and Otto Klotz come back from Nanthel, where they have spent the day. Lerne is probably joyful. He is going to resume his fertile studies on grafting, whose aim—whose sole aim—is the benefit of humankind. But Klotz, in love with Emma, wants to give this research another, profane objective, motivated, above all, by money: the transplantation of brains. Without a doubt, he has proposed that objective—which he could not pursue at Mannheim for lack of money—to my uncle, without result.

The assistant has his own Machiavellian plan, though. With the help of his three compatriots, altered in advance and hide in the bushes, he knocks the professor down and ties him up. He locks the man whose wealth and independence—identity, to put it another way—he covets in the laboratory.

He wants to take advantage of the physical vigor that he is going to surrender one last time, however, and he spends the night with Emma.

The next day, before dawn, he goes to the laboratory, where Lerne awaits him, hidden from view. His three trusted accomplices put them both to sleep, and graft Klotz's brain into my uncle's skull. As for Lerne's brain, they content themselves with stuffing it behind the forehead of Klotz, who is no more than a cadaver, and they hastily bury the lot with the anatomical debris.

So there is Otto Klotz, behind the mask, reclad in the desired appearance, costumed as Lerne, master of Fonval, Emma, the work: a sort of hermit-crab sheltered by the shell of the creature he has killed.

Emma sees him emerge the laboratory. He comes back into the château, pale and doddery, overturns the routines of everyday life, and has the intersecting paths of labyrinth constructed. Then, certain of his impunity he begins his terrible experiments in his unapproachable lair.

Futile experiments, fortunately! The body-snatcher had expired too soon, without having reaped the fruits of a larceny of which he was the victim, since the heart disease that had just carried Klotz away was actually the property of Lerne's body. The thief of a house is punished thus when the roof collapses upon him.

I understood now why that face had resumed my uncle's true physiognomy! The German's soul was no longer behind it to give it his own expression.

Klotz was Lerne's murderer, rather than Lerne having murdered Klotz! I couldn't get over it. That was one confidence the double individual had omitted to make to me! Vexed at having been his dupe for such a long time, I told myself that, had I been living alone with him, I would probably have perceived the deception, but that the society of people as gullible as Emma and accomplices like the assistants had drawn me into the delusion, in the wake of their own error or pretence.

Oh, Aunt Lidivine, I thought, *you're right to smile with your pastel lips. Your Frédéric fell into an odious trap nearly five years ago, and the spirit that has just quit this body is not his. Nothing foreign remains within it now, save for an empty brain, a carnal mass as banal as the liver. It's really your excellent husband that we're watching over, while the other has just died and is paying his debt....*

On that thought, I sobbed my heart out beside the astonishing corpse—but the sardonic rictus left behind as the wicked soul fled, like a stamp, still hindered my self-expression. I effaced it with the tip of my finger, modeling the hardened, scarcely malleable mouth to my own taste.

As I drew back to consider the effect, someone scratched softly on the door.

"It's me, Nicolas...Emma."

The innocent girl! Should I tell her the truth? How would she react to such a twist of fate? I knew her. Scorned so many times, she would have reproached me for trying to trick her. I kept quiet.

"Go to bed," she said, in a whisper. "Barbe will take your place."

"No thanks. No, leave me alone."

I had to continue my vigil at my uncle's side. I had accused him of too many sins, and I needed to ask forgiveness of his memory, and that of my aunt. That's why, in spite of the bacchanal of the storm, we talked all night long: the dead man, the pastel, and me.

When Barbe came at daybreak, I went out into the cold of the morning, which soothes the fever of vigils on the skin.

The autumnal grounds exhaled a faint cemetery odor. The great wind of the previous night had plucked all the leaves, and my footsteps crackled on their thick couch; there were none to be seen any longer on the skeletal trees, save for a few here and there, and it was difficult to tell whether they were leaves or sparrows. In a matter of hours, the grounds had made their preparations for winter. What would become of the marvelous greenhouse, as the frosts drew near? Perhaps I would be able to get into it, by virtue of the death that had dispossessed the Germans.

I veered in that direction—but what I saw at a distance caused me to accelerate my steps. The greenhouse door was open, and an acrid sooty smoke was coming from it, as well as from holes in the glass.

I went in.

The rotunda, the aquarium and the third hall were a scene of destruction. Everything there had been overturned, smashed and set alight. Heaps of rubbish were piled up in the idle of each of the three halls; all mixed up there, I saw broken plants with shattered pots, shards of crystal and sea anemones, soiled flowers next to slaughtered beasts—in brief, three massive compost-heaps in which the tripartite exhibition-hall saw the end of all its marvels, delightful, poignant and repulsive alike. Rags were still burning in one corner; in another, on a heap of ashes, a few branches—the most compromising—were completing their consumption in hissing embers. Charred bones stank to high heaven.

The assistants had obviously devoted themselves to this pillage in order to obliterate every last trace of their work, and only the storm had prevented me from hearing them—but they would not have stopped there, in such determined progress...

To make sure, I visited the charnel-house under the cliff. There was nothing there, in a gaping hole, but various animal bones and carcasses, the former without skulls and the latter without heads. Klotz was no longer there. Nelly wasn't there either.

The sack of the laboratory seemed to me to be a masterpiece. It demonstrated the innate aptitude for such work of men in general and certain nations in particular. I had the run of the buildings, all the doors of which were clicking and banging at the whim of the wind. In the courtyard, nothing remained but living animals that had not been subjected to treatment; I only discovered the others later. Here, therefore, there were no signs of destruction. The operating theaters, by contrast, enclosed an indescribable chaos of broken bottles, whose mingled liquids inundated the floor-tiles with a pharmaceutical lake. The massacre of books, labels and notebooks was dispersed throughout the holocaust of twisted apparatus. Finally, the majority of the surgical instruments had been stolen.

The scoundrels had made off with the secret of the Circean operation and the equipment necessary to carry it out. Their lodgings, in fact, with their empty cupboards and chests of drawers, and their furniture turned upside down, informed me that the three conspirators had gone for good.

As I left the ravaged living quarters, my attention was caught by a thread of blue smoke rising up behind the building's left wing. It was coming from a heap of semi-charred detritus, the cadaverous odor of which made me nauseous.

I approached it nevertheless and, one of the items of detritus having moved, pulled it out of the pestilential pile. It was a miserable rat, lame and scorched— which, having gone mad, leapt at me. Its head, trepanned in the round, laid bare the bloody brain.

Seized by horror and pity, I finished the last of the monsters' victims off with the heel of my boot.

XV. The New Beast

Under the influence of an apathy entirely understandable in the circumstances, the official physician did not carry out any examination or checks. I told him about my late uncle's fainting fits, and my uncle's diagnosis of his own heart disease—and he gave me permission to have him buried.

"Doctor Lerne is certainly dead," he said "And our present task will, with your permission, stop at that ascertainment. As for the rest, it's not for us to undertake causal investigations that might lead us to contradict such an eminent master and make him die in some fashion other than the one he anticipated."

The funeral took place in Grey-l'Abbaye, with no pomp and no audience— after which I spent ten days clarifying the affairs of that inconceivable duplicity, the unparalleled amalgam of murderer and victim, Klotz-Lerne.

In the course of his phenomenal existence—about four and a half years— he had not made a will. That proved to me that, in spite of his funereal prognostications, death had come upon him entirely unexpectedly, for, in the opposite case, he would doubtless have taken the trouble to disinherit me. At the back of a secret drawer in the writing-desk, I found my uncle's will, as the letter of long ago had told me I would. It left everything to me—but Klotz-Lerne had overladen the estate with mortgages, and contracted many debts.

My initial impulse was to appeal to the law, but the absurdity of the case struck me, and all the upsets that such a substitution of identities might import into the juridical order: the crimes of a sort unforeseen by the Code, the fraudulent sales, the usurpation of a heritage that was unnatural as well as illegal. It was necessary to resign myself to all the consequences of a mind-numbing fraud, and not breathe a word, for fear of worse insinuations.

Taking everything into account however, accepting the succession still left me in profit and I had already decided to rid myself of Fonval, by sale at auction, foreseeing that it would henceforth be nothing to me but a nest of bad memories.

I went through all the stacks of papers. Every line of those of the true Lerne confirmed his medical honesty and the purity of his research on grafting. Those of Klotz-Lerne, easily recognizable by the alterations in the handwriting an often blackened by Gothic script, were the object of a meticulous sorting process, and were incinerated as irrefutable testimony of numerous crimes, in which there was nothing to disprove the involvement a certain Nicolas Vermont, resident at Fonval for six months. Under the pressure of the same concern, I searched the grounds and the surrounding commons. When that was done, I gave the livestock to the villagers, and dismissed Barbe.

Then I summoned help. Large trunks were stuffed with family possessions, while Emma packed her suitcases, torn between regret for her lost chimera and the pleasure of going to Paris with me.

Since the death of Klotz-Lerne, eager to return to the tumult of society and the comforts of wealth without the transitory constraints of setting up house, I had written to one of my friends, asking him to rent me an apartment more spacious than my bachelor pad, appropriate to lodge an amorous couple. His reply delighted us. He had found lodgings for us in the Avenue Victor Hugo: a small house made as if to measure and furnished to our taste. Domestic staff, carefully recruited by him, awaited us there.

And the moment came to leave Fonval forever. I wandered through the house devoid of furniture and the grounds devoid of foliage. It seemed that autumn had stripped them both naked simultaneously. The old perfumes were still floating in the abandoned rooms, charged with melancholy memories. Oh, what charm the musty and the locked-up sometimes have! The tenacious silhouettes of unhooked pictures and mirrors, sideboards and wardrobes, were still visible on the walls: patches in the faded wallpaper that remained quite new, shadows of magnificent things left by them to the familiar wall, vivid stains destined to pale themselves over time, along with the memory of their absence. Now empty, some rooms seemed to have shrunk, and others seemed more capacious, without any obvious reason. I revisited the entire dwelling, from top to bottom; by courtesy a skylight and the glimmer of an air-vent I explored the attic and the cellar—and I did not weary of wandering through the décor of my youth, like a living being haunting a phantom place.

Oh, my youth! I felt that it was the sole inhabitant of Fonval. In spite of their importance, the recent dramas paled by comparison, Donovan's room and Emma's no more than mine or my aunt's. Had I been right to put Fonval up for auction? That doubt accompanied me as I bid my farewells to the grounds. The meadow became a lawn again, and the Minotaur's summer-house only reminded me of Briareus. I made the grand tour, following the cliff. The clouds were so low that one might have thought them a ceiling of grey cotton wool perched on the circular crest.

In that wintry interior light, the statues, derived of their green togas, displayed their time- and rain-ravaged concrete; their noses flat or their chins cracked, some among them were crumbling. One, with a Bacchic gesture, extended a mutilated arm whose hand, supporting a bowl, was only connected to the elbow by its armature, an iron bone dreadful to look at. They would continue their poses in solitude. A hint of wilderness, of which only vague indications were perceptible, was already beginning to show. A hawk was sharpening its beak on the summer-house weather-vane. A marten crossed the pasture with tranquil bounds.

Unable to resolve to leave, I re-opened the château; then I went back into the grounds. I heard my footsteps rattle on the floor-tiles of the corridors and rustle in the leaves on the pathways. The silence increased by degrees; as I broke it, I experienced certain difficulty. It sensed that was going to reign as master and, as I paused in the middle of the state, it tested its omnipotence.

I remained there for a long time, dreamily: the human center of the enormous circle and of a round-dance of thoughts. In answer to my summons, the faces of yesteryear and yesterday, fantastic and real, fictional and actual individuals, came in a cyclone and whirled around me in a frenzied crowd, making the basin into a Maëlstrom of memory in which the entire Past rotated.

But it was necessary to go away, and leave Fonval to the ivy and the spiders.

Emma, dressed for the journey, was impatiently standing guard in front of the coach-house. I opened the door. The automobile was parked at an angle at the back of the building. I had not seen it since the accident, and could not even remember having put it away. Moved by a belated sense of obligation, one of the assistants had doubtless put it in as best he could.

In spite of my negligence, the engine started willingly at the first electric contact. Then I brought the car out as far as the semicircular esplanade, and closed the symbolically sobbing gate on so many memories, putting an end to the terrifying history of Klotz, thank God, but also to the years of my youth.

I imagined that the act of keeping Fonval might have the power to prolong them. "We'll stop in Grey, at the lawyer's," I said to Emma. "I'm no longer going to sell. I'll only rent it out."

We set off. I took the straight road. The rocky walls became lower. Emma prattled.

The automobile purred lightly to begin with. Even so, I wasn't long delayed in regretting having given it so little care. There was a sudden jolt, followed by several others, and its progress was soon no more than a sequence of abrupt spurts, as soon slowed down as projected.

I've already mentioned that the car was the very model of automation, its pedals and handles reduced to a minimum. Such a machine has one inconvenience; it needs to be perfectly in order before setting off, for, once *en route*, one has no more influence on it than that required to accelerate or moderate its regimen, and cannot fortify it by dosage or running repairs.

The prospect of a having to stop made me frown.

Meanwhile, the car continued its jerky progress, and I couldn't help laughing. That manner of advancement reminded me, comically, of the excursions I had taken on foot in company with Klotz-Lerne, and the capricious slowness of my false uncle, always stopping and starting again. Hoping that it was a temporary indisposition of the engine, perhaps due to an excess of oil, I allowed the automobile to go on. I tried to make out, from the noise of the engine, which of its functions was defective and was causing the periodic inequalities in transmission, which became increasingly marked with each deceleration. Some of them were, in fact, so accentuated that we almost came to a momentary halt. My ridiculous comparison became more emphatic, and that amused me. *Just like that rascally professor*, I thought. *That's funny!*

"What's the matter?" asked my beloved. "You don't look very happy."

"Me? Get away!"

Strangely enough, that question had an impact on me. I would have thought that my face was quite calm, but on the contrary! What reason did I have for not being calm? I was annoyed, that's all. I was simply wondering which of the organs of this "great body"—as the professor called it—was suffering, and unable to figure it out, on the point of stopping, I...I was annoyed—yes, that was all there was to it! I listened in vain, with an experienced ear, to the bangs, clicks and stifled knocks; but no characteristic sound revealed a malady of the headlights, the valves or the crank-shafts.

"I'll bet it's the clutch that's slipping!" I cried. "And yet the engine's quite regular..."

"Look, Nicolas!" Emma said then. "Should that thing there be moving?"

"Ah! That's what I said! You see!"

She had pointed to the clutch pedal, which was moving of its own accord, while the machine's somersaults corresponded to its displacements. That was definitely the problem!

While my gaze was fixed on the pedal, it remained fully depressed, then it extended again, abruptly. The pedal had sprung back.

A certain unease was tormenting me. To be sure, there is nothing as annoying as a car that won't go, but even so, I couldn't remember ever having been so strangely affected by a breakdown....

All of sudden, the horn began to sound by itself...

I felt an irresistible need to say something, no matter what; my dumbness redoubled my apprehension.

"It's a general breakdown," I declared, forcing myself to speak in a detached tone. "We won't get there before nightfall, my poor Emma."

"Wouldn't it be better to repair it right away?"

"No, I prefer to continue. When one stops, one never knows when one will be able to get back on the road again. There'll still be time...perhaps it will warm up again..."

But the horn drowned out my voice with a loud clamor—and my fingers suddenly clenched on the steering wheel, for that clamor, having diminished in volume, became an extended continuous note, which became rhythmic as it sang, and took on inflections...and I sensed a tune emerging from that cadence...a march. Perhaps, after all, it was me who was imaging it...but the tune became clearer and, after a few hesitations, like those of a singer testing his voice, the automobile intoned it resolutely in its copper throat.

It went *rum ti tum, ti tum.*

To the accompaniment of the German song, a host of suspicions stirred within my anxiety. I had an intuition of a fantastic and mysterious monstrosity— again! Terror gripped me. I tried to cut off the gas, but the switch resisted; to declutch, but the pedal resisted; to brake, but the lever resisted. A superior force rendered the unmovable. Losing my head, I let go of the steering wheel and tugged at the diabolical brake with both hands, with the same result—except that the horn made a gargling sound and fell silent, after having utter a sort of snigger.

My beloved roared with laughter, and said: "There's a trumpeting clown in there!"

Personally, I had no desire to laugh. The train of my thoughts ran on vertiginously, but my reason refused to sanction my deductions.

Was not that metallic automobile, in which wood, rubber and copper had been proscribed, not a single component of which was made of previously-living matter, *an organized body that had never been alive?* Was not that automatic mechanism a body endowed with reflexes but completely devoid of intelligence? Was it not, in conclusion, according to the theory in the notebook, the sole possible receptacle for a soul in its totality? That receptacle which the professor, without thinking about it, had declared non-existent?

At the instant of his *apparent* death, Klotz-Lerne had doubtless been carrying out an experiment on the car reminiscent of that on the poplar; but, having been distracted for several weeks, perhaps he had made a fatal mistake, not anticipating that his soul would slide into the empty vessel in its entirety and that, once the pedicle was broken, his human form would be no more than a cadaver, which the laws of his discovery would prevent him from re-entering.

Or perhaps, weary of pursuing his ungraspable fortune, Klotz-Lerne had acted deliberately, and committed a sort of suicide by exchanging my uncle's substance for that of a machine.

But why should he not have quite simply wanted to become the new beast predicted in his eccentric lecture: the animal of the future, the lord of creation, which organ-replacement would render immortal and infinitely perfectible, according to his lunatic prophecy?

Once again, however accurate this interior discussion was, I did not want to accept its conclusions. A resemblance of gait between the automobile and the professor, a probable auditory illusion, and the possible sticking of a lever could not be sufficient to prove that enormity. My anguish required a more decisive proof.

It got one without delay.

We were coming to the edge of the forest—that boundary to which the defunct maniac had unremittingly limited his works. I understood that the matter was about to be settled and, on the off chance, I warned Emma.

"Hold on tight," I said. "Lean back!"

In spite of our precautions, the automobile's abrupt halt plunged us forward.

"What's the matter?" said Emma.

"Nothing. Stay calm..."

To be frank, I was undecided. What should I do? To get out might be perilous. On the back of the Klotz-automobile we were, at least, out of its reach, and I did not want to be charged by it. I tried to move it forward. As before, none of the controls would obey my orders. I struggled with every one of them, but the rebellion would not make any concession...

We were in that awkward situation when, unexpectedly, I feel the steering wheel turn in my hands; the levers and pedals were activated, and the automobile, having moved off, made a U-turn and began to take us back in the direction of Fonval. I was lucky enough to be able to turn it round again, by surprise, but as soon as it was pointed in the right direction, it became utterly determined not to go any further, by so much a single rotation of its wheels.

Emma finally realized that something unusual was happening, and urged me to get out, in order to fix the "breakdown".

A few seconds before, however, my fear had been transformed into rage. The horn cackled.

"He who laughs last laughs longest!" I muttered.

"What's the matter, then? What's the matter?" my companion repeated.

Paying her no need, I took a steel rod from the luggage-rack which served me as a defensive weapon and, to Emma's profound amazement, I struck the mulish car with it.

Then the scene became epic! Under the formidable volley of blows, the heavy vehicle behaved like a recalcitrant horse, rearing up, jerking sideways and bucking, it did everything it could to saddle us.

"Hang on!" I cried to my beloved. And I struck harder.

The engine groaned, the horn howled in pain or roared with wrath. The sharp blows rained down on the sheet-metal of the hood, and the racket made the woods echo with a fabulous din.

Suddenly, uttering the trumpeting sound that elephants make, the metallic mastodon bounded forward, made two or three attempts to catapult us out, and then dashed forward with lightning speed—bolting!

I was no longer master of the situation. The madness of a runaway monster was dictating our fortune. We were almost flying; the eighty-horse-power machine fled with the rapidity of a fall; the rushing air was no longer breathable. Sometimes, the siren screamed stridently.

We went through Grey like a lightning-flash. Chickens and dogs beneath the wheels; blood on my goggles. We were going so fast that Maître Pallud's coats-of-arms gave me the impression of a gold streak. At the exit from the village, the highway made a hedge for us with its plane-trees; then the long hill opposed its slope to our celerity. There, giving signs of a fatigue that I noticed in it for the first time, the decelerating automobile allowed itself to be steered.

I had to thrash it frequently to get it to take us as far as Nanthel, which we eventually reached without any hitch. As we passed over a curb, however, the copper mouth uttered an exclamation of pain, and I saw that the jolt had just broken one of the springs in the right front wheel. When we reached the courtyard of the hotel, I tried to fit a new spring to the rim, but did not succeed in doing so; my attempts drew such moans from the horn that I had to abandon the repair. It wasn't urgent, anyway; I had decided to complete the journey by rail and send the recalcitrant machine back on a goods train. The future would decide its fate. For the moment, I confided it to a garage, among the double phaetons, saloons and limousines, and withdrew in haste, knowing that the round eyes of its headlights were glowing behind me with a hostile gaze.

While I reflected on the details of this incredible phenomenon as I drew away, a passage from a scientific article I had once read, and which had made an impact on me, came to mind. I was not a little surprised to find in the words some sort of vague explanation of the prodigy and the promise of further miracles just as disconcerting: "It is possible to imagine that there is an intermediate state between those of living beings and inert matter, just as there are entities intermediate between animals and vegetables."

From the outside, the hotel gave every sign of luxurious comfort. An elevator bore me up and I was taken to my room. My partner had preceded me. Having been cloistered for such a long time, she was gazing at the street, the swarming people and the shops lit up in all their splendor with a sort of avidity. She could not tear herself away from the spectacle of life, and, while changing her clothes, returned incessantly to the window, parting the drawn curtains in order to look out again. I thought she seemed less affable with respect to me, and that the world interested her more than I did. My strange conduct in the automobile must have surprised her, and, as I had decided not to offer her any explanation of it, I suspected that she regarded me as a lunatic, not yet cured of his insanity.

At dinner, at a little private table lit by candelabras whose soft light was that of a boudoir, Emma, surrounded by men in suits and women in low-cut dresses, exhibited a misplaced exuberance. She ogled the former and looked the latter up and down, sometimes admiringly and sometimes contemptuously, expressing loud approval or laughing ostentatiously, a source of amusement and astonishment, ridiculous and delightful. She wanted to chatter away to the entire audience.

I took her away as soon as I could—but her desire to return to worldly life was so ardent that it was necessary for us to go immediately to some public place. Of the theater and the casino, only the latter was open; that evening, it was playing host to the finals of a wrestling championship organized in imitation of those in Paris.

The little hall was crammed with shop-assistants, students and hooligans. A cloud floated within it, a mixture of proletarian and petty bourgeois tobacco-smoke.

Emma displayed herself proudly in her box. A crapulous popular song, played by a shameless orchestra, made her ecstatic, and as her ecstasy was scarcely discreet, three hundred pairs of eyes turned to face her, attracted by the windmill movements of a fan and the feathers of a hat that were beating time just as boldly. Emma smiled, and subjected the three hundred pairs of eyes to a military inspection.

The fights—and especially the fighters—filled her with enthusiasm. Those bestial humans, whose heads—all massive jaws and tiny brows—seemed destined for the guillotine-basket, excited the most unseemly frenzy in my beloved.

A hairy tattooed colossus won the contest. He came forward to make his bow, awkwardly bobbling a myrmidon's head with porcine eyes atop a titanic body in order to do so. He was a local man, and his fellow citizens gave him a standing ovation. The title of "Bastion of Nanthel and Champion of the Ardennes" was bestowed upon him. Emma, standing up, applauded him and cried "Bravo!" so loudly, and with such insistence, that she provoked scandalous laughter in the crowd. The champion blew her a kiss. I felt my face blaze with shame.

We returned to the hotel and exchanged bitter words, precursors of a chaste night—chaste, but restless. Our apartment happened to be above the arched entrance and edit, through which automobiles were passing all through night...which caused me to dream of misfortunes and absurdities.

Awakening brought me real ones. I was alone in the bed.

Bewildered, I tried to interpret my beloved's absence in terms of the most excusable domestic activities, but her place was cold and that disconcerted me. I rang for the bellboy. He arrived, and gave me this letter, which I have kept, and whose lined paper, spattered with smears and ink-blots, I now pin to my blank sheet:

Dear Nicola,

Forgive me for the payn but Must better that we part, I found my first Love, who I fought for with Léoni, Alcide. Hes the hansome man was winner yesterday. I gowith cos I done him wrong. Definate cant quit that life but for enormamous money, like lerne Promise. And then Idve made you unappy And then Idve cheated on you, for you see you only mad me fly twice, first when the bull fetch you one in the neck with its horn in the little wood, And then the time you ran away after, in my room, the Rest was not the same. I wanta realman. Isnt your fault, anI hope it wont cause you payn.

Gooby forever.

Emma Bourdichet[38]

Confronted with a categorical indication on this point, formulated in a language almost as barbarous as that of legal jargon, there was nothing to be done but concede defeat. In any case, were nor the sentiments of which Emma was giving evidence exactly those that had attracted me to her? Had I not loved, above all else, that great thirst for love-making, the cause of her bewitching beauty and the reason for her infidelity?

I had the strength and the wisdom to put off the rest of my reflections until the following day. They would only have drawn me to weakness. I enquired about the first train to Paris, and sent for a mechanic who might take responsibility for driving my eighty horse-power, or, if you prefer, Klotz-automobile. I was soon notified of the man's arrival; we went to the garage together.

The car had disappeared.

As you will imagine, I did not hesitate to link the two defections together and suspect Emma of a secret complicity, but the hotel manager, believing that it was the work of daring thieves, went to the police station. He returned with the news that an automobile bearing the number 234-XY had been found in a sub-

---

[38] Renard inserts a long footnote here, attributed, like his earlier note, to "the transcriber"— the narrative voice of the prologue. "At the first communal reading we made of *Doctor Lerne*, the form, and especially the style, of this note appeared to us to be in flagrant contradiction with Mademoiselle Bourdichet's habitual language. Mediocre as it may be, that language is, in fact, less defective than this style (see chapter VII, where the difference is more obviously manifest). Gilbert immediately called attention to this disparity, claiming that it was superabundant proof of Cardaillac's deception, which—according to him—had not been able to maintain to the end the integrity of his female character. Someone replied that he ought, for the moment, to assume Cardaillac's good faith; in that case, the note constitutes an irrefutable document, a direct emanation of Mademoiselle Bourdichet, while the sentences attributed to her, scattered through the course of the narrative, are only quotations. They come to us, therefore, via the memory of Monsieur Vermont, who, not being a professional writer, reports the spirit rather than the letter. (See how he renders exchanges of insults with more vivacity than the long passage in Chapter VII—which is because he recalls the exchanges more clearly, *because they are brief*.) These remarks are sufficient to shake Gilbert's argument. An experiment that Marlotte made destroys it completely. Having asked a few demi-mondaines to honor him with a love-letter, he was amazed to see that almost all of these young women, whose language is polished by their frequentation of well-educated men, write like serving-maids."

urban side-street, abandoned—according to him—by thieves for lack of oil; the reservoir had run dry.

Of course! I said to myself. *Klotz has tried to run away. He didn't reckon on the exhaustion of the oil, and is now paralyzed!*

I kept the true version of the incident to myself and instructed the mechanic to push the car to the train, without trying to start the engine. "Promise me," I insisted. "It's very important. It's time for my train—I must rush. Go—and above all, don't replace the oil!"

XVI. The Enchanter Dies Conclusively

And now, here I am in this house in the Avenue Victor Hugo, rented for Emma. But I'm alone with my strange memories, since she preferred to sacrifice her intoxicating and lucrative beauty to Monsieur Alcide. Let's not mention that again.

It's the beginning of February. The fire is burning behind me, crackling like a flapping flag. Since my return to Paris, having no work to do and no inclination to read, I've been writing the narrative of my singular adventures every evening and morning on this round table.

Are they finished?

The Klotz-automobile is here, in the coach-house, in a box that I had specially constructed for it. In spite of my instructions, the mechanic from Nanthel replaced the oil, and my new chauffeur and I have had all the difficulty in the world in bringing the human car here, for it has been impossible for us to turn the stopcocks to drain the reservoirs. He began by destroying his replacement, a 20-horse-power machine, the latest model.

What could I do with the accursed Klotz? Sell him, and expose my peers to his malignity? That would be a crime. Destroy him, killing the professor in his final transformation? That would be murder. So I imprisoned him. The box has high walls of oak and the door is securely bolted.

At first, the new beast spent his nights blaring out his dolorous and menacing scales, and the neighbors complained. Then I had the delinquent horn dismantled, in my presence. It was extraordinarily difficult to remove the screws and bolts, and we observed that the apparatus had, so to speak, welded itself to the car. We had to rip it out, which made the entire machine shiver. A sort of yellow liquid, with the odor of gasoline, spurted from the wound and leaked in droplets from the amputated section. I concluded from this that the metal has reorganized itself under the influence of the infused life—hence my fruitless efforts to fit a new spring on to the wheel, that operation now being a sort of animal graft, as impractical as the transplantation of a wooden finger on to a living hand.

Deprived of his oral apparatus, my prisoner nevertheless continued his nocturnal racket for a week, launching himself at the door like a battering ram.

197

Then, abruptly, he fell silent. It's been nearly a month now. I think the gas tank and the oil reservoir are empty. Even so, I've forbidden Louis, my mechanic, to enter the ferocious animal's cage I order to make certain of it.

We're at peace now, but Klotz is still there.

Louis has put an end to the philosophical considerations that were ready to escape from my pen. He's just arrived precipitately, and said me, with his eyes wide: "Monsieur! Monsieur! Come and look at the 80 horse-power!"

I didn't ask him anything else, but went out at top speed.

On the stairway, the servant confessed to me that he had taken it upon himself to open the garage door because a bad smell had been coming from it for some time. Indeed, even the atmosphere in the courtyard was nauseating. Almost admiringly, Lois said: "Tell me whether that's nice, Monsieur!" And he ushered me into the box.

The car presented such a bizarre appearance that I did not recognize it at first.

Sunk in a heap on its softened wheels, it was deformed as if it were a half-melted automobile made of wax. The levers were limp, curved like rubber bars. The shapeless headlights seemed to be deflated and their blue sticky lenses resembled the leucomas on dead eyes. I saw suspicious stains eating into the aluminum, and holes corroded in the iron. The steel, having become porous, was crumbling, and the copper had taken on the spongy consistency of a mushroom. Finally, the majority of its parts were marbled by reddish or greenish leprosies, which were neither rust nor verdigris.

One the ground, the vile compost-heap was surrounded by a disgusting syrupy pool that had gushed out of it, gleaming with a murky iridescence. Strange chemical reactions were causing heavy bubbles to burst from time to time from that putrefying metal flesh and there was an intermittent flatulence gurgling in the mechanism's interior.

Suddenly, falling dully like cow-dung into mud, the steering-wheel collapsed, smashing the chassis and, by reaction, the hood. An unspeakable broth was seething there, and the horrid stench of organic decomposition made me recoil—but I had had the time to observe, in the depths of the shadow, the swarming of grave-worms.

"What lousy workmanship!" declared the mechanic.

I tried to make him believe that jolting sometimes dissociates metal, and can cause such molecular modifications therein. He did not appear to lend much credence to my assertions. In order to understand and accept it, knowing the even more incredible truth, I have been forced to satisfy myself by putting it into precise verbal form internally, in order to affirm and explain things in the same way that a mathematical problem in worked out by means of precise figures.

Klotz is dead. The automobile is dead—and the beautiful theory of an animalized mechanism, immortal by virtue of the replacements of its parts and infinitely perfectible, has died with its author. The gift of life is, at the same time, the gift of death, which is its implacable sequel; and to render inorganic objects organic is to condemn them to a more or less imminent disorganization.

Contrary to my expectation, however, the fantastic creature did not die for lack of gasoline, exsanguinated. No—the tanks were half-full. It is therefore, the soul that has killed it—the human soul, that corrupting soul which so rapidly wears out animal constitutions healthier than our own, and had rapidly reached a reckoning with that pure metallic body.

I've given orders for the disgusting heap of refuse to be thrown away. The sewers will be Klotz's tomb. He's dead! I'm rid of him. He's *irredeemably dead*...finally DEAD! His spirit is with those of the dead.

He can no longer hurt me. Ha ha ha! DEAD! The filthy beast!

I should be happy, but I'm not. Oh, it's not because of Emma! The silly little girl certainly caused me "payn" but that will fade away, and to admit that a grief is consolable is to be consoled already. My unhappiness comes from memories. It's what I've seen and felt that torments me: the madman, Nelly, the operation, the Minotaur, Me-Jupiter, and so many other horrors! I dread eyes that stare at me, and I lower my eyes in the presence of keyholes...that's the source of my misery.

But I'm also fearful of a terrible possibility...

What if it isn't over? What if Klotz's death isn't the end of the story?

I don't care about him, since he no longer exists; even when he comes to torment me wearing Lerne's face or that of a phantom car, I know that it's probably only a dream or a hallucination of my feeble eyes. He's dead, and I repeat that he doesn't worry me at all.

It's the three assistants that worry me. Where are they, and what are they doing? That's the question. They have the Circean formula, and must be making use of it for their own benefit to traffic in personalities. In spite of his defeat, Klotz-Lerne had met several people willing to submit to his surgical witchcraft and barter their souls for someone else's. Every day, the three Germans must be increasing the number of these wretches, desirous of money, youth or health. There are men and women in the world who are, unsuspected by others, not themselves.

I can no longer be sure of anything. Faces seem to me to be masks. Perhaps I should have noticed it before, but there are certain people whose physiognomy reflects a soul opposite to their own. Others, virtuous and honest, offer glimpses of unprecedented vices and unexpected passions, as frightening as prodigies. Do they have the same souls today as they had yesterday?

Sometimes, a strange gleam comes into the eyes of someone to whom I'm talking, an idea that isn't his; he will soon retract it, if he has expressed it, and he'll be the first to be astonished that he was able to think it. I know people whose opinions vary from one day to the next—and that's quite illogical.

Finally, something imperious often invades me, a brutal ascendancy forcing me back within myself, so to speak, enjoining my nerves and persuading my muscles to reprehensible actions or regrettable words for the duration of a slap in the face or a curse.

I know, I know; everyone experiences these thoughtless impulses and always has—*but the reason for them is becoming increasingly obscure and mysterious to me.* Just as they cite calculation, hypocrisy or diplomacy as the causes of custom and etiquette, people cite fever, anger or stupidity as the causes of the sudden revelations whose frequency I have observed among my peers, and which are, they say, only the lack of those greater things, or rebellions against them.

Might not the science of an enchanter be the real instigator?

Evidently, the mental state I'm in is exhausting me, and requires soothing. Now, it's maintained by my obsession with my sinister sojourn in Fonval. That's why, after my return, having clearly understood the necessity of losing the memory of it, I set out to write it all down—not, great gods, with the ambition of writing a book, but in the hope that, one it's on paper, it will be less in my head, and that putting it outside will be sufficient to get rid of it.

That's not the case. Far from it. I have on the contrary, brought it more vividly back to life as I have recounted it, and some mysterious magical compulsion has occasionally obliged me to write a word or a sentence contrary to my intention.

I've failed in my intention. I have to force myself to forget the nightmare, by getting rid of anything, however trifling, that is capable of reminding me of it. Soon, various items will be annihilated. Certain overly intelligent calves might be born in the vicinity of Fonval; Io, Europa and Athor must be bought back and slaughtered. Fonval and all its furniture must be sold. I must live! Live by myself, no matter how ridiculous or stupid a person I might be, but original, independent, uninfluenced and free—oh, free of memories!

These abominations, I swear, are passing through my brain for the last time. I'm only writing that down in order to swear it more solemnly.

And you, felonious manuscript! You, *Doctor Lerne*, which perpetuates beings and facts whose existence I shall henceforth refuse to admit—to the fire with you! To the fire! To the fire! To the fire!

André Couvreur: *An Invasion of Macrobes*

Une Invasion de Macrobes, *here translated as* "An Invasion of Macrobes," *by André Couvreur (1863-1944), was originally published in four parts in November 1909 in the weekly literary supplement of L'Illustration, then reprinted in book form, in a revised version, the following year by Pierre Lafitte.*

"André Couvreur" was born Achille-Émile-Henri Couvreur, but he signed his early literary works, all of which intended for the theater, "A. Chils." By the time his play Le Secret de Polichinelle *was produced in 1893, he had qualified as a physician, receiving his degree in 1892, slightly belatedly, perhaps because he had been pursuing his literary ambitions in parallel with his studies. His doctoral thesis explored the relationship between pulmonary tuberculosis and tubercular tracheobronchial adenopathy. His father and older brother were both doctors, and he had doubtless been encouraged to follow in their footsteps, perhaps a trifle reluctantly, but it must have been obvious by 1892 that medicine offered him better opportunities to make a living than literature, and he doubtless made a firm commitment to make a decent living when he married in 1893. Nevertheless, he never surrendered his literary ambitions, and when his novels began to appear, he was quick to join the Société des Gens de Lettres.*

André Couvreur first introduced the character of Dr. Armand Caresco, a conscienceless surgeon carrying out medical experiments, in Le Mal Nécessaire *[The Necessary Evil] (1899).[39] His most evident literary precursor was Dr. Gael from Louise Michel's* Les Microbes humains *(1886) and* Le Monde nouveau *(1888),[40] who is introduced as a conscienceless researcher casually carrying out experiments in human vivisection and surgical modification, but is ultimately recast as a physical and intellectual superman whose discoveries might enable humankind to take a great evolutionary leap forward after the cataclysm that is scheduled to destroy the corrupt capitalist world order. Caresco also sees himself as an intellectual superman whose discoveries might enable humankind to take a leap forward. This daring book dared to broach such shocking topics as the methodology and occasional necessity of hysterectomies.*

Caresco next appeared in La Graine *[The Seed] (1903),[41] one of the most shocking works of its era, one that attempted more fervently than any other to push back the boundaries of the conventionally-unmentionable, such as contra-*

---

[39] Black Coat Press, ISBN 978-1-61227-253-5.

[40] translated respectively as *The Human Microbes* and *The New World* and available in Black Coat Press editions, ISBNs 978-1-61227-116-3 and 978-1-61227-117-0.

[41] *Human Seed*, Black Coat Press, ISBN 978-1-61227-880-3.

ception, abortion and eugenics, illustrated through the lives of the 18 children of the Grignon family, afflicted by the social disasters of syphilis and alcoholism.

Caresco last appeared in Caresco, Surhomme *[Caresco, Superman] (1904),[42] in which the brilliant mad scientist rules the body-shaped island of Eucrasia whose inhabitants have been transformed by advanced surgical techniques. The natives are addicted to sensual pleasures, subservient to the will of Caresco, whom they call the "Superman," for fear that he will castrate them.*

In 1909, Couvreur embarked on a second series of adventures featuring yet another mad scientist, Professor Tornada. Une Invasion de macrobes *is the nearest thing to a conventional thriller that he ever wrote, and for much of the horrific climax—especially the scenes in the sewer—it is easy to forget the story is actually a comedy; its graphic action is very effective, because rather than in spite of its garishness. Although it is not a thriller or a horror story, the same is true of the second story, in that the author becomes genuinely wrapped up in his thought-experiment, fascination frequently taking precedence over satire.*

Tornada returned in L'Androgyne *[The Androgyne] (1922),[43] in which he turns a man into a woman;* Le Valseur Phosphorescent *[The Phosphorescent Waltzer] (1923),[44] in which he creates a phosphorescent android;* Les Mémoires d'un Immortel *[Memoirs of an Immortal] (1924),[45] which tackles the concept of immortality;* Le Biocole *(1927),[46] in which he achieves a form of immortality through organ replacement and becomes the creator of a utopian enclave called Biocolia; and finally,* Le Cas de la Baronne Sasoitsu *[The Case of Baroness Sasoitsu] (1939),[47] in which the now-reformed mad genius solves a baffling murder by using his psychovisor which translates thoughts into images.*

B.S. & J.-M.L.

I

I shall never forget the evening of May the eleventh. It marked the beginning of an event so extraordinary that our posterity, when it remembers it, will have the right to wonder whether an entire people might not have been carried away by madness at a particular moment of its social history. However, what I

[42] Black Coat Press, ISBN 978-1-61227-254-2.

[43] In *The Exploits of Professor Tornada* (Volume 1), Black Coat Press, ISBN 978-1-61227-279-5.

[44] In *The Exploits of Professor Tornada* (Volume 2), Black Coat Press, ISBN 978-1-61227-280-1.

[45] In *The Exploits of Professor Tornada* (Volume 2), q.v.

[46] In *The Exploits of Professor Tornada* (Volume 3), Black Coat Press, ISBN 978-1-61227-281-8.

[47] In *The Exploits of Professor Tornada* (Volume 3), q.v.

am going to consign to this memoir, I lived through, suffering frightful emotions, and if I was mad, along with everyone else, at least I am sincere in writing.

I was then in charge of a laboratory at the Institut Pasteur, and I had just become engaged to Mademoiselle Suzanne Vernet, the daughter of the celebrated biologist Vernet, a member of the Académie des Sciences. Suzanne was a young woman of the elite, nobly raised by a father who had been widowed for a long time. Her ash-blonde hair would have been sufficient to render her remarkable even if the regularity of her features, the limpid flame of her blue eyes and all the harmonious grace of her person had not added a surplus of beauty that everyone admired. We had adored one another since adolescence—which explains how delightful that initial familiarity was, in which propriety permitted us to hold hands, when she ceased to address me ceremoniously as "Monsieur Gérard" in order to call me Jean, while I responded by calling her Suzanne.

Oh, that exquisite spring evening! I remember that, in order to escape the compliments of the habitués of the house, we had gone into the garden and sat down on a bench. A pale moonlight inundated us; the lilacs, asleep in the warmth, sent us their perfumes; and there was a universal caress. Although the open window allowed us to overhear the conversation of Monsieur Vernet's guests, we were only listening to one another.

There were, however, many interesting people among those who had come to my future father-in-law's weekly gathering: scientists, artists and political men. They included Commandant Junisseau, the pilot of the dirigible *France*; the chemist Serviat, a member of the Institut and the inventor of fracassite, an incomparable explosive; General Gramont of the artillery; Dardant, the editor of the *Parisien*, the great twice-daily paper; Vigueur, the Undersecretary of State for Posts and Telegraphs; and others equally notorious. But what did those celebrities matter, compared with our simple love? Was all of human glory worth as much as one of Suzanne's smiles? Was all that enlightenment as dazzling as her soft gaze—touched, at that moment, one might have thought, by a celestial tint? And what eloquence could match that of our future projects?

I must admit, however, that one name, suddenly pronounced by the others, extracted us from our delicious intimacy. I don't know what frightful presentiment made us prick up our ears when it was pronounced. It even seemed to us that the evocation of Tornada, the individual who was mentioned, threw a malaise equal to ours into the salon, for silence fell abruptly as soon as the chemist Serviat, the inventor of fracassite, resumed speaking, in order to denigrate that man he had just named, violently.

"Tornada—what a strange name![48] Do you know him?" my fiancée asked me then.

---

[48] Slightly strange, indeed, as a name for a scientist (but no more so than Caresco). A *tornada*, in Occitan literature, is a supplementary stanza to a lyric po-

"I do, indeed, know him, my dear Suzanne," I replied. "This Tornada is a scientist who is as eccentric as he is rich: an unorthodox worker whose research, toward whatever branch of science he directs it, has always been marked by a hint of genius. He has occupied himself successively with telepathy, the problems of unknown forces, biology, astronomy and everything connected with the occult. Notably, we owe to him the discovery of a certain microbe living in alkaline environments, which he named *Micrococcus aspirator*—a discovery denied by Monsieur Serviat, who is speaking at present. But what has put his name in lights most of all is a paper on 'The Abnormal Development of Organisms Favored by Culture Media,' which generated a lot of discussion in the scientific world, and even in the newspapers when he presented it at the Académie des Science."

"Abnormal Development?" queried Suzanne.

"That language is incomprehensible for you, isn't it? What it means is that, according to Tornada, one can transform certain organisms, such as microbes, causing them to grow to extraordinary dimensions, simply by placing them in conditions of life and nutrition appropriate to their development..."

"Making giants with microbes?"

"I don't think that's Tornada's ambition," I replied, smiling, "but he seems to be promising that. In any case, the paper made the learned assembly to which it was submitted sit up. It was considered as the work of a maniac who had yielded himself to a Darwinist fantasy—and it's precisely because of the kind of anxiety provoked by his very special intelligence that Tornada was denied a seat at the Académie when he offered himself as a candidate last year. Since then, he's disappeared, swearing that he'll have his revenge."

"Yes, I remember now," Suzanne said. "Papa was very sorry about his failure. Unlike Monsieur Serviat, he appreciates Tornada's inventive genius, and he had supported his candidature..."

We would have liked to get back to our amorous conversation, but the suggestion of the individual haunted us, and we went back into the drawing room to listen to the discussion that had sprung up on his account. His bad temper was being assessed there without indulgence. Monsieur Vernet was the only one to defend him, and to protest against the jesting calumnies suggesting, on the part of some, that he has succumbed to an attack of furious madness and, on the part of others, that he had gone to China to stir up racial hatred.

Suddenly, however, the voice of Commandant Junisseau rose up: "Permit me, Messieurs, to tell you what has become of Tornada."

---

em, which sometimes served in the days of the troubadours as a kind of "punchline," sometimes as an explanatory footnote or dedication, and sometimes, especially in Italian Renaissance adaptations—perhaps most significantly, in the present context—as a fresh voice commenting on the substance of the lyric.

He was surrounded, and in absolute silence, he continued: "Do you know the forest of Rosny, near Mantes? There exists therein, not far from the Seine, a region little known to holiday-makers. No road takes automobiles there, and an entire estate, hidden in the trees, attached to the Château de Chambure, is invisible—one might even say inaccessible. It's there that, three days ago, passing over it in my dirigible, I was surprised to see a large building, occupying about ten thousand square meters, about a hundred meters high, which had risen up as if by enchantment. Extremely intrigued, I landed, and made a tour on foot of a kind of hangar. I observed that it was closed everywhere, except for one place where there was an enormous iron door. I then sought information from the local peasants, and bit by bit—for the people seemed to be afraid of saying too much—I got it out of them that the edifice had been constructed in secret by an individual whose description fits that of Professor Tornada."

"Is it plausible that such an edifice can sprout from the ground without the press finding out about it?" protested Monsieur Dardant, the editor of the *Parisien*, shrugging his shoulders skeptically.

"My dear Monsieur, that's precisely what renders the thing interesting—that you haven't even suspected it. It's high time that you put the dirigible at the service of your reporters. Know, then, what I heard from a reliable source. The materials of the gigantic hall were ordered from abroad: the iron from America, the cement from Holland, the bricks from England, the wood from Norway—even the workmen, who were introduced in gangs, weren't French. Having arrived by steamer, they went home the same way, without making contact with the indigenes, of whose language they were, in any case, completely ignorant. The proximity of the railways and the Seine facilitated these transportations."

"It's very improbable...." someone else objected.

"What is even more improbable," Junisseau went on, turning toward his interlocutor, "is that unknown machines comparable to laboratory apparatus—giant laboratory apparatus, for Titans—have been brought piece by piece and assembled in place as soon as the construction was finished. Commentaries, naturally, have taken wing; the rumor has gone around that Tornada has installed a distillery; and the locals—who are, I repeat, terrorized—haven't been able to learn any more, for the massive door, functioning by means of a electrical mechanism, is always closed to their curiosity."

"But Tornada isn't living in his hangar on his own?" queried Monsieur Serviat, again.

"So it's believed."

"It's a fairy tale!" the chemist scoffed.

His irony was aborted by the sound of voices. What did it all mean? Was Tornada completely mad, or an utter genius? Was he attempting his promised vengeance? Monsieur Vernet recalled, in order to excuse him, that it was after having lost his wife and daughter—both of whom he adored—in a single night that the inventor had shown the first signs of strangeness.

And it was while a few instances of that strangeness were being cited that that a manservant opened the drawing room door and announced: "Monsieur le Professeur Tornada!"

II

There was a stir. One might have thought that the bizarre name fell upon the room like the announcement of a catastrophe. Instinctively, obedient to a protective impulse, I moved closer to my fiancée.

The sight of the newcomer was, in any case, conducive to some malaise. He was a short, simian man, of whom one only noticed at first the black beard, so thick that it hung down in two carefully-combed sections all the way to his legs. By contrast, the head was almost completely bald, and the polished cranium permitted observation of the abnormal conformation of the head, which one might have thought kneaded by the Devil, undulating with excessive bumps that must have lodged a particular intelligence. The rest of the physiognomy, when one took inventory of it, did not attenuate in the least the surprise provoked by those first impressions. The ears stuck out like the appendages of a wolf, twitching at the slightest sonorities. The exceedingly dark eyes, very small and mobile, filled with flashes at times, and retreated behind the eyelids at others. Finally, numerous tics, some more singular than others, continually shook the head, the arms and the legs, testifying to incessant convulsions beneath that Hoffmannesque exterior.

Nevertheless, my future father-in-law welcomed Tornada deferentially. He introduced him, not without malice, to the influential individuals present who had just been heaping their criticism on his inventive genius. The little man accompanied each handshake he gave with a snigger. When it was Monsieur Serviat's turn, he turned away with a manifest disgust and immediately came toward Suzanne and me.

I was surprised then by the transformation that had overtaken him. His nervous phenomena seemed suddenly to have calmed down. He gazed with an undisguised and thoroughly paternal admiration at my fiancée's lovely face. He took us to one side and complimented us with a softness of voice all the more surprising because we might have expected to hear nothing other than inarticulate sounds issuing from such a scarcely human face.

He questioned us about the tenderness of our idyll, and seemed very sensitive to it. He confided to us, wiping away a tear, that his daughter would also have been of an age to get married, if destiny had not snatched her away. Then, to dissipate that sadness, he offered Suzanne a book of verses that he had composed for her—and I recall that my fiancée, seduced by the gesture, requested silence, and read a few agreeably-turned lines, which drew applause addressed as much to the reader as to the poet.

That incident had effaced the bitterness and malevolence of the words that had preceded the professor's arrival. Tea was served, and he accepted it, like everyone else, with a good grace, while elegantly stroking his beard. He even made a few witty remarks. And the rest of the soirée would have gone by normally, in an inattention salutary for everyone, had it not be for the fact that, exactly at midnight, at the first stroke of the clock, Tornada began to show signs of anxiety.

He grimaced several times; his legs launched kicks into empty space; his hands described a very particular gesticulation, which I compared to the ameboid movements of certain animalcules. One sensed that a crisis was brewing. Although the conversations continued with an apparent indifference, the attention of the entire salon was nevertheless fixed on him.

Finally, at the last stroke of midnight, he uttered a more resounding snigger, bounded on to a sofa, and declared: "Messieurs, it's exactly a year since I was rejected by the Académie. Illustrious, jealous individuals—you were one of them, Serviat—considered my paper on 'The Abnormal Development of Organisms Favored by Culture Media' as the work of a poorly equilibrated mind. Come on, look at me—do I look like a madman?"

His tics had returned, more frightfully. Taking pity on him, fearing an attack that might cause him to fall down, I made a movement as if to catch him in my arms, but the particularly alarming expression of his eyes at that moment stopped me.

He went on: "No, I'm not mad! I'm merely a misunderstood and insulted genius. And I'll have my revenge, my good friends! I'll savor a terrible revenge! Look! It's beginning at this moment. In an hour's time, I'll open the door, and they'll go forth, they'll go forth! On your way, my lovely macrobes! On your way! Feast! There's flesh! There's blood! Flesh, and blood!"

He was shouting. Dolorously amazed, we were already thinking about putting him in a straitjacket—but he calmed down somewhat, in order to address himself to a few of us for whom he seemed to have a particular hatred.

"You, Commandant Junisseau, heave been spying on me: prepare your dirigible for flight! You, Dardant, your paper has ridiculed me; do you think you can laugh much longer? It's my turn now! In a week's time you'll no longer have a single one of those readers whose minds you've perverted. You, Duverdon the banker, you've supported my competitors with your influence: quickly, close your counters, for you'll have no clients...and in any case, the Bourse will be destroyed! You, Minister Vigueur, no more posts, no more telegraphs! You, Serviat, ha ha! you... prepare tons of fracassite! My children are going to eat you, Serviat On your way! On your way! They're going forth! They're going forth! On your way, my lovely macrobes!"

Everyone around him had fallen silent, shivering with an instinctive fear, resulting not from the incomprehensible threats that the orator was uttering but from the malady that had afflicted him to such an extent. Monsieur Vernet tried to calm him down. He helped him to get down from the sofa and drew him gently toward the door.

In any case, Tornada had suddenly calmed down again, and I was not far from thinking that he was trying to attenuate, by a reasonable attitude, the amazement and alarm that he had read on my fiancée's face. As he went out he beckoned to us, and we followed him into the antechamber, drawn as if by a magnetism.

There he put his hands together to make a plea.

"My children, and you, Vernet, are the only ones I want to spare, so listen to my advice and follow it. I'm lucid, and I'm fonder of you than you can believe. Listen to me. Within a week, Paris will be devastated. There won't be a single Frenchman left alive in a fortnight's time. Flee! Flee! Arrange your affairs swiftly, and leave by the first steamer. Flee tomorrow! The day after, it will be too late!"

"My good friend, would you like me to take you home?" Monsieur Vernet proposed.

"He thinks I'm mad too!" Tornada lamented. "Oh, if I didn't love you" Look, you know me, right? Reread my book. You know that my *Micrococcus aspirator* lives in alkaline environments, and that my culture media enable it to develop abnormally. So, then, what do you think, eh? If, all of a sudden...ha ha!"

He became furiously exited again, brandishing his umbrella. "In an hour they go forth! Flesh screams! Blood flows! Everything crumbles! Flee!"

He slipped away, without our being able to make a move to stop him and care for him. He plunged into the dim light of the boulevard. We went to the door and saw him go to an automobile without a chauffeur, into which he bounded, and drove off furiously.

We went back to the drawing room, dolorously impressed. People there were laughing, without any commiseration for that brain afflicted with disequilibrium. Monsieur Serviat declared that a madhouse would collect him before much longer. Then we finished taking tea, talking about the threat of a railway strike that was causing Undersecretary Vigueur far more anxiety than Tornada's predictions.

III

As soon as the soirée was over I went home. My apartment was in the Chaussée de la Muette, in the delightful quarter of Paris bordering the Bois de Boulogne. I plunged into my sheets, but although I was very tired, I could not go to sleep at first. A nagging thought was running through my head, which one word dropped into Tornada's rambling summarized in its entirety.

What was the meaning of the term "macrobe," which he had pronounced several times? Not that I had any trouble establishing its etymology. *Macrobe* was obviously the term opposite to *microbe*, signifying very large, in the same way that the latter term signifies very small. It wasn't necessary to be much of a Hellenist to deduce that. But how big had those animals been able to grow, assuming that the scientist really had developed them abnormally? Would they have a destructive effect as phenomenal as his sinister prophecy indicted?

No! It would become slightly unhinged oneself even to dream of it. And I strove to drive away that stupid anxiety. As it did not cease to recur, I thought about my fiancée, and then about my automobile, which I had just changed in order to buy a more powerful one. My imagination placed Suzanne in the vehicle by my side, while Monsieur Vernet was in the back seat, and I finally departed for a delightful excursion that occupied my entire slumber.

The next morning, I woke up feeling very spry. It required the perception of my newspaper to remind me of the incidents of the previous day. I opened it unhurriedly, without even searching for some sensational headline. Anyway, the rag contained nothing new, except that the railway strike was still threatening. I got dressed and had breakfast cheerfully, and went out under a radiant sky in order to go to the Institut Pasteur on foot.

I felt less enthusiasm than usual to devote myself to my customary tasks that day. Those who love the atmosphere of a laboratory know the veritable satisfaction one experiences in going into rooms bathed with light, putting on the long white smock that is like a uniform for pupils and their masters alike, and sitting down amid the greetings of comrades at the glass-topped table garnished with the hundred various utensils whose precious mechanism and ingenious complication aids bacteriological research. In truth, I felt that I was a very small and very modest cog in the vast factory of health to which the great Pasteur gave the initial impetus, but it seemed that the scientist's memory encouraged my efforts, and that his glorious past was prolonged in my humble labor.

That day, as I said, I took longer than usual to make the journey. I would gladly have let myself idle. The weather was so conducive to dreaming, and nature was putting such seduction into everything! The young leaves on the trees had never been as green, the air was calm, as fluid as the celestial spaces. Everything was vibrant with the joy of spring, and the Seine, which I crossed by the Pont de la Concorde, deliberately extending my route in order to savor the terrestrial beauty more fully, was nothing but a vast crucible in which a thousand diamonds were glittering, given birth by a breeze that was adorable to breathe.

My hopes as a fiancé came into unison with the tenderness scattered over the city; I saw myself a few months older—our marriage was arranged for the middle of August—holding Suzanne in my arms, walking beside the river, initiating her into the marvels of the great liquid way, renewed at every hour of the day, adopting, in accordance with the influence of the light—mist, sunshine, darkness, even rain and storms—such diverse and ever-seductive appearances. The quays silent or animated; the water peaceful with the slumber of boats, or noisy with the bustle of barges, the smoky and whistling passage of steamboats;

the bridges crowded of deserted; the reflections of grave monuments or the pure profiles of domes, towers, belfries—yes, the whole river was a poem that I would read with Suzanne, and no power in the world, save for death, would be able to prevent me from traveling it with her.

But I perceived that I was late. I hailed a cab; and, rapidly transported to the Institut Pasteur, I went through the door and reached my laboratory.

As I went in I was surprised to find a highly unusual animation there. Twenty students were surrounding one of my colleagues, who was leaning over a microscope, listening to him pronounce words whose meaning I could not grasp, but to which bursts of laughter replied. I advanced toward them. It was only then that the name of Tornada, which was stimulating their gaiety, reached my ears and reminded me, with a disagreeable—even painful—sentiment, of the previous evening's scene, to which I had not given another thought, so much had my thought built me an ivory tower inaccessible to the actions of others.

"Here's Gérard!" exclaimed my colleague, perceiving me. "You've arrived just in time, my dear friend, to give us your opinion. Put your eye to this microscope..."

I did as I was asked; taking his place, I interrogated the field of the apparatus, which was extremely powerful. I saw there, moving between the two transparent slivers of the preparation, several animalcules of a form that was unknown to me. Magnified a thousand times, they presented a swollen central section with seeming extremities, one a tail and one a head, the latter rather elongated and endowed with a few vibratile movements. The ensemble was, moreover, rather confused, for one can imagine how tiny an animal is that has to be magnified to that extent for one to begin to make it out.

"Do you recognize that dirty beast?" joked my colleague, addressing himself to me.

"No."

"What might it be?" he asked, again.

I consulted the objective again.

"I don't know."

"Well, no, my dear chap; it's the famous *Micrococcus aspirator* of alkaline environments described by Tornada, which we're trying to fatten up by means of his method. I believe, in truth, that we've only succeeded in making it thinner..."

At the tone of his response, and the laughter that broke out around me, I thought he was trying to trick me, by presenting me with one of those microorganisms that abound in nature but that science has not yet classified. Although my research was not orientated in that direction, I did not want, even so, to appear ignorant, and I joined in with the gaiety. However, a sharp interior disturbance contradicted the amusement on my lips, and it was further accentuated when my knowledgeable comrade went on, more seriously: "Yes, that wretched little beast has remained inexorable to all our attempts; we've cared for it and pampered it for months on end, rigorously following Tornada's method—but nothing; it gives its belly the cold shoulder; our cooking isn't to its taste, and I firmly believe that Tornada's paper is nothing but a joke in rather poor taste."

He turned to the students. "Messieurs let's not waste any more of our time on this joke; let's go on to other exercises. If I ever see Tornada again, I'll ask him whether he's making fun of the Institut Pasteur. To work, Messieurs!

A few further ludicrous reflections by the pupils saluted the definitive burial of that research. One offered the straight-faced suggestion that the scientist ought to be trepanned in order to discover the microbes that were inspiring such delirium in his brain. Another proposed extracting therefrom a serum usable in the treatment of madness, although wisdom was also a very tedious malady. A third, finally, regretted the failure of the experiment, because it would have been amusing and lucrative to exhibit the *Micrococcus aspirator* in a menagerie.

"Shutting Tornada in with it dressing him as an animal-tamer, eh? What receipts!"

A new order from my colleague extinguished the juvenile jokes pitilessly, however. Soon, there was nothing to be heard in the room but the discreet noises of a laborious anthill.

For my part, the failure of the scientist's method, and the buffooneries that had been its consequence, had dissipated the malaise and the puerile presentiment that had oppressed me briefly. I started to smile at the vague dread to which the threats of the madman and Commandant Junisseau's revelations concerning the giant laboratory had given a kind of logical consistency.

I resumed my ordinary occupations serenely, and at six o'clock in the evening, satisfied with my day, I escaped from the Institut, like a bird drunk on liberty, in order to go to Monsieur Vernet's house the Boulevard de Sebastopol, where I was to dine.

I was scarcely in the street when I heard a special edition being advertized. I approached the crier, and was able to read in the huge characters of the headline news that stupefied me:

A scientific phenomenon! Public danger! Appearance of giant man-eating animals near Mantes!

I could scarcely believe my ears. I bought the paper and discovered, in no time, quite simply what the newsvendor had just been howling. The paper gave no further details, and the few lines that related the circumstance would have passed unnoticed if the headline had not printed them in such large letters.

I must confess that a little frisson ran through me at first, but the idea occurred to me at the same time that Dardant, the editor of the *Parisien*, had heard Tornada's declaration, and that he was occasionally wont to print "hoaxes"—a hoax excusable on this occasion, to deflect attention from worries about the impending strike. Those reflections reassured me.

I took the Metro, and became even more confident when, having reached the great boulevards, I observed that my opinion was shared by the public. On the sidewalks, on the terraces of the cafés, everywhere, people were reading the newspaper and welcoming the dispatch with bursts of laughter and shrugs.

I bought a bouquet, and it was with a light heart that I crossed my future father-in-law's threshold. I kissed my fiancée's hand and gave her my flowers, and we sat down at the dining-table. That family meal, with its admirable intimacy, distanced me so completely from the external world that it was only at dessert that I thought of unfolding the *Parisien* to show her the news.

It produced the same effect on Suzanne as it had had on me. It seemed to her to be an amusing invention, significant of Dardant's prodigious mercantile talent. But as Monsieur Vernet remained pensive, I was surprised, and asked him what he was thinking.

"Who can tell?" he replied. "Perhaps Tornada isn't completely mad. His paper has merit..."

"So you believe, Monsieur Vernet...?"

"I don't believe anything, my friend; I don't know anything. But..."

He concluded his thought with a vague gesture, which was not very reassuring. As Suzanne was becoming anxious, I said: "Doesn't your friend Marceline Colais live in Mantes? Couldn't she tell us something? Would you care to telephone her?"

"Right away! Right away!" Suzanne approved.

The apparatus was brought to the table, and I obtained a connection easily. My fiancée took one earpiece while I put the other to my own ear. An anxious attention attached us to the apparatus. Suzanne spoke,

"Hello! It's Suzanne Vernet who's telephoning. What's this that the newspapers are saying about anthropophagic animals in your region?"

A burst of laughter replied to us. The young woman did not know anything, had not heard anything, and made fun of our credulity. Just as she said goodbye, however, Suzanne and I went pale. We had heard, quite clearly, a very singular sound coming from the earpiece. It resembled the whistle of a siren, which was followed by a noise similar to that produced by a collapsing house—all dominated by a scream of terror, the sound of a woman panicking.

We were stunned. What drama was unfolding out there, on the other end of the wire?

"My God! What can have happened?" asked Suzanne, shivering.

Then, after a pause that we employed in looking at one another interrogatively, she continued: "My friend's scream...that racket... it's all inconceivable... don't you think so?"

"Try to restore the connection," said Monsieur Vernet.

I tried to interrogate the apparatus again, in vain. Three times, in a nervous voice, I begged for the connection to be restored, but the operator told us that it was impossible to obtain one. A fourth appeal met with the same response.

That episode had bowled us over. We strove, however, to find a reassuring interpretation. We criticized the incompetence of the switchboards and the improbable noises that were heard crackling on the line even in times when they were functioning normally. In truth, out explanations were only designed to make us feel better. The dinner was concluded without enthusiasm, and Suzanne and I bid one another goodnight, with the emotion of lovers whose tenderness is threatened by an evil destiny.

"If ever something happens," she confided to me in a whisper, "come here quickly to find me..."

I promised her that. Once outside, I wanted to clarify the matter. In the splendid nocturnal weather, a trip to Mantes in my forty horsepower Motobloc was a simple excursion. I would therefore go to Mantes. I turned into the boulevard, heading for the Metro that ought to take me to the Chaussée de la Muette. The great artery immediately filled me with anxiety. At a distance, I heard ominous noises, and I saw an agitated crowd swelling. When I arrived at the location of the tumult, however, I found that it was only a demonstration by strikers.

It passed by, and life became normal again at that spot. The theater audiences were spilling out during the intermissions; the display windows of the cafés were ablaze. Some displays imposed their luxury in an orgy of electricity. Open air phonographs and cinematographs in windows gathered spectators. Nothing had changed. It was nocturnal Paris, the elegant good humor of which was not even eroded by the strike.

I went home. I dressed for the road and went to the garage next door to my apartment. My chauffeur, his day's work completed, had gone. At first, I hesitated to undertake the excursion on my own, but, incapable of resisting my curiosity, I switched on two powerful headlights, took my place in the driving-seat, and sped away in my machine, which was soon beyond the toll-booths.

The Bois and the hill to Suresnes were traversed in no time. My powerful and docile vehicle, which had recently been delivered to me by the famous manufacturer Page, carried me along with a magnificent surge, and I listened delightedly to the palpitations of its mechanical heart, as calm and regular going up the hills as coming down them. I passed through the pretty towns on my route— which form an almost uninterrupted border of gracious houses all the way to Saint-Germain—like a whirlwind. After going through Saint-Germain I perceived that I had unwittingly taken the road to Poissy. I was in the middle of deserted woodland, framed by two walls of trees split overhead by a palpitating sky.

No one who has not undertaken such nocturnal escapades can imagine the emotions and the fantastic suggestions imposed by the landscape—to which my obsession gave a particular force. I required all that preoccupation not to get carried away and to retain a measure of composure, and the full glare of my headlights not to mistake for extraordinary animals the foliage that I went past on my route, and the air stirred up by the speed of my passage for their breath. The moon was hidden; I could only see the obstacles revealed by my headlights, and when I had gone past them I thought I was leaving behind an immensity populated by phantoms.

I arrived in Poissy at about half past eleven. I was very glad, after traversing a few silent streets, to come into the middle of a party. A musical competition was keeping the town awake; multicolored illuminations were running along the façades; the main square was animated by an open air ball; and a brass band, playing on a stage covered with garlands, was guiding the gesticulations of uniforms and bright dresses. The sight of that enthusiasm and gaiety made me appreciate the puerility of my fears. Would these people be amusing themselves in that fashion if danger threatened them? Could they be unaware of it?

I stopped my auto in front of a tavern, in order to draw off some moral rearmament more than to warm myself up with a cup of coffee, and I hesitated briefly as to whether to continue my journey. However, as I had promise myself to dissipate my nightmare completely, I got back into the driving seat and stepped on the accelerator again, making a detour in order to rejoin the direct road from Saint-Germain to Mantes.

Now, let me collect my impressions, because the next hour became stupefying, and it was at that moment that I entered veritably into the drama. I remember perfectly that I had completely forgotten the macrobes, and that I had no other thought than savoring the charm of nocturnal tourism, when I arrived within six kilometers of Mantes. My first anxiety was in observing that there were no lights indicating the location of the town—a sign that led me at first to think that I had missed my way.

Surprised to have gone astray on a road that I knew very well, I had stopped to consult my map when a strange echo, coming from a few kilometers away, interrupted my research. It was the roar of a siren, but a very particular roar, deeper in the middle and more highly pitched at the end than the sound produced by the warning devices fashionable to indicate the approach of automobiles. The clamor reminded me exactly of the one I had heard over the telephone. A short silence followed, more frightening than the din, which held me in suspense. Then a second blast burst forth, soon followed by a third, then a fourth, then five and then ten, twenty, in an enormous, frightful concert.

No, there could not be as many automobiles as that. And a terrible suspicion took possession of my mind again. Shivering, I turned my machine round, dimmed my headlights, and climbed up on my seat, directing my eyes toward the enigma of the obscurity. I waited, ready to flee.

I did not have to wait long. My senses, their acuity multiplied tenfold by an anxious curiosity, soon enabled me to perceive that an extraordinary phenomenon was occurring in the vicinity. The roaring had ceased, but it was replaced by sounds that I had great difficulty at first comparing to sounds that I knew. I heard: *Frott...! Frott...! Frott...! Frott..! Frott...!* as if immense iron brooms were being swept over stone. Yes, it resembled gigantic sweeps of a broom clearing the distant ground—and it was getting nearer, without any obvious great rapidity.

Frott…! Frott..! Frott…! the air repeated.

What was happening out there? What hallucinatory horde was raking the terrestrial crust like that? What monstrosities were approaching?

To interrogate the mystery, I knelt down on the seat of my vehicle, and, with my hand clutching the back, I looked in bewilderment in the direction of the town whose lights were extinct.

I had not discovered anything there when my eyes, adapting slightly better to the gloom, distinguished some three kilometers away, surging from a place where I knew there was a dip in the terrain, a confused phosphorescent form, moving unevenly off the road, sometimes to the right and sometimes to the left.

It was impossible for me to estimate the dimensions of the moving object at that distance, but it was certainly very large. In sum I could only compare the visual impression to the one that a green mist would have given me, seen from a long way off, at the moment when it emerged from the ground in order to displace itself by performing zigzags.

In the limpid firmament, the stars stood out without losing any of their brightness—which proved to me that the radiation of the mass as not very vivid. The glimmer sank into a dip in the terrain, then reappeared, closer and more extended, accompanied by several others, whose number gradually increased until I counted a dozen of them. Finally, the entire horizon was occupied by those phosphorescent presences, and the rumble that they allowed to be heard, heavier and more sonorous, soon demonstrated to me that I was dealing with colossal solid displacements.

To describe my terror is an impossible task. The most elementary prudence would have advised me to flee, but an invincible need to know attached me to the unreal spectacle. The creatures drew nearer. The more distinct they came, the more convinced I was that a kind of gigantic arm emerging from them was accomplishing circular gyratory movement, reminiscent of those described by an elephant's trunk, very rapidly.

They were still a good kilometer away, and yet I thought that I could already perceive their breath—unless it was an improbable displacement of air provoked by the rotations of their appendages. And I stayed there, paralyzed and stupid, entirely focused on their luminous progress, only retaining the vaguest consciousness of the fact that they were now approaching with greater rapidity.

Yes, I was still there, hypnotized, when suddenly the sky was filled with the fall of an immense green bolide, which came to land fifty meters away from me, to my right, while I was deafened by the roar of a siren, and a violent blast of air nearly tore me out of my seat.

Then, finally obedient to terror, conscious that I had just escaped death, but that death was still threatening me, I turned round, stamped on the accelerator of my Motobloc and, clinging to my steering-wheel, sped away frantically.

How did I not crash twenty times during that flight at a hundred kilometers an hour? How, with the feeble glare of my dimmed headlights, was I able to avoid ditches and avoid running off the road at bends? It was a pure miracle. Fortunately, French roads are admirable. My whole machine was quivering, creaking and lurching. One might have thought that my panic had infected it.

I went through several silent villages. I remember slowing down, as I passed a belated peasant, and shouting at him: "Run! The macrobes are coming!" But he looked at me uncomprehendingly. He must have thought I was mad. Had I not thought Tornada was mad myself? And I resumed my flight. The road seemed to sink behind me, becoming a gulf as soon as I had passed over it.

Before arriving at the forest of Saint-Germain, however, I was ashamed of my cowardice and wanted to make amends with a little humanity. Confident in the advance I had over the fantastic animals, I took the turning toward Poissy again, in order to raise the alarm. Oh, what a fatal inspiration! It must have been half past one when I got there; the nocturnal fête was coming to an end, the dances were languishing, the illuminations going out. Recognizing a gendarme in the middle of the crowd I asked him to take me to the Maire.

I shall never forget the indignation of that honest municipal officer when, disturbed in his legitimate slumber, he appeared at his window still half-asleep, wearing a red headscarf.

"What do you want?" he growled.

"I need to talk to you urgently, Monsieur le Maire," I replied. "It's a very serious matter. The life of our fatherland might depend on it."

"Have you put our hand on a spy?"

"No, Monsieur le Maire, it's much more serious, much more serious..."

I divined that he was hesitant, but the presence of the gendarme undoubtedly reassured him, for he closed his window in order to open his door to me soon thereafter, holding a candle-tray in his hand. I followed him into a banal drawing room, and the only memory I have of it that that a Japanese tapestry hanging on one wall immediately attracted my curiosity. It represented a warrior with bristling moustaches aiming his spear at a fantastic animal, the silhouette of which, by an apposite freak of chance, adopted the form of a *Micrococcus aspirator* to which a thick furry pelt had been added. In the state of preoccupation that I was in, that coincidence frightened me, and I spent the entire beginning of my visit—all the time that the Maire took to light an oil lamp—hypnotizing myself with that exotic work of art, not without noticing that my attitude was making the good bourgeois anxious, for he stopped several times to look at me from the corner of his eyes.

"I'm listening," he said, finally, offering me a chair protected by a dust-cover, while he sat down on a sofa, hiding his bare legs under the flaps of a vast dressing-gown.

"Monsieur," I began, forcing myself to speak calmly, "I regret to disturb you at this undue hour, but the peril is at your gates; the macrobes are coming, and as they might invade your town at any moment..."

"The macrobes?"

No, you cannot imagine the physiognomy that the honorable representative of the citizens of Poissy adopted at that moment. I do not know any actor, the funniest of all the buffoons of out theatrical stages, or the most tragic tragedian among the great stars of drama, who could have imprinted his features with such a mixture of bewilderment, stupor and terror. Yes, terror—not of the danger that I had just related to him, but of me. That is, moreover, understandable. I was trembling like an alcoholic; my hair retained the disorder of my flight in the auto, and my eyes were hallucinated by the Japanese tapestry. I must have looked as if I had just emerged from a straitjacket.

"Let's see!" he said, getting up and prudently putting the table between us. "What are macrobes?"

"They're giant animals, Monsieur le Maire, quite similar to the one your tapestry represents---there, you see, on the wall..."

"And where are these animals?"

"Halfway along the road from Mantes to Poissy."

"You've seen them?"

"Just now. I was in my car...my car...I had to turn round. You do believe me, Monsieur le Maire?"

"Certainly, my good friend!"

"And you'll warn your fellow citizens, advise them to flee?"

"Certainly—right away..."

How did I not guess that the stupid old man was not planning at that moment a means of immobilizing me? He took a few more steps around the table, still to get away from me—for in my ardor to convince him I had attempted to get closer to him. Then, suddenly, he bounded outside, saying: "Wait here, I'll warn them...I'll be back!"

And he disappeared, turning the key in the lock on the door. Stupefied, I remained patient for a moment; then, finally understanding my interlocutor's intentions, I became indignant, shaking the door violently. The sound of footfalls responded to my anger. The door opened again; three gendarmes grabbed hold of me, and would not let me go.

A grave individual with long hair, his expression clouded by sleep, was accompanying them. He examined me, looked at my pupils, took my pulse, listened momentarily to the arbitrary vociferations that the arbitrary violence was causing me to utter, and then, taking a few steps back, he held a discussion with the Maire. I could hear what they were saying.

"Yes, yes, he's very excited. A fit, probably, perhaps *delirium tremens*..."

"What shall we do, my dear Doctor?" the Maire asked, anxiously.

"Put him in a safe place! We can't let him go...he might be capable..."

"Where, in a safe place? We don't have a hospital."

"I can only think of the prison."

"Obviously."

"Obviously."

"You'll make your report tomorrow, won't you?" the Maire concluded. "You'll not that we were obliged to lock him up because he's a danger to public safety?" Turning toward me, he added: "Poor fellow."

His testimony of pity did not pacify me. On the contrary, I covered the municipal officer and the physician with the most violent imprecations, which increased their certainty that I was quite mad. The gendarmes shook their heads dolorously. I tried to escape their grip, in vain. The more I struggled, the tighter the vice of their fingers became. I had to confess myself defeated, and allow myself to be tied up with a cord whose knots dug into my flesh. Finally, I was lifted up on to the shoulders of a gendarme in order to be carried to a cell.

The prison was next door to the Maire's house, so we only had a short street to cross. My guardians opened a massive door, dragged me along a corridor and threw me into a square redoubt reeking of ordure and brightly enough lit by a gas-lamp for me to make out a drunkard snoring on the straw.

"Isn't it dangerous to leave them together?" asked the Maire.

"Have no fear," said one of the gendarmes, "given that we've tied him up like a chicken for the oven."

"As for the other, he's out for the count; he'll sleep until tomorrow," added a second uniform.

"And then again, if one of them kills the other, it'll be no great loss to society," the doctor philosophized.

"In that case, my friend, let's go to bed," the ministerial officer concluded, serenely.

The lock grated, my despots' footsteps drew away, and I was left alone with the drunkard.

All these incidents might seem amusingly picturesque to those who are reading them, but I can assure you that I retain an exceedingly melancholy memory of them. During the first few minutes in which I found myself claustrated in that infamous company, my anger dissipated to give way to an anxiety, of which Suzanne and her father, as you can imagine, were the sole objects. I anticipated that I would be locked in that cell for at least a day, the time for a medical investigation to repair the gross error of the Poissy practitioner. What would happen during those twenty-four hours of detention? What formidable events, the menace of which was sweeping the ground out there, in the direction of Mantes—events inaccessible to human will—might prevent me from rejoining my pure fiancée and my venerable friend.

I reflected, fearfully. All the incredible things that I had seen on that sinister evening returned to stand out with irrefutable clarity on the screen of my memory.

Obviously, the mystery still subsisted, with its frightful horror, but there was no doubt that I had been close to those phosphorescent monstrosities; that they were solid bodies of incalculable dimensions; that their whistling, like the noise of a siren, signified an enormous displacement of air; that their progress was accomplished without great rapidity.

One sole point left me hesitant, with regard to that last remark, which was that one roaring mass, the one that had determined my flight at the moment when I perceived the others, had seemed to me to fall from the sky, as if a trampoline had projected it to land beside me. I had then had the deafening sound of its fall in my ears; I remembered having felt the earth vacillate. Did not that fact permit the conclusion that the fantastic animals were, at certain moments, capable of speed, of progressing by means of prodigious bounds?

But those few seconds had gone by in such confusion, and a legitimate terror had attenuated the veritable impression to such an extent, that on reflection, I no longer dared affirm that fall, and that the apparition might, instead of descending from on high, have surged forth from below, when a caprice of the terrain had hid it from me. No, I no longer knew. In my uncertainty, I preferred to rally to the latter hypothesis, inasmuch as my need for personal tranquility also concerned the two dear distant beings, Suzanne and her father, whom my absence tomorrow was bound to torment.

My absence? Why could I not find myself close to them? Why could I not demand of my ingenuity, and my muscular strength, the means of escaping, of getting back to them? My eyes made a tour of the cell; I sounded the thickness of the walls that isolated me from the rest of humankind.

No chance of escape that way; Hercules himself could not have shaken the imposing resistance of the massive stones; a pick-ax, which I did not possess, would have taken days to bite into them.

As for the narrow window that I observed above my head, its orifice was defended by iron bars so voluminous and so solid that I could not even think of separating them—and in any case, the rope that bound me from head to foot was reminding me dolorously of my impotence.

No, before thinking about getting through the door, the only issue that I recognized as possible, it was first necessary for me to get rid of my bonds, and they were laboring my flesh violently enough for me to recognize that there was nothing for me to do but bow to fatality and await the implacable unfurling of events.

I lay my head on the straw that served me as a bed, and a long shiver of distress, as might be caused by the fall into an abyss, ran through me.

"Want summat?" growled a quavering voice, at that moment, beside me.

It was my drunkard. He had just woken up, and after having propped himself up on his elbow, he was looking at me with a blissful smile. He was clad in a dirty, threadbare chestnut-colored costume, some cast-off from a well-to-do wardrobe. His graying hair sent dusty wisps in all directions. His wild and un-kempt beard was varnished, under the chin, by a trickle of drool.

"Y'thirsty?" he asked, again.

I turned my head away, sickened. Was I, on top of everything else, to be subjected to the amiability of that repulsive individual?

He seemed, in fact, to be full of the most fraternal intentions toward me. He was still smiling. He belched. Then, interpreting my silence in favor of his sentiments, he tried to move closer to me. He got up, fell back on the straw, and attempted a new thrust, which brought him on to all fours—after which, holding on to a ring sealed into the wall, he succeeded in standing up. Tottering, with his hands in his pocket like a satisfied landowner, he came over to me, studied me for a moment, rejoiced noisily in the inferiority that retained me tied up at his feet, then hiccupped: "Yer a bugeois, no? Not on the social? Me, I am. But so what? All brudders. Ever'thin' aff t'turn upside-down for us all t'be equil. Eh? Get it, m'dear—no mo' bosses...no mo' workus...equility f'r all! And feet for'ard! Eh? What'yer say?"

Oh, that ignoble language, which might perhaps have moved me to pity on any other occasion, but which took on I don't know what prophetic significance that night! Evidently, if the nightmare that I had lived near Mantes for intense minutes were ever realized, if I were not dreaming, if I were not mad, all the democratic ambition of my drunkard, the great social leveling that was the ob-session of the humble, was about to be accomplished before long, as the normal conclusion of a biological adventure. Evidently, from one moment to the next, the classes might no longer exist, wealth no longer differentiating people, and parallelism would be established under the threat of a common danger. Would they be effective, then, the theories that I had heard emerging from other mouths than those of libertarians, when sociologists had predicted in my presence that science would accomplish the egalitarian work rejected by charity? Alas, could I imagine that the hour might offer itself so precociously, in circumstances so dramatic, under the influence of a laboratory discovery?

And once again, I was brought back to thinking about Tornada by the di-vagations of my cellmate.

I decided, however, that I ought to be obedient to circumstances, and per-haps make use of my occasional philosopher. I turned my gaze toward him. He was pitiful, repulsive and terrible. In the gaslight that struck his face, the expres-sion of his physiognomy was suddenly modified. His smile was transformed into a rictus; he passed from affection to hatred. His beard bristled, his eyes filled with an evil gleam. I understood that I had become the focal point of a long ran-cor.

"Bastard!" he howled, raising his fist. "No mo' bugeois! Absint' for ev'ry cit'zen, f'rever!" Drawing closer to me, he added: "Say: death t'cops!"

And when I remained obstinately silent, he repeated the order: "Gwan, say death t'cops!"

I would certainly have granted him that exclamation in order to have peace. I even began to pronounce it, when my complaisance froze on my lips. The drunkard, obedient to his interior rage, had just taken out a knife, and was leaning toward me. I confess that I felt a rather disagreeable frisson pass through me.

"Y'don'wanter? Well, I'm gwant'bleed yer."

He made the gesture. I saw the flash of the blade heading toward my immobility.

But the knife, fortunately misdirected by the alcoholic, missed its target and lodged instead in the gap between my torso and my arm, while the effort projected my would-be murderer on to the ground, from which he tried in vain to get up again. Fearful, nevertheless, of a further attempt, using the only means of avoidance permissible to me, I rolled over and over for several meters—and at that moment I had the particularly intoxicating impression of being liberated from my bonds.

It had in fact, been the case that, while my adversary's weapon had not succeeded in stabbing me, it had severed the rope that wound around me, in such a fashion that, by a blessed hazard, instead of annihilating me, his action had freed me.

I conceived such gratitude for the drunk that my first sentiment, once I was untied, was to put my hand to my fob-pocket, in order to recompense him generously for his failed crime—but I did not have to carry out the intention; the drunkard had fallen asleep where he was, arching his lips into a new smile, as if the soul of justice were translated on his face.

From then on, my escape plan was easy to conceive and carry out. At daybreak, when one of the gendarmes came to check on the condition of his two prisoners, I pounced on him and, planting my head in his chest, sent him flying into the corridor. I stepped over the representative of order, without taking pity on his groans, and found myself running in the open air.

A few peasants arriving for the market saw me pass by with amazement. Needless to say, they put down their baskets in order to pursue me, for the mentality of the crowd is so formulated that any man running without a reason immediately inspires the idea that he is a criminal, but I had a sufficient start on them to give myself the infantile satisfaction of breaking a few windows in the mayor's house; after which I leapt into my Motobloc—which, fortunately, was still parked under his windows—and took the road to Paris without worrying any further about sparing such stupidly-governed citizens from the disaster.

Amazingly, the great city was waking up in absolute calm. In the Chaussée de la Muette, the shops were opening as usual, the little people were setting off for their customary work. I parked my auto at the sidewalk, ran to buy the newspapers, and observed with surprise that they had no information. Even the *Parisien* had fallen silent about the event and had retracted the news that it had published the day before, attributing it to the work of a practical joker. On the other hand, it devoted a great deal of space to the railway strike, and I learned thus that the Nord, the Est and the Orléans had suspended their departures for lack of staff.

"The work of a practical joker!" I sniggered, crumpling the newspaper

Those words immediately dilated before me with a sinister amplitude. I could not leave them with the banal significance that the reporter had wanted to give them, and they provoked a new bitterness within me. A practical joke was, indeed, about to be played on the nation, but what a joke, concluding with what consequences!

The silhouette of the man who had planned it sprang forth again in my memory. I saw him again, coming into my future father-in-law's drawing room, devoting himself during the early part of the evening to placid conversation, welcoming the homage of those who venerated his science, shunning his detractors, offering my fiancée, in the form of poetry, the adornment of a mind that was able to detach itself from the arid problems of biology, and also seemed to be accessible to charm, tenderness, pity and dolor—and suddenly, at the moment when the clock had announced the opening of another day, rising up like a horrible prophet, declaiming to a elite with an incoherence of language, a dementia of gestures, at which, alas, I could to longer be content to smile pityingly.

Yes, it was a joke: a horrible joke.

I could not free my memory from it. I gazed with dazed eyes at the unfortunate traders who had no suspicion of the menace, and who would soon become its victims. The street, whose picturesque bustle ordinary offered me so much attraction at that hour, when the great city placidly prepares for its daily work, filled me this time with an unprecedented dolorous melancholy.

While I generally held the effort of those laborious shopkeepers in high esteem, deeming a social benefit their promptitude in rising early, running to the Les Halles, making their purchases and coming back just as rapidly to display their wares, organize their deliveries, decorate their windows and satisfy the needs of their clientele; while I admired their tenacious economy, their savings acquired sou by sou, which, converted into shares and bonds, constituted the fortune and strength of our nation relative to foreign nations; while they confirmed the impression in me that the fate of a people is subordinate to the work of the humble, and that the initiative from below takes precedence over everything that radiates from above—that morning, by contrast, their tranquil energy exasperated me. Were they not about to be the turkeys of that formidable practical joke, tomorrow, or perhaps today?

Veritably, their gait seemed to me to have taken on something turkey-like: they were heavy and flat, waddling like poultry—and if they had been warned, they would certainly have started uttering the incredulous clucking of a poultry-yard!

I remained on the pavement momentarily, in that disconcerting contemplation. An open bakery dispatched the flavorsome aroma of fresh warm loaves in my direction. I breathed it in without allowing myself to be tempted. I soon saw a shopgirl come out, her hair tousled, her expression still clouded by sleep, holding a piece of paper in her hands, wrapped around a few croissants just out of the oven. She was graceful; she characterized in her modest garments the elegance particular to young Parisiennes. Simply by the way she tucked up her skirt, she testified to the artistic character of her race.

She considered my appearance with astonishment—my animal skin and the dirt on my face. Before stepping off the sidewalk to cross the road she paused beside my auto and examined the bodywork with a knowing expression, approving of it with a nod of the head. One last glance that she darted at me seemed to demand a place in the vehicle, evocative of open spaces, rapid travel beneath the blue sky, through landscapes caressed by the sun. The she drew away, hurrying to work.

Little shopgirl, if you had known the terror that reigned within me, would you have implored me with that tacit prayer?

I consulted my watch. It was not yet seven o'clock. A sentiment of reserve, incomprehensible in the circumstances, a dread of disturbing my friends so early, advised me to put off for a little while the moment when I would arrive to throw fear into their peaceful intimacy. I sat outside a café and ordered a glass of milk, which I forgot to drink.

Weary of the earth, of everything that moved upon it and everything that was in preparation for it, I looked up momentarily at the sky. What a contrast! Up there, everything expanded in a delightful fluidity. A blaze of dawn light flowed from the adorably blue infinity over the rooftops, bringing out against a golden background the jutting balconies of a recently-constructed tall building, proud of its novelty among others more ancient. Would that order still subsist tomorrow? Would that architectural décor, terminating a centuries-of esthetic tradition, edified by the genius of a people, be standing much longer? Would it not crumble, collapse and fall apart, like Messina in its recent convulsion,[49] under the brutal effect of monsters?

But no; that was implausible, and I had to smile at my dread. And I focused, as the objective of my illusions and my hopes, on a little curly cloud drifting in the celestial softness. Its tranquility comforted me. I could not imagine disaster surging from such placid harmony, beneath such a reassuring firmament.

I swallowed my glass of milk; I called the waiter to settle up with a ten franc piece, and while waiting for him to bring me my change I picked up my newspaper again in order to confirm my quietude—for it seemed implausible to me that a calamity as redoubtable as the one whose advent I dreaded could be unsuspected in its columns.

---

[49] The city of Messina, in Sicily, was almost completely destroyed by an earthquake on 28 December 1908.

Again, my search was in vain; all the reportage, from the masthead to the stop press, was taken up by calculating the effects of the rail strike. And I became indignant that the Nord, the East and the Orléans had suspended their traffic for lack of personnel.

"It's truly a fine time for those animals to go on strike!" I could not help saying to the waiter, who came back carrying a saucer containing coins.

He looked me up and down. I judged him to be a rude and frustrated citizen, one of those people who judge the enemy by the cut of his waistcoat and would make a meal of a well-dressed man. God knows, however, what my costume looked like! But my auto was there, testifying to my wealth and the privilege of my class.

The waiter cleaned the marble table-top with swipe of a dish-cloth and riposted: "Isn't it always the moment? Demands have no time limit. The longer the proletariat waits, the more they'll suffer. Why shouldn't they profit from the occasion, citizen?"

"What occasion, my friend?"

I expected a response that related to my inner anguish.

"Well, the occasion..."

"Again, what?"

"You want me to spell it out? You know very well."

"I don't know anything," I insisted.

"Citizen Bitard, secretary of the C.G.T. has been arrested," he declared.[50]

"Oh, my friend, he's not the one that it's necessary to arrest!"

He expressed his surprise with a violent swipe of his dish-cloth. "Who, then?"

"It's them."

"Them?"

"Yes, them... the others... out there!"

I remember his disdainful, indignant expression, and the manner in which he expressed his opinion of how I had spent the night, simulating the gesture of drinking to imply that I was drunk. I neglected to make him revise his sentiment, for I got up abruptly and abandoned the table, forgetting to pick up my change.

The railway strike suddenly appeared to me as a further complication aggravating the probable situation. The social catastrophe, even if it did not spread to other lines, would immobilize and paralyze an entire city just at the moment when an exodus might become necessary. What would become of those people without a means of flight at the time when it was necessary to flee? What an untimely obstacle, due to the imbecilic pressure of a few troublemakers!

I felt the need to get back to my fiancée as soon as possible. Having climbed back into my vehicle I took the quickest and least encumbered route to

---

[50] La Confédération Générale du Travail was—and still is—one of the principal trade unions in France.

reach the Boulevard de Sebastopol—but I had reckoned without the vicissitudes that still awaited me.

Thinking that the streets would be deserted at that early hour I was going along the Seine, intending, once I reached the Châtelet, to make a turn that would bring me directly to the house of my future father-in-law, when, having reached the level of the Quai d'Orsay railway station, I ran into a violent crowd that the police were having difficulty containing. I don't know how many thousands of hotheads were there, inflamed by anger and alcohol, thundering imprecations and raising arms at the ends of which cudgels where twirling, while, in the distance, a black mass disposed in six ranks—a cohort of the central brigades—were waiting to be given orders by a short Prefect of Police surrounded by a general staff of peace officers and conferring with them.

My car had reached the outer eddies of that crowd, and, perched in my seat, I contemplated the spectacle with all the more passion because I wanted to find therein a confirmation of my secret dread, to believe that I was facing a people conscious of the danger that threatened them and preparing the resistance. But I soon had to abandon that idea when I had interrogated by a gamin who, having climbed up on to a street-light, was encouraging the demonstration with his acidulated clamors. Just as he was about to reply to me, I saw him suddenly go pale, direct his arm westwards and shout: "There they are! There they are!"

I turned round, expecting giant apparitions, but I only perceived a sparkle of helmets dominating the stature of war-horses. It was the dragoons, summoned to bar the strikers' route as they were preparing the cross the Seine and sack the Quai d'Orsay station. Their mass, projecting the flashes of weapons, soon stopped behind me, an opaque and menacing animal barrier, toward which the central brigades, suddenly going into action, began to drive the demonstrators, herding them with a reckless savagery—with the result that I was trapped between the two parties, cursing the fury of both, watching, with the sole desire to escape as quickly as possible from the pitiless impacts of whirling sabers and cudgels, the cries of the wounded, the falling bodies and the splashes of blood that thrusts directed at heads and faces caused to spring forth.

Soon, a frantic revolutionary brandishing a stick at the end of which hung a red handkerchief leapt on to my car to rally his companions, and I became the center of the battle. Fortunately, the agents could only succeed in making roads into the first ranks of the crowd; an armor composed of ten human tampons protected me from their ranks. My mudguard and headlights gave way under the pressure, I heard their splintering mingled with the vociferations, and I was already fearing for the more precious mechanisms of my engine when, before a more desperate charge by the strikers, the police yielded, broke ranks and retreated. I took advantage of it to back up slowly, heading toward the dragoons, who were charging in their turn, and who, when they reached me, divided their ranks in order to let me through.

From then on, I was uninterested in the outcome of the collision. I scarcely noticed it when a fanatic with the face of a boar grabbed a horse by the nostrils and unsaddled the rider, who was trampled by other horses, and when a peace officer of giant stature, shaking off a cluster of hooligans intent on destroying him, was cut down by a saber-thrust that a maladroit dragoon had intended for one of his adversaries. I had only one urgency: to escape as quickly as possible and get back to my fiancée; and after having turned the vehicle round, I was about to depart, leaving those stupid energies at odds when a female voice emerging from a group of spectators planted on the sidewalk called to me: "Monsieur Gérard! Monsieur Gérard!"

Your name, shouted from the middle of a crowd—especially a crowd subject to such a delirium—is always somewhat impressive. I turned round.

"You, Madame Danielli!" I exclaimed.

I had just recognized a celebrated pythoness. Madame Danielli hosted a famous salon simultaneously frequented by naïve spiritists, skeptical scientists and a few artists and satirical writers. One could not, however, resist her elegant youthfulness and her tragic mask, afflicted by numerous successes of second sight. Combining cleverness and distinction with her remarkable gifts of mediumship, she was welcomed in the best society, and fished for her clients in the troubled open waters of worldly credulity. She announced everyone's destiny after reading the lines on their hands, and, it was said, the fate of peoples did not escape her when she consulted the reflection of the stars by night in the transparency of a lake she owned in Italy. She adapted to her prophecies the phenomena and the instrumentation of recent discoveries in science; radium was in her domain; she applied it by some unknown method to the materialization of the perispirit and the astral body.[51] In sum, she offered a curious complication of good faith and trickery that I had detected on the two evenings when I had allowed myself to be dragged to her house by one of my friends, a professor in the Faculté de Médecine.

"You here, Madame?" I repeated.

"Do you blame me for having got up early to come and observe an event that I had predicted a long time ago?"

She was triumphant; her physiognomy did not reveal any compassion for the outrages that were being perpetrated before her eyes. On the contrary; her teeth were dazzling in a radiant smile, all the more so because a flattering approval, emitted by the snobs surrounding her, was supporting her victory.

---

[51] "Perispirit" was a term frequently employed French spiritism, having been invented by its most influential pioneer, Allen Kardec. It refers to a hypothetical "fluid body": a subtle substance improvised by a spirit in order to connect with the sensory perceptions of observers. Basically a refinement of the idea of a ghost, it has some kinship with the Theosophist notion of an "astral body," which was a later invention than Kardec's and was more widely popularized.

"Ah! You predicted it!"

The most suspicious intelligences pass through phases of credulity. It is at moments of sentimental crisis, when nerves tensed for too long leave you in a kind of psychic inferiority. You then become prey to a confidence for which you will criticize yourself in calmer moments; you allow yourself to submit to puerile investigations of your self—and history reports such weakness among great captains and the most notorious political schemers. Suddenly, that was my case.

"Is this the only event you predicted for the present epoch?" I asked her, awaiting her response with such an expression of interest that she understood immediately that I was about to fall under her influence.

"No."

Then, taking a further step, I said: "Can you tell me something I know, which perhaps I'm the only person to know, which will be manifest today or tomorrow?"

"Certainly," she affirmed, with conviction.

"I'm listening."

With a gesture, she asked her entourage to move aside. She seemed to isolate herself from the external world. Her features dressed themselves with mystical suffering. Her gaze widened, became hallucinated, and penetrated mine. It also seemed to me that my brain received some kind of fluid discharge sent by hers, and I shivered.

"What I have to tell you," she murmured, her lips almost joined, leaning her suddenly-stiffened silhouette toward me, "is that it's necessary for you to get out of Paris as soon as possible, taking those who are dear to you with you."

"Why?"

"A peril is in preparation for you....it's coming...it's getting closer..."

"What?"

"An incredible event...yes, truly incredible..."

"Once again, what?"

She hesitated. Her throat appealed for air as if a hand were blocking its entrance. I noticed that the veins of her neck were distended, tracing blue lines beneath the nacre of her skin. Her eyebrows coming together, her forehead furrowed, she continued: "What? I can't tell you, exactly. It's a phenomenon so unfamiliar, so strange..."

"I want to know," I insisted.

"Well, I see large arms reminiscent of elephants' trunks...but are they really arms? Can arms terminate in shocks of long hair divided in two? I can see them, though; they're agitating...they're agitating in front of a green terrain...but a green that isn't that of nature...one might rather take it for a green fog...and I can see little animals...yes, tiny, very tiny...as tiny microbes running over a sofa...in a drawing room where a young woman is smiling..."

"Go on! Go on!" I begged, observing that her nervous exaltation seemed to be coming to an end.

.

227

I did not obtain anything more. Suddenly, she went pale, and her eyes wandered. She tottered, and her companions only just had time to leap forward to catch her in their arms. That was the way that her divinatory crises usually concluded.

I did not stay to care for her. Subject to the suggestion of her prediction, in which I detected, among the incoherence of its imagery, a confused fraction of truth, I fled; I spend toward the Boulevard de Sebastopol, going via the Place de la Concorde and the main roads.

I have often reflected since then about the curious oracle of the young py-thoness. I do not believe in occultism or any supernatural manifestation, but it is certain that an order of divinatory phenomena exists, which science is already attempting to explain, and of which it will succeed one day or another in unraveling the threads of the mystery.

With regard to my own case, I believe I can confirm that Madame Dan-ielli—who, it will be noted, told me nothing that I did not already know—had extracted the elements of her prediction from me. How? Simply by reading the thoughts that my disorientated mind had delivered to her as easily as a book re-counts an individual's sentiments. Endowed with a particularly sensitive nervous system, the perspicacity of which is not attenuated by the location or the circumstances, she penetrated my soul, received its impressions by means of the same mechanism by which wireless telegraphy puts two distant poles in communication; she only repeated back to me what she had discovered within me.

That conviction is also inspired in me by the disjointed and baroque fashion in which she translated the images which, at that emotional moment, were vibrant within my skull. When she embellished the microbes' trunks with "shocks of long hair divided in two" it's probable that I was thinking at that moment about the characteristic shape of Tornada's beard, and that the seeress only glimpsed that particularity, which she grafted on to the appendices of the giant animals. In the same way, the green terrains and green fog that she had mentioned were a confusion of two impressions I had retained from my nocturnal excursion, one resulting from the monsters' phosphorescence, the other from the extent of the ground over which they were moving. And the same explanation appeared to me to attach to the final phrase of her discourse, for the "tiny microbes running over a sofa in a drawing room where a young woman is smiling" doubtless derived from the memory I hastily invoked, while she was reading me, of the original soirée of the drama, when my fiancée and I had discussed Tornada's scientific pretensions and the madman had announced their realization by bounding on to a sofa in the middle of my future father-in-law's drawing room.

In order to make the matter even more comprehensible, I will say that my mind, at the moment when the pythoness was documented it, was similar to a disordered cinematograph, turning at such a speed, and so incoherently, that the

228

person reading its impressions could only transmit them in the form of blurred visions superimposed on one another.

At any rate, what the young woman had said had troubled me strangely. I added it to all the supernatural aspects of that frightful adventure, and began to feel an indescribable distress. It seemed to me that my reason was tottering on the brink of an abyss, and I began to wonder seriously whether the diagnosis of the physician who had had me locked up in the prison at Poissy as a madman might not offer some appearance of logic after all. The sentiment that persisted from that descent into doubt was fear, an atrocious fear, which made my hand tremble on the steering-wheel of my auto, distilling a cold sweat on my temples.

I passed furiously through the Place de la Concorde, the Rue de la Paix and the great boulevards. At the corner of the Boulevard Sebastopol I scraped another automobile; it was a miracle that I did not reduce my vehicle to smithereens. I greeted the accusations and insults of the people who witnessed the collision with a snigger; I passed on, and finally arrived at my friends' house.

I found Monsieur Vernet and my adorable fiancée there, well rested by a good night's sleep, finishing their breakfast. What a sovereign peace there was in that interior, where those two elite individuals lived! What comfort and consolation there was in that familial vision! Succeeding the anxieties that I had just traversed, and preceding a drama whose horror I could foresee, I knew the price of the gentle intimacy of that hearth. I went into it with the wonderment of a disaster-victim escaping from devouring flames or engulfing waters.

The table was set in the dining room; a clean tablecloth with red stripes forming rectangles, covered the tabletop; the white bowls and metal receptacles exhaled the flavorsome odor of milky coffee; crusty bread-rolls rounded their backs in the vicinity of delicate butter; the silverware gleamed placidly. Around the meal there was a restful ambience: a Provençal dresser dormant beneath its centenarian patina, supporting red-tinted copper pans; a bread-basket like a cage with lustrous bars; the antique clock, with the regular tick-tock of its swinging pendulum; the preciously polychromatic plates decorating the walls; the modernized chandelier still opposing its candles to the electric switch; and the deep, shaggy, soft Orient carpet, into which the feet sank, easing the difficulty of walking, making you forget that elsewhere, it was necessary to crush in order to advance in life...

There, in that limpid décor, my friends were inaugurating their day. Suzanne had tied back her hair in a hasty torsade; a mauve peignoir liberally espoused her harmonious figure; she was imparting the confidences of her young heart to her father with a happy loquacity: the impressions of a fiancée's happiness, which the night had cradled and appeared in the morning fresher and even more radiant.

Monsieur Vernet, already dressed in order to give his lecture, attenuating by the gentleness and bounty of his venerable face the austerity offered by his costume of frock-coat and black cravat, was listening, with his elbows on the

229

table, reflecting in the adoration of his eyes the charm to which he was subject. Oh, how far they were from the implausible peril with which I was about to poison their conversation, when I irrupted into the dining room, and threw myself, utterly exhausted by fatigue and emotion, on to a chair that Suzanne offered me.

I stammered my odyssey; I recounted my frightful night, my adventure in the darkness, my peril in confrontation with the phosphorescent monsters; and the tragic voice of the sirens, and the fall of the green bolide, which must have been a monster's leap; and my return amid the abysm of the roads, and my sojourn in prison.

I glimpsed an anxious interrogation in their eyes; I understood that they too were beginning to doubt my mental condition.

"Come on, my boy, are you quite certain of what you're saying?" Monsieur Vernet asked, to begin with.

"Unless I've gone mad," I objected.

"Oh no, it isn't that, thank God, that I'm supposing...but you might, while accomplishing the journey that you've described to us, have been influenced by a suggestion from the previous evening. The mysterious troubles the bravest, and the imagination is exasperated under the influence of fatigue. It's a physiological phenomenon noted by science, and it has been observed that dreams are thus transported into reality. Come on, think hard: ask yourself whether you were not asleep in the seat of your car when you stopped before Mantes?"

"It's possible...it sometimes happens, in sleep..." Suzanne added, trying to soften the impact.

When I sketched a negative gesture, Monsieur Vernet continued.

"I remember that during the war of 1870, one night when I was posted as an advance sentinel, I went to sleep under the exhaustion of overwork. In my mind, haunted by the invasion, a suggestion was then produced in which I mingled the enemy—who, however, were not occupying the département in which we were camped. I saw an entire Prussian army pass by in the moonlight, and imagined that it was accomplishing a flanking movement with the intention of surrounding us and crushing us.

"I only experienced that dream for about five minutes, during which I remained upright, with my back against a tree, but when I woke up, the impression of it was so clear, so persistent, so absolute that I confused my orders with my imagination and fired a rifle shot to warn my companions of the danger; after which I flew to the advance posts, where I recounted with the greatest sincerity—as you have just done, my friend—what my mind had created during my brief slumber. The regiment moved off, ready to do battle, but it was observed the following morning that no Prussians were there—any more, I hope than monsters were there last night, in the vicinity of Mantes."

"No!" I exclaimed. "I swear to you that I have not been the victim of a hallucination of that kind! I had full mastery of my brain when I saw what I've reported to you."

I resumed my story; I put so much effort into convincing them, brought forth so many plausible details, so many precise memories, and supported them with scientific reflections establishing so clearly the integrity of my faculties, that they finally allowed themselves to be infected by my anguish.

We discussed the consequences of the event at length. They did not seem to me to be as frightful as I had been led at first to imagine them.

"In the twentieth century, damn it, it would be very surprising if people couldn't defend themselves against animals!" asserted Monsieur Vernet, raising his head with a challenging expression.

"Evidently, we have cannons whose force of projection is incalculable," agreed my fiancée.

"We have explosives that can blast through the walls of fortresses and the steel of armor-plate," Monsieur Vernet insisted.

"We have toxins, we have all the treasures of chemistry!" I enthused, adding another dimension of possibility to the measures of destruction.

"The government will take action!" the scientist affirmed.

"Has it even been alerted?" I said, doubtfully.

"It seems implausible to me that it hasn't, my friend."

And, deciding the employment of my morning, which I had intended to spend waiting with my fiancée, the worthy man gave me his advice: "Go to the Ministry of Posts. See Vigueur on my behalf; demand the truth, which he might perhaps be hiding from the public, and get him to tell you exactly how grave the danger is. We'll decide what to do thereafter."

"But what if it's too late?" I objected.

Nevertheless, I did as the scientist said.

My driving costume, which I had not had time to change, caused the ushers some disquiet; I had a great deal of difficulty getting as far as the minister. Fortunately, a cabinet attaché recognized me under my animal-skin and had the doors opened for me.

I was had only just arrived in the minister's office, and had begun to tell him about my adventure, to which he was listening with the pitying indulgence that the language of lunatics provokes, when a communication from the telegraph office informed us that after Mantes, communication by wire with Le Havre had been cut off.

"There must have been a storm," said the minister, with absurd confidence.

"No, Monsieur, it's the macrobes."

He looked at me with even more pity. This time, however, I was convinced. I no longer had the right to doubt my reason. Was not the interruption of telegrams a further proof that had just been added to all those I had accumulated during my mysterious nocturnal encounter?

I left the minister, searching feverishly for a means of escaping the terrible approach. It seemed to me to be utterly imprudent to await events and to depend on human resistance. Was it not a legitimate egotism that commanded me, first of all, to ensure the retreat of my future family, and my own?

Spurred on by the memory of what Tornada had said—"Flee! Flee without losing a minute! Flee tomorrow!"—and regretting that we had already lost one day, it was under the lash of a whip that I returned to my fiancée's home.

Suzanne was alone, Monsieur Vernet having thought that he ought not to miss his lecture at the Collège de France. I had never seen the dear child so tenderly emotional, and simultaneously so resolute in the face of the decision to be made.

"Listen, my dear Jean," she said, "I don't know what these macrobes are, or what real danger they pose, but my heart—and you know very well what renders it vigilant—advises me that we should leave. At the rate at which you tell me they're advancing, they probably won't reach Paris for two days. We still have time, therefore. Would you like us to leave together, tomorrow?"

"This evening, Suzanne, this evening!"

"Well, all right then, this evening! It will be our anticipated honeymoon voyage, and I'll easily convince Papa to leave..."

She smiled, adorably sad. Confident in her good sense, I asked her: "In what direction shall we go, my dear Suzanne?"

"Southwards, eastwards or northwards, since the west is occupied by the enemy."

"Alas, Suzanne the railways to the north and east are on strike."

"The P.L.M., then," she said, trenchantly. "We'll meet at seven o'clock in the buffet at the Gare de Lyon, shall we? We'll take the nine o'clock express to Marseilles."

I accepted enthusiastically. If she had been taking me toward Mantes I would still have followed her. Each of her words was a command, which I accepted while blessing her.

IV

Immediately after leaving Suzanne, I went in haste to the garage in which I had put my car a short while before. I wanted to be ready for any eventuality, and I had a notion that my auto might be useful.

The garage was not far from my apartment, and I had hired a compartment therein reserved for my exclusive use. Do I have any need to say that Jules, my chauffeur, was one of those ingenious and shady Parisians, of whom automobilism has cultivated so many? But he adored his car, and made it a point of honor to look after it in such a way that it was always ready to take to the road. Every morning he cleaned it and checked the engine, and as the task was generally finished before ten o'clock, I hoped to be able to count on my machine that day.

It was a great disappointment to me when I found my mechanic still hard at work. Clad in a blue smock, his arms bare and his face stained with grease, he had taken off the dashboard and was striving to repair one of the components. As soon as he saw me he raised his arms in the air.

"There you are!" he proclaimed. "I don't know what Monsieur was doing with his auto last night, and I don't know where Monsieur went, but Monsieur must surely have run into a few ditches. All the bolts are loose, the float isn't working..." He pointed at the rear of the vehicle: "And Monsieur had broken a spring!"

I was on the point of telling him about my nocturnal excursion and the extraordinary surprise that had motivated my flight at a hundred kilometers an hour, without headlights, along dark roads, to the point that he would be surprised that my machine had not been completely demolished, but an instinctive prudence, compounded out of egotism and lack of confidence in my servant's discretion arrested the confidence on my lips. Anyway, was I sure of what I had been about to tell him? Had I not undergone a fantastic adventure of which I was still in doubt myself?

My story would only have aroused the incredulity and laughter of the workers surrounding me. Everyone is aware of the camaraderie, the kind of freemasonry, that unites the workers of the sport, and my revelations would not have taken long to be passed around, covering me with ridicule. I had too much to repent of my loquaciousness in Poissy; that first experiment had been too fertile in disappointment, and I was still aching from it. So I preferred to keep silent, while resolving to take Jules with me.

"How long will the repairs take?" I asked.

"They'll require a good two or three hours, Monsieur; and that's not counting the spring, which will probably take me all afternoon. Strictly speaking, though, that can wait until tomorrow, if Monsieur isn't taking passengers."

"But I'm taking Monsieur and Mademoiselle Vernet, Jules, and we're leaving for a long journey?"

"Monsieur can't put it off?"

"That's impossible."

Desperately, I turned my anxiety toward the other mechanics, nodding my head in their direction. "Will they help you? I'll pay what's necessary."

"Monsieur can see that they're all busy."

I lowered my head—but what my chauffeur said next caused me to raise it again instantly.

"Then again," he said, "I don't know what's going on...it's definitely the day for things to go wrong...two of my mates who left for Rouen with their bosses and should have returned this morning haven't come back. They've probably had a breakdown."

I had a frightful vision. In spite of my uncertainty, my ignorance of the reality of the dancer, and the confusion of my nocturnal impressions, I immediately created a frightful legend. I imagined the unfortunates encountering the monsters, and being subject to assaults whose nature I could not conceive, but in

233

which were mingled effusions of blood and the crushing of flesh, as Tornada had announced in Monsieur Vernet's house during his fit of prophetic madness. That thought contracted my physiognomy to such an extent that my chauffeur perceived it,

"Is Monsieur in pain?" he asked.

"Yes, Jules, I'm not very well."

"Monsieur would do better to rest instead of wanting to go out on the road."

"Rest? No, Jules, I can't, because..." I didn't finish. An atrocious anxiety, even more than an interested reserve, caused me to change the tenor of my reply. "You're right, Jules; I'll go to bed." And one last time, I urged him: "Hurry up, my friend, hurry up!"

I left and headed for home. Not being able to depend on my car, I decided to take a fiacre to the Gare de Lyon at the appointed hour. In the meantime I would have time to pack my bags and repair the heavy insomnia that was weighing down on me. I went along the street slowly, without thinking about getting something to eat in a restaurant, although it was lunch time.

What astonished me most of all was the placidity of people who were continuing their indolent existence, when so much anxiety was eating me up inside. They didn't know anything, then? They didn't suspect anything? They were going past me, rubbing shoulders with me, with an air of indifference. Some were reading their newspapers; others were walking dogs; others were displaying themselves in open carriages and deeming it normal that their coachmen were not whipping the horses in order to flee, that their chauffeurs were filling up their gas tanks in order to reach distant regions.

I had a temptation to run to them, to shout at them to get ready to leave, to protect their loved ones. I was like a drunken man irritated by the tranquility of the crowd, an anarchist awaiting the disaster who also wants to let the secret of his vengeance explode. A fat woman who was putting on airs beneath a mauve umbrella annoyed me to the point that I wanted to slap her face. When my concierge called to me to hand me my letters as I passed her lodge, I shuddered and looked at her with a fearful expression.

"Monsieur didn't come home last night," she said, suggestively, with an indulgent smile.

I reached the elevator and pressed the button for the third floor. Curiously enough, the fact of being lifted off the ground caused my ideas to change. Once I was in the cage, I gradually yielded to a confidence as calm as my fears had been agonizing a minute before. No, it wasn't possible that the century that utilized electricity so easily as a means of transport, which challenged distance by the manipulation of steam, perfected destruction by inventing terrible weapons, and reckoned with air and water by the simple use of gasoline-powered propellers, could be incapable of responding to an invasion of animals emerged from a test-tube in a laboratory. Oh, how illogical I was being, given my science! My cerebral mechanism must have been disrupted by insomnia and emotion!

Having reached my apartment I was glad to observe the absence of my domestic, and also irritated by it. Remembering that I had given him orders that would keep him out all day, I went to the lumber-room, seized a leather trunk of respectable dimensions, dragged it into my room and got ready to start filling it.

But what should I put in the trunk? Where were we going? How long would we be away? Would we be cold or hot? Oh, a curious engagement voyage. I piled in clothes at random. One detail, which makes me smile now, and demonstrates the extent to which Suzanne was occupying my thoughts: I equipped myself, in anticipation of a long sojourn in her company, with three pairs of silk pajamas in pastel shades, which I had bought to adorn the coquetry of the first days of our marriage.

Nevertheless, while occupying myself with these garments, my mind never ceased to envisage the cruel problem of the moment. From time to time I stopped, went to stand in front of my mirror, and considered the lines engraved in my face by worry. I was pale, my forehead striped by two furrows; sweat that was not engendered by the temperature moistened the roots of my hair; a feverish tremor agitated my fingers. I no longer recognized in that image the calm fellow who, two days previously, had counted so radiantly on the future embellished by the promises of his marriage.

I was in the middle of my preparations when I heard carriages passing by heading for the races at Saint-Cloud. That exodus in the direction of the danger returned all my uncertainty. I could not conceive that, in twelve hours, and event of such importance had not reached the ears of Parisians, when Mantes was scarcely fifty kilometers away from the capital. Obviously, the strike on the westbound railway, the interruption of the telephone and telegraph wires, went some way to explaining the slowness with which the news was traveling, but were the roads not teeming with numerous excursionists? Did not a continuous coming-and-going of private couriers, local trams and even pedestrians establish a kind of chain between those two points, capable of transmitting such grave information? Were there not dirigibles, and carrier pigeons?

I reflected on that with an insistence near to obsession. I strayed over those ideas to the point of calculating the time it would take for a good horseman to bring a dispatch from a prefect to the government. Veritably, nothing seemed simpler. Then why—yes, why—this silence?

Of course! Because the couriers, the autos, the trams, the pedestrians and the riders—the entire chain of communication—had been broken by the monsters! Because the latter had a destructive radius of which I envisaged the full amplitude; because they had absorbed or paralyzed everything that moved, everything that transmitted social life.

"We're doomed" I couldn't help murmuring at my image in the mirror.

"No, we have time to escape," the same image replied, "because our enemies are only moving with an appreciable slowness. Even supposing that their progress were less rapid, and that they were only advancing, in a straight line, at three kilometers an hour—the pace of a slow walker, taking into account the unevenness of the terrain—wouldn't they already be at the gates of Paris? Wouldn't our ears be deafened by their roars, at least? Come on, Jean my friend! Calm down; finish your packing calmly, and then replenish your energy with a few hours sleep!"

Those reflections by my double calmed me down. I comforted myself with a light snack, and, overcome by fatigue, threw myself on to my bed fully dressed, in order to get a little salutary sleep before leaving.

V

At four o'clock in the afternoon I was woken up by a tumult in the street. I went to the window and saw people running and shouting, in an extraordinary disorder. Autos went by, and then large carriages, crammed with people.

As soon as I went down into the street to make enquiries, I learned that in the middle of the horse races at Saint-Cloud, the news had arrived that the macrobes had been seen in the forest of Saint-Germain. Descriptions of the animals were being given that were obviously exaggerated—magnified, I assumed, by popular imagination, It was said that they were as tall as the first platform of the Eiffel Tower, equipped with three long gyratory arms and endowed with a veracity that did not spare anything, swallowing livestock and people alike.

I concluded that the tales were implausible, but the progress of the monsters, more rapid than I had thought, alarmed me. Could I not change our plan of escape, and go to the Boulevard de Sebastopol by car in order to carry away those who were dear to me in a vehicle as rapid as the train?

I returned to the garage and found that my chauffeur had dismantled two of the most important components, and that the reassembly would take several more hours. Disconcerted, unable to think of any other course of action than to attend the arranged rendezvous at the railways station, I wasted time telling him to hurry, stunning him with futile words, in order that he would not interrupt his work to listen to the noises in the street. But as, in any case, he would not be able to finish before the end of the day, I left him to return to my apartment. I loaded my baggage into an odious fiacre, and took my place therein as well, without becoming too indignant at the fact that the coachman demanded fifty francs for the trip, paid in advance,

My carriage progressed with difficulty in the midst of an excited crowd filling the street. As soon as it had crossed the Seine, by the Pont Henri IV, I found the causeway invaded by an extraordinary melee of vehicles trying to reach the railway station, and the sidewalks were no less cluttered with a population of travelers of all conditions, the majority carrying parcels as if moving house. The news of the invasion must have spread like wildfire and inspired everyone with the same idea as us. To get out of Paris and flee was the sovereign determination of that entire crowd.

I felt a vivid annoyance. Would we get a seat on the train? I could see other carriages racing from everywhere, and the express was not due to leave for two hours, so I abandoned my fiacre, leaving the coachman my trunk by way of a tip. Furnished only with a small bag, which permitted me to cleave a path through the crowd, I succeeded, with infinite difficult, in reaching the station buffet. I saw Suzanne and her father immediately, sitting at a table. They seemed consternated.

"Do you know what I've just heard?" declared Monsieur Vernet, immediately. "The trains aren't leaving! A P.L.M. strike was called this afternoon at the Bourse du Travail!"

"What are we going to do?" asked Suzanne, anxiously.

"Well," I replied, "we'll leave by automobile."

I had already drawn up a plan of my route and mentally traced the route that we would follow, drawing away from the enemy, to reach the south of France. I had driven around the suburbs of Paris so extensively, and knew the slightest by-roads so well, that the map was, so to speak, encrusted in my memory.

"My forty horse-power ought to be ready. I'll go fetch it and come back to collect you."

"No! Don't leave us, we'll lose one another," she objected, tenderly fearful.

My proposal has reassured my friends. They got up in order to follow it, and we went back into the crowd. It was becoming increasingly dense and increasingly hostile. We understood that news of the strike had spread. We saw fists raised, faced grimacing their hatred. Voices were shouting: "Death to the strikers!" at a uniformed employee who was trying to calm them down—in vain, for his supplications had no effect on the stupidity of hooligans who were beginning to smash innocent baggage-carts and set fire to them.

The arrival of a flock of newsvendors suspended the tumult, however. Imitating everyone else, so powerful was our curiosity, we bought several evening editions at inflated prices. They related frightening details about the macrobes. In spite of contradictory descriptions of their origin, their form, their size and their color, they were in accord in recognizing their voracity and their taste for human flesh. There was talk of hecatombs. They had destroyed Mantes, consumed Poissy, and it was said that their weight was so colossal that no monument could resist them, that they crushed or toppled everything in their path. And the papers reported other rumors too; they announced a council of ministers, urgently convened, to organize defenses against this new kind of invasion.

Those stories distressed us deeply.

"Let's hurry to the auto!" Suzanne begged.

But how could we get back to the Muette quarter? How could we get out of that crowd, for a start? The entire population, it seemed to us, was outside, rushing futilely toward the station, agitated by contrary currents that were swirling toward the inaccessible Metro, while carriages, immobilized, stagnated in the middle of that human sea. We saw a child crushed in front of us, and I had to protect Suzanne, who was suffocating. Love rendered me ferocious; I would have knocked down the people who were daring to crowd my fiancée and hinder her progress.

Finally, with extraordinary difficulty, we escaped from the brutal turbulence and headed for the Seine in order to take a boat. Alas, there was another hitch when we got there; there was a queue at the pontoons for the departure to Charenton, but the steamboats for the Point-du-Jour had suspended their service. An empty fiacre, which we hailed, went past us at a fast gallop, without the coachman even turning his head. We decided them to get to my quarter by means of our own resources, and set off at a hasty walk, following the Boulevard Saint-Germain and the quays.

Night was falling already. A lamplighter, faithful to his task, was automatically spreading light over the almost-deserted streets. In the sky, the firmament exhibited a grave and limpid purity.

We were pressing our pace when, before crossing the Pont d'Iéna, uniformed officers appeared in the dim light. We followed them momentarily, and understood from what they were saying that they were a commission appointed by the Minister of War to go to the top of the Eiffel Tower in order to reconnoiter the macrobes' positions and project fire at them.

"What's the point of going up?" said one of them. "The electrical workers have stopped work. We won't have any light."

That reflection inspired us with an even greater desire to reach our liberating vehicle. But one might have thought that destiny was against us. When we went into the garage, exhausted by our journey, the automobile was no longer there. My chauffeur had disappeared, taking it away. My greatest dolor was observing Suzanne's despair.

"What are we going to do now?" he said.

We were in the road, facing my garage. The street was almost entirely deserted, save or certain places where panicky merchants were shuttering their shop windows, while others were trying to shift their furniture, as if they were afraid that it might fall victim to the macrobes' rapacity. An old woman went by, using a flap of her mantle to protect a cage occupied by a parrot. We also saw an entire family, including young children, collapse on the sidewalk. The little ones were carrying their toys, with fearful gestures. Everyone was protecting the things they loved in their own fashion. And that general desolation was in complete conformity with the sadness that reigned in us.

"I'll go ask a policeman is any measures have been taken," I proposed, feeling a need to do something.

I went to a policeman who, faithful to his orders, was on patrol outside the railway station at the boundary. He was a man of terrifying aspect, his forehead bulging, his lip barred with a thick moustache, clad in a badly-fitting uniform. Before even listening to me he cut off my question with a weary gesture and ordered me to move on.

"He doesn't know anything," I said, when I returned, crestfallen, to my friends.

"What are we going to do?" Suzanne repeated.

"Let's not lose our composure, my children," Monsieur Vernet advised. "Let's wait until tomorrow to make a decision, given that the gas is now going out too. What could we do in the dark, weary as we are?"

"Yes, I'm tired—very tired," admitted my fiancée.

"In any case," Monsieur Vernet went on, "are the macrobes as much to be feared as interested journalism proclaims? How do you expect these animals, emerged from a culture broth, as vastly developed as one can imagine, to nourish themselves on human flesh?"

"And to possess tissues sufficient compact to topple houses?" I added.

"It's pure fantasy, my future father-in-law insisted. "There are limits to science, and credulity also ought to exist therein. Let's not allow ourselves to be carried away by the folly of others. Moreover, I'd like to believe that our protection is being organized by our government. Let's have confidence in them, and offer ourselves hospitality, my dear child."

"Gladly!" I agreed.

I understood well enough that the scientist's rather banal reflections had been intended to reassure his daughter. I was of the same mind, and I hastened to take them home and offer them the honors of my domicile, with which they were not yet familiar.

The visit to my apartment, the presentation of family trinkets with so many precious memories attached to them and the organization of sleeping accommodation for the night soon provided a diversion for our obsession. My home emitted a kind of radiation from which my guests and I derived the greatest benefit. I had lit the candles in the candlesticks; their soft light threw golden glints into my fiancée's hair, and Monsieur Vernet's head was haloed by an even more respectable whiteness. We could not repress a smile when he agreed to quit his frock-coat in order to put on my indoor jacket in Pyrenean wool, whose sleeves were too short.

A dear family intimacy for which I had so often wished was inaugurated, restful in its little pleasantries, even in the midst of a tragic ambiance. I was not so far from feeling grateful for the events that had procured it for me.

"You can take my bed, my dear Suzanne," I proposed. "As for you, Monsieur Vernet, forgive me for only offering you the drawing room divan—but it's comfortable..."

"What about you?" the young woman asked.

"I'll be content with my manservant's bed, given that he hasn't come back. Would I not be comfortable anywhere, when it's a matter of blunting the cruelties of fate for you? And am I not the humblest of your servants, my dear Suzanne?"

I gave some plausibility to that last declaration by going to find something for them to eat. In the kitchen I discovered the remains of a ragout, dry bread and half a bottle of Bordeaux: the remains of my meal the day before last. I set the table; I put on an apron in order to warn up the food over a wood fire, and refused the aid that Suzanne offered me, having also put on an apron, with an adorable grace.

Our accoutrements inspired us with such good humor that we dined almost cheerfully, deliberately omitting to talk about the menace that was approaching from the west.

At ten o'clock, we parted, and I learned later that my fiancée slept heavily. I must confess that my slumber arrived rather belatedly, and was troubled by Tornada-like tics.

VI

I was already no longer asleep when an unusual sound of wheels, coming from the street, reverberated in the panes of my window at daybreak the next morning. I got dressed in haste and when downstairs to see what was happening. On the doorstep, in front of the concierge's lodge—deserted, like the rest of the house—I encountered Monsieur Vernet and Suzanne. They were already in conversation with General Gramont, whom I had met in their house many a time. He was a small, stiff, nervous man, notoriously energetic, whom the Ministry of War was sending to meet the enemy with two batteries of artillery. Monsieur Vernet had stopped him in order to question him, as he was passing by, taking his cannons to Mont-Valérien.

I went up to him. "Well, General?"

"Well, this is a strange business!" proclaimed the warrior, caressing the neck of his horse with his riding-crop. With a smile, he continued: "How could I have thought, my dear Monsieur, on the day when I was complimenting you on your engagement, that that epileptic specimen"—he meant Tornada—"had such a surprise in store for us in short order? To depart on campaign against macrobes, to mobilize the army, bring out our artillery, to destroy infusoria, that's out of the ordinary! Until now, for lack of a war, they've been using us as police; are they going to make us sweep the streets now? Oh, the twentieth century promises astonishment to those of our grandchildren who embark on a military career!"

"What news is there?" I asked, after having acquiesced to the generalities the general had pronounced.

"News? Rather curious, and even incomprehensible, if one can judge by the information that has reached the Ministry of War, which comes from a reconnaissance service ordered especially—for the observation post on top of the Eiffel Tower isn't functioning."

"Incomprehensible in what way, General?"

"In the sense that the danger that was menacing us solely in the west now seems to have circumscribed Paris. Yes, the macrobes have carried out a flanking maneuver and drawn a circle around the city. Their presence has been ascertained at Saint-Germain, at Saint-Cyr, at Versailles, at Palaiseau, at Corbeil, at Raincy and beyond the forest of Montmorency. A veritable investment, I tell you. And it's that plan of attack on their part which stupefies me, for it's a strategy, there's no doubt about it! So, one wonders what brain is communicating its orders, what genius has the inconceivable power to direct them, to organize them!"

"And one thinks of Tornada," said Monsieur Vernet, confessing the thought that was oppressing all of us.

"Of Tornada, obviously."

The sinister evocation silenced us for a few seconds. We contemplated the military apparatus that society was opposing to the beasts, the silhouettes of horsemen dancing with the trot of their mounts, the members of the gun crews shaken by the rude jolts of the ammunition-carts in which they had been placed and the menacing profiles of the cannons whose gray maws had been dispossessed of their covers. Hoofbeats, rumblings, threat; it really was war.

"They're advancing with an extraordinary speed, then?" Suzanne asked, tearfully.

"Everything leads us to think so, my child. Everything leads us to believe that they'd already be in Paris if their inconceivable discipline hadn't retained them long enough to besiege us."

"Are they as terrible as the reports indicate?" my fiancée persisted.

"They seem to be. I've been told that they're carnivores. Carnivores! Can you imagine that, Monsieur Vernet? It's amazing! Can you imagine that a squadron of cuirassiers sent against them in the direction of Raincy has disappeared in its entirety, with the exception of a few cavalrymen and the physician-major, who were manning the field hospital? Placed in the rear, they were able to escape, thanks to the restraint of the macrobes, which appeared not to want to surpass an attack zone. I met the major at the Ministry this morning, and held his report in my hands."

"What did it say? How do they operate?"

"He claims that the monsters possess a kind of cloaca underneath their abdomen, which opens to absorb their fodder. Once introduced into them, it's crushed, triturated and emptied of all its nutritive elements, while the non-alimentary substances—breastplates, for example, which are certainly rather indigestible—are expelled through the same cloaca, which opens again to reject them."

Monsieur Vernet interrupted the warrior. "That procedure," he remarked, is scarcely in accord with the idea I had formed of *Micrococcus aspirator*. If what Tornada told the Académie is accurate, the microbe possesses, by way of a nourishing arm, a kind of long appendage planted at the front of the individual."

Turning to me, he interrogated me with his gaze. I confirmed with a nod of the head that that detail was indeed what I had observed the night before last.

"I must admit," Gramont went on, "that the major was rather reserved concerning the accuracy of his report. You'll agree that it's a rather difficult time to make scientific observations when one is threatened with being sucked into the belly of a monster. A Jonah can't easily stand in for a Claude Bernard. One sees oneself more as *cuvé* than Cuvier!"[52]

On another occasion we would have appreciated the joke; on this one, it slid past our anxiety.

"The newspapers assert that their proportions are colossal, that they can crush houses beneath their weight?" I queried. More urgently, I added: "Is that true? In what fashion do they move in order to achieve such destructive effects?"

"One second, my friend," the general prevaricated. He leaned toward his orderly and shouted an order; the latter set off at a gallop to transmit the command to the head of the column. Soon, the cohort stopped; the members of the troop relaxed and the cannons ceased their deafening metallic rattle. We were more easily able to collect the general's information, which he transmitted to us while puffing nervously on a cigarette.

"I'm giving them a little rest," he explained. "The poor fellows spent the night on their feet, ready to saddle up at a moment's notice." Then, in reply to my question, he said: "How do they move? That's rather special. It's by rolling transversally—at least, so the major says. He also claims that the mode of progression in question hasn't yet been observed in nature."

"Pardon me!" said Monsieur Vernet, "but we know of some microorganisms that move in that fashion. I've seen them under the objective of my microscope. But again, that doesn't correspond with observations of *Micrococcus aspirator*, General."

"Then it's necessary to conclude, my dear Master, that the macrobes are other animals than those you believe to have been cultivated by Tornada."

---

[52] This pun does not translate, obviously; *cuver*, of which *cuvé* is the past participle, refers to fermentation, with specific reference to wine-making; feminized, it become a noun referring to the vat in which such fermentation takes place, whereas the common noun *cuvier* refers to a copper washtub; the proper noun, of course, refers to the great biologist Georges Cuvier.

That discussion of theoretical taxonomy scarcely suited the warrior. He preferred positive phenomena, obstacles that shells could attain and damage. While twirling his cigarette, however, he went on: "In any case, that explanation confirms the destructive power of the monsters. It's by rotating themselves, by virtue of their excessive mass, that they crush and flatten everything they encounter. Yesterday, at Mont-Valérien, where I'm going, the annihilation of the Château de Saint-German was observed through binoculars, and the town itself, through which we've all passed, where we've all paraded our reveries, collapsed and was flattened like a mere sand-dune."

"Will we ever stop them?" sighed Suzanne, veiling her eyes, as if to protect them from the image of that scene of ruination.

The general resumed smiling, with fine confidence. He threw away his cigarette and gathered up the reins of his mount.

"Certainly, my child. Artillery has been sent in all directions. You're going to hear the growling of new pieces, and you'll see how they comport themselves against the macrobes. We're going to puncture those bladders as easily as cutting through butter. Ours is a new therapeutics—mechanotherapy! Melinite—the medicament of the century, eh? Who would have believed it?" As Monsieur Vernet shook his head, worriedly, he went on: "You don't believe that we can smash them? Do you want me to show you? It's worth the trouble, I can assure you. We won't see a war as original as this for a long time..." And still joking, at the scientist's expense, he added: "Unless, my dear Master, you can grow a few infusoria yourself to attack the others?"

The proposition of accompanying the general to Mont-Valérien was seductive. What else did we have to do, anyway? We consulted one another with our gaze, admitting our temptation. What an appetite is greater than curiosity? Before the attraction of the spectacle, we lost all fear of danger. Furthermore, the combatant's final words had revived our courage.

"We'd like nothing better than to see the battle," said Monsieur Vernet, but how are we going to get there? How can we go with you?"

"I have two bicycles," I proposed. "One for you and the other for Suzanne."

"I don't know how to ride one, my boy."

"I can give you a place in an ammunition-cart."

"In that case, let's go."

We were soon ready to depart. Orders shouted at the top of the voice brought the weary men to their feet. A clink of sabers was mingled with the whinnying of the animals. Then the ground rumbled, the column moved off in martial fashion, and we left with that unexpected caravan, in the midst of the blinding dust raised by the heavy machines.

That whole suburban region, first the Bois de Boulogne, and then the hill of Suresnes, though which we passed to reach Fort Mont-Valérien, was abandoned.[53] We passed over a drawbridge, went through an old fortified wall and then, separating from the artillery, which took another path in order to position the guns, we followed a path leading to a barracks, which, once traversed, finally permitted us to reach, via a narrow staircase, a broad terrace from which the view extended all the way to the hills of Saint-Germain. Our eyes did not take long to savor the splendor of the panorama bathed in solar radiation, and the blue-tinted patches of terrain emerging from the mist.

We looked immediately for the fearful enigma, avid for information, but at first we could not see anything. The appearance of the region seemed normal.

"I can see them!" Monsieur Vernet suddenly exclaimed, his eyes glued to a pair of binoculars.

I seized his apparatus immediately, and inspected the horizon in my turn. Indeed, in the direction of Bezons, confused masses, melting into the gray background, had stopped behind a bridge newly built over the Seine, visible in that location in the middle of a devastated landscape. Their volume at that distance was inappreciable; they seemed, however, to be twice as tall as the only house that remained standing.

Their form was that of an elongated oval, with one extremity that seemed to be the head, and another that might have been the tail. At the level of the head section, an appendage sprouted, of a dimension at least equal to half the length of the body, and it seemed to me that the appendage in question terminated in a wider section, waving limply in the air, idly raised like an elephant's trunk.

The animals did not have any other apparent limbs, and I was wondering how they could move forward when I saw one extend its prolongation, set it on the ground in order to obtain a point of support there, and—probably fixing itself by means of some kind of suction mechanism, drag the rest of its body after it, which elongated and then became compacted again. Their progress was thus a little like that of a snake whose body was obedient to a tentacle, and the physician's report, which General Gramont had mentioned a little while before, was erroneous in all points. On the contrary; the disposition adopted really was the one of which I had retained an impression in the wake of my nocturnal excursion.

I counted ten similar monsters.

"But it really is the *Micrococcus aspirator* of alkaline environments described by Tornada!" exclaimed Monsieur Vernet, his scientific interest coming to the fore in spite of everything. Then he added: "That's prodigious! The man is

---

[53] Fort Mont-Valérien is of some symbolic significance in this context because it had played a major role in keeping the Prussians at bay for some time during the 1870 siege, withstanding heavy artillery bombardment. Its surrender was a key clause in the armistice signed in January 1871; it was effectively bartered for the food supplies that Bismarck let into the city to save the population from the threat of starvation.

a genius! Now it's a matter of ascertaining whether the animal's appendage also serves to nourish them."

"Alas! As long as it's not at our expense..." Suzanne murmured.

I was about to reply when rapid orders shouted beneath us compelled us to silence.

A battery prepared to fire. The distance was calculated and I saw the officers lean over the apparatus. Then a din deafened us. Fortunately, I had advised my fiancée to block her ears, and she closed her eyes as the blast passed through the air.

The moment became tragic, anguishing. What would the shell do to the animals?

With my eyes to the binoculars, I took note of the effects. I saw the projectile land on the house that was still standing and hollow out a breach in it. Almost immediately, a second shot was dispatched, falling directly on to the bridge, which was half-demolished.

"Victory!" cried Monsieur Vernet. "They can't get across!"

What illusion! The scientist had scarcely prophesied than the macrobes moved into the water, which did not even cover two-thirds of their bodies. Their immersion caused the river to overflow and produced distant eddies. They stayed there for a while, as if bathing. Some of them plunged their trunks into the liquid, and launched torrents as they pulled them out again.

Finally, the first emerged, then a second, and a third was following them when another shell, more successfully aimed, landed on it. The extraordinary thing was that the shell, instead of striking it, slid over its tegument and went to burst against a tree on the other bank.

At first we thought the device had been badly-constructed, all the more so because something else very peculiar happened at the same instant. Just as the shell exploded, we saw an orange flash about a hundred meters above the enemy troop, so vivid that it eclipsed to solar radiation, and so strangely distributed in the sky that it was reminiscent of a firework rocket launched in broad daylight, of a previously unknown intensity.

I did not understand those phenomena at all. I attempted to reason them out by attributing them to defective powder being used by the artillery, but that explanation could not be true, for the shots that followed were no more fortunate. The projectiles touched the carapaces of the monsters, and the carapaces caused them to rebound.

"They're invulnerable, then!" Monsieur Vernet exclaimed. "Their consistency disrupts all my hypotheses!"

And it was true. All the more stimulated by the impacts they received, seemingly obedient to a mysterious order, the macrobes increased the rapidity of their progress and undulated more precipitately in our direction.

"My God! My God!" stammered Suzanne, seizing my arm. "They're coming!"

"Indeed..."

"Let's run! Run!"

"One more second," I said, my attention riveted by that unreal spectacle. But did I really see what followed? Did the binoculars, trembling in my hands, not deceive me? Did I really see that the colossi were employing a different fashion of movement, and that they were now proceeding by means of successive bounds, obtaining a point of support on the ground by means of their trunks and describing in the air, a long way from the ground, an enormous somersault, like the leap of a carp when it emerges from the water—and which caused them to advance hundreds of meters at each jump?

Our terror, following the failure of the artillery, was indescribable. We ran away, tumbling down the stairs any old how and running through the courtyard, and we found ourselves outside the fortifying wall. Officers, soldiers and civilians alike were frantic, stampeding. The guns had been abandoned in order to flee more rapidly.

The general tried in vain to organize an honorable retreat, but his voice was drowned out by the din. I saw his furious mouth howling incomprehensible orders. Nothing could have opposed the torrent of the panic.

I had not forgotten my dear Suzanne, however. I had taken care to put her on her bicycle and to support her during the descent of Suresnes. She was calling madly for her father when the scientist caught us up. He was fleeing at a rapid trot on a horse that he had mounted in haste. He had never learned to ride and was going downhill with his hair blowing in the wind, clinging to the saddle and the animal's mane, offering a spectacle that would have been hilarious if we had still had a sense of humor.

We found ourselves back in the Chaussée de la Muette without my remembering exactly how we got there. I dismounted just in time to catch Suzanne, who was about to faint. The dear child was exhausted by fear, fatigue and hunger.

I immediately thought of finding something for her to eat, but I had exhausted my provisions the previous evening. The quarter was deserted, none of the shops any longer being inhabited. I was cursing my impotence when hazard came to our aid.

The last runaways had scarcely disappeared into the Rue de Passy when a refrain sung in a tenor voice rose up behind us. The tune—*Viens, poupoule, viens!*—was familiar to us; it was one of those odious popular songs that invade the country like epidemics of stupidity from time to time.[54] The words, however, had been adapted to circumstances, and the parody "*Viens, macrobe, viens!*" rose with a stupefying insistence in the solitude of the place.

---

[54] The song in question, whose title and chorus is roughly translatable as "Come, baby, come," was made famous by the popular music hall performer Félix Mayol. He can still be seen and heard singing it, thanks to YouTube.

We turned round and perceived the singer. It was a little man with a hilarious physiognomy, dressed in the fashion of a Montmartre cabaret singer in a gray frock-coat and flared trousers. Installed before a display of brioches and licorice water, he was waiting for clients and seemed to be ironically enjoying the situation we were in. I went over to him, lured by his provisions.

"Just in time!" I said. "You're very philosophical..."

"Fatalistic, Monsieur," he replied. "Long experience of events has taught me that it does no good to get excited. It's necessary to await the course of destiny while singing. It's very French."

"And you're not afraid to stay here? You know that they're not far away?"

"Where would I go? Under the bridges? I'm familiar with them, thanks! They've sheltered my poor anatomy all too often. It's true that my place was marked out for me at the Élysée...perhaps you don't know that there's been a change of government, and that I was offered the Undersecretariat of Fine Arts...but no, I refused. The position isn't sufficiently fruitful. I prefer selling brioches and coco, to cocos of your sort."[55]

And as my eyes were shining in response to the bait of suggestive bread rolls, with a golden patina that was already several days old, he added: "You want some?"

"Yes—how much?"

"Two hundred francs for three."

"Oh!"

"The macrobian price, Monsieur. And I'll throw in the nectar too!"

"Done," I said, exchanging two lovely banknotes for the brioches and a liter of the beverage.

I brought them back to my friends, and the singer retired, informing us that we were "mugs." I blessed him nonetheless.

VII

Hunger appeased, we discussed our distress. Who would save us? Having the good fortune to be a friend of the Voisin brothers, the constructors of the famous tailed biplane,[56] I thought briefly of going to their nearby factory to procure one of their aircraft, in order to carry us away. Their ingenious apparatus

---

[55] Another untranslatable pun; *coco* signifying both "licorice water"—also known in England as sugarelly, although the beverage has faded from popularity to such an extent that the term is no longer current—and "coconut," the latter being used as an argot term with the same implication as "blockhead.".

[56] Gabriel and Charles Voisin bought out their collaborator Louis Blériot in 1906 in order to establish the first aircraft manufacturing company at Billancourt, accessible from the Chaussée de la Muette in Passy without too much difficulty, by bicycle or on horseback.

was familiar to me; I knew that they were now using aerial transport of proven security in several places, capable of long journeys without renewing contact with the ground. But a major aviation show in the Midi, I remembered, had attracted all of their available machines, and my desire was incapable of realization.

That further disappointment plunged us back into melancholy. The destruction of the incredible invaders appeared to us to be increasingly improbable. The cannon fire that we could now hear in all directions was scarcely reassuring; we knew its impotence. And we were allowing ourselves to go on to more cruel anticipations when a faint noise overhead caused us to look up.

Then our hearts dilated, for we had just perceived the presence in the sky of Commandant Junisseau, in his dirigible.

He had recognized us too. He came, with a consummate mastery, to hover ten meters above us. Very excited, he shouted to us, his voice vibrant: "I've followed all the vicissitudes of the artillery battle and observed the vain results of melinite. I'm going to employ the fracassite recently invented by Serviat. Unfortunately, I lack an aide. Would you like to come with me, Monsieur Gérard? It's for the fatherland!

Oh, the cruel hesitation! To abandon my friends at such a moment! To leave Suzanne! I was about to refuse when my fiancée's gaze ordered me to depart.

"Go, Jean, go! You owe it to your country! We'll wait for you in your apartment. My heart won't leave you."

A rope hoisted me up. In order to reach the nacelle I had to accomplish a few gymnastic movements to which I was no longer accustomed, and which I executed with a certain difficulty. Encouraged by Junisseau, however, I succeeded, and we departed.

I shall not waste time describing the vast apparatus that carried me away, or explaining how the fabric envelope inflated by a gas lighter than air supported, by means of a network emanating therefrom, the cage set on an armed beam that had collected me. Nor shall I linger over an explanation of the role of the air-balloon, the stabilizers, the automatic valves, the pressure vent, the multiplier, the equilibrator, the bolt-rope and the suspension. In any case, such machines fly over every day, and the dirigible has lost the favor of curiosity since the airplane has completed the conquest of the fluid that we breathe. Let it suffice, therefore, for the reader to know that the nacelle was surrounded by an iron wire mesh stopping at a support-rail, and that I perceived at my feet, on the perforated floor, two carefully-stacked piles of shells.

Detaching my gaze from those destructive engines, I then observed the luminous circle described by the propeller in the play of the sunlight; then, after an empty space, the raised catwalk on which Junisseau was standing, close enough for conversation between us to be possible. Standing with superb authority, he was presiding, thanks to movements transmitted by a steering-column, over the evolution of his apparatus, while at the rear, a single assistant, the mechanic, was manning the engine, obedient to the orders that the commandant whistled to him by telephone. All these dispositions would have interested me prodigiously at another time, for it was my first ascent, but for the moment, I only retained the impression of a magnificent instrument utilizable in the defense of those I loved.

"Stay there, don't move, and understand clearly what I expect of you!" the aeronaut shouted to me from his catwalk, in the midst of the various sounds produced by the dirigible's flight.

He scanned the horizon with an imperious eye, and then communicated to his servant the orders that, once executed, produced a lurching that caused me to feel some nausea. I soon realized, however, that we had caught a favorable air current, for it appeared to me that we were moving faster, and my stomach settled. Looking down at my feet then, I perceived the ground through the gaps in the floor, drawing away beneath us. The branches of the Bois de Boulogne flew past confusedly, in a green harmony. Soon, the gray ribbon of the Seine was surpassed.

Junisseau's voice tore me away from that spectacle.

"In brief, this is what I want you to do. I've seen the futile contest of the artillery; I've observed the macrobes at length, and I've understood that there's only one means of thwarting them."

"What's that, Commandant?"

"It's blinding them."

"Blinding them?"

"Yes. I've noticed on their carapace, not far behind their appendage, a kind of circular patch, with two concentric rings, which seems to constitute the monsters' cyclopean eye. It's by that means that I think they're accessible. Although projectiles slide over and ricochet from their teguments—and see how nature protects them, since their visual apparatus is shielded by the invulnerable trunk!—our perpendicularity gives us the hope that we might get to them simply by depositing the explosive at the portal to the cerebral system. Can you imagine the purée that half a pound of fracassite will make of their insides!"

He rubbed his hands and pinched his nose, then remarked, with a loud laugh: "The anarchists haven't yet found anything like it, eh?"

"But what's my role, Commandant?" I asked. "How can I be useful to you?"

"You're brave, aren't you? You're not chicken? You won't tremble? You're not myopic?"

I reassured him on all these points. Then he continued: "You, my good friend, have simply, if I might express it thus, to put the salt on the sparrow's tail—in other words, to let the projectile fall on to the macrobe's eye at the moment that I cause the dirigible to hover above it. It's a game of massacre, an amusement for pretty ladies, and I truly regret not having invited any to partake of this new kind of sport. Once the first macrobe is destroyed, we'll pass on to the second, then the third, and so on, until the complete extermination of the race. I can stay in the air for ten hours and in my hangar at Moulineaux I have a reserve of five hundred shells, as many loaded with melinite as with fracassite, so it will be easy for us to restock."

What he said gave me pause for thought. I thought that handling bombs was a perilous business, and that I had thirty of them at my feet.

"Isn't there any danger at the moment of the explosion?" I asked. "I'd very much like to know."

"No—not the slightest! And then again, so what? It's for the fatherland!"

"Yes—for France!" I cried. And silently, I added: "For Suzanne." A noble heroic enthusiasm exalted me. I felt as brave as an ancient god taking to the serenity of the skies in order to smite the dragons delivered to my blows by another celestial power rivaling my own.

Entirely intent on the role I was to play, from then on I took a passionate interest in the movements of my two bold companions, ingeniously maneuvering the dirigible. The captain, consulting a compass, gave curt orders that his aide carried out phlegmatically. After having flown straight up into the sky, we allowed ourselves to descend with a vertiginous lightning rapidity. I could have sworn, however, that we were not moving, and that our balloon was suspended by an immense wire attached to a hook somewhere high in the sky.

Suddenly, the engine was not throbbing as rapidly. I understood that we were stationary, and leaned over the side.

"Rueil!" Junisseau specified.

How small the world seemed! And how derisory those monstrous gray masses were, that I had feared so much a little while before! I was surprised not to feel more distressed by the sight of them. They had changed location slightly, moving back in the direction of Rueil, and after having destroyed and pulverized everything in their path, they were taking a rest before tackling the rising ground that extends from Rueil to Suresnes and Mont-Valérien.

We drew closer still, and I was able to see that the idea I had formed from a distance had given me a reasonably exact idea of what they really were. They reproduced in colossal proportions, which I estimate to be thirty meters in height by ten broad and fifty long, the *Micrococcus aspirator* of alkaline environments described and depicted by Tornada. I saw that their carapace was constituted by overlapping scales, so harmonious in form that I thought that the scales, hardened by their special culture, must represent the cells of a tegument whose discrimination the microscope did not permit in tiny specimens, although there was no reason why it should not exist.

As for their gyratory tentacle, I confirmed that it served both as an organ of locomotion and if nutrition, as the baleful scientist had announced, for a poor field-worker who was obstinate in not fleeing, was caught by one of them before my eyes, and absorbed as a breadcrumb might be by a human mouth—or, to offer a better representation, sucked in by a current of air determined by the trunk while producing the siren-like sound, now significant for me as the roar of a vacuum-cleaner. The man disappeared head first, gesturing stiffly, reminiscent of one of the marionettes of a Punch-and-Judy show dragged off their miniature stage by an invisible string. He disappeared, and I heard his horrible screams...but the sentiment of my liberating mission filled me too much for me to pity him.

I was no longer thinking about anything but the strange destinies of the science capable of transforming the world in this fashion. Were these macrobes not the masters of the world? Oh, it was high time they were destroyed—that I directed my explosive vengeance toward that lidless eye, whose stupid pupil, round and black, with a green-tinted rim, seemed to be looking at us at that exact moment. And I calculated that I could let my projectile fall upon it without difficulty, even if their immobility did not last long.

We drew even closer. We were no more than a hundred meters or so above the leading macrobe when Junisseau said to me: "Look, Monsieur Gérard— there's another enigma! It's that indefinable entity that I observed for some time a little while ago, and which leads the macrobes in battle, whom they obey like a leader. Can you see it there, at the rear?"

I turned in the direction indicated by the Commandant, and did indeed perceive, unfortunately too far away to be able to make out its nature precisely, a kind of reddish animal, with the vague form of a little human whose upper body and head had been replaced by a sponge taller than it was wide, and equipped with an arm. Yes, a sponge-man, moving on two thin legs, running to the right and left to herd the giant animals, as a sheepdog does with a flock of sheep. It was steering them without making any sound, from a distance, making gestures like a sprinkler of holy water, and its orders were executed, it seemed to me, with the same fearful docility with which sheep obey the commands of the dog.

I confess that that little general of colossi intrigued me greatly, and I would gladly have lingered to watch its maneuvers if Junisseau had not raised his voice again.

"Pay attention! The time has come!" He pointed at the shells carefully stacked at my feet. "Take the first one from the right-hand pile, which is composed of fracassite. Place it on the exterior bar...carefully, without tilting it... it's a delicate operation."

A tremor ran through me, which he perceived, in spite of my attempt to repress it.

"Are you scared?"

I stiffened myself. "Not at all, Commandant."

And, with all my muscles tense, all my nervous strength deployed, I took hold of one of the voluminous steel cones, which weight approximately fifty kilos, and lifted it up to the rim of the nacelle.

"Have you a clear sight of the monster's eye?"

"Yes, Commandant."

"You won't miss the target?"

"I hope not."

"It's necessary not to hope, but to be sure. If the device falls anywhere but into the optical orifice, it's us who'll be blown up, my friend...and I'd rather it was them!"

"Me too, Commandant," I agreed, with a pale smile.

I was scarcely at ease. I was having infinite difficulty maintaining the explosive on the rail, all the more so as I had placed it on the very edge, in order not to miss the precise instant of release, and the fifty thousand grams were pulling on my nervous arms. The Commandant whistled into his telephone; the mechanic moved a lever. The engine throbbed less rapidly. We dropped toward the monster.

"Wait! Stay cool!" ordered the Commandant.

Another blast of the whistle resounded; the propeller stopped turning. This time, I perceived the colossal grey mass directly beneath my feet, the optical patch displayed thereon.

"Wait!"

I was only waiting for the word when the dirigible suddenly tilted, while a roar, two which an oath from the aviator replied, burst forth beneath our floor. We had made the mistake of not worrying about the seemingly-lazy trunk of the animal, which was swinging limply at the level of our mooring rope, and the monster had grabbed the rope, drawing us toward it with an improbable force.

Our vessel lurched. We were doomed.

"Above all, don't let go!" Junisseau shouted.

As he spoke, he launched himself off the catwalk. I thought at first he was making the move to escape the danger, to flee, at the risk of killing himself as he abandoned us, but my indignation was soon converted into a boundless admiration. Oh, what courage! What audacity! I saw him hang on by one arm to the iron framework like a veritable acrobat, above the void, and then seize with his other hand a knife that he was clutching in his teeth, and cut the rope. His liberating gesture, aided by the intelligence of the mechanic, who has restored thrust to the engine, caused us to rebound out of the monster's reach. We were saved.

"Commandant, that's admirable, what you did!" I shouted, when his athletic agility had brought him back to his steering-column.

Well, yes—he scarcely cared about my appreciation. In any case, he could hardly hear me amid the renewed purr of the engine and the propeller determined by our new thrust. Very calmly, he controlled his equilibrator, transmitted his instructions to the mechanic again with blasts of his whistle. Under the guidance of its helm, the dirigible circled around, bringing us back over the enemy. Junisseau's courageous deed had inspired me with a noble emulation. This time, it was without trembling that I approached the first macrobe, still motionless.

The maneuver was repeated with the same precision, and when I judged that I was situated vertically above the circular patch, I looked at the Commandant.

"Go!"

I relaxed my taut arms. I saw the steel thunderbolt reach the enemy. Then, for a second of intense emotion, I waited for the noise consecutive to my action.

What a surprise! Nothing! No bang! The detonation did not take place. And when, in spite of the maneuver that had taken the dirigible precipitately out of range of the anticipated explosion, I saw what had become of the shell, I perceived that it had slid over the monster and fallen on the ground without bursting.

"A dud! Another! Another!" Junisseau shouted at me, bringing us back to the battle.

"Another!"

With a new rage, I lifted a second device on to the rail. We approached again, and I propelled it into the void with the same care to aim exactly. Alas, once again the result was implausibly negative; all that I heard exploded was the Commandant's oath.

"Fracassite doesn't explode!" he said, with a cold wrath. "It's another one of Serviat's hoaxes!"

And, leaning on the equilibrator so hard that I thought we were going to crash on top of the monster, he added: "Get the melinite! It's the pile on the left! Perhaps, in the eye...the artillery shells didn't hit the eye...!"

I did as I was told. I got ready for a third time. Again the dirigible hovered above the enormous carapace.

"Let go!" Junisseau howled.

"Smack in the eye!" I exulted.

A frightful detonation accompanied my cry of victory. The floor, hit by shrapnel, was holed almost beneath my feet. Acrid fumes, which gripped the throat, enveloped us as we were carried sideways by a rapid thrust. It took perhaps a minute to dissipate the mist.

"This time, Commandant, I think..."

"This time? Look, my friend!"

Surprised by the irony of his tone, I leaned over the side to observe my massacre. What a disappointment! I had proclaimed the triumph too soon. My device had indeed hit the target, but the monster had not sustained the slightest damage. On the contrary: the shock seemed to have given it pleasure, as if tickling it, for it was continuing to swing its tentacle indolently.

Then, we realized that the "eye" was simply a variation of the carapace, something like an ornament, a beauty spot, as fantasists call them. At any rate, the invulnerability of the macrobes became a proven fact after we had attempted—from a greater height, in order to avoid the shrapnel—further shots at a second one, and then a third. The results were the same. They were definitely indestructible. A ferocious snigger, uttered by the sponge-man, who had drawn closer to us and had witnessed the duel, convinced us further still. Where had I heard that laughter before? Oh, why hadn't I thought of destroying that one?

I was overwhelmed. I hardly heard Junisseau ordering the return to Paris. What would become of us, now that combat was definitively impossible? Would the Commandant take pity on us? Would he be humane enough to take Monsieur Vernet, Suzanne and me away in his dirigible?

I was about to beg him to do that when a pain in my wrist suspended my request. Examining the place that was causing me to suffer, I saw that it was bleeding, with a gray-tinted body in the middle of the wound. I had been wounded without realizing it in the heat of the battle.

I took out the foreign body, and, after having observed that it was a fragment of a macrobian scale, a horny tissue as hard as iron, I bandaged my arm with my handkerchief and turned my imploring eyes toward Junisseau.

"Commandant! Commandant!" I begged, finally.

He had anticipated me. He shook his head, declaring that the engine was fatigued, that he could not overload it, and that his duty called him elsewhere, to the national defense.

Perhaps he also understood, by the anger in my eyes, that I was capable of a crime, capable of throwing him overboard in order to take possession of his dirigible. But what could I have done with it? I did not know how to fly it; and a circular glance cast over the region we were overlooking had just told me that Paris was surrounded on all sides by the gray masses, into the midst of which my inexperience would doubtless have steered us.

Furthermore, our enemies were progressing with prodigious rapidity. A curve that the pilot had described having brought us over Saint-Cloud, I saw that the town was already threatened with ruin. Its square was swarming with fugitives, and in a matter of seconds, its railway station, its bridge, its church, the entrance to its park and the taverns planted along its shore—an entire sunlit décor, picturesque, amusing, evocative of so many Parisian Sunday excursions—were nothing more than dust.

Then I lowered my head and waited for Junisseau to drop me off in the Chaussée de la Muette. He left without saying another word. With him, my last hope disappeared, as his dirigible paled and vanished in the azure.

VIII

I found Monsieur Vernet and my fiancée in my apartment. As soon as she perceived that I was injured, Suzanne threw herself into my arms, weeping. The dear heart! I would gladly have been hurt, more grievously, twenty times over to receive the dolorous charm of such an impulse.

"Oh, my dear Jean," she said you me, "here you are at last! If you knew what I'd gone through! I was mad with anxiety! The hope I invested in your expedition, of the annihilation of the macrobes due to your courage, couldn't dissipate my anguish! And Papa was no less troubled than me! We've spent the entire time of your absence leaning out of the window, looking at the horizon, listening for the noises that might have reached us from that frightful battle...and nothing! Nothing reached us, except once...three distant explosions. We understood, alas, when we did not hear the explosions repeated, that the battle was lost..."

"She ought to have added, to tell you everything," Monsieur Verne remarked, "that the silence of the explosives was even more difficult for her to bear than the echoes of the engagement..."

Suzanne placed her hand gently over her father's mouth, to stop the confession—but Monsieur Vernet continued: "Didn't she imagine that you had fallen prey to the monsters? I tried in vain to demonstrate the impossibility of that, by reason of the altitude accessible to the dirigible and the facility of the maneuvers favorable to your escape, but she didn't want to admit it. She objected, with a certain logic, that the leaping of the animals, which we observed a little while ago through the binoculars, was capable of carrying them within range of you. She could already see you..."

"In truth," I interjected, "it was very nearly true."

And I recounted, terrifying them with my story, how one of the animals had, at one time, seized the aerial vessel's mooring-rope, and how we had only escaped its attack thanks to the incredible gymnastic feat accomplished by Commandant Junisseau. Evidently, my language must have been imprinted with all the force of the sensations I had experienced—and never, I thought, had a storyteller been obliged to give such color, interest and sincerity to his story, for to every one of the episodes of the adventure, Suzanne responded with a facial expression of greater distress, and the tighter pressure of her mutually-clasped hands. I had to relate the same details ten times over, and retrace the silhouette of the monsters a hundred times, to satisfy curiosities that my own exhausted emotion no longer permitted me to envisage calmly. The incessant interjections of my friends continually suspended my confidences, and I scarcely had time to answer one question before another was posed.

"Are they really as big as that?"

"Is it conceivable that fracassite isn't able to damage them?"

"How long is their appendage?"

"What diameter?"

"Do they make a noise as they suck things in?"

"In sum, do they have the form of a leather bottle?"

"Of an elongated leather bottle?"

"Of a leather bottle whose anterior prolongation is their aspirator arm?"

"Their tentacle widens at the tip, doesn't it, like a conch?"

"And their carapace, let's talk about that—it's made of scales, like a crocodile's, you say?"

"Can you explain why their movement isn't jerky?"

"They crawl, then?"

"They crawl *and* they bound?"

"And the sponge-man—what can it be?"

"It's prodigious!"

"It's terrifying!"

I did my best to content their breathless curiosity; I reread in them all my previous alarms. The listened to me with wide eyes, their hearts palpitating, and my explanations confirmed the proverb alleging that the truth can be stranger than fiction. In the fervor of my narration, I began to gesticulate, and in response to one movement my wrist started hurting and began to bleed. I could not suppress a whimper; my nervous system found its trigger in that physical dolor.

"How uncharitable we are, Father! Look, our poor friend's pale...he's hurt!"

Indeed, I had to sit down. A mist clouded my eyes. Mastering their fear, Suzanne and her father hastened to help me. They untied the handkerchief that I had hurriedly put over the wound.

I had a long cut, such as might have been produced by the edge of a sword, with astonishingly neat edges. The separated tissues revealed the nacreous trajectory of tendons, which, mercifully, had not been severed.

The conviction that my wound would have no further consequences, and would allow me to use my arm—at the cost of some pain, it is true—gave me strength, and permitted me to reassure my fiancée who had gone pale in her turn.

"It's nothing—nothing at all—my dear Suzanne...a mere scratch. In a few days it'll be completely gone."

"Are you sure?" asked Monsieur Vernet, "that the injury was produced by a splinter of a carapace?"

"Of course," I said, holding out the projectile, which I had put in my waistcoat pocket.

It was a precious piece of evidence, of which the scientist immediately took possession. He examined it, felt it and turned it over repeatedly, with a veritable avidity. Assuredly, none of his anatomical specimens, in which the power or bizarrerie of life was manifest, had ever procured him such joy as he manipulated it. He consulted its opacity, its color, its form. He took a magnifying-glass from his pocket and studied its contexture. A gem worth a million could not have put more emotion into the heart of a coquette.

"What's inconceivable," he ended up admitting, in a tone mingling delight and surprise, "is the consistency of the tissue. I wonder what elements it's composed of. I'd never have believed that an anatomical parenchyma could acquire such cohesion in such a short time. No, that's never been observed in nature. Diamond, which is the most resistant substance known, is only carbon crystallized by the centuries...but centuries have passed over it, whereas a year, at the most, has transformed and solidified the epidermis of *Micrococcus aspirator*. It's a prodigy, my children. Ought we not to admire it...?"

But he fell silent. Our physiognomies had admitted that his enthusiasm seemed to us to be pure blasphemy. Holding the debris between his fingers, he went to the window and ran the cutting edge of the fragment over the pane.

"Ha! My word, it scratches glass! You see, my children—it scratches glass!"

Feverishly, his hand traced two words, and I realized that he was simply translating his scientific wonderment into those two words, because what he had written was: *Tornada genius*. He even took his enthusiasm so far as to remove from Suzanne's finger the superb solitaire that I had slipped on to it on the day of our engagement, and run the edge of the fragment over it.

"And that's more extraordinary still! My children, it scratches diamond!"

"Oh, Papa!" Suzanne protested.

Perhaps for the first time in his life, however, he became indignant. "What! A man has had conceptions vast enough to surpass the work of time, and you criticize me for checking its effects with what I have to hand? In what way does that diminish your affection? It has never been given to anyone to experiment with such a phenomenon! Damn it! Leave me to my admiration, my children! I'm free to admire! I'm the master of my veneration! Evil has its beauty, and its grandeur too! And I revolt, in the end, on observing that you don't appreciate, as I do, the creative power of a brain that has thrown down this challenge to nature! For he has created, one must admit...while we scientists have been content to translate and deduce, Tornada has created, at a stroke, formidable life! And that it scratches diamond, I can hardly believe!"

Soon, however, his daughter's distressed expression returned him to a more reasonable appreciation. He calmed down completely at the spectacle of his daughter completing the dressing of my wound, after having washed it with an antiseptic solution. He placed the projectile in his wallet, and began pacing back and forth with long strides—but he evidently continued in private the enthusiastic monologue that our dolorous task had interrupted—and when my wrist was finally bandaged, he did not wait any longer to give free rein to an interpretation that his scientific logic had inspired.

He turned to me: "Well, my friend, that patch that you mistook for the monster's eye, do you know what it is? It's the trace of the original segmentation of the macrobe."

"What does that mean?" Suzanne asked.

"To put it more prosaically, their navel, my dear child. These animalcules, which have been poorly observed at the Institut Pasteur, multiply by binary fission. They give live by virtue of their own resources. They bear their perpetuity in themselves alone. Hence, one can deduce their pullulation when one thinks that they have only to divide into two to make two individuals, and that those segmented fragments constitute, in their turn, individuals capable of multiplying themselves. And that's rather frightful...and quite interesting. Yes, prodigiously interesting. Oh, that Tornada!"

A plaint from Suzanne extinguished his admiration. The poor child went pale. Valiant as she had shown herself to be thus far, she could not resist the exigencies of hunger. For my part, I was no longer listening to my rancor against Tornada, already the cause of so much suffering and calamity, inasmuch as my fiancée's hunger had reached me, and my stomach, like those of my companions, was remembering that it had absorbed nothing in the last eighteen hours by a single brioche and a glass of licorice water. But where could we find something to eat? How could I get into the deserted shops, where provisions must still exit?

I went down into the street to search. I knocked on the iron shutters, which remained deaf to my appeals. Then, understanding the futility of my attempts, I went to my garage and equipped myself with a full set of burglar's tools, which I used to force the doors of the apartments in my house. I rushed to the larders; they were empty. On the fourth floor, however, I discovered a bag of chocolate in a bedroom, which I pocketed; and in the concierge's lodge, which I did not neglect, there was the remains of a cheese, some jam and stale bread. I brought it all back to my friends, and we feasted on it.

Then we went out, cocking our ears toward the west, without perceiving any abnormal noises. It was four o'clock in the afternoon. A delightful sun bathed that frightful day with its gentle warmth. No, the sky had never opposed such delights of spring to so much terrestrial devastation. We went along the Rue de Passy and headed toward the Seine.

Monsieur Vernet, aching from his unexpected morning ride, advanced with difficulty, his hand on his hack. Taking pity on his suffering and his white hair, Suzanne and I each lent him a supportive arm. On the way, haunted by the proximity of the macrobes, we discussed their ravages again, and their fashion of leaping into the air, crushing houses with their colossal mass as they fell back. We were surprised that the rapidity of their action had not yet introduced them into Paris. What were they waiting for? Why were they pausing before falling upon that colossal prey of two million inhabitants? Were they already sated? What order of suspension were they obeying? We could only imagine...

The danger, as frightening as could be, caused us to imagine the utility of our terror in escaping their reach.

"In a cellar!" Suzanne proposed.

"No," I said. "Their tentacle is long, and would surely suck us in."

"Of course! Let's go up the Eiffel Tower!" Monsieur Vernet exclaimed, pointing at the monument, which was nearby. "The appendage of the animals can't reckon with its solidity, and won't reach the first stage!"

We headed in that direction, swiftly, but on the Pont d'Iéna we were stopped by a battalion of infantry. Conserving their marvelous discipline amid the general panic, the troop had formed a barrage around the Chap-de-Mars. We tried in vain to negotiate a passage. We learned that the tower had been reserved for studies of the defense, and that the government had already appointed a committee, chaired by ministers, which would function up there, after having installed offices and a supply of paper.

"That puts the lid on it!" sniggered Monsieur Vernet, shrugging his shoulders.

"Let's go into the Metro," I suggested. "I think it will be safer underground than in the open, as long as we stay away from the tunnel openings."

My plan was agreed, and we resumed our route toward Marbeuf station. There, once again, our despair and indignation increased, when we found that the Metro, like the tower, was under military guard and that no one was allowed in.

Then, consternated, reduced to wandering without shelter, anticipating the end of everything, but nevertheless driven to seek out a crowd by an appetite of curiosity, a need to combine our misery with that of others, we went along the Champs-Élysées toward the Place de la Concorde.

The splendid avenue was less abandoned by human presence. In the gathering dust we observed a certain movement. There was traffic moving through open coaching entrances, carts waiting on the sidewalk; a dispute had just begun. That life, succeeding the solitude of my own quarter, warmed our hearts. We experienced the egotistical impression determining that the sight of the misery of others offers solace to our own.

We drew nearer, and I went up to a group of three individuals, of somewhat disquieting attitude, who were agitating around piled-up items of furniture. I thought that they had received instructions from a property-owner to clear a house whose vestibule announced a certain sumptuousness.

"What are you doing, my friends?" I asked. "How are you wasting your time? Do you realize the peril that threatens us? Since you have the good fortune to possess a carriage, only load it with yourselves, and leave!"

I hesitated for a moment before continuing. An absurd hope attached me o the fate of those fanatics, whom I would have avoided with horror in normal times. I was reckless enough to consider them as possible liberators, to envisage fleeing in their company, on their cart, through a countryside that I wanted to suppose practicable, free of enemies.

"Leave!" I risked. "Leave as quickly as possible—and if you have a spark of humanity, take us with you."

With a gesture, I indicated the location of my wallet, to signify that I was willing to pay for their services.

"One might perhaps see..." said one of them, with a sly smile whose significance, unfortunately, I did not suspect.

The three individuals stepped aside and began to confer. We waited, tremulously, for the conclusion of their discussion. Then one of them approached us. I remember that he was a big, solid fellow, wearing a cap with several flaps, whose mouth was partly deprived of teeth. He reeked of alcohol, and his hands, which he spread in order to converse, were covered in scratches that were still bleeding.

"For sure, my mates and I would like nothing better than to work for worthy bourgeois. It all depends on the price...if there's a means of reaching an understanding. How much do you have on you?"

I took out my wallet, which, in anticipation of an analogous expense, I had taken care to furnish copiously. I counted in front of my interlocutor the sum that I found there, without noticing that the rustle of the bills provoked a particular gleam in his eye. When I had finished my calculation, I confided: "I have three thousand francs. Is that sufficient?"

"For sure, that'll do me!" he said, taking possession of the wad and stuffing it unceremoniously into his trousers.

He turned to his companions, and all three burst out laughing.

Slightly surprised by their attitude, but expecting nevertheless that they were about to execute the agreement, the price of which I had paid in advance, we waited for them to unload their cargo. By contrast, we saw them continuing to heap up the rest of the objects that were on the sidewalk.

"Hey! Aren't you forgetting us?" I exclaimed to my debtor.

He turned round and planted himself in front of me, swaying slightly, his massive silhouette looming over me by a head. With a further smile, full of bestiality, he caused the fangs that still remained behind his lips to gleam. I would never have thought that a human face could acquire such a satanic expression, and my indignation was further increased by the insult.

"What? What?"

"You're loading your cart. It's us who ought to be taking our place there!"

"That's agreed," he said, extending his hand. "But you'll have to wait for the next trip."

"Wretch!"

I had been cheated. His attitude indicated that he would have laid me out with a blow of his fist. I had no hope of any restitution from the nauseating bandit. Oh, if I had only had my revolver! I believe that I would have put a hole in his ugly head without a scruple.

But Suzanne pulled me sleeve. "Let's go...what does money matter? Let's go!" she begged.

"Come on!" her father insisted.

We drew away. All along the avenue we encountered no one but other members of the lowest criminal classes, similarly occupied. All those people were looters, alas! Assured of impunity in a city devoid of police, they were calmly robbing houses of their riches. We saw works of art of the greatest beauty being carried away, sacks full of jewelry, inestimable tapestries: an entire booty of marvels that had been heaped up pell-mell on carts with emaciated horses. The criminal faces of the thieves, their breath heavy with alcohol, their eyes avid, their coarse delight in enriching themselves, inexplicable in those menacing hours, were repulsive, and caused us to hasten our pace toward the Place de la Concorde, and then the Rue Royale, where people had gathered.

Oh why had we entered that human tide that was flowing along the boulevards, and which immediately absorbed us, took possession of us and carried us away!

There was an indescribable swarming, a pressure such that we were suffocated by it at first. One might have thought that the circulation of Paris had flowed back toward its heart, doubtless out of the same need for community in misfortune that we also experienced, and the whole of the vast city seemed to be concentrated in that place.

One cannot form any idea of what that crowd was like. It was not even a crowd, for a crowd is elastic; determination permits it to be escaped; this was a condensation of all the men, all the women and all the children, amassed and compressed between two insurmountable barriers, the walls of houses, subject to surges, eddies and whirlpools provoked by the exasperated gestures of those attempting to make room. For as far as the falling dusk allowed us to distinguish that scene of disorder, we could see nothing but a seed-bed of heads, the majority hatless, a swell of raised arms, brandished canes, frantic gestures, dominated in places by children set on the shoulders of their parents, striving to get them out of the crush.

The ground floor of the buildings opposed implacable resistance to that anarchy with lowered iron shutters, but on the entresol and all the upper floors, crowded windows were disgorging, one might have thought, the living substance of houses filled like anthills. The Place de la Madeleine, the church that erects the antique order of its columns there, the roofs and the chimneys—everything was covered with the human swarm; it seemed that people were stacked one on top of another; clusters caused the trees to bend; and we saw a balcony, succumbing under the weight, plunge into the crowd, introducing death and disaster thereto. As for the howls, the imprecations, the blasphemies that accompanied the fury, I dare not record them.

"We're doomed! Link arms! Squeeze together!" I had shouted to my companions at the very beginning, as soon as I realized that it was impossible to go back. And we had seized one another, knotted ourselves together, in such a way as not to allow ourselves to be dissociated, taking care to place Suzanne between Monsieur Vernet and me, to barricade her delicate person with our tense muscles. I sensed her grip imploring my strength. She did not say anything, she did not cry out; she submitted to the assault of pursed lips, palpitating nostrils.

As for me, all my humanity, my fraternal pity bequeathed by centuries of civilization, had vanished at a stroke; I felt myself repossessed by the savage impulses that engaged our remote ancestors to the ferocious egotism of self-preservation; I would have committed murder to defend us. And I pushed, and pushed back, with a cold rage.

And yet, at times, just as the wind stops blowing and destroying in the midst of a tempest, calms were produced; the human tide stagnated, a relative respite leveling out the crowd—above all, when news arrived, coming nearer and nearer. The cries died down then; the fury declared a truce; a wave of emotion, gaining the anxiety of the people, calmed the delirium. The street-rumors in question were, however, highly improbable, even inadmissible; and what surprised me most of all was that the drama that had unfolded a few kilometers from Paris, and was now displaying its menace around the fortifications, was unknown to the majority.

At times, it was announced that the macrobes had been destroyed by the artillery, and explicit details were given about their anatomy, for it was put about that their autopsy had been carried out by the scientists of the Muséum. I remember that in the midst of the silence, a young man who wore the white smock and black skullcap of a hospital intern shouted details of the scientific examination to us from a window.

"Their stomach," he affirmed, "is as big as a dining room where twenty-four guests could eat in comfort. People have been found there alive who were swallowed two days ago, including a great wood-merchant from Mantes, who had to introduce himself to the deputation, and a peasant pushing a wheelbarrow full of carrots. Yes Messieurs, those poor folk had lived on those vegetables! To tell the truth, the effect of gastric juices had left them in a rather sorry state...they presented the same lesions that burns would have produced, but their lives are expected to be saved..."

A ludicrous invention: delirium or joke? The people welcomed those words open-mouthed, immediately passing them on, and those absurdities passed like a consoling breeze. It would not have taken much for us, who knew the unreality of such fables, to have accorded confidence to them, by virtue of a sort of appetite for reassurance, in order to dissipate momentarily the horrible nightmare of our impotence.

But what astonished us more was hearing, from another window, a grave gentleman who looked like a magistrate, wearing the ribbon of the Légion d'honneur, shout to us: "Don't worry! It's all over! The danger is averted! Tornada is nothing but a vulgar usurper; he had no other purpose than to take possession of the government. And that's now done; the president has resigned. Tornada is installed at the Élysée." He added: "Everything will be restored to order...go home in peace!"

I could not imagine that such implausibilities were being pronounced with so much seriousness.

They reflected, moreover, a state of social enervation, which the present situation could not help but exasperate, and of which trouble-makers were bound to take advantage. I had that conviction when, a few meters further on, I collected the report of events that, on this occasion, appeared to me to offer more truth, by virtue of the fact that were more appropriate to the mentality of a people at bay.

Those rumors were confided to me by one of the journalists of the *Parisien*, Dardant's paper. I knew him; we had studied together, and had not run into one another for a long time when the turbulence suddenly brought us face to face. Having entered the crowd in pursuit of material for a sensational article than he hoped to publish the following day, like us, he had been unable to get out. Cramped, jabbing with his elbows, fighting, without ceasing to hold his notebook in one hand and his pencil in the other, he shouted at me:

"Well, what do you think? This is new! Half of Paris is in revolution, did you know that? There's talk of the Commune! I don't understand anything anymore. Do the anarchists want to seize power? What can you expect, with such a government?"

But a surge of the crowd separated us. I saw him dragged away by the countercurrent, compressed and lifted up, then swallowed up, still finding a means to scribble notes in his book. He waved his arms briefly, as if to swim toward me, and then vanished.

In any case, on our side, a sinister band, mingling men and women, foaming at the mouth, their eyes bulging, jostled us. The cohort in question was howling:

"Death to the bourgeois!"

"Down with the Republic!"

"Long live Anarchism!"

"A blood-letting, to save the people!"

"No more rich!"

"No more owners!"

"Filth! Death! Hou! Hou!"

Evidently, our decent clothing made us an objective of their hatred. They surrounded us, they stifled us; and amid the gesticulations of the fanatics, I thought I saw the gleam of a weapon—a revolver or a knife; I no longer know. I only retain, as a certain impression, my fiancée's fearful expression as she turned toward me, and the memory of letting go of her arm for a moment in order to throw a punch and crush the lip of a hooligan who was trying to lay his hands on hr.

That was an imprudence, for my action immediately determined a red rage on the part of the bandits. And I wondered whether we would be able to get out of it, and what massacre might have succeeded my recklessness if, by a strange opposition of popular sentimentality, a procession of students—oh, how invariably insouciant and cheerful that age is—had not interposed themselves between our aggressors and us. The young people arrived, dragged in a crazy saraband, perforating the crowd, so to speak, drunk on noise and youth, shouting, as if in the midst of a fairground, that inept song of which circumstances had definitely determined the fortune:

263

"*Viens, macrobe, viens!*"

They did not break the block of our knotted arms. They passed by, carrying the anarchists away, whom their passion guided elsewhere, away from us; and that distance, limited to a few meters of separation, was worth as much as an immensity in the circumstances. The clamors of revolt were mingled momentarily with the inanities of the song, dissolving into them, each translating the base psychology of the crowd. Soon, other angers, other threats and other fears arriving from all directions, caused us to forget them.

And the tide took possession of us again, hugged us, dragged us away, tossing us once again, in the radiant heat of thousands and thousands of people. Squeezed against one another, arms still enlaced, we allowed ourselves to be carried along by a wave that incessantly brought us back to the same place.

It took us, I think, three hours to cover the distance between the Opéra and the Rue Drouot. Night had fallen completely; we could only distinguish the swarm of people by the light of the rare resinous torches that the police had attached to occasional lamp-posts. After areas of dim light, we passed into frightening shadow, in which abominable actions inspired by exasperated instincts were carried out. In order to protect Suzanne from them as much as possible we kept as close as we could to the border of houses.

Occasionally we passed cafés that were still open, but barricaded, and saw customers inside drinking by the light of candles set in bottlenecks. They looked back at us, immobilized and fearful. Once, there was a veritable charge of the crowd toward a brasserie where people were eating. We heard the sound of breaking windows, revolver shots and women's screams, but we got out of the way in time not to have to witness the pillage of the restaurant.

Twenty paces further on, another spectacle immobilized us again. A cinematographic display flickering at the corner of the boulevard announced that it was about to show scenes of the combat of the artillery against the macrobes—but it did not show any of the sinister animals, and concluded its session with an advertisement for a laxative pill. Then the light abruptly went out.

We had just fallen into darkness again when a clamor rose up, while a human flood carried us away, crushing us, bringing us toward a focal point that we could not perceive.

"My God! People are fighting!" Suzanne shouted to me in the torment. "Let's get out of here!"

Her energy, so terribly put to the proof since we had entered into the torment, seemed to me to be on the point of exhaustion. I could feel her weakening. Was she about to fall into a faint there and then?

"If ever..." I began to say to Monsieur Vernet—but I did not have time to finish the recommendation I was about to give, concerning the way in which we ought to protect the fragile child. The riot got worse, inflating the thunder of voices and causing the people to thrash around in an indescribable confusion.

Not letting go of the person with whom I was primarily concerned, estimating that her father, on the other arm, was an additional burden rather than a support, I exasperated my resistance with the sentiment of my dual responsibility. Beside myself, losing all the sympathy that I normally felt for the unfortunate, even if they were strangers to me, I resisted, shoved back and struck out.

Alas, what did I accomplish during those savage minutes? What terrors did I provoke in order to remain standing? What flesh did I trample in order that mine might subsist, in order that my companions should not come to harm? I dug my heels into people who had fallen; I penetrated torsos, crushed limbs and kicked—alas!—I kicked imploring children out of the way.

And the strangest thing about that odious melee in which everyone was led by circumstances to sacrifice his neighbor is that it had no cause. That murderous crowd was obedient to an irrational panic comparable to that which grips a theater audience when a practical joker shouts "Fire!" although nothing is burning. If all those people had kept still, they would certainly have been content with the restricted space that bound them together. The formidable pressure was compounded out of thousands of individual gestures.

I was soon convinced of that, and felt remorse, when I saw the mob suddenly calm down, as waves calm down when a few drops of oil are poured on them. It only required a policeman standing on the shoulders of another, aiding himself with a small electric torch, to begin reading a government proclamation.

The tumult was extinguished; only a quivering, anxious curiosity replaced the clamors of disorder and the fighting. As we were quite close to the official messenger, I did not miss a word of what was emitted through a bushy moustache, whose coarseness was emphasized by the glare of the torch. And this time, the news, at least in substance, seemed to me to be accurate.

"The government," I heard shouted, "meeting in Ministerial Council, is communicating the latest information concerning the danger threatening Paris, and the measures adopted to remedy it. The public ought not to be unaware that the situation is grave, the macrobes occupying the entire periphery of the city. Their movements, precisely monitored since last night, imply that they are following a plan of investment, the strategy of which will, to all appearances, defeat all the measures taken in anticipation..."

"Hou! Hou!" growled the crowd, at the last, evidently maladroit phrase—but as if the heads of State had anticipated that protestation, the policeman continued:

"Nevertheless, the progress of the macrobes has been temporarily suspended, and nothing suggests that they will resume their march before serious protective measures have been undertaken. The government is pleased to announce that a committee of scientists, with Professor Serviat, a member of the Institut, at the head had succeeded in crossing the monsters' zone of occupation and has penetrated into the laboratory from which the animals originated. The committee informs us by wireless telegraph that, having discovered the process of their de-

265

velopment, it has already found, within the resources of chemistry, the means of destroying them scientifically..."

"Ah! Ah!" the crowd responded to that promise—whose simplicity, however, worried me.

The agent went on: "The government therefore engages the population to remain calm, and not to yield to the actions of the enemies of the Republic, avid to profit from an exceptional situation to disturb social peace. These troublemakers, by creating further disturbances, can only disrupt the calm of mind that is, at present, more precious than ever to the ministers, in order to calculate the danger and confront it. Measures of extreme rigor will, in any case, be taken against agitators of disorder, and the first, for which the government has taken the initiative, is the declaration of a state of siege."

Cheers, mingles with whistles, greeted that announcement, but the policeman signaled by his gestures that he had not yet finished. His voice rose up again in the silence.

"Although able to guarantee the normal reestablishment of security, as much with regard to political troubles as the invasion of the macrobes, the government nevertheless advises the population to take refuge in the subterranean areas of Paris. Access is authorized to the Métropolitain, the Catacombs, the sewers and the tunnels situated beneath the Opéra. The cellars of the Hôtel de Ville, several monuments and certain churches, lists of which will be pinned up in the Mairies, will, by prefectorial warrant, be delivered to the public. A system of food supply will be organized tomorrow by the municipality..."

"Ha! We'll believe that when we see it!" shouted a street-urchin, in the midst of the silence that fooled the end of the sentence.

Oh, the Parisian people! How fickle they are! Laughter underlined that childish gibe—and that was a good thing, because it downed out the end of the proclamation, which made a further demand for the confidence of the people and announced that the police were on the track of Tornada.

"That manifesto is signed by Durand-Tartapian, the Minister of the Interior," Monsieur Vernet breached, in the momentary calm. He added: "Notice that he's only inspired by political concerns. Isn't that typically modern? So I only grant him a very limited credit. The annihilation of the monsters seems to me to be increasingly improbable. I prefer to retain from that statement only the article that permits us to hide. But where shall we go, my children? You've seen the state of this crowd—its lack of restraint, of wisdom. You've seen its fury. And then, going down into the Metro—will that be possible?"

"Isn't it more prudent to try our luck in the Catacombs?" I asked.

"Evidently, the Catacombs are less well-known, but they're a long way away—the entrance is in the Place Denfert-Rochereau...and my poor Suzanne..."

"I feel capable of going as far as that, Father."

"Let's go then, let's go!"

266

We were just in time; the crowd was going crazy again. Bawling, scream-ing and revolutionary songs burst forth not far away. An immense flame, sudden flaring up in the vicinity, revealed that the sedition had not been quieted by the government's fine words. We turned round and saw a column of fire, plumed by millions of sparks, shoot up behind the rooftops of the houses.

"What's burning?" people were asking.

"It's the Opéra!"

"No, it's the Crédit Lyonnais."

"No, it's further away—it's the Printemps or the Thêátre de l'Athenée..."

The guesses were drowned out by the rumors. A horde grouped around a black flag prolonged its stir as far as our group, and suddenly, the terror of a sin-gle man dominated the tumult for an instant. I heard the cried of a tortured beast and, standing on tiptoe, I saw in the uncertain light of the distant fire that they were murdering the policeman who had just read the official message. Oh, those clamors that grabbed your guts, that slaughter of a worthy man!

"Run! Let's run!" Suzanne begged.

All our energy from then on was consecrated to moving obliquely to the right, in order to take the Rue Richelieu, which was nearby. The crowd was shoving, stifling us, proffering its futile, desperate rage from a hundred thousand mouths, shouting: "Death to Tornada! Death to Tornada!" The roadway was nothing but a roaring furnace, fueled by hatred. Oh, how urgently we strove to get out of it! What blows we gave and received! What savage precipitation!

Finally, after further actions that I dare not remember, we were finally moving into the desired street when a cry from Suzanne immobilized us.

"There he is! The wretch! The wretch1"

At first, I thought she had gone mad. But on observing the object that had unleashed her anger, I was petrified. There, inside a café, I saw Tornada!

It was him; there was no doubt about it. It was him, because of his ravaged face, agitated by tics, because of his vast beard hanging down to his belt, which his nervous fingers were occupying in buckling and then unbuckling. It was him, sitting in front of a peppermint cordial, the reflection of which, projected by a candle-flame, tinted his sardonic laughter green. It was him, watching with im-punity, triumphantly, his vengeance of genius!

At first, anger invaded me, a temptation to launch myself at his abominabb person, to break the glass that separated me from him, to wind his long hairy beard around his neck and squeeze, strangling him with it! But a wisdom, a council of moderation that I read in the attitude of my companions, immediately put a brake on my rage. Ill-placed as we were to exchange our sentiments in the midst of that frightful tumult, those clamors stifling our voices, I understood from the gestures of Suzanne and her father rather than their words that they wanted me to get to the madman, and to get him to put an end to the cataclysm.

They would have attempted it themselves, with more chance of influence than I had, if two insurmountable obstacles—firstly the crowd, and then a large barricade of barrels protecting the glazed window—had not separated them from the criminal. I saw Monsieur Vernet's mouth open to shout a recommendation to me, but I could not hear his voice. Then he indicated to me, by lowering his finger, a possible route through an open ventilation-shaft to the kitchens, and with another gesture, his resolution to remain where he was until the negotiations were concluded.

I shivered at those mute orders. Would I ever find them again? Deprived of my support, would they not be borne away?

After that hesitation, which any fiancé will excuse, I released my arm from Suzanne's, cleaved through the human border encrusting the walls, and plunged into the ventilation-shaft, which was only just wide enough to permit the passage of a human body.

IX

I plunged, it is necessary to say, arms outstretched and head first; and it is a pure miracle that I was not badly hurt in that somersault, which an acrobat would have refused to execute. It is certain that great emotions count among the best anesthetics, for, like a soldier who does not feel the bullet that has passed right through his body, I felt neither the violence of my fall nor the tearing of my wrist when my hands encountered the flagstones of the kitchen. Furthermore, my movement of propulsion toward that dark and unknown place was so rapid, so irrational that I dare not affirm that it ended on the floor. It is possible that I encountered obstacles that attenuated its brutality, and that I fell on to sacks or baskets of comestible provisions. In truth, I no longer know.

At any rate, the kitchen was not deserted, and curses greeted me as soon as I stood up again. Directing my gaze toward a corner of the room where an oil-lamp was spreading a light so feeble that it was indistinguishable from outside, I saw half a dozen people sitting around a table covered with victuals, occupied in eating with a serenity and an appetite that appeared to me not to lack irony.

It was a kitchen household of the classic type: the obese man clad in white with a cloth cap tilted over his ear; the fat woman with three chins collapsing toward enormous breasts; in the company of four apprentices as thin as their seniors were blossoming with fat.

"No one can come in!" the man commenced by shouting at me, brandishing his fork.

"It's not allowed!" said his companion, supportively, pausing in her mastication.

"Does Monsieur have his invitation on him?" chaffed one of the apprentices.

"Don't disturb yourselves, my friends," I replied.

That dialogue, whose flavor would have been appreciated by a vaudevillian, but which only revealed a perfectly natural emotion in either side, did not cheer up the diners. At first they affirmed their intention of sending me back by the same route that I had arrived, but they doubtless feared that my example might be followed by others, for, after a conference whose details were inaudible to me, the man got up to go and close the ventilation-shaft by means of a solid iron lid. He cursed at the same time, declaring to me, with irritated eyes, that he was going to lack air now, and that he detested "eating while stifling."

"I beg your pardon," I said, humbly, when I thought he had calmed down slightly. "Excuse me—I'm just passing through. Will you allow me to go and join one of my friends, who is waiting for me in the café?"

But he shook his head. "No one goes through—I told you that, Monsieur. It would take no more than that for us to open the doors to customers. We'd no longer be at home then."

"Listen," I said. "The meeting I have upstairs is important. Do you know who you have upstairs? Do you know who I've just seen, from the street? Tornada!"

"Tornada?"

"Yes, Tornada."

"Who's that?"

"What! You don't know! You don't know the name of Tornada?"

Thinking that I was the object of his mockery, at the height of irritation, I had folded my arms.

"Tornada?" the man repeated. "Unknown, Tornada. Me, I live quietly."

"We only know *tournedos*," confided the female cook.

"But what about the macrobes?" I howled. "You've heard mention of them? Well, Tornada, their inventor, their creator, is upstairs!"

This time, Homeric laughter welcomed my declaration. Oh, the macrobes! What a joke! No, the story of the macrobes was for others! They knew perfectly well that it was only an invention of the revolutionaries, made to deceive the people, to whip them up, to drive them along, as the barking of dogs directs a flock of sheep to a determined point, and no serious man would ever be naïve enough to attach any faith to it. And the apprentices, infected by the chef's explosion, laughed uproariously, clutching their bellies.

"That's fine," I said. "Retain your absurd confidence. I'm not going to waste my time convincing you—but I need to go through and I shall. Show me the way."

I must have looked intimidating, because the man's gaiety suddenly died down. Cowed, he opened a door for me and pointed to a dark stairway. I groped my way up the steps, and, guided by the noise, went through another door and reached the common room.

Immediately, I recognized the madman enveloped by the halo of the green liquid. I slid through the crowded ranks of the customers and joined him.

I paused momentarily to look at him. He seemed even stranger than before, more firmly in the grip of his dementia than during our previous meeting. Folded in two on his chair, having buttoned his jacket over the threads of his beard, it seemed to me that he had scarcely recovered from a convulsion that had furrowed his brow terribly and was still agitating his right arm. The candlelight, gliding over his cranium, emphasized its improbable bumps, and his cheekbones, crimsoned at present, were jutting in the midst of the green tint of the rest of his face.

He stretched, sniggered and stammered a few words; then, picking up a piece of paper that the fit had caused him to drop, he began scribbling on it, and soon seemed to be nothing but a peaceful mathematician or a mild philosopher, transporting through the disaster the passion of a metaphysical problem.

"Monsieur Tornada! Monsieur Tornada!" I said, in a voice that would have softened the heart of a Chinese torturer.

He did not raise his head. He continued to draw the tip of his pencil over the sheet of paper. Leaning toward his work, I perceived that he was drawing a map of Paris, around which a number of little crosses had been marked. In less tragic circumstances, I would certainly have attempted to identify the positions of those crosses, which obviously related to the present calamity, and I would have discovered the emplacements of the monsters investing us. But the moment scarcely inspired my mind to curiosity, and I was intent on another liberating concern.

"Monsieur Tornada! Monsieur Tornada!" I repeated, this time touching him on the shoulder.

He flinched, as if he had been touched by an electric discharge. He covered his drawing with his fully-extended hand, then screwed it up, rolled it into a ball, shoved it in his mouth, and started masticating it. Only then did he look at me, and I judged by his wild expression that he did not recognize me. His breathing accelerated; three times, his eyes disappeared beneath his eyelids in such a fashion as only to show the whites; his hands described a few movements imitating the extension and subsequent retreat of a tentacle, and after having spat out the ball of paper, he finally resumed a normal expression.

During that further fit, I had had time to finish observing the alteration of his features, noting their satanic expression, increased by the surprise of hearing his name spoken aloud. The extension of his vibratile ears, the planes and hollows sculpted in his visage, and the prognathism of his jaw had adopted such reliefs that, in truth, his physiognomy no longer looked human.

"Who are you?" he demanded, in a distant voice, which the ambient noise made even fainter.

"You don't recognize me?"

"No."

"I'm Mademoiselle Vernet's fiancé."

I perceived that that name, thrown into his mind, immediately acquired such an influence there that I thought at first that I could count on its evocation. Tornada must have been going through one of those psychological states in which delirium is still semi-conscious, in which the inspiration of a fact, or a person, can be sufficient to modify the current of a determination, when the brain takes possession of it. His face as imprinted with a very particular softness; tears flowed from his eyelids.

"Oh! Yes, Suzanne...Suzanne..." he stammered. "How glad I am to have advised her to flee! She's far away now. She and my worthy friend are far out of range of my darlings!"

"No!" I protested, violently. "They haven't fled! They're here, nearby. You can see them from here, jostled by that furious crowd! For pity's sake, Monsieur..."

"Yes, I'm glad," he affirmed, rubbing his hands.

He was no longer listening to me. At the same time, I had sown the seeds of another upheaval in his mental ferment, and he was surrendering to it, completely forgetting the first. I thought it prudent to allow that new eruptive lava to flow away before returning to my supplication, and I listened to his rambling words.

"But the others! Oh, the poor people! Are they miserable enough? Look at them! This is a good place from which to observe them. You've never seen anything like it! I had to be born for that! The elements have never given any idea of such a cataclysm! They're mightily imbecilic, the elements! They make the ground tremble, they parade cyclones, stir up tidal waves...but what's that, compared with what I've created? What is it, in truth? An entire people...the most beautiful of peoples...the French people...!"

He laughed sardonically. Then, accentuating the lines on his forehead, clenching his fists, he panted, with such profusion that that I had difficulty divining what kind of ideas corresponded to each of his statements: "Me, in my laboratory...a culture, a simple culture...darlings...soda and chalk combined...atmospheric demi-pressure...and yellow, yellow, yellow...! And then, I had to fix the acidity...then, every day, a little more...I caressed them...I held them in the palm of my hand...oh, what a thrill! What a thrill, my darling!"

He punctuated his speech with special gestures, translating the entire evolution of his phenomenon. Sometimes his hands described circles, sometimes zigzags; sometimes they seemed to be palpating substance, sometimes stoking spines. But he became suddenly suspicious of me, and looked at me warily.

"If you ever repeat...."

"No, no," I protested. "Trust me! You know how much admiration I have for you, for your work...and the bonds that unite me with Suzanne..."

"Have they gone to the Midi?" he asked, anxiously.

It was the moment, propitious once again, to soften him, to remind him of two friends, whom the torment was bringing closer to us. I could, in fact, see through the window that the shadows outside were agitating more violently; the eye of the popular cyclone was moving toward the window of the café. A strident cry that I thought I recognized as that of my fiancée was a more imperious

271

appeal for the rapid execution of my project to save us from death by means of the murderer himself.

"Listen," I said to him. "Listen carefully…leave your dreams for a moment. You love Suzanne like your own daughter, don't you?"

"Yes, my daughter, my poor child!"

"And Monsieur Vernet, you love him too, you hold him in esteem?"

"He's the only brain in the Institut," he affirmed.

"Well, both of them…"

I was unable to go on. A formable crack resounded from the front of the café. The barricade of barrels that was forbidding access had just given way, thunderously. A hurricane of cries, the last plaint of those who were choking and trampled underfoot, unfurled, accompanied by the sound of glass panes shattered by the rush. The human sea invaded our refuge, sweeping away the tables of the original customers, driving as far as the café's counter in an indescribable disorder. A thousand terrified faces, a thousand howling faces, were dancing before my eyes—and among them I recognized, fearfully, the most dear of faces: Suzanne, alone, struggling in the torment, extending the imploration of her hands and the agony of her gaze toward me.

Then, I forgot Tornada, who had just stood up, uttering a burst of insane laughter. I precipitated myself toward my fiancée, and reached her, by means of I don't know what prodigy of force and ferocity. Then, after having drawn her to me, encircling her with my arms: "Your father, Suzanne?"

"Separated! Carried away! Lost!"

"Where? Which way?"

"That way! That way! Oh, let's search for him, Jean, for pity' sake! Let's find him! Him first…"

I drew her toward the outside. Fortunately, a counter-surge facilitated our exit, and we were able to slide along the wall, avidly interrogating the atrocious melee that the sentiment of individual defense was still driving to the worst actions.

To describe my fiancée's despair to you would be impossible. A thousand times she called out to her father in the torment. A thousand times, retained by my hand, she whirled around in the same space of ten square meters, stiffening herself against the tide of men, women and children. We were no longer thinking about Tornada, nor of revenge. We were interrogating the swell of heads frantically, without the beloved white head showing itself therein. Futile efforts! Soon, a more forceful mob swept us back into the street that we had decided to take before being separated from Monsieur Vernet.

"Don't worry, my dear Suzanne," I said to her. "We'll find him again at the Catacombs."

In tears, fearful, in despair, she obeyed me. We had only to allow ourselves to be shoved along the Rue Richelieu. Lighting had not been provided there, unlike the boulevards; the conflagration did not project any light there, and it was pitch black, the haunted night of murders and crimes. Oh, what a terrible odyssey, what instincts, in that darkness! I still shiver at the thought.

Outside the Bibliothèque Nationale, however, I suddenly felt Suzanne stop holding on to me. She weakened; she collapsed in a faint. I took her in my arms and carried her, utterly limp, thinking that I was no longer holding anything but a corpse. The flood threw me out, with my precious burden, in the Place du Palais-Royal, where a torch was burning. Seeing that the crowd was battling furiously to reach the entrance to the Metro, I made a detour and took refuge in the Place du Carrousel, which was dark and relatively deserted. I reached the Gambetta monument and deposited the object of my adoration, who was just coming round, on the stone. I was out of breath, incapable of any further action.

"My father? Where's my father?" Suzanne asked, faintly.

I strove in vain to console her. She wept, and through her tears she stammered the same question, incessantly. Sitting beside her, I rested her head on my shoulder. At that moment, I knew all the distress of hearing her suffer and remaining impotent. Mothers who watch their children die must experience those sharp emotions.

Gradually, however, Suzanne's plaints became spaced out. Soon, I could not perceive anything but regular breathing—child-like breathing. Exhausted, she had fallen asleep. I felt a horrible fatigue myself, which went so far as to dominate the sharp pain in my wrist. I no longer had the courage to do anything but lay my fiancée on the ground and cover her with my jacket.

And under a sky whose implacable darkness was spangled with stars, like a funereal awning, I went to sleep in my turn.

X

The next day, as soon as the livid daylight appeared, the fresh air and the pain in my wrist woke me up.

Was it, in fact, really those factors that recalled me to the ambient reality? Was it not rather a song that pursued me momentarily in my sleep? At any rate, when I opened my eyes, I fund before me an indescribable presence. I would have smiled, on any other occasion, on recognizing the man who was singing *"Viens, macrobe, viens!"*—the same individual who, the day before, had sold us old brioches for an exorbitant price. His Neptunian hair covered by a flat-brimmed hat, his nose reddened by cold, his replete body shivering in a long gray frock-coat, he was strolling with a artificial gaiety through the desolation of others; and with his pipe in his mouth, he never ceased to continue the success of his song. I even believe I remember that he was staggering slightly.

I turned my eyes away with dignity in order to gaze at my fiancée, lying beside me. She was adorably pale, continuing her child-like slumber.

Then I looked at the Place du Carrousel. In that magnificent space, as in the sumptuous perspective of the Jardin des Tuileries, there was nothing but a succession of groups formed by people who had imitated us; the ground was strewn with exhausted people, still asleep. Only might have thought it a desolate field where all afflictions were united, parents with children, husbands with wives. Some were waking up and stretching. Sobs rose up behind me, on the other side of the grille surrounding the Gambetta monument. It was lamentable...

An usher from the Colonial Ministry, recognizable by his blue coat with gold buttons, came down from the Pavillon de Flore and advanced through the heaps, stepping over bodies. Allowing Suzanne to sleep, and without losing sight of her, I went toward the man, as others did, who were surrounding him already.

"Well, what's the news?"

"You're in luck, Messieurs. We possess fresh intelligence, for the telephone service as just been reestablished."

"So, what do you have to tell us?"

"Nothing very cheerful. They're ferocious; they've destroyed the Élysée, taken the Hôtel de Ville, blown up the bridges surrounding the Île Saint-Louis and massacre the troops sent against them—and it's said that they've set fire to the warehouses at Ivry. I noticed a gleam, yesterday evening..."

"What do you mean? Are they setting fire to things too?"

"Oh, they won't deprive us, the monsters!"

"It's their leader, doubtless?"

"A famous scoundrel, Monsieur! He declared the Commune last night! What will become of us, the honest functionaries...?"

"Tornada has...?"

"Tornada!" said the man, looking me up and down, angrily, beginning to think that I was making fun of him.

Only then did I understand that the honest functionary in question had no other concern that informing me of the triumph of the Revolution in Paris. Anarchy had sprung forth from the danger threatening the city; the sectarians had taken advantage of the confusion to change the government. And his first, his gravest preoccupation was what was going to become of his position and his salary, comfortably acquired by eight hours of daily idleness, in consequence of the social upheaval. The other danger did not exist, in the face of that personal anxiety.

"But what about the macrobes, my good man?"

"The macrobes? Well, they're still there."

"Are there any details?"

"No. They haven't budged during the night."

"You're talking as if their presence around Paris doesn't worry you?"

"It might worry me, if Monsieur Serviat, the great chemist, weren't occupied with them, but with him, one can rest assured. Oh, he's a clever one, Serviat!"

"Why? What has he done?"

274

"You don't know? It's odd that you're so ignorant."

"Speak, speak, my god man!" I pressed him, panting to know.

"Well, he's succeeded in getting into the macrobes' cave out there at Rosny, near Mantes..."

"That was proclaimed, indeed, but I thought..."

"It's not necessary to think; it's necessary to know. Me, I know."

"Speak! Speak!"

He hesitated. The confidences he had imparted so easily in talking about the revolution seemed to grip him at heart now that he had to surrender information of much greater interest. Perhaps, in fact, he did not know anything at all, and was talking to make himself seem important.

He smiled blissfully. "This is it: Serviat has returned, and it appears that he's found a secret to destroy the vile beasts—a kind of chemical product that he's gone to offer to the new government, to curry favor. Oh, he's a clever one, Serviat...he doesn't forget, he's thinking about his situation."

From his parted lips the usher expelled a little jet of saliva. Then, pushing his cap toward the back of his occiput, he said: "Me, Monsieur, I wouldn't have been so confused. I know what I'd have done, if I'd been the government. Yes, it wouldn't have taken long."

"What would you have done, my good man?"

"I'd have gathered all the honest folk underground, and left the surface of the communards."

"And then?"

"Then I'd have sent the army against them—a well-disciplined, strong army, with cannons. We pay enough taxes for that."

"And?"

"Then, naturally, the communards would have been chased out of Paris."

"Naturally," I agreed, with a certain pity.

"And what would have happened?"

"Yes, what would have happened?"

"The macrobes would have wolfed the lot, M'sieu...and that would have been a good thing, M'sieu!"

And the honest functionary, as soon as he had revealed his strategic plan, drew away, rubbing his hands.

I have taken the trouble to record that conversation with the usher, not because of the interest it presents in itself—for in truth, it was rather puerile—but because it is very significant of the mentality that animated an entire people in those hours of fear. It is curious to observe the paltry considerations can result from the instinct of conservation, which is generally believed to be purified, and magnified by centuries of civilizing atavism.

Although the very existence of society was compromised, and a giant ring surrounded Paris, ready to stifle it, the predominant concern among thousands of citizens was to modify the social order, to change the formula of government, and to base individual hopes on political calculations; while thousands of other citizens only envisaged the dispossession with terror. Yes it was expectable, the panic of all the poor people dominated in spite of everything by obsessions of an inferior and purely self-interested order; and every heir having to think about his inheritance, while every businessman was already planning the speculations that the disaster would allow him to stir up. It is said by a reliable source that when Messina began to collapse after a subterranean convulsion, as soon as the news broke, avid businessmen took the train to the destroyed city, running the risk of further quakes, with the sole aim of buying cheap the land diminished in price by the cataclysm—like birds of prey flocking to charnel-house without noticing the rifles aimed at them.

Well, with regard to the drama through which I lived, the same disconcerting psychological observation was recordable. Certainly, in many circumstances, evidence of admirable abnegation compensated for the vileness of the general egotism. Certainly, there were heroic parents, devoted children, spouses and fiancés, whose altruism was sufficient in itself to ornament the story of such a calamity with the most beautiful nobility—fortunately for human dignity. But I repeat, the vast majority no longer took advice from anything but the dryness of their hearts; the people who were no longer dominated by the fear of the gendarme, and the gendarme too—an honest functionary, in essence—all, I have reason to think, were only obedient in that enormous adventure to the impulses of an eminently shabby self-interest.

That was for me an incomparable lesson in philosophy, and I would certainly have taken longer inspiration therefrom if my anxiety had not brought me back to Suzanne. I went to rejoin her, my heart suddenly calmed, only wanting to remember from the usher's words the intoxicating hope of our imminent liberation. I thought that the pause in the macrobes' progress had been inspired by Tornada, and that the madman, finding his vengeance sufficient, had used his mysterious power over the monsters to prevent them from advancing. A further contribution to the accreditation of that sentiment, moreover, was the presence of Tornada, observed by me the previous evening, which I wanted to consider as a safeguard. Would he expose himself to the risk of being crushed or devoured along with everyone else?

Vibrantly, I came back to Suzanne and woke her up in order to tell her what I knew, and what I had concluded from the usher's words.

"Oh, if it's true, what a liberation!" she sighed. "Only let me hug my father in my arms, and I'll forget this entire drama!"

"Let's go, Suzanne. No doubt we'll find him soon."

Fragile hope! A terrifying noise responded to that remark, and plunged us back into the frightful reality. Oh, that was the moment when we entered more cruelly into that improbable drama. What a frisson suddenly ran through me—for I was too well aware of the significance of the *Frott...! Frott...! Frott...!* that we could hear not to begin trembling, manifestly enough for Suzanne to experience the reverberation of my emotion.

She did not even have time to question me. An incredible racket, produced by the collapse of houses, burst forth in the surroundings, as if an earthquake had shaken the whole city. The horrified clamor of a people was mingled with it, dominated most of all by the roaring that revealed the proximity of the monsters. They could be heard arriving from every direction: from Les Halles, from the Saint-Germain quarter, from the great boulevards, from the region of the Hôtel de Ville. Yes, everywhere! From all directions the deadly hordes were running, sacking, swallowing, at the very moment when we were counting on the pity of their creator. By virtue of what incredible accord were they making that unanimous irruption, surrounding the center of Paris with a destructive circle?

To begin with, we ran toward the Jardin des Tuileries. Then we stopped, like hunted animals, uncertain of which way to go. paralyzed by the roars that were bursting forth from all directions. I took hold of Suzanne's trembling hand. A common, infinite distress stupefied us. We stared at one another, awaiting the event that would annihilate us.

A few minutes were eternalized in that unspeakable terror. Then I saw—did I really see it? was I not delirious? am I not delirious now in recounting it?—an enormous mass, like an elongated gray rock that had surged from the entrails of the earth, fill the sky while accomplishing a forward roll, and fall directly upon the buildings of the Finance Ministry, which collapsed under its weight.

The light of day had been suddenly diminished by it. Dust billowed up from the crushed building, continuing the artificial demi-obscurity, with the result that the macrobe that had just introduced itself so fantastically began its devastating work without me being able to distinguish it clearly. It finally emerged from its cloud, and I estimated, in spite of my terror, that it was a little taller than the level of a fourth floor, and that the area of the Cour du Carrousel permitted it just enough room to crawl along, dilating its body and then shrinking it again. Meanwhile, its trunk, projected in all directions by a rapid rotation and endowed with an incalculable force of suction, collected on the wing, if I might put it thus, all the wretched, tiny people who were running along the ground and drew them into it.

Oh, the unforgettable nightmare! The macrobe went back and forth, turning and roaring—and we stood there contemplating it, a cold sweat on our temples, our limbs limp, petrified, involuntarily uttering little inarticulate squeaks, which we could not repress. We sensed that it was about to suck us in like the others, but we did not budge.

It accomplished a rush to the right, and then it came back toward the Gambetta monument, and stopped there. That pause was lucky for us, at the same time as it signified a new threat for the future. I had thought, in fact, after the failure of the bombs, that Tornada's creatures were blind and moved toward their fodder by means of a simple sniffing of their tentacle, but I was obliged by

277

what I saw then to be convinced that they were endowed with sight in some part of their body that I could not identify. It is impossible to interpret otherwise the act that followed the macrobe's hesitation.

In fact, the latter sniffed the statue of the orator forcefully; then, observing that the bronze did not respond to its attractive force, seized by rage, it wrapped its trunk around it and tore it free. It held it for a moment; then, finally recognizing its error, hurled it into the air prodigiously. I followed the trajectory described by the projectile, and even before the thought occurred to me that it might annihilate us, I saw it fall five meters away from us, digging into the ground and flattening, with a red splash, a poor man dressed in a gray frock-coat, who was singing, in accordance with the whim of a parodist of whom history ought to speak: "*Viens, macrobe, viens!*"

That crushing, so close to us, rendered us all our terror. We fled then, recklessly. Pursued by the whistling of the tentacle, by the broom-like swishing that the carapace made, our ears ringing, carried on by the gallop of others, we reached the flower garden of the Tuileries, and then the bank of the Seine.

I do not know by virtue of what miracle we escaped at that moment. Lifted up twenty times by the air current that the trunk produced, and dropped to the ground twenty times, we struggled with our last reserves of energy against the fury of the torrent of suction. Alongside us, galloping like us, we had already seen the ministry usher disappear, and then a curé who dropped to his knees, and then women, children and a hundred others. It was amazing to observe the facility with which the monster snatched them up and caused them to fly into the flared conch that constituted the tip of its appendage. One might have thought that a magnetic current was drawing them in.

In any case, my senses were so confused at that moment, and my preoccupation to maintain my fiancée next to me so vivid, and my blood, hastened by running, was making such glimmers dance before my eyes, that I dare not affirm anything further about that frightful minute. Certainly, however, other things must have happened during that flight, which took us along the edge of the Place de la Concorde and then the Cours-la-Reine, at the speed of a runaway horse.

I do remember that when we arrived at the Pont d'Alma, after stopping momentarily, and noticing that no macrobe was in view on the other bank, I shouted to Suzanne, in a suffocation: "To the Eiffel Tower! Across the bridge! To the Eiffel Tower!"

For the moment, I was truly inspired. The monster, in fact, did not follow us. Its gray mass continued to snake along the other bank, crushing the trees, disemboweling the buildings, swallowing the unfortunates who had not imitated us.

It seemed to us that we were quitting the torments of Hell to enter into a paradise of solitude. Humans, you who ordinarily walk at a measured pace, you will never know how delightful it was for us to advance with less haste, to let ourselves ease our breathing momentarily, all the more so as we had taken for the objective of our relented course the liberating tower, the summit of which we could see, installed in the warmth of the nascent sun, and we had the certainty that its tall framework would soon be disengaged from its girdle of troops, because the horses of the Republican Guards, relieved of their riders, were galloping toward us. I felt the hoof of one of them brush me, like a caress, as it passed by.

Will I be able to recount what followed without hating destiny? When we arrived at the tower, the situation was scarcely any more enviable. Our last refuge was inaccessible. An entire population was battling to climb up it. Men were killing one another like ferocious beasts, in order to reach safety. The stairways and struts of the edifice, from a few meters above the ground, were black with people, bristling with human clusters. They formed the swarm of an anthill, a feverish swell, rising to the most elevated positions. I saw people hanging on to columns letting go and falling on to their fellows.

As for myself, I no longer knew any chivalrous sentiment, or any pity. Dragging Suzanne, I rushed into the melee, and knew the horrible intoxication of thrusting people aside, striking out, perhaps killing...I can no longer remember. But I retain since that time, the greatest indulgence for crimes engendered by the instincts.

And I shoved, and I struck out, in order to reach the first marble step of the southern stairway; and I was about to reach it when a roar burst forth a hundred meters away from us, and then a second, and then others.

Of course! I was stupid not to have realized that those twenty million preys perched on the tower would tempt our engulfers!

And the macrobes came running from all directions; their gray mass surged forth; their prodigious bounds filled every sector of the horizon, and then landed on the nourishing heap, while their avid trunks, whirling and roaring, ate into the crowd.

Oh, to flee, to flee again! Alas, we no longer had that possibility; the crowd paralyzed us, froze us with its far, by the very suspension of its fratricidal actions.

Momentarily, I had a flicker of hope, for the pressure threw us toward the Pont d'Iéna and I thought it was free and launched myself toward it...ah yes! One last monster, the one that had been pursuing us a little while before, moved on to it.

Then, there was nothing else to do but await the hecatomb. I darted one last glance of distress and love at Suzanne, to which she responded with an unexpected expression, as her face brightened with the celestial exaltation of martyrs.

"It's over, Suzanne! This time, we're doomed!" I stammered, with a shiver.

"Well, let's die in the river—together!" she shouted.

Yes! Any death at all rather than the monsters' tentacle!

In a few bounds, we tumbled down the stairs that led to the jetty. The river, an image of serenity in the face of the disaster, was rolling magnificently. The idea of disappearing into it enveloped me with a sovereign tranquility.

I drew my fiancée against me, and, passing her all my heart in a first and final kiss, surrendered myself with her to the Lethean wave.

XI

I no longer recall exactly what happened during the minute that followed our leap into the Seine, for I was at the end of thought and suffering, and I no longer had any idea in my head but finishing it, and holding Suzanne in my arms. I retain the memory, however, that the coldness of the water seemed beneficent to me, and that my ears filled with a splashing that replaced the noisy clamors from without.

Then...was it the instinct of preservation, superior to my will that brought me to the surface and, in spite of the weight of my garments, forced me to utilize the current that was bearing us away? Was it me who sustained Suzanne, or was it her who, with a hesitation equal to mine, maintained herself intelligently on my shoulder while I swam? I cannot say. I cannot specify anything apart from the moment when, after having traversed the entire width of the river, I saw the people on the quay on the other bank who were making signs to me. I have the perception that someone threw me a rope, and that the rope was terminated by an anchor, which remained on the surface of the water.

With the aid of chance, and also my skill, I succeeded in hooking the spike of that anchor to my fiancée's dress. Without seeing it, for I was now too busy resisting the current, I divined that someone was pulling her ashore and hoisting her up on to the quay. Then someone threw me the anchor, to which I clung, in order to be lifted up in my turn. I vaguely recognized the large wall on which the Pont d'Iéna is seated, and finally fainted, out of strength, into a gentle oblivion.

The dolor of the wound on my wrist, which had reopened during the preceding events, reanimated me. My first perceptions were strange, and continued to give me the impression that I was living in a dream. What could I see, then? What was that dark room, feebly lit by a smoky lamp, in which people were leaning over me, watching my awakening with interest?

What amazed me most of all, though, was to observe that the light was playing over the breastplate of an ancient suit of armor, looming up in front of me. I remained in that vague hesitation, my ears assaulted by noises emanating from the far side of the room. Then, as an individual leaned toward me, I saw on his face the features of Monsieur Serviat, the chemist, the friend of my future father-in-law.

I have not said enough about Monsieur Serviat, who plays a preponderant role in this story. Monsieur Serviat was, as I have already said, a highly placed official scientist whose career had been singularly favored by circumstances and chance. He was also haloed by a legend, and during gala days at the Élysée he never failed, as he pointed to the commander's cross pinned to his lapel, to declare that twenty-three years before, he had only been a humble pharmacist's errand boy, sweeping the shop and delivering bottles of medicine all over the city. One fine day, in the middle of an epidemic—it was a good day for pharmacists—he had stood in for the sick apprentice, crushing potassium chlorate and adding julep syrup with such joy that his employer had been amazed and, having taken him under his protection, had sent him to study the art dear to Monsieur Purgon.[57]

No one suspects the fortune that a man thus launched into science might acquire. Knowing that he is unsupported, everyone takes an interest in him; devoid of protection, everyone protects him; and devoid of esteem, everyone admires him, and admires themselves at the same time. If the sons of Papa succeed easily, the sons of many Papas have even greater chances of success. No one will be astonished, therefore, that the député for Carcassonne, from which young Serviat hailed, obtained a bursary from the city for him, and that old ladies clubbed together to add the dessert dishes to the city's beefsteaks. There was a Serviat Committee, and the child of Carcassonne, glorious in his examinations, became the glory of the entire Midi when, a little later, appointed a professor of chemistry, he praised the alimentary vale of alcohol—but, it goes without saying, the good alcohol, the sole inoffensive alcohol, that the vintners distil. From then on, having become a great citizen of the region, all meridional political influences coalesced to aid him to pass through the doors of the Institut while still young.

Never did any man wear the green coat so valiantly. He put it on for all occasions. When anyone had need of that color to embellish a wedding or garnish a table, he immediately came running. He paraded himself, strutted, put on airs and flirted merrily. He did not lack, moreover, either the appetite for work enjoyed by those who have begun work too late to have used up their intellect, nor the faculty of assimilation the brains possess which are spared the multiple and confused registrations of childhood. He gave lectures; he was a kind of commercial traveler of science. His few discoveries got a lot of publicity, without being absolutely new—but they passed for such, in consequence of the fortunate death of a few insignificant collaborators. And we know the results of the fracassite, which he had invented without anyone's aid. All things considered, a charming man.

Well, my friend, are you feeling better?" he asked me, as soon as he discovered the reactivation of my gaze.

"Yes...but what has become of Suzanne?" I asked, immediately.

"Have no fear, the young woman is here," he replied.

---

[57] A character in Molière's *Le Malade imaginaire* (1673), physician to the hypochondriac who gives the play its title.

I sat up, and distinguished my fiancée lying on the ground in the middle of another group, in the halo of another lamp. She woke up just in time to send me a sad smile with her lips, and began asking for her father insistently. At that moment I lost consciousness again.

A little later, the energetic flagellations of a wet cloth on my face rendered me the use of my senses definitively. Then, my eyes adapting to the place, I recognized that I was in a kind of stonework gallery between fifteen and twenty meters long and about three wide, about one and a half times my stature in height. On one side, to my right, the tunnel opened to the outside, so far as I could judge by the daylight filtering through the base of a grille placed over a door; while on the other side, to my left, the conduit plunged steeply into the earth, extending into an obscurity disturbed by clamors. A confusion of voices was buzzing in that refuge, dominating a sound of water that I could clearly hear running in the darkness when the voices died down. When I extended my led to stretch it, my foot collided with something hard, like a rail.

"Where am I, then?" I asked Monsieur Serviat, who had just addressed a few words to the heroic armor.

"You're at the entrance of the sewer that opens on to the Quai de Billy, my friend."

That response allowed me to get my bearings. I had, in my time, visited the underground regions of Paris, and I knew that there exist in places, communicating with the Seine, galleries known as "outlets," facilitating the clearance of sewers. By that means, the sandy debris that accumulates in the drains can be collected and transferred to boats which transport it some distance away. The same conduits, in addition, permit collectors to disgorge their overflow into the river in times when abundant rains provoke sudden floods.

That explained all that I had just glimpsed, including the illumination of the wan service lamps, the presence of rails under my feet, and the nearby wagons. It was an unexpected freak of chance that the plunge into the Seine that Suzanne and I had made had terminated just at the entrance to one of those galleries, and that we had had the good fortune to be picked up there.

Good fortune? Was it necessary to give so much thanks to fate? Should we not rather, on the contrary, have cursed it for having snatched Suzanne and me from the oblivion to which we had reconciled ourselves? What would become of us in the midst of these people that hazard and fear had assembled in this subterranean duct? Who would feed us? What would permit us to wait until our enemies had gone away? Would they ever go away? Would Tornada, taking his vengeance to the ultimate limits of cruelty, employing his mysterious power over his creatures, ever order them to retreat? Even supposing that he avowed the same hatred against the rest of the nation that he had heaped upon Paris, and that he launched his army on further ravages, would he not organize matters in such a way as to complete the extermination of the capital by leaving a rearguard of monsters there? Would there not emerge from his powerful brain—had he not already anticipated—a means of clearing out the places in which the residue of the people, thus far spared the gluttony of the macrobes, had gone to ground? I could suppose anything of such a terrifying individual.

A thousand other considerations were still jostling in my imagination, already exhausted by so much anguish. The physiological inferiority in which I found myself gave them a confusion of which terror was the principal agent. I supposed, by turns, everything that one can invent of the most deadly and the most salutary. Soon, however, only one obsession subsisted, the tenacity of which ended up oppressing me. I saw Suzanne and myself, and our companions in distress, chased from our refuge by virtue of the air suddenly having become unbreathable, Tornada having arranged to project toxic elements into each issue of the sewer.

In truth, I expected no more than that logical conclusion of a great crime, the methodical destruction that would precipitate us outside in the fashion of rabbits chased from their warren by ferrets. I believed that I could already sense the action. And now I think about it, I think that idea was suggested to me by the unhealthy emanations with which the atmosphere of the sewer was charged. How many thousands of lungs were respiring there, in that obscure and narrow network?

My head was aching; I could feel the pulsations of my heart throbbing in my temples. Overcoming the faint that still threatened, I dragged myself over to Suzanne, who was lying a few paces away. The people who had supervised our rescue had stood aside momentarily. I extended my hand toward her, and her wet clothes, clinging to her flesh, initially gave me the most painful impression—but my distress increased further when I observed the diminution and the weakness of her poor body.

She tried to speak; her voice barely vibrated. I understood, however.

"It's you, Jean, isn't it?"

"It's me, Suzanne."

"I'm not dreaming? You're really there?"

"You're not dreaming, and I'm really beside you."

"Why did you save me just now? We were sinking...it would have been very easy to die."

"It would have been frightful to be separated, Suzanne."

"Those who love one another aren't separated by death."

"I still wanted to believe there was a chance!"

"Oh, chance!"

"I wanted to cling to a hope."

"Oh, hope!"

"It's necessary."

"I have no more chance and no more hope. My father..."

After lifting herself up slightly on one elbow, she had just let her head fall back on to the ground, betrayed by her strength. That movement permitted her to receive the vague light of a lantern hanging on the wall; and I found her so livid, with the bone-structure of her face so evident, that I thought of the physiognomy that she would acquire once dead, and I understood the vanity of the words that I was employing to reassure her. To attempt further explanations, to invent other hypotheses of salvation, would only increase her disappointment, for the time being, adding a further torture to the anticipations that her common sense established clearly through her weakness. Anyway, she no longer seemed disposed to talk. She was at the limit of exhaustion, and her hand, of which I had taken hold with the precaution with which one touches fragile objects, was cold and soft in mine; only occasional nervous tremors revealed the persistence of life therein.

I also succumbed to numbness and think I would have fallen asleep if singular noises, which soon took on the amplitude of a din, had not been produced in the more remote part of the sewer. In my demi-torpor, I saw four individuals come to place themselves in front of me. They conferred in low voices, and I heard their words, which seemed at first to be rather incoherent.

"No pity," said one. "Pity's all right when..."

"Better to let them be!" growled a second, who wore the blue smock and wide-brimmed hat of Les Halles.

"We could roll dice for the guard?" suggested a third, whose clothing, with metal buttons, must have been some kind of military or watchman's uniform.

"For sure! Then it's not always the same ones to strike!" approved a fourth, whose silhouette I could not make out.

And all four of them repeated in chorus: "No! No pity for anyone!"

But a revolt of voices, coming from a distance, interrupted their conspiracy. They were shouting:

"Leave us alone!"

"We have as much right to be here as you!"

"We were here first!"

"Back!"

"I warn you that I'm armed!"

"I want to pass!"

"Back! Back!"

Then the protestations were lost in a furious scuffle. A detonation burst forth, which suddenly quieted the tumult. The noise of a mass falling in the water occupied that temporary silence—after which an irritated voice proclaimed: "I have enough for five!"

And the plaints, maledictions and exclamations of hatred resumed, duller and more attenuated.

I understood then what was happening, and I don't repent of having felt my generosity awakening. In other circumstances, perhaps, I would have appointed myself the champion of the unfortunates who, less fortunate than us, had found their retreat in the collector itself, while we were occupying a relatively spacious diverticulum. Oh, the poor people! Coming from the gallery directly below ours,

I could hear the poignant expression of their distress and bitterness. How could I dare to complain when, on reconstructing accurately enough the ovoid structure of the sewer, I knew that they must be cornered at the side wall, perched on a narrow sidewalk forming a border to the drainage channel; and that they were only protected from falling into the water by a fragile rail—all that in the horror of darkness!

Soon, I no longer had to wonder why they stayed there instead of coming into ours, which was connected to theirs by a small iron ladder. Nothing would have been easier for them to lodge there, for there were no more than twenty of us, and, furthermore, another tunnel, leading from out refuge to the outside, gave access via a few stone steps to a fairly large space constructed immediately beneath the road surface, and which, to judge by the voices I could hear arriving from there, was not overcrowded. But the feeble reflections of a lamp revealed to me that some of our companions in adventure had gathered in front of the steps leading to the conductor, and their egotism was opposing the sharing of our space.

Implacable in their cruelty, I saw them strike redoubtable blows again, and throw back into the sewer a poor man who tried to join us by climbing up the shaft of a hoist near the iron stairway, which facilitated the removal of sand. I heard the unfortunate man's body fall into the water, amid cries of hatred exchanged between the people in our gallery and those filling the sidewalk of the collector tunnel.

Nevertheless, my natural generosity soon dissipated in the face of the present contentment of still being alive and having Suzanne, also alive, by my side.

I was huddled against her, and I passed through a new, rather pleasant cerebral phase, doubtless resulting from the torpor succeeding the unusual physical expense demanded by recent events. I rested from thought, anticipation and attempting to comprehend what was happening around me. I think that I even slept for a while. Then, my annihilation dissipated progressively; the ambient phenomena recovered their value, and I surrendered to my curiosity. I sat up, with my back to the wall, and found that I was next to Monsieur Serviat.

The great scientist was very absorbed at that moment with an individual clad in ancient armor, the breastplate of which I had perceived when I awoke. He was making noble gestures as he spoke to him; he seemed to be letting his words fall from the height of a pulpit, and his southern accent acquired the amplitude of a declaration of doctrine, with the particularity that he adopted simultaneously a nuance of respect and sympathy whose motive I could not comprehend. I was obliged to tug on the flap of his frock-coat twice to attract his attention to me and for him to satisfy my need to know by virtue of what sequence of events the sewer had also collected him.

"My dear Master," I began, "you've saved us: what gratitude!"

"Don't mention it, my friend," he protested. "But let's confess that hazard sometimes works for the best, since it was at the very moment when I was risking a last glance at what was happening on the far bank that I perceived you as you threw yourselves in the water. That act of audacious despair, to which the events, surprisingly enough, only seem to have inspired you, had the interest for me that any struggle incites. Although urged to come back in here by those surrounding me, I could not take my eyes of the couple who were fleeing so bravely."

"Oh, my dear Master, bravely..."

"But yes! Yes!"

"We wanted to die..."

"I approve of your having sought death elsewhere than in the stomach of monsters. At least Tornada won't have had your skin!"

He did not hold back the expression of his old rancor in the manner in which he pronounced that last sentence. I detected therein all the rage of scientific rivalry, improbably persistent at that moment when danger had cornered us.

"The swine, eh? Can you believe it?" he added. Then, dismissing the hated image with a gesture, he went on: "Yes, I was there, on the bank, watching the plunge without being able to identify the plungers, when I suddenly recognized you. It was then that I ordered that someone throw you an anchor. Oh, you were very skillful in catching it, my friend—it was a veritable feat; and that Tornada..."

He did not finish. He understood that his insistence was about to become distasteful, and seemingly decided to revert to good manners. I thought I divined that his respect was commanded by the presence of the ancient suit of armor, which had just drawn closer to us and was listening to us.

"But you, my dear Master, how is it that you found yourself here? So many various rumors have been circulating in your regard that I don't know what to think. Has it not been proclaimed that you had found a means of breaking through the circle of monsters and reaching Tornada's laboratory? There, it was affirmed, you had discovered the secret of the macrobes' creation—a secret that has no connection with what our enemy has published—and that you had brought back a method of destruction that your first action was to submit to the new government. Is there any truth in what has been said? Excuse my impatience, and pardon me for interrupting your conversation with Monsieur..."

I pointed at the ancient armor, but Serviat paid no heed to my pause. If my questions were pressing, he seemed to be in just as much haste to inform me.

He raised a finger in the air. "Fantasy!" he said. "Everything that has been communicated—fantasy! The governments, both the former and the new, were making use of my name in order to reassure the public. In truth, I haven't moved from Paris. I had no need to penetrate into Tornada's laboratory to figure out his macrobes, and I had only to remain in mine to conceive a means of destroying them—and it's done, my friend...*Eureka!*"

Carefully, he removed from the pocket of his frock-coat a bottle that was creating a bulge there, and raised it into the air. I was able to make out that the bottle did not present any tragic appearance. It was filed with an opaline liquid, which reflected in blue the rays of the lamp before which he held it up. Immediately after having exhibited it, however, he replaced the bottle in its hiding place with the same precaution.

"*Eureka!*" the scientist repeated, buttoning up his frock-coat. Then, suddenly gripped by anger again, frowning ferociously and shaking his jowls, he exclaimed: "Oh, it's high time I avenged myself on that blackguard! It's time I put an end to his machinations! He's behaved toward me like the worst of fraudsters. He's stolen from me, Monsieur! He's stolen my discovery!"

"What discovery?"

"Why, *Micrococcus aspirator!*"

"I thought, Master, that you denied its existence?" I dared to suggest.

"You need to understand—I haven't denied anything!" he protested. "on the contrary, long before Tornada presented his paper to the Académie, I was the first to claim that all bodies are capable of giving birth, or, at least, favoring the evolution, of parasites specific to their species. That is, moreover, a general law; it's sufficient to look at what happens in nature to convince oneself of it. It's evident that the life of some is grafted on to the death of others...yes, that life is engendered by death..."

It would have been easy to adapt that philosophical phrase to our present situation, but it did not provoke any retrospective despair or lamentable anticipation, for the chemist did not leave us time to reflect upon it, continuing: "I had, therefore, foreseen this *Micrococcus aspirator*, and I can thus affirm that Tornada has robbed me."

It is, assuredly, an excessive pretention that assimilates a rather vague and quite commonplace general idea to a discovery that is more than ingenious, but the scientific mores of our era are accustomed to these arbitrary procedures, and I did not comment on its injustice, inasmuch as another question was burning my lips.

"All right," I conceded, indulgently, "But what about his other discovery?"

"What discovery! I deny it! Tornada is incapable of discovering anything!"

"However, Master...!"

"What?"

"His abnormal development favored by..."

"I deny it!"

"Damn! However..."

"I deny it! I deny it!"

"Ah! I could swear, myself..." I completed my sentence with an abrupt gesture toward the exterior ravages.

The scientist became conscious of the ridicule to which his obstinacy was giving rise. He suddenly calmed down. He turned to the person in the armor and bowed, with a smile. Then he addressed himself to me.

"When I say that I deny it, it's necessary to understand what I mean. I don't deny the phenomenon, of course—you'd think I was as mad as Tornada! But I deny that he has found the principle of it. Long before him, I and Dar..." He interrupted himself, and then resumed: "I and Darwin thought about anatomical modifications capable of presenting themselves in transplanted organisms. It only remained to find the method. That was the affair of a good workman, not a genius. Certainly, I don't refuse Tornada the qualities of a good workman, but the idea isn't new. Oh no, it isn't new!"

He rubbed his hands, delighted at having made things clear.

"Assuredly," I approved, meekly. "But my dear Master, your own discovery? Your method for saving us from the monsters?"

"Ah! There, I've got it!" he announced, proudly, radiant this time. He spun toward the individual encased in iron and bowed again. He said, mistaking his designation, doubtless in the heat of his revelation: "Listen carefully, Madame. What I have to tell you is quite prodigious."

He turned back to me. "You listen to me as well, Gérard, and remember this date, for it will be celebrated tomorrow. When I found out that Tornada had launched his macrobes against Paris, I said to myself: 'Serviat, people are obviously going to count on you; what can you do for these worthy people?' Then, quivering with the hope that I inspired, I went to my laboratory and shut myself up there, alone—all alone, that's my best fashion of creating. Then, my friends, I thought of it! Ah, what a seething there is, beneath this cranium. What accolades of neurons! What accolades, my good friends!"

He fanned his forehead, doubtless to calm the ardor still simmering there, and then went on: "Yes, everything is vibrant behind there; all the hypotheses racing tumultuously; and I had to choose from among a dust of ideas, as an astronomer has to select a single star from the Milky Way. I had rapidly eliminated from that confusion the cumbersome notions, and I remained in confrontation with two solutions—two, no more. And my ingenuity had been to borrow them from biology."

Privately, I approved of the Master's admission of his borrowing. It was probably the first time he had admitted to having borrowed anything.

He continued: "Being a chemist, I could easily have thought of something else, but I thought about biology. For, with what phenomenon were we dealing? A biological phenomenon. And also pathological. Follow me carefully."

I thought I was back on the school benches, so professorial was the tone of voice he had adopted. He pinched his nose and declared: "What are these macrobes? Large microbes, my friends, nothing else. How does one destroy microbes? Yes, how does one destroy them? You know, Gérard, but you, Madame"—again he was mistaken in his appellation!—"you, Madame, don't know."

And, raising himself up to his full height, sticking his thumbs in his waistcoat, he went on: "One destroys microbes in several ways. I'll pass over the mechanical and antiseptic methods. I'll even pass over the agents favorable to phagocystosis.[58] And I arrive immediately at the new therapeutics..."

"An antimicrobial serum?" I exclaimed.

"Ah, my good friend Gérard, that's where I was quicker off the mark than you! What is the serum of malady? It's a liquid taken from the blood of healthy animals, resistant to the malady, or sick animals previously immunized by an infection or a vaccination, isn't it? And the hypothesis was, indeed, elegant, of making an antimicrobial serum. Ha ha! Not banal...not banal..."

He swelled up with pride at the idea, and continued: "But how could a serum be injected into those dirty beasts? Can you see me setting out, syringe in hand, to confront those giants and saying to them: lend me your scale so I can introduce something into it? *Viens, macrobe, viens!*" He ventured a smile, and then resumed his gravity. "And then again, a serum isn't manufactured in twenty-four hours. Then I thought, quite simply, of a toxin."

"A toxin isn't manufactured in twenty-four hours either, Master."

"My dear Gérard," he said, swelling with pride, "for me, twenty-four hours is sufficient."

He took out his bottle again. He consulted the troubled fluid amorously, and said, with great simplicity: "And here it is."

"What toxin?" I persisted. "Is it a derivative of albuminoid? What is its molecular grouping? Is it radioactive? Does it contain mineral materials, manganese...?"

"That, my friend, is my business," the academician riposted, his expression suddenly firm. "That's chemistry, and it's my business. Let it suffice for you to know that with a few drops from this little flask, I have enough to poison a kilometer of the Seine. It's a violent destructive agent, which I've extracted from my brain, and I intend to distribute it in the river when the monsters come to slake their thirst there."

He put the bottle back in his pocket, with the same jealous care, without further explanation.

He adopted his easy-going attitude again, and added: "And that's when, emerging from my laboratory, I was surprised by the arrival of the macrobes. Slightly anxious, I admit, I precipitated myself into the mouth of a sewer that happened to be open—and do you know to whom I had the honor of offering my hand in order that she might descend at the same time as me? My old and great friend, the Baronne d'Abila, to whom I introduce, in these strange circumstances, Mademoiselle Suzanne Vernet and Monsieur Jean Gérard."

---

[58] Phagocytosis—the process by which a phagocyte engulfs a solid particle—was named and described by Élie Metchikoff on the Institute Pasteur in 1882, initially observed in single-celled creatures, although the possible importance of the process in the working of the immune system was gradually realized.

Suzanne had stood up to listen to the scientist's explanations. Amazed, we turned our eyes toward the person indicated to us by our interlocutor. In truth, we hesitated at first to bow, for we had just realized that the armored knight was a woman.

Now that those frightful hours have passed, I can smile at the baroque idea that the Baronne d'Abila had had, in the hope of protecting herself against the macrobes, of putting on an ancient suit of armor ornamenting her antechamber. Her considerable breasts and stout calves were escaping in adipose pads from the iron plates that she had precipitately placed over her chemise, whose fabric surpassed them. Plant on that warrior apparel a little tousled russet head, which would have been obliged, half a century before, to put on the make-up then generously reparative of the outrage of the years, and you will have a picture of the caricature that Monsieur Serviat was offering to us. Nevertheless, we were not unduly astonished. We knew that the Baronne was very eccentric, often celebrated by the newspapers for her sporting achievements and dangerous voyages of exploration, and we were at a moment when such details do not surprise you. Although she bore the name of a purgative water,[59] and perhaps by the very reason of that particularity, she was very popular in France.

She greeted us politely with an inclination of the head and a gesture with the helmet that she was holding under her arm.

"Alas, Madame," I felt obliged to say to her—for one feels constrained to condolences in all the frightful events of life—"what a frightful adventure!"

"But no!" she protested. "I find, on the contrary, that it's very amusing. I was nearly collected a little while ago by a macrobe, and it was the most exciting moment of my life. I've never experienced anything similar, even on the day when cannibals took me to their grill-room in order to feast on me..."

"Ha ha! They had good taste!" quipped Monsieur Serviat.

"Oh, shut up, Master!" said the Baronne, coquettishly, slapping him gently on the hands.

Soon, however, the chemist's discovery having rendered us some hope, our natural curiosity, invincible in spite of the gravity of the moment, drew us toward the people who were our companions in distress. The majority, plunged in the darkness, were unrecognizable, but by the dubious clarity of a sewerman's lamp, recently hung on the wall, I distinguished among the nearer ones, first, a female collector for the Salvation Army, wearing the distinctive cap of the sect, who seemed to me to be very pretty; then a clean-shaven actor with a sonorous voice, emphatic in his gestures; then an American clad in a loud suit, who was

---

[59] This slightly cryptic reference probably refers to solutions made from the plant *Citrullus colocynthis*—commonly known as bitter apple or vine of Sodom—used as a purgative since antiquity and commonly harvested in the vicinity of Abila in Jordan, although the Baronne's name is more likely to refer to Avila in Spain, the name of which was occasionally rendered as Abila.

pluming his drooping moustache with puffs of smoke from a pipe stuffed with Richmond tobacco; then a concierge who was weeping unstoppably; then a sewerman shod in boots and dressed in waterproof cloth. There were others, too, whose status was difficult to define—including an astonishingly dark-haired elegant man of the "old rake" variety, and a very young blond man—all exhausted, and supporting very lamentably, to judge by the bitterness of their conversation, the menace of the microbes.

But how dare we criticize the attitude of others when Suzanne and I felt so desperate ourselves? My poor fiancée, her garments still soaked from her immersion, was shivering, and although I drew her close to me, I was unable to warm her up. Fortunately, moved by pity, the sewerman had the inspiration of lighting a coke fire that was prepared in one of those perforated braziers that road-menders use for making macadam. The smoke it gave off provoked protests at first, but, the heat it radiated soon being appreciated by everyone, we were able to dry ourselves there without remorse. In the end, I was obliged to give thanks for the devotion of which people are capable, for the brave man shared a bread roll with our group, which gave us some comfort. His alms were inappreciable, and he refused the louis that I offered him.

And the time went by, immeasurably long. When I was not employed in consoling Suzanne, I could not help being invaded by a philosophical astonishment that the attitude of my companions inspired in me. I judged, in total lucidity, how irreparable and inveterate the poisoning of our civilization is. We had not been in that tunnel for half a day, and social life was already recommencing its work, with the same motives, the same passions and the same defects, as if events assured us of our continued existence. A glance was sufficient to convince me.

Monsieur Serviat was playing the gallant with the influential Baronne d'Abila; and while the young recruit of the Salvation Army, as pretty as an angel who might also be a demon, started preaching and collecting, the American, comfortably installed on a bed of sand provided to him by one of the small wagons, never ceased smoking, and demanding whisky, proclaiming that he would give his fortune to have a glass. His offer seemed to me to be as extravagant as his passion for alcohol. Did he not inform us, the next moment, that he was a billionaire in consequence of a trust in calves? He was, he affirmed tranquilly, "the emperor of veal."

After that, I heard the concierge bragging about the tyranny she had exercised over her tenants, before those "satanic pimps"—as she called the macrobes—made their appearance, and the actor declaring that Monsieur Guitry could not hold a candle to him.[60]

---

[60] The reference is to Lucien Guitry, father of the eventually-more-famous Sacha, who left the Comédie-Française in 1902 to become director of the Renais-

Perhaps, though, those boastful things were only said superficially, in order to counter intimate dread, for, although we supposed that we were protected from the monsters' devouring rage, and could no longer hear anything overhead that revealed their presence—neither roars not the creaking of carapaces—we could not suppose, even so, that their work was concluded. Sometimes, too, the name of Tornada was pronounced, and there was then a further consternation, a hatred proclaimed by all mouths. Then everyone fell silent, listening, in anguish. We feared those giant leaps, which, by provoking the collapse of our tunnel, would have given access to the gluttonous giants.

At other times, news, transmitted along the human chain filling the collector and communicating with the entire subterranean network of Paris, reached our ears, confirming the total destruction of the city, the annihilation of its people.

Suddenly, however, what a contrast! What a breath of liberation!

"They're destroyed! They're destroyed!" transmitted voices arriving in tumult from the tunnel below our own.

One might have thought it a rumble of triumph, a thousand clamors welcoming the birth of a god.

And almost immediately: "Long live Serviat! Long live the savior!"

"Have I saved someone, then?" the chemist asked me.

That was the exact moment when the actor, shouting more loudly than the others, came to tell us the news.

"Yes, Monsieur," he said, addressing himself more specifically to the chemist. "Yes, Monsieur, Serviat has saved us!" And raising his arms to the heavens, his mouth wide, he went on: "Serviat is a genius, you hear, Monsieur! Serviat is the man of the century!"

"Thank you," said the scientist, swelling up with pride, "But..."

"And let no one contradict me!"

"I wouldn't dream of it...but what has he done, your Serviat?"

"He's found a lethal malady, which he's transmitted to the monsters."

"Ah! What is it?"

"The plague! Yes, Monsieur, a sort of plague! And they're dying of it, they're dying of it!"

"Really?"

"Really."

"Well, Monsieur, tell these poor people to wait a little before shouting. They're going too quickly. Certainly, the nation can count on Serviat..."

"A man of genius!"

"Indeed, but who hasn't yet had the opportunity to make use of his invention."

---

sance, where he established his reputation as the leading French exponent of contemporary drama.

"How do you know, Monsieur?"

"I know."

"Because?"

"Because, Monsieur, I am Serviat...that's me!"

I have no need to insist on the actor's confusion—a confusion that rebounded on the ambient frenzy, reached the human cordon transmitting the news, extinguishing the cries of enthusiasm with the same rapidity, to replace them with tears.

And the bleak wait resumed.

Like the others, I had allowed myself to be taken in momentarily by the illusion of deliverance, although I did not know yet what to make of it. It is curious to remark how contagious the puerility off a crowd at bay can be. Is there is that circumstance a manifestation of cerebral anemia?[61] Possibly. But I was obliged, like the others, to bow down to the reality, and I soon had no other resource to occupy my mind, relaxed by drowsiness, than to interest myself in the dramas unfolding at the two issues of our tunnel, where the macrobes were not threatening people directly and were allowing them to deliver themselves to scenes of abominable violence.

To be sure, I only saw those scenes through a dim light, and I was too weary to philosophize about their psychology, but for which I would not have failed to endorse the verity of all the ages that might makes right. Did the poor people imploring us from the bottom of the stairway leading to the collector not have as much right as us to share our space? Did we ourselves not have the right to take the few steps leading to the subterranean room that was only occupied by a few individuals? No: on either side, a ferocious guard was maintained, arbitrarily limiting everyone's right of abode, and distributing blows of a cudgel to those who wanted to exceed its limits. I saw the powerful market porter devoting himself to that task with a particular mastery.

"No one passes!" he howled. And his fist, raised to the level of his hat, fell upon a skull. The noise was audible, the crash of the body, which fell with a splash into the water.

At one time, weary of striking out, he detaching himself from his group and came over to me.

"It's time the idlers did some work," he said. "Your turn!"

I refused. His fist clenched; I feared his crushing blow, and assumed a defensive stance. I could have crushed me between his fingers, but Suzanne threw herself upon me, making a rampart of her weakness, and the brute relaxed his fist, and went away, grumbling.

---

[61] The distinctive features of crowd psychology, developed at such length in this narrative, had become a hot topic of debate in fin-de-siècle France because of the pioneering investigations of the subject carried out by Gabriel Tarde and Gustave Le Bon.

How can I continue to translate those long minutes of anxious uncertainty? Silence was progressively established; everyone rested in their own distress. Suzanne had gone back to sleep, babbling vague words testifying to her nightmare. I took advantage of that to stretch my legs a little, and started pacing back and forth, like an animal in a cage with other animals.

My room for maneuver was by no means comfortable to travel, as can easily be imagined. I was hindered by recumbent bodies, which I had to step over, by the presence of wagons blocking the tunnel to the extent that it was necessary for me to slide along the wall to get past them. As for risking myself at the external opening overlooking the Seine, where daylight, visible through the bars of the closed gate would soon be replaced by terrifying darkness, I truly did not dare. For the moment, all the menace seemed to me to lie in that direction, and, not knowing what surprise that orifice might reserve for those who approached it, I judged it more prudent to keep my distance.

Soon, it was completely dark outside. Our redoubt, in the wan light of the lamp, took on a particularly lamentable aspect. Silhouettes stood out in a fearfully suggestive imprecision. Faces could no longer be seen; their angular contours, their sculpture of distress and dolor, could only be divined.

At times, there was a fulgurant glimmer in the shadow; that was the American, the "emperor of veal," relighting his pipe. "Whisky? Whisky!" he demanded, with an insistence neighboring on delirium. And the atmosphere filled with the perfume of his tobacco, while the young collector for the Salvation Army, his neighbor for the moment, waved the smoke away from her nostrils with indignant protective gestures, similar to those of the astonishingly dark-haired old gentleman and the very blond young man.

"As if it's permissible to poison the air like that!" agreed the concierge, with disgust, sweeping the air with her apron. And she added: "Just try that in my house! I'd have a policeman on you in three minutes, and out you'd go, Englisher!"

That "Englisher" summarized all her ethnographic notions, all her age-old hatred of the invader. She had, besides, already heaped that denomination on the "satanic pimps"—and Tornada for her, was also an "Englisher."

"Necessary not to get your blood up for so little, Mother," said the worthy sewerman, placidly. "Necessary to think how lucky we are to be here."

That consolation had no other result than reestablishing the concierge's flood of tears, and the apron dabbed her eyes to collect the moisture therefrom.

In another corner, I observed the truly warm friendship, emerging from the disaster, that was being established between Monsieur Serviat and the Baronne d'Abila. Would they have thought of finding one another charming in normal life? My God, what admirable resources the genius of the species has! Yes, while everything around us was collapsing, perishing in a frightful cataclysm, those two individuals were embarking upon a regular flirtation. I saw them, each as picturesque as the other—I say picturesque because of their social status, although I could as easily have employed a less indulgent expression—him, the great scientist, the national glory, with his bottle making a bulge in his frock-coast; her, the grand dame, squeezed into her stifling suit of armor, using all the graces, flatteries and coquetries they would have deployed in a drawing room during a formal reception. My word, did the member of the Institut not push seduction to the point of opening a box of candy and offering a piece to the explorer?

"It's not the toxin this time, Master?"

"No, trust me."

But, as the fingers clad in an iron gauntlet could not take one, I believe I remember seeing the scientists seize a bonbon and place it in the Baronne's lips. I heard the latter's teeth, still pretty—perhaps an artificial beauty, but let's not dwell on that—crunch upon the delicacy…which issued a violent appeal for the satisfaction of my hunger.

"Oh, give me one! Give me one!" I had a desire to cry out. But I was timid, still reserved, and I dared not think about my starvation, and Suzanne's, and turned my gaze away from the temptation in order to interest myself in other psychological states, which the situation unveiled, as malady lays bare the soul of an invalid.

Among all those poor stranded individuals whom destiny had accumulated in that subterranean tunnel, I had not failed to be intrigued by the appearance of one particular individual whose silhouette remains astonishingly clear in my mind, although the circumstances had scarcely caused my gaze to pass over him. He was a man of indeterminate age, nothing about him indicating whether he was young or old. He was neither fat nor thin, neither tall nor short, wearing garments of a respectable cut, gloves and decent shoes. Everything about him would have made him one of those neutral individuals whose paths one frequently crosses in the streets without noticing them, had a certain eccentricity not been acquired by the aristocratic quality of his face, in which a monocle and an extraordinarily fetching beard, trimmed with absolute symmetry, with not a single overlapping hair, reigned triumphantly.

To judge by the care that he took of that superb beard, by the worshipful manner in which he raked it incessantly with a small pocket comb, one divined that it was his sole claim to fame, and one forgot that it was dominated by a commonplace nose, eyes devoid of brightness, and a restricted forehead, half of which was covered by a gray felt hat.

Imagine, moreover, that the individual was striving to give the beard and monocle thus planted in a banal face an air of superior irony—that he often mingled in groups occupied in discussing our frightful situation, but that, without saying a word, once the news was acquired, he retired, shrugging his shoulders, accompanying his retreat with a satisfied clucking and a pressure of his hands, one against the other, so energetic that the joints of his fingers cracked.

And yet, a manifest need to talk gripped him; that was evident from his attitude. Doubtless, on the other hand, he did not want to confide his noble reflections to common mortals.

After a long hesitation, he apparently judged me worthy of receiving them, for he began to prowl around me, and soon, without my having given any signal to provoke his testimony, he came up to me and engaged me in conversation with a quiet, colorless voice.

"My dear Monsieur," he said, "this is a very strange event, and for myself, I'm curious to know what its consequences will be. Don't believe, however, that I'm as distressed as the others by the dire fate that is reserved for me! Oh no, that base terror is by no means mine!" Accentuating the cracking of his knuckles, he added: "I am, on the contrary, delighted by what is happening."

"What! You're delighted by this disaster?" I exclaimed, without moderating my surprise and indignation. "Can you confess that at such a moment?"

"Understand me clearly. Listen to me with deference. I don't confide my thoughts to just anyone. If I've chosen you for a confidant, it's because I don't know you, and because I can believe you to be of a moral caliber superior to that of the others."

He caressed his beard with both hands, with the back of one and the palm of the other, and then continued, sententiously: "I find in this adventure of the macrobes a supreme lesson in energy. I was waiting for the time that would finally permit me to express my sentiment, and I deliver it with all the more satisfaction because I predicted this catastrophe."

"What! You anticipated that Paris would one day be delivered to the voracity of these monsters, Monsieur?"

"Understand me clearly: I don't mean that I foresaw that a scientist would one day bring the disaster out of a culture medium, I simply mean to express that I was counting on a great public calamity to regenerate our people, which is truly in need of it. People no longer make war, my dear Monsieur, because the nations fear the bloodshed and the destruction; they no longer tremble before epidemics, because hygiene stops them with sterilizers; they're protected from heat and cold; and mechanical tools do the work of arms. Add that a legion of humanitarians has invaded our globe, that savages are being civilized and that the tsar bows down before the Duma. So, what means remain for Immanent Cruelty to do its work? What means remain for the soul to draw the elements of virtue from dolor? Alas, humans no longer have to relax into the egotism of their happy lives; they go to sleep without enjoyment, with the concern of cultivating the heart, and there is a universal decadence. Well, no! It's too much! Bless the lesson of fear! Lift up hearts! Let us fortify ourselves! Let us become virile!"

In the ardor of his discourse his monocle had escape from his eye; he was sketching broad gestures; and I listened with amazement to the strength prophet. A thousand objections, inspired by my present distress, rose to my lips, and I would have presented them to him had I not sensed that his flood of words still had some way to expand.

In a voice suddenly transformed, which hissed with envy, he continued: "I tell you that the present moment is eminently salutary! Let us obtain the confirmation for that, if you wish, from the study of all those around us, who have gravitated to this sewer. Let us observe them in turn. I have some of them at my fingertips; to every lord his honor. Let us look first at Serviat, who is pretending not to recognize me, although we have collaborated in the past. He's a man of science honored to the point that, on gala days at the Élysée, he sports decorations and sashes of ever color and form, so numerous that, finding no more room to pin them on his chest, he's obliged to hang them over his buttocks! Come on, Monsieur, I ask you—is it decent to pose like that in a display of tinsel?"

I saw that he was caressing the lapel of his jacket with the tip of his finger, and leaning over, I noticed that his own modesty prevented him from wearing anything except a little red ribbon, which I mistook at first for the Légion d'honneur.

He continued: "Alas, Monsieur, Serviat has invented fracassite. Has he invented it? No matter. At any rate, once his discovery was made, he dared to deliver it to the artillery, with the result that now, if what is said about the power of that explosive is true, war will become impossible, and we shall be deprived henceforth of a source of necessary calamity. What would you have done in his place, Monsieur? What did I do, myself, when I discovered the formula of my own explosive? I hastened to bury it in a drawer, imitating my disinterest on the day when I found the serum for tuberculosis. Ah, that's the way I am!"

His momentum carrying him away, he had dropped his monocle again. He was obliged to search for it on the ground for some time. He finally discovered it, after groping around, and replaced it in the orbit.

"And that Baronne, whom I've encountered many times in society, and who is also pretending not to know me, doubtless because I haven't spared my sentiments in her regard in my newspaper..."

"Your newspaper?"

"Yes—you've surely read the *Justicier*, my weekly publication?"

"Certainly," I acquiesced, obligingly, although I was completely ignorant of the rag in question.

"Well, that Baronne, let's talk about her! Would you believe that she takes baths in goat's milk? That she covers her entire body in beauty cream at sixty-six francs a pot, and that she has devised a system of suspenders with which she stretches her face at night in order to avoid wrinkles? She poses as a charitable woman! She's president of the Association for the Protection of Feeding-Bottles—to replace the milk in her baths, perhaps. She sits on the committees of twenty societies, each more benevolent than the last to vicious infancy and spoiled old age—and she explores Africa in order to care for the ophthalmia of little cannibals! Wretch! Wretch!"

He shook his fists.

"Well, Monsieur, I tell you this: charity is baleful work. To the proposition that work should be given to the poor, I consent; but the proposition that they should be maintained, I reject. It's contrary to dignity, to social intelligence! It's also contrary to the will of Nature, which wants everyone to develop strength in the service of the instinct of conservation! Let us follow the example of Nature does! Let us follow the example of Death! They are excellent selectors! They are being disturbed in their harmonious dispositions; the prey they have decided to sacrifice is being snatched from them; the swing of their scythes is being paralyzed—and it's evil work to oppose them. I understand that so well that when I was sought out to be placed at the head of the Association of Bone-setters, even though my position, my name and my antecedents designated me to do that work triumphantly, I flatly refused, Monsieur; I slammed my door in the faces of the delegates who were imploring me; and there was an almighty fuss!"

"Oh, I thought...?" I said, interrogating the color of his decoration more carefully; noticing this time a minuscule yellow stripe bordering the red of his ribbon. It was the distinction of some negro king.

He divined my astonishment at seeing him ornamented by it, and, wanting to dissipate the deplorable effect of my discovery, he added: "I refused the Légion d'honneur. They squander it too much."

Proud of that further gesture of disdain, he took a small comb from his pocket clad in a leather sheath, opened it, and engaged it delicately in his beard.

"And the others, Monsieur! That concierge, who was once mine and with whom I quarreled because she made her lodge a hospital for all the stray cats in the street! And that actor, who has seen me many a time applauding in the front row of the orchestra stalls—with a certain sincerity, I must admit, for he's not denuded of tradition—but whom I couldn't go to see again after the day when he interpreted the plays of Brieux![62] And that dainty child who wears the costume of the Salvation Army, and whom I had to threaten with the police one day for wanting to slip me her newspaper, which I consider as a kind of begging. Yes, all of them, Monsieur, all of them, I consider as baleful servants of a benevolence contrary to the broad designs of Nature, which demands that one experiences strife, that one suffers, for the greater elevation of character!"

He concluded his diatribe with an expression of anxiety, which I thought at first attributable to the problems that were agitating him. It was nothing of the sort, however, and I soon perceived that his preoccupation was engendered by a

---

[62] Eugène Brieux (1858-1932) was the leading realist dramatist of his era in France. His play *Les Avariés* (1901; filmed in English as *Damaged Lives*), public performance of which was banned by the censor, but which was read by the author in private to a select audience, followed hot on the heels of Couvreur's *Les Mancenilles* (1900), which similarly deals in a didactic fashion with the danger to society posed by syphilis.

personal detail, for, having caressed his beard, he had just observed that its elegance was opposed by the defective alignment of a few hairs. This time, he brought out a pair of scissors from his pocket and snipped the undisciplined hairs—and his physiognomy resumed its fine implacable tranquility.

I was then able to get a word in.

"I find you unjust, Monsieur. To struggle against evil, in whatever form, is the finest employment of the civilizing faculties. In my own case..."

"What do you do?" he interjected, immediately.

"I'm in charge of a laboratory at the Institut Pasteur..."

"The Institut Pasteur! You're at the Institut Pasteur?" he cried, thrusting me away with a manifest horror. "You've gone astray in that place? You work on serums? On vaccines? Have you no shame?"

"No, Monsieur."

"You ought not to be proud of yourself, my friend. The Institut Pasteur is an abominable factor of decadence. It's me who's telling you this!"

I was beginning to get indignant. "But who are you, Monsieur, who find it so easy to heap such criticism on humankind?"

He took off his hat. I expected to hear him pronounce the name of some important Parisian personality.

"I'm Célestin Lebon."

"And what is your business?"

"Insurance, Monsieur."

After which he turned his back on me, in order to go and snigger somewhere else.

I had soon forgotten his ramblings. I took some pleasure in conversing with the sewerman, possessed of a candid soul, in complete contrast to the one whose bile I have just been respiring. He talked to me about the macrobes with a surprising tranquility. He was brave without being boastful. He listened to the story of my nocturnal expedition to Mantes, and seemed surprised that the monsters were phosphorescent.

"What's happened certainly isn't ordinary," he concluded, when I had finished.

At about ten o'clock a new racket began, which woke Suzanne. Once again, the illusion of deliverance was being passed along. As my fiancée no longer believed it, the sewerman, who had decidedly taken a liking to her, proposed to go out and ascertain whether the monsters had retreated.

He was surrounded.

"It's dark; you won't be able to see anything..."

"But yes, since they're green, the darkness..."

And the brave man went to the door that gave access to the Quai de Billy, opened it, stuck his head through, inspected the bank, and then came back in. And I shall never forget the joyful fashion in which he shouted to us: "For sure, because there's nothing more to scoff, they've gone!"

With what irony destiny was playing with us, in making the worst realities succeed the most cheerful hypotheses! The sewerman had not taken four steps away from the door, which he had just carefully closed behind him, when the door, pulled from outside, exploded furiously. At the same time, an invincible current of air extinguished our lamp, and the celestial shadow disappeared from the orifice of the tunnel to be replaced there by a green phosphorescence.

"Get down! Get down! Lie down!" I shouted to Suzanne, forcing her to flatten herself on the ground beside me.

I understood what had happened. One of our engulfers, evidently on watch in the roadway above our heads, must have been attracted by the imprudent reconnaissance of the sewerman. Sniffing the man, it had lowered its appendage toward the entrance, and, not being able to get into it by virtue of the narrowness of the orifice, it had applied its conch to the opening, like a sucker, in order to produce a vacuum in our tunnel and such in anything that was there.

I was even more convinced when I heard the fatal roaring, to which the inter-collision of wagons responded as they slid along their rails, like children's toys, toward the monstrous tentacle, and were then rejected by it when they were found to be inappropriate for alimentation.

That gigantic suction had provoked a formidable displacement of air, which I sensed that Suzanne and I, placed among those nearest to the door, would be unable to resist. Although we were still clinging to the ground, the improbable force rolled us over at times. It was a cyclone unleashed over our few cubic meters with all the furious impetuosity of the great unleashments of nature. We felt people passing over us like projectiles, going to be engulfed by the green phosphorescence. And we would have been subjected to the same fate if my hand had not been fortunate enough to encounter a mooring ring sealed into the wall, and had I not clung to it with a desperate energy, while my other hand prevented Suzanne's displacement.

Then the phenomenon vanished as quickly as it had appeared. Darkness resumed possession of the orifice of the tunnel, and we heard nothing more. One might have thought that nothing had happened.

It had, though. When the lamp was lit again, and when we counted ourselves, some were missing. Five victims—five immolated individuals—had served as prey for the monster. The sewerman and Célestin Lebon were among them, and the American had left us too. Oh, the poor devil wouldn't be demanding his whisky any more. We found his pipe, still smoking.

Night set in above us, in consternation. We had gathered in the most distant corner of the tunnel in order to escape any similar attempt, in case it was repeated. Nevertheless, sitting against the wall and huddled together, Suzanne and I succumbed to fatigue.

It might have been two o'clock in the morning when we were woken up by the noise of a collapse nearby.

"It's the Pont d'Iéna crumbling!" guessed Monsieur Serviat.

We went back to sleep. We had arrived at a certain fatalism.

XII

A sob uttered by Suzanne snatched me from my heavy inertia. I cannot describe the sadness that the plaint in question caused me, combined with the malaise of waking up in the cold and damp. The fire had gone out some time ago for want of fuel.

My flesh felt bruised and mortified. A glance toward the livid dawn showing through the entrance to our tunnel further increased my torment. My entire horizon was limited to a stretch of river drowned by rain. There were tears in nature, as in me, as in the still-closed eyes of my fiancée. What cruel dream must the poor child be going through, for her sweet face to be manifesting such anxiety? Her parted lips were stammering incomprehensible words; her hands, folded over her body, lying on the ground, were trembling; her entire being testified to a horrible interior drama.

I woke her up to extract her from it. I strove to offer her a reassuring smile. With the aim of replacing her alarm with a more immediate and less grave preoccupation, I asked her to adjust my dressing. She lent herself to the task with the bravery of a young nurse.

Around us, the first impression of that morning was quite different from what I expected. Our companions stretched their limbs first, and loosened themselves up by swinging their arms. Then—I don't know why, perhaps because of that incomparable character unique to Parisians—they began to crack jokes. A few humorous rockets were rapidly transformed into a veritable firework display for which the attitude of the Baronne provided a pretext.

The latter, her bosom being decidedly too cramped, had taken off the breastplate of her armor and handed it to Monsieur Serviat, who had put it on over his frock-coat to warm himself up. But as she was in her chemise beneath her protective disguise, and as she had retained her helmet on her head and her thigh-guards on her legs, I confess that her accoutrement did not lack hilarity, and that the grand dame on the one hand, and the great scientist on the other, were rather reminiscent of two clowns in a vaudeville theater.

Inspired by the example, the actor turned his jacket inside out and started composing verses about them, which the audience repeated in chorus. Cases are cited of nervous, almost demented gaiety, at the most tragic moments of history. The funniest thing of all was that the chanted refrain followed a tune that had been adopted, with other words, into the repertoire of the Salvation Army, and the pretty follower of General Booth joined in ardently. She thought we had been converted!

I observed that she had, at least, inspired the religion of her beauty in two of us, and that the old excessively dark-haired old gentleman and the very blond young man were deploying a furious rivalry in adoring her as their new idol.

301

The hostile glances that they darted at one another were harshly appreciated by the concierge. The latter, sitting apart in a corner, superb in her dignity in the midst of the racket, opined that all those people were well worthy of living in a sewer; she could not even conceive that they had been born elsewhere.

Soon, however, that artificial gaiety melted away. We had had no more news of life outside, nor of the macrobes, when terrible information reached us thanks to the unfortunates who had taken refuge in the nearby collector. The poor people, still prevented from joining us by those who had posed themselves at the stair-head, opposing a human barrage to them, were uttering more emphatic plaints.

I deplored all the peril of their situation. I, the rare moments of silence, when they ceased to cry out, we heard the current of the water, increased by the external downpour, flowing more impetuously. The level was riding in the corridor, and a particular odor was emitted by it, fetid in the extreme, the reek of which also filled our tunnel, scarcely combated by the air from outside. We attributed that odor to the detritus that the rain had brought into the drains, subsequently drawing it into the sewer, which was making the entire network a veritable charnel-house.

We soon had proof of the verity of that explanation, for toward midday, as he concierge was proposing that it might be possible to extract something to eat from the things that the collector was carrying, a mocking voice emerged therefrom, replying:

"Madame is hungry? Let Madame permit me to offer her breakfast..."

At the same time, an object wrapped in paper as thrown up to us from the gulf. There was a battle around the projectile, but when its envelope was removed, a cry of horror went up. What had been sent to us was the hand of a little child, still bearing a modest golden ring on the ring finger.

"Alas, what mother must have had the despair...," Suzanne murmured, turning her eyes away.

From then on, the certainty of danger resumed its full value within us. The memory of that human debris had dissipated the gaiety and the appetite of the captives. Two live rats, which had been captured when the more impetuous waters chased them out of the collector, were also disdained. We knew only too well, alas, on what they had been nourished!

The result was that the day, the third since the appearance of the macrobes, ended in pangs of hunger. Dusk fell on the bank visible from the orifice; the twilight darkened, and eventually disappeared.

I hollowed out a bed for Suzanne in the sand in one of the small wagons, and installed her in it. Still fearful of an attack by the monsters that the vehicle and its precious contents might have attracted, I took care to moor it with a powerful iron chain that was passed to me from the chamber communicating with the roadway. And night reigned in absolute obscurity, for we saved the few drops of oil still remaining in the lamps, in case their light became useful later.

That was a night of terror, which I traversed initially without being able to sleep, occupied in watching over the repose of the object of my adoration—a night haunted by phantoms, of which the water growling in the collector echoed the lugubrious, melancholy song. Then, as the surface of the great city fell silent, I allowed myself to be borne away into a reparative oblivion.

I scarcely dare remember my first sensation of the following day, so atrocious was it. I was woken up by a clutching hand posed upon my stomach and, one might have thought, uprooting it. I truly discovered, that morning, what the starving endure—but, disdaining my own suffering in order not to think about anything but Suzanne's, I got up and leaned over her bed of sand.

At first, my anxiety was extreme, when I thought I had discovered nothing more than a cadaver, so inert was her body, so silent her lips and so icy her hand. To dissipate my horrible dread, at the risk, if she were only asleep, of causing her to quit the slumber that was soothing her existence, I shook her gently.

"I'm hungry…! I'm hungry…!" she moaned, in an exceedingly wan voice.

She repeated her plaint, with a childish insistence. I had never cursed the genius of Tornada and the cruelty of destiny, which were submitting my beloved to such an ordeal, as I did at that moment. And my rage was further increased when daylight, imposing itself on the orifice of the tunnel, showed me the adorable contours of her face, suddenly so thin, so slack and so corroded.

"Today, my beloved, today we'll eat," I assured her. "This situation can't go on! The monsters will go away. Hold on! Can you hear what people are saying? They're saying that the macrobes are drawing away, eastwards."

A more vivid gleam in her eyes persuaded me that she was smiling at that hope. I refrained from dissuading her from that, although I remained convinced of the improbability of such a retreat.

I imagined, on the contrary, how terrible our death would be in that redoubt, which was increasingly filled by the fetid odor. I recalled the description of a long agony given by the survivors of a mine disaster occasioned by an explosion of firedamp. Alas, were we going to perish, like them, in the tortures of starvation? Were we going to look at our neighbors, with eyes searching for the place to bite? At least we had the advantage over the miners of being able to move out into the open! A few steps to take, and we could disappear into the river that had spared us two days before!

I anticipated that that would be our end.

However, the macrobes had not given any sign of their presence for about thirty hours, since the moment when the formidable sound, heard the night before last, which we had assumed to be the Pont d'Iéna collapsing under their mass. Logic, however, forced me to agree that if the retreat of Tornada's creatures had taken place, we would already have heard cries of deliverance, and seen the people who had taken refuge on the Eiffel Tower spreading out joyfully over the opposite bank.

I confided my impression to the Baronne and Monsieur Serviat, and they approved with nods of the head—but as their lips were moving without them speaking, I was seized by a sudden suspicion.

"Have you found something to eat, then?" I demanded, abruptly.

"They're cocaine pastilles that we're sucking," the Baronne ended up confessing, after some hesitation. "The Master had a few of them, because of his stomach..." At the same time, she patted her fat bosom. "It's calming, but I'd rather have a truffled turkey."

That gastronomic evocation immediately reanimated my torture. After having obtained a pastille for Suzanne, not without supplication, which I immediately transmitted to her with the prudence of a man confiding a stolen treasure, I declared our situation intolerable, and that it was finally time to go and see what was happening outside.

Monsieur Serviat approved my project. Then he affirmed, brandishing his bottle of toxin, that he was still waiting for the moment to poison the Seine.

"It's necessary," he concluded, "that someone devotes himself to the common cause. Let someone inform me as to the position of the *Micrococci aspiratores!* They'll surely end up drinking, after having eaten so much! An then..."

He seemed sure of his fact. Everyone looked at him. Yes, who would sacrifice himself? The Baronne declared that she would willingly volunteer. She had seen others do it, during her expeditions among the savages. But then, what if it were necessary for her to jump into the water in the hazard of a pursuit?

"Well, Baronne," said Monsieur Serviat, "can you swim?"

"Yes, when I'm not wearing leg-armor."

"What's more simple than to take it off?"

"Well, my dear Master, I don't have anything else on down there."

That was true. She only had a chemise on under her armor! And modesty attached her to the shore. I did not even have the heart to smile at the idea of that more-than-plump Valkyrie departing with her chemise flapping, to reconnoiter the terrain.

As no one else offered, I turned to my fiancée.

"I'll go, my dear Suzanne. I owe you the risk..."

"What danger you'd be running, Jean!" she refused, tremulously. "I beg you..."

I convinced her, however, to let me go.

The kiss she offered to my lips posed there like a powerful cordial, and I hastened toward the exit, my heart pounding.

As soon as I emerged, I stopped, marveling at an unforgettable spectacle.

After the previous day's rain, spring had returned. The river, sparkling in a few eddies, was flowing with a majestic indifference. The opposite bank was blossoming in the sunlight. To the right, the panorama extended as far as a veil of mauve mist extended over the distant hills; while to the left, the Pont d'Iéna, contrary to what I supposed, was intact, still projecting its powerful contexture between the two banks.

No monstrous presence; no threat; one might have thought it the awakening of Paris on a splendid morning. But on raising my eyes toward the Eiffel Tower, I saw it still swarming with people, and a dirigible, which I recognized as the *France*, was detaching itself at that precise moment, and started flying into the azure, toward the west.

Those observations persuaded me right away that the macrobes had not left Paris. I would have gone back right away to announce the sad news if the ardent desire to bring back some nourishment for Suzanne had not inspired me with the temerity to go on. I therefore started climbing the stairway leading to the Pont d'Iéna.

Having reached the top, the possessor of a vaster horizon, I was finally able to take account of the disasters caused by the giants. In fact, improbably, the right campanile of the Trocadéro had collapsed, and its central dome was staved in. I calculated fearfully the height of the leap accomplished by the monsters, and their formidable weight in falling back, in order that such a monument could be smashed to that extent. On the other side of the Seine, the devastation was similar; all the houses were reduced to rubble, exposing lamentable fragments of walls, to which morsels of masonry still clung in places.

I shivered before that spectacle. I hesitated to take my perilous adventure any further. What could I do, what could I find among those ruins? Would I not be exposing myself quite needlessly? Furthermore, signals were being addressed to me from the tower whose exact significance I could not understand, because of the distance, but which were certainly not encouraging me to continue.

However, as the image of Suzanne, dying of hunger, did not cease to obsess my mind, I plucked up my courage, crossed the bridge at a gallop, went around the foliage framing that side of the Champ-de-Mars and reached the Avenue de La Bourdonnais. My idea was that I would end up finding something to eat there. It was impossible that an entire quarter could be devoid of provisions and that I would not succeed in unearthing some from beneath the rubble—all the more so as I remember the presence of a grocery near the beginning of the long artery.

I was soon forced to retract my hopes, though. The road was virtually non-existent; there was nothing but an extraordinary confusion of heaps of stone, wood, twisted iron, windows and chimneys, mingled as if every house had been dynamited. Shading my eyes with my hands, however, I saw in the distance that the Galerie des Machines, which had not yet been destroyed, was still standing, and that in the middle of the avenue, one single-story building—only one—also subsisted, spared by the scourge. Its shop-front, painted bright blue, sprightly in the sunlight in the midst of the disaster, immediately became my objective, and I headed toward it, going around obstacles, and sometimes jumping over them in order to go more rapidly, immediately getting to my feet again if I tripped.

And still no macrobes on the horizon. Nothing. It was a solitude that troubled me as much as the giant apparitions. I can say without boasting that I showed proof at that moment of a certain courage, given that the silence of the people perched on the tower, by whom I felt that I was being observed, also frightened me.

Oh, what a journey! Well, would you believe that I was not the only one making it? Suddenly, I perceived accompanying me, disappearing only to appear again, an adorable little dog, one of those spirited black English terriers, as amiable as can be, who are in ordinary life better than friends to us. At times it stopped in front of me, and stood on its hind legs, bringing its front paws back against its torso, begging. I can assure you that with its upright ears and its shining eyes visibly inspired by a soul, it was pleading the cause of its famished instinct irresistibly.

Irresistibly? No, alas, for I lacked humanity on this occasion. I called to the charming little animal with my most encouraging voice, but my secret design was not to nourish it—quite the contrary!

It must have divined my ferocious intention, however, for it ran away just as I was about to seize it. Then I continued on my way toward the blue shopfront.

When I reached it, I observed that it bore the sign of a wholesaler of wines and vinegars. Unable to account for the fact that it had been spared by the scourge—perhaps because of its lesser dimensions, after all?—and astonished by the contrast between its fresh paint and perfect alignments and the surrounding collapses, I introduced myself into the building without difficulty. After having passed along a corridor I found a bourgeois dining-room, to which a kitchen was adjacent. I ran into it, and there, in the larder—O marvel!—I found food.

No, the miser recovering possession of his money, the near-dead shipwreck-victim who sees the savior vessel appearing, the criminal who hears his acquittal pronounced—what do I know?—none of those fortunate individuals ever blessed circumstances as much as I did before my discovery. Imagine it: on that bourgeois shelf there were two cold roasted chickens, half a ham, languorously pink, red wine, butter and bread! Yes, bread too—stale bread, but bread! Oh, the truculent emotion!

And I began "stuffing myself up to here!" I started chewing, chewing voraciously, and drinking, drinking recklessly. O Suzanne, my beloved, forgive me; I believe that I forgot you in that paradisal minute. Forgive me, on learning that it was for you, immediately my hunger was satisfied, that I put two chicken-wings in my pocket; for you that I heaped the rest of the provisions into a basket; for you again that I made a rapid tour of the shop, and stole at hazard six bottles of white wine with which I completed my provisions.

Infinitely pleased with that booty, I loaded the basket on to my shoulders and headed back outside. That unexpected meal had completely transformed my psychology. I found the sight of the rubble cheering. The street was so calm, so deserted, and I was now astonished by the facility of my expedition. And I started marching briskly, vivified by a new energy, listened to the bottles clinking merrily on my back, and thinking joyfully about the joy that I was about to cause, when, perhaps a third of the way along the avenue, a familiar sound—a hated sound—made me turn my head.

Frott...! Frott...! Frott...!

It was coming from the direction of the Galerie des Machines.

They were still there, alas. They had discovered me!

Climbing on to a heap of rubble, I saw them in the distance, coming out one by one from the vast hall, which they had doubtless adopted as a lair, where they must have been lurking like dogs in a kennel after breaking down the doors. They were coming, crawling, raising their tentacles, roaring, their frightful gray mass scarcely impeded by the border of rubble.

I got down again immediately in order to run away. Turning my head again, I could only see one of them, for the others were masked by the formidable dimensions of the first. Nevertheless, I sensed ten behind it—ten that were about to surround me, to seize me, to swallow me.

Then I started a mad, reckless race, far more terrible and perilous than the one I had undertaken three days before, along the quays, for this time I was alone, the only prey. I bounded over the rubble with the agility and skill of a gymnast, and took advantage of the open spaces to recover my momentum, and ran in a vertigo, obedient to the illusion that I was gaining ground. I had not let go of my basket, though; I kept it stuck to my shoulder by a miracle of equilibrium, and I heard the bottles bumping into one another, accompanying with the gaiety of their clinking the frightful rumble of the monsters, who were gaining on me.

And what irony! Suddenly, a bottle broke, and I felt liquid inundating me from head to toe—and, surprised by a strong acidic odor, I perceived that it was vinegar that I had carried away, not wine.

Damn! The monsters were going to eat me *à la vinaigrette!*

Realizing that escape was impossible, I put down my basket and waited, with sufficient composure still to witness a poignant drama that unfolded fifty meters away from me. The little dog that I had wanted to kill a little while before had come back, frightened and trembling, as if hypnotized, into the middle of the street. It stood on its hind legs, pulled back its forepaws, and started begging in front of the macrobe, with an attitude of delightful supplication.

Futile graces! I saw it lifted from the ground, and, still maintaining its adorable attitude, fly into the aspiratory tentacle. I was all the more upset because its disappearance signified my imminent fate. In fact, I could already feel the violently-displaced air causing me to oscillate.

Then the tentacle came closer. It was whirling. I contemplated its frightful gray gyration, stupidly. My last thought reached across space to the tunnel where Suzanne was waiting for me.

XIII

By virtue of what inexplicable phenomenon did the monster suddenly veer away from me, as if my presence inspired the same horror in it as it did in me? Was it caprice? Was it the disdain of a satiated animal? But in that case, the ones that were following it would not have spared me, and my death would have been no less certain.

Utterly terrified as I was, I had hardly had time to ask myself that question, and to observe that my first pursuer had executed a leap into the air that left the way clear for the others, than a second macrobe surged forth. It sniffed me, less avidly than the preceding one, and then seemed to be repelled by my person, by virtue of the same invisible force. It retreated backwards, allowing me to hear the collision of its carapace with those of its fellows; then it disappeared.

And seven other macrobes presented themselves thus before the prey that I was, then vanished in the projection of their entire mass, accomplishing a perilous leap, and subsequently falling back deafeningly in the vicinity. From the direction of the racket, I understood that they were fleeing toward Grenelle.

I remained alone.

Stupefied, having no explanation for my incredible immunity, with a mad bound, I resumed my race toward the Pont d'Iéna. I tumbled down the stairway leading to the quay and went back into the tunnel. A sublime cry from Suzanne welcomed me; her arms wrapped around me frantically. The sweet recompense for my audacity! I would have liked to respond by reassuring her, and promising her imminent liberty, but I had to confess, to her and to the others who were pressing me with questions, that the danger still persisted. Then, as they noticed the odor of vinegar on me, I was obliged to give the explanation, recounting my adventure, and the breaking of a bottle of that liquid on my shoulder. It was unbelievable, and yet, in spite of the implausibility of what I said, those minds debilitated by hunger believed me.

Finally, waiting until my interlocutors had been distracted by the Serviat-d'Abila flirtation, which was being closely observed, not without malice—oh, the genius of the species; everything gives way before it!—I handed my fiancée the two chicken wings that I had taken care to pocket. She was so imprudently hasty in raising them to her mouth that she was seen. First the actor, then the concierge, and then the disciple of the Salvation army, and others, threw themselves upon her like wolves, mouths agape, to snatch the victuals away from her. I did my best to defend her property, striking out at the gang of marauders, trying brutally to drive them away; it was no good. She was knocked down and dispossessed before even having been able to swallow two mouthfuls.

That brutality inspired me with the most vivid rancor against the humans assembled there. I judged them well worthy of their fate, and I promised to avenge myself on them and to disdain all sentiments of compassion in future.

That incident, that violent battle over a scrap of food, had only served to inflame the appetite of others. The most ludicrous and unrealizable projects to procure something to eat were proposed. Eyes were gleaming, and the young Englishwoman from the Salvation Army ate dirt before my eyes.

"My God!" the Baronne suddenly said. "Why not demand from the sewer that which Heaven, truly too unjust, refuses us at present..." Then she added, making her teeth grate a little more: "I believe that once, when I was living among the cannibals..."

I turned to Suzanne. She was on the brink of fainting. I could not, however, allow her to die of hunger. I equipped myself with a bucket and, parting the ferocious guardians of our gallery, went down to the bottom of the iron stairway leading to the collector.

It was the first time I had ventured that far, and I was able, by the light of a match, to convince myself of the privilege of our situation, those of us who were living in the broad corridor.

As far as the light of my match dissipated the darkness, I could see people sitting on the ledge above the channel of the sewer. The majority, huddled against the cement wall, were asleep, exhausted, their legs dangling in the water. Others were moaning, and I saw some who were already in advance of us, biting into pieces of flesh pulled out of the black water at hazard.

What impressed me the most, however, was the odor that filled the place. Whereas, in our location, the air renewed by the vicinity of the exterior was relatively breathable, here there was an unspeakable atmosphere, vitiated by the crowding of people, and by all the horrors that the sewer, swollen by rain, was carrying.

Not lingering over those sensations, I plunged my bucket into the current, without catching anything at first. I repeated the maneuver and, encountering resistance, pulled harder, and eventually found myself loaded with a heavy booty.

I went back upstairs, but, having reached the summit, I ran into new difficulties, for those who had appointed themselves the owners of the tunnel no longer wanted to let me back in.

First, I negotiated in vain; I invoked justice, right and reason. Then, as they remained deaf to my arguments, I ended up flying into a frightful rage and declared that I was determined to throw into the water, along with myself, any inhuman individuals who continued to oppose my passage. Then the latter stood aside before my threats, and I finally returned to my friends.

Oh, what we pulled out of my dipper then! I cannot think about it without shivering. There was a human foot, a fragment of shoulder, a vertebral column and a few other items of quivering flesh. My fiancée turned away from them in horror, and I no longer care to remember that the actor devoured a piece of sausage that was lying in the bucket with those anatomical specimens.

"Listen, Jean," Suzanne said to me, her eyes dilated with distress. "Listen: I can see that we're condemned to die of hunger. It's frightful, and I want no more of it. Let's hasten our agony, shall we? Ask Monsieur Serviat, who possesses a violent poison, to give us a few drops—and let's drink them together, my Jean!"

The poor child! It was the only time, very excusably, that she lacked courage. I tried at first to dissuade her from her project, to make her envisage a possible deliverance—but she was obstinate, and I consented.

I transmitted my request to Serviat, who refused flatly, on the pretext that individual interest had to cede to the salvation of all, and that he would not surrender an atom of his precious liquid.

When I returned to Suzanne after that discussion, I perceived than she had fallen into a kind of torpor due to weakness and emotion. Then I lifted her into the wagon and laid her down on her makeshift bed, and, having covered her with sand to shield her from the cold, I waited for darkness, which returned, atrocious and eternal.

Around me there were plaints, gasps and delirium. As he went to sleep, the actor declaimed the story of Theramenes.[63]

The next day was the fourth of our claustration. Our despair, on awakening, foundered before our exhaustion. We were no longer thinking; we were no longer anything more than anemic whimpering animals. I calculated that human resistance has limits, and that several among us would undoubtedly die that day. Alas, would my fiancée also be subject to that fatal decision of fate? I anticipated the blow that I would suffer, that would strike me down over her body.

She was lying in her bed of sand, her eyes closed and her hands joined, like a wax Madonna. Her lips were employing their scant breath in calling to two individuals whom she confused in the same devotion, the last glimmer of a heart in the process of extinction.

"Papa...! Jean...!" she repeated.

Oh, that poignant appeal, the anguishing litany of her virginal tenderness! I picked up her head gently, like a precious trinket, and drew it to my shoulder; I talked to her, and I was surprised by the widening of her gaze, which searched for me without seeing me. The poor child! How I adored her, that morning!

But I must get back to the tragic adventure, and the fashion, as extraordinary as everything else, in which it ended.

I remember that Suzanne had fallen unconscious again, which permitted me, with the aid of the triumphant daylight at the orifice, to measure the weak-

---

[63] Theramenes was an Athenian statesman and general continually caught up in political upheavals in which he apparently attempted to play a moderating role; he was eventually executed for his troubles, remaining a highly controversial figure after his death, whose actions and motivations created a dissent among historians that continues, albeit esoterically, to the present day.

ness of the other disaster-victims. It seemed to me that the same instinct had reckoned with the sentimentality of all of them. Faces emaciated, features drawn by suffering, they were no longer attentive to anything but their hunger. Their eyes admitted that they would have devoured one another.

I heard the actor and the concierge proposing, as if it were perfectly natural, selecting by drawing lots the person who would serve the others as nourishment, and I wondered whether the covetousness of the excessively dark-haired gentleman and the very blond young man, still directed toward the pretty collector for the Salvation Army, was still addressed to her charms or to the delicate snack that she promised.

Monsieur Serviat was slyly sucking his last cocaine pastille, and the Baronne d'Abila, the only one who was still striving to find the situation amusing, had just tightened her leg-armor by two notches, declaring that she would come out of it with an admirable figure.

Yes, we were at that point when, suddenly, someone directing his gaze toward the exit shouted: "Look what's happening in the Seine!"

We drew a little nearer to the orifice, still haunted by the fear of tentacles, and perceived that an enormous wave, propelled in the opposite direction to the current, like a tidal bore, had suddenly raised the level of the river. The water, which we had been unable to see a little while before because it was framed by the quays, was now visible; foam was seething on its surface, and we estimated that it must have risen by about a meter. We expected to see it fall back again, or at least remain stationary, but on the contrary, it continued to swell, to the extent that it soon reached the bank, over which it began to extend, turbulently.

Alarmed by that phenomenon, so seemingly unnatural, but for which I found an explanation without difficulty, I turned to Monsieur Serviat.

"Is it, perhaps, the macrobes?"

"Go and see, my friend! Go and see!"

Forgetting the danger of risking myself outside, so impassioned was I by the other danger, I bounded on to the quay. And what sudden anxiety! To the west, the direction from which the flood was precipitating, shortly before the Pont du Passy, a giant floodgate was blocking the Seine. One of the animals was lying across the bed of the river and filling it almost entirely.

If I had not been familiar with the monsters I would willingly have compared the one that was bathing to a metal dam disposed for a subfluvial endeavor, two-thirds submerged, whose upper part, heaving adopted the form of an elongated dome, dull gray in color, was surmounted by a mobile chimney—the animal's appendage. I saw the tentacle plunge into the liquid, sucking in a considerable quantity, and raising it up again, squirt the jet a hundred meters. My fear increased further when I observed that other macrobes were coming from the direction of Grenelle, ready to imitate it.

"This time, it's the end," I came back to say to the scientist. The animals are bathing. One has already invaded the Seine and the others..."

"Well, perhaps it's time to offer them a little liqueur!" exclaimed Monsieur Serviat, brandishing his bottle of toxin.

He had scarcely announced his plan when a second wave disturbed the river, overflowing the bank and projecting a torrent into our tunnel. A horrible human clamor, mainly coming from the collector placed beneath us, where the mass of liquid had found its natural direction, responded to the voice of the roaring wave. The imprecations of men and the desperate screams of women rang out; there was a frightful din compounded of all the noises reverberated by the cement walls along the dark tunnel.

I understood that another macrobe had plunged into the river, upstream from the first. That explanation, however, did not serve to moderate my terror, because I foresaw that, even if the other animals had decided to take up their positions behind the first, we would be no less condemned to perish submerged, given that the river would not stop In its inexhaustible course, and that its elements, repelled by the monstrous barriers, would inevitably accumulate between the quays where the drain was hollowed out. Indeed, after having dropped momentarily, the level was already rising again, less impetuously but without respite, and we had water up to our knees.

All that formidable chaos, that panic in the face of disaster, those plaints and gasps, had extracted Suzanne from her inertia. She raised herself up in her wagon, gazed at the tide dazedly, and turned her hallucinated face toward me.

"Jean!" she stammered. "Is it possible? Is it true?" Then submitting to the reality, she held out her arms to me, with the distress of a child at the end of so much suffering, after seeing fate play with her, and me, so stubbornly, before carrying us away. I seized her swiftly, and pressed her to my heart.

"Oh, Suzanne!" I cried. "My Suzanne, don't forget..."

But a third wave cut me off, passing furiously through our refuge, and went to be engulfed in the collector, definitively extinguishing the lamentations of the unfortunates who were down there.

Oh, what agonies there were in that black liquid! And what a spectacle in our tunnel, where people, howling their terror, were struggling to resist the current that already possessed us up to the waist!

And what I saw then, unconsciously, in a last glimmer of observation, before preparing to die myself and to feel Suzanne dying in my arms!

First there was a mother who, escaping from the collector and having reached the top step of the iron ladder, incapable of opposing any longer the forces dragging her away, holding out her child toward men who disdained her plea. She begged someone to take the child, that at least her treasure might be saved. She was swept away, disappearing along with her poor burden.

Then, in an extraordinary confusion, in a haste paralyzed by the water, there were people striving to reach the other stairway, the stone steps departing from the middle of our tunnel toward the roadway. Reaching the bottom, they ran into the implacable egotism of those who were already occupying the steps, who, further delaying the danger of going outside, defended their position with terrible actions, hitting, stabbing, strangling.

I saw the collector for the Salvation Army, her whole face illuminated with an ecstatic joy, open her mouth and intone a hymn, while the actor, suddenly going mad, was gripped by inextinguishable laughter. I saw the Baronne strip off the rest of her armor once and for all, and get ready to start swimming, beside Monsieur Serviat, who was taking the stopper from his bottle with a tremulous hand.

As for me, all my energies deployed toward the sole possible issue, I gripped Suzanne tightly in my arms, and resolved to attempt a last near-impossible salvation, to reach the submerged quay, then the steps to the Pont d'Iéna, and then the streets. Briefly, I gave her a few last instructions, recommending her to hang on to my shoulder without impeding my movements. She was scarcely listening anyway; her eyes, dilated by fright, were still protesting, more than any possible speech, against the imbecilic cruelty of destiny, which was obstinate in battering down the door of our happiness.

She must have judged, as I did, the futility of our efforts, suspecting that, at the exit from the tunnel, the fatal current would carry us away, to steer us toward the macrobes' tentacles. Even if we were spared by the fury of the waters, even if we reached dry ground, was our end not assured by the voracity of the monsters?

And the water rose, rose incessantly, under the inexhaustible momentum of the river. Stiffening myself nevertheless. I took a few strides toward the exterior light.

I had arrived very close to the exit, but a fourth wave, more impetuous than the others, immobilized me. A fourth macrobe had just plunged into the river, again upstream of the preceding ones.

The liquid mass swirled and foamed, and then leveled off, leaving me shoulder-deep in the water, while Suzanne, whom I was carrying, was waist-deep. I took a few more steps, and arrived in broad daylight, before the unforgettable spectacle of the flood, agitated by the swell of the successive gigantic immersions.

"Look out! Don't swallow a drop! I'm poisoning the Seine!" shouted Monsieur Serviat, who had followed us, hanging on to the Baronne at the moment when she plunged bravely into the torrent.

He was solemnly brandishing his murderous bottle. Although I was conscious of the puerility of his action, thinking that he would condemn us to be poisoned too, given that one cannot ask a swimmer not to open his mouth, an absurd hope nevertheless invaded me at the sight of what was about to happen.

"I'm poisoning! I'm poisoning!" he repeated, excitedly, his vessel unstoppered, both arms raised.

"It's futile, my poor Serviat!" a voice replied to him, coming from our left. "My lovely macrobes adore your toxin!"

313

Oh, that voice! That accursed voice! Where was it coming from? I thought I recognized it, and yet, was it possible that it came at that moment to insult our misery? What macabre joker was emitting it, then?

I turned my gaze toward the place from which it was echoing, and what I saw inspired the most emotional moment of the entire adventure, fertile as it was in *coups de théâtre*.

Standing in a rather frail dinghy, which was moving alongside the wall of the quay, was an improbable individual. Was it really a person? Was it not rather an unreal apparition, engendered by my delirious brain? Everything led me to believe so, for no human being had ever been decked out thus. The phantom was, in fact, covered, from the occiput to the toes, even hiding the face in such way as not to leave room for anything but the eyes and a long black beard, by a chestnut-red envelope similar to those rubber fabrics that are manufactured in order to make artificial sponges. And the improbability of the costumes was completed by the object that he wore slung over his shoulder: a bucket like those used by bill-posters, equipped with its brush.

Quite at ease, in spite of his burden, he brought his dinghy forward by pressing with his feet on two pedals that doubtless controlled the thrust and orientation of some kind of automobile engine.

Then I remembered something: I had seen that spongy silhouette before, from the height of the dirigible *France*, on the day when Junisseau had pointed out the individual guiding the macrobes with the broad sweeps of a holy-water sprinkler. I was, therefore, in the presence of the Almighty of the monsters, the genius that controlled them and led them to destruction!

And suddenly, after having recognized a tic that had just convulsed one of his free arms, I launched toward the apparition a stupefied cry: "Tornada!"

It was Tornada! It was the god of the macrobes, their creator, their inspirer, so deadly to Humankind! It was Tornada, at the height of his madness, taking a boat trip on the Seine, doubtless in order to savor, in the spectacle of his work, the intense voluptuousness that maniacs experience in the realization of their crime. And the more we looked at him in terror, the more he laughed, and the more agitated his tics became.

"How little scientific intelligence you have, my poor Serviat!" he contrived to shout, nevertheless, above the fury of the waters.

Stupor had stopped the chemist's gesture of salvation. He considered Tornada, in bewilderment. I remember that he unthinkingly replaced the stopper in his bottle, but continued to hold it up in the air, probably preserving it for his moral enemy. Then, suddenly, seized by rage, he stammered:

"Just wait, scoundrel! I'll take away your appetite for the Académie!"

Drunk with wrath, forgetting that he could not swim, he came forward, cleaving through the flood, toward the madman. But the latter did not even seem to notice him. He had returned his interest to the group formed by Suzanne and myself, to my efforts to resist the inundation, which was reaching us again, coming up to my shoulders.

He was moved to pity. "What! It's you, my dear children! It's you, imprudent little ones! You didn't follow my advice, then? You stayed in Paris?"

"Oh, Monsieur!" my fiancée implored, in a sudden surge of hope. "Save us! Save us!"

I saw that that appeal had suddenly softened the strange individual. Using his skill and a surprising strength, he brought the boat closer to us, and with a firmness of grip that one would not have suspected in such a small man, he first grasped my fiancée, lifted her up and drew her into his boat. Then he extended his hand to me, in my turn. That was fortunate, for the river was continuing its inexorable rise, the turbulent waters had already exceeded human height, and I was on the point of succumbing to the engulfing flood.

Then, as soon as we were in the dinghy, Tornada picked up the brush contained in his bucket, and sprinkled us with a liquid that had a strong odor of vinegar.

"Wretch! Wretch!" Monsieur Serviat was still howling, hanging on to the boat with one hand and trying to climb into it.

Tornada did not seem to hear him. He was sitting down next to Suzanne and gazing at her with a profound tenderness. His eyes filled with tears, but I was unable to determine whether the cause that provoked his emotion was the fact of seeing my fiancée so exhausted, with the lividity of a corpse, or whether, on the contrary, the acid vapor given off by his receptacle and his clothing was irritating his eyes and determining the apparent sadness.

He remained thus, unmoving, contemplating her, for several seconds, which seemed to me to last for an eternity.

"Speak, my child," he said, finally—and that last word took on an extraordinary softness on his lips. "Speak, and you alone I will obey."

"Halt the disaster, Monsieur!" Suzanne moaned. "Save those you can still spare!"

"Even Serviat?"

"Yes, him too! All of them! All those who remain!"

That request seemed to make him hesitate. He began grimacing again, and his limbs sketched further convulsions. A last supplication from Suzanne who had thrown herself on her knees, finally made up his mind. He gripped his rival, who was still clinging on to the edge of the boat, by the wrist and pulled him in.

"You! If you move...!" he said, dumping him on to a banquette, like a parcel.

In response to an ardent prayer from Suzanne he repeated his maneuver for the Baronne, just as a fifth bore, produced by the irruption of a fifth macrobe into the river, had descended upon her and was about to drag her away. The socialite was in quite a state! Her wet chemise was clinging to her vast flesh, her long hair was loose and sticky. Oh, I swear to you that it was not a pretty sight!

But how much more dolorous was the disaster that had swept over our erstwhile companions, who had all drowned, annihilated by the irresistible flood. The orifice of our refuge was invisible now, alas!

Trembling with horror, I sat quietly in the boat, hugging Suzanne. The drama had taken such a stupefying turn that I no longer knew what to think. Tornada's conduct promised us salvation, but what enigmas did it still reserve for us? The madman was liberating us, after having destroyed an entire people, but what was he going to do with us now...inasmuch as the macrobes had detected us?

I saw their colossal masses moving sinuously along the driver, toward our freely drifting boat. On the other hand, more were arriving, bounding from every corner of the sunlit space, accumulating on the bank, raising their frightful roaring conches. Tornada, however, did not seem to be alarmed by their approach. He planted his little sponge-silhouette in the boat, derisory before so many monstrosities encircling us, and he spoke.

"Serviat," he said, "You're a pretentious idiot and an incomparable ass. Do you still deny the presence of *Micrococcus aspirator* in alkaline environments?"

"I don't know..." the scientist stammered.

"You don't know? And yet I'm showing them to you, the darlings! Look around you—they're visible enough. And do you still deny that they can develop abnormally, in an appropriate culture medium? Eh? Do you still deny that?"

He twitched triumphantly. He clucked, in a victorious snigger.

The chemist, as frightened as us in seeing the circle of animals draw tighter, did not reply.

"Monsieur!" Suzanne begged. "They're arriving! They're here! There!"

"Have no fear, my child."

Our boat continued its atrocious drift. It had arrived about fifty meters from the first immersed macrobe; seized by the eddies produced by its mass, it spun, contrary to the direction of the river's flow, imposing on us successively the view of all the giants circling us—but which, however, remained on the bank, trunks elevated, held back by an incomprehensible dread. Our anguish reached its extreme. How were we going to escape them? By means of what magic power was the genius of Tornada going to save us from the monstrous horde? Or was he simply bringing us to the hecatomb, with a refinement of cruelty?

I thought so at first, at the further signs of evident dementia that Tornada was then showing. He had picked up the brush from the receptacle suspended from his shoulder, and began sprinkling us again, like a priest blessing the dead, while his lips murmured obscure words. What did that action signify, after all? What power did it have over our destiny? Was it merely a macabre ritual prior to the sacrifice?

The fabulous circle was still tightening. In every direction, there was no longer anything to be seen but raised trunks, prolonging their horrible whistles.

Nothing, this time—no divine or terrestrial power—could enable us to avoid the fatal air current. I gave Suzanne my last glance of adoration. Around us, the thousand sunlit facets of the water were palpitating.

"Watch carefully, Serviat!" proclaimed the madman.

He resumed his position at the pedals, and activated them with a few light pressures. The boat moved off, going up the Seine with an amazing rapidity. We seemed to be flying over the water, whose surface was now flooding the quays, with the result that, whichever way we turned, we perceived the lamentable expanse of devastated Paris, while the macrobes, attracted to the banks by our presence, directed their progress in our direction. Pitiful heaps of rubble, and fragments of the walls of palaces, the Chambre des Députés, the Légion d'honneur and the Gare d'Orsay filed past.

Between the Pont des Saints-Pères and the Pont des Arts, however, the boat suddenly stopped. What an astonishing contrast! The Cité had been spared; the towers of Notre-Dame, the Palais de Justice, the Sainte-Chapelle, defied the abolished city with their splendor, and the crushed Louvre opposed its ruins to the still-intact Institut.

What did Tornada want? Why that sinister excursion? Did he want to contemplate, one last time, the cupola that the incredulity of men had refused him? Did he want, one last time, to carry away the vision of his disastrous power, or to pass his magnificent and fatal army in review? It was there, arranged along the two banks, having immobilized at the same time as us, and yet, it seemed to me, still retained by I knew not what mysterious power.

"Look, Serviat!" howled the maniac. "Look at the Institut! If I wanted, eh? In pieces, the Institut. But there's Vernet...where has he gone, then, Vernet? And then, there's his daughter...oh, oh, oh, my daughter, where is she, too? My daughter!"

He sniggered. He spat in the direction of the monument. Then he leaned on his pedals again, and the boat, still accompanied by its formidable cortege, resumed its route toward the Trocadéro. Soon, we found ourselves back at our point of departure. The waters, further increased, were swelling around the masses installed there.

"What is life, if it isn't oblivion?" reflected the madman, aloud, twisting the two halves of his beard together.

Mad—yes, indubitably, he was mad. Unhurriedly, he took from the inside pocket of his strange garment a small pistol barely twenty centimeters long, like a child's toy. He secured it in his hand, and pointed it at the nearest macrobe in the river. I observed that he was aiming at a fairly distinct patch situated beneath the monster's tentacle, which I had not noticed until then. Was it with that vain implement that he expected to breach the mass that fracassite had been unable to scratch?

"*Vade retro, macrobe!*" he pronounced, pressing the trigger.

317

The shot was fired. A light smoke evaporated in the firmamental purity. And the miracle was accomplished: as soon as the animal was touched by the projectile, we saw it quit the water, turning a prodigious somersault, Instead of carrying it forward, however, the leap took it backwards, with the result that the colossus, having obstructed the sky momentarily, fell back toward Grenelle in a clap of thunder.

"And one!" Tornada counted.

The water displaced by that immense void had drawn us toward the second macrobe. After an instant of further peril provoked by the unstable equilibrium of our boat, when the level had stabilized again, Tornada raised his arm again and subjected the second animal to the same fate as the first.

This time, the leap finished on the Pont de Passy, which resisted, and the gigantic carcass remained there, motionless, belly up, its tentacle hanging down. We could no longer doubt the mortal power of the projectiles.

"I bow down, Tornada!" cried Serviat, as stupefied as us. Then, lowering his head, he added. "Yes, I'm defeated. You're the Master! Explain it to me now, Tornada—explain it!"

"How did I do it? Oh, my poor fellow!"

He turned to Suzanne. In truth, it was to her that he replied; it was her that he attempted to dazzle. He disdained his rival—and that disdain spared us necessarily abstract scientific reasoning. While taking aim methodically at the other animals, which his boat, skillfully maneuvered, passed along the river's edge, periodically reloading his ammunition clip –whose cartridges, each enclosed in a brass detonator, were constituted by thick glass ampoules, he continued.

"It's to you that I'm addressing myself, my child, for, if I except your father, the brain of an academician is too obtuse to comprehend. This is what I've done. I cultivated in special media, entirely appropriate to their growth, microscopic animalcules that I had discovered in bicarbonate of soda. I had the idea that they would develop there abnormally, and that I would be able to make them do so rapidly, by subjecting them to appropriate conditions of air, light, nourishment and social exigencies—yes, social exigencies too, for a chemist must double as a sociologist. As I said, I had the idea that I could subject them, within a year, to the transformations that Darwinism attributes to centuries of evolution. What? Does function not create the organ, eh? Ha ha! I made functionaries! Who do not belong to the Institut!"

He paused to take aim, extending his arm.

"Leap, macrobe! Bang! *De profundis!* Yes, out there in my laboratory at Rosny, I plotted a tasty revenge against those cretins. Out there, I grew these villainous beasts. If you knew what voluptuousness there was in seeing them, every day, growing larger—and my joy increased too! Bang! *Ave macrobe!*

"And destroying them, now, I can confess to you that it's breaking my heart—bang! I kill you too, lovely macrobe!—and it required, my child, your meek suggestion, and the imperishable memory of my daughter, which your grace has reawakened—bang! will you, macrobe, ever reawaken?—for me to decide to immolate my pretties. Bang!... Bang! Bang! Bang! Bang!"

Gripped by a destructive rage, with an extraordinary skill, he now accelerated his fire, which was succeeded by the immeasurable leaps of the macrobes, and the thunderous din when they fell back, out of our sight. Perhaps fifty had already been carried away by their agonized leap, and the bank was now free of them, while only one remained in the water, which continue to block the watercourse, and that one was still too far away from us to be an immediate preoccupation.

But what was he going to do about the others, the scientific genius? How was he going to get to them? Already my imagination was setting off on a hunt, in Tornada's wake, through the streets of the devastated city, or rather the surrounding plains that were also subject to their ravages—and that pursuit, favored by an evident security, was already making me smile when my attention was absorbed by a new maneuver of the man clad in sponge.

"Pass me that object," he said to me, pointing to a long case on the floor of the boat, which I had not previously noticed.

I held it out to him; it was rather heavy, in spite of its restricted dimensions. As soon as it was in his possession he held it up vertically; then he pressed a spring that gave birth to the three limbs of a tripod, which he established solidly on the floor. Another pressure on a second spring caused a kind of little metal tube to emerge at the upper extremity, surmounted by an ampoule similar to those he had employed to destroy his macrobes. Without him even having to touch it again, a succession of sparks set the base of the tube ablaze; then an almost insignificant explosion occurred, which launched the ampoule into the air.

"Close your eyes!" Tornada ordered, at the same time.

I made the mistake of not obeying him. Curiosity made me look up into the sky, following the supposed trajectory of the ampoule, until an extremely vivid flash of light seared my retinas. Although blinded by that extraordinary radiation, I nevertheless retained the impression that its color was an orange-red and that its form was akin to the spray of a firework.

That light, so special, and its expansion in the form of a bouquet, was not new to me. I remembered having observed it several times before, from the height of Mont-Valérien, on the day when the Committee of National Defense had made a fool of itself with the plan to destroy the macrobes with cannon fire. Why was Tornada reproducing it? In what interest?

I soon had an explanation from the words with which the inventor accompanied his maneuver, and once again I had to admire the more than ingenious fashion in which the whole affair had been planned.

"Run, my lovelies! Run, my darlings! He murmured, addressing himself to our invisible enemies, which were incapable of hearing him. Then, in a louder

319

voice, gesturing toward the deserted banks, he added: "Run! Come! The light is calling you! Don't you recognize your light of orig..."

He suspended his phrase, but I had understood. Their light of origin! That was it! Tornada had made use of an orange-red light to cultivate his microorganisms, and that was doubtless the reason why the experiments carried out at the Institut Pasteur, for lack of that detail, had failed. And that orange-red light, he was reproducing in their air with an exceptional intensity; he was making use of it to rally his creatures, to attract them, as if by a magnetic fluid, to the sacrifice to which his new pity commanded him.

Indeed, at his celestial command, the bank soon resonated with a formidable *Frott...! Frott...! Frott...!* and was garnished once again with a host of gray enormities.

All the rest of the flock was there, fifty meters away from us, roaring, brandishing their tentacles, and yet, still retained on the bank but I still knew not what terror of their shepherd.

Meanwhile, Tornada continued to direct his weapon against the successive targets offered to his skill. It was no longer anything but a continuous crepitation, and to every one of his infallible shots, a formidable leap responded, an obscuration of the sky soon followed by the distant fall of a monstrous cadaver. We were no longer counting his victims, but he seemed to have the number in his head, for he proclaimed, at a certain moment:

"Seventy-two! Keep coming, my darlings! Come! Bang! Bang!..... And Bang!

"For pity's sake, explain," Serviat groaned. "Explain!"

But Tornada continued to address himself to Suzanne, while reloading his weapon.

"How inferior he is! What a nonentity he is! It's true that he's a member of the Institut! But you, my child, you, who aren't, tell me: how does one neutralize acids?"

"Acids?" asked my fiancée.

"Yes, acids."

"With alkalis."

"Of course! She knows! She isn't a member of the Institut! And she knows, too, that acids are the enemies of alkalis! So, you can grasp, Serviat, you utter ass, that in order to destroy creatures emerged from alkaline environments, it requires...what? Bang! Bang!...it requires a few drops of acid...simple vinegar! And bang! Bang!...and that it's sufficient to strike there, at the original cell, the vital navel of my lovely microbes, their only vulnerable spot. Bang! Bang!...that it's sufficient to strike there, to kill them, the poor darlings! And to think that Serviat has prepared a toxin! A toxin! Ha ha ha! Bang! Bang!"

He was no longer clucking; he was growling; he was uttering howls toward his hecatomb.

Then, a flash of revelation shot through me. I understood then why I had been spared by the monsters, two days before, in the Avenue de La Bourdonnais; why they had even moved away from me in evident horror. Fate had aided me singularly, by inundating me with the immunizing liquid, the vinegar from the bottle broken in the haste of my flight. I understood, too, everything that had previously seemed inexplicable to me: Tornada's costume, a sponge steeped in acetic acid; and his actions in sprinkling us religiously; and method of herding the macrobes by inspiring them with the terror of the murderous fluid. All that I had put down to the count of incoherence became the logic of a powerful brain, and I criticized myself, in my spirit of scientific deduction, for not having suspected it.

Mad, however, Tornada was! It was sufficient to contemplate him at that moment, rolling his wild eyes, intoxicated by his murderous gestures, shouting and howling, to be convinced of it.

Nevertheless, he soon relented his fire; he no longer launched his projectiles without hesitation. He proclaimed the repeated "Bang! Bang!" that accompanied the death of his creatures more faintly. His final shots were spaced out.

Our boat had brought us close to the macrobe that still occupied the river, the waters flowing around it to resume their course beyond it, after having passed over the height of the quays, giving it the appearance of a gray rock in the midst of a tormented sea. As soon as it saw us, its tentacle began to gyrate.

"We're at ninety-nine," said Tornada, in a whisper. "That's the last!"

He was weeping. To destroy his work like that, for a child's grateful smile—was that not a sacrifice to which it is necessary to attribute a certain measure of grandeur? Had Suzanne not extracted from him the testimony of his genius? Was it not his brain that she was tearing out of him, at the same time that she was forcing him to extinguish his creation?

And Tornada's hand trembled, when he aimed his weapon for the last time. Nevertheless, he hit his target, and an enormous displacement of the river, companying the monster's leap, after nearly causing us to overturn, finally signified our liberation.

I cannot describe our jubilation here.

"All! All! Adieu, my pretties!" sobbed Tornada. Then, turning to Suzanne: "You see, my child, what I've done for you! Will you now forgive a poor, desperate man who wanted to rediscover his daughter in you?"

He held out his hand to her—but she shivered with such fright; she had, at the memory of the distress that hand had accumulated, the disasters it had engendered, the innocent deaths that it had caused, experienced such a surge of disgust that Tornada understood that he had committed irreparable sins. He grimaced, and twisted his beard. He convulsed in a tic that was reminiscent of the tentacular movement of his monsters. Finally, he took another revolver out of his pocket, and before we could do anything to stop him, he applied the barrel to his temple.

"Bang!" he repeated.

And he collapsed, in a red splash. The madman disappeared with his work.

But now that I am finishing this story; now that, having relocated Monsieur Vernet—among what transports you can imagine—Suzanne and I are married; and I can hear, interrupting the joyous sounds that those little devils our children are making, the ringing of the bell that is announcing the arrival of Monsieur Serviat and the Baronne—can you imagine that they're married!—now, truly, on thinking about it, I wonder whether everything I've recounted was real, and whether Suzanne and I, and everyone we know, an entire people, were not atrociously delirious for a week...

Jacques Spitz: *Dr. Mops' Experiment*

L'Expérience du Dr. Mops [Dr. Mops' Experiment] was released by Gallimard in their prestigious literary NRF (Nouvelle Revue Française) in 1939. It was the ninth but last of Spitz's novels that they published and was perhaps a prophetic portent of what was to come.

Jacques Spitz (1896-1963) was born in the town of Ghazaouet in what was then French Algeria. His father was in the French military. He eventually went on to graduate brilliantly from the famous Ecole Polytechnique and subsequently lived in Paris, single, working as a freelance engineer, spending much of his time writing. At the start of his literary career, Spitz was influenced by the Surrealist Movement and penned several mainstream novels in that vein, as well as a dark and cynical play about a comical, dystopian future, Ceci est un drame *[This Is A Tragedy], published only in 1947.*

In 1935, Spitz turned to science fiction with L'Agonie du Globe *[The Agony of the Globe]. In total, Spitz wrote eight major genre novels over the next ten years, becoming a worthy successor to Maurice Renard and J.-H. Rosny Aîné, and heralding future luminaries of the 1950s and 1960s such as René Barjavel and Pierre Boulle.*

In L'Agonie du Globe, *Earth is bisected into two hemispheres, one of which eventually crashes into the Moon. The novel established the characteristics of Spitz' style: the use of realistic, scientific details, put to the service of a wild and surrealistic imagination and a pessimistic view of humanity, the result being a tragicomic satire on a "cosmic" scale. His concerns were primarily about the society of men, and in that, he anticipated the "New Wave" writers like J. G. Ballard and Thomas M. Disch by 30 years.*

His next book, Les Evadés de l'An 4000 *[The Escapees from the Year 4000] (1936), is about a new ice age which drives men underground where they fall prey to a scientific dictature; eventually, some more enlightened characters escape and flee towards Venus.*

It was followed two years later by La Guerre des Mouches *[The War of the Flies] and* L'Homme élastique *[The Elastic Man] (both 1938). The first featured the conquest of Earth by mutated flies animated by a gestalt intelligence. It is a particularly dark and pessimistic work, containing some fierce satirical observations about mankind, its foibles, and, ultimately, its utter impotence before its implacable enemy. The few survivors end up in a zoo.*

By comparison, L'Homme élastique, *with its means to compress and decompress atoms, enabling the creation of tiny super-soldiers and flaccid giants, is almost tame, but its handling of the theme of miniaturization is as ground-breaking today as it was when it was written.*

L'Expérience du Dr. Mops (1939) and L'Oeil du Purgatoire (1945) both explored the theme of farseeing into the future. In the latter, Dr. Dagerloff's unhappy guinea pig, the painter Jan Poldonski, sees not the real future, but an increasingly aging present, where death and decay ultimately become overpowering sights. L'Oeil du Purgatoire is a dark, introspective novel, a reflection of the notion of time and aging, certainly unique in the annals of science fiction.

Spitz' final genre works included La Parcelle Z *[Particle Z] (1942) and the somewhat more hopeful* Les Signaux du Soleil *[The Signals from the Sun] (1943), in which Martians and Venusians, unaware of our existence, discuss their plans to mine Earth's atmosphere through sunspots. Their communications are deciphered by the hero. Fortunately for Earth, the aliens stop once they realize that our planet is inhabited by intelligent life. This is accomplished by encrypting pi into the ionization of the atmosphere.*

Two more genre novels remained unpublished during Spitz' life: La Guerre Mondiale No. 3 *[World War III], which was finally published posthumously in 2005, and* Alpha du Centaure *[Alpha Centauri], which was either unpublished or pulped upon publication when its publisher was seized by the Germans (stories differ).*

After 1945, Spitz, who had fought during two World Wars and had received the Legion of Honor for his bravery, abandoned science fiction and wrote only semi-autobiographical and surreal pieces.

J.-M.L.

I

If the month of April had not been so rainy in Paris that year, nothing would have happened, or something else would have happened. But what good is it going on about the role played by incidental circumstances in life's great events? I no longer believe in causes and effects now—the laborious explanations that one forges after the fact in order to take account of a chain of events. All that is of no importance whatsoever, and it is only for the sake of vain mental satisfaction that one imagines a logical sequence in the course of events.

I had just returned to France to spend a year's leave there. One has to stay for three consecutive years in the Pacific islands—the Philippines, Timor, Bali—to understand what a return to France might mean. To rediscover trees, dairy produce, cool nights, mosquito-less slumbers, women whose eyes gleam and actually seem to signify something, old houses, ancient landscapes without scorpions, snakes or insects, and people whose language one understands effortlessly...

My first fortnight in Paris was delightful—for it was in Paris, naturally, that I began. After a fortnight of all kinds of folly, however, I woke up from the kind of intoxication into which that return had plunged me to become aware of the fact that it was raining perpetually, and that I felt chilly. My sojourn in the tropics had rendered me sensitive to cold. I could no longer set aside my fur-lined coat. Two weeks of rain had sufficed for me to be repossessed by nostalgia for the Sun that I had cursed for three years in the equatorial regions. The remedy did not require any great effort of the imagination. I was alone, free to go where I liked; I followed the traditional current that draws idlers southwards, and I woke up one morning in a couchette on a train moving along the Côte d'Azur. I got off in Monaco, because I had just finished my breakfast at that moment, and almost everyone had left the carriage. I could just as easily have stopped at Nice or Menton, but it happened to be Monaco.

The first day was execrable. Although the hotel was comfortable and the Sun high in the sky, I found around me nothing but people over 70: little invalid carriages; plaids; blankets over every knee; old mottled and twisted hands with swollen veins and outmoded rings; bottles of mineral water on every table; and, everywhere, the empty, discolored gazes of old people, awaiting death beneath checkered caps like those worn by American millionaires.

The following morning, to distance myself somewhat from that asylum of excessively rich old people, I took a stroll along a road that followed the coast through the pines and palm-trees overhanging the walls of villas. As I approached a little inlet, I perceived one of those tiny cars that one only finds in Europe, going along the road leading down to the sea. The road was little more than a pathway, and the badly-jolted vehicle had to be steered through the difficult sections with great care. It succeeded nevertheless in reaching the beach, and when the driver got out, I observed to my surprise that it was a woman—a young woman, to judge by her slenderness and the smoothness of her gestures. From the car's trunk, she extracted a bizarre instrument, which I recognized as one of those tricycles that move on the water, of which one sees a large number on the coast. Then, throwing off her robe, under which she was clad in a bathing costume, the young woman leapt nimbly into the saddle and began pedaling out to sea. One might have thought it an aquatic spider, a plaything like those sold by street-traders on the sidewalk.

When I arrived at the water's edge, she was already some distance away. After a moment's hesitation, I decided that my underpants could take the place of swimming trunks, and set forth in my turn into the transparent water.

I had no specific intention of joining the siren on the tricycle; I was merely giving way to a juvenile impulse to play in the water, as an example had been set for me on that sunny morning. I was a good enough swimmer not to have any fear of introducing myself in those conditions, and even of taking delight in a certain vanity—but the water in the cove, already warm, caressed my cheek so pleasantly that I was soon thinking about nothing but swimming. To be sure, the prospect of an adventure always occupies the mind of a man of my age when he has nothing to do and a year's liberty of which to dispose, but what adventure could match the simple pleasure of merely being in the infinite expanse of water, as clear as in the tropics?—and which, moreover, offered itself as far as the eye could see, without the barrage of steel nets that protect Oceanian beaches from sharks, I was free to go as far out to sea as I wished, my eye at the level of the horizon, cleaving the soft expanse with my arms...

If European seas have no sharks, though, they offer other inconveniences.

A motor boat arrived to pollute the essence of my marine surroundings with its horrible noise and odor. Returning to the surface, I found myself 50 meters from the young woman, who was still pedaling, high above the water, now steering for the shore.

The motor boat's wake struck the flank of the tricycle, whose floats were lifted up. I saw the apparatus sway. Its occupant tried to steady it, but was finally tipped into the sea. At first, I laughed—but a scream soon reached my ears, and I saw and arm waving as if appealing for help. I swam toward the overturned tricycle. One of the young woman's ankles was caught between the chain and the frame; stuck in an inconvenient position, she was unable to swim. I held her up with one hand, while bracing the other against the inverted machine, and she pulled free.

"Thank you," she said. "Just in time, I think."

A few strokes took us to the shore, pushing the apparatus ahead of us. I looked at her: the oval of her rubber cap outlined a very young face with exceedingly pure features. But women always look attractive thus, I said to myself, thinking of nuns and aviatrixes. Then I recalled the damp, firm figure that my arm had enfolded while I freed her.

"It's lucky you were there," she said, finally, in an entirely natural voice, which no longer retained the slight breathlessness of her cry for help. "I might not have been able to get out of it on my own."

She rubbed her ankle.

"Are you hurt?" I asked, with some hypocrisy, for I saw it as a pretext to touch her bare leg.

"A slight graze," she said, drawing away slightly. "It was the chain that trapped me."

My gaze moved back from the ankle to the face. With an abrupt gesture she liberated her rubber-clad hair: a surge of blonde curls, slightly damp around the nape of the neck, blossomed in the sunlight. As soon as she had shaken her head in order to permit her hair to resume its natural shape, I was able to estimate her age—about 20.

"I was trying it today for the first time," she explained, picking up the tricycle with both hands in order to reload it into the car, "and I haven't gotten used to it yet."

As I manifested some slight surprised at see her making preparations to leave so quickly, she said: "I've interrupted your swim. Forgive me." And she started the car.

I remained alone on the beach, rather disappointed to find the adventure cut short. Obviously, I had not expected her to throw her arms around my neck, telling me that I had saved her life, but she didn't have to leave so suddenly, without shaking my hand, or even uttering one of those polite formulas which at least permit the hope of a further meeting...

Lying in the Sun, I was meditating on the ingratitude of young women, while accusing myself of not having been able to take advantage of the situation, when two blasts of a horn made me lift me head. Having reached the cliff-top, the unknown woman had stopped her car and was sounding the horn to attract my attention. She waved her hand twice in a friendly gesture, then set off again.

That fashion of taking her leave, which revived my regrets, seemed to me a trifle perfidious. *She's a little tease*, I thought. I thought her lost forever. I didn't yet know that the Côte d'Azur is no more than a large village.

All afternoon, I dragged regrets and a morose state of mind though various dives in Nice. That evening, back in Monte Carlo, after having hesitated between roulette and the Russian ballet, I opted for the latter. Although the auditorium was mostly filled with the old people whose appearance I found depressing, the audience was elegant and my neighbor, in particular, set me dreaming. All that I could see of her was a fine, intelligent profile, but her perfume, which enveloped me rather insidiously, gradually effaced the memory of that morning's failed adventure. In the darkness, I let myself lapse into the game that consists of substituting for the nagging impression of a woman the presence of the one who might perhaps take her place. An already-dulled past regret was mingled with a not-yet-too-sharp future curiosity. My neighbor was veritably embalmed, and her slender hands, virginal of rings, were delicately taking hold of the reins of my reverie when I suddenly recognized, three rows in front of me, the golden hair that had glistened in the morning sunlight on the beach.

Instantly, I only had eyes for that blonde nape. From various slight movements, I understood that she was accompanying her neighbor, whose bald head reflected a fraction of the stage-lighting into the gloom. I was already assuming that he could not be a very serious rival.

This time, it was necessary not to let the opportunity escape.

During the interval, good luck helped to bring me face to face with the couple in the corridor leading to the boxes. I needed no further ruse; the unknown woman came up to me smiling, holding out her hand.

"Father, I can introduce you to my savior," she said, laughing, "but I don't know his name."

I gave my name; the bald gentleman murmured a name that I didn't catch.

"And this is my cousin Narda," she continued, indicating a slightly awkward young woman of about 17, who was standing to one side.

"Since you have saved her life," the father said to me, straight away, "I can entrust her safety to you. I must absent myself momentarily—don't wait for me."

He was speaking with a slight foreign accent, and his extraordinarily bushy eyebrows contrasted with his close-shaven head, which I had thought at first to be bald. He disappeared into the crowd. I went into a corner of the foyer with the young women. The morning's incident furnished a ready-made topic of conversation.

"A scratch that one can scarcely see through a stocking," she replied, still smiling.

My suit must have inspired more confidence than my swimming-costume, for amiability showed through the banality of the words. I learned that young Narda had arrived straight from her Swiss boarding school for the Easter vacation.

"...And she prefers going to the theater to going swimming with me," she added, teasingly.

To which Narda replied, in an almost child-like voice: "Yvane doesn't understand that the water of Swiss swimming-baths is much calmer."

I smiled, and turned back to Yvane, whose name I had finally learned. "If you wouldn't mind my company, I'd gladly accompany you on your next nautical experiment."

"We'd need a tandem," she replied, lightly, without giving any answer to my proposition.

The interval elapsed without my being able to obtain a firm engagement, which I could not solicit overtly. The bell rang and we had to go our separate ways. With a furrowed brow, disappointed once more, I was returning to my solitary seat when Yvane came toward me again, cutting through the crowd.

"I forgot to ask you to come to tea the day after tomorrow," she said, rapidly. "We live in the Château de la Colle, a few kilometers from Nice on the road to Vence. Ask for the house of Doctor Mops—my father-in-law—and you'll find it without any difficulty." Then, with a friendly nod of the head, she allowed herself to be borne away by the tide of spectators.

I had agreed without saying a word. The belated invitation reminded me of the adieu launched from the cliff-top. Was it typical of her turn of mind to return to unsettled situations? Or should I see these intentional postscripts as a demonstration that she was merely giving way to the obligations of politeness? I was thinking about that, recalling her words, when I was suddenly caught up by the term "father-in-law." I would not have thought that she was married, and, on leaning that she was, all the ideas that I had already formed in her regard were revealed as misleading. Nothing in her gestures or her costume—her simple long white dress and the absence of jewelry—indicated that she was in the power of a husband. As the curtain went up again, however, she turned her head slightly toward the auditorium and, meeting my gaze, made me a sign so manifestly ingenuous that I understood my error. "Father-in-law" has two meanings.[64] Her mother must have remarried Doctor Mops.

I was in possession of a baggage of impressions sufficient to give rise to pleasant dreams. After leaving the theater, instead of going to bed, I went to the hotel bar to get gradually merry. Full of assurance, I then found the means of buying a car from an Italian marquis of sorts, who had just been cleaned out at the roulette wheel, and who was drinking beside me. Anyway, a car would doubtless be useful. And in the juvenile delight procured for me by the slimmest possibility of intrigue offered that day by a precious hazard, I went to sleep on the threshold of drunkenness.

II

My entry to the Château de la Colle was greeted by the barking of two Great Danes, fortunately enclosed in a kennel, which split my ears for nearly five minutes before the front door was opened by a Javanese servant. My surprise in confrontation with this Asiatic face, which I had scarcely expected, was redoubled by the sight of the colonial souvenirs—panoplies, trophies, wooden sculptures and masks—that cluttered the drawing-room into which I was shown. Even the window-panes were made of the alabaster-tinted translucent seashells that are used in Manila instead of glass. I found myself abruptly transported to the Dutch East Indies or the Philippines, when I had thought that I was in Provence.

I was still utterly displaced when the door opened on Yvane, whose blonde and blue apparition fortunately brought me back to myself in space and time. She understood the meaning of the grateful smile with which I welcomed her.

"What an idea to usher you into the midst of all this bric-à-brac!" she exclaimed. "My stepfather, who is Dutch, has spent many years in Batavia." She accompanied her explanation with an ironic gesture addressed to all the Oriental ironmongery encumbering the walls. "Come on, we'll be better off elsewhere."

I followed her on to the terrace situated behind the main building, which overlooked a little valley. An olive-grove climbed the slope that was facing us, and vine were discernible behind the curtain of cypresses extended over the first ridge. It was an abridged version of the Provencal countryside.

"Here, I find you again," I said to Yvane.

Very simple in her dress of coarse blue fabric, she adopted a charming gaucherie, tinted with lassitude, in order to furnish the customary explanations.

"The property comprises some 20 hectares, but it hasn't been well-maintained. I ought to occupy myself with it, but I lack the resolve."

"Are you the mistress of the house, then?"

---

[64] Like the French *beau-père*, the English "father-in-law" can, indeed, mean "stepfather," although that meaning is almost obsolete.

"Yes, since my mother's death two years ago. My stepfather leaves all the domestic details to me. As I have a horror of giving orders, that works out rather badly."

I assured her that even though I was an architect, I preferred untidy houses, with weeds growing in the pathways.

"Oh, you're an architect!" she said. Abandoning herself to the first association of ideas, she went on: "The gardeners have been pestering me to have the reservoir refilled, and I don't know how to do it..."

"Well, my visit won't have been useless," I said, laughing. "I'll give you a consultation."

We climbed the slope of the olive-grove, hollowed out at the summit of which was one of those large reservoirs open to the sky, such as one finds in Provence, and which, opening at ground level, are reminiscent of swimming pools. The reservoir was dry; the bottom was in need of concreting over.

"I'll contact a contractor and give you an estimate...but I scarcely expected to be talking business."

"Me neither," she replied, so sincerely that we both laughed.

"I'll change the subject, then, and pay you compliments," I went on.

"Why?" she asked, innocently, turning her large eyes toward me, which were the same color as her dress but which had the varnished gleam of Delft pottery.

"Because you speak French very well," I replied, caught off-guard by so much naivety.

"But I am French. My mother was French before she remarried a Dutchman. My name is Yvane Suyter—that's a Flemish name."

When we got back to the terrace, the tea was being served beneath a plane-tree, and various individuals were already busy about the table.

"Delighted to see you here, Monsieur Delambre," Dr. Mops said to me, with a briskness that I now knew to be Dutch.

In keeping with his status as a country landowner, he had coiffed his cranium in a Panama hat and was smoking a cigar. I was introduced to a relatively young man, Dirk Linard, who was his secretary. Narda was also there, engrossed in connecting the electric wire of the toaster to a power cable running along the balustrade of the terrace.

"You'll get your hands dirty," Yvane said to her.

"Well, I'll go wash them," she replied, with the imperturbable logic of a child.

As Yvane handed the doctor a cup of tea, he declared that he would prefer beer. "Here," he said, "it's not hot enough for warm drinks to be refreshing."

"That's a physician's theory," I said.

"No, a beer-drinker's," he replied, laughing. "Besides, that sort of medicine doesn't interest me. I'm a neurologist—but I won't bore you and all these young folk with the story of my research. It's quite enough that Dirk has to suffer my speeches."

Without saying a word, Dirk lost himself in the contemplation of a cricket that had strayed on to the table. Narda was now peeling the plane-tree, whose bark had been separated by the heat. All that was quite banal, but collectively, these various individuals gave a rather odd impression—which, nevertheless put me at ease. Instead of forming a more-or-less closed family circle, which always resists the intrusion of a new face, everyone here appeared to be following their own train of thought. Everyday companions did not seem to count for any more than a newcomer like me. I therefore had the impression of inserting myself painlessly into the middle of a cordial disunity.

Out of politeness, I made vague comments appropriate to the occasion. The doctor replied. By the manner in which he was holding his cigar between his teeth, I had already observed that he wore dentures. The care with which he smoothed his eyebrows, the only hairy parts of his face, indicated a certain affectation, which prevented me from taking him seriously, but when the servant brought a few letters on a tray, he put on his spectacles in a purposeful way that revealed a studious man, while his myopic gaze, circled with glass, acquired an undeniable intelligence.

"Well," he said, casually, "I'm going to go back to work with Dirk. On another occasion, Monsieur Delambre, I'll show you some unusual things that might perhaps interest you."

His departure seemed to lighten the atmosphere. Narda continued nonetheless to scatter pieces of bark under the table.

"Come on, stop it!" exclaimed Yvane.

"I hear you using the voice of a mother issuing a reprimand," I said to Yvane, while darting an amused glance at her young cousin. "What age difference is there between you?"

"Five years. Narda's 17, but she's been badly brought-up at boarding-school. She's an orphan, the daughter of one of my mother's brothers." Yvane offered this explanation in a low voice. "My stepfather accepted responsibility for her too."

There was a slight sadness in her tone that surprised me a little. I didn't press the point. We got up to take a turn around the property.

When we finally found ourselves back beside my car, she planted herself in front of me and said, brusquely: "I'm afraid you were bored."

I assured her of the contrary.

"Nevertheless," she said, not listening to me, "I'm putting myself in your place. I meet a young woman in the sea, go to her aid and pull her out of a perilous situation, then meet her again by chance at the theater—all that is bizarre enough, and sets my imagination working. I imagine a sporty fairy, some kind of star leading a luxurious existence, of a fantastic environment worthy of a woman

331

fallen from the sky, and I find a poor girl living prosaically with her stepfather, almost alone in an old house. If I were you, I'd be disappointed."

"And the young woman, who also has a right to dream—what does she say when she only finds a great devil of an architect who promises to get her reservoir repaired?"

She laughed, tilting her head back, and the bursts of her laughter, which sounded young and fresh, lifted up her tanned throat. "Oh, I can see now that my reflection was indiscreet," she declared.

"The young woman remains more mysterious than she believes herself to be," I assured her.

Seeing her there in front of me, in fact, upright, simply-dressed, without make-up, with her eyes and hair bright, I found that she participated in the mystery of limpid entities and denuded artifices. She invited speculation, but in a truly magnificent fashion, as a pebble shining buy the roadside, a stem reaching up toward the sky, or a wild animal free in its movements encourages speculation about the enigma of existence.

"May I, as a good friend, come to collect you tomorrow in order to take you out in my turn—perhaps to Cannes?"

"With Narda?" she asked, after a moment's hesitation.

"Of course," I declared, starting the engine.

Having traveled a certain distance along the road, I stopped the car in order to light a cigarette.

The whole thing had been simple and rather odd at the same time. I looked at myself in the rear-view mirror. "Curious, curious," I murmured. I smiled. I no longer recognized myself.

When I presented myself the following day at the agreed time, I found Yvane in conversation with a gardener in the main pathway. "Narda can't come," she told me, immediately.

"I don't think that will alter our program. Your stepfather won't see anything improper in your going out with me, I hope?"

"Why should he?" she replied, in a surprised tone. Her tone and expression seemed decisive enough.

"I'd love to drive," she said, opening the door.

I yielded the steering-wheel to her, and she set off with a great deal of assurance. She weaved her way through the little crowded streets of Cannes rather skillfully. Authoritatively, she selected one of the best-known dance-halls in the town, and we parked on the quayside. When I praised her decisiveness, she replied, bizarrely: "I'm just struggling against my inferiority complex."

"One of your stepfather's terms?" I remarked.

"No—all the idiots are talking about their complexes just now. Haven't you noticed?"

I confessed my ignorance, and the recent date of my return to France. She listened distractedly, while dancing. She danced well. Secretly, I compared her with the women present; in the middle of all those faces made up with applications of cream and powder, her freshness and youth were imposing. The heat was stifling, though, and the orchestra really was making too much noise.

"Are you enjoying yourself?" I asked her.

She looked at me, searching in my eyes for the correct response, and replied: "No." We went back to the car and, abandoning the pleasures of the coast, set forth at hazard inland. A shared taste directed us toward deserted and honest places. By the side of the road a small inn appeared, whose terrace overlooked the region all the way to the sea. There were we able to drink lemonade in an arbor.

Her bare hand was lying on the corner of the table. Playfully, I covered it with mine, as if to compare their dimensions.

"My skin is darker than yours," she declared. "After two years here, I have the right to a certain advancement."

"If you'd met me in shorts on Bali, I'd have beaten you for suntan. I was no longer a white man in any but name."

She paused thoughtfully, and then declared: "Why do you think that I'm not curious about your past? Anyway, it's the same with everything. It's bizarre, at my age, but I don't experience any curiosity. The world doesn't tempt me. At times, I think that it's an illness."

I noticed that, without my being aware of it, the hand I had superimposed on hers had folded up to imprison it entirely. I didn't move a muscle, but I sensed that her gaze was lowered, like mine, upon our immobile fingers. She remained mute.

"I didn't do it deliberately," I said.

"I know that. It's like the tendrils of a vine. Have you seen vines in spring, creeping along a trellis? The tendrils only take a few hours to wind around the supportive wires; one might think that they were little conscious hands, and yet they don't know what they're doing, and more than your fingers knew…"

"Perhaps it's all the more revealing? The expression of a profound natural instinct…"

She looked me in the eye and said: "I know what you're thinking. You think that what I said doesn't mean anything, and that I'm deliberately misinterpreting a gesture that might have made a commitment you didn't intend."

"You read thoughts well," I admitted.

"Give me a cigarette," she said, then, abruptly enough for me to understand that she only wanted me to let go of her hand.

"Tell my stepfather," she continued, in a different tone, "that I can read thoughts. He'll be jealous—that's his great ambition."

"Is his research really serious, then?" I said, slightly disconcerted by the intrusion of the stepfather into the conversation.

"I think so," she replied, with some gravity. As I held out a match for her, she exclaimed: "I'm glad you don't have a lighter. I can't bear people who use lighters."

"Me neither—that odor of petrol, and the vulgarity of that movement of the thumb over the flint-wheel..."

Her expression brightened, and she added, precipitately: "Yes, yes—but I've discovered the real reason. Fire is a noble thing, and making fire is an operation so sacred that we must respectfully employ both hands to give birth to the flame. When, with a lighter, you light the wick with excessive familiarity, it's a veritable blasphemy, a punishable triviality, like celebrating a mystery in a garage. The Sun, and fire are my personal gods..."

I listened to her with a half-smile on my lips. It was getting late. In front of us the Sun was hollowing out longer shadows in the rocky hillsides. The facades of small farmhouses scattered on the terraced fields were tinted in gold. In the pine-tree above our heads, crickets were singing. For a long moment, we watched the Sun setting on the plain in silence.

"The Virgilian hour," I murmured.

In a whisper, I heard her say: "*Majoresque cadunt...*"[65] As I looked at her in surprise, she explained, with a hint of irony directed at herself: "I have my baccalaureat."

The Fiat was waiting for us in front of the inn. I asked her if she still wanted to drive. She shook her head. Her mood seemed to have changed again; she remained silent. I could no longer sense anything of her but the hip that sometimes made contact with mine as we went around bends. Troubled, I could find nothing to say. It seemed that we were making a proof of our silences—the most redoubtable of all.

When I stopped the car in front of the gate of the property, the silence of the motor rendered ours even more perceptible and weighty. Noiselessly, for I can find no other word to render the significance of the movement that might, I sensed, release an internal storm within her, she turned toward me. Our faces found themselves so close that our lips touched lightly. She opened the door and, having leapt to the ground, opened the gate without looking back.

III

The next day, if the weather had been less beautiful, less sunny, with less spring in the air, I would have found myself almost reasonable. A nice shower would have set me squarely on the right road, bringing me back to an awareness of the necessary greyness that is the background of any well-conducted life. But with all those colors—there were armfuls of flowers in every room in the hotel,

---

[65] *Majoresque cadunt altis e montibus umbrae* [The Shadows of high mountains grow large] is a popular quotation from Virgil's *Eclogues*.

and the casino flower-beds were nothing but living mosaics—my head still felt lacking in solidity.

No new rendezvous had been arranged, but the reservoir in need of repair furnished me with a pretext to manifest myself whenever I wished. Before the morning was out, I had already telephoned a contractor in Nice.

Then, as I was passing the casino, I happened upon Dr. Mops, who was climbing into his large Mercedes, driven by a Malay chauffeur.

"Gambling already?" I asked, in a familiar fashion.

"No, not yet. I'll probably try it in a few days' time."

"What?" I said. "Since you've been here, you haven't yet tried your luck?"

"I wasn't ready. I'm only here to measure the interval separating two plays at the same table."

Not caring whether or not I understood him, he replied with that slightly naïve seriousness that had already struck me in his regard. I thought that he was preparing some kind of system.

"Be careful," I told him, "the mathematics are precise, and chance has laws that can't be subverted."

This time, he did not furnish an explanation, contenting himself with asking: "Can I give you a lift to La Colle?"

As the opportunity was there, I took my place in the big car.

The influence of spring was evidently not making itself felt in me alone, for the doctor's cordiality became even more expansive as we went along the road.

"Oh, Monsieur Delambre," he said to me, with the sharp accent that gave his words a child-like manner, "you're lucky to be young! When I think of my youth, though, of all the stupid things I did…would you think, to look at me, that there was a time when I thought I could photograph souls?"

I had scarcely expected that sort of youthful stupidity, and I burst out laughing.

"Yes, I occupied myself with psychic research; I photographed auras, vital bubbles. By night, I laid out sensitive plates to obtain the imprints of the states of my soul; I even slipped into my friends' homes. I wasted three years of my life in India studying the secrets of indigenous magic! And I won't mention spiritualist séances, daggers to cut through emanations, electrical recordings of prayers, of the *expir* and the *inspir*…

"My first wife was to blame. I married too young; I was in love. My wife was a theosophist; out of love, I devoted myself to the same follies as her. The worst of it was that we were both very wrapped up in the little circle that we formed, and my medical studies had given me an impressive vocabulary and an authority. How could one not be stupid at that point? That's youth…

"In our Northern lands, one does not mature as quickly as in your country, and one also remains young for longer. Then my wife died—she threw herself out of a window on a day of great inspiration; the *inspir* ought to have saved her.

My eyes were opened. Afterwards, I read August Comte and Le Dantec,[66] to mention only your philosophers, and I burned that which I had adored, reverting to sane ideas. The brain secretes thought as the kidney secretes urine. *Der Mann is was er ist.* Everything is inscribed in matter. There's still a lot of naivety in that, I grant you, but I resumed my studies, this time seriously. Science has completed my formation by submitting me to its discipline. I was one of Berger's pupils at Jena for six years.[67] I became passionate about his work on the electricity of the brain, before taking flight on my own wings."

I listened distractedly to this tale, which brought a smile to my lips with its extreme volubility. I had to say something.

"In my profession, we only have to deal with stones—it's less dangerous."

"A fine profession nevertheless," said the doctor. "A profession of artisans and artists..."

With these words he appeared to have exhausted the possibility of a discourse on architecture, for he continued without transition: "I'm glad that you've made the acquaintance of my girls. They don't see many people, and my company is scarcely agreeable. I make an effort from time to time to steer them this way or that, but everything that amuses most people bores me, and inversely..."

He followed this declaration with hearty satisfied laughter, which relieved him of all bitterness. As we were arriving, he suggested that I accompany him to his study on the first floor while we waited for lunch. I couldn't refuse, and I followed him into a sort of vast library, very comfortably furnished, with a wholly Dutch orderliness. Colored panes in the windows contributed to giving that interior the appearance and intimate atmosphere of a painting by a minor master.

A large photograph was standing on the desk. "My first wife," the doctor explained. Taking the photograph between his thumb and index finger, he made it pivot on its support. Another female face was framed on the other side. "The second," he said.

I did not linger over the comical aspect of that juxtaposition, moved though I was by finding Yvane's features echoed in the new face: there was the same nose, small and delicate, the same slight projection of the cheekbones, and the same obliquity of the features, which gave the face an expression reminiscent of a nervous hind.

"Whisky?" asked the doctor, abruptly. He added, perhaps by way of excuse: "An old colonial habit."

---

[66] Félix Le Dantec (1869-1917) was a biologist and philosopher who wrote several books on evolution and one on atheism, taking a positivist approach derived from Comte.

[67] Hans Berger (1873-1941), the director of the Jena Psychiatric University Clinic from 1919-1938, pioneered the use of encephalography in human beings, working on the correlation of brain activity with consciousness.

I accepted. He pulled a little wheeled bar toward him. Suddenly, he uttered a curse and rang for a servant. A bare-footed Malay came in, and he spoke to him harshly in Dutch. Without saying a word, the servant went to move a large standard lamp that stood in one corner of the room five centimeters to one side.

"I can't bear the objects in my study not being in exactly the right place," the doctor told me. "The slightest modification of position upsets my thought-processes. For ten years, I've been working in unaltered surroundings. When I think that, one day, Yvane took it into her head to bring in a bouquet of flowers! It's the only time I lost my temper with her, the poor child!"

That little scene had made a slightly painful impression on me. My embarrassed gaze scanned the room. Half-hidden behind a movable staircase, something reminiscent of a grand plan of Paris was hanging in front of the books in a bookcase. The encounter with that familiar image gladdened my heart.

However, the doctor said: "It's an anatomical illustration, considerably enlarged, representing the internal face of the right hemisphere of the brain. It has hung there for ten years. I haven't been able to resolve myself to taking it down, and it remains in my lair like a sorcerer's owl."

Whisky in hand, he went to stand in front of the image, and laughed. "Nothing is as beautiful as a brain, truly. Every sinuosity, every groove of the pallium, has its meaning. And to think that I know all of that by heart! What a marvel of a labyrinth, in which one does not get lost! Now, Monsieur Delambre, if you like such things, here's a rather nice item..."

He lifted the lid of a varnished box, which revealed a solidified mass on a black marble pedestal, which I recognized this time as the lobes of a brain.

"A fine molding," I said, with a layman's slight nausea.

"A molding! It's an anatomical preparation, hardened in formaldehyde—a success that cost me rather dear, although I was able to make a good job of it. It's the brain of my second wife."

I could not repress an exclamation.

"I had asked that an autopsy be carried out on the cadaver," the doctor told me. "Wasn't it the least I could do to reserve a choice morsel, the favorite object of my studies? Preserve it in alcohol? Never! A slow petrifaction has made it into this work of art...

"In your architect's office, Monsieur Delambre, perhaps you have a view of the Parthenon, Rheims cathedral or the Empire State Building—what do I know? As an architect of the brain, why should I not give pride of place to a perfect encephalum?—the encephalum of a woman that I was pleased to imagine perfect for a long time. Others might have kept her heart, but we must abandon that organ to the symbolic significance that it has in the popular imagination. For us, who are much closer to the secrets of the flesh, a brain is much fuller of memories. You know, I often think that here"—he touched a region of the grey marble with the rim of his glass—"in the striated zone bordering the calcarine fissure, images of me reflected in my poor Gilberte's eyes formed many times over. The impulse that drove her arms, her beautiful bare arms, to fold around me, came from that frontal ascendant circumvolution, on the edge of the fissure of Rolando—and there in the region that extends from the mesocephalum to the rachidian bulb, where the 'central self' of that adorable being resided, along with the supreme regulator of all the physical functions, the entire personality of the departed doubtless remains, obscurely inscribed in the petrified fibers. What was she but a fragment of organized matter?—a cleverly-ordered atomic ballet; a bundle of cells ruled by this superior structure of which I conserve her very being, in a far more authentic fashion, much truer than within the vain memories in my own mind, or the superficial images that photographic prints evoke for us."

He had got carried away, perhaps slightly intoxicated by the alcohol, forgetful of my presence. The lunch-bell sounded opportunely, freeing me from the necessity of furnishing any reply. I felt rather ill-at-ease. When we met up with the young women in the hallway, their presence was a great relief to me. Yvane shook my hand in a comradely manner, perhaps with a slight hint of detachment. Dirk sat down at the table after having greeted us be clicking his heels. The doctor, at whose side he took his place, was the only one to offer him his hand.

During the meal, my uneasy impression dissipated gradually. The greater part of the conversation was abandoned to more-or-less overt attempts by Narda to obtain authorization from her uncle to remain at La Colle instead of returning to her Swiss boarding-school after the vacation. I appointed myself as her advocate. We finally obtained a "We'll see" from the doctor, which was almost a consent, and won me a covert smile from the young cousin. Entering into that little family comedy amused me, but I wasn't there to play the big brother. As we got up from the table, I asked Yvane to take me to the reservoir that I had to have repaired.

I had been looking forward to being alone together for a while. It was almost disappointing at first. She remained thoughtful, but gradually confided in me.

"Last night, I thought about the walk we took yesterday, and behind my thoughts, as if from a misty background, I saw the frightful 'What's the point?' that has pursued me all my life appear once again. The thought of your amity hasn't caused it to vanish…"

That sadness contrasted so strongly with her youth and the dazzling health of her body that I could easily have refused to believe it, but her tone was sincere. She was not acting out some comedy of coquetry, but seemed, on the contrary, to be surprised by what she was saying.

Far from being put off by her gloomy disposition, I experienced instead a desire to get closer to her, to help bring her out of herself, to force her to blossom freely and happily. It was akin to a devotional duty, a good deed to be done. I affected a great optimism, spoke with assurance, put on a display of vigor and will-power, in order to give her an exemplary tonic.

We were walking slowly, having forgotten the pretext for my visit. At the rear of the property, a little summer-house stood on the hill. I asked her to take me to look at it. The three rooms, on one floor, were surmounted by a *loggia*, which was reached by means of a ladder, and which looked out on to the mountains of the hinterland.

"Have you never had any desire to live here?" I asked.

"Well, no—you see, that's the sort of idea that doesn't occur to me spontaneously." She added, with a hint of bitterness: "The ideas that come to me spontaneously aren't good ones."

She sat down on the rim of the *loggia*, with her back to the column. Was it the shadow that the roof projected over her? Her eyes seemed to me to be brighter, bluer, and larger. A very vague smile floated sadly over her face. I had the bizarre feeling that I recognized it, and perceived that she was duplicating the expression her mother wore in the portrait that the doctor had kept. But the horrible memory of the anatomical specimen enclosed in the varnished casket was superimposed over her living image, and I had to make an effort to put it out of my mind.

She began speaking, in a deliberate and slightly strained voice, as if she were reciting a prepared text: "A gentleman goes for a stroll on the Côte d'Azur. Thousands of gentlemen go strolling on the coast. Why *this* gentleman? What difference is there between the day when, while taking a dip in the sea, one meets this gentleman, and all the other days when one takes a dip in the sea? The gentleman has certainly met a great many ladies who were also taking dips, in the sea or elsewhere. And is this gentleman asking himself: 'Why *this* lady?'" In a sharper tone, she added: "Yes, why should that meeting take on a serious significance, when nothing distinguished it, when it occurred, from all the other meetings in the world?"

"My word," I began, not knowing quite what I was going to say, "if it was a matter of chance, why complain about it? The clouds in the sky, the stars, life itself—everything is a matter of chance."

She sighed, raising her hand to her forehead. "Yes, yes—I'm very stupid when I let my poor head run on."

By way of protest, I had also moved my hand discreetly toward the head that she was slandering. Gently, like a trusting animal, she leaned forward to rest her forehead in the palm of my hand. It was the first time I had touched her face. Emotionally, I was allowing my fingers to model her temples and come into contact with the curve of her brow when the memory of the atrocious relic preserved by the doctor came to mind again. I felt that I had a duty to remove her from a depressing atmosphere and a deadening influence—the causes of the anxiety to which her thoughts gave testimony.

She raised her head again—the entire scene had lasted no longer than a few seconds—and said, in a changed and cheerful voice: "You have cool hands; you've cured me."

As we went back down the *loggia*'s ladder, an idea suddenly crossed my mind and, without further reflection, I exclaimed: "Would you rent this summerhouse to me?"

She was momentarily nonplussed. "What an idea!"

"Quite seriously," I said, "I like the place. It reminds me of those bungalows in India that are open to the cool night air. You're not doing anything with it; for my part, I could live in it as easily as the hotel. If I have the impression of being in my own home, I would be more willing to stay on the coast for some time."

"But you'd be very badly lodged—the rooms are uninhabitable."

"It wouldn't take much to get them back into a proper state."

"Do you think so?" she cried, suddenly, with a childish spontaneity. "Oh it would be chic then!"

We began to study the place methodically. She brought to the domiciliary visit a zest and gaiety that she had not yet shown that day.

"Do you really think that it's possible?"

"Why not? If your stepfather will accept me as a tenant..."

"Oh, it will be perfectly all right with him."

I was sincere in my desire to rent the summer-house; the picturesque quality and the tranquility of the place, the olive-grove outside my door and the view of the mountains all attracted me. When I raised my head to interrogate the crumbling plaster of the ceilings, however, I nevertheless thought: *I'm in the process of putting a noose around my own neck.* But I thought it with some contentment, even delight. She seemed so pleased!

We went on to study the possibilities that I would have of reaching my home without passing through the property. There was a pathway along the estate's enclosing wall, which led directly to the main road. A door—long sealed up, admittedly—opened on to the path; all that was required was to find the key. Once the bundles of firewood that were encumbering it were cleared, the debris of a neighboring shed would furnish a garage for my car sufficient for the summer. Like children in the depths of a park, we were playing Robinson Crusoe. The intimacy between us was increased.

IV

None of what we had imagined proved impossible. Instead of putting the contractor's laborers to work on the reservoir, I sent them to the summer-house. I went to supervise the work every day. A week later, I was almost ready to take up residence.

If I had feared finding myself too close to the inhabitants of the château by renting the summer-house, that fear would immediately have proved vain. They exercised the greatest discretion in not disturbing my comings and goings. I had refused the items of furniture that the doctor had offered me, preferring to buy a few chairs or rustic accessories at random during my visits to the antique-dealers of the inland villages. Whenever I happened to meet Yvane, I asked her to accompany me on my excursions. Our searches amused her, I could tell. Once, she sighed: "And to think that these things would overwhelm me with boredom if it were a matter of my own house!"

There was a semi-admission in that, whose charm derived from her casual personality; it was an observation that she made innocently and unguardedly, whose real significance seemed to escape her.

I asked her to call me Pierre, since I called her by her first name. She did so immediately, without any reluctance. On occasion, she even addressed me as "tu" inadvertently, without anything ever having happened between us that justified a greater intimacy. That gave our relationship an air of pleasant comradeship, which would have been a trifle puerile if I had not found her grave and tormented on other occasions. Sometimes, her gaze became so vague that, plunging into her pupils, I had the impression that no matter how far I might go, sinking infinitely into the mists and blue-tinted heaths of her internal world, I would never succeed in catching up with her. But these sudden changes of mood prevented our meeting from becoming habitual, and the interest that I brought to them was ever on the alert. I could see her again and again without any monotony tarnishing her individuality.

One day, I was coming back from Biot with a consignment of earthenware pots that were destined for the decoration of my future dwelling, when I saw Dirk on the road, returning to La Colle on foot. In the course of the recent meals at which he had appeared, he had not opened his mouth. I wanted to be friendly and as I drew level with him I proposed that he get in. He did so without hesitation.

"Were you taking a little walk?" I asked.

He took some time before replying: "I was an assistant to a stockbroker in Amsterdam before entering the doctor's employ."

"Oh yes," I said. "I forgot to ask you. You haven't always studied medicine, then?"

"I'm primarily occupied with assisting in certain experiments, and spend a great deal of time in conversations in which I do nothing but listen."

"I was wondering what sort of collaboration you engaged in with the doctor."

"You'll have to give me a light, then," he declared.

I turned toward him to hand him a box of matches, but to my surprise, he had nothing in his mouth.

"A funny way of asking for a cigarette," I said. "Look, there are some in the pocket on your side of the car."

He took a cigarette for himself and lit it. "You're right," he said.

"About what? Never letting go of the steering-wheel? One can never be careful enough, and I have a whole lot of pottery there."

He seemed to be a million miles away, and his remarks were disjointed to the point that I suspected him of some secret intention. Where was he heading? Was it that my presence at La Colle near the young women had awakened a certain jealousy within him, which was responsible for his strange attitude toward me?

"She's very beautiful, and worthy to be loved," he declared, abruptly.

I started, and immediately brought the vehicle to a halt.

"Come on, my dear Dirk," I said, deliberately, "there's no need to play games. Who are you talking about? Are you talking about Mademoiselle Yvane?"

He drew on his cigarette awkwardly. His large round eyes were staring at me in astonishment.

"You've put it into third gear," he said.

The car had stopped. He was either mad or playing the imbecile. Irritated, I shrugged my shoulders and, without persisting further, engaged the clutch again—but, disturbed by what he had said, I did indeed go into third gear, and the motor stalled. I swore, pressing the starter again. The doctor's company must have unbalanced the poor fellow's mind. I abstained from speaking to him again during the few kilometers that we still had to cover, and I decided privately that, instead of dropping him at the château, I would leave him on the road, where the little path that led to the summer-house branched off.

He undoubtedly understood my intention, for even before I decelerated, he said to me very politely: "Thank you for having spared me a little of the road. I'd prefer to go back in discreetly now, without mentioning that I met you. I beg you not to mention it yourself. Goodbye, and thanks."

We were still 300 meters from the junction. He was a little premature in bidding me farewell. Having reached the path, I let him down. He bowed to me again, very amicably, but without saying a word.

Still under the influence of that bizarre scene, I arrived at the summer-house. Yvane was on the doorstep with a large armful of carnations.

"I hope I'm not being indiscreet," he said. "I came so that the vases wouldn't remain empty. Nothing is sadder, or even more ill-omened, than an empty vase."

Setting the flowers down on the window-sill, she came to help me unload the car.

"Don't you find Dirk truly bizarre?" I asked her.

"I don't know—I scarcely pay any attention to him," she replied.

"I'm wondering whether he hasn't conceived a grand passion for you," I continued, without meaning any harm.

She blushed violently. "What makes you think that? It's certainly not true, but the thought of it makes me ashamed. Yes, the most respectful homages, wherever they come from, seem to me to be a diminution of myself." She made a sort of angry gesture, and continued in a hurried voice: "I'd like it if no one ever noticed me, never gave me a thought, even of mere sympathy. That's why I live a solitary existence, not seeing people of my own age. It's an assault on my liberty for anyone to presume to dispose of me thus without my consent. It soils me—don't you think so?"

Visibly very emotional, she stood with her arms hanging loose, in complete disarray, as if struck in a sensitive spot.

I reproached myself for me abruptness, my misunderstanding of the extreme modesty of which she gave evidence. I was too awkward, too heavy-handed for that exaggerated sensitivity. She did not appear to hear my excuses, but she collected herself gradually.

"No," she said, "it's me who's ridiculous in letting myself go like that, but I can't control myself—forgive me. Just give me your hand for a moment, without saying anything."

I took her hand. We were leaning against the carnations lying on the window-sill. In front of us, the setting Sun was touching the horizon. The bleating of a goat rose up from a neighboring field, and all around us, the toads were already sounding their solitary note. In the calm air, the odor of flowers became more insistent.

We held hands like two well-behaved children. I respected her silence, which, as it became prolonged, gave a more serious significance to what I had thought to be only a caprice, which I did not understand. I looked at her: her eyes lost in infinity, her face turned toward the setting Sun seemed to be calling out to the languor of the evening, to the clouds stretching across the sky, to the fatigue of living. Little by little, in the rising shadows, I thought I saw her lose consciousness, becoming the soul of the night, distant and impalpable, barely alive. Becoming more emotional, I increased the pressure of my fingers. She shuddered, finally return to herself, and spoke. Her words, murmured in a soft, slightly sad voice, took on a strange sibylline resonance within the vast frame of silence that had preceded it.

"It's getting dark. I came to put flowers in the vases, but I won't have time to arrange them."

The dinner bell sounded on the far side of the little valley. She took a few paces. "I can't believe," she went on, "that you're going to live here."

"Yes—tomorrow evening, I assure you, I shall be here."

In my mind, these words only had the import of a polite reply, but on hearing them in the silence, after the long preceding scene, I was struck myself by the somewhat solemn character that they took on. It was like a promise, an engagement.

Yvane received it without saying a word, and seemed to bear it away beneath the silvery foliage of the olive-trees.

V

Faithful to my promise, the next day, I made arrangements to leave the hotel. I had just paid the bill and emerged on to the casino plaza when I noticed the doctor's Mercedes among the parked cars.

He gambles, then, whatever he might say, I thought.

In fact the doctor, flanked by Dirk, appeared shortly afterwards. He offered, once again, to take me back to La Colle. Dirk sat beside the chauffeur, and I took my place inside. We had scarcely moved off when the doctor declared: "We had a good morning..." Taking a thick wad of banknotes from his pockets, he specified: "422,000 francs."

I uttered an exclamation. "Take care not to lose them," I added, at hazard.

"I can't lose—I'm betting on certainties."

"What! I'd really like to know..."

He shrank back into a corner in order to stare at me ironically. "You challenged me to find a system. It's a good thing that science is occasionally useful for something."

My curiosity was unsatisfied. Until then it had been rather difficult to take him seriously, but the wad of banknotes obliged me to revise my initial impression. I did not hesitate to press him to be more precise. He was reluctant to do so.

"It's a rather long story that requires appropriate explanations. Will you consent to accompany me to the laboratory?"

Desirous of clarifying the issue, I accepted the invitation. He doctor gave an order, and on entering La Colle, the car went around the main building to deposit us by a side door in the left wing. A little stairway climbed up to the first floor, opening directly into a sequence of whitewashed rooms exclusively furnished with scientific apparatus.

Very deliberately, the doctor began by putting on white smock with short sleeves. Then he donned the classic skull-cap of the surgeon. "My dear Monsieur Delambre," he said to me, "you are not unaware that the activity of the brain is accompanied by electrical currents that are quite easy to detect?"

"My God," I said, without allowing myself to be intimidated by the solemnity of these preparations, "I have a strong suspicion that electricity must have something to do with what goes on therein..."

He smiled at this admission of ignorance, and rang a hand-bell. A Javanese in a white smock appeared, to whom he said a few words in Malay.

"We're going to begin with a classic experiment," he said.

The Javanese came back, holding a large rabbit by the ears.

"Watch this animal," said the doctor. "First I'll put it to sleep."

He injected the contents of a syringe beneath the rabbit's skin; it fell unconscious on the marble table-top.

With a few strokes of a razor, rapid and precise gestures, he shaved the top of the animal's cranium. Then he arranged his victim on a wooden block, immobilized its head, and, having connected an instrument like a dentist's drill to the electric current, he applied it to the exposed area.

"This marvelous little apparatus permits any skull to be made into a skimmer," he said. "Look, I'm making a few openings in this animal's cranium." Indicating a milky membrane reminiscent of the dome of a jellyfish in the middle of the hole he was cutting, he added: "And now you can see the *dura mater*."

That kind of operation always has an effect; I grimaced as I watched.

"The animal is obviously ready," the doctor declared. "You can see that it doesn't take as long as making a stew."

The Javanese, who was serving as an assistant, then transported the animal to an apparatus fastened to the ceiling, from which various wires hung. The doctor took one, which he introduced into the animal's ear; then he pointed out a sort of clock-face situated in front of us.

"The mirror of this galvanometer will inform us about the electrical currents running through the circuit."

A second wire was placed in direct contact with the brain of the rabbit, and the little mirror began to oscillate.

"Alpha waves in the occipital region," murmured the doctor, speaking to himself. Pricking the rabbit's paw, which caused it to shiver, he added: "Now we excite the animal. See how the motive impulse is accompanied by an electrical current indicated by a considerable deviation of the galvanometer."

In my incompetence, I thought it was going to a great deal of trouble to make a mirror quiver on the end of a ire, but I feigned great interest. "Have similar experiments been carried out on humans?" I asked.

"Of course!" he cried. "The cranial cavity isn't opened, of course; one simply puts the electrodes in contact with the scalp. What's more, I have a specialized premises for the study of encephalograms."

Abandoning the rabbit to the Javanese, to whom he gave a number of further orders that I did not understand, he preceded me into another large room in the middle of which was an armchair surmounted by a sort of crowd or helmet somewhat reminiscent of those which serve to perm feminine coiffeurs.

"I've acquired sufficient experience to be able to operate on myself," the doctor said. "The experimental apparatus here is a little more delicate, but is broadly the same as the one you saw just now. If we light this little flame, its image, reflected in the mirror of the oscillograph, will be projected on to this screen, and render the pulsations of the current visible."

Going over to the frosted-glass windows, he suddenly pulled down a black screen, which plunged the room into semi-darkness. Then, lifting off his white skull-cap with a rapid hand-movement, he sat down in the armchair and put his head inside the helmet.

"Don't move," he said to me. "I'll keep quiet for a few minutes to let the murmurs of my cerebral activity die down; then I'll make the contact, and you'll see luminous oscillations on the screen corresponding to the rhythm of the Berger currents that are running through my encephalum."

Meekly, I fell silent. I was intrigued, as in a cinema, torn between a muted anxiety and the satisfaction of being initiated into the esoteric scientific mysteries. The doctor did as he had said, and after a few minutes, the luminous dot began to describe broad oscillations on the screen.

"You can see, now that I'm speaking to you," the doctor said, "the effort of attention that I have to make in order to slow down the rhythm of the oscillations that are muffled by other currents nascent in the zone of articulate language."

The displacement on the screen had indeed slowed down; it returned to its initial amplitude when the doctor had ceased speaking.

"The experiment is particularly striking when one performs it on oneself, for one witnesses it from outside and inside at the same time, if I might put it thus. Do you want to try it?"

"It doesn't do any harm?" I asked.

"None—it's just like being in a seat at the theater."

I took his place. He gently applied my head to the head-rest, and I felt two little pieces of metal come into contact with my skin behind the ears.

"The blunted electrodes pass through your hair and won't prick you. Relax, and don't think about anything, as if you were going to go to sleep."

I obeyed. In the dark and silent room, the luminous dot gradually began its swaying. It was agitated by regular frissons, interrupted by calmer periods.

"Now begin a mental operation," the doctor whispered to me. "Recite the alphabet backwards."

I began internally: Z, Y, X... I was surprised to see the quivering of the dot on the screen die down. As I searched for the letter that ought to come after X, without finding it, the luminous dot became completely motionless, making my mental effort manifest. Before finding the letter, I had to recite the entire alphabet forwards—A. B., C, etc.—and the oscillations resumed during that facile listing. Then I resumed with W, V...and hesitated again before recovering U and T—which provoked a further interruption of the pulsations.

The doctor was right; the experiment was quite striking. The variable efforts of attention were materialized on the screen by the quivering of the dot. It was as if one could see inside one's own head—something more impressive than seeing one's own heart beating. To make the little will-o'-the-wisp that represented the spark of thought dance on the screen, it was sufficient to try to think, or not to think. No command more tenuous and more direct could ever have permitted the external development of a phenomenon. I was like the god of that dancing patch.

"We not only have the possibility of detecting the Berger waves that reflect the activity of thought," the doctor told me. "We can also reveal the specific currents due to affectivity."

I felt him moving some sort of metallic comb through my hair in order to push it to the right side of my forehead, where he seemed to be searching carefully for a suitable location. The luminous patch began to describe a little circle in the middle of the screen.

"Relax."

The luminous patch became almost motionless. Then, very softly, he breathed in my ear: "My dear Monsieur Delambre, what are your sentiments with regard to my step-daughter Yvane?"

A surge of blood rose to my face, and I started in the armchair. On the screen, the little circle enlarged to the point of touching the edges, leading an extravagant dance.

"I don't see what that has to do with anything," I said, at hazard, my throat dry.

"Are you in love with my step-daughter?" the doctor persisted.

"You'll permit me to keep my sentiments to myself," I replied, with deliberate insolence.

"Alas, I fear that's impossible," said the doctor, whose eyes never left the screen on which the saraband of the luminous circle had lost all restraint.

"That's treachery!" I cried, furiously, removing all the instruments sounding my skull with a single thrust.

"Calm down, my dear Monsieur," said the doctor, removing the screens that were obscuring the windows. "My question is easily explicable. I don't seek to uncover secrets that do not belong to me without good reason. If you were only to be a temporary friend, I would owe you the consideration due to friendship, and nothing more, but if the interest you feel for my family responds to a more profound sentiment, it's perfectly normal for me to have confidence in you and furnish you with supplementary explanations regarding my work, under the seal of secrecy. Indeed, it would displease me now to be seen in your eyes as a person who earns his living gambling..."

My anger was not diminishing greatly.

"I don't know how I feel myself..." I began.

The doctor made a gesture, accompanied by a smile.

"I don't need anything more from you—what I've seen is sufficient. But everything that we've done to date is very little compared with what remains for me to tell you. You were curious to know my betting system, Monsieur Delambre, and your curiosity will be satisfied. Would you care to accompany me to my study? We'll be able to talk more comfortably there."

VI

That session in the laboratory left me furious and somewhat at a loss. The situation had been turned around. Dr. Mops, whom I had treated until then in a casual manner, had seized the initiative from me. I felt diminished, ready to submit to his ascendancy even though I forbade myself to do so. The thought that I might have been lured into some kind of trap also occurred to me. As soon as we had quit the experimental laboratories, he abandoned the rather solemn tone that he had adopted, quite seamlessly, to recover the polite and cordial appearance he normally manifested. That abrupt change of attitude only served to confirm that his customary joviality was an affectation, and that I had to be even more on my guard.

"A little Hollands gin?" he proposed, once we were in the study. "Schiedam is our Bordeaux, and carries the renown of the Netherlands throughout the world! My word, it's worth as much as Rembrandt!"

I swallowed the alcohol, and felt more secure on my foundations. The doctor lowered himself into an armchair, folded his arms, and began by caressing his hairy biceps a few times beneath the short sleeves of his white smock.

"I told you, Monsieur, that I don't want to have secrets from you. That will oblige me to remind you of certain histological data. They might not interest you, but they have their importance. A long time ago it was remarked that, unlike the ordinary cells that make up our organism, nerve-cells do not multiply. You are born with all your-nerve-cells and, their number being incapable of augmentation, they accompany you to your death. Thus from birth onwards, the material structure of the nervous system, which will support every psychophysiological edifice of your personality, is ready to play its role, to be loaded with all the knowledge that you will acquire. In other words, your brain is a blank slate that will be inscribed as you advance through life, and from which you cannot erase anything, since the particles that constitute it are always the same. That particularity of nerve-cells is rich in significance for the nature of human personality. There is no need to make any appeal to a supernatural soul to justify the conservation of the self in the midst of the general flow of things; the permanence of the cells is sufficient to explain it.

"I shall now pass on to the other extreme of philosophical speculation. I've already made you a profession of materialist faith. I believe that everything that happens in the universe, and everything that will happen there, depends on material factors, the evolution of which is regulated by immutable laws. Everything has been written since the first day of creation, and nothing can modify in any manner whatsoever the unfolding of the initial program."

After the scene in the laboratory, this philosophical conversation was somewhat anodyne—and, all things considered, I preferred it to experiments in which I served as the subject. I made a gesture of polite condescension, as if to reserve my opinion, and contented myself with drinking a mouthful of gin.

"What I've just told you is not essential to the consequences that follow whatever hypothesis one adopts, but it explains the orientation I have given to my research. I have been able to localize in the cerebral cortex the zones that preside over the organization of memory, and I have been able to detect, as in the experiments we have just made, the electrical currents associated with the activity of these zones.

"Just now, if you had not abruptly interrupted me, I would have shown you a curious but well-known experiment on the rabbit with the open skull, which consists of artificially imparting a rhythm to the electrical oscillations of the cortical currents. It is sufficient to submit the animal to periodic excitations, such as a lamp that goes on and off before its eyes, for the pulsations of the cerebral currents to reproduce the artificial rhythm of the lamp. Now, pay close attention to me..."

He got to his feet, extended a professorial finger to emphasize an important part of the speech, and continued: "Here is a subject. I localize the cerebral currents corresponding to the zones of memory. I impart an accelerated oscillatory rhythm, which has the effect of giving the nerve-cells of memory a more intense and more rapid activity than normal. I thus *age* the cells artificially, pushing them temporally, in terms of duration, to a point in their evolution that is ahead of the other cells. But these memory cells do not have two ways of aging. If, as I have told you, the film of the world's evolution is recorded at all times in the archives of the future, if what is going to happen is already contained within what had already happened, the cells age as they would normally age, but more rapidly—and, as a result, the hard-driven activity of my subject's memory precedes him in time, thus revealing to me the future that is already recorded, which nothing can modify. I finally obtain a subject who has a memory of the future...

"That subject, as you have deduced, is Dirk."

I sat there somewhat petrified, my head tilted back in the armchair so as not to quit the doctor's eyes, for I now mistrusted his every gesture. But the memory of Dirk's strange attitude during our last meeting came back to mind.

"Dirk," he continued, "who remains entirely normal with regard to his comportment, is presently living mentally one minute and 12 seconds ahead of the present. His life is unfolding in two parts: his body keeps company with ours, and he makes all the gestures he needs to make at the right moment, but his thoughts preceded it by 72 seconds, and from time to time, he says what he ought to have said 72 seconds later!" He accompanied these final words with a triumphant snigger.

"Did Dirk consent to this experiment?" I stammered.

"The question is irrelevant," the doctor said, dryly. "Now, you will easily comprehend the consequences. One only has to know how to take advantage of a 72-second advancement in the knowledge of the future. The average interval that separates two spins of a roulette-wheel is 70 seconds. Above the gaming table, after each spin, a figure lights up indicating the number that has just come up. I place myself, with Dick, so that I can see the signal. Twelve comes up and lights up. I ask him: 'Which number is lit up?' He replies: '28.' I know that 28 will come up on the following spin, and I bet the maximum. If he doesn't reply, it can only be because the interval between one spin and the next will differ from seventy seconds. This morning, I obtained four responses, which is four coincidences. Result: 400,000 and some francs. In a week, the principality has poured 12 million into my pocket.

My bewilderment was tempered by a prudent smile.

"That's your fortune made..." I said.

"Not yet," said the doctor. "My little ruse couldn't last forever, and this very morning I sensed that there were four inspectors of the gaming police spying on me. They can't prove anything against me, but they can ban me from the gaming rooms, under one pretext or another. I've collected 12 million in passing, but in reality, my ambitions are much greater."

I frowned, gripped once again by anxiety.

"Let's leave it there, if you will," said the doctor. "As for the rest, I don't want to go any further before being certain—selling the bear's skin before it's shot, as they say in France. I hope that you won't ask any more of me, and that we're still friends..."

My thoughts were utterly confused within my head. I got up, shook the hand that he extended to me mechanically, and went out.

I only came back to myself somewhat when I found myself in the open air again. I had taken too strong a dose of the doctor, unless it was the gin...

In any case, my first clear impression was an irresistible desire to go as far away as possible as quickly as possible. Everything that happened here seemed troubling, vaguely dangerous. I had committee a folly in wanting to install myself in the dependencies of the château. To set sail as soon as possible was the wisest course.

Little by little, however, the cool air under the trees in the grounds calmed my agitation. At the corner of a path, I happened upon Narda, in company with two Great Danes.

"Do you know that my uncle has given me permission to stay here?" she said. "I'm very glad not to be returning to Switzerland. If you hadn't been there at lunch the other day, I wouldn't have dared say anything."

It did me good to hear her frank girlish voice. It occurred to me to appeal to the judgment of her innocence regarding the matter that preoccupied me.

"Narda, what do you think of your uncle?"

"Him? He makes me laugh," she replied, laughing herself.

A happy age! I thought. *But who knows—perhaps she's right and one ought to laugh?* Her company brought me back to a saner view of things. I listened to her chatter. She told me, incidentally, with the precision that a child's words have, that Yvane was at the hairdressers in Cannes. Extraordinarily, I had not given any further thought to Yvane—but my mind was immediately invaded by her. Could I flee and abandon her?

From the summer-house, where I pursued my meditations, I could catch glimpses between the branches of the olive-trees of the left wing of the châ-teau—the one with the laboratories—a few hundred meters away. It was a sordid patch in the landscape, like a muted threat. Truly, I felt that prudence commanded me to tear myself away from this place. On the other hand, though, thinking of Yvane, I found that there was no immediate peril, that I could still wait to see how things went. In spite of everything, I remained undecided.

I cast an eye over the interior of my dwelling. The divan, comfortable beneath its bright cretonnes, seemed welcoming. In the entrance-hall, the flowers that Yvane had brought were slowly dying in the vases. The promise I had made the previous day returned to my memory. On due reflection, my malaise stemmed mainly from a vague dread of discovering secrets that I ought not to know, of finding myself an accomplice of deeds of which I would rather remain ignorant. And poor Dirk—what role was he playing in all this?

All things considered, I could not bear the idea of going to sleep so close to the doctor. He might have been able to influence my dreams, to devote himself while I slept to God knows what experiment upon me. Before nightfall, I leapt into my car and went to sleep in a hotel in Nice.

When one has a house, it's much funnier not to live in it, I said to myself, by way of an excuse.

VII

When I woke up in my hotel room, the events of the previous day had settled down somewhat in my mind. My fears seemed exaggerated. I had a house waiting for me in the foothills; what was I still doing in a hotel, in that scorching town, when I hadn't seen Yvane for two days? Going through the market of the old town, I filled my car with flowers and, strengthened by that justification for my sojourn in Nice, I took the road to La Colle.

All was silence in the summer-house and its surroundings. The *loggia* was charming in the fresh morning sunlight. I began to unpack my belongings. Someone rapped on the window; it was Yvane, wanting to know how I had slept. I confessed to not having gone to bed there. She seemed distressed.

"What disappoints me more than anything else," she said, "is that yesterday evening I imagined you here, in your house, and I thought that I could see you here...and now I find out that it was false! I'm not used to my thoughts being mistaken. There was nothing in the house where I thought I could see you. How extraordinary that is!"

Although those sighs might seem rather puerile, it was impossible for me not to be moved by the inflections of her voice, in which the very essence of her being seemed to be distilled: a disarmed and disarming sincerity in confrontation with life.

To console her, as one consoles a child, I told her that I had found a little five-meter boat for sale in the old harbor at Nice, and that we might perhaps be able to buy it between us. My idea did a marvelous job of chasing away her disappointment. The "we" that she repeated had something clandestine and chaste in her mouth, which delighted me. She wanted to go and see the boat immediately. I yielded to her desire.

Confronted by the boat, it was necessary to try it out. I had to pardon myself for my inability to speak; I consented to everything. We refused the assistance of the sailor who offered to accompany us; the sea was calm, we could easily steer it by ourselves.

Yvane was charmingly unskillful, in spite of her docility in following my advice. The departure was rather laborious, but we got out to sea as best we could. Once the first period of activity was over, we finally found ourselves side by side, hands on the tiller. Then the thought occurred to us both that, for the first time, we were truly alone—for we exchanged a smile at the same time, which had that meaning.

She let herself loll backwards on to the false bridge, the nape of her neck in the gap, her eyes challenging the brightness of the sky, and her hair floating over our wake.

"It's as if I'd fished up a siren," I said.

Her little hand as resting on the tiller, brown and nervous; it no longer seemed to form part of her stretched-out body: a forgotten hand, sagely following the movements that I imposed on the rudder; a hand so alone, with a bone-structure so delicate, that it was heart-melting. I leaned over and I kissed it for a long time, in the valley hollowed out by the roots of two fingers.

"You're kissing me in September," said her voice, singing over the sea. As I didn't understand, she added: "You know how one counts the months on a closed fist: 31, 30 days...you're kissing me in September."

"Come closer," I said to her. "What are you doing so far away?"

She sat up again. "I was forgetting. That's what I was doing—forgetting."

"Forgetting what?"

"Everything. That's my dominant impression, for the moment: forgetfulness. And it's infinitely refreshing. As if I had left everything behind, to be elsewhere."

"Having left me behind with everything else?"

"No, not you—but me, I've left myself behind."

"Give it to me, then, and I'll look after it while you're not here."

With the gesture of an obedient little girl, she came to rest her hair on my shoulder. The sail carried us on silently, effortlessly. "A pretty self," I murmured, "brown and gold, perfumed with sea-salt, a self as light as a morning sky."

A sharp movement of her head, rolling on my shoulder, indicated a mute negation.

"A self that wearies me and makes me despair," she said. "I never know where it's going, what it will do—a self that drags me into dreams in which I lose myself... It looks me in the face: 'Is that me? Is it possible that there are so many differences between the self that you see from outside and the one that I see from inside?'"

"Then it's the one inside that it's necessary for me to look after."

"No, that's a wild, intractable animal," she replied. "I'd better give you the other."

"I want both of them," I said.

She shook her head pensively, but came back to huddle against me.

I too forgot everything. At that moment I was very far away from La Colle, the doctor, his frightful logic and his somber experiments. My usual indecision had given way to a certainty: the thought that, out of the entire life that I had been leading for thirty years, also without understanding very much, there was nothing to retain and carry forward but that very simple and marvelous thing, the living being pressed against me.

I steered into an inlet where the water was so calm and so transparent in the rays of sunlight that at twenty meters' depth one could make out the patches of sand and algae on the sea-bed. Leaning over the edge, Yvane said something that I would remember for a long time: "What strange and marvelous land-scapes! Why are the drowned the only ones who have the right to stroll there?"

"What about divers?"

She protested against that prosaic notion. "There are landscapes in which it is necessary to go naked, caressed by the algae, one's hair at the mercy of the waves, one's eyes exposed to the sea. Ys, the city of Ys... those are my initials, you know. Y. S. I would love to walk the streets of my drowned city, the city of Ys..."

"I thought that I had fished up a siren!" Alluding to our first meeting, I continued: "From the first day, I should have known that..."

It was the first time that I found myself evoking a memory that we had in common. I asked her what she had thought of me that day.

She caressed the contour of my cheek with her hand. "Nothing. I couldn't know that you would be so indulgent to all my caprices, so welcoming to all my girlish ways. I've often been told that I'm no more than 12 years of age. I'd love that to be true—but I'd rather have an ageless mind. There's no one but you with whom I can say what I think."

The wind had changed and a slight swell was getting up. The boat's movements sometimes threw us into contact with one another, as if for a lesson in salutary rudeness, to remind us of our bodies made of muscle and bone. I hadn't the heart, however, nor the force of mind, for exacting gestures.

I was no longer a child, nor even a young man. Many times, it had been granted to me to enjoy the company of women who were said to be agreeable. In those past circumstances, the obligation to play a role, to be attentive to the impression I might be producing or to expected tasks, had always marred the pleasure of those encounters. In this instance, there was nothing like that. For the first time, I let myself go without thinking about it, without worrying about a game-plan—not because I let myself be led, but because everything proceeded of its own accord. "With you, I can say what I think," she had said. "And I too," I could have replied, "have only ever felt with you this impression of effortless wellbeing."

We did not return until the evening. And that evening, for the first time, I slept in the summer-house. The attraction of a virgin heart had borne away all the troubles and dangers that seemed to be roaming the pathways of the grounds. The event took on a symbolic value, and marked a step toward the acceptance of a situation that, sooner or later, would demand an official approach. It was, however, to take me nearly a week to decide to speak to the doctor.

VIII

I asked to see the doctor one morning. The painful impressions felt during my first visits assailed me once again as soon as I went into his study. Every object was occupying its immutable place, and if the stained glass panels in the windows were not projected their colors on to the carpet, it was because that morning's leaden sky was becoming stormy.

"It's some time since we've had the pleasure of meeting up," the doctor said, cheerfully. "One only needs to be neighbors not to see one another." I wanted to get to the point of my visit as rapidly as possible, but the doctor did not give me the opportunity. "Is your dwelling suitable for work? As for me, I haven't been wasting my time." He paused deliberately before announcing to me, with greater emphasis: "Dirk is 48 hours in advance..."

Everything that I had intended to say suddenly stuck in my throat, unable to compare with this extraordinary declaration. Having wanted to forget that entire frightful experience, I found myself brutally plunged back into it, and was gripped, my breath cut off as if by a jet of cold water.

"We weren't going to stop short after obtaining the first encouraging results," the doctor continued, apparently desirous of taking advantage of my surprise to proffer his confidences. "The treatment by artificial excitation seems to be acting more and more rapidly as we progress further. The difficulties encountered, would you believe, are of a much more trivial order—they relate to the measures that have to be taken to remain in contact with the subject. I anticipated the measures in question, but I did not imagine that they would have to be applied so delicately. In fact, not only can Dirk only talk if his surroundings are identical to those in which he will find himself 48 hours later, but it's also necessary that he situation of his interlocutors be that which will be reproduced the day after tomorrow. Only in these conditions is the connection made between the two components of his person, between his body and his mind, and, in consequence, the possibility of expression. Otherwise, he's out of phase, if I might put it thus, and says nothing.

"Do you understand now the importance I attach to the permanence of the décor around us? A simple bouquet of flowers on my table would suffice to paralyze Dirk. Moreover, as the questions that I ask him must be those that I will ask him the day after tomorrow, I'm constrained to keep a very strict timetable, scrupulously repeating myself every day—otherwise I could only rely on fortuitous connections.

"You seem incredulous, but I'll convince you. It will soon be 10 a.m., the time of my first daily interview with Dirk. In order that he will accept you as an interlocutor it's necessary first of all for you to promise to come and see me again the day after tomorrow, at the same time, dressed as closely as possible in the same manner. On that condition, he will tell you today what he ought to tell you in two days' time. Do you promise?"

Mechanically, I nodded my head.

"In any case, I'll find out immediately whether you'll keep your promise. If he recognizes you, it's because you'll come."

He got up, went to the door at the back of his study, and, with his eyes glued to his wristwatch, waited until it was exactly 10 a.m. to call out: "We're going to work, Dirk—will you come down?"

"Yes, Monsieur," said Dirk's voice.

"Those are our ritual phrases," the doctor explained, as I heard the noise of footsteps on an interior stairway.

Dirk appeared, calm and casual in manner, more at his ease than during our last encounter.

"Bonjour, Dirk," I said, in a slightly strangled voice.

"Why, Monsieur Delambre—I'm glad to see you."

The doctor addressed a glance of satisfaction to me, doubtless to thank me for the visit that I would pay him in two days' time. Going over to a window he opened it to the sky.

"What do you think of the weather, Dirk?"

"Bright sunlight," said Dirk. "A glorious day."

It had never been so black; the storm seemed to be about to break.

"Now you know what the weather will be like on the day after tomorrow," the doctor said to me. "Have no fear of thinking aloud—Dirk might hear you, but he won't make it manifest if it's not in the day after tomorrow's sequence."

"Do you really think it's fine?" I asked Dirk. "Don't you see any clouds?"

"You're joking," he replied. "The sky has never been so blue."

At that moment, there was a lightning flash; thunder reverberated, and I observed that Dirk had shivered.

"Did you hear that?" I asked him.

He didn't reply.

"Your question isn't one of those that will be asked in two days' time," the doctor explained. "The subject is disconnected—but my dear Monsieur Delambre, you must be aware that if I'm pushing this young man into the future, it's not merely to find out what the weather will be like, in order to get my umbrella ready in good time. As we have no more secrets from you, we shall continue the sequence of our daily labors in your presence."

He placed in Dirk's hands a long, rather narrow strip of paper, then went round to the other side of his desk and sat down, with a pencil in his hand. "You can begin, Dirk," he said. "Don't go too quickly."

"Central Mining 4215. Geduld 1700. Union Corporation 1,80. Areas 355. Anglo-American 511. Goldfields 698. Royal Dutch 6957. Rio 2486..."

I realized then that the paper strip from which was reading was one of those sheets that are unrolled by the apparatus recording share prices on the Bourse. The doctor noted down the figures.

Imperturbably, Dick continued: "Rosario 4250. Quilmès 5390..."

After a quarter of an hour, Dirk stopped reading.

"Do you understand?" the doctor asked me, then. "The figures on the roll are yesterday's share prices. This morning, as on every other morning, they were brought to me from the local branch of the Crédit-Lyonnais at Nice. I have them read by Dirk—who, in his former capacity as a stockbroker's clerk, never ceased to interest himself in financial matters. What he reads are not yesterday's prices, however, but tomorrow's. The consequence is easy to grasp. In a little while, I shall telephone my instructions. I can't say that I'm gambling, because I'm buying and selling on a basis of certainty. And my dear Monsieur Delambre, in the share market, we no longer find inspectors to forbid us entry into the gaming-halls!"

A diabolical flash of lightning made his gaze glitter behind his spectacles. He seemed to be waiting for some exclamation on my part. I refused him that pleasure.

The session was concluded. Dirk came to shake my hand. I felt an enormous pity for the poor devil.

"Au revoir, Dirk," I said, squeezing his hand for a long time.

His lips moved, but no sound came out.

"Evidence that the day after tomorrow, at 10:35 a.m., you'll already have left my study," the doctor said. "Your visit will be briefer than today's..."

I got to my feet and went out without saying a word. As on every other occasion that I had paid the doctor a visit, I found myself at first in the same state as a compass crazed by a magnetic storm. I no longer knew what to think or do. "Oh, if he thinks that I'll go back, he's mistaken!" I began by exclaiming. To thwart the assault on my liberty, it required no more than that. To start with, I would go away...

Extrapolating the hypothesis of a precipitate flight, however, I asked my-self where I was going to go. I could pay a visit to my brother-in-law in Cairo, or go in search of an old girl-friend in Cambo—a souvenir of my last leave—but neither of these prospects seemed very inviting. As for resuming the vagabond life that I had led previously, that would seeking adventures that would certainly be less strange than the one I had found here...

The deluge of rain that began to fall cleared my head somewhat. In spite of its scientific pretensions, this entire story was shady. The fashion in which Dirk was being treated made me particularly indignant. Not that I had any particular sympathy for the poor fellow, but it's difficult to see a human being treated as a guinea pig without raising a protest. I had not been forceful enough. Of all those living in the doctor's entourage, I was the only one who could stand up to him. If I were gone, who knows what his tyranny or influence might do to those who were abandoned to him? But who knew, too, whether he might be using his stepdaughter to lure me into a trap, in order to attempt some other experiment on me?

Well, I would not retreat—and, since I was in the game, he would have to reckon with me. To begin with, would tell him that I would not tolerate a man being crippled in order to make money on the stock market...

I mulled over reflections of this sort throughout the following day. Yvane was absent. Gripped by a fit of energy, she had gone to Marseilles to obtain cus-toms clearance for some packages that had arrived from Holland.

I was ready for anything when I found myself, at the appointed time, in the doctor's study.

The scene was repeated with a haunting fidelity.

"We're going to work, Dirk—will you come down?"

"Of course, Monsieur."

Dirk appeared,

"Bonjour!" I cried.

He did not reply.

"Which shows that your visit will not be repeated in 48 hours' time," said the doctor, mockingly.

Then there was the scene at the window.

"What do you think of the weather, Dirk?"

"Already very hot for the time of year."

"So the weather won't be any different the day after tomorrow," the doctor concluded.

"So you don't see any clouds, Dirk?" I said, glad to find that he saw the sky as blue as it really was—but I had forgotten that he couldn't reply to me, since I wouldn't be there two days later.

The doctor put the Bourse prices into his hands.

No sound emerged from his lips.

"It's Friday," he doctor explained. "Tomorrow, Saturday, the Bourse will be closed—therefore, he can't say anything. I'll leave the paper in his hands, however, in order not to lose the rhythm of our regular employment."

Familiarized with the atmosphere, I was less affected than before. That was the moment that decided to intervene. I took the doctor to one side and began point-blank: "Have you not abused your powers by constraining Dirk to engage in this horrible adventure?"

The doctor raised his head in surprise, to stare at me through the lenses of his spectacles. I met his gaze resolutely. He could see that I was firmly decided.

"I might ask you what right you have to interfere?" he replied, dryly.

"I can't tolerate someone being tortured in front of me, whatever more-or-less scientific motives are invoked."

The impassivity affected by the doctor finished up making me angry. My fists clenched involuntarily. The doctor uttered a sigh.

"My generous impulse," he began, "has betrayed me, as is generally the rule. You want an explanation; here it is, although it will pain me. The man to whose defense you are leaping took advantage of the hospitality that he found at my hearth to seduce my wife. Yes, Monsieur, this young rascal has dishonored me. Not for the sake of love, but out of vanity. Furthermore, he dared to plot my own demise. His criminal conduct was the cause of Gabrielle's death. He knows that one word from me, and he would be in the hands of the Law. Over him, I have the right of life or death, and I could legitimately dispose of him according to my whim—but I have not imposed any conditions on him. He was the one who, in order to redeem himself, demanded that I use him as an experimental subject. I would have preferred to send him away, never to see him again...

"Oh, I don't know whether you have ever loved, Monsieur Delambre, whether your confidence has ever been betrayed. As for me, I have loved, loved stupidly, blindly, faithfully...but let's get on...

"The frightful revelation left me a wreck. It was an internal collapse, a visceral laceration, a desire for oblivion that submerged me. At 40 years of age, Gabrielle had conserved all the naivety of childhood. Even motherhood had not succeeded in weighing her down with gravity and anxieties. She was like an incarnation of eternal youth; her candor was prodigious...that was why I loved her. Perhaps I astonish you. It's extraordinary that the equilibrium of our serious and diligent lives should rest on such slender supports, so delicate that the slightest tempting voice can cause them bend. Conceivable or not, that's the way it is. She...she was not guilty; she couldn't understand; she abandoned herself to some sort of game. When she understood, she died of it. But him, the wretch...

"And at every hour of the day, it's necessary that I have before me the face of that man, the lips that were placed on...the hands that have...oh, it's frightful. In jealousy, the precise images that flesh retains are particularly tormenting. The source of those images is there, constantly before my eyes. Between him and me, the one who has more grounds for complaint is not the one you think. It was three years ago, and I haven't yet forgotten any of it...

"After that blow, what remained to me? My work. My research. I threw myself into it with the ardor of desperation; it was the sole link that attached me to life. And it is also to distance myself from that man, the constant reminder of my misfortune, that I drive him in front of me into the future, further and further still..."

This confession left me nonplussed once more. The entire offensive that I had planned was overturned. Instead of finding myself in the presence of a more-or-less obscure machination, I merely discovered a lamentable and banal story of marital misfortune. For the moment, I could find nothing more to say. But from these confidences, I retained especially, with an egoism that was a match for the doctor's sentimental deceptions, that which concerned the mother of the woman who had captured my heart. In the brief portrait that he doctor had painted of his Gabrielle, I was surprised to find the moral equivalent of her daughter, and even more astonished that the reasons that had motivated the doctor's attachment—the charm of a certain innocence, a certain candor—were the same as those that had seduced me in Yvane. Such an identity of sentiments prevented me from smiling at an unfortunate and rather comical coincidence between the two experiences. More than that; in that replication, produced over successive generations, and in that commonality of instinct which ensures that men are always moved by the same thing, I found a certain mechanical, obligatory quality that diminished, it seemed to me, the scope and value of my inclination toward Yvane. Whereas I had believed, naively, that I had chosen her because of what she was, and because of what I was, and our meeting had appeared marvelous because she seemed unique, I had only been yielding to the obscure solicitations of heredity and general instinct that govern the heart of every male. I had been nothing but a plaything, a cog-wheel. Was the doctor right, then, when he claimed that everything is ineluctably inscribed in advance in the material depths of the flesh?

It also seemed to be a kind of rule that, after each of my interviews with the doctor, the feelings I had for Yvane were seemingly undermined, and that it was necessary for me to see her again, and spent a few days with her, before all the mysterious little threads that attached us to one another were woven together again.

Was she aware of it? Probably. Never was her presence more discreet, more delicate, than at those times when I distanced myself from her in thought—as if she had divined that that was the best means of getting me back.

I had decided not to interrogate her straightforwardly about the doctor's confidences. It seemed to me that precise questions would have broken the charm and delicacy of the atmosphere in which our relationship was unfolding. What happened between us ought only to be concerned with ourselves. I also decided—and perhaps that was my greatest error—to keep our intrigue completely separate from the thoughts that continued to occupy me at other times, which were concentrated on the doctor's activities. When I was with Yvane, I was with her exclusively; I did not want to see in her any but the person that she wanted to be for me, detaching her and cutting her off from her connections and roots—from the entire frame within which she had lived. I regarded her as a sudden apparition, which one does not seek to explain, in order to allow myself to be more completely seduced by the magic of her gratuitous presence. In her, too, it must be admitted, there was something that invited that manner of procedure. It seemed that she demanded, in order to be fully herself, not to be attached in any excessively narrow and precise fashion to the world that surrounded her. It was in her destiny to play the fairy, and one should not lift the veils of mist the float over the heaths of fairyland.

I still had hours of solitude, however, in which to reflect in a more down-to-earth fashion on the doctor's confession. Once the initial surprise was past, it appeared to me that I had only heard his version of events—a version that seemed to me to be suspicious in more than one respect. Another testimony was necessary, and I could only obtain that testimony from Dirk—who had become invisible, maintained in strict secrecy. By dint of thinking about it, I eventually persuaded myself that a meeting with Dirk was indispensable, and I gradually formulated a plan to achieve that end.

IX

Dirk was definitely resident in the château, since the daily sessions were taking place in the doctor's study. The presence of the dogs forbade any nocturnal investigation. It was impossible for me to trust the Malay servants to take him a note. There remained the simplest solution: to take advantage of an absence of the doctor during the day to reach the place where Dirk was kept, as a more-or-less voluntary prisoner.

It was necessary, however, to discover the location of that place as precisely as possible beforehand. For once, my profession as an architect would be useful to me, in permitting me to reconstitute, from what I could observe of the château's exterior, its interior layout. It had two floors, not counting the raised ground-floor in which no one resided. I knew, from having been here, that the doctor had his study, and the rooms the served as his laboratory, on the first floor. When he had called Dirk through the little door in his study, I had heard the latter coming down a flight of stairs, so Dirk must live on the second floor. On the side facing my summer-house, the façade of that floor had no less than fourteen windows On the other side of the building, the observations that I was only able to make while passing by in the afternoon had to be more discreet. The number of windows was the same, some of them occasionally being open: the servants' rooms, and, perhaps, Dirk's. The difficulty was to determine the situation of the latter, in order not to enter one of the Javanese servants' rooms inadvertently.

The young women lived in the right wing, which was to my left when I was observing from my summer-house; the doctor, on the other hand, lived in the left wing. Dirk had to be lodged not far from him, which left me a choice between seven windows on each façade. The main staircase, which I had taken to go up o the doctor's study, occupied the middle of the building and led to a long corridor on the first floor which ran from end to end, on to which opened, among others, the door of the study. Remembering the colored glass that ornamented the study windows, I was easily able to locate the three windows corresponding to that room on the façade.

The interior stairway that led to Dirk's room had to terminate above those windows, and could not lead to the other façade of the château if, as I supposed, a median corridor ran the entire length of the second floor, replicating the disposition adopted for the first floor communications—which was probable, given the symmetry of the building. That only left me a choice between two windows on the second floor on the facing façade. Supposing then that the stairway leading from the first to the second floor was in the middle of the building, I calculated that, having reached the second floor landing, I had to turn right and walk perhaps ten or twelve meters before finding myself in front of a door opening into Dirk's apartment.

As I carried out this analysis, the house gradually lost its mystery for me, which was a moral advantage for the success of my enterprise. But now that I think about all those calculations again, and all the time I wasted attempting to discover what I needed to know, of which I still had no suspicion, I am inclined to wonder whether, in so doing, I was not the plaything of a superior will. At any rate, let's pass on…

I could only operate by day, of course. From time to time, the doctor had himself driven to the coast, and I was fortunate enough to have a signal of his absence when the Mercedes was not in the garage. Even better, the noise of the heavy vehicle on the gravel of the driveway carried as far as my retreat, alerting me to his departure while I was at home. It only remained for me to wait for a favorable opportunity.

On May 24—that date was to acquire a terrible importance—I was mulling over my plan, lying in a hammock at the entrance to the summer-house, when the characteristic sound of the Mercedes warned me that the doctor was just leaving. I knew that Yvane had gone to Nice to take Narda to see the dentist. The way was entirely clear. I decided to take my chance.

I went rapidly down through the olive grove, in the clothes that I happened to be wearing—a royal blue flannel suit and espadrilles—and then climbed up to the terrace of the château, going around to the right. A passing glance at the open door of the garage confirmed that the Mercedes was gone. I reached the steps of the main façade and tried the door-handle. The door opened. I was inside.

Affecting a casual air, in case I were to run into a servant, I took the large staircase that led me to the first floor. Thus far, all had gone well. I paused momentarily in front of a reproduction of *The Anatomy Lesson*,[68] which decorated the landing. Then, not hearing any noise, I set foot on the stairway leading to the second floor. I began to feel that my state of mind was that of a burglar. The stairway, narrower than the other, was displaced three meters to the left, which modified my calculations. On the second floor, I found myself confronted by a rather narrow corridor, where a surprise awaited me. All the doors opening on to that corridor were on the same side, facing me—corresponding, in consequence, to rooms whose windows were on the principal façade. All my calculations fell into the water.

Somewhat disorientated, I retraced my steps and knocked on the door of the doctor's study on the first floor. There was no response. I tried the handle, but the door was locked. Two analogous attempts on the neighboring doors were no more successful. The doctor had taken his precautions.

Gradually, the anxiety that has accompanied my initial steps gave way to a sentiment of irritation, which gave my actions more audacity. After sitting down in a rattan armchair on the first floor landing, in order to resume my deductions at leisure, facing *The Anatomy Lesson*, I went back up to the second floor, counted out 14 meters—11 meters plus the three meters of the stairway's displacement—along the corridor extending from the landing, then, facing a partition wall in which there was no door, I knocked twice with my fist. There was no response. The wall sounded solid. I was about to repeat the action when I was surprised to hear a muffled sneeze, and then a second. The noise seemed to be coming from the floor. There was no doubt that someone was there, who could not be anyone but Dirk—but it was necessary for me to be able to enter into communication with him.

I was going back down to make a further attempt on the first floor when I noticed, half-way down the stairway, a door hidden in the wooden paneling. It opened without difficulty to a mildly forceful push, revealing a narrow corridor illuminated at floor level by the tops of the first floor windows. The story had been divided at mid-height over a certain extent, which I had not anticipated, and it was in one of the rooms thus constituted that the prisoner had to be lodged. The corridor ended in a spiral stairway, which, after a few ascendant steps, was blocked by a vault of recent construction. I was able, however, to distinguish in the gloom of the stairway—which was not directly lit—some sort of panel opening in the wall. I opened its battens to reveal a rather narrow opening, like those used to transmit plates from a kitchen to a parlor. I extended my arm, and by groping around found a shutter at the back, which I pushed. A little

---

[68] *The Anatomy Lesson of Dr. Nicolaes Tulp* was painted by Rembrandt in 1632.

room, ill-lit, appeared at a lower level. On a corner divan, I made out an elongated form.

"Dirk!" I called.

The form stood up. I recognized Dirk by his silhouette rather than his face, so dark was the room. He came toward the opening and raised his arms, as if to receive something that I had held out to him. It was by this route that his nourishment must be brought to him, and he was repeating a familiar gesture.

"Dirk," I said to him, "it's me, Pierre Delambre. I've been looking for you; I wanted to see you in the doctor's absence. Isn't there some means by which I might get to you comfortable?"

His lips moved, but no sound came out. Evidence confuses you by virtue of its evidential character, all the more so when one has not anticipated it. There, I encountered the capital obstacle to which, in spite of all my reflections, I had not given a moment's thought in the planning of the expedition. How could I enter into communication with Dirk, given that the poor fellow's thoughts were no longer occupying the present moment?

I persisted, though. "Make an effort, Dirk, I beg you. Can't I have a conversation with you? I didn't know that you were being held prisoner like this. Whatever wrong you did, the treatment to which you are being subjected is inhuman—worse, of a deliberate cruelty that I find repulsive. I'm your friend, Dirk, ready to do everything I can to help you. Answer me—tell me that you can hear me."

My voice took on a plaintive tone. I could not extend my head very far through the hole, but I could pass my arms through. Dirk, standing on tiptoe, had seized the hand that I held out to him and shook it with an energy in which I thought I could see the mark of his despair at not being able to express himself. The blue sleeve of my jacket seemed black in the gloom. I had the appearance of leaning out of the window in a carriage door, saying goodbye to a friend who was remaining on the platform at a railway station.

The grip of Dirk's hand was sustained for some time, and suddenly, I heard: "My dear friend, you have my every sympathy! Poor Yvane—that strange, atrocious death! Drowned! Drowned in such circumstances…"

At first, I didn't understand. Then, suddenly, I was struck in the heart. I uttered a bestial cry and withdrew my hand brutally.

"Dirk!" I cried into the opening. "Repeat what you said, Dirk. What are you saying? Yvane…Dirk, what did you say? Repeat it?"

I howled, threatened. He did not breathe another word, and even retreated to his divan before my insults.

I fell silent. I was inundated with sweat. Mechanically, I took a few steps along the corridor. No, it wasn't possible; I was mistaken. And yet, with an intensity and a precision that the memory of a sound had never assumed in me before, I heard his words echoing once more: "*Poor Yvane—that strange, atrocious death! Drowned! Drowned in such circumstances…*"

Half way along the corridor, I made a half-turn to come back toward the opening, to try to repair the thread that my cry had broken. I begged again, imploringly, but nothing came of it. Dirk did not even move.

"*That atrocious death! Drowned! Drowned in such circumstances...*" The words were buzzing in my head. My mind still refused to accept their full significance. I collapsed into an armchair in the hallway, resolved to watch out for the doctor's return, waiting for him with an impatience compared with which, the impatience I had put into watching him leave was derisory. What was he doing? I had to see him immediately...

I don't know how much time went by like that. Finally, I heard the car drawing up before the steps. I ran out.

"Doctor! Doctor!"

"What's wrong?" he said, confronted by my haggard appearance.

"Oh, doctor..."

He drew me rapidly into the study, some distance away from the chauffeur, who was unloading the vehicle.

"Dirk," I said, "Dirk...tell me, first...how much time is here? How long is his advancement?

"29 days and six hours," he replied. "Why?"

"29 days and six hours," I repeated. "29 days and six hours..." I cried, in protest: "No, that's not possible!"

"Come on, explain yourself!" he demanded, with understandable irritation.

I told him everything, without omitting anything: the suspicions I had conceived, the manner in which I had spied on him. I told him every detail of my afternoon expedition, hiding nothing.

When I pronounced the words that Dirk had let escape, I saw him grow pale. Without him saying a word, tears began to run from his eyes.

"No, no!" I exclaimed. "Tell me that I'm mistaken, that it's not true! You don't believe it; you can't think it. I have no other hope but you; it can't be true. Dirk is making a mistake; he sometimes speaks at random."

The doctor shook his head. Softly, he demanded: "Repeat the words you heard."

I repeated them.

The doctor bowed his head silently, and hid his eyes behind his hand.

"But after all," I cried, again, "we shall fight, now that we've been warned. Now that we know, we can take our precautions in consequence... The boat, the boat that we were going to buy, I know now what I have to do. I have to keep her away from the coast, night and day. Since we know, thanks to you, thanks to your experiments, we must be able to get out of it."

He shook his head and replied, sadly: "We also know that the world rotates, but we can't stop it, for all that. What you hope to do is as impossible as immobilizing the Sun."

That resignation made me indignant. I got up, and thumped the desk hard.

"Well, as for me," I said, "I don't accept it. I accept the challenge. I shall save her; I have to save her...don't you understand that I love her." I was shouting in the doctor's face, which had become impassive again. "I've loved her since I first saw her. I've never said so, admitted it, either to her or myself, but I love her. I won't allow the woman I love to be snatched away. Yvane, Yvane..."

I no longer knew what I was saying.

The doctor watched me in silence. "Calm down," he said. "You're not telling me anything I didn't already know. But we men ought to be strong. If a physician had told you that a fatal illness would carry you away, wouldn't you be able to control yourself?"

"But an accident can be avoided. Drowned, drowned—her! When I think that, only the other day, leaning over the edge of the boat, she said, with regard to the sea-bed...oh, it's frightful! But I shall fight, I shall fight, I shall get the better of you, of your experiments, of everything...I don't believe it, anyway. I tell you this to your face—I don't believe in what you've done."

He came toward me and took me by the shoulders. "Yes, my poor friend, don't believe it—I might have been mistaken."

It was obvious that he as only saying that to allow me some hope. I let myself fall into an armchair, repeating: "But I love her...I shall fight, shall fight...help me..."

"Yes," he said, "I'll help you. But don't warn her—that would be too atrocious. Speak vaguely about a presentment, if you wish, and then, with her sensitive nature...be on the alert, watch over her. Let's see, this is the May 24. Twenty-nine days—that gives us until...let's see, does the month of May have 30 days or 31?"

With these words, the memory returned to me of her pronouncement: "*You've kissed me in September.*" I couldn't hold out, and let myself dissolve in tears. Eventually collecting myself, a little calmer, I murmured: "Perhaps I'm mistaken; perhaps I was misled by similar sounds. What if you were to try to bring me together with Dirk again?"

The doctor seemed to be reflecting.

"The scene that you've described, during which a connection was formed between the décor and Dirk's mind, in an entirely fortuitous fashion, obviously reproduces a farewell scene on a railway platform. At this moment—which is to say, in 29 days' time—you're in the train; you have left Dirk, and are far away from him. It's therefore impossible for a new connection to be forged between you and him, for the time being."

The calmness and lucidity with which I could see that he was reasoning made me indignant, and restored all my feverishness. "But we have to do something, even so! Don't accept, search!"

"You see me as crushed as you are, my friend. Yvane is the sole affection that remains to me on Earth, the last link that still connects me to my poor Gabrielle. When I look at her, I think I'm seeing her mother alive again...you love

365

her, you couldn't find a more delicate and more precious individual....I'll think about it—but I confide her to you, Pierre..." And he added, pushing me gently toward the door: "Who knows what love can do?"

X

I didn't want to lose a moment. I went to take up a position next to the gate to watch out for Yvane's return. Anxiety was gnawing at me. Who could tell? Perhaps, already...

When I saw the little car appear on the road, I hurried out in front of it.

"Yvane! Yvane!" I shouted.

I leapt on to the running-board, took hold of Yvane and threw myself upon her cheeks, covering them with kisses. I had got her back—she was alive, really alive! My behavior contrasted so strongly with my habitual reserve that she was utterly nonplussed.

"What's wrong?" she asked, her voice as calm as ever, but nuanced with surprise.

"What's wrong?" I said, collecting myself. "Nothing, nothing—it's just that I'm so glad to see you again!" Turning toward Narda, I added: "You too." And, to put Yvane off the scent, I tried to take her in my arms and kiss her too.

"No, not on the cheek," she said. "My tooth's still hurting." She turned her head to get away, and my lips brushed hers.

"Come on, Pierre, why these sudden manifestations?" Yvane demanded.

"It's such a long time since you left—I've had a frightful dream. Yvane, come with me immediately—Narda can put the car away."

As soon as the car had gone, I put my arms around Yvane again. I didn't let go, in order to assure myself of her presence, to touch her body, her muscles, to feel her next to me, robust and full of life. There really was no affection in the gestures.

"One might think you were a puppy greeting its master," she said, in an amused tone.

"Yes," I said, "that's it. That's it, exactly."

I didn't want to waste another minute before putting her on her guard, but I hadn't prepared any lie.

"Yvane, promise me...or, rather, I beg you to promise me...It's a favor that I'm imploring of you...listen, it's very serious: you must promise me on everything you hold most dear...so much the worse if it seems bizarre..."

"What a preamble! What's up with you this evening?"

"I want you to promise not to leave La Colle for a month, not to go near the coast, and not to take a boat out for any reason whatsoever."

"How bizarre! Why?"

"You mustn't ask me for explanations. It's very serious, I assure you...very serious for me."

We were walking along a side-path; gradually, I recovered my composure. The little smile that she had had on her lips during my demonstrations was frozen into a slight grimace that seemed to have been forgotten on her face by her preoccupied mind. I didn't want her to reflect—it seemed to me to be so easy to deduce. I wanted her to accept my conditions as a bizarrerie of my character.

"It's a trial that I have decided to impose upon you—but I beg you to grant me what I ask of you, stupid as it might seem."

At the tone of my voice, which must have seemed quite anguished, her beautiful face became grave.

"Yvane," I continued, "all that I'm shutting up in my heart, all that I cannot bring myself to say, but which is as plainly visible as the sun in the sky...Yvane, since you know that you are the only thing on earth that counts for me..."

She put a finger on my lips. She was right; it was better for me to shut up. I stammered another: "My love"—or, rather, my lips articulated the syllables on her lips. We were standing in the midst of impassive cypresses. My two hands were sustaining her shoulders. From head to toe our two bodies were touching. For the first time, I held her against me, no longer like a large flower found by the roadside, but as the only creature in the world. I hugged her to my breast, like the other half of my heart—the heart that I could feel beating through the light fabric, the heart which, perhaps, was already counting the beats that separated it from silence...

Then began the most agonizing and the most marvelous days that I had ever known.

While I was with Yvane, touching her with my hands, never taking my eyes off her, discovering in her adorable face a thousand hidden retreats into which I went to lose myself in dreams, wandering amid all the secrets of her nape and her hair, testing with my lips the caress of her lashes, the cool corners of her eyelids, rediscovering on her cheeks the perfumes that allowed all the flowers of May to escape into the air, I forgot...I forgot everything.

Having spoken, having put an end to my stupid hesitation, to my internal reticence, I had opened the way to a tide of affection, which escaped me in torrents of joy, causing me to shiver with happiness, giving me an infinite confidence in the forces of love.

But when night came, and I found myself alone with myself, the atrocious anguish gripped me again. I saw her under the atrocious threat. Thinking that the greatest regret of the living is not to have loved enough, not to have told those who have departed that they loved them often enough, I wanted, at least, to escape that remorse, to tell the living Yvane over and over again of a love so great, so immense, that it could overwhelm her eternally.

Then, insomnia developing, I forged insensate grievances against myself. "Coward," I said myself, "you didn't speak, you only committed yourself because you found out that she's going to die. That love isn't the kind that can vanquish death. It was before you knew that you should have declared yourself. Don't hope to snatch her away from the destiny that awaits her."

At dawn, as soon as the last demands of convention permitted it, I ran to Yvane's windows. I didn't want to lose a single minute. Still entirely possessed by my nocturnal errors, I thought her dead, and every time, my first kiss was like a kiss that one deposits on a lifeless face in a mortuary chamber. And I had the indescribable joy of seeing that face come back to life, of feeling two arms of flesh entwine around my neck, of finding Yvane as true as ever.

She had meekly given in to my demand that she not stray far from La Colle, and not to approach the coast on any pretext. No more excursions by boat, no more sea-bathing. I pretended to be jealous; I wanted her all to myself, to be with me every moment of the day.

One night, I woke up covered in an anguished sweat; while half-asleep, I had just remembered the reservoir that I had forgotten. Level with the ground, it was a permanent threat. I got up immediately, went to open the drainage tap, and did not leave the place until the reservoir was dry.

To be sure, it's commonplace to associate death with love. But in this instance, it wasn't a question of literature, and never were those two divinities interlinked as intimately and as authentically as they were for me as the days went by. The thought of death stirred in my heart as if to extract, with an unexpected intensity, all the passion of which a human being might be capable. I was in love, so much in love that I might have died of it myself.

Gradually, the days were passing by, and I recovered hope. As I was distanced from the moment of the horrible confidence, as I saw Yvane, happy and very much alive, trusting in the infinite affection that I evidenced for her, I began to doubt, to forget. All my precautions had been taken. I mounted a vigilant guard. The nightmare became less painful. I maintained a strict consistency, striking out each passing day on my calendar, the bearer of a black accolade extending from the May 24 to June 22. The days passed without incident. The month of June was delightful, in its light and coolness.

"Will you hold me prisoner much longer?" Yvane asked me, during the long pale evenings when the Sun seemed unable to decide to disappear.

To tease me, she proposed a little excursion by car on the coast road, but when confronted by the effect that any such proposition immediately had on me, she did not persist, only murmuring: "A bizarre trial, like no other..."

I only lived for her, and with her. I refused to see any other resident of the château; I did not want anything to disturb the dream in which we were taking refuge. Forgetting the external world gave me more confidence in the powers of the heart. Yvane was there, always there. Her supple figure, which I felt like a firm and living liana at my side, was a certainty that helped me to chase away the somber torments of the night. Calmer, less anxious regarding the immediate, I could watch her live, with more curiosity about her mind. It appeared to me that her thought-processes, which had always been rather mysterious, did not allow themselves to be enveloped in the immense affection that I draped around her body and her heart. On the contrary, as if assured that someone—who was partly herself—was standing guard over her flesh, freeing her from the concern of maintaining everyday contact with reality, she seemed to be using the possibilities of her leisure to extend her dreams toward more distant horizons, where I had difficulty following her. Silently, I remained half-way to those heights, like a shepherd who allows his flocks to frolic on the summits, sure that when evening comes he will find them again on the path to the valley.

"Is happiness—the thing is more mysterious than the word—a closed shelter or a trampoline that facilitates bouncing?" she mused, aloud. "Being happy, I never felt so light, so disposed to bounce...beyond my happiness, if I might put it like that. As in dreams, I could almost believe that it would be sufficient for me to extend my arms to fly like an arrow into the sky, to become a skylark, or a cloud..." Meanwhile, her hand was playing with my hair. "Pierre, Pierre, with a name so hard, how can you be so tender?"

The strange thing is that it was necessary to hear that, the significance being in the intonation, almost as a reproach, as if the word "affection" signified carelessness or laxity...

In the course of one of the walks by means of which I tried to make her forget our seclusion, I sat down on the side of a hill. She came to wedge herself between my knees, lying back against my breast—in her armchair, she said—and I inclined my head over her neck, tasting in the cleavage of her blouse the savor of her warm and supple flesh. My arms were folded around her breasts.

"Nothing, nothing can tear her away from me," I whispered, in the shadow of her hair.

After a long silence, I heard her murmur: "It's beautiful, beautiful—as if I were about to die..."

I cried out in protest.

"Why?" she went on. "Happiness is so much greater than life, that when one confides oneself entirely to someone, one surpasses life, and death no longer has any meaning."

"No, Yvane, that's a blasphemy. You mustn't tempt the gods."

She reflected for a while. "You value my flesh more than I do," she said. "Isn't the person who loves the most the one who goes furthest, driven by happiness?"

So great was the power of the spell that several times, on the evenings of those days, I forgot to strike out the elapsed day on the calendar. The second fortnight of June had begun. We decided that we would make an ascent of a neighboring mountain on the day of the summer solstice. On the longest day of the year, we would see the last sunset of spring, and we would walk all night to reach the summit and see it reappear at dawn: the summer sun, already fleeing from us....

Narda drove us in the car to the foot of the mountain, treating us as lunatics because we had refused to take anything with us.

"I want to walk with my arms free, aware of nothing but my own weight," Yvane had said. "Every precaution, every preparation, is an insult to the landscape, a weapon against nature…"

We started along the path at 8 p.m. The day was still warm. I let her walk ahead of me to set the pace, which was more than slothful, and to keep her in sight, like a spectacle of which I never wearied: the sway of her figure, the play of her long bare arms, naïve in design. Sometimes, she passed over an obstacle with a rapid bound, revealing a pale calf beneath her short dress, chaste and hollowed by the effort. With the hands that she had wanted to liberate she caressed the berries of arbutus trees as she passed by, or tested the tips of aloe-leaves, turning round abruptly to reassure herself of my presence, and replying with a smile to the smile with which I accompanied her every gesture.

The last lizards were abandoning the place; the vegetation was becoming sparser, the path narrower. With our backs to a section of a wall of rock, still warm, we watched the sunset. The view extended through the depths of the valley to the sea, grey and shin in the distant mist: the sea, my secret enemy, sullen within the décor illuminated by the red earth of the mountains, as if I had snatched away the prey that it hoped to claim. With the satisfaction of a victor, I took the bare arm of that prey, who was standing silently beside me. It had been grazed in places by the dry branches of juniper bushes. To erase the white marks are restore its natural polish, I caressed it with my palm, as one does an object made of precious material.

"So you, too, don't think it necessary to consent to the marks imprinted by life?" she asked.

I took time to reflect before replying: "The same life that inflicts them also erases them, better than our ministrations."

She had tilted her head back toward the zenith, which was already turning a dark violet. "The clouds don't soil the sky," she said.

Darkness rose in the east. There were no more birds. A belated sparrow-hawk passed below us, fleeing toward the valley.

"Well be the only two living, thinking beings on the mountain this evening—that's a great responsibility," she said, ironically. "Here's the night—I can feel it coming, warmer…" She turned toward me and added: "The first night when we shall be together." Then, abruptly: "I'm glad; there'll be moonlight."

A pale clarity became visible on the peak facing us.

"You divine everything," I observed. "You see everything before me. For myself, I only want to see you…but it's as well that you're in advance, interrogating things, like my infinitely sensitive watchman."

She put her arms around my neck and laid her head on my shoulder. "Carried by you, I see better and further—alone, I would never have come so far.

And everything here is so calm! What are we going to find at the top of the mountain? What if we meet angels?"

"Are you happy?" I asked.

"Enough to forget to live," she replied.

We resumed our march. Our mountain had nothing immense or painful about it, but it had a peak, and its inoffensive slope brought us closer to the stars. The air became still and the rocks retained around them a little of the warm atmosphere of the day, impregnated with thyme. Little by little, in the lunar light, forms lost their excessive precision. The world of the night was born around us.

She put her mouth close to my ear to murmur: "Listen—in its progress over the earth, the night is marching from summit to summit, and I'm sure that we're going toward the place where its bare foot will rest…"

I knew that in her, excitement took the form of a return to childhood. I too felt myself gradually entering into the enchantment. A diffuse fatigue inclined me to follow all the solicitations of the imagination, and I was able to see the elves gliding between the pools of moonlight, in good faith.

I proposed a halt.

"No, higher up," she said, "higher still."

I followed her white shadow, which scaled the final scree-slopes at a run.

"The summit!" she said, stopping suddenly, open-mouthed before the fantastic décor of standing stones that crowned the plateau we had just reached. She was breathing hard. A moonbeam, catching one of the crystal buttons of her dress, shimmered like a pale star.

"You'll have a heart attack, child," I said, placing my hand on her breast.

"It doesn't matter. Poor heart, it's carried me this far. It's yours, keep it. Me, I belong to the night."

The night surrounded us with its infinite silence. Very close to my ear, a murmur became audible: "I shall never consent to cease being happy. Now, I'm so happy, so intoxicated to have come so far, so high, that I'd like to dance, to dance solo for the night."

I scarcely recognized her voice.

She tore herself away from my arms, bounded a few paces away, and, abruptly taking off her dress, seemed to flee into the starry sky.

A white form in the moonlight, leaping from stone to stone, momentarily motionless, slender beneath the immense sky, then bounding through the shadows to reappear at the far side of the darkness beneath the dark blue vault, sometimes pausing on an altar of stone, sometimes gliding more smoothly between the grey monsters of crouching rocks…

One might have thought her the priestess of some strange cult, understood and celebrated by herself alone. What spirit emanated by that antique earth had taken possession of her body thus? What sacred flame, reborn from the ashes of the past, had returned to life in her? A chaste Bacchante, in love with the great secrets of nature, she seemed to be offering herself to the caress of the heavens...

The queen of the elves danced on the mountain that night. A spark of flesh bounded within the confines of the earth and the sky. My eyes saw her, beneath the stars that cannot see at all.

I dared not intervene. Something there surpassed me, whose gravity I felt more than understood—something, however, of great and profound significance.

I received in my arms and rested on my knees an exhausted form, half-unconscious with fatigue, streaming with perfumes of the earth and juices distilled by her flesh.

Like an obscure acolyte of some great mystery, I piously gathered from her temple, amid her sticky hair, the sweat poured out by that body as a libation to the spirit of the night. The heart that had been abandoned to me was still palpitating with the emotions of an excessively mad endeavor; I cradled its repose gently, until the return of the dawn.

By the light of the paling sky, mauve rings were visible around her closed eyelids. Her hollowed cheeks took on ivory tints. The new day revealed to me another face, which I scarcely recognized: a perishable face, but one whose very frailty made me love her even more than hers glorious image even more. I loved her in a way that touched the utmost depths of human affection, delirious with joy.

She opened her eyes, and, confronted by the silvery, more distant stars, murmured: "It's ended, already..." before burying her face in my bosom.

I wrapped her in my jacket. The first coolness of the day was threatening us. We began to descend. She walked with closed eyes, leaning on me like a sleepwalker. "How far it is!" she sighed. I wanted to carry her in my arms. To march at dawn, carrying the object of one's love! In my intoxication, I would have lifted up the world...

When the summer Sun rose, I looked at it with pride, as an equal.

I did not leave her until we reached the threshold of her room, in the shelter of the familiar frame. One last time, I hugged her as if to stifle her. Happiness was streaming through me, impregnating me to the most distant fibers of my being. I went to throw myself down on the divan in the summer-house, to resume the dream...

Later, while I was half-asleep, I heard a voice calling: "Pierre! Pierre!" I sat up. It was Narda's voice. I raced to the threshold. Narda was running up the slope toward me.

"Pierre!" she cried. "Come quickly!"

"Why? What's wrong?"

"Yvane—come quickly! Yvane, in her bath—she's not moving. She's very cold."

Dream or reality? I tottered. Abruptly, facing the midday sun, I understood, and collapsed, unconscious.

XI

The medical examiner requested an inquest, which returned a verdict of accidental death. An electric hair-drier dipped into the bathwater had provoked an initial electrocution, whose work had been completed by a prolonged immersion of the body in the cold water. On emerging from my faint, I had not wanted to see the woman who was no more. No image of death ought to tarnish her memory. I didn't want to see anything or hear anything, but to continue to dream.

I decided to go away, to leave the summer-house forever. I was taken to a railway station. I got on to a train. When the train stopped, I got off in a city. For two days I lived in a world that I no longer recognized. There was nothing; nothing remained. I could not extract myself from my hallucination. I said to myself: "Do I need to eat? Oh yes, I need to eat. So what? I need to eat." Or "Sleep? Do I need sleep, then?" But slumber would not obey me. If, by chance, I succeeded in becoming drowsy for a few hours, my awakening was all the more atrocious. "What's wrong, then?" I asked myself, for long minutes, having lost all memory. Then I remembered the horrible appeal; I thought I heard Narda's cry for help. Every time, there was the same shock to the heart, the same fall into the void, the same gulf to the bottom of which I was precipitated. The broken thread could not be reattached. My mind remained astray. An individual is measured by the void they leave behind. With Yvane gone, the void was so great that it swallowed the world.

I could not continue to live like that. I returned to the summer-house. There, at least, I recovered memories; there, shadows were still floating beneath the branches, with which I could hear myself, and which might perhaps invite me, little by little, to accept that to which, with all my forces in revolt, I still refused to submit.

I rarely went out, awaiting the hours disdained by humans, the hours of complete darkness, or dawn, to deliver myself to pilgrimages of a sort, in the course of which I reshuffled dreams endlessly. I feared no ridicule. I went to find the dogs in their kennel to talk to them about Yvane. Those animals, which I could scarcely go near before, now accepted me as their companion, as if they understood.

I slipped into the garage to revisit the little car in which I had seen her for the first time. I caressed its seat and its steering-wheel, pressed my lips upon the handgrip of the gear-stick that had been polished and worn by the palm of her hand, and, with my eyes closed, clutching that cold, absent hand in mid-air, I worked my way through the rosary of memories associated with her: her tanned hand on the table of the inn; her movement, always with the left hand, to push back the rebellious wisps of hair behind her ear; her hand on the tiller of the boat; or, again, her fingers extended as if to catch hold of the distant notes of a keyboard, gripping her forehead—that was the day when we went up on to the *loggia* that revealed the red mountains...

At the turning of a pathway, a gust of honeysuckle stopped me in my tracks; I thought I heard her voice again, saying: "I prefer it to all the orchids on Earth." She was about to appear, her white socks rolled down over her ankles, well-secured in large yellow shoes, her blonde curls escaping from her headscarf to float over her sunburnt nape, all of her beautiful face bright, transparent, illuminated by her pale blue eyes...

On finding a glove that I thought was hers beneath a garden table, I thought I would faint, and my distress as so visible that Narda, whether it was true or not, protested loudly that the glove was one of hers.

I recreated her, initially determined to add nothing that did not belong to her, but also not to conserve anything of her but that which we had in common. A form lighter, more diaphanous, easier to manipulate in my dreams, with which I could continue to pursue the dream in which I had lived. Thus a sleeper snatched from slumber tries, with all the resources of his awakened imagination, to reconnect the broken thread of the dream that had enchanted him. Fragments of our conversations came back to mind. Little by little, I invented others, imaginary ones, in which I asked questions and made replies, guiding myself by the intonations of her voice remaining in my memory to find the words that she would have pronounced. It often happened that I cursed the makers of legend, but I was forced to recognize that certain individuals compel legend-mongering.

On seeing my dream-Yvane develop, I understood a little better that she had been unable to live in a real, complex world, demanding too much calculation. A certain physical awkwardness (what would have happened, the day of the tricycle, if I had not turned up?) a certain forgetfulness of her body, a disgust for its activity, the versatility of her moods—in brief, everything that made her a delightful and charming individual—was out of step with the world. Too delicate to live. Who knows? Perhaps, even when she was alive, I had already loved her as one loves a dead woman, ideally. But what good was this world, then, if the only precious individuals that one meets here are also the only ones who cannot live in it?

I knew full well that the first distraction of my thought, the first relaxation of my effort of will, would bring me back into contact with the reality: "She's dead"—and the aerial phantom into which I was trying to breathe life would collapse. The frailty of my dreams by comparison with the implacable density of the real was thus a constant reminder of the harshness of the world. And the doctor's arid philosophy, the implacable aspect of destiny, gradually imposed itself upon me. He was right; everything was written; nothing could be done about it. Had not Yvane been conscious of it herself? Did not her passivity in confrontation with things, and her refusal to take decisions, demonstrate submission in advance to an invincible fatality?

Gentle summer rains accompanied these reveries. The château's residents respected my solitude and my follies. For my part, I had developed a complete indifference with respect to the doctor and his research. So far as I was concerned, it had exhausted its possibilities at a single stroke. The future was of no more interest to me than the present.

One day, I spotted my host at a distance in the grounds. I noticed that he had become more severe—more careworn, it seemed—but I made a detour so as not to meet him. From various symptoms, I deduced that there was a great deal of activity in the laboratories; the windows remained illuminated for much of the night and sometimes, the howls of martyrized animals reached me. It was of little importance; I was a stranger to the universe, as far astray in my own fashion as Dirk might be in the future, thanks to the effects of the doctor's magic. In my case, there had been no need of any scientific apparatus; the mere memory of Yvane had sufficed to bear away my mind, to carry into the past, leaving nothing in the present but an empty body.

Sometimes, I happened to run into poor Dirk. Although I did not know why, the kind of captivity in which he had been held for a long time seemed to have been relaxed. As he was always mute, he did not disturb me. He fell into step with me, stopping when I stopped, going away when I showed signs that his presence was becoming tedious.

One day, in the pine-wood, we were sitting together on a fallen trunk. In the distance, a crew of woodcutters was working in an area that had recently caught fire, and axe-blows punctuated the silence at regular intervals.

"What a horrible war..." he murmured.

I thought at first that he was talking about a battle between ants that was unfolding at our feet, toward which I directed a vague gaze; then I remembered that his words could not be referring to the present. I had an opportunity to report them to the doctor, who surprised me one morning in the garage. His face seemed fatigued, with a slightly haggard nuance in his eyes that was new in him. A certain abruptness of word and gesture punctured his desire always to seem affable.

"The confidence is interesting," he said. "Dirk is nearly a year in advance at present. He must be referring to a European war. For several days, I haven't succeeded in getting anything out of him, and now I know why: the era in which he's living is disturbed by events, and the possibilities of forming connections with the calm atmosphere in which we live are rarer."

"Oh, a war..." I said.

I said it mechanically, fundamentally indifferent. The doctor misunderstood the meaning of my reflection.

"The fact that he spoke to you should reassure you as to yourself, and establishes that, whatever happens, you'll still be alive a year from now."

I made a gesture of detachment. The logic of the deduction irritated me— and I thought all these more-or-less obscure pronouncements about the future rather childish. They reminded me of the predictions of fortune-tellers, and such tea-leaves didn't interest me any more by virtue of their scientific pretensions.

"Don't be surprised if you hear a certain amount of noise," the doctor said to me then. "I'll probably be obliged, during the coming sessions, to fire a few rifle-shots in order to create an atmosphere."

It was after we had parted that my thoughts returned to the assurance he had give me: "You'll still be alive a year from now." Thus, in a year, I would still be the same person, having eaten and slept regularly, having continued the monotonous game of life, perhaps having forgotten. One comes to love one's pain, to the point of dreading uneasily that it might one day go away. The prospect of eventually forgetting wounded me deeply. Thus, that brief conversation with the doctor had awoken my rancor at a stroke. The same rebellion that had taken hold of me at the announcement of Yvane's death gripped me again. "Oh! I'll still be alive a year from now!" What right did he have to dispose of me thus? And my free will, what became of that? The impression of fatality under which he had made me live had become intolerable. I felt that I was at the limits of a kind of madness, but that it was no longer in my power to command myself.

A chaotic mass of thoughts and feelings was seething within me: my pain, the memory of Yvane, a rebellion against fate, against life. Suddenly, I thought I glimpsed a possibility of vengeance against the universe, against the doctor, against his pronouncements. "You'll still be alive a year from now." It had been a bold move to advance that prophecy. If it was impossible to prevent death from doing its work at an appointed hour, with life one must still be able to act in its stead. Me, alive a year from now—that remained to be seen...

Sliding down that slope, in the atmosphere of semi-madness that was then mine—and the only one in which I could live—I eventually came to think that, if I succeeded in inflicting a falsification upon the doctor, I would ruin his entire theory, and, in consequence, the death of Yvane would be negated. That unsustainable idea nevertheless appeared to me to be more luminous with every passing day. Oh, he would fire rifle-shots! Well, I too had a revolver...

I had been ripened by all the bad habits of solitude...now it seemed that Yvane was appealing to me. If, in creating her legend, I was not obeying a pure fantasy, but yielding to her invitation, was it not the case now that she was inviting me to join her, in the indescribable places where her memory was perpetuated? Yes, it was really her that was calling me...

From that moment on, threatened on the one hand by an implacably progressing universe, and solicited on the other by the most gracious phantom ever borne aloft by the light air of those summer nights, could I hesitate much longer?

When a warm and placid evening arrived, so similar to the evening on which we had left together for our last excursion that I thought I could hear the sound of the car that had taken us outside my door, I could resist no longer; I slipped my revolver into my pocket, and I set off for the mountain.

Carefully, I followed in her footsteps once again. I had forgotten nothing—nothing at all. Every pebble, every blade of grass, was etched into my memory. As I passed by, I caressed the same leaves that she had stroked. At the first halt, beside the wall of rock, the same Sun plunged into its bath of molten gold, and in the empty space my hand passed back and forth for a long time over the arm that was no longer held out to me. A final hesitation still gripped me, but when the same sparrowhawk, recalled by the evening to its nest on the plain, plunged into the valley in front of me, I no longer doubted what awaited me on high. The meaning of the strange scene, in the course of which she had escaped from my arms to bound into the night, now seemed clear to me. With a marvelous prescience, while alive, she had arranged a rendezvous with me in these mysterious places where life overlapped death. Her phantom was still dancing; I only had to go to meet it.

I could have continued on my way with my eyes closed. I went up the scree-slope again and reached the summit. The rocks were there, standing to attention, faithful to their strange forms. I sat down at the place where I had taken her in my arms and awaited the miracle. The Moon was slowly following its path through the stars; my eyes grew weary interrogating the reflections and the shadows; my heart was crying out within my bosom, but there was no reply in the silence.

I understood the meaning of that heartbeat then: one last step remained to be taken. I breathed in deeply, inflating my chest to the maximum for the last time. I closed my eyes, greeting with a welcoming smile the other night that was already descending within me, which a radiant apparition was about to illuminate. I put the barrel of the gun to the very skin of my breast, and pressed the trigger.

There was a click; the weapon had jammed.

I swore, and threw the revolver to the ground. Thwarted! I had been defeated. The doctor had won. Even the right to kill myself had escaped me. Yvane was dead, really dead. I had advanced to the very threshold in the attempt to rejoin her, in vain: the ultimate door remained closed. I remained alone, sober now, on the rim of the abyss, and I felt the long crisis of dementia, in the course of which I had attempted to bring her back to life, unravel within me.

While recognizing the insane aspect of the adventure, however, while now understanding with perfect lucidity what crazy reasoning had driven me to want to kill myself that she might live, I still would not consent to be dominated by fate. Undoubtedly, nothing could make destiny turn back on its past decisions, but if I had not been able to kill myself for Yvane, I could at least kill myself to prove that I was, in spite of everything, free.

It's strange to commit suicide twice for entirely different reasons. Groping about, I searched for the revolver in the heather. Very deliberately, I dismantled the loading-chamber, replaced it and cocked the hammer to arm the weapon. I smiled again, but out of hatred for the doctor.

"You've won twice—now it's my turn!" I cried. I put the barrel to my temple this time, and even more deliberately and more determinedly than before, I squeezed the trigger.

Revolvers don't jam twice.

XII

It was white, brighter than white, like a star of silver or polished metal. Blue glints were woven into the rays that emerged from the thing for me, guiding me to the crossroads of light in order to permit me to reach the thing itself, the silver star that also seemed to be a diamond destined to serve as a lodging for my gaze. I had never seen such a marvel, brilliant, suspended, motionless, attractive. Never had any rising star or crystalline drop surprised in the morning dew shone with so pure a gleam. My indolence, wandering in dark space, escaped the darkness in which it was content, and in that dazzling and icy flame that I had suddenly discovered at the limit of my vision, I witnessed that extraordinary miracle, the revival of my curiosity. Light, true light, caused the rebirth within me of the glimmer of intelligence; the one gave birth to the other, and my consciousness, reanimated by that spark, which extracted it from limbo, discovered itself at the moment of its awakening, to lend its unreal magic to the magic of reality. I remained in suspense for a moment, as if at the confluence of two worlds: that of things and that of their comprehension, immobile on their sparkling frontier, hesitant to choose, to renounce the pure and simple marveling of the conscious gaze alone—but an already-awakening intelligence did not leave me any further leisure, pushing me into the infinite network of its mute interrogations to capture the object of my initial surprise, which, amid a thousand memories of anterior experiences, asleep and forgotten, scattered in the debris of my memory, it was finally able to recognize and to identify as being a nickel-plated tap.

The magic ceased abruptly with that realization, but the repose that followed the seething activity thus regenerated was no less delectable for that. In order to savor it, I closed my eyes, returning momentarily to darkness. When I opened them again, there was an angel on the wall. Perhaps I was waiting for him.

The angel did not say anything, paying less attention to me than to a young man who was clutching his arm. He was an extremely handsome angel, in truth, whose harmoniously-formed wings descended to the ground, and I admired the way that he bore them with such ease, like the tails of a coat put on for eternity: an angel with long blond hair, too long for my memories...yes, definitely too long...

At the same moment, thanks to that exaggeratedly-expansive hair, I understood that I wasn't dead, and that the angel was part of a picture hanging on the wall of my room.

I wasn't dead, and the colored plate above my bed told the story of a young man miraculously saved by his guardian angel, whose apparition was holding him back from the edge of the precipice. I had already encountered the engraving in the books of my childhood. Here, more pretentious in its gilded frame, it participated in the strange charm of aperitif advertisements on the walls of village cafes. But I wasn't dead. Why, then, had I to make that observation, which is not usually one of those that imposes itself on awakening?

A woman in a nurse's uniform came in, bearing a breakfast-tray. She seemed surprised to hear me ask her questions, and came back in company with a man in a white smock, whose face brightened when he heard me. My very ordinary reflections were, however, solely concerned with the fine sunlight that was shining that morning. They withdrew to let me eat. Later, the door opened again.

"Narda!" I exclaimed.

I watched her coming toward me, as brunette as the angel was blond. She took one of my hands in hers. "Pierre! How glad I am! You recognize me! You recognize me!"

The sound of her voice completed my return to myself, and permitted me to reconnect with memories of the past. In a flash, I reviewed the château, the summer-house, my departure, the night on the mountain.

"But where am I?" I asked.

"In a hospital in Switzerland, near Lausanne. We brought you with us."

"But why? What's happened, then? How long have I been like this?"

"Tomorrow, it will be six months since the day when you were found on..." She stopped, fearful of bringing back painful memories.

"Six months!" I exclaimed, unable to believe my ears. "What? I've been in this state for six months!"

"The wound healed quickly, but the rest took longer to put back in order," she explained, with a discretion of expression that was touching. "When they telephoned this morning to tell me that you were talking, I didn't want to lose a minute, I came right away. I never lost hope, but the doctors didn't want to give any guarantees..."

The novelty had not yet passed, and in my confusion, it was a very trivial thought that came to my lips: "For once I get a year's leave, and I spend six months unconscious—just my luck..." But I was still in need of explanations. "Who takes care of me?"

"We do," said Narda. "My uncle, the doctors..."

"Has your uncle been looking after me?" I asked, suddenly anxious.

"No, don't worry," she said, laughing. "But we didn't know who to inform. I've written to addresses found in your papers; we've had a reply for Cairo, from your sister. She offered to accommodate you out there, but the climate..."

"Why, in fact, am I in Switzerland?"

"One of my uncle's ideas. The sojourn in Provence had ceased to please him. You'll never guess why—he's afraid of a war. We've moved to Switzerland, lock, stock and barrel—and you came with us."

"I see, I see," I murmured, having become pensive since mention of the doctor had entered into the conversation. "I owe you an infinite debt, my dear Narda. It's truly admirable that a solitary individual always finds, in his hour of need, devotion at his service..."

An interval of forgetfulness that lasts six months, even when one has not been conscious of it, creates a situation in which one looks back the man one has been with new eyes. I recovered possession of myself as if of an abandoned apartment; I recognized the general disposition of places and objects, but the affective links that bound me to them had changed. I was a stranger in my own dwelling. On passing my hand over my forehead, I encountered a scar near my temple, the first new thing that I had found within me. It was also the last of the man that I had been. There, in fact, was the junction between my successive selves. In the old me, that scar had had a profound spiritual significance, but I no longer acceded to its gravity. Now, for the new me, it was no more than a little sinuous line, losing itself in the roots of my hair, and I limited myself to following it with my finger, with an almost amused curiosity.

In a few days, I recovered full rational possession of myself. I was able to leave the clinic, to go out for walks in the town, and, after the brief intoxication of convalescence, to retrieve the petty annoyances of life. Politeness, for want of any other sentiment of gratitude, obliged me to pay a visit to Dr. Mops. I could not make up my mind to do it—not so much, I thought, because of memories of a past that was well and truly dead, but because it displeased me to present myself to him in the somewhat ridiculous role of a failed suicide. Day after day, I put off my visit, letting myself drift, in the mild Swiss ambience, from breakfast to lunch, and from lunch to dinner, without making any decision.

In the course of the visits Narda made, I expended treasures of diplomacy in declining the invitations she addressed to me on her uncle's behalf.

"We're living not far away," she told me, thinking to soothe me. "Nothing has changed—you'll see."

"Yes, yes," I said, distractedly, knowing very well for what reasons nothing had changed. Giving in to the succession of memories, I added: "By the way, what's become of Dirk?"

"Still the same, still just as mad. He doesn't talk anymore, so to speak. He hasn't forgotten, but he gets everything mixed up. A little while ago, he greeted me with a 'Bonjour, Madame Delambre'—which surprised me greatly. I hardly expected to hear your name emerging from his mouth."

In spite of myself, I let the impact show.

"What's wrong, Pierre? You're very pale."

Immediately, I felt myself blushing and tried to turn away to avoid Narda's gaze.

"I'm sorry," she said. "I'm too stupid. I didn't intend to remind you of the past—but the harm's done now; don't hold it against me. And since I'm so awkward, I'll leave you…"

It was obvious that she attributed my distress purely to the memory of Yvane. As for me, my emotion did not derive so much from Dirk's new prediction—which I felt capable of falsifying, now that I was strong from top to toe, no longer paralyzed by any sentiment—as from the idea that the experiment, whose interference with my life had already had such consequences, was still going on, and that it was threatening to draw me in again.

The decision that I had hesitated to take was immediately set aside. Utterly resolved to draw a line under the entire story and not to set foot again in the doctor's home, who could think what he liked of me, I would leave for Paris the following day.

The next day, with my bags packed, I was about to have them transported to the station when a note was handed to me. It was from Narda.

Things are happening here that are making me anxious. I need someone to help me, but I don't know who to turn to. Could you possibly ask one of the doctors who has cared for you, and in whom I can have confidence, to come here on some pretext or other? He must ask for me first. Sorry to inconvenience you by asking you to do me this favor. It's rather urgent.

I had ten minutes to think about it before the car left for the station. My first impulse was not to modify my plans at all. Then it seemed to me that I had time to telephone the chief physician of the clinic in which I had been looked after, to pass on Narda's request. However, I did nothing. Was it not cowardly on my part to abandon a young woman of 18 to difficulties that I sensed to be rather acute, since I was fleeing them myself? Not to mention that I owed her my life, since she was the one that had directed the search for me toward the mountain…

On the other hand, it was also too stupid to start playing the St. Bernard dog again, and I had had it up to the ears with this whole story, and that entire family. I had decided to leave, and I had only to do it…

I re-read the letter. It was not a call for help; at any rate, it was indirect and very discreet. In spite of its brevity, it contained several spelling mistakes, which touched me.[69] It was those spelling mistakes that made me put off my departure to the evening train…

A little later, that same morning, I rang Dr. Mops' doorbell.

---

[69] As rendered in the text I am translating, Narda's message does not, in fact, contain any spelling mistakes. It is possible that they have been corrected by an editor. At any rate, I decided that it would be inappropriate to introduce any, in spite of the inconsistency.

XIII

"Bonjour, Delambre—glad to see you again."

The doctor had come into the room while my back was turned. He came forward. I scarcely recognized him, so much older did he seem to have grown. His voice, harsher still, broke on the final syllables. His tone was still trying to be patronizing, but it was forced, and missed its effect.

As Narda, to whom I had asked my arrival to be announced, opened the door in her turn, he said dryly: "Give us a moment, my child—I'd like to talk privately to Monsieur Delambre."

Narda obeyed without any response, but before disappearing she shot me a glance whose meaning I could not quite decipher. She seemed to be begging me to be circumspect.

The doctor's abrupt manners were perhaps intended to get the upper hand on me, but no longer having any need to be wary of him, I felt myself ready to respond tit for tat.

"Would you care to follow me?" he asked. "Here, I mistrust the walls."

We found ourselves back in the eternal study, where the right hemisphere of the brain was hanging in its accustomed place. The old décor no longer impressed me, but it had an unexpected effect on me: for the first time since consciousness had returned to me, I started thinking about Yvane again. Not that I had forgotten her, but her remembrance occupied a region of my memory that I had forbidden myself to revisit until that day. But now, solely as an effect of the disposition of the furniture, that entire voluntarily-obscure zone of my memory lit up, became animated—not, as before, as a life that was bound intimately to mine, but as an image lit from behind, whose outline revealed a familiar face. It was no longer the living Yvane, but a portrait of Yvane, awakening more curiosity than profound distress. A portrait that made me think, all the same...

"My dear chap," the doctor began, having given me a long time to install myself, "you see before you a man who is finished, empty, clapped out. The mainspring has broken, a few days ago."

In truth, his voice had become miserable; the mask of authority with which he had greeted me had fallen away, leaving a flaccid face with distressed features, and a dull, weary gaze. Far from feeling pity, however, I experienced a slight repulsion instead.

"I'm not exaggerating," he continued. "Dirk is dead."

"Ah!" I said, slightly disconcerted by this news. Aside, I thought: *So that's what has troubled Narda.* Aloud, I continued: "And you probably fear annoying inquiries—but I imagine that you can easily find explanations."

"I've killed the goose that laid the golden eggs," he continued, ignoring me.

I should certainly have anticipated that he was not a man to be moved to it by the death of an experimental subject, and that he was only deploring the loss to his interests.

"Anyway," he said, getting to his feet, "you'll see."

"No, no," I protested. "I don't want to." I preferred not to get mixed up in the affair, which might become awkward—but as he did not seem to comprehend my refusal, I added a vague explanation: "The sight of dead bodies, you know..."

"What? The sight of dead bodies? What do you mean?"

"Well, you've just told me that he's dead."

"You've misunderstood," he said. "He's dead, but he's as healthy as you or me."

Bewilderment must have been painted on my face.

"I thought you remembered," the doctor explained. "I was pushing Dirk into the future. He was eight years ahead when, suddenly, within the last week, all possibility of communicating with him was broken off. I tried everything before giving in to the evidence. He fell silent because, in eight years, he will quite simply be dead. But while waiting for the eight years to elapse, he's here, solid and very much alive. You can judge for yourself."

He got up then, went to the little door, and the scene I knew so well began again.

"We're going to work, Dirk—will you come down?"

On hearing Dirk's footsteps on the stairway, the indifference that I had felt until then gave way to a vague anxiety. What was the phantom that was about to appear?

Dirk came toward me, his hand extended. I had to vanquish a slight hesitation, but I shook the hand. It was vigorous and warm, like a true hand.

"Come on," I said, turning to the doctor. "Are you sure that he's..." Dirk's presence prevented me from pronouncing the word.

"Alas," sighed the doctor. He went to tap Dirk on the shoulder; then, without any inhibition, he said: "Dead, dead—he's really dead, I assure you. In the long run, it was certainly to be expected, but who would have thought that that, in eight years, this stout fellow would already be clapped out? He's solid, though—look at him. I thought he was good for another thirty years, and I continued fearlessly, gaining several future weeks every day. With an advance of only eight years, I thought I still had a healthy margin in front of me, but *crack!* He's come apart in my hands..."

A sort of despairing wrath returned some animation to the doctor's face. He strode back and forth, while continuing his lament.

"At the very moment when I was in the process of learning, thanks to him, some astonishing things about the treatment of cancerous tumors by cosmic rays! As you can imagine, with an advance of eight years, I was no longer playing the stock market—a mere initial amusement; in any case, there were difficulties...

"No, what interested me was deciphering the science of the future. I was directing the experiment to its true goal, realizing the dream of all scientists: to know the next episode of the great serial of discovery, the state of science for future generations. You'll recall the words of your Renan: 'I would give everything that I know to be able to read the little textbook that will educate the schoolchildren of the next century!' And now the dream that I was in the process of realizing has suddenly collapsed, because of the death of this imbecile. It's my entire life's work that's come to nothing..."

Dirk was listening, as if it were happening to someone else. The scene was curious. Ever suspicious, I ventured a few objections. "What tells you that he's dead? He isn't talking to you anymore, but perhaps it's you that will be dead in eight years?"

"I thought of that, but I have irrefutable counter-proofs. The microphone installed in his room continually records on tape, day and night, everything that he lets slip. What he says in his sleep, take note, is independent of the external surroundings, since every night resembles any other night in the past or future. Until the last few days, the tape recorded fragments of nightmares, but for three days, there's been complete silence, after one last night that it isn't difficult to recognize as a night of death-throes. Look, I'll play it for you..."

"No, no—I believe you. There's no need."

My eyes never left Dirk, who seemed to be following the entire conversation, turning his head from one interlocutor to the other, smiling, and sometimes passing his hand distractedly over his cheek. An interested movement had made him sit up when the doctor proposed that we listen to the night of his death-throes—but more sustained attention permitted the recognition of the automatic nature of these gestures, and a certain absence in his facial expression might have revealed the living dead man.

In spite of my determination to stay out of the whole story, I could not help being affected by the interesting nature of the scene. Beads of sweat formed on my forehead. I mopped my brow; in fact, I felt very ill-at-ease. With the insensitivity of an executioner, the doctor continued to give me details in a loud voice. I wondered whether, in spite of everything, Dirk did feel and understand something.

The doctor only felt sorry for himself. "Twenty years of study, ten years in the laboratory, two years of daily cares devoted to bringing a marvelous subject to perfection, an experiment to which I have sacrificed everything—much more than you can suppose—and it all disappears at a stroke! What do you think I can do with my life now? All that work was my reason for living. I have nothing left—nothing! Start again? I'm too old, and one doesn't find such a subject every day. I thought I had reached the extremity of distress once, with my marital misfortunes—today, it's even worse. I've fallen back to zero, with nothing to hold on to. All hope has left me. The real dead man, in this story, is me. He's all right—look at him…"

The scene was becoming painful. The doctor was getting carried away, and his face was going purple. As I made no response to his plaints, he was raging in a void, like a damned soul.

"This central heating is truly pitiless!" he suddenly exclaimed. "It's stifling in here."

Marching toward one of the stained-glass windows, he opened it wide with a single thrust. A gust of fresh air irrupted into the room, and a marvelous mountain vista appeared in the window-frame. Beyond Lac Leman, the view extended to the great chain of the Alps. Above the lake's mists, in the clear pale blue sky, the dazzling whiteness of snowy peaks rose up, seemingly suspended miraculously in space. It was a magnificent winter day, illuminated by a low December Sun, cutting out the contours so clearly that no detail escaped the gaze. One might have believed that one could touch the summits by reaching out an arm. The large surfaces of glaciers reflected the sunlight in places like convex mirrors. Elsewhere, light translucent clouds rose up over the eastern slopes, toward the shadow. The entire panorama of the high mountains was empty, devoid of dwellings and human beings, as immense and pure as a gigantic snow-crystal, in which nature seemed to be contemplating itself. The icy air that came to bathe the temples drew thoughts irresistibly toward dreams of altitude. The doctor had stopped speaking; a release-valve had been opened in our minds. I took refuge in the contemplation of the landscape.

"Whisky?" the doctor suddenly proposed.

He handed me a glass of whisky and soda, offered one to Dirk, and let himself fall into the depths of an armchair, holding his glass in his fist and agitating a piece of ice. In the silence of the room, nothing was audible but the crystalline sound of the ice knocking on the wall of the glass.

It was then that something extraordinary happened.

"Hosanna! Hosanna!" said a loud voice.

I turned toward Dirk; his mouth was still open and the liquid was swaying in the glass that he was holding.

Startled, the doctor dropped his, which broke on the parquet. "Did you hear that?" he asked me, in a low voice.

"He can speak, then," I said.

Without seeming to attach any importance to our stupefaction, Dirk drank a mouthful of whisky, put down his glass and then, gripped by a frisson, cried: "Hosanna! Hosanna!"

"You see, he's not dead!" I exclaimed, triumphantly, glad to score a point off the doctor for the first time.

My triumph was facile. The words "stupefaction" and "bewilderment" were insufficient to describe the doctor's expression. Mouth open, his eyes quite round, fixed on Dirk, his intelligence seemed to have quit his face conclusively. In a low voice, he murmured: "He's dead, dead—I'm sure that he's dead."

An idea suddenly crossed my mind, and I exclaimed, on a whim: "Well then, he's in Heaven!"

I expected a burst of laughter on the doctor's part. I saw him go green.

"In Heaven?" he said, in a pitiful, stammering tone. "No, that's impossible. There is no Heaven. There's only death, nothingness, oblivion…"

As in the course of a combat in which one is mysteriously alerted to the adversary's secret weakness, I sensed at that moment that the moment of my revenge had come. I took full advantage.

"What do you know?" I proclaimed, drawing myself up to my full height authoritatively. "The décor, always the décor—that snow, that purity of atmosphere: he's found himself at home. He's in Heaven, in Heaven… This is the moment when the experiment will become truly interesting, and we shall learn what no one has ever been able to learn. At this moment, he's singing the praises of God…"

And for the third time, Dirk uttered his double "Hosanna!" I was almost convinced by it myself. Excitedly, I turned back to the doctor, and cried: "Do you understand? He can see God!"

I did not have to go on. The doctor's eyes turned up, his upper body stiffened in shock, and then he collapsed like a dead weight on the floor.

XIV

I lifted him up again, laid him on the leather-clad divan and bathed his temples with whisky. Dirk continued drinking, as if nothing had happened. I was looking for a hand-bell to summon help when the doctor came to.

"The fresh air caught me unawares after that heat," he said. "Will you close the window, please?"

His speech was slurred, and the pallor of his face against the background of brown leather was striking. A continuous tremor shook his right hand, which was extended alongside his body.

"Who should I call?" I asked.

"No one," he replied. "I'll be better momentarily."

"Nevertheless," I persisted, "A physician…"

"I know what it is." He tried to raise his left arm to the back of his neck, which must have been causing him pain.

I slipped a cushion under his shoulders.

"Awfully sorry to put you out," he muttered. With all his might, he tried to collect himself. "Take Dirk back, I beg you," he asked, then.

When I returned, I found him sitting on the divan. He had made an effort to get up; he was still grimacing.

"Danger of hemiplegia on the right side," he murmured. And he gave voice to a little click of the tongue to emphasize the gravity of the diagnosis.

"I'll ring for someone to carry you to your bed," I decided.

"Never, never," he protested. "I don't need anything; I don't trust anyone. It will all be better momentarily. If you want to oblige me, sit down. Let's have a chat to try to see things clearly. You'll help me to think—my head still feels heavy."

He closed his eyes and passed his left hand repeatedly over his face, which was creased like the skin of a pachyderm.

"You said something very stupid in speaking of Heaven just now, Pierre..."

I knew full well that that was the irritant point, but I wasn't going to abandon a dominant position out of pity for his condition. He had taken a beating, physically and morally, but I sensed that he was still tough.

"How, then, do you explain that Dirk is dead, but that he can speak?" I asked him.

"I can't explain it yet; that's why I need to think." He laughed mockingly. "Heaven! But that's the opposite of what I've thought my entire life. I've never ceased to turn my back on it, on Heaven—and I won't, for the sake of a few exclamations let slip..."

"But the experiment," I persisted. "Your experiment...people find what they weren't looking for—that's almost the rule in any scientific investigation."

When I pronounced the word "experiment," he opened his eyes again and fixed me with a long round-eyed stare. He wanted to see whether I was speaking seriously, whether I might be seeking to deceive him by latching on to his weakness. He was committed to his "experiment," the old fox, and he found himself caught in a dilemma: either cease to believe in his experiment, or accept its conclusions.

He shook his head. "It's scarcely probable that I shall ever believe in Heaven. I make mock of it, of Heaven—it's the Earth that interests me."

He was, however, far from presenting a fair countenance to the Earth.

Forthrightly, with an authority all the more definitive because it was a matter of indifference to me, I declared: "Then the experiment is concluded."

A twitch ran across his face. His heart must have been hurting, for he raised his good hand to his breast to forage inside his waistcoat. There was some cruelty on my part in torturing that old man with diminished power of thought, whose pride was—I sensed rather than thought—suffering, because he had become my plaything, and saw me adopting a casual attitude toward him. I was about to stop exploiting my success and abandon the game when a sharper stab of pain caused his head suddenly to jerk backwards.

He began: "Yvane. It was..." Then a second fainting-fit caused him to lose consciousness for a few seconds.

"A drink," he said, on coming round.

I filled a glass, which I had to hold up to his lips.

"The tablets in the little box, there on my desk."

I followed his indications.

"Two," he said.

He took them, and swallowed them with a mouthful of water. His eyes never left me, staring at me in a jaundiced and malicious fashion. He resented me more than ever; I could feel it...but of what was he resentful? Perhaps being able to move freely, being healthy, and fundamentally indifferent to his physical and moral torment. The most curious thing was that he still refused to let me call anyone, and insisted that I remain alone with him.

The tremor in his right hand, which he had concealed in the pocket of his jacket, was incessant. It had even reached his head, even though it was support-ed by the back of the divan, and a slight periodic creaking of the leather broke the silence of the room, like a cricket in the woodwork.

"How droll life is," he murmured. "One gets used to things, to people, without perceiving them. Through the house runs a little animal, lively, amus-ing, silent, a well-behaved child, whom one suddenly sees coming to a halt in doorways, wondering if she might come in. Once, going along a corridor, I stood on her doll's plates. There was a flood of tears; I picked her up and put her on my knee to comfort her. I caressed her head, her fine hair, tied up in a red ribbon...that must have been when it all began."

He was mumbling, in a thick voice that I had difficulty following. I thought he was becoming delirious, but he opened his eyes and he gaze fell upon me, harsh and very keen—a gaze that made no appeal for pity, and before which I instinctively put myself on guard.

"Yvane," he said, without taking his eyes off me. "It was me who killed her."

I succeeded in remaining impassive. The hostility of his gaze had warned me that it was necessary to expect a direct blow. Not one of my eyelashes quiv-ered. To tell the truth, I didn't understand immediately, and before the full meaning of the confession got through to me, I only realized why I was still there, what obscure force had kept me in the presence of that half-dead old man. Now I knew, and my first impression was almost one of relief.

He had closed his eyes again before my impassive face. He went on, stammering, searching for his words.

"A rival is born—that's something from a novel. It doesn't matter—there's truth in it. The same image revives, fresher and younger, next to the old one, which fades away without one being aware of it. The little hand that disappears into the large paw that one holds out grows bigger day by day. The voice be-comes nuanced, the mid becomes more precise; something entirely new is there, in a bud that will blossom. It's a recommencement, one is gripped again by things that one held fifteen years before. One is unaware of one's own aging—and then, one asks for nothing, save for a presence, and that diffuse impression of contentment, of lightness, that the mere sight of a gracious face procures. One is also without suspicion.

"She lifted up her hair to braid it in spirals behind her ears. It was her first grown-up hair-do; she asked me if it suited her. Everything suited her; my smile was my reply. That was in a boat; we were coming down the Rhine during the holidays, leaning on the rail. Her ear, bitten by the cold wind, went pink. We were making the voyage together, a philopena that I had lost.[70] I'd bought a large umbrella, of which she made fun.

"One doesn't know, one never knows anything of what is happening, fundamentally. What was I searching for in books, in the laboratory? I forgot to live in trying to divine the secrets of life. But others were living in my stead, and to watch others live, when one loves them, is sufficient. We had our first secrets—it was me who covertly gave her money to buy her first car. One day, when she was preparing for her baccalaureat, she came to ask me to explain the nervous system to her, in a few words. She was preparing for the oral, and was afraid, so timid was she. The nervous system, in a few words!"

He opened his eyes to say: "She was sitting where you are, listening with a touching good will to explanations that had never been so confused. It pained me to see her forehead furrowed attentively because of my clumsiness in expressing myself. Those wrinkles hollowed out between her eyebrows were still child-like; that was the only sign that my words could awaken in her face...

"When death determined that we remained alone, I kissed her through the veil of mourning, I knew the taste of her tears. For myself, I didn't weep, I wasn't in pain. I wasn't aware of a displacement of affection. Life went on. Every day I was struck by the increasing resemblance to her mother. It wasn't only her arms and her gait, but the expressions on her face, her little habits, the way she threw her hat aside when she came into the hallway, the same musical intonation in long words, her liking for the same flowers, the same delight punctuated by hesitations and reticences, and an occasional bizarre sadness in her gaze. The woman I had always loved was still present. She kept the house with a touching application. We scarcely talked to one another—I didn't know what to say to her. Certain attentions, filial in inspiration, charmed me. When you appeared, I hated you immediately, for it was only at that moment that I began to understand. It was necessary for me to fight; I fought.

"I fought. I never recovered from finding the sickness so profound and deep-rooted for such a long time. I employed every possible means: reasoning, moral rigidity, obsessive work; I went so far as to treat myself, in order to sterilize certain zones of my sentimental imagination! Why did I continue to refuse to accept the inevitable? Without mentioning insurmountable obstacles, I was old, and my prestige was too fragile by comparison with a single youthful smile.

---

[70] Philopena (*philippine* in French) is a question-and-answer game in which the loser must pay a forfeit.

I fought. Nature laughs heartily at our determination. The more I shut myself up in the laboratory in order to forget, the more the sickness tormented me. What miseries are hidden beneath the most indifferent appearances! An old fool with the soul of a child! A horrible jealousy devoured me. My last chance in life was escaping me without my being able to prevent it. It was necessary. I had to consent to it. Why, then, did you come to tell me what was going to happen?"

I listened in spite of myself, sickened and as if crushed by a particular kind of horror. With the pronouncement of Yvane's name, I had felt all the memories engraved in my mind come to life again. The image that I had believed dead, or distant, regained its presence, the flesh of my flesh. And if I still did not react more extravagantly, it was because my whole mind and body were no more than a confused and dolorous mass, and because the awakening of that pain occupied me entirely.

"I fought. In doing so, I came to consider you as a savior. You were helping me, without knowing it, to fight the good fight. I encouraged your meetings. I hoped that things would work out, that, sensing that she was more attracted to you with every passing day, seeing her acquire from someone else a happiness that I could never hope to give her, I would get used to it...

"I didn't get used to it. The jealousy, far from being extinguished, became even more unbearable. I was not so much jealous of you, nor of her, but of the youth that you both had, of the youth that authorized you to show your sentiments in broad daylight and without shame, while at my age, under pain of being an object of repulsion and disgust, they had to be buried.

"Yvane no longer even saw me; I bored her; she scarcely appeared at meals. She withdrew from my life. I could not reconcile myself to that void. I came to think that I would have preferred to see her die...why, then, did you come at that moment? Why did you notify me that it was going to happen? You revealed to me what I was going to do, which I didn't yet suspect myself...and once I knew, what point was there in fighting? What was the point of my anguish? I was marked for the frightful task,[71] I had to succumb. There was nothing to divert me, to tempt me. From that day on, I stopped fighting. It was you who pushed me over the edge, you who pronounced the sentence of destiny upon me."

So, not content to display his ignominy, he was claiming...

"You're vile!" I shouted at him.

"I know," he said. "I don't care." And his half-paralyzed face creased into a sort of smile. But why was he smiling?

He had succeeded in plunging me back into a nightmare. I was the one who, horrified in the face of his monstrous calmness, at the idea of a possible

---

[71] I have translated this phrase literally, but it is worth noting that the French *tâche* [task] is phonetically identical to *tache* [stain], a tacit double meaning emphasized by the use of the term *marqué* [marked].

culpability, felt a criminal anguish squeezing my heart. He was humming now, and, believe me, his voice took on a near-triumphant tone.

"I loved her, I killed her, as they say in the assize court. "With a few nuances, I could say as much—and you, too, could say as much. Our means were different—but dead, she belongs as much to one of us as to the other. She belongs to anyone who can evoke her memory, and I hold a trump card that you don't have. Dirk is dead—in Heaven, you say; well, my dear Pierre, he'll give me news of Yvane before you..."

I could not restrain myself. I passed from horror to disgust, from repulsion o the desire to use both hands to wring the wrinkled neck from which that frightful confession had emerged, with rattles in the throat and expulsions of phlegm. I got to me feet abruptly. For an instant, I hesitated. Then I slapped him twice, with all my strength. His head wobbled from right to left and from left to right against the back of the divan. I marched to the door. Behind me, a raucous sound rose up within the room.

He was laughing.

XV

I slammed the door, and fled into the corridor. I no longer wanted to see anything or hear anything. The mud that had just been stirred up never ceased to give off noxious poisons. It seemed to me to be saturated with them, to the utmost depths of my being. That which I had treasured more than anything else in the world would henceforth be utterly soiled. When I had believed that I was living on a level a little higher than the ordinary, I awoke floundering in a muddy pool and nameless horrors.

A hand was placed on my arm; I shook it off.

"What's the matter, Pierre?"

Narda was trying to stop me as I passed by. "Where are you going? I was waiting for you—I wanted to talk to you..."

"I'm going away," I replied, brutally. "I'm going away—don't ask me for anything more." And almost running, I went out on to the road beyond the gate, in order to flee as quickly as possible.

She followed me. "At least tell me what happened! One would think that you were afraid."

"I'm going away. I don't want to have anything to do with this place any longer. Your uncle is a monster. If I have any advice to give you, it's to do as I do. Find relatives or friends to take you in—don't stay in this house for another hour."

I spoke without turning round, as if I were being pursued. She trotted along beside me.

"Come on—I need an explanation," she declared.

391

It was difficult for me to give her an explanation as complete as was necessary. I could at least say something, though. While striding on at a rapid pace, I told her the whole story of Dirk, the roulette, the Bourse, the doctor's experiment, everything that I had seen and everything that he had told me.

And then a sentence emerged from that naïve mouth which brought me to an abrupt halt.

"And you believed him?" she said, ironically.

"What?" I stammered. "Did I believe him? I had to..." At the same time, though, for the first time, doubt sprang forth in my mind like a lightning-flash. Why had I not asked the question that Narda posed so candidly before? Had I allowed myself to be deceived, like the worst of imbeciles?

"I'm almost sure that he's never won at roulette or on the Bourse," Narda went on. "I receive the mail, and I've never found any evidence there that he's acquired the fortune you attribute to him. Without being constrained, our situation is far from being as brilliant as one might believe."

That simple factual information, given in a frank voice and with a smile, shook me again. I had never actually witnessed the gains that the doctor had told me he had won at roulette. On reflection, however, the hypothesis of a deception was impossible. "But after all," I protested, "there are other things. I've witnessed experiments. I've seen your uncle operate. His knowledge and sincerity are beyond doubt."

"Oh, I've had abundant opportunity to observe that he doesn't doubt it," Narda went on. "I believe that he's sincere, but he's deceiving himself. That's what I wanted to discuss with you, and that's why I asked you to come. Gradually, he's convinced himself that he can know the future. The future! Come on—that's impossible! I don't understand all the scientific explanations at all. That he's rendered Dirk stupid is certain—but what's also probable is that the ease with which the poor fellow is amenable to suggestion has done the rest, and has permitted my uncle to delude himself. The interest that you've appeared to take in his studies might also have provoked him, with all the sincerity in the world, to deceive you. He's been acting out a comedy, and he's ended up believing it himself."

"But then..." I said.

"Yes," she said, "I think he's mad, possessed by a curious folly. He's become the prisoner of his simulation—or, if you prefer, he's gone mad by virtue of being able to believe in his experiment. I wanted him to be examined unawares by a specialist physician. You could have introduced, as one of your friends, a doctor in whom we could have confidence."

I stood there, by the side of the road. The doctor was mad. That seemed almost obvious now. By the same token, that madness removed any value from his frightful confession, and his accusations. He had been delirious while speaking to me a little while ago. I began to breathe more freely. At the same time, listening to Narda speak procured me a curious impression of relief. Her common sense brought me back to reality. It was admirable that a head not yet twenty years old had seen clearly at first glance, which such convincing lucidity, in a situation in which I had sunk into the mud.

"In truth, Narda, what you say would explain many things. I should have thought of it sooner. But what led you to think that...?"

"It seems quite natural to me. While you were ill, I talked to the physicians that were in charge of you. I also saw other patients. I noticed that mad people almost never appear to be mad...and I made the connection."

It was, however, necessary to make sure. Now I was the one who wanted to proceed urgently to the psychiatric examination that Narda had suggested. I didn't lose a moment. I took one of the doctors at the clinic where I had been cared for to one side and explained the case to him. That afternoon we returned to the villa, on the pretext of paying a friendly call on Dr. Mops.

A strange noise greeted us at the entrance. One might have thought that it was an accordion of harmonium. The servants seemed to be absent. I took Narda's place marching at the front and headed for the first floor. The noise became clearer: music composed of percussive notes, a sort of brisk dance, wild and refined at the same time, evoking the spirits of the air: a ballet of sparks. Where had I heard music like that before?

Without knocking, I opened the double door of the study, and a gust of incense hit me in the face. The room was full of thick white vapor. Gradually, the air current dissipated it. In one corner, two Javanese men were crouching in front of their xylophones, tapping out as hard as they could the Balinese tunes with which the cremation of cadavers is accompanied out there. But a large organ was suddenly unleashed in the smoke. A voice, in which the doctor's timbre was recognizable, began to sing:

"Au ciel! Au ciel! Au ciel!
"J'irai la voir un jour...."[72]

Then we perceived Dirk in the midst of the smoke, sitting in front of a bottle of whisky, and finally, the doctor himself. He had turned up to the maximum a gramophone that was playing a record by Franck. Having put on a long white smock over his clothes, with his head tilted back toward the ceiling, he was reeling off all the religious songs he knew:

"Esprit sain, descendez en nous..."[73]

---

[72] This is the first couplet of a popular French religious song; the person that the singer is looking forward to seeing in Heaven is the Virgin Mary. The song's composer is unknown; its accompaniment here by the music of César Franck is presumably cited in the interests of deliberate incongruity.

[73] This is a deliberate misrendering of the first line of another French religious folk-song. The actual version begins *"Esprit saint"* [Holy spirit], but omitting the t renders the phrase reminiscent of the common expression *sain d'esprit* ["of sound mind", or simply "sane"]. The subsequent reference of the beatitudes (the

As the Javanese had ceased striking their instruments at the sight of us, he noticed us, and aimed a revolver at them. "In the name of God, play!" he roared.

The *Béatitudes*, howled in a furious fashion, continued to rend our ears. The odor of incense was unbreathable.

"There's no need to see any more," the physician whispered in my ear.

I exchanges glances with Narda. The expression on her face was striking. It rendered the sentiment I inspired by the scene exactly: a resigned sadness. Her calmness had not been mistaken; she had found the right note instinctively.

It was necessary to draw closer to the maniac, whose back was turned to us. Suddenly, he perceived me. "No, no" he cried. "No murderers in Heaven!"

The words were lost in the brief struggle that followed. Soon, a special vehicle took Dirk and the doctor away.

After that abrupt denouement, I found myself alone at the hotel where my suitcases were waiting for me. The thoughts that had inevitably been displaced somewhat during the afternoon's comings and goings return to assail me. The doctor's insanity threw glimmers into the past that completely altered its lighting and significance. If he could be regarded as an irresponsible madman, the measure of involuntary responsibility that I had had in the events increased in proportion. "Murderer"—the last word that he had hurled at me, echoed for a long time within me. In that horrible adventure into which I had been dragged without understanding any of it, my role was revealed as frightful. I had been lacking in judgment and suspicion, to the point of directing the maniac toward his victim. Of what blindness had I given proof! I had seen nothing, sensed nothing of everything that was happening between the individuals with whom I had lived for weeks. Like an ignorant child, I had passed by the frightful secrets resident in other hearts without being aware of them, without being alerted to them, too egotistically wrapped-up and sequestered within my own sentiments. I had not wanted to see anything other than Yvane; I had only had eyes and thoughts for her; now I had to pay the price.

It was around Yvane that all those obscure forces were gravitating, to her that I returned again. Her phantom pressed me more closely than ever. And more than anything else, the thought broke my heart that, while I believed I was giving her all the love of which I was capable, I had only marked her for death. I horrified myself. The significance of my sentiments, the very ones that I had thought the noblest, appeared to me to be deceptive and frightful.

In spite of everything, it all remained obscure, as if too complicated for me. What parts of truth and falsehood were mingled in the doctor's words? Had he wanted to avenge himself on me by torturing me with terrible confidences invented wholesale, or had he confessed the truth in one last fit of lucidity? His

---

blessings contained in two speeches by Jesus recorded in *Matthew* and *Luke*) is not to the words of the song; Mops is mixing up lines plucked at random from various sources.

madness did not explain everything. In the play of secret powers that we had all unleashed—me in allowing myself to be guided by my heart, the doctor by his mad research—Heaven and Hell seemed to lose their colors, to play their parts indifferently.

The fact also remained that certain predictions made by Dirk were strangely verified. Was it not to escape a new prophecy that I had decided, the previous evening, to flee? Might not Narda's rectitude of thought and cold lucidity, which had pleased and reassured me, be one more trap? Why had I promised to help her? Where was the error? Where was the truth? The excessively clear explanations that she gave left out too many things, too many nuances to which, in spite of everything, I felt attached. And was she not prowling around me like a new threat? I no longer knew what to think; I was frightened. Living in that atmosphere, I felt that I was in danger of ending up like the doctor. It was necessary to abandon everything, to renounce seeing clearly, to leave, to have a change of scene, to forget.

XVI

Three months passed; my leave was coming to an end. After a few days in a rest home, where inactivity had done me more harm than good. I embarked on a tiresome winter crossing to the Canaries, then accompanied a friend I had made on an automobile journey across the Sahara. I saw many faces, many horizons, deserts and seas, but I could not forget. Remorse pursued me incessantly. The entire human race seems always to be carrying out a duty of expelling from its bosom that which honors it. But even I, no more than anyone else, in spite of all my love and what I thought to be a sophisticated understanding, had not been capable of saving the most delicate and most marvelously sensitive creature that had ever seen the light of day. More than that, I had been chosen, as if by the gods, to be the instrument of her annihilation. I could not get over that.

Although, with time, my despair had taken on a less precise and lees acute form, less attached to those details that the memory retrieves to pierce the heart, and I had moved on to vaguer, more abstract considerations, the memory of Yvane still occupied my thoughts fully, like an infinite chain of mountains, so imposing that no matter how far one moves away from them, they nevertheless mark the entire landscape with their character.

I had anticipated that a certain pride would enter into that desire to compose a great dolor for myself, but taking account of it did not signify any progress toward a cure. Whatever attitude I took, the fact remained that I had met the most exquisite of creatures, and that I had killed her. I was infinitely guilty. A certain dread of life, and a certain mistrust of myself, still paralyzed me. Every action seemed to engage my beyond my intention. I would have preferred not to leave the desert or the four walls of a room.

It was, however, necessary that I return to Paris in order to make my return journey to the Far East. One morning, I was about to collect my mail from the American Express office when a tall brunette girl came toward me in the hall.

"Narda!" I said, surprised at first but then immediately embarrassed to see her again after the abrupt fashion in which I had left Lausanne—but she did not appear to be disposed to hold me to account for that. She accompanied me, chatting all the while, as far as the sidewalk of the Opéra. She explained that she was about to leave for South America, in the company of a Dutch family, and gave me abundant details of her future situation. Discreetly, she avoided any reference to the past, but one question was burning on my lips. I asked her for news of the doctor.

"He's in a nursing home—quite calm, but there's little hope of ever seeing him leave it."

"It's better thus," I said, becoming thoughtful again, "for he might be dangerous."

"Dangerous?" she said, in surprise.

It was my turn to be astonished that, with the sureness of judgment with which I credited her, she had not been alerted to that. After various allusions that, although clear, were not understood, I said straightforwardly: "After all, he was the one who killed Yvane."

"What?" she said. "What are you saying?"

"I'm only repeating what your uncle confessed to me." I added: "In order that Dirk's predictions should not be found at fault, he did not hesitate..." In spite of myself, my voice broke.

"But Pierre," she said, placing her hand on my arm, "what you say is impossible."

"He told me himself, and gave me reasons that I cannot repeat to you."

"His mind must already have been disturbed, and perhaps it was his bad conscience talking. He's a lunatic, but he's not a criminal. I'm absolutely sure that he didn't..."

Blushing with emotion, she could not finish her sentence. In the midst of the noise of the traffic, in the open area in front of the Opéra, that conversation took on a strange character.

I regretted having spoken, having dispelled the illusions of an innocent soul again. Decidedly, everything I did turned bad. But Narda resumed: "He didn't kill Yvane, since..."

"...It was an accident," I finished, evasively.

"No," said Narda, looking me in the eyes. "It wasn't an accident. Yvane killed herself."

A bus could have emerged from the entrance of the Metro and I would not have been so amazed. It required all the credit that I gave to Narda's precocious intellectual maturity, not to believe her, but to be persuaded that she really had pronounced the words I had just heard.

"Killed herself! Come on, that's impossible!"

"Yvane killed herself," Narda repeated, very calmly. "I know that because she left me a letter. The version of the accident having been accepted, I preferred to keep the secret to myself, but after what you've told me, you need to know the truth."

I shook my head again.

"If you'd care to accompany me to my hotel," she proposed, "I'll show you the letter."

I followed her, without seeing or hearing anything. When she said: "Here it is," I stopped, and let myself fall into a chair in the hallway.

She brought out a letter: a piece of white paper, folded in four. The large, irregular handwriting, with exaggerated capital letters, was definitely Yvane's. The sheet trembled in my hands, and I was obliged to lean my elbows on the table.

I read:

My darling, I'm dying because I want to die. I shall never come down from the mountain. When one has reached the summit of happiness, one can no longer accept going back. Don't weep, I have nothing to lament. I have seen and felt everything that it is necessary to see, and it's with an indescribable delight that I depart. Never have I been so happy. Be kind to Pierre. You are both of the race of the living. Yvane.

Facing me, pinned to the wall, was a poster for a shipping company depicting an African woman laden with bananas beside the bow of a ship. Through the open door, in the little street on the Left Bank where the hotel was located, I could see hatless women passing by, all carrying identical waxed-cloth bags, from which vegetables protruded. It was morning; a market must be close by. "It's truly curious," I said, "that all the women in a quarter resemble one another." At the desk, the manageress, a plump blonde, was rubbing the plate of glass in front of the counter with a rag, moving the telephone and a stack of papers from one side to the other in their turn. The bus going past in the neighboring street made the electric light-bulb hanging from the ceiling vibrate. I raised my head; fortunately, it was not directly above me. I uncrossed my legs, and the wicker armchair creaked under my weight. An old American woman presented herself, politely and modestly, and greeted the manageress—who, after a glance at the pigeon-holes, shook her head: there were no letters, no more today than yesterday, probably. Then I heard the sound of a vacuum cleaner on the upper floor, coming down the elevator shaft. The elevator wasn't working, in need of repair. On the rattan table that separated me from Narda, a large yellow ash-tray bearing an advertisement for an aperitif caught my eye. Yielding to the imperious solicitation, I lit a cigarette. Finally, I said: "Yes, yes..."

Thus, in that décor which I had not chosen, which I would never have been able to imagine, but which imposed itself upon me with a reality and a solidity that I had been unable to recognize in the surrounding world for many weeks, I felt the insistent phantom whose company held me prisoner in the past abandon me, at the same time as remorse. What relationship had the present décor of the world to the words of that poor letter, which I read once again? To what point in a vanished past was it trying to attach itself? The mountain, happiness—that was far away, far, far away beyond the sea. The residue of the stormy perturbation was fleeing into my internal sky. A great wind was blowing, bringing with it the quotidian daylight. The familiar, the banal and the ordinary resumed possession of my life.

Narda was still talking.

"...like my Aunt Suyter, her grandmother, who also killed herself—perhaps you knew that? An oppressive heredity weighs upon the family. Poor Yvane, she was already bizarre as a child, and had to be put in a nursing home on several occasions. In her, fits of terrible depression followed instants of great excitement. After her mother's death she gave rise to great anxieties. My uncle had decided to keep her close to him, but his company was not designed to make things better. I had arrived at La Colle too recently to take clear account..."

Her voice resembled the noises of the street. Her hair was as black as the telephone-stand. The cretonne cushion of the armchair also gave the impression of a family-member with a corsage, because of its embroidered flowers. She went on talking. Her common sense was overwhelming and contagious. The clock opposite showed that it was 12:25 p.m.

"Well, shall we have dinner together?" I asked, abruptly.

She accepted without needing any persuasion. At the corner of the street, I took her arm. It was smooth and muscular.

"I know a little Italian restaurant..." she began.

The idea of that little restaurant suddenly illuminated me. I was hungry. I was aware of that for the first time in many months.

"An Italian restaurant?" I said. "I remember, one day in Boulogne...hang on...I ate...what was it called? It was marvelous...a mixture of pasta and vegetables...oh! It was *lasagne verdi*."

"Well, I believe that I saw the exact same thing on the menu!" she said, in a joyful explosion.

I was holding on to that arm very firmly; it was allowing itself to be held. "No! They have it!" I replied, laughing. "Then I love you!"

I was not, however, to marry her until much later, after the war. That erupted so abruptly into our lives that the entire drama that I have just recounted slipped away into the past before I could form a clear idea of it. In any case, I have been trying for a long time not to think too intensely about it, and the war at least had the merit of aiding me in that task. Thus, caught between so many proposed explanations, I have never been sure exactly how Yvane died, and why. Similarly, with respect to the doctor's experiment, I have never been able to determine with certainty how much truth was mixed in with the simulation. All things considered, I prefer not knowing. I've reported the facts; I shall leave to others the pretention of seeing them clearly and interpreting them. For my part, I limit myself to the disillusioned opinion with which I began: everything that happens is of no importance whatsoever, and it is only for the sake of vain mental satisfaction that one imagines a logical sequence in the course of events. There are so many equally plausible ways of representing things that I flatly refuse to adopt any one of them. And what I have seen during the war could not modify my way of thinking—or, rather, of not thinking.

www.ingramcontent.com/pod-product-compliance
Lightning Source LLC
Chambersburg PA
CBHW020254030726
47499CB00001B/205